D1355518

Peter James was educated at Charterhouse then at film school. He lived in North America for a number of years, working as a screenwriter and film producer before returning to England. His novels, including the number one bestseller *Possession*, have been translated into thirty languages and three have been filmed. All his novels reflect his deep interest in the world of the police, with whom he does in-depth research, as well as science, medicine and the paranormal. He has produced numerous films, including *The Merchant Of Venice*, starring Al Pacino, Jeremy Irons and Joseph Fiennes. He also co-created the hit Channel 4 series, *Bedsitcom*, which was nominated for a Rose d'Or. He is currently, as co-producer, developing his Roy Grace novels for television with ITV Productions. Peter James won the Krimi-Blitz 2005 Crime Writer of the Year award in Germany, and *Dead Simple* won both the 2006 Prix Polar International award and the 2007 Prix Coeur Noir award in France. *Looking Good Dead* was shortlisted for the 2007 Richard and Judy Crime Thriller of the Year award, France's SNCF and Le Grand Prix de Littérature award. *Not Dead Enough* was shortlisted for the Theakstons Old Peculier Crime Thriller of the Year award and the ITV3 Crime Thriller Of The Year award. He divides his time between his homes in Notting Hill, London and near Brighton in Sussex. Visit his website at www.peterjames.com.

ALCHEMIST

Peter James

An Orion paperback

First published in Great Britain in 1996
by Victor Gollancz
This paperback edition published in 1999
by Orion Books Ltd,
Orion House, 5 Upper St Martin's Lane,
London WC2H 9EA

An Hachette UK company

Reissued 2005

Printed and bound in Great Britain by
Clays Ltd, St Ives plc

The Orion Publishing Group's policy is to use papers that
are natural, renewable and recyclable products and
made from wood grown in sustainable forests. The logging
and manufacturing processes are expected to conform to
the environmental regulations of the country of origin.

www.orionbooks.co.uk

'There is one thing stronger than all the armies in the world; and that is an idea whose time has come'

Victor Hugo

PROLOGUE

Israel. February 1991

Utter conviction was the Englishman's only luggage.

He sat in silence on the lumpy seat in the back of the lurching Mercedes taxi that smelled of greasy vinyl and old cigarette butts, immersed in his thoughts.

Alpha and Omega. The words repeated like an old tune in his head he could not shake free.

I am the Alpha and Omega, the beginning and the end, the first and the last.

Yahweh.

Not any more you bastard, he mouthed silently.

The air conditioning was not working. He stared out of the open window at scenery that had looked much the same for the past hour. Hot, arid air riffled his hair. A plastic thermometer stuck to the dash registered close on 120°; every few moments there was an irritating 'ping' as a Star of David suspended from the interior mirror struck it.

Occasionally he noticed the smells of the desert outside; mostly a milky sweetness soured by occasional sharp tangs of salt. They passed through a village, through a stench of sewage, then thick sweet smells of grilling meats and roasting nuts. A child waved at them, but he did not wave back.

I met a traveller from an antique land.

Shelley, he thought. Ah yes, Shelley. *He* understood. Shelley, Byron; they knew the secret, they had tried to share it, tried to live it.

Sometimes,

The Devil is a gentleman.

He smiled.

Twenty minutes later the taxi halted abruptly. 'You walk from here,' the driver said. 'No good, the road.'

But to the Englishman the road looked no worse ahead than

it did behind: still a scar in the sand, fly-blown, strewn with boulders and loose stones, shimmering in the heat.

He paid the driver: 'Half now and half when I come back.'

The driver was staring at the mountains at the end of the scar with frightened eyes. 'Come back,' he said as if it were an echo. 'Tomorrow. Ten o'clock I waiting here.' He already had the Mercedes in gear and was gunning the engine.

Then the Englishman was alone under the metallic blue sky with the drifting plume of the taxi's dust. He shivered, feeling just a fleeting doubt as he stared across the pink, yellow and cream hues of the desert sand, strewn with the occasional oil drum from past wars.

He had travelled three thousand miles by aeroplane and by taxi. Now he had the hard part ahead, the walk on foot alone to the end of the journey. And to a new beginning.

He felt suddenly awed by the power he had come to meet, and he knew that the taxi driver had felt so also; knew that was why he had refused to go further. This was a land where history held the evidence for legends, where the proof sought by the rest of the world still lay locked away, where a secret could remain untouched in the mountains for centuries. For millennia. Or could be lost for ever like the Clavicle of Solomon. And had been.

He put his hat on, shouldered his small bag and began walking. He carried no map but he knew where he was going, did not even need the track that stretched out beyond his shadow in front of him. He knew, because something was drawing him forward like a magnet. Drawing him to his destiny. Towards the closest-kept secret in the world. His time had come and he was prepared.

The wind brushed against his face, like a sign.

He walked due west. Thoughts came to him, tumbled into his mind, jostled for space. The hailing frequency had been opened and he was here to listen, to be instructed; to receive. To receive the gift that was above all others. Moses had led the children of Israel through this desert. Now he too was being led through this same desert, walking in time's footsteps, and soon he would be standing on the shoulders of a giant. The

2

Sermon on the Mount had been delivered on one of the slopes that lay ahead. The history of Christianity belonged in the granules of sand that coated the terrain.

Silicon came from sand. From two bits of dust came the Big Bang – all Creation. From a few grains of sand came the silicon chip. Chemistry. Chemistry was everything. Now you could have a computer that was smaller than a grain of sand. *And I will show you something different from either / Your shadow at morning striding behind you / Or your shadow at evening rising to meet you; / I will show you fear in a handful of dust.*

He walked for two hours at an unfaltering pace, passing several flocks of sheep and goats tended by Bedouins in tatty black and white robes, preparing himself all the time, the way he had been taught. Opening up the channels. Sweat sloughed off him, drenching his white silk shirt, gluing it to his skin, spreading dark stains under the arms of his linen jacket. He always wore a suit and tie and it had not occurred to him to wear anything less now. A camel train moved across the horizon like a mirage, but his inner concentration was such that he barely noticed it.

The Alpha and the Omega, he thought. The words repeated in his head like a mantra as he walked. *The Alpha and the Omega.* He smiled; it gave him strength, warded off the fear that he still felt with every step that it could go wrong, so terribly wrong. It had been known to go wrong before. He paused to drink from the water bottle he carried in his bag, then walked on.

The mountains were closer now. He could see the sheer faces of sandstone rising into the sky like shadows, and could feel in his bones the inky darkness of the cave that was steadily reeling him in. But he had no fear now, only a growing elation. Above him, a lone hawk cruised high overhead, and somewhere else in the sky an unseen bird cried a single low call that reminded him of a gull.

The sun was beginning to sink down towards the peaks, lengthening his shadow ahead of him, and he felt tired for the first time as he started the climb. There was no track now, no signposts or markers, no hint that man had ever been here before, just the ever-steepening wall of rock that was both rising above him and dropping beneath him into the valley.

Then finally as he continued his long traverse, he saw a figure above him, sitting motionless like a statue. Standing silently beside it, he could make out the tethered goat. They were here; he had come to the right place; he chided himself for having had momentary doubts, then his pace quickened with a new energy.

He walked along a narrow ledge, the mountain dropping sheer away to his left; the wind came out of the darkness of the cave to greet him: dank, cold air. The seated man did not move as he approached, did not turn his head but just stared ahead into the narrow entrance of the cave that stretched back miles into pitch blackness, as motionless as the wooden stake beside him to which his goat was tethered.

Dressed in a dirty white jellaba, the goatherd was skeletally thin, with the Semitic features of the region that could have passed him for a Jew or a Palestinian. His small dark eyes were glazed and devoid of all expression.

The Englishman eyed the goatherd carefully. He was about twenty; personally he would have chosen someone a bit younger and stronger, but he would do, he supposed; anyone in their prime would do. He walked on past him into the darkness of the cave itself, without acknowledging him.

In the dim edges of light he could see the pentacle carved as finely as a tomb into the floor, and the ornate stone chair that stood like a throne in its midst. He put his bag on the floor then sat in the chair as he had been told, folded his hands in his lap, closed his eyes and meditated for an hour.

As he opened his eyes again, the first rays of the setting sun came through the opening in the five-sided lodestone that hung beneath the roof of the cave. Minutes later the whole orb of the sun was visible, dazzling, but the Englishman stared at it, imposing his will against it, and remained silent.

The sun slid directly down behind the back of the goatherd, until it seemed that he had absorbed all its light and the Englishman could see nothing but his shimmering silhouette against the sky. Then darkness came rapidly outside.

4

The Englishman waited patiently as if all time had stopped for him, waited until the signal came into his mind, then he began to speak the words of the incantation he had been learning, rehearsing and reciting every day for ten years.

They were behind him, somewhere, in the darkness. He had not seen them and they made no sound but he knew they were there, all of them standing in their ordained positions, except for the old man who would be lying on the stretcher on which they had carried him. After two hours he finished the incantation. The last echoes of his words died.

Now he had to wait again.

All time was really suspended now. All time was his. The Englishman could see and hear nothing; he stared ahead blindly, dimly aware of the chill air numbing his body. He felt more calm than he had ever been before in his whole life. More ready. It was coming and it would be here soon.

The first signal came from the goat. A tentative bleat, then another, more insistent. He heard a hoof shuffle on the stone floor, then a stamp, the rope of the tether creaking against the stake. Then more bleats, rising fear.

The first icy tongues of wind licked the Englishman's face hungrily, teased his hair, ruffled his clothes. They came in fast, unannounced, strengthening in intensity every second, getting colder, rougher, pushing him around on his chair, buffeting him.

He heard a rumble like an approaching tube train, followed by a faint tremor. Now! It was coming now. Travelling across all time to meet him. It was an appointment he had always known, from the day he was born, that he would one day keep. Here it was!

'Ayaaaaaayaaaaaaa!' The goatherd's cry of terror rang out and was swept away in the vortex of wind that exploded like a bomb inside the cave.

The Englishman was catapulted from his chair, hurtled across the floor and slammed into a wall. Wind screamed around him, pressed on his ears as if it were going to shatter his drums, implode his head; for a moment his faith left him and he tried to blot out the pain, bit his tongue to prevent himself from screaming out loud.

The wind caterwauled around him; it carried voices, foreign tongues, strange sounds, chants. It lifted the Englishman up, sent him tumbling across the floor, lifted him again, dropped him, gashing his head on the stone chair. He groped the floor wildly with his hands.

Stay inside the pentacle.

The instruction, had to obey the instruction, the first rule. He felt for the lines carved into the floor; the floor heaved, shook, tipped him sideways.

Then there was complete silence.

He lay still. The wind had gone completely. There was nothing now, nothing at all except for bitumen blackness and the silence.

Somewhere a light flared. He smelled the smoky warmth of burning paraffin. Flickering lights on the walls, growing in number, in intensity. He looked behind him: a row of lit torches stretched the full two hundred yards' width of the cave. He could see the silhouettes behind them but not the faces. There was no need to see the faces; many he already knew; the others, in time, he would meet.

He turned to look at the goatherd and the goat. He saw the frayed fronds of the snapped tether first; then one of the goat's hooves and a section of the leg. Beside it lay two human arms torn off at the elbow, the fingers interlinked as if in a final gesture of prayer; they were partly covered in a ragged strip of bloodstained cloth. A coil of the goat's intestines glistened in a slimy heap on the floor near them.

He saw a human foot, then the goatherd's head and the top part of his torso crudely severed at the breastbone; close beside lay the head of the animal severed at the neck and tilted at an angle, with one ear raised as if cocked to listen. Blood, strips of flesh, fragments of organs lay scattered across the floor and adhered to the walls as if hurled by an explosion.

The silence seemed as if it would last for ever.

It was broken finally by the old man's voice; the old man they had carried here on the stretcher. He spoke in sure, quiet tones filled with the authority he had held for so many years:

6

Nema. Olam a son arebil des
Menoitatnet ni sacudni son en te.
Sirtson subirotibed
Summittimid son te tucis
Artson atibed sibon ettimid te
Eidoh sibon ad
Munaiditouq murtson menap
Arret ni te oleac ni
Tucis aut satnulov taif
Muut munger tainevda
Muut nemon rutecifitcnas
Sileac ni se iuq
Retson retap.
Hail the new emperor of the Grand Grimoire!

The Englishman bided his time before replying. He stood up, restored himself in his chair, and sat facing away from the torch lights and out into the night. He breathed in slowly and deeply, filling his lungs so that his voice would carry, then braced himself: 'Hail Satan,' he said.

The echo came back in unison: 'Hail Satan!'

1

Reading, England. November, 1993

Only one of them would survive. They raced through the darkness, guided solely by instincts handed down through three billion years. And each of them had less intelligence than a clockwork toy.

Just one survivor out of sixty-five million. Strength would have something to do with it but mostly it would be luck. The right place at the right time. Like life itself.

Sixty-five million wiggling, tadpole-like creatures inside a soup of chemicals, ejaculated into the woman, freed and doomed simultaneously. Ripples of contraction joined with their own efforts and propelled them forward in tiny tramlines through the mucus, at a rate of one inch every eight minutes, up towards the uterus. Each elbowed the next, as they fought their way through the prickly follicles of hair that blocked their path and which entwined them like tentacles, some getting no further. The rest moved on, propelled by a primal urgency they were not equipped to understand, and with no concept of what failure meant.

Unaware of the turmoil deep inside her own body, Sarah Johnson stared up at her husband's face in the glow of the bedside light and smiled. 'Don't move,' she said. 'Stay there, it feels so good.' She reached up and kissed him.

He kissed her back then softly nuzzled her ear. 'How was it?'

'Nice.'

'Just nice?' he said, a little flatly.

'Very nice,' she said, and kissed his upper lip.

'That's all?'

'The earth moved,' she said teasingly.

'Not the whole universe?'

'I think the whole universe probably moved too,' she said

quietly. She felt him contract and she clenched him with her muscles, trying to hold him there for longer. Their eyes danced with each other. They had been married for four years and were still wildly in love.

She pulled her fingers through his thick, wavy hair, her heart still racing; he expanded then contracted a fraction inside her and fresh aftershocks of pleasure resonated through her. She breathed deeply, the pounding in her heart only slowly beginning to subside.

'God, I love you so much, Sarah,' he said.

'I love you too,' she said.

Over sixty-four million of the sperm were dead now, but most of them still carried on with their journey, travelling as fast as the ones that were still alive, propelled like flotsam on a rip-tide by the contractions of the uterine muscle.

A mere three thousand were still living when they reached the mouth of the Fallopian tube. A further two thousand died, either crushed, asphyxiated, or exhausted in the next inch of the journey. One solitary sperm, alive and healthy, finally reached the egg ahead of the rest.

From its mouth it spat an enzyme that acted like a paralysing anaesthetic on the cells surrounding the egg, enabling it to push them apart. From its feet it excreted a glue that enabled it to bond to the outer zone of the egg. Then it began to tunnel through the heavily protected protein shell. Finally it reached the egg inside and began to fuse with it.

The sperm's task was nearly over. Its long, stringy tail dropped off and was discarded. The sperm's nucleus entered the egg and within minutes the egg had begun to divide. The sperm and the nucleus each carried twenty-three chromosomes – a half set. Each chromosome carried between 50,000 to 100,000 genes, which carried between them three billion units of DNA. Like all eggs, this one contained an X chromosome. The sperm contained a Y.

By the time Sarah Johnson had fallen asleep, she was pregnant with a baby boy. Neither she nor her husband, Alan, had any forebodings that night. They had no way of knowing then, as they lay in each other's arms, that the child they yearned for so much would kill her without ever having spoken a word.

2

Georgetown, Washington. September, 1994
The bird hung motionless in the sky above the small boy, its wings outstretched, as if suspended by invisible threads. Slowly, like the blades of a helicopter, it began to rotate on its own axis: a giant, black predator scouring the landscape beneath it for quarry.

Suddenly it side-slipped, as if the threads had been severed, stopped and steadied for one fleeting moment; then it began to zigzag downwards, half flying, half plummeting, like a shadow chasing itself, its wings flapping clumsily as if they were clawing the air.

Seconds later it alighted on the ground only a few yards from where he stood, with a thud. Its head jerked sharply up, and seemed to stare straight at him in surprise.

The boy stared back for a moment in sheer disbelief. 'DAAAADDDDDDYYYYYYY!' he screamed. 'DAAAADDDDYYYY! DAAADDDYYYY! DAAAD-DDYYYY! DAAADDDYYYY! DAAAA –'

'Honey, it's OK, honey. Mummy's here, your mummy's here!'

Then the face of the bird dissolved into bright light.
Silence.

Conor Molloy opened his eyes, stared up at the glow of the pearl bulb in its familiar plain shade. Then he saw the bookshelves lined with his old comics, annuals, children's encyclopaedias, his tiny microscope . . .

The room was as he had left it a decade and a half ago; the same flimsy curtains, the dull red carpet, the white chest of drawers. The bed he now lay in was the same bed that he had outgrown some time in his teens, but which had never been changed.

'Conor, you all right?'

His mother's face was peering at him anxiously, her slender fingers glinting with the base metals of far too many rings, and in an instant nothing had changed. Fifteen years, more, were stripped away like bedclothes. He was a child again, a small boy saved from a nightmare by his mother.

'Honey, darling, are you all right?'

He swallowed the lump that was in his throat and nodded.

'You were hollering your head off.'

'I'm sorry.'

'The dream? Was it the dream?'

He was quiet for a moment, wondering whether to admit it, aware of the rebuke it would bring once more. But he knew there was no point in trying to hide anything from her, she could always see through him. She could read the inside of his head as clearly as if it were beaming out to her from a television screen. 'Yes,' he said.

She was fifty-six and still beautiful. Her long dark hair was flecked with occasional grey strands, but they looked more like highlights than age. Her blue eyes were still set in a fine classical face, barely different from the one that he had seen staring out from the host of mail-order catalogues and magazine ads she kept crammed away in a cupboard.

However much she might have embarrassed him as a child with her strange behaviour in front of his friends, he looked at her now and knew that he had never ceased loving her. He admired her for all that she had given him as a mother.

'You want to go back to sleep or you want a drink?' she asked.

Conor glanced at his watch; it was ten past three. But tomorrow was the last day he would see her for a long time. 'A drink would be good, Mom. Sorry to wake you.'

'You didn't – I haven't been to sleep.'

He slipped out of bed and pulled on his dressing gown. As he padded towards the kitchen he heard the kettle starting to boil and smelled the sweet smoke of a freshly lit cigarette. The ranch-style house had grown in keeping with his mother's prosperity over the years. It had started as a modest bungalow in an area that just qualified for a Georgetown address. Appearances had meant a lot to his father – he preferred to live in a small property with a good address, rather than a larger house elsewhere. His father'd had strong, intractable views on pretty well everything.

His mother made some herbal tea, ignoring the fact that Conor loathed the stuff, then took it through to the old living room that was now only used when his mother was frightened about something. In his early childhood, the room had been a conventional family centrepiece. But over the years his mother had changed it dramatically. She had had the walls and the ceiling panelled in oak, giving it a rather claustrophobic air that was further enhanced by two of the walls being covered floor to ceiling in bookshelves – packed solid with occult reference works and grimoires. Also arranged along the shelves, making access to some of the books tricky, was a vast assortment of rock crystals fashioned into bizarre shapes, and eerie bronze and stone gargoyles.

Heavy crimson drapes, permanently drawn, kept the outside world at bay. Two Burmese cats sat like sentinels either side of a gas coal fire in a crenellated hearth. This was kept burning, along with two joss sticks, day and night, all year round. A massive woven pentagram hung on the wall directly above the fire, flanked on each side by two tall black candles.

His mother had eased herself into one of the two comfortable sofas and sat serene in her long black robe. Behind her was the small wooden table where she had done her sittings. A crystal ball, a small glass pyramid and several other artefacts were laid there. On the far wall a row of voodoo masks stared menacingly down on to her computer workstation, from which in less affluent times she posted occult news on to the Internet, gave tarot readings by fax and eMail, and communicated messages for psychic healing.

A locked door between the two walls of bookshelves led into her inner chamber, where she had conducted her seances and practised ritual magic. Conor had never been permitted inside the room; and although frequently as a child he had stood with

12

his ear pressed to the door, he had never heard anything other than meaningless chanting.

His mother drew hard on her cigarette and blew the smoke at the panelled ceiling, which was covered in carved occult symbols. 'Conor, I know you say your mind's made up, but I want you to reconsider one more time. I've lost too much in my life. I don't want to lose you.'

'You're not losing me – I'm at the end of a phone, we can eMail each other every day – and I'm going to be just a plane ride away.'

'You know what I mean,' she said, her tone becoming sharper.

He said nothing.

'You just don't know what you're getting into. Maybe I've taught you too much, given you false confidence. Believe me, I've seen it for myself, I've experienced what they can do. Think again while you still have the chance.'

'Mom, I'm going.'

'You don't have to go. There are other companies – right here –'

'Mom! We've had this out a thousand times. I have to do this.'

'You're as stubborn as your father.'

'I'm his son,' he said simply.

3

London, October, 1993

'What you have to realize is that in the past one hundred and fifty years the pharmaceutical industry has gone from selling snake oil to controlling the future of the human race. The problem is, it's still run by the snake-oil salesmen.'

Oh Christ, Montana Bannerman thought, staring at the television monitor up above her.

'Thieving, unscrupulous bastards, the whole lot of them!'

Her father thumped the coffee table, and the female interviewer beside him looked a little flustered.

Dr Bannerman was a giant of a man in every way; both physically tall and powerfully built, and a towering genius in science. But with his bald dome rising from a mane of greying hair, his semi-permanent rig of denims, Chelsea boots and a checked lumberjack shirt, he looked more like an ageing rock star than a molecular biologist.

Monty had tried to stop her father from drinking before he'd gone on air, but he had gulped down two large whiskies in the Sky News hospitality suite and he was now in full flood. The Rastafarian leader of the Afro-Caribbean rap group which was due on next nodded his head in enthusiasm. 'He's right! The man is right! Wow, is he right!'

Monty smiled politely through gritted teeth. Her father was not doing much right now to endear himself to the pharmaceutical establishment on whom he depended for his funding. On whom they both depended.

'Don't you think, Dr Bannerman, that the pharmaceutical industry has made human life very much more comfortable? It's eliminated an enormous amount of pain, it's eradicated or brought under control countless previously incurable diseases. How do you argue against that?'

'All that is a by-product. The pharmaceutical industry is interested in one thing and one thing only: profit. If it happens to help a few people on the way, fine, so be it.'

'And that's what you really believe?' the interviewer said.

'That's what I was told, verbatim, by the chief executive of one of our largest pharmaceutical companies when I was a young research student. All this do-gooding stuff is crap. Look at the Nobel Prize. Alfred Nobel made his fortune out of inventing dynamite. He followed that by establishing an annual prize for peace. How much more cynical can you get?'

'If that's the way you feel, why did you accept a Nobel Prize for Chemistry?'

'Sometimes I wish I hadn't.' Bannerman shrugged his shoulders. 'I'm afraid in my line of work we have to be whores, selling ourselves to anyone prepared to put up cash for the next three years' funding.' He smiled and the true warmth of the man fleetingly shone through the storm cloud of his expression. 'Nobel Prizes make good calling cards.'

Plug the book, Daddy! Monty thought, staring at the fat hardback that lay on the table, angled at the camera but out of focus. *That's why you're there – to plug the book – not to slag off the pharmaceutical establishment!*

The interviewer shifted position and leaned closer towards him. She was about the same age as herself, Monty thought, late twenties, a pretty brunette with hair in a neat bob and a businesslike suit. The tone of her voice emphasized the change of subject.

'You are the first molecular biologist to have cracked the secret of switching on and off human genes. This has been acclaimed by the scientific world as one of the most important breakthroughs of all time. Up until now scientists have been able to identify certain genes, those related to disease and ageing, but they've not been able to do anything about them. None of the gene-therapy attempts with cystic fibrosis sufferers, for example, have yet totally succeeded. In your position most scientists might have tried to keep their work secret, but you've refused to patent your discoveries and have published them for all the world to see in your new book, *The Gene Bomb – The 21st Century Holocaust.*'

The camera zoomed in on the jacket. *Good girl!* Monty thought.

'Why have you done that, Dr Bannerman?'

His voice was big and deep, with a slight Transatlantic accent, reflecting his obsession with Americana. 'Because no one has the right to patent human life by patenting genes. Genes will ultimately give scientists absolute control over life, but who will control the scientists?' He thumped his fist hard on the table again. 'Not governments – they'll be bought off. No, it's going to be the pharmaceutical industry. An industry so secretive they don't even allow you in the door. Is that because they're worried about you stealing their secrets? No! They're worried you might find out how much money they're all making, and how much money they're paying out as *baksheesh*. Did you know that in 1988 the top eighteen US pharmaceutical companies paid out one hundred and sixty-five million dollars in bribes to doctors?'

The interviewer flinched. 'Do you have evidence of that?'

'Those are figures published by the US Government,' Bannerman said triumphantly.

There was a ragged cheer from the rock band who were glued to the monitor. Monty groaned silently. But the interviewer, failing to grab a good story by the nose, rapidly changed the subject once more. Monty sighed her relief.

'I would imagine, Dr Bannerman, that at this moment you must have every pharmaceutical company in the world beating a path to your doorstep to offer you funding.'

'And they can turn round and go straight back home, the bastards. They ignored me for thirty years and now suddenly I'm everybody's best friend. We share seventy per cent of our genes with slime mould – but I think in the pharmaceutical industry the percentage is even higher.'

Monty closed her eyes and groaned again. *The book, do the book, Daddy – we need the money!*

Sure, her father had a valid axe to grind, he had a right to be bitter against an industry – and a succession of governments – that held scientists in such low esteem that it forced them to emigrate, or to spend much of their working lives scrabbling around for funding instead of concentrating on their real work. But neither was Dick Bannerman an easy man to work with or to deal with. One of the true *enfants terribles* of science. In spite of his genius, over the years he had not helped himself as much as he might have done; he was nudging sixty now, and age had not mellowed him one bit.

'How did I do?' It was always the first question he asked Monty after any interview or speech, a sudden childlike innocence appearing in his brown eyes, as if knowing he had done wrong and not wanting to face up to it.

She backed her MG carefully out of the bay, then drove slowly towards the exit booth of the underground car park. 'How do *you* think you did?' she replied with a smile.

'Four out of ten?'

'Maybe five,' she said.

16

'You're being generous.'

She paid £2.50 to the attendant at the barrier, then drove into the falling darkness of the South London rush hour.

'The interviewer was a child,' Dick Bannerman said, as if in his own defence.

'At least she'd read the book, which is more than most.'

'True,' he said, sounding distant. 'Very true.'

Monty recognized the signs of her father lapsing into his own deep thoughts. 'I think you should call Sir Neil Rorke back,' she said, continuing a discussion they'd been having before the interview.

'Think he'll still want to speak to me?' he said wryly.

'If he wasn't watching Sky News.'

Sir Neil Rorke was Chairman of the Bendix Schere Foundation, the third largest pharmaceutical company in Britain and ranked high as a world player. In addition to its main business of manufacturing prescription and over-the-counter pharmaceuticals, it had a massive baby-food division, a worldwide chain of fertility clinics and a group of prestigious private hospitals. Bendix Schere had been one of the first pharmaceutical companies to invest heavily in genetics research and was the largest single provider of research funds for genetics in the country.

For the past thirty years Dick Bannerman had refused to go to the pharmaceutical industry for funding, because he was passionately against the whole concept of patenting. Knowledge should be shared, he believed, and it was a principle he rigidly adhered to at Bannerman Genetics Research sited on the campus of Berkshire University. His funding came partly from the university, partly – and very sporadically – from the government, and even more sporadically from a handful of charitable organizations – in particular those supporting research into genetic-linked diseases, such as the Imperial Cancer Research Foundation, the Cystic Fibrosis Trust, and the Parkinson's Foundation.

But with the constant expense of keeping up to date in technology, combined with the increasing desire of funders to see a return on their investment beyond pure research results, the pressure in keeping the labs running, with their staff of twenty, was taking its toll. Whenever Monty thought about the breakthroughs her father had made despite all the handicaps, she wondered how much more he could achieve with better funding. Sir Neil Rorke might just be the answer. 'I've never heard anything good about Bendix Schere,' Dick Bannerman said.

'What have you heard that's bad?'

He pushed a toothpick into the side of his mouth and bit on it. 'Nothing specific. They're obsessively secretive.'

'So's the whole pharmaceutical industry.'

'Rorke's not going to offer any funding without wanting his pound of flesh.'

'Patents aren't that terrible, Daddy – and they don't last for ever. Seventeen years in the UK – that's not long.'

He looked at her with his head slanted. 'Seventeen years will see me out.'

'I hope not.'

'Well – you'll be pushing me round in a wheelchair, and I'll be gaga.'

'And still scratching around for funding.'

The remark silenced him, and she knew the barb had struck home.

He was getting tired of the fight for money; and he knew that time was running out on him. They'd had a letter from Berkshire University telling them, with regret, that their funding was going to be halved for the next three years; it had added that with Dr Bannerman's recent achievements in genetics there should be little difficulty finding funding from the commercial sector. The government had been making similar hints. He was going to have to go cap in hand to the pharmaceutical industry one day, and right now he was riding high. The timing had never been better.

'You have nothing to lose by meeting Sir Neil,' Monty said. 'If you don't like what he says, then fine.'

'Yup, OK, fine, we'll meet, see what's what. Will you come too – help assess him? Maybe you can charm some loot out of him.'

'Sure I'll come. Whenever I've seen him on television he always looks very friendly.'

Dick Bannerman removed the toothpick and twisted it in his fingers, examining the tip. 'Cobras always smile before they strike.'

4

Berkshire, England. October, 1993

On Tuesday nights Anna Sterling's husband Mark went to rugger practice, followed by a drinking session then a curry with the guys. Monty Bannerman and Anna usually had supper together or went to a film.

They had been meeting up like that, weekly, for as long as Monty could remember. Anna was her oldest friend, and she was also one of her few remaining pals who did not have children. Monty was aware that was probably the main reason nothing had changed between them.

With her own thirtieth birthday looming up next April, and still single in spite of some past close relationships, to her irritation the thought of children often preyed on Monty's mind. She liked to think she was stronger than other women, that she wasn't simply a prisoner of her genes and sentenced, by the mere lack of a Y chromosome, to broody emotions about washing nappies and wiping bums.

There were some days when she successfully convinced herself that she really did not like children, that they were loathsome little creatures, rating on her own list of desirability only marginally higher than being suspended upside down in boiling oil. But there were other times when her defences were blown away and she would find herself sucked into an emotional whirlpool of longing.

Monty and Anna had been at school together and had gone on to the same art college. Anna was a genuinely gifted sculptress, and her talent was evident. She had already had successful exhibitions, and was getting many commissions. Monty considered herself to be a moderately proficient landscape painter, but no more. She had hoped for a career in the art world, either in restoration or valuation. But halfway through her second year at college her mother had died, and she had taken a few weeks off to help her father who had been devastated by his loss.

Sarah Bannerman had died of breast cancer within a year of the disease being diagnosed, and her husband had felt a deep sense of guilt and failure that, despite all his work, he had not come up with any kind of gene therapy in time to save her – feelings that had since been heightened by the announcement that scientists in America had found a way of detecting the cancer gene.

Dick Bannerman, although a brilliant scientist, was a hopeless businessman and had depended on Monty's mother, who had been his secretary, PA, and book-keeper. Monty had intended helping him out just until she could find a suitable assistant for him, and now, nine years on, she was still with him and had become his right hand.

Although sometimes regretting that she had abandoned her art, her biggest love in life, Monty enjoyed the challenge of her work and was fiercely proud of her father. Largely as a result of his own enthusiasm, she had gone from being profoundly uninterested and ignorant about science, to having a fascination and deep respect for it.

Anna and Mark Sterling lived in a tumble-down Georgian farmhouse on the edge of a Berkshire village, ten miles from Monty's cottage, and Mark brought in an increasingly large salary as a lawyer in a London practice. Anna had always been a character who liked to be in control of every situation, and even tried to organize her friends' lives, but recently Monty had begun to notice that in spite of her growing success she seemed to be losing some of her grip.

Normally strict with her pets, Anna allowed her new puppy, a boxer named Buster, to run around unchecked. As they sat in the untidy kitchen, Monty watched as the dog emptied the contents of the wastebin on to the floor without a word of admonishment from Anna, who simply refilled their glasses with white wine and ignored it.

Monty studied her, a little alarmed at the changes she was

noticing. Anna was an attractive girl, but she put on weight easily and she was definitely doing so at the moment; although parcelled as she was in a sloppy joe and shapeless trousers, it was hard for Monty to tell quite how much.

'Anna, you don't look happy,' Monty said. 'What's wrong?'

Her friend shoved the bottle of Australian Chardonnay along the pine table as if moving a chess piece. She stared morosely at the table. 'I'm infertile. I can't bloody conceive.'

'I – I didn't know you wanted to,' Monty said, taken aback.

'We've been trying for two years. My period started this morning – three weeks late. I really thought that this time was it.' She pursed her lips tightly.

'Have you been to see anyone?'

'I've had a checkup – they've looked at my tubes, everything seems to be working fine. Mark's had his sperm count done – he's producing enough to impregnate the entire population of China.'

'Why didn't you tell me about this?'

'I don't know.' She slopped some more wine into her glass. 'It just makes me feel so bloody inadequate. I was hoping to surprise you with the really good news that you were going to be a godmother.' She shrugged. 'We have to take my temperature every day, fill out a chart, pick the right days of the month to make love.' She looked at Monty forlornly. 'I'm worried I might never have children.'

'I don't think you should start worrying yet,' Monty said. 'There's tons of things you can do – infertility treatments are very sophisticated now.'

Anna nodded. 'The doctor wants to put me on a drug called Maternox.'

'Maternox?' Monty repeated. 'Yes – that's the one everyone takes these days. It's meant to be the best. That's probably all you need.'

Anna stood up and opened the door of the oven. The tantalizing aroma of lasagne filled the room. She closed the door and sat back down. 'Another ten minutes. Anyway, how's you?'

'I'm OK.'

'Listen, there's a friend of Mark's I want to try to get you

21

together with – his wife has just left him – and he's really nice, I mean seriously nice. Very dishy.'

'So why did his wife leave him?'

'She's a bloody fool. I'll arrange a dinner party some time in the next month – I think you'd like him.'

'What does he do?'

'He's a laywer – one of the big City firms.'

The prospect did not immediately appeal. Although Monty was hugely fond of Anna and liked her arty friends, she invariably found Mark's friends dull and only interested in themselves. 'Sure,' she said flatly.

'He's fun, you'll be impressed. You will!'

'What's his name?'

'Martin Meads.'

Martin Meads. Monty repeated the name silently in her head. It did not do much for her. *Mrs Martin Meads*. That did even less. *Mrs Monty Meads*. No better. 'Sure,' she said. 'Why not?'

'Hey, by the way,' Anna changed the subject abruptly, 'I saw your father on television on Tuesday – switched on Sky News and there he was. He seemed on pretty good form, slagging off the pharmaceutical industry. Actually, the book sounded quite interesting, I might give it a try. Is it as impenetrable as *A Brief History of Time*?'

'Only in parts. There are some good chapters – you'd get through it.'

'How is he?'

'Not easy; he's very stressed at the moment. Things are really tight. All the staff at the lab have agreed to take a ten per cent pay cut to avoid redundancies.'

'I find that incredible with all the acclaim he gets for his work. I don't understand why you have such a hard time getting funding.'

'If he'd agree to let the pharmaceutical industry fund us, we'd have no problem.'

'And he still won't because of his views on patenting?'

'I think he's coming round a little. We're meeting the Chairman of Bendix Schere on Monday. Hey, I just realized – they're the company that makes Maternox!'

'Maybe you can get me a discount . . .'

'I'll ask!' Monty grinned and clinked her glass against her friend's. 'Cheer up. I want to come to a christening in a year's time.'

5

London. October, 1993

'What time are we meeting these shysters?'

'One, Daddy,' Monty said, through clenched teeth as she coaxed the clapped-out fax machine into accepting the letter she was trying to send to Washington. 'We should leave in half an hour.'

At least her father was wearing a suit; that was something. Charcoal grey, single breasted, the cut flattered his burly physique, made his shoulders look straight in spite of the years spent slouching over his experiments. But he was pacing around the office restlessly, like a schoolboy in his Sunday best waiting to be dragged to church.

Bannerman Genetics Research occupied a crumbling Victorian building that had originally been built as a laundry. It was on the fringe of the campus, tucked away beyond the main car park of Berkshire University and for the past three years had been subjected to a constant bombardment of noise and dust from a new science block under construction only yards away.

Monty shared the dingy first-floor office with her father. Every year she thought it was a miracle that their laboratory got its certificate from the Health and Safety Executive without a major review. That was definitely on the cards. All it needed was a new, vigilant inspector and they'd be in for tens of thousands of pounds of expenditure.

She looked fondly through the dividing glass that revealed the main laboratory with its scientists, students and technicians at work. The older generation in their white coats, the younger one in jeans and sweatshirts. Some of these people had been with her father all their working lives. Walter Hoggin, their chief technician, was one of them.

She watched him walking ponderously across the lab now, a gentle giant of a man. He must be nearing retirement, she thought sadly, not looking forward to the day when they would lose him. So long as Walter was there, applying his scrutiny to everything, she knew that in spite of their antiquated premises and equipment the safety of their staff would never be compromised.

'ON LINE TRANSMIT,' appeared in the window of the fax machine. The letter began to feed in, then suddenly slipped sideways, and there followed a series of warning bleeps. Panicking, Monty grabbed the page and tried to retrieve it. It tore in half.

'Damn you!' She glared at the machine in fury and saw an error code number appear in the window. They had spent a hundred pounds having it serviced less than a week ago. The engineer had warned her that it was fit for the scrap heap, but Monty had hoped she might be able to eke another few months out of it.

She opened the cover and carefully retrieved the torn and crumpled remains of the other half of the letter, which she had just typed for her father, accepting an invitation to talk at Georgetown University next autumn. Then she sat down and reprinted it on her equally clapped-out word processor. Money, she thought. God, they needed it.

The forty-nine-storey windowless monolith that housed the headquarters of the Bendix Schere Foundation was situated on the Euston Road in London, dwarfing the building of one of its fellow giants and rivals in the pharmaceutical industry, Wellcome plc and the Wellcome Foundation.

Even in an industry not widely noted for its openness, the Bendix Schere Foundation had a unique mystique; it combined a wide range of public activities, including billions of pounds and dollars donated to medical research charities, with an obsessive secrecy about its ownership and an internal organization that had defeated the investigative attempts of some of the world's most persistent journalists.

From the turnover figures made public in order to satisfy the requirements of the American Food and Drugs Administration and the British Department of Health and Social Security, Medicines Division, Bendix Schere was currently ranked in sixth place among the world's pharmaceutical giants. The company was registered in Liechtenstein and its stock was entirely held in bearer bonds rather than registered share certificates, making the identification of its stockholders as impenetrable to outsiders as access to its buildings. .

The engine of Monty's MG rumbled as a security guard inside a mini fortress checked for authorization, then handed her two green lapel clips and opened the high steel gate in front of them.

She drove into the vast parking lot and headed, through the ranks of immaculate-looking cars, towards the visitors' bay against the far perimeter.

'Doesn't anyone ever drive these cars?' her father murmured. 'They're all bloody spotless.'

He was right; the cars looked as if they'd been driven straight from the showrooms; it was only the registration letters that gave away the fact that they weren't all new.

'Maybe someone'll clean this for us while we're inside,' Monty said, staring at the grime on the white bonnet. She had bought the MG second-hand ten years ago and still loved it dearly. But pressure of work during the past year, and the strain of always juggling their resources, had left her with not even enough free time to give the car the thorough clean and polish it deserved.

The Bendix Building, as it was called, looked as if it had been hewn from a single block of electric blue steel. It rose steeply into the sky, a sleek complexity of razor-sharp lines and dark recesses that gave it, from some angles, the hint of a medieval fortress. Walking across the lot towards the main entrance, Monty could not decide whether she liked the architecture or not, and recalled the controversy when the building had first gone up.

It had its own white sound acoustics equalizers, an artificial daylight system combined with ionizers, which the architects claimed gave a better *feelgood* factor than any natural sunlight environment, and which had been proven to increase productivity. And there had been the sinister rumours. Why, people had asked, had Bendix Schere felt the need for a headquarters without windows? What did they want to hide? Was it simply a design statement? An experiment in futuristic architecture? Or were they performing macabre animal experiments behind those sculpted walls?

It was a mild autumn morning, and neither Monty nor her father wore a coat. She had been debating for several days how to dress for this meeting. In the end she had settled for her black velvet jacket, a white silk blouse, with a jungle-print Cornelia James woollen shawl, a black short skirt and shoes with a medium heel to give her a little more height. She had been described in a newspaper, several years back, as her father's 'petite' daughter. She had tended to avoid flat shoes ever since.

At five feet four inches, there were many times when she wished she was taller, but she had no actual quarrel with her legs. She had been blessed in that department and knew it. It was her hair that was the least predictable part of her appearance: a mass of tangled blonde tresses that buried her shoulders, and which was naturally frizzy. There were some days when it looked great, dynamite even, but there were others when it acted like someone had sprayed it with weed killer.

Monty had inherited almost all her features from her Norwegian mother and after even the lightest exertion her complexion became a picture of Scandinavian health and vitality. But she knew only too well that after months of a long wet winter it could look horribly sallow and pasty.

She was aware of so much she had inherited from her mother, not just in looks but in tastes also. Most was welcome, but one thing was not: ever since the diagnosis of her mother's illness, Monty had carried at the back of her mind the knowledge that one particularly unwelcome gene might have come with the bundle handed down to herself. But she rarely dwelt on it, allaying her fears with the hope that advances in genetic science might find a way of dealing with it before anything happened.

Almost everyone who met Monty enjoyed her company. An intensely positive person, she carried an air of expectancy in her stance, and a sparkle of humour in her face that seemed to touch a chord in people's better natures.

As father and daughter walked up a row of white marble steps, electronic doors slid open and they entered an atrium the height of a cathedral. The white marble theme was continued throughout, giving a subdued neoclassical air. The only colour came from some tubs of evergreen plants.

The far side of the lobby was cordoned off by a line of electronic turnstiles flanked by a long security counter and a battery of monitoring equipment, behind which three uniformed men sat. As they walked over to the counter, one of the men looked up and smiled politely.

He was black, but his face was drained of any depth of colour by some ailment that was clearly affecting him badly. He looked as if he had once been strong and quite tall, but had now lost both height and weight. 'May I help you, please?' His voice had the nasal sound of someone with a cold.

'Yes, we have an appointment at a quarter to one with Sir Neil Rorke.'

'May I have your names, please?'

Monty gave him both their names, which he entered on a keyboard. A printer whined and a moment later he handed them two computerized lapel badges. Monty and her father looked down at the green badges they had been given outside and had already clipped to their breast pockets, then added the new passes. The guard studied the keyboard again, selected another key, and watched the computer screen. Then he smiled at them a second time.

'I'll take you up there.'

He waved them through the turnstile, then led them to the atrium's twin banks of lifts. When he pushed a card into a slot, the nearest doors opened immediately and in almost complete silence. Monty found the absence of noise slightly disconcerting as she stepped into the plushly carpeted and mirrored interior. She noticed, with some surprise, that there was no panel of buttons.

The guard waited courteously for her father, then followed them in, looked up and gave a single nod. The doors began to slide silently shut. Monty followed the direction of his gaze up to a tiny glass sensor above the doors; except it wasn't a sensor, she realized, it was a lens.

Moments later she and her father found themselves delivered by the guard into a palatial anteroom. There were pilasters along the walls and a colour scheme of shades of grey; it gave Monty the sense of having walked on to the set for the closing scenes of *2001: A Space Odyssey*.

An elegant brunette in her early thirties seated behind an island desk in the centre of the room took over from the departing security guard and said pleasantly, but slightly robotically: 'Good afternoon, please have a seat. Sir Neil will be with you in a moment.'

What a place! Monty thought. Gazing around from a grey leather sofa, she noticed that there were several large abstract paintings on the walls, by artists she felt she ought to recognize. Not her taste at all, although no doubt a wise corporate investment, she acknowledged. She compared this palace to their own premises. Bannerman Genetics didn't even have a waiting room; visitors had to stand awkwardly between the desks of the accounts department, shoehorned into a space barely larger than a broom closet.

God, the money here! She eyed her father, wondering what was going through his mind. *Give it a chance, Daddy*, she thought. *Please*.

She had butterflies in her stomach; she wasn't nervous of meeting Sir Neil Rorke, she was frightened of her unpredictable father expressing his disgust at the ostentation of this place and storming out. He was already looking around with a frown on his face.

'Have you noticed – there's nothing here that says anything about the company at all? If I had this kind of space, I'd damned well use it to show off some of my products.'

He sounded in positive humour. *Stay that way*, she thought fervently. *At least just long enough to get a proposal from them!*

She glanced at the brunette who was typing on a keyboard. Monty wondered if the monitor in front of her showed the inside of the lift, and if it was she who controlled it. Then a door opened at the far end of the room and the unmistakable figure of Sir Neil Rorke appeared.

'Dr Bannerman! Miss Bannerman! How very good to meet you!'

The greeting was cheery and friendly, and his voice had the warm, baritone delivery of a seasoned after-dinner speaker. He was dressed in an amply cut chalk-striped suit and his head of thick wavy hair was left flamboyantly long. His face was mapped with broken veins, carrying in its fleshy creases the aura of panelled dining halls, fine wines and the owners' enclosures at race courses. He had about him an air of avuncular cuddliness. In those first moments, it took an effort of concentration for Monty to remember that she was in the presence of one of the world's greatest captains of industry.

He held out a hand that was large and pink. Monty shook it, and was a little taken aback by the power of his grip: it was hard as steel. And at the same time, she felt a spark of something as she met the twinkle in his deep, hazelnut eyes. Not a sexual *frisson*, or anything of that nature, it was more a sense that he understood her, that he knew exactly why she had come here and the problems she faced with her father, and that he wanted to communicate the message to her that he was on her side, that he was in the conspiracy with her and she could trust him.

As he released her hand and turned to her father, she was left with the feeling, from that one fleeting moment, that she had known him all her life. She began to understand now why it was that people warmed to him: in just a few seconds he had become her favourite uncle, they were going to share a special treat together, he was going to take her to the pier and buy her candy floss and a huge ice cream with a chocolate flake sticking out of it.

She glanced surreptitiously at her father, but his face gave nothing away.

'Come through to my office and have a drink. Dr Crowe, our Chief Executive, will be joining us for lunch in a few minutes.' Rorke led the way and Monty walked into a long, plush corridor lined on both sides with more bizarre canvases.

'You once wanted to be a painter, didn't you, Miss Bannerman?' he said, walking beside them, hands behind his back.

Monty frowned, wondering how he knew that. 'Yes – a long time ago.'

'But you're a traditionalist.' He parted his hands and gestured at the abstracts. 'I don't think these are your scene at all.'

She looked back at him, unsure what to reply, surprised and puzzled. 'I – I never got as far as studying abstract art,' she replied, not wanting to be rude.

Rorke smiled benignly, and his voice became melancholic. 'Ah well, you see, life for all of us is full of unmade journeys.' He turned to her father and said pointedly: 'I am sure you would agree, Dr Bannerman?'

I like this man, Monty thought. *I really like this man.*

6

Barnet, North London. 1940

The bedclothes were ripped away and it seemed that the electric light came on simultaneously. The small boy in striped pyjamas, hands folded across his navel, blinked, startled awake from a deep sleep.

'May the Lord forgive you, Daniel Judd.'

His mother's voice. A bony palm struck his cheek, the blow knocking his head sideways, cricking his neck. The cold night air chilled his thin body as his mother glowered down at him, her face framed by grey hair pulled straight and flat into a tight bun, the muscles of her bare neck tense with rage and protruding from her woollen dressing gown.

As the second blow struck he saw his father, also in dressing gown and slippers, glaring at him from the door. Reedy tall, his face leathery, cadaverously thin, tightened further with anger.

'Lord forgive our boy,' his father said, 'for he knows not what he doeth.'

The boy stared up at his parents, blinking against the harsh glare of the bulb. His mother's hand, hard as iron, gripped his wrists, forcing his hands violently apart. 'We've told you!' she said, her voice quavering. 'How many more times do we have to say it?'

He tried desperately to mouth a question, to ask her what she meant, but his throat – constricted with fear – allowed no sound to escape. Another blow struck his face.

'Eternal damnation,' his father's voice intoned. 'That's what you are courting, you evil boy. The Lord our Father in Heaven sees all our sins. To be carnally minded is death; we have to save you from yourself, from the wrath of the Lord.'

'You filthy, disobedient, evil sinner,' his mother's voice raised to a shriek and the boy flinched in fear. And confusion.

'Don't you remember the words of our Lord, boy?' his father said. '*Although they claimed to be wise, they became fools and exchanged the glory of the immortal God for images made to look like mortal man and birds and animals and reptiles?*'

The boy stared, bewildered. No, he did not remember. He was six years old.

'*Therefore God gave them over in the sinful desires of their hearts to sexual impurity for the degrading of their bodies with one another. They exchanged the truth of God for a lie, and worshipped and served created things rather than the Creator – who is forever praised. Amen.*'

The boy stared in silence.

'Amen!' his father said again, more loudly. '*Amen*, boy!'

Daniel Judd warded off another blow from his mother by meekly mouthing, 'Amen.'

There was a brief lull. He lay, terrified, hands by his sides, beneath the seething fury of his parents. Then his mother spoke, her eyes half closed, as if she were in a trance and receiving her instructions from a frequency into which she had just tuned. Her face softened from anger into a serene smile.

'Those who live according to the sinful nature have their minds set on what that nature desires, but those who live in accordance with the Spirit have their minds set on what the Spirit desires. The mind of sinful man is death, but the mind controlled by the Spirit is life and peace. Because the sinful mind is hostile to God, it does not submit to God's law, nor can it do so. Those controlled by the sinful nature cannot please God.'

'You understand that, Daniel, don't you?' his father said, his voice gentle now, pleading.

The boy nodded meekly as his mother continued without pausing for breath. 'You are controlled not by the sinful nature but by the Spirit, if the Spirit of God lives in you.'

'Does the Spirit of God live in you, Daniel?' his father asked.

The boy was silent for a moment then nodded.

'Are you sure, boy?'

'I'm sure, Father.' It came out as a frightened squeak.

'You want to please God, boy?'

'Yes, Father, I want to please God.'

'If anyone does not have the Spirit of Christ, he does not belong to Christ,' his mother said. 'But if Christ is in you, your body is dead because of sin, yet your spirit is alive because of righteousness.'

'Do you understand that, boy?' His father's voice had lost its gentleness.

The boy did not understand, the logic was beyond him. Yet he knew the answers that were expected, knew the only way to get peace, to avoid another slap, to avoid being thrashed or locked in the unheated shed in the garden all night. He nodded, and gave a weakly mouthed 'Yes'.

'You want the Spirit to be living in you, boy, or do you want eternal damnation?' his father said.

'Spirit,' the boy mouthed.

'Speak up, Daniel, I can't hear you and your mother can't hear you, and if we can't hear you the Lord our Father cannot hear you.'

'Spirit,' the boy said again, more loudly, choking on the tears that guttered down his cheeks.

32

'For if you live according to the sinful nature,' his mother continued, 'you will die; but if by the Spirit you put to death the misdeeds of the body, you will live, because those who are led by the Spirit of God are sons of God.'

The father pressed his face close to his son's. So close the son could feel the warmth of human breath, could see chin stubble.

'You do not want to commit any misdeeds of the body do you, boy? Assure your mother and I and, above all, assure our Lord.'

'No mm-mm-middeeds,' the boy said in terror.

'For you did not receive a spirit that makes you a slave again to fear, but you received the spirit of sonship. And by him we cry, *Abba, Father.* The Spirit himself testifies with our spirit that we are God's children.'

'And you want to be one of God's children, don't you, boy? Not one of Satan's?'

'God's children,' the boy mouthed.

'Now if we are children, then we are heirs – heirs of God. Like Christ. And if we share in His sufferings it is in order that we may also share in His glory.'

His parents fell silent. Daniel watched their faces in turn; cold eyes raked him. He had let them down again, even in his sleep, in some way he did not comprehend.

'Do you want us to save you from the Lord's wrath, boy?'

Daniel stared at his father and nodded meekly. He saw his mother slip out of the room.

His father asked again. 'Are you sure you wouldn't rather enjoin with Satan? Suffer the eternal fires of damnation in Hell?'

The boy shook his head.

'Shall we say the Lord's Prayer together, boy?'

Daniel nodded.

'Our Father which art in Heaven,' his father began.

'Our Father which art in Heaven,' the boy repeated as his mother returned to the room with two long leather straps. As they continued to recite the Lord's Prayer, she bound his left arm tightly by the wrist, then tugged it down the outside of the bed, looped the strap tightly around the outside of the metal

33

frame and secured it. Then she did the same with his right arm so that he was lying on his back with his arms pinioned down the outside of the bed.

'It's for your own good,' his father said more gently when his mother had finished. 'To save you from yourself in the eyes of the Lord. To save you from being tempted to touch your forbidden parts.'

'To save us all from the Lord's wrath,' his mother added in her sour, loveless voice. 'To save us from your sins.'

Then they turned the light off and closed the door.

7

London. October, 1993

The Directors' dining room on the forty-ninth floor of the Bendix Building felt so light and airy it seemed to Monty almost impossible to believe that it had no hidden windows with natural daylight streaming in.

The décor was the same Regency grey and white colour scheme as the anteroom; it was furnished with a traditional oval mahogany dining table and matching chairs, and the walls were hung with Impressionist paintings, which was the school she loved most. There was a Degas still life on the wall behind her father, and she found herself unable to stop looking at it. *An original Degas. Not a print or a copy. She was eating her lunch in front of a real Degas!* She had never seen one outside a gallery before.

The menu was superb: grilled scallops, followed by fillet steak, and an exotic fruit salad, along with fine white and red wines.

At least her father had behaved himself so far. In fact, he had been remarkably good company, tucking into his meal and chatting convivially, mostly about genetics, more as if he were at a dinner party with favourite colleagues than at an interview on which his future might depend.

Rorke ate and drank with gusto as well; in contrast, Dr Crowe cut his food one sliver at a time, his slender fingers manipulating his cutlery with surgical deftness. Almost as a foil to Rorke's cheery ebullience, he sat quietly, whilst studying Monty and her father with alert, steely eyes that missed nothing.

He was a lean, sharp-featured man of fifty-two, with a narrow equine face, and his eyes were abnormally close together, giving an intensity to his gaze that Monty found rather unsettling. His lips were strange also, she thought. They were very thin, with a vermilion hue that stood out against his alabaster complexion, their effect being to make him look rather effete.

She had done her homework on Crowe and had been impressed by his background. It was rare in the pharmaceutical industry to have a chief exec who was a scientist, and Crowe undoubtedly could have had a very brilliant career in research if he'd chosen. He had graduated from Cambridge with a double first in biology and pharmacology, then gone to the United States where he had done his masters at John Hopkins on the immune system.

Back in Britain he'd spent three years as a research fellow at the Imperial Cancer Research Foundation. He'd then joined the Clinical Trials division of the Bendix Schere Foundation and become head of it after two years. At the age of thirty-six he was made the youngest main board director in the history of the company. Ten years later, in 1986, he was appointed Chief Executive on the sudden death of his predecessor, who was killed when the company jet crashed in mysterious circumstances during a routine visit to the Bendix Schere manufacturing plant in the Philippines.

Whilst Rorke was a man who had clearly reached the top through inborn leadership quality and force of personality, Crowe struck Monty as more of a manipulator. She had not taken a dislike to him, but at the same time had not warmed towards him in the way she had to Rorke. Yet she knew there were big advantages for her father in having a fellow scientist at the top of the company, because at least they could talk the same language.

Dick Bannerman pushed a wedge of cheese into his mouth, chewing ruminatively. 'Sir Neil, one of the things that's always struck me as curious is the obsession with secrecy that your company – foundation – seems to have.'

Monty looked at the three men anxiously. This was the first hint of hostility from her father. Crowe impassively snapped a biscuit in half; in the silence it sounded like a gunshot.

Rorke smiled, and opened his hands expansively. 'A very reasonable query, Dr Bannerman.'

Monty had noticed that, in spite of the conviviality of the luncheon, their hosts had made no overtures about relaxing the formalities and moving to first-name terms.

'You see,' Rorke continued, 'in our industry we encounter opposition from a great many sources. People object to the mark-ups we make on prescription pharmaceuticals, forgetting that the cost today of developing a new drug and bringing it to the market is upwards of one hundred million pounds, and that we only have a limited patent life in which to recoup those costs. And there are some very unpleasant fanatics among the Animal Rights lot – quite frankly as dangerous as some political terrorist groups. We keep information about our company secret to protect the shareholders, the directors and our staff. Simple as that.'

'Would you be prepared to divulge the shareholders to me?'

After a brief exchanged glance with Crowe, Rorke smiled amiably. 'We're going to put a proposal to you today, Dr Bannerman. If you accept it, I'm sure you'll find there are no secrets kept from you.'

Dick Bannerman leaned back in his chair and looked at the two men in turn. 'So, what is the proposal?'

'We'd like to give you a short tour first, show you some of the work we're doing here and the facilities we have – if you can spare the time?'

Rorke went to the door and opened it. As Monty walked through she sought Rorke's eye and he winked.

They went back into the lift they'd come up in. Rorke looked at the lens above the door and enunciated clearly: 'Sixth floor.'

The door closed and the lift sank swiftly downwards.

'How does that work?' Monty asked.

'A combination of visual and voice recognition,' Crowe said, with a smile of satisfaction. 'Computer identification security. It matches the face of the person giving the command to the image in its data base, combines it with the voice print, then accepts the command. Or denies it.'

The lift stopped and they stepped into a wide corridor with emerald carpeting and pale green walls. One side was much brighter than the other, as if bathed in rays of sunshine streaming through invisible skylights. The doors boasted elegant brass handles, and with the exception of the small observation windows cut into a few of them, and the faintly acrid smell, it felt more like the corridor of a modern five-star hotel than a laboratory.

Rorke inserted a card into a slot, punched a sequence of numbers on the key pad, then courteously ushered Monty and her father into another, equally plush corridor, which stretched into the distance. There was a row of notice boards on either side, with graphs, Department of Health and Safety regulations, and various posters, giving it a slightly more familiar air to Monty, and the acrid smell she always associated with molecular biology labs was stronger here.

'On this floor and the next two above we do pure genetics research,' Crowe said, 'and we also co-ordinate the results from our research campuses in Reading, Plymouth, Carlisle, Bern, Frankfurt and Charlottesville.'

'You're in the process of building new labs at Slough, aren't you?' Dick Bannerman said.

'Yes,' Vincent Crowe confirmed. 'We're building a completely new research campus from scratch. When it's completed in three years' time it will house the largest transgenics laboratory facility in the world.'

'And it's all underground, isn't it?' Dick Bannerman pursued.

Crowe stiffened fleetingly, then smiled. 'The transgenics, yes. I wasn't aware that was public knowledge.'

'Twenty-seven acres of underground labs, I believe?' Bannerman said, then stopped, momentarily distracted by a computer screen on the wall that was an electronic notice board. The screen was headed: **BENDIX SCHERE NEWSNET**, and a flashing announcement beneath it read: **MATERNOX-11 RECEIVES FDA APPROVAL**.

'Twenty-*eight* acres,' Crowe said.

'Why underground? Security?'

'Precisely.'

'And you think that kind of environment will be conducive to work? To getting the best out of people?'

'How do you find the atmosphere in here, Dr Bannerman?' Crowe asked.

'It's very impressive,' he said. 'I have to admit that. I find it hard to believe there aren't any windows.'

'It won't be any different at Slough. There's no magic formula about daylight – in fact much of daylight, as you know, is highly corrosive. We've simply applied science, sifted the good qualities and filtered out the bad. Productivity here in the Bendix Building is thirty per cent higher than in conventional working environments.'

'I'd like to see how you arrived at those figures,' Bannerman said sceptically.

Monty gave him a cautioning glance. It was all going so well, she want him blowing it now with a sudden display of temper.

'Happily,' Crowe said. 'We are so convinced by the figures that we are installing artificial daylight environments in our new hospitals, and we believe they'll cut a substantial percentage off recovery times.'

The innovative ethos of Bendix Schere excited Monty. She was experiencing, in this rather futuristic building, in the presence of these enormously powerful and influential men, the sensation of being a privileged insider at the very cutting edge of science.

Rorke led them into a vast lab that left Monty speechless with envy. She had simply never seen any laboratory, anywhere, so well equipped and so orderly: rows and rows of white work surfaces brimming with state-of-the-art lab technology. The staff, all wearing white coats, seemed to have a luxurious amount of space and through the air of concentrated

38

efficiency Monty could almost feel the progress that was being made.

Her father pointed to a television camera above the door. 'What's that for?' he said suspiciously.

'Safety,' Crowe replied. 'If someone's working here on their own late at night or over a weekend, and they have an accident, they might need help. This way Security can keep an eye on all the labs in use and act swiftly.'

Rorke led them on through more labs, some even larger, some much smaller, all equally well equipped. Monty compared all this to their own dingy Victorian premises. They could have fitted Bannerman Research Laboratories into a single floor of this building a dozen times over, and as she thought of their hopeless struggle to survive she began to feel increasingly angry. Angry at governments which had ignored the importance of scientific research for decades, angry at all the organizations and foundations which had made her father beg like a dog for every scrap of money. She looked at him now, hoping against hope that some of the excitement of this place was rubbing off on him also.

'Ah, Mr Seals!' Crowe said, raising his voice suddenly to hail a long-haired man in a white coat who had just emerged from one door and was about to go through another. When he realized it was Crowe and Rorke, he straightened his shoulders and immediately walked up to them.

'Mr Seals is Chief Lab Technician for our genetics department. This is Dr Bannerman and his daughter, Miss Bannerman.'

Monty watched Seals' face as he gave her father a look of recognition and admiration, and then said politely: 'Very pleased to meet you both.'

He was in his mid-thirties, with lank brown hair that tumbled across his forehead and rested on his shoulders. When he tossed it back with a practised motion a single stud was revealed in his left ear. He would have been very good-looking if it wasn't for the ravages of teenage acne that had left his skin slightly pockmarked.

'You have quite a set-up here,' Dick Bannerman said.

'Thank you. I'm afraid a lot of the techniques we're

employing are based on your own work in your published papers.'

'Nothing to apologize for,' Bannerman said. 'That's why I publish them – to share knowledge. Do *you* share it too?' he asked pointedly.

Seals reddened. 'I'm afraid that's not my decision.'

'I guess you have a lot of bricks and mortar to pay for here.'

'Modern equipment *is* very expensive, Dr Bannerman, as I'm sure you appreciate.'

Monty admired the way the young man first held his ground, and then became increasingly animated as he explained the new generations of gene-sequencing machines they had just got up to speed. She saw in him a lot of youthful energy and a sense of purpose, of mission. Without realizing it, she found herself comparing him to their elderly plodder of a Chief Lab Technician, Walter Hoggin, for whom computers continued to remain a mystery, and anything hi-tech was something to be regarded with suspicion. And she knew that however fond of Walter she might be, it was people of the calibre of this Seals character that they really needed – but could not afford.

A squat gold frog, the size of a football, occupied centre stage of Sir Neil's massive desk. Monty wondered if it was a trophy and thought, irreverently, that it was not dissimilar to Rorke's own shape. She disliked frogs and this one had a reptilian smile that made her shudder when she glanced at it.

There were few other items on the desk: a leather blotter, a silver receptacle for pens, a dictating machine and telephone, and a computer terminal. There was not a single sheet of paper in sight anywhere in the office, and she suddenly realized that she couldn't remember seeing any paper in any of the labs either.

To the right of the desk was a tall, white machine that Monty at first thought might be connected with the air system. She had noticed similar machines in all the downstairs labs. Then she recalled seeing such a machine in a movie recently, and realized what it must be: a paper shredder.

The four of them were seated at a conference table, ready to drink the tea just poured by Rorke's secretary. Rorke picked up his spoon and began to stir his cup, then he spoke.

'Dr Bannerman, let's be direct with each other. I know your views about patenting scientific discoveries, and in particular human genes, and I'm not unsympathetic. But in the real world, money has to come from somewhere, and our profits at Bendix Schere come from the manufacture of pharmaceuticals on which we hold patents.' He raised a hand. 'The life of a patent in the UK is only twenty years. We have exclusivity for that period. But considering the resources we have to invest in developing our products, it's really a very short time.'

Monty wondered if her father was going to launch into one of his antipatenting polemics, but to her relief he sat impassively, staring back at Rorke. He had obviously been impressed by what they'd been shown that afternoon, and whilst he might have strong opinions, and contempt for the establishment, he was no fool. And what he had seen today was a display of the finest research tools that money could buy.

'We could kick some funding into your laboratory in Berkshire,' Rorke went on. 'But I don't think we'd get the best value for our investment that way, and frankly I don't think, even with proper funding, that you can reach anywhere near your true potential with your current set-up. Dr Crowe and I both believe you're the finest genetics scientist in this country, and probably the world. And you still have a great many highly productive years ahead of you, whether we do business together or not.'

Bannerman smiled, waiting for the crunch.

'If you were given the right facilities, and the right funding, I think you could achieve very much more – and that's not to demean all you've done to date.'

'What kind of facilities?'

'The kind you've seen down on the sixth, seventh and eighth floors here; the kind we have at our UK plants in Reading, Birmingham and Edinburgh. Or overseas in Bern, Frankfurt and Charlottesville.' Rorke paused and picked up his teacup. 'Our proposal is very simple: we'd like you to join the Bendix Schere Foundation as head of our entire worldwide genetics research programme.'

Bannerman shook his head. 'I'm very flattered, gentlemen, but I'm a scientist not a businessman. I want to do research – not run an organization.'

'I think perhaps Sir Neil hasn't made it quite clear,' Crowe said. 'Research is exactly what we *want* you to do, and nothing else. You would have the entire human resources and all the facilities in the Bendix Schere Foundation to utilize in any way you wanted.'

Dick Bannerman didn't miss a beat. 'I couldn't abandon my own staff.'

'I don't think that would be a problem,' Rorke said, looking expectantly at Crowe.

'No,' Crowe said, a little hesitantly. 'I'm sure we could keep your key people.'

'*All* my staff are key people,' Bannerman said. 'It's damned hard getting work of the kind they're specialized in. I'd want an assurance from you that there wouldn't be one single redundancy before I even considered any proposal. And I'd want your assurance that my daughter could continue to work as my right hand.'

'I'm sure we could give such an undertaking,' Rorke said genially, ignoring the warning signal Crowe was trying to communicate with his eyes.

There would have to be some give and take over staff, Monty knew, but she was thrilled by the proposal, and encouraged that at least her father had not rejected it out of hand.

'Could you tell us exactly what budget would be available, and what remuneration we'd receive?' she asked, eager to have the details made concrete.

Crowe smiled and produced, seemingly from thin air, two identical documents, one of which he handed to Monty, the other to her father. They were the first actual pieces of paper Monty had seen in the building.

The bold wording at the top said: **RESTRICTED CIRCULATION: MAIN BOARD DIRECTORS ONLY. FROM THE CHAIRMAN'S OFFICE.**

Beneath was the heading: 'Proposals for the Acquisition of Bannerman Genetics Research Laboratories.'

'They are buggers, these people, aren't they?' Dick Bannerman said as the lift sank rapidly down towards the ground floor.

Monty raised a finger to her lips, looking warily at the lens above the door. 'They might be listening,' she whispered.

He shrugged, but said nothing more until they were outside the building and walking towards the car.

'Why did you say they are *buggers*, Daddy?'

'Laying on that fancy lunch – thinking I'm going to be impressed by something like that.'

'*I* was impressed,' she said. 'I was very impressed with the company and with them.'

'They've got some decent kit,' he said. 'A few gizmos we could do with.'

'A *few*?'

'I can see the plus points,' he said. 'But I can also see one hell of a lot of minuses.'

'I can't see any minuses,' she said. 'None at all.'

8

London. Saturday 22 October, 1994

DR BRUCE KATZ. MR DUNSTAN OGWAN. INTERNATIONAL FACTORS. MRS V. ALASSIO. MR JOHNSON – FORD MOTOR COMPANY. R. PATEL. A. COHN. CROSSGATES TRAVEL. MR OBERTELLI. MISS REDMAYNE.

Conor Molloy surveyed the battery of signs that greeted the passengers exiting from the customs channels into the arrivals concourse at Heathrow, then stopped when he couldn't see his own name amongst them. He leaned on the brake bar of his baggage cart, scanned the sea of faces and handwritten placards more carefully.

In his early thirties, at a shade over six feet tall, with his short black hair fashionably gelled and shovelled haphazardly backwards, even red-eyed with jet-lag he cut a striking figure, and several of the people waiting to greet passengers looked at him, wondering if he was a movie star they ought to recognize.

Both his outfit and his face shouted *Entertainment Industry*: he was dressed in an open-necked denim shirt over a white t-shirt, washed-out cotton chinos with rugged boots, and a suede bomber jacket. His face had elements of both Tom Cruise and Tim Robbins but was an improvement on each. Conor Molloy possessed, by almost any criteria, drop-dead good looks. Much of his charm came from the fact that he was unaware of this. In fact, in his chosen profession, looks did not matter at all; he would have made exactly the same progress if he had been born the Elephant Man.

His eye was eventually caught by a man pushing his way through the jostling crowd, and he realized that this was his driver.

'Conor Molloy? Charley Rowley! We're going to be working together. Fucking awful traffic this morning – thought I was going to miss you!'

'The flight came in a little early, I guess. Pilot said we had a strong tailwind,' Conor replied, taking an instant liking to the man's cheery nature.

They shook hands. Although Charley Rowley was also only in his thirties, from the way he was puffing and perspiring he seemed badly out of shape. Ignoring Conor's protest, he wrestled the baggage cart away from him and began pushing it across the concourse.

The American hurried along in pursuit, holding his shoulder bag, containing his laptop computer, which he had not let out of his sight on the journey. 'It was good of you to come – you needn't have worried – I could have taken a cab.'

'The Directors wouldn't hear of it! BS is very big on the personal touch. You've heard the slogan "The World's Most Caring Company"? Well, that applies to its staff as well as its customers.'

Conor detected the note of cynicism. 'Yeah, well, it's still good of you to give up a Saturday morning.'

Rowley sniffed and said with a grin, 'Yah, I think so too!'

As he accompanied Rowley through the exit and into the car park, Conor was careful not to say too much. No one was to be trusted. *No one*. He had waited twenty-five years for this opportunity, had worked himself into the ground to get the qualifications, and finally pulled off what he had once thought to be an impossible goal. He was aware that his mother's fears for his safety were wholly justifiable, and he did not underestimate the intelligence, the resources and the sheer power of what he was up against. He knew that with just one slip he could lose his chance for ever – and very probably his life.

'Shit!' Conor looked around his apartment with a broad grin. 'This is all mine?'

Charley Rowley nodded.

Conor walked across the living-room floor and stared out of the window. He could see right across Hyde Park to the hazy silhouettes of South Kensington beyond. The morning sun glinted like foil on the dewy grass; he saw a jogger, and a woman walking a string of assorted dogs. Traffic poured down the Bayswater Road beneath him. It made a different sound from the traffic in Washington; there it was the tramp of rolling tyres, here it was the grinding roar of trucks, and the diesel rattle of idling taxis.

'Great view!' He stifled a yawn and wished he hadn't drunk so much on the plane, nor smoked so much. Nerves. His nerves had got to him on the flight. Now his brain was muzzy and a sharp band of pain ran down the centre of his forehead. He felt unwashed and grungy, and was aware of the smell of his body through his crumpled shirt; his trousers had rumpled and his feet felt sweaty from spending the night inside his insulated boots. But in spite of that he was on a high right now, adrenaline running.

He fancied strong coffee and a cigarette, but decided to be careful about the cigarette; Charles Rowley might not smoke and he didn't want to start off giving a bad impression. At least that was one compensation about living alone: he no longer had to worry about someone else's health fascism.

Since splitting up with his live-in girlfriend eighteen months back, he'd been enjoying the luxury of not having to sneak out into the street whenever he fancied a smoke, or write down the units of alcohol he drank in a daily log. He looked forward to the possibility of a sexual fling with someone in England, but not an emotional relationship. He was going to need all his wits about him in the coming months, and wanted minimum distractions.

'That view gets even better in mid-summer,' Rowley said, 'when the crumpet lies out there topless.'

Conor grinned. 'Think I can hang on to this place until next summer?'

Rowley yawned, as if he had been infected by the American's tiredness. 'Someone from Human Resources will be along to see you on Monday about finding a permanent pad.'

Then he eyed the two heavy suitcases in the doorway with their dog-eared Washington baggage tags, and the Duty Free carton of Marlboro beside them. 'OK, I'd better leave you to get settled in. You must be knackered.'

'Want a coffee first?'

Rowley squinted at his watch and wavered. 'Yah, OK, thanks, just a quick one. The kitchen should be stocked – there's a woman who looks after the BS apartments and she'll get you anything else you need.' He checked his watch again. 'I have to pick my girlfriend up – going to a charity ball down in Dorset this evening, otherwise I'd have suggested doing something.'

'I'll be fine. I'm going to crash out for a few hours then take a wander around – try to see some of the sights. Might catch a movie if I can stay awake.' Conor nodded at the thick envelope packed with magazines and papers he'd just been given. 'And you've left me enough reading material on the company to keep me occupied most of the weekend.'

They went through into the kitchen, which looked as if it had never been used, and searched their way through the fitted units for the coffee and cups.

'Got any friends over here?'

Conor shook his head, and gave the answer he'd been

rehearsing for months: 'A few ancestors kicking around some place in Ireland; we're not a very tight-knit family.'

'Irish ancestry?'

'Yup – but we don't make any big deal about it.'

'You're not married, right?'

'Nope.'

Rowley grinned. 'Next question: couldn't help noticing the carton of cigarettes – do you smoke?'

'Uh huh,' Conor said guardedly.

'Brilliant! Join the Bendix Schere Speakeasy!'

'What do you mean?'

Rowley pulled a pack of Silk Cut from his pocket and offered one to Conor. 'Bendix Schere's a no-smoking company.' He clicked a gold Dunhill and held it up to give Conor a light.

Conor inhaled. 'We have plenty of those in the States.'

'As extreme as BS?'

'Extreme?'

'You're not just forbidden to smoke on the premises, you're forbidden to smoke at all, anywhere . . . ever.'

'You don't mean at home?'

'At home, on holiday, on Mars.' Rowley began opening and shutting cupboard doors searching for a substitute ashtray. He finally settled for a saucer.

'Any other regulations I ought to know about?' Conor began to fill the kettle.

'You mean they didn't send you a list?'

'Maybe I didn't read the small print.'

Rowley shook his head. 'The Bendix Schere bylaws are seriously unreal; there's pages of them; it's written into your contract of employment that you learn them by heart. You didn't read that?'

'I saw the clause but I don't remember seeing a copy of the actual bylaws.'

'They probably didn't want to scare you off. You don't drink, do you?'

Conor looked alarmed. 'Drink? Alcohol? Sure I drink.'

Rowley wagged a finger reproachfully. 'Naughty boy. Drinking is strictly *verboten*! No one is permitted to enter company premises within twenty-four hours of having consumed alcohol.'

'That *is* unreal!' Conor said indignantly.

'If the Thought Police catch you, you're out; for good.'

'The who?'

Rowley sniffed again. 'S'what I call them. Security.'

Conor said nothing.

'You want me to go on? Your car, right – you'll be getting a car on Monday – it should have been ready for you today, but there was a cockup. You *have* to keep that car clean. The Thought Police patrol the car park. They see a dirty car belonging to a staff member, they take it away and they return it a week later with an eighty-nine pound bill for valeting. Docked from salary.'

Conor stared at him. 'You're not serious?'

'I'm serious. You want the honour of working for Bendix Schere, you play by their rules. Everyone who works for BS knows there's a long queue pressing up against their back, waiting for their job. They pay the best, they have the finest equipment and some of the finest people. Their gameplan is to become the largest pharmaceutical company in the world and that's where they're heading. I've met a lot of folks who are actually shit scared of this company.'

'Employees?'

Rowley glanced around the kitchen, sizing it up. 'Yah. And outsiders in related industries. BS has long tentacles and they're spreading all the time.'

'A lot of subsidiaries, right?'

'You can't believe what they own. In a couple of years they'll control the world baby-food market. They own half the over-the-counter pharmaceutical companies in this country, in Europe and in the States, and they're buying up generics companies around the world in a kind of feeding frenzy.'

'I heard,' Conor said.

'Did you also hear about their retail operations?' Rowley said, his voice dropping a fraction.

'Retail?'

He nodded. 'Retail pharmacy. They own PriceSave Drug-Smart, one of the largest pharmacist chains in Britain.'

Conor frowned; PriceSave DrugSmart were also one of the largest mall pharmacist chains in the States, but his research into Bendix Schere had not revealed any connection to them. 'I didn't know that,' he said.

'You're not meant to.' Rowley unscrewed the cap from a jar of Nescafé, as the kettle hissed. 'You're also not meant to know that they fund the United States Herpes Association, the World Psoriasis Group and the International Arthritic Association – among other leading charities.'

'A lot of pharmaceutical companies give charitable donations, surely?'

'Sure – *donations*. With BS it's more than just donations. They actually fund them. *They* control them and *they* appoint the trustees.'

'So these charities all recommend Bendix Schere drugs in their newsletters?'

'Exclusively. And they trash all the competitors' products.'

'Even if they're better?'

'Especially if they're better.'

Conor began to wonder how much more about the company his research had failed to show up.

Rowley raised his eyebrows, and added, a trifle defensively, 'They're not doing anything different from their competitors – except perhaps doing it better.' He held up the coffee jar. 'One spoon or two?'

'Two, thanks.' Conor tapped ash off his cigarette, his mind working hard. The kettle rumbled as it came to the boil then switched itself off, and he poured the water into their cups.

'Best thing to do, Conor, is not get too stressed about it. They pay well and there are a few OK people amongst the dross. Just keep your head down and get on with it, and before you know it you'll be sixty-five and collecting your pension!'

Conor blinked slowly. *You might be*, he thought. *But not me, baby*.

With that, Charley Rowley stubbed out his cigarette, took two gulps of coffee, tugged on his battered Barbour and shook Conor's hand. Wishing him luck, he told him he looked forward to seeing him on Monday.

'Oh – by the way,' he said. 'When we meet in the office I'm *Mr* Rowley and you're *Mr* Molloy, OK?'

'Sure,' Conor said, a little surprised.

'Another rule,' he said. 'No first-name terms between staff at any time. Under the terms of our contracts I could be sacked for calling you *Conor* in here.'

'Lucky no one's listening,' Conor said.

Rowley gave him an odd smile. 'Don't bank on it.'

'You mean that?'

He shook his head. 'Not so much here – but be careful in the office – you never know when the Thought Police might be eavesdropping.'

'Great!'

'You get used to it. We all seem to survive!' Then he sloped off down the corridor towards the lift.

Conor closed the door, sensing the void Rowley had left behind. He was alone now, really alone for the first time, in a foreign country, and the extent of his task seemed to have grown. He looked around the apartment, walking from room to room, checking it out, and wondering if it really might be bugged. But there was nothing anyone was going to pick up from him with a microphone.

Three bedrooms, one really sumptuous and each with bath and shower. Designer kitchen, and an amazing living room the size of a football pitch . . . bare parquet floor scattered with oriental rugs; big soft sofas, stark chromium lamps and chairs that looked like they'd been lifted from the Museum of Modern Art. This pad had *style*. Like something out of a commercial. It disgusted him.

He poured himself a second coffee, then unpacked his Macintosh PowerBook, opened the lid and switched on. While it was booting up, he unwound the modem lead, slipped the plug into the rear of the computer, then knelt down on the floor, pulled out the phone jack from the wall, and inserted the modem jack in its place.

After a further thirty seconds the machine was ready. He opened the eMail program and checked for messages. There were two. The first was from a long-time associate-cum-pal, Dave Schwab, who now worked at the US Patent Office, wishing him good luck in his new job. The second had no sender identification and was entirely encrypted into seemingly meaningless letters and digits.

Conor opened his encryption program, moved his cursor to the box marked 'Decode' and clicked on it.

9

Monday 5 September, 1994
Alan Johnson woke with a start. The smash of breaking glass. His chest felt as if it were caught in a wrench. Sarah . . . thrashing about beside him. Screaming.

'Do something! Alan, for God's sake *do* something!'

She was shaking, convulsing, her body twisting from side to side. His right arm sent the clutter on his bedside table to the floor, his glasses amongst it; found the light, pressed the switch, turned to look at her.

Oh, God!

Her face was bloated one side, hideously contorted and distended like a rubber mask the other; her eyes, encased in black rings, were bulging and focusing wildly. Her skin was clammy, complexion opaque, except for the red spots and dark scabs where the livid ravages of the burning rash were attacking her.

She thrashed to the right, the left, howling like someone possessed. Her stomach rose up under the bedclothes; she twisted again, seemingly in mid-air, fell on to her swollen belly, rose, fell down again, chewed the pillow in her agony, shuddered with a convulsion that crashed through her like an aftershock, tearing a moan from deep inside her.

'Darling,' he said, anxiety constricting his voice. 'Darling, what's happening – is it starting? The baby coming? I'll call the doctor.'

She spun round on to her back. He pulled the bedclothes off and stared wide-eyed; it was as if the baby she was carrying

51

had gone berserk, was trying to bash its way out through her stomach. It was punching her, kicking her. He could see where sections of her skin had stretched, shrunk; her stomach extended so far he thought for one ghastly moment the skin would burst and a hand or a foot would come through.

He jumped off the bed, grabbed the phone, hunting in the address book at the same time, and dialled the doctor. Eight and a half months: she wasn't due for another fortnight but she had been so ill with the rash, nausea, headaches. And no one had been able to do anything. They were scared to give her painkillers in case they harmed the baby. And they didn't know what was wrong. A virus, they said. Unidentified viruses do sometimes strike, Dr Humphreys had explained. The phone rang, then gave way to a bland cold voice at the other end.

'Dr Humphreys, please,' gasped Alan.

'Dr Humphreys is not on call tonight. I can page Dr Anselm for you.'

'It's an emergency!'

'I don't know how quickly I can get him. If you're very worried, you had better call an –'

The rest of her sentence was drowned by a horrendous scream from his wife. 'Doooo something! Alan, quick! please do –' Her voice dissolved into a choking gargle.

He turned and the wrench around his chest tightened. 'No, God, no. Sarah!' Blood was spewing from his wife's mouth, spattering the pillow. He depressed the phone cradle with his hand and dialled '999'. Pressed his free hand to her clammy forehead. 'Be OK, going to be OK, going to be fine.' It was just like she was plugged into an electrical socket, shimmying, pulsing, then contorting.

Alan Johnson stood watching his wife stretched out on the metal table in the cramped Casualty resuscitation room, surrounded by emergency paraphernalia and figures in green surgical scrubs – attaching lines, hooking up tubes, adjusting monitors.

He had married relatively late, at thirty-seven, largely due to his shyness with the opposite sex. A slightly built man of old-fashioned values, he worked as a junior accountant in an engineering firm and had met Sarah at Bible study at their local church. She was a quiet, gentle girl, who had worked as a book-keeper with a pharmaceutical research laboratory until five months into her pregnancy when she'd become too unwell. She had a straight bob of light brown hair which she normally kept immaculately neat, and which was in keeping with her shy demeanour. Her screams were as out of character as the tangled hair matted and plastered to her face. His heart heaved as he watched a nurse standing over her, holding an oxygen mask to her face; they had tried to get an endotracheal tube down but all her muscles had gone into spasm, rejecting everything, as if her body was trying with every ounce of remaining strength to expel the baby.

He squeezed his wife's cold, sticky hand, but there was no response. He tried again, looked pleadingly at her eyes for some sign but they were closed. He stared wildly around the room: at the anaesthetist who was busy changing a bag on to a drip stand; at the obstetrician who was bleary-eyed from being dragged out of bed at three in the morning.

'Is she going to be all right?'

Experienced grey eyes stared back at him from above the mask. The voice was deep and soft, with a reassuring tone to it, but could offer little to go on now. A finger pointed to the jagged orange graph-line on the foetal heart-trace monitor. 'Mr Johnson, that's showing us the baby is hyperactive, with prolonged episodes of bradycardia. The heart rate is consistently below eighty, and the baby is suffering severe foetal distress.' A hesitation. 'We're going to have to do a Caesarean if we want to try to save the baby, but there's a real possibility your wife might not survive the anaesthetic; she's extremely weak. I'm afraid you are going to have to make the decision.'

'Decision?' Alan Johnson echoed, barely comprehending. He questioned the obstetrician's calm eyes, and his voice began trembling. 'Wh-what d-do you – you advise?'

The obstetrician broke it to him as gently as he could. 'Mr Johnson, I don't think your wife has any chance of surviving unless we operate; the baby will kill her if this goes on. There is a chance if we operate that she will live – and that the baby will also.'

Alan Johnson wrung his hands. Slowly he nodded. 'Go ahead, please, you'd better go ahead.'

They allowed him into the operating theatre and he stood at the rear, in a gown, mask and white clogs, beside the anaesthetics machine, his eyes switching from his wife's motionless face to the dials of the monitors. He was thinking of the cot in the small upstairs room of their home, with the yellow walls and blue skirting board that he'd painted himself, and the paper frieze of nursery rhymes that he and Sarah had put up together . . . the pram, and the toys and clothes they had bought although they had not known whether it would be a boy or a girl.

Until the past few months their marriage had been utter bliss. He had never felt so happy in all his life. He should have realized, he knew, that there was a price to pay. God never gave without asking for something in return, although sometimes it was hard to understand the reasons behind His requests. But God was always right, and they knew that whatever pain He put them through, He loved them both as dearly as they did Him.

God had tested them for the first three years of their marriage by not permitting Sarah to get pregnant, in spite of their regular and passionate love-making. They understood the value of this test was to make them realize that human life could not be taken for granted, nor could the right to create it. Dr Humphreys had prescribed a course of a fertility drug called Maternox, and within three months of starting to take it, Sarah had fallen pregnant.

Alan could remember the joy as they had sat together in Dr Humphreys' small surgery and he had confirmed the news that she was indeed expecting a baby. He thought back with tears in his eyes to those early days of her pregnancy. Apart from the small growing bump, Sarah had hardly seemed affected. None of the symptoms you read about, like morning sickness or strange food crazes. Then she had lost colour from her face and suddenly started feeling very tired, drained of energy. Anaemia, the doctor had told them, nothing to worry about; he had prescribed a course of vitamin supplements and for a while afterwards she had seemed fine.

Fine until she had learned the company she was working for was being taken over and rumours were rife that there would be redundancies. A week later the first attack of the rash had struck. Just a small, localized reaction on the right-hand side of her chest and over the top of her shoulder, which Dr Humphreys had diagnosed as shingles, brought on by the stress of fearing about her job. But even he had been surprised how quickly it had faded.

It was a few weeks later that she had complained of the first headache; he remembered her lying in bed, clamping her skull between her hands and fighting back tears. Then the nausea and the vomiting. Dr Humphreys had become alarmed. For a month she had been able to hold down very little food and he had suggested she should be admitted to hospital. But Sarah was an independent creature and had not wanted that.

So Alan had taken time off work to look after her, nursing her night and day, exhausting himself, applying ointment and damp towels to the painful rash that had returned with a vengeance in the past month. And which now lay, like burn blisters, in large swathes across her body. Dr Humphreys had had Sarah examined by a dermatologist, who suspected a virulent form of psoriasis, and had taken a biopsy for laboratory analysis. But the rash matched no known strain of psoriasis. The dermatologist's final diagnosis was that it was a symptom of an unidentified virus that had infected her. He explained that such viruses attacked at random, and there was no other cure than medical supervision, and time.

'I've never seen a viral rash like this,' the obstetrician said quietly to Alan. 'Have you been abroad somewhere?'

'No one's identified it yet,' Alan Johnson said. 'The Centre for Tropical Diseases thin –'

His voice was cut short as his wife's belly seemed suddenly to stretch in three different directions at once; for an instant the bare skin looked like molten lava bubbling in a volcano. The obstetrician stepped back to her side and the team of medics closed in around Alan's wife, blocking his view.

He still stood at the back of the small theatre, fearfully

scanning the readouts on the digital gauges. He identified the pulse monitor, watched with sickening despair as the orange waves and troughs seemed to be getting smaller and smaller. He pressed his hands together and closed his eyes, whispering quietly: 'Please God, don't let her die, don't let my darling Sarah die, let her live, please let her live.'

Then he said the Lord's Prayer, followed by more prayers, then the Lord's Prayer again. Prayer sustained him during the next few minutes, then he swayed giddily, and had to steady himself against a tiled wall. *Can't pass out, not now, can't.*

There was a sudden flurry around the operating table. Two orderlies had wheeled in a large box of apparatus on wheels. He heard the sharp hiss of compressed air. Then again, then a silence. He opened his eyes and the room slid past him as if he were viewing it through a train window. A hand took his arm, he heard the obstetrician's voice, gentle but weary.

'I'm sorry, Mr Johnson.'

He looked down at his wife through tear-filled eyes. One of the nurses was already turning off the drips that had been sustaining her. Another was disconnecting the wires from a monitor. Her belly still thrashed wildly and Alan found himself having to comprehend in a single moment that his wife was dead but that their child was still alive inside her.

Then the surgeon made an incision down Sarah's navel. A band of blood followed the blade's path.

'I —' Alan mouthed. 'I – she's – she's –?' His voice trailed and no one noticed that he had spoken; they were all concentrating now, two nurses clamping back the cut skin, the surgeon pushing his gloved hands inside the opening, a third nurse swabbing. His view became blocked.

Then a surgically gloved hand raised into the air a tiny, wriggling creature trailing a long white cord.

Alan Johnson's spirits lifted a fraction. The creature was moving. Sarah's baby! *Their* baby. Their baby was born! God had made this bit go right!

He pushed his way through the forest of green gowns, barely registering the sudden eerie silence, not seeing the frowns above the masks.

Then he froze. Stared in disbelieving horror. At the creature. The child. His and Sarah's child.

No. Oh God, please *no*.

The tiny human shape coated in wet blood and vernix was thrashing like a hooked fish. He made himself study the head, where the face should be except there was no face; just a mass of hideously twisted and misshapen flesh; blank skin; no nose, no mouth; just one eye at an odd angle in the centre of what might be the forehead.

'Jesus,' someone behind him said.

'It's alive,' someone else said. 'It's alive.'

'Male.'

Alan stood transfixed; a cowl. He had read somewhere that babies were sometimes born with one; they would take the cowl off in a moment and it would be fine. *He* would be fine; *their son* would be fine.

The surgeon turned the baby round; its back was dark. As Alan looked closer he realized the skin of the baby's back was covered in thick matted hair.

He let out a moan. Someone caught him as his legs buckled. Two nurses helped him towards the door. He tried to walk but his legs would no longer support him. They helped him sit on a chair in the corridor. He saw a fire extinguisher and a hose reel on the wall, felt a cold draught blow on his face. A moment late the obstetrician with bloody gloved hands was standing in front of him, addressing him in a lowered voice.

'I'm afraid the baby is terribly deformed. The little chap doesn't have a face at all. It's a version of a rare malformation caused either by an extra chromosome or possibly the deletion of a small chromosome segment. We don't have sufficient knowledge of DNA to understand the exact cause yet.' He paused for a moment. 'It's called Cyclopism, or Cyclops Syndrome.'

'Just a cowl. Isn't it just a cowl? Can't you remove it?'

The obstetrician shook his head slowly. 'I'm afraid it's not a cowl. I wish it was. Cyclopism happens very occasionally and we can't pick it up from the scans. He's alive now but once we sever the umbilical cord he'll be unable to sustain himself. I think it would be kinder to let him die rather than put him on to life support.'

Alan Johnson shook his head slowly from side to side. 'Can't you do anything? Plastic surgery – can't you –' He was rambling, he knew, clutching at straws.

'It would be best not to do anything,' the obstetrician said quietly but firmly.

Alan sank his face into his hands. He tried to imagine what Sarah would have wanted if she were still – still – he pictured the baby turn in the gloved hand, saw the vernix, the blood, the thick hairs on its back. A tremor shook him, then another. He looked at the surgeon helplessly pleading, beginning to weep, silently at first, then with deep gulping sobs.

10

London. Tuesday 25 October, 1994
At eight in the morning beneath a flinty sky Conor Molloy, harassed after getting lost and taking longer than anticipated, turned his small new BMW across the traffic flow along the Euston Road. He joined one of the lines of cars crawling through the metal security gates alongside the Bendix Building, and showed his ID card to the guard who nodded him through into the car park. In spite of the early hour, it was almost full.

He climbed out of the car, casting a cursory eye over the immaculate grey paintwork. It would be several days before he needed to worry about getting it washed, he thought, mindful of the penalty that Charley Rowley had warned him about.

Rules and regulations. This place had more rules than an institution, and it seemed like every few minutes he discovered another one. He had spent most of his first day at work, yesterday, encountering and learning them whilst getting to know the geography of the building under Charley Rowley's guidance. He had not appreciated when Rowley had met him at the airport that he was the Sectional Manager of Genetics, rather than just a mere colleague. But after only one day with him, Rowley felt even more like a colleague than a boss, and Conor fully intended to cultivate their budding friendship.

He had learnt that Bendix Schere was organized into five directorates: Production, Marketing, Research and Development (R & D), Finance and Secretariat (F & S), and Security – with a maze of sub-divisions within each. Leisure facilities consisted of a luxurious staff canteen, and a very impressively equipped health hydro in the basement, complete with personal training programmes, squash and tennis courts, and an Olympic-size pool.

Rowley had taken him to almost every floor, except for the top three which were off-limits: the forty-ninth was the Directors' enclave, and the two below, which Rowley called the Pentagon, housed the global command centre of security for the entire Bendix Schere Foundation.

Conor had been introduced to a number of heads of department, and he had privately assessed each one as to whether he thought they were loyal company people, or potential rebels like Charley Rowley. To his disappointment almost all of them struck him as zealously dedicated to the Bendix Schere ethos. With a few exceptions within his own department, Group Patents and Agreements, almost all the employees he'd met seemed to be sharply dressed males and females who greeted him with power handshakes accompanied by piercing eyeball contact, and glib phrases of welcome delivered like a foreign language learned by rote.

He noticed also that there seemed to be no unattractive, handicapped or overweight employees, and that the only non-whites were either in Security or menial jobs. There was a uniformity, as if everyone had been hired from a restricted intellectual, personality and appearance band. Or maybe it was the artifice of the building's interior that had this effect on employees after a length of time?

Although just at the start of his second day, Conor had already begun to doubt whether anyone other than Charley Rowley, and a long-haired lab technician called Jake Seals, had any spark of individuality about them. If the science of cloning were more advanced, it wouldn't take a big leap of imagination for him to believe almost everyone else had been cultured in a laboratory from a specific formula.

Conformity, Conor thought as he buttoned his coat against the biting wind and hurried across the lot. Science was about discipline; about systematic observation, experiment and measurement. And yet medicine was always acknowledged as being such an inexact science. By dressing the company up with strange rules and tough procedures, perhaps Bendix Schere felt it could convey the impression to the world that its particular knowledge of medicine was more exact than it really was.

He glanced up at the sculpted windowless edifice of the building, and felt a certain respect despite himself. Then he walked up the marble steps, through the electronic doors and into the white marble interior of the lobby atrium, which was almost deserted. He showed his ID to another guard, swiped his smart-card on a security turnstile and walked across to the lifts.

They were all in use, and as he stood waiting he tried to make out his reflection in the burnished copperplate of a lift door, and checked the knot of his paisley tie.

He was dressed smartly but conservatively, in a plain navy double-breasted suit, white shirt, and navy Crombie great-coat. His hair had been rearranged by the wind and a couple of gelled locks were standing vertically. As he smoothed them down with his hands, he was suddenly conscious of being stared at by a young woman in her late twenties. She was standing beside him, watching him with a look of amusement.

He shuffled his feet and dug a hand in his coat pocket awkwardly. She was quite a bit shorter than him, with a fashionable frizz of long blonde hair and an assertively pretty and intelligent face. A lift announced its arrival and they stepped in; several more people followed. The young woman smiled at him a little triumphantly as if she knew she had caught him out, but there was a hint of interest also. As the crowd jostled them closer together, he smelled the musky scent she was wearing and found it distinctly sensuous.

He looked at her again. Gorgeous greeny-blue eyes full of warmth and humour. She stood out, she was definitely from a different mould. 'Rebellion' was stamped all over her.

The lift stopped on the fifth floor and two men in white overalls got out. The doors closed again. Conor found himself trying to sneak a glance down at her legs but her trench coat blocked his view. 'Like it here?' he asked her.

'In the lift?'

He was slow this morning, the jet-lag seemed to be knocking him and it was a second before he got the joke and grinned. 'Sure – I guess the lift's pretty special. How about the rest of the place?'

'So far. We're still just moving in at the moment. My father and I.' She had a nice voice, confident, punchy.

A couple of people frowned at them. Staff were advised not to converse in the lifts. Security; you never knew who might be in there with you.

She glanced away from him, distracted by some thought that seemed to be troubling her, then caught his eye again and they exchanged a brief silent smile. He shot a surreptitious look at her hands and noticed she was wearing no wedding or engagement ring. Then they stopped at the eighth floor, one of the genetics labs, he remembered, and he watched her step on to the green carpet and walk jauntily away, his eyes staying on her until the door closed. *Nice*, he thought. *Very, very nice. Sparky and approachable.*

The car began to rise and a few seconds later halted at the twentieth floor, which was to be his home for the foreseeable future. The door of the lift opened on to a small reception area staffed by an attractive but frosty young woman who was seated behind a row of monitors on a console, typing.

'Good morning, Mr Molloy,' she said, without even looking up from her screen. Good looks, but cold as ice. He smiled and tried to sound as pleasant as possible.

'Good morning – ah –' Her name momentarily escaped him. Then he remembered. 'Miss Paston.'

Bendix Schere operated a system of anonymous secretaries. Some offices were already equipped with voice-activated word-processor systems, but most correspondence and document generation was produced by secretarial pools with whom the rest of the staff rarely had contact.

The system, Rowley had explained, was simple. There was a dictation icon on your computer terminal screen. You clicked on it and dictation controls appeared. You then dictated a letter or document the usual way, before keying in a command to send it down to the secretarial pool. A short while later, the typed letters or documents would come up on your screen and you could key in any changes or corrections yourself. Any letters would be automatically signed for you by the computer and your copy would be stored on disk.

Miss Hoity-toity still hadn't looked at him, and he walked past her desk, inserted his smart-card into the door behind her, then punched in his code. The lock clicked and he pushed the door open.

Each directorate was colour coded. Group Patents and Agreements (GP & Ags) came under Research and Development and therefore shared the same emerald-green carpeting and pale green walls as the laboratories. But in contrast to the futuristic feeling of the rest of the building, the Group Patents and Agreements Department looked as if it had been there for ever.

It was a labyrinth of narrow corridors lined with cramped offices, and open-plan areas with desk cubicles squeezed too closely together. Despite being spread over three floors, the Department was urgently in need of more space. And although it had all the computerized equipment it needed, most patent work was still carried out on paper and there were filing cabinets wall-to-wall, many of which were decades old. Whole areas were shelved like libraries, and crammed with reference texts.

Even some of Conor's new colleagues looked refreshingly old-fashioned: serious, sedate men in various shades of grey suits with various shades of greying hair, and ties of the wrong colour and width. It seemed to him that any fashion sense in the Department was vested with the women, who looked smart and elegant. And like all patent offices, its studious atmosphere belied the fact that this was the hub around which global fortunes revolved.

GP & Ags was presided over by a team of British and international patent lawyers and patent agents. No product that Bendix Schere invented, developed, bought or tried to sell was of any use to it unless it owned and controlled the patents worldwide, and the Department's role was to get the most comprehensive patents it could – both to protect the company's own products and to block the competitors'. This meant not only rigorously defending the patents, but also using every trick in the book to get their life extended. In extreme cases from time to time they obtained new patents on old products by carefully reformulating those products.

In most countries the limit on patents ranged between seventeen to twenty years, but with annual profits of over £500,000,000 coming in from each of its most successful patented pharmaceuticals, every extra year that could be gained meant massive extra profits for Bendix Schere.

Conor's office was next door to Charley Rowley's, and as he passed by he could see the open briefcase on the desk, indicating that his colleague had beaten him to it. He would apologize later for his time of arrival, he thought, as he stood outside his own office, punching in the code number. Virtually every single door in the Bendix Building had a security combination lock: to reach restricted access areas, such as the laboratories, and the Group Patents floors, a smart-card had to be inserted into a slot as well. From his experiences yesterday, Conor was already finding moving around the premises a real bore.

His office was not much bigger than a cupboard. A gerbil would feel pretty claustrophobic in here, he thought; but at least it was better than open plan, which meant no privacy. He hung his coat and jacket on the rear of the door, squeezed past three steel filing cabinets and the paper shredder and eased himself behind his desk.

For security purposes, wastepaper baskets were strictly forbidden. All unwanted paper had to be fed into the shredders. Bulkier items had to be put into black garbage bags and pushed into a chute, on each floor, down to the basement incinerator. It was a sackable offence to leave any paperwork whatsoever, other than incoming correspondence, on a desk in an unattended office.

The only extraneous items on Conor's desk this morning were a fresh Manila envelope addressed to him, and a crimson leather-bound book, which was embossed with a gold line-drawing of a small boy under a halo, kneeling in prayer. The accompanying wording read: 'The Bendix Schere Creed'.

Conor had looked through the book yesterday in disbelief. All new employees were meant to read it from cover to cover. It told the story of how the company's founder, Joshua Bendix, had made his first fortune peddling invisible ink made from lemon juice. There was even an illustration of the original bottle.

It went on to detail the deeply Christian ethos in the formative years of the company, back in the 1880s. Conor had read that there used to be regular morning prayer assembly for all employees. And Joshua Bendix had decreed that ten per cent of all profits should be donated to charity, a practice that was continued to this day.

What the book did not reveal, Charley Rowley had told Conor quietly, when they had slipped out for a pub lunch, was that such funding was used exclusively to set up and control charities dealing with the specific chronic diseases and ailments for which Bendix Schere manufactured pharmaceuticals.

He picked up the envelope, which had already been slit open. He had been informed of this practice, and he wondered if there were security teams employed to read everything that arrived. Somehow he doubted it. The envelopes were probably opened to discourage any correspondence of a personal nature being sent to staff, or between staff.

He shook out a wodge of estate agents' particulars, together with a note from the Relocation Officer who had visited him briefly yesterday – an awesomely efficient young woman called Sue Perkins, who'd discussed the kind of apartment he could afford on his salary. She had first identified on a map the areas that would best suit him. She had then pointed out, to his amazement, the shaded zones that marked the parts of London where Bendix Schere employees were encouraged,

64

but not contractually bound, to live. She'd advised him, however, that it was likely to become mandatory to live in these areas at some point in the near future.

Now, already awaiting him were twenty potential apartments from which he could draw a shortlist. He put the envelope into his briefcase to read at home that night, switched on his computer terminal and logged in.

The first thing that appeared on the screen, as it would do each morning, was a sinister form titled: 'Colleague Data Sheet.' In it were boxes on which everyone was supposed to enter the names of their immediate colleagues, and further boxes for them to tick – assessing those same colleagues on neatness, confidence, competence, how they handle themselves with other people, and company loyalty.

He debated what to do for a moment, then entered Charley Rowley's name and gave him a couple of points short of the maximum possible, not wanting to appear to be either sucking up or too indiscriminate. After this he clicked on the icon to open his internal eMail box. There was one message waiting: **'9.15 meeting. 20th floor Boardroom. Pick you up a few minutes before. CR.'**

His mind returned to the blonde who had got out at the eighth floor, and he thought about her for a few minutes. He'd ask Charley Rowley who she was. *Just moving in at the moment*, she had said. Her father and herself. There shouldn't be too much of a problem identifying her – Charley Rowley seemed to be a walking encyclopaedia on the place.

Yes, she would definitely be worth tracking down.

11

Bill Gunn walked slowly around the forty-seventh floor ops room of the Bendix Building, completing his regular daily check on all the equipment. He had a team of thirty technicians beneath him, many of them university graduates, but the Director of Security still liked to inspect everything himself. Old habits died hard.

This particular habit went back to his early days as a wireless operator in the Signals Corps of the Paras. Never trusting any piece of electrical equipment on which his life might depend, he would dismantle and reassemble it himself prior to any operation; that was the only way he could be certain it would give no trouble. And for the same reason, he always unpacked and repacked his own parachute.

A thick-set forty-eight-year-old of below average height, he had an impassive face with *military* stamped all over it and brown hair cropped only marginally longer than a crew cut. Somehow he always looked out of place in a suit, despite having worn one for the past twenty years. Like many trained fighting men, he had tunnel-vision loyalty to his paymasters, but at Bendix Schere there was something else, quite different, bonding him to them.

He had been recruited into the SAS and then into GCHQ at Cheltenham, the eyes and ears of the British Government's Intelligence Services. There he had been involved in anti-terrorism: setting up, operating and improving surveillance systems of the foreign embassies based in Britain, as well as of key buildings in potentially hostile countries like Russia, Iran and Iraq. It had been invaluable for his learning curve. When Bendix Schere had quietly head-hunted him nine years later, he was one of the most informed surveillance experts in the world.

Both the forty-seventh floor and the one above looked like space stations, bristling with the most sophisticated eaves-dropping and satellite tracking technology, most of which was used more for monitoring staff for internal security than it was for spying on the competition.

Gunn halted next to the vehicle-data tracking system. In front of him was a vast panel of some five thousand tiny red lights, each with a number beneath. About two thirds of the lights were off, the others were winking brightly. Each light represented a company vehicle, and the winking ones in-dicated those actually being driven at that moment.

By typing the number of the light into the computer screen

beside the panel, Gunn could bring up full details on any company vehicle, anywhere in the world, and compass coordinates of its position accurate to within ten feet – together with a written description of its location and a road map to any desired scale. The computer also recorded a log of all the vehicle's journeys for the preceding four weeks, and compared it against a log of the previous twelve months to show any significant change in pattern.

Another system on this floor was Gunn's own invention and he was particularly proud of it: 'Retrace'. Every time an employee swiped their smart-card or inserted it to move through a door, a signal was transmitted to Gunn's database. The computer would analyse each employee's movements over the previous month and compare it to the pattern of the previous twelve months, and alert Gunn of any significant variations that should be checked out.

Less sophisticated aspects of Gunn's monitoring set-up included the ability, from his own office, to listen in on any telephone call made to or from any Bendix Schere building, and the ability to eavesdrop on any conversation taking place on company territory. Additionally, all laboratory activity could be observed through closed-circuit television.

Satisfied that everything was running smoothly, he returned to his comfortable lair on the forty-eighth floor, closed the door, sat down in front of his battery of screens, and turned to the next item in his unvarying weekly routine: *new employees*. He tapped a key and brought up the list.

The name 'Conor Molloy' was one of three on the list of twenty names that was highlighted. Gunn tapped in the command for Conor's computer log and saw there had been very little activity. One eMail, from Charley Rowley, this morning, and one Colleague Data Sheet filled in. He activated 'Retrace' and checked Conor's movements yesterday. It looked like a pretty thorough introductory tour. No worries. Then he called up the Colleague Data Sheet and looked at it carefully.

Only two points short of the maximum. He frowned. Charley Rowley had been on his danger list for a long time as someone with an attitude problem. It was improbable that anyone of sound judgement would award him such a ludicrously high score. It indicated either that Conor Molloy's character-assessment abilities might be suspect, or that he was trying to suck up, or that he had simply made up the score.

It wasn't uncommon for new employees to give high marks out of fear of retribution. They needn't worry about that – the comments were kept completely confidential, but of course they had no way of knowing that. Conor Molloy had done nothing serious by his action, not lit a warning beacon or anything as dramatic as that, but it was, all the same, just one tiny mark against his name. Sometimes, Gunn had found, enough tiny marks would start, eventually, to point to something. And Gunn already felt a slight unease about the new American patent lawyer.

There was nothing specific, no colours he could nail to a mast, but from his years of surveillance he had developed an instinct for people who were up to something, and that instinct was telling him to watch Molloy.

He called up Conor's original application details and read through them carefully. The American had an impeccable background, that was for sure. Biochemistry degree cum summa from Harvard. Masters at Stanford in Organic Chemistry. Two years in Molecular Biology at Carnegie Mellon. Three years back at Harvard at law school, taking his bar and then Patent Office exams. Finishing Harvard, he had been head-hunted and grabbed by Merck, where he had spent two years in the patent department.

Merck was the fourth largest pharmaceutical company in the world. They were good employers and good payers. So why had Molloy switched horses? The reason was right there on the application form: Molloy believed that Bendix Schere had a more progressive genetics programme. Fine, that was true, Gunn had no quarrel with that. Bendix Schere offered the best genetics opportunities in the world. Also, Merck had wanted to send Molloy to California, and he didn't want to live on the West Coast. A perfectly acceptable explanation. Bendix Schere offered him the chance of a couple of years working in England. Conor Molloy had liked the idea of that. No problem there either. The man was single, heterosexual, wanted to see a bit of the world before settling down. All the reasons Conor Molloy had given were solid.

So what the hell was it about him that just did not quite add up?

12

Monty Bannerman's anger boiled over into fury as she held the letter in her hand and read it through yet again.

What bastard had done this? And on whose authority? She glanced at her watch. 10.30. Her appointment with Sir Neil Rorke was for eleven. Well, he would have to sort this out, good and proper! She drew in a deep breath, trying to calm herself; she'd been in a rage ever since the letter had arrived at their old laboratory yesterday morning, even waking several times during the night and fretting about it.

Thank God she had been there and had opened her father's post. If he'd seen this, he would've gone berserk. As it was he had wondered where Walter Hoggin, their Chief Lab Technician, had been all day, and she'd had to lie, telling him he was off sick.

The takeover by Bendix Schere of Bannerman Genetics Research had finally been agreed and signed eight months ago, but the transition was not proving easy. Numerous experiments *in situ* were too delicate to be moved, making the relocation from Berkshire University to the Bendix Building in London a laborious process that would go on for several months yet.

Mountains of paperwork needed to be gone through for Bendix Schere's Group Patents and Agreements Department, currently the bane of her life. And all because the patent agents and lawyers needed to see and read, in some semblance of order, virtually *every* scrap of paper relating to *every* experiment that had ever been carried out at Bannerman Genetics. So almost everything that had been filed at her father's lab now needed entering on to the Bendix Schere computer system. There was a clerical pool available to do this tedious work, but so much required untangling and deciphering that Monty was ending up finding it easier to do much of it herself.

Since late February Monty and her father had been dividing their time between their old lab and their sumptuous new premises on the eighth floor of the Bendix Building. Monty had found it to be a very strenuous period, in which she'd had to draw constantly on all her resources of courtesy and diplomacy, not least because she found the Bendix Schere team less helpful than she'd expected. Rather than welcoming the arrival of someone of Dick Bannerman's calibre, many of the staff gave the impression that they resented the intrusion of outsiders.

And her father had been continually testing the nerve of the Board of Directors, to see how far he could push them. So far, every request for the purchase of equipment sent to Accounts for authorization had come back approved – even if the £300,000 for Cray gene-sequencing computer hardware had taken a month and several tricky meetings. Bendix Schere was not into wanton spending binges, but it was prepared to throw money at anything that had a real chance of producing results and beating the opposition.

Up until now, the company had not put a foot wrong in its dealings with Dr Bannerman. Tetchy as he had been at the start, and filled with misgivings about their bureaucracy, he'd had to admit that Bendix Schere had behaved honourably.

He even confessed to Monty that it was a relief to have a regular pay cheque instead of continually scrabbling to find the money every time a bill arrived at home. In fact they were both on reasonable salaries now – with the added bonus for Dick Bannerman of a percentage share in any profits resulting from his work. And Monty was earning more than double the subsistence wage she had previously been eking out of Bannerman Genetics.

So what was behind the letter? Was it simply a mistake? Some goof-up of internal communications? Or was this where the glib promises of Sir Neil Rorke and Dr Vincent Crowe all terminated? The end of the line.

In half an hour she would find out.

She put the letter in her handbag, then turned her attention to the stack of CVs on her desk. Her father was busy hiring, increasing the size of his team during the next twelve months from thirty-five to two hundred. He had made up a hit list of graduates, postgraduates, postdocs, and research fellows to head-hunt. And he was obviously enjoying himself; it made a big change from turning people down or, worse, letting staff go because he couldn't afford them. For the first time since her mother's death Monty considered him happy, and she wanted it to stay that way.

At five to eleven she put on her double-breasted navy jacket and picked up her handbag. She still hadn't got used to the luxury of an office of her own. It wasn't big by any standard, but the only fault she could really find was not having an external window. The temperature was pleasant and the air did feel fresh, even vibrant, but she had the same slightly claustrophobic sensation she always experienced when inside enclosed places.

She walked past the male security guard seated at his console in front of the lifts. But these lifts went no further than the forty-eighth floor, and only a Director with a smart-card could summon the express lift which went beyond. She had been instructed to ask the guard to call it, which he did.

God, the Directors are paranoid! she thought. *What are they frightened of? Industrial espionage? Terrorists? Animal Rights? Cranks?*

As she waited she thought fleetingly of the American who had travelled up in the lift with her that morning, and smiled privately to herself, remembering the expression on his face when she had caught him preening himself.

He was a good-looking guy, but no doubt typical of the men whom she had met here so far. There seemed to be an abundance of rather precious types who took themselves far too seriously, as if working for Bendix Schere had elevated them quite beyond the status of ordinary mortals.

A sharp ping announced the arrival of the lift and she stepped in. Moments later, the bronze doors opened and she was back in the same anteroom, with its weird abstracts, where she had come with her father for their first meeting with Rorke and Crowe.

A door opened as she waited in the reception area and Rorke's private secretary, a draconian-looking woman with flame-red hair, informed Monty that Sir Neil was ready to see her.

Rorke came to the door of his office himself, hand outstretched, and a smile which instantly made her feel he was genuinely glad to see her.

She shook the fleshy hand warily, remembering from past experience the steely hardness of his grip. 'Good morning, Sir Neil – I appreciate you taking the time to see me.'

'Always time for you, my dear.' He gestured her to sit in one of the comfortable chairs grouped casually around a coffee table well away from his desk, making her feel a little thrown by the informality. It had been several months since she had last seen him, but he was unchanged, his face just as rubicund, his black hair as flamboyantly long as before, and he was dressed in one of the loud chalk-striped suits and kipper ties that seemed to be his trademark.

'So tell me,' he said. 'How's it all going?'

'Well,' she said hesitantly, not wanting to start off by launching straight into her proposed attack, 'it's been going extremely well. Although the whole process of the move is taking much longer than we thought.'

He brought his hands together and interlocked his fingers. 'I understand from Dr Crowe that everyone's very happy this end.' He paused and smiled wryly. 'Your father certainly knows how to spend our money.'

'It's all necessary equipment.'

'Of course! I'm not complaining – we're delighted by his enthusiasm.'

Monty smiled back politely, preparing her next words. Then her eyes fell on the large gold frog on the onyx plinth on Rorke's desk, and she shuddered slightly. Today, the frog seemed to be gazing, with a hostile glare, straight back at her.

She took a breath. 'There is something specific, Sir Neil,' she said, opening her handbag and removing the letter. 'This came yesterday, addressed to my father. It's from our Chief Lab Technician, a man called Walter Hoggin, who's been with Daddy ever since he started. In it he says that he's received a letter from Bendix Schere's Director of Human Resources, informing him that due to his age he has been made redundant, that he is not to come to the company premises again and that all personal belongings will be delivered to his home.' She stared challengingly and noted, with some satisfaction, the look of concern on the Chairman's face.

Rorke leaned forward thoughtfully. 'Due to his age? How old is he?'

'Sixty-six,' she said.

He leaned back. 'Ah,' he said. 'I would imagine that's the answer. That's a year past retirement.'

'We've never forced people to retire at any age,' she said testily.

Rorke's expression hardened a fraction; the change was barely perceptible, but it was enough for Monty to see a glimpse of the Chairman's tough side. 'Unfortunately, Miss Bannerman, *we* do have rigid rules about retirement age.'

She kept her calm, in spite of her rising anger. 'I understand that, Sir Neil, but, as you know, the safeguarding of our staff's jobs was one of my father's biggest concerns – and mine. At that very first meeting we had with yourself and Dr Crowe, you both gave your assurances on that score. It was one of the basic conditions on which we entered into the agreement with you.'

He nodded. 'Well, we certainly don't want to break an agreement, that's not the way we do business. I'll have a word with Dr Crowe and see what we can do about this.'

'I'd appreciate that very much,' she said. 'As a matter of urgency. Walter is extremely distressed. It's just not the way we treat people.'

He watched her carefully. 'I'm sure we can make an exception – perhaps find something for him at our Slough campus.' He raised his eyebrows.

'Thank you.' She replaced the letter in her handbag, feeling relieved.

'We're a large company, and we have a very big heart too.'

'That's good to hear,' she said.

'I value you and your father very highly. I certainly don't want anything to sour our relationship, or your views about Bendix Schere. If there's anything else on your mind, you will please tell me, won't you? My door is always open.'

'Thank you, Sir Neil.'

He walked her back to the lift himself. As she stepped in, he said: 'Miss Bannerman, I do mean it. We may be a global organization, but I run a tight ship. If you or your father are unhappy about anything at all, you must come directly to me. Promise me that?'

She promised.

13

Barnet, North London. 1946

Daniel Judd lay on his back in the darkness for the fourth night running with his arms pulled down each side of his bed and strapped tight to the legs with leather belts. The hard edge of the metal frame dug into the same raw weals made on his wrists last night and the night before.

His bottom and back were bleeding from the separate thrashings he had received from his parents: from his mother for refusing to say his prayers before he got into bed last night, and from his father because he had not said grace properly before supper.

His nose was blocked and he wanted to blow it, but could not do so without his hands. He also needed to urinate badly but was too afraid to call out for his parents, and yet he was frightened of the punishment if he wet his bed.

So he lay snuffling and helpless, eyes stinging with tears, his distended bladder shooting sharp pains up the left side of his stomach; he could only watch the darkness of the room with open-eyed fear.

They had tails and stings like scorpions, and in their tails they had power to torment people for five months.

Scorpions!

Scorpions got you if you did not have the seal of God on your forehead.

He had never seen a live scorpion, only pictures in an encyclopaedia, and a dead one in a cabinet in a museum; it was smaller than he had thought, the size of a large beetle. Black and hard. He imagined the floor covered in them now, marching their way over to the bed, reaching the bottom of the legs. Then swarming up, gripping the vertical sides of the mattress with their black claws. Gathering at the end of the eiderdown.

And he did not have the seal of God on his forehead to protect him.

His parents had told him of the seal, but they said that he was a sinner and that was why he hadn't got one. Even so, he had gone to the bathroom mirror to check himself, and to his dismay had realized they were right.

He could not see the seal on either his mother or his father's forehead either, but they said that once you had it, it became invisible. And you would *know* when you had it.

His mother had read a passage about scorpions tonight.

. . . when he opened the Abyss, smoke rose from it like the smoke from a gigantic furnace. The sun and sky were darkened by the smoke from the Abyss. And out of the smoke locusts came down upon the earth and were given power like that of scorpions. They were told not to harm the grass of the earth or any plant or tree, but only those people who did not have the seal of God on their foreheads.

They were not given power to kill them, but only to torture them for five months. And the agony suffered was like that of the sting of a scorpion when it strikes a man. During those days men will seek death, but will not find it; they will long to die but death will elude them.

His mother had told him the scorpions would get him if he had impure thoughts in the night. If he thought about touching himself. If he thought about touching his *dirty thing*.

And yes, he had thought about touching it, was thinking about touching it now, about holding it and letting the urine

75

flow, letting it gush out and getting rid of that terrible pain in his tummy.

And that meant the scorpions were going to get him. For sure. He listened hard, listened for the sound of claws on the carpet, tiny scrapings, clackings, making their way up the bedclothes any moment.

He listened in clenched silence. He could hear them! His bed felt alive, teeming with insects; he held his breath in the darkness, trying to sense movement beyond the coursing of his own blood. The movement of insects. He bit his lip. *Something.* There was something crawling up the counterpane. Now.

Scratch. Scratch-scratch. Scratch. Pause. Scratch-scratch-scratch-scratch-scratch.

His mouth was dry with fear.

Scratch-scratch-scratch.

Closer.

Scratch-scratch-scratch.

He stifled the first cry, swallowed it, choked it back. Could hear the sound of the claws scraping against the shiny cotton, slithering as if they were on ice. Then gripping! Scratch-scratch-scratch.

Something touched his arm.

Something pressed against his pyjama sleeve; a tiny indent then another, then another. He could feel the pricks of the claws through the thin material. Moving up his sleeve, past his elbow. Could imagine the small black thing, tail held high, curled forward over its spine. He swallowed. It was OK if you stayed still, that's what you had to do, *stay still*, not let it know you were frightened.

It reached his shoulder. Then something touched his neck, something cold, hard, quivering; next he felt the first claw dig in, sharp as a needle; his body was shimmying with terror. Felt the legs digging harder in, making their purchase on his skin; traversing his neck and over his Adam's apple, each step a needle prick. Up the base of his chin, touching his lower lip. Over his mouth; he could smell it now, a vile rancid smell. It moved past his nostrils then began ascending his cheek, climbing towards his eye.

76

It was going to sting him through the eye . . .

'Mother! Mama! Daddy!' he screamed, thrashing in terror, breathing short hard bursts, spinning his head wildly from side to side. 'Mother, Father, oh help me oh help me oh help me!'

The light came on, momentarily blinding him. As he blinked, something blocked his right eye; something hard pressed against the ball. A shadow swept down; he sensed the flick of a finger; something moved on the carpet to his right; a creature on its back, wriggling its legs in the air; dark brown, about an inch long.

Then his father crushed it on the bare floorboard with his slippered foot.

'Scorpion,' Daniel whispered, barely able to breathe now.

'What a fuss to make, you stupid little boy,' his mother said. 'Scorpion?'

'It's not a scorpion, it's a cockroach.' His father picked it up between his fingers and held it over his son's face. Two of its legs flexed and slowly released; orange gunge was oozing from its split belly; an antenna quivered.

'It's a sign,' his mother pronounced. He stared up at her, wrapped in her woollen dressing gown, face stark white and clammy with cream, her eyes hard with anger. 'It's a sign from God of your impure thoughts.' She slapped him hard across the face. Were you thinking filth?'

He shook his head in fear. She slapped him again. 'You're lying! God sent you a cockroach first; a scorpion will be next. You must repent, boy; every time you do not repent the anger of our Lord increases.'

Daniel began to sob. 'Why is God so horrible to me?' he said.

His mother slapped him again, harder. 'Our most merciful Father who art in Heaven you call *horrible*? How dare you?'

'I hate God,' he sobbed. 'I hate Him! I want to kill Him!'

His mother screamed at him, yanked his hair, spat in his face, then slapped him repeatedly on both cheeks. She went out of the room, came back with a bar of soap and tried to ram it into his mouth. 'Wash your mouth of your blasphemy! You will go to Hell for ever!'

His father dropped the cockroach into the wastebin. 'Repent, son,' he said. 'Before it is too late.'

Daniel said nothing.

His father picked up the Bible from the bedside table and began to read aloud.

'The heads of the horses resembled the heads of lions, and out of their mouths came fire, smoke and sulphur.

'A third of mankind was killed by these three plagues of fire, smoke and sulphur . . . The power of the horses was in their mouths and in their tails, for their tails were like snakes . . .

'The rest of mankind, that were not killed by these plagues, still did not repent of the work of their hands, they did not stop worshipping demons, and idols of gold, silver, bronze, stone and wood – idols that cannot see or hear or walk.

'Nor did they repent of their murders, their magic arts, their sexual immorality or their thefts.'

Then his parents went out of the room, closing the door. 'You'll sleep with the light on so God can see you more clearly; so you can understand it makes no difference whether it is dark or light. *He* sees everything.'

Daniel lay still, staring up at the bare light bulb, at the spidery brown stain on the ceiling where water had once leaked; at the black night through the curtainless window; at the crucifix on the wall to the right of it. Hatred burned inside him. Hatred for God. Hatred for Jesus on the Cross.

He concentrated on the crucifix. *God so loved the world, that he gave his only begotten Son, that whosoever believeth in him should not perish, but have everlasting life.*

He looked at the naked man with the outstretched arms, the bent legs and sagging head. Then he thought about himself, lying here, with his arms outstretched. They were the same as each other!

God had allowed his son to be crucified. God had killed his only son. To save mankind. God had not treated Jesus any better than he was being treated now by his own parents. The anger inside him increased, roared like a furnace. He felt himself becoming hot. He began to sense a strange energy coming into his body. A sense of strength and power that began in the pit of his stomach and radiated outward through his chest, his arms, his legs. His eyes stayed locked on the crucifix, he could see it so clearly, as if it were not twelve feet away across the room, but inches from his face.

He could see the agony there. The twisted muscles, the fingers curled and dying like the legs of the cockroach. The crucifix began to tremble. Just a few tiny vibrations at first, then more. Daniel willed it to vibrate harder; harder still.

Suddenly, with no warning, it dropped straight to the floor with a loud report, like a gunshot.

Daniel saw the two small holes in the walls where the nails had fallen out; and the flesh-coloured shadow in the shape of a cross that lay etched in the grimy ochre paint of the wall.

Then he grinned.

He had made it do that. He had made the crucifix fall from the wall just by thinking about it! His eyes flicked to the Bible on the table beside him. He concentrated his stare on it. *Burst into flames*, he thought. *Go on, burn!*

He focused hard, locked everything else from his mind, brought the strength and power back to a peak. Concentrated. Concentrated. *Burn, damn you, ghastly horrid book.*

BURN!!!

There was a tremendous bang, then the tinkling of falling glass. The window! It had turned to a mass of cracks and was imploding before his eyes; a few small shards at first, then the whole pane buckled and fell in glass daggers on to the floor.

His door hurled open and his parents came storming in. 'What in the –?' his mother began, her voice drying mid-sentence as she was confronted by the broken window; then the crucifix on the floor.

His father stared, bewildered, then tested the straps that held his arms pinioned. His parents glanced at each other; his mother tested the straps as well.

'Daniel,' his father pronounced, 'if you do not have the seal of God on your forehead, then you have the mark of the Beast.'

'He is an evil child and he must be saved,' his mother said.

'Do you understand what it means, Daniel?' his father said. '*If anyone worships the Beast and His image and receives His mark on the forehead or on the hand, he will drink of the wine of God's fury, which has been poured full strength into the cup of His wrath. He will be tormented with burning sulphur in the presence of the holy angels and of the Lamb. And the smoke of their torment rises for ever and ever. There is no rest day or night for those who worship the Beast and His image, or for anyone who receives the mark of His name.'*

'Is that what you want, boy?' his mother screamed. 'You want the mark of the Beast?'

Daniel looked up at his mother and said nothing.

14

London. Wednesday 2 November, 1994
You are one ugly bastard! Conor Molloy thought, staring at the poor black and white photograph inset into a research paper. 'Gastric Brooding Frog', said the caption beneath. *'Rheobatrachus silus.'*

'Rheobatrachus silus is a rare aquatic frog of eastern Australia. The female ingests the eggs after fertilization and broods them in the stomach until fully formed. "Gastric brooding" takes place in the fundus and proximal part of the stomach, which dilates to accommodate the growing young,' he read, wondering what this paper was doing in the midst of Dr Bannerman's research, although nothing much surprised him any more about the work of the Nobel-winning scientist.

During the past nine days he felt as if he had got to know Dr Bannerman intimately, without having actually met the great man yet; he had lived and breathed him almost every waking moment, poring through his life's work document by document.

Bendix Schere wanted to file patents in Britain, Europe and the US on as much of Bannerman's work as possible, and Conor's brief was to report on what patents might be obtained in the US. Dr Vincent Crowe, the company's Chief Executive, wanted to see the report himself within ten days.

Conor knew he was on trial and had been thrown in at the deep end. Patent applications were expensive and time-consuming. If he recommended filing any applications that failed, it would reflect badly on him. Equally, if he missed any opportunities it could cost the company millions, or even billions, in lost revenue – not that he would lose any sleep over *that*.

To obtain a patent, you had to convince the Patent Examiner that nobody had made public enough details of the invention, or scientific discovery, to enable anyone else to reproduce it. However, Dr Bannerman had published copious papers detailing virtually every single aspect of his work, for the whole world to copy. Conor's report was going to make grim reading if Bendix Schere had been hoping to cash in on Bannerman's work to date.

Conor smiled. *I haven't met you, Dr Bannerman,* he thought, *but I like you. I like you a lot.*

His door, which he had left ajar, opened suddenly and Charley Rowley stuck his head in. 'How's it going?'

'OK, I guess.'

'I wondered if you were free on Friday night? Having a little dinner party – thought you might like to meet some normal people?'

Conor caught the look in his eye and acknowledged it. He'd been out to the pub for lunch a few times with Rowley, and had remarked on the apparent lack of any social contact between staff members of Group Patents and Agreements. Rowley had told him it wasn't just GP & Ags – it was the same throughout the whole company, and it was deliberate policy: staff were not encouraged to mix during office hours, or to socialize in private. It was a total reversal of the corporate bonding ethos found in most large corporations. 'All part of the mystique, the secrecy,' Rowley had said. *And the paranoia,* Conor had almost replied at the time.

'Sure, I'm free on Friday; sounds good.'

Conor was free every night. He had not even become acquainted with anyone else in the company yet, although he now knew a number of names and faces, with whom he exchanged polite greetings. And most of his free time had been spent working through the Bannerman paperwork, punctuated by the occasional unsuccessful foray of apartment hunting.

'About eight o'clock?' Rowley said. 'I'll eMail you the address and directions – just over the river in Wandsworth.'

Conor was just trying to recall from the map the Relocation Officer had shown him whether that was an approved residential zone or not, when he was saved the trouble.

'Dead easy to find. Parts of it are even approved BS zones,' Rowley said with a mocking expression. 'Though fortunately not my particular street, so you'll be slumming it with the outcasts.'

'As long as smoking's permitted, I'm sure I'll just about get by,' grinned Conor. The idea of meeting people appealed; he fancied a break from his own solitude, and Rowley seemed like the kind of guy who would know some decent unattached females.

Rowley flipped through a stack of unopened magazines on Conor's desk, which had all arrived in the morning's post. *Monitor Weekly, Doctor, Prescribe, BMJ, Genetic Engineering News, Human Genome News*. 'Didn't take long for these guys to cobble you on to their mailing lists.'

Conor had already dumped most of yesterday's pile into an incinerator bag and dropped it down the chute. 'I don't know how anyone gets time to read them.'

Rowley became serious suddenly. 'You are going to be OK for Dr Crowe's deadline?'

'No sweat. I just have a few gaps to plug in the work on psoriasis, and there's some stuff I can't figure out. I'm going to need to spend a few hours going through it with Dr Bannerman – that should do it.'

'He can be a bit of a tricky bugger,' Rowley warned. 'Doesn't approve of patenting – if you catch him in the wrong mood he can go nuclear. And he's not that easy to get hold of – your best bet's his daughter.'

Something rang a bell in Conor's head: last Tuesday, his second day here, the blonde he'd seen in the lift and who'd spoken of, '. . . *my father and I*.' He'd been meaning to ask Rowley about her and now he wondered if this was the same young woman.

Rowley continued. 'Works as his PA – and she's bloody efficient – knows where everything is.' He gave Conor a lascivious grin. 'She's also bloody gorgeous.'

Monty had been feeling happier since her meeting with Sir Neil Rorke, and she'd been impressed at the speed with which he had acted. Not only had Walter Hoggin been reinstated within twenty-four hours, in the Quality Control Department of one of Bendix Schere's manufacturing plants only a few miles away, he had also been informed that he would be receiving a bonus of six months' salary as compensation.

Monty had been left with the distinct feeling from Rorke that someone's head would roll over this affair, and she thought it would be very nice if it was Dr Vincent Crowe's – but somehow knew that was unlikely.

From her desk she could see through the partition window straight into the corridor whose plush doors led to the fourteen laboratories under her father's control. Some were tiny rooms, purpose-built for one specific function, but eight were substantial general research labs, the largest of which was directly opposite her.

The equipment her father had ordered was arriving daily, together with some of the experiments in progress from their Berkshire University site. Even as she watched, four workmen were awkwardly manoeuvring a massive crate, plastered with 'FRAGILE' warning stickers.

Then she saw the lanky figure of Jake Seals, the Bendix Schere Chief Lab Technician, who was in charge of their move. He strode past, rapped on her door, then opened it using his electronic pass card – as usual without waiting for her to answer.

He wore a sweatshirt and jeans beneath his white coat, which was contrary to the Bendix Schere dress code, but his slovenly appearance and a certain attitude problem belied a sharp brain, a comprehensive knowledge of his field and a willingness to work hard, all hours, without complaint. Monty respected his abilities.

'Morning, Mr Seals,' she said pleasantly. 'How are we today?'

He tossed his shoulder-length hair back, then closed the door behind him and sat down at the chair in front of her desk. 'Got a minute?'

'Yes – but only about a minute – someone's on their way down to see me.'

He held a thumb up in front of him and examined the nail for a moment, staring at it while he spoke to her. 'You don't like this place, do you?'

She was genuinely surprised by the question. 'Whatever gave you that impression?'

'It sucks, doesn't it?'

'It's too early for me to have formed any kind of opinion,' she said, guardedly, not sure what he was driving at.

He lowered his thumb, glanced at the ceiling as though he were checking for bugs. 'You know what I mean – except you don't know the half of it.'

'The half of what?'

He stood up, tossed his hair back again and dug his hands into his coat pockets. 'We'll have a longer talk some time. Away from here.' He went out and disappeared down the corridor.

15

A small black Christmas tree sat beside each of the thirty-four names the Director of Security was scrolling through on one of the screens in front of his desk. It might have seemed an innocent enough symbol to outsiders, but there was nothing innocent about its significance here: these were people whose loyalties to Bendix Schere were uncertain, and Bill Gunn kept them under close scrutiny.

It was his Wednesday morning routine to scan the computer summaries of their activities, and he had been paying particularly close attention today to Jake Seals. The Chief Lab Technician's pattern of activity had altered significantly during the past three months. Firstly the usage of his car had gone up dramatically, and tracking back his journey paths had revealed that he had made three visits to one of BS's principal rivals: Cobbold Tessering. Two visits to their London head office and one to their research campus in Buckinghamshire.

Head-hunting by competitors was a major problem – although Bendix Schere were just as guilty of it themselves – and Cobbold Tessering were a particular worry. From their own industrial espionage operations, in which Gunn was actively involved, BS were aware that Cobbold Tessering was almost certainly the second largest player in the field of genetics research next to themselves. Jake Seals' position gave him access to an awful lot of research information for any one employee. And if they lost him to Cobbold Tessering, it would be a major disaster. The whole Board knew that.

Secondly, Seals' movements around the Bendix Building itself had altered recently.

Gunn leaned back in his chair, fingers intertwined, his stare fixed on one of the row of monitors in front of him. Occasionally he would disentangle his fingers and stab a symbol on his keyboard to scroll forward, as he studied the comparison graph of the subject's movements around the building for the past three months, compared with the previous three, and then against the previous year.

'What are you up to, you little shit?' he said quietly, squeezing his fingers so hard the bones hurt. After some moments he reached for the polystyrene cup on his desk, sipped some coffee, then keyed in the command to run a program giving him a more detailed analysis of exactly where in the building Seals had been going.

The program showed that the main difference was that instead of spending most of his time on the sixth floor, where he was based, Jake Seals was now spending most of his time up on the eighth. Gunn felt a twinge of disappointment. Since Seals was in charge of the Bannerman move, it was hardly surprising he'd been spending his time there.

His internal phone rang. It was on a network that only operated within the two security floors and could not be tapped from the outside. He swept the receiver to his ear. 'Yes?'

'Just picked up something interesting, Mr Gunn.'

It was Norbert Ricks. The kid was like a robot; Gunn felt sometimes that Ricks' brain was wired into his job. He was twenty-six and nerdy-looking, but he could do any job within his field, which was voice-analysis systems, brilliantly. And other than Gunn, whom he treated the slavish way a dog treats his master, he had no communication with anyone else in the company. In line with most of the hand-picked team Gunn had assembled during his tenure, Ricks suffered from a personality disorder. In his case: Aaitkhcken-Yeltz Syndrome – an inability to interact with his colleagues.

All staff under Gunn's command in Security worked in similar isolation. Divide and rule – like Adolf Hitler's policy. Bill Gunn had read every word ever written about Hitler and the Third Reich. Organization, manipulation, control. Those were the watchwords.

You selected your team carefully: you chose brilliant but damaged, inadequate people, you divided them, isolated them into pockets, fired them up with dreams of gain, and then you spread fear among them – so that they would only, ultimately, communicate with and trust one person. Bill Gunn.

And this was not simply the way Gunn chose to run his team, it was also his own personal insurance policy: no one at Bendix Schere could ever get rid of him – unless they wanted to watch the whole internal security fall apart.

'Yes, Mr Ricks, what is it?'

'Something you should listen to. Got it on Voice-Ac just now.'

Voice-Ac was a voice-recognition monitoring system. Through the microphones planted in every office and in the common parts of the Bendix Building, Voice-Ac could distinguish the voices of the thirty-four people under close surveillance and automatically record anything the said. The system was not activated by any other voices, so it was a relatively easy process for Ricks, who was trained in fast-forward listening, to trawl the suspects' conversation for anything that might be significant.

'Patch it through,' Gunn said.

'Coming on Channel Three.'

Gunn stabbed the button on the control panel and listened. Almost instantly he heard the clearly recognizable tones of Jake Seals, and a woman whose voice he did not know:

'You don't like this place, do you?'

'Whatever gave you that impression?'

'It sucks, doesn't it?'

'It's too early for me to have formed any kind of opinion.'

'You know what I mean – except you don't know the half of it.'

'The half of what?'

'We'll have a longer talk some time. Away from here.'

There was a click, then silence. Gunn still had the receiver in his hand. 'Who's the woman?'

'It's that Miss Bannerman. The conversation took place at ten thirty-four this morning.'

Gunn glanced at his watch. It was now twelve o'clock. 'Good boy,' he said, then hung up.

There was a slightly bitter taste in his mouth which he tried to swill away with a mouthful of lukewarm coffee. He activated the replay button and listened in a couple more times. The woman sounded innocent enough but that wasn't the point.

The Bannerman acquisition had been vital to Bendix Schere's long-term plans, more so than they had ever let on to the scientist himself in all the negotiations that had taken place. Gunn had made it his business to be fully aware of all this; of how difficult it had been to get Bannerman. And he knew the last thing anyone wanted was for Bannerman, his daughter, or any of their old team to learn things that would put them on their guard. But Seals was obviously going to spill *something*, soon, and was planning to do so safely away from the premises. In his mind at least.

He called up the Bendix Building staff list on the computer screen and added a Christmas tree symbol to the right of Montana Bannerman's name. Her conversations would also have to be monitored from now on. Then he picked up his internal phone and set in motion a home phone tap and twenty-four-hour surveillance operation on Jake Seals.

16

Shortly after half past ten, a wodge of files tucked under his arm, Conor enunciated 'Floor Eight' and felt the lift respond. He checked out his reflection in the bronze mirror, adjusted his tie, and smoothed the gelled tangle of his hair. Then the doors opened and he walked out into the green-carpeted foyer of the genetics research floor.

'Miss Bannerman, please,' he told the security guard, his eyes picking up the camera directly above the oak console.

'Room 814, fifth door on the right down the corridor,' the guard said, with a glazed look, as if he had already given the same directions a thousand times that morning.

As he walked past, Conor glanced round to see what the guard was watching on his monitor screens. One showed a blank stairwell behind what was presumably a fire-exit door. Another showed an empty corridor. A third showed a large lab with several people working in it.

Ahead of him, two men in the corridor were negotiating a crate on a porter's trolley through a doorway. And on the door directly opposite was the number '814'. Through the window he could see a frizz of long blonde hair and his spirits rose as he realized it *was* the same young woman he had already met; she was seated at her desk surrounded by stacks of unopened packing cases and cardboard boxes. He rapped on the door which was ajar.

'Come in.'

He felt an instant attraction the moment he entered; hair the colour of winter wheat cascaded either side of a welcoming face, and clear blue eyes sparkled up at him with life and humour. Their owner looked elegant and businesslike in a bottle-green suit with a white, open-neck blouse.

'Hi,' he said. 'Conor Molloy – we met before, right?'

'Good morning, *Mr* Molloy.' She put emphasis on the 'Mr' as if to remind him of the regulations, but also to convey that she could not take the formality too seriously.

She gestured to one of the chairs in front of her desk and he sat down, holding the files on his lap, feeling good in her presence and enjoying the tease in her eyes. He noticed the tiny dimples in her cheeks and the almost perfect whiteness of her teeth. *Miss Bannerman*, he thought; *you are seriously gorgeous.*

'Would you like some coffee?'

'Sure, thanks.'

She stood up. 'Black or white?'

'No milk or sugar.'

He watched her as she walked out of the office. She was short, no more than about five foot three inches, with a slender figure, and she carried herself with a carefree air that exuded sensuality. It took him several moments after she had gone to collect his thoughts on the paperwork he had brought, and the questions he needed to ask. Then he glanced around, looking for clues about her.

It was a pleasant office, flooded with the illusion of natural light and with the hi-tech furnishings that were standard throughout the building. There were a few personal touches, but not many: a couple of potted plants on the floor; a framed photograph of a man he recognized as Dr Bannerman with a woman who looked like an older version of Montana Bannerman; and a Burberry mackintosh hung from a hook on the door.

He looked up at the ceiling with its built-in light and climate-control panels, and the ugly nozzles of the fire sprinkler system, wondering darkly what else might be concealed up there.

Yes, she was a rebel, this young woman, he thought. No question about it. She would need a little coaxing along; *gently, gently catch a monkey.* But if he played his cards right he had a feeling he could win himself a powerful ally. And she was perfectly positioned; her father was now effectively masterminding the entire Bendix Schere genetics research programme; there would be very little information to which she would not have access.

She came back with two Styrofoam cups. 'I'm afraid the coffee isn't too brilliant on this floor.'

'Now she tells me,' he said with a smile, accepting the cup.

She sat back down. 'You're in Group Patents? A patent agent?'

'Uh huh. I'm a patent attorney – kind of the American equivalent.'

'Where are you from?'

'Washington. Ever been there?'

'Yes,' she said. 'A few times. My father's given several talks at Georgetown University.'

'That's where I was an undergrad. It's a good place.'

'We're going over in a few weeks – he has to do a short promotion tour for his book. It's just come out in the States.'

'What's it about?'

'It's called *The Gene Bomb – The 21st Century Holocaust*.'

He looked at her and quietly tested the water. 'Sounds controversial?'

'Very. My father tends to be controversial. Rather too much for his own good.'

'I've kind of noticed – reading through his published papers – he doesn't seem to have too much truck with a lot of the conventions of his profession.'

'No, he doesn't.'

'How about you?'

'I do my best to keep him on the straight and narrow.'

'You don't go along with his view that patenting is wrong?'

She shook her head and he saw a trace of sadness in her expression. 'My father is a genius, Mr Molloy, but like a lot of geniuses he doesn't always live in the real world. I understand his feelings about pooling knowledge, particularly with genetics, but I actually believe in the patenting system. I believe in this company – I feel a great sense of privilege to be here.'

Conor's spirits dropped a fraction as he read the sincerity in the expression that accompanied her words. She wasn't just saying it to impress.

Give me time, he thought. Give me time and I'll change your mind about this company. I promise.

17

Reading, England. Tuesday 13 September, 1994
Tiny balls of rainwater rolled around on the glistening bonnet of the small blue Nissan. The inside of the car reeked of polish; the vinyl dashboard and the parcel shelf were buffed to a gloss, the carpets freshly shampooed. The last time he had been in his father-in-law's car, Alan Johnson reflected through his misery, it had been a tip, littered with old newspapers, sweet wrappers, yellow Post-it notes. He must have had it specially valeted for the funeral.

The wipers swept an arc in front of him, but he saw only a blur of rainwater that was indistinguishable from his tears. They were pulling up outside the house now; the late roses still in bloom in the front garden were bowed beneath the weight of water. Sarah's roses; she had watered them, tended them and she would never see them again. She would never see any more flowers.

Gone.

Dead.

Not coming back. Ever.

Five o'clock and it was growing gloomy. The sparse grass looked sodden and forlorn; a sapling cherry supported by a stake stood in its midst. All the windows were dark. No lights on. Sarah always told him it was important to leave lights on when you went out; she was practical, much more practical than himself. She did the shopping, paid the bills, juggled their bank balances and their overdrafts, organized the essentials. He stared at their home, barely a year old, modern, cosy, newly decorated. Sarah had chosen the colours, the curtains, the furnishings, the kitchen units. She had made it warm and cheery; now it looked dark and forbidding. And empty.

God, it looked empty.

He turned to his father-in-law. 'Will you come with me – I don't think I can face going in there alone.'

'Of course, of course,' Hubert Wentworth said quietly, pulling on the handbrake and switching off the engine. He leaned back, looking exhausted from the strain of the day and took a deep breath. 'You – ah – can stay with me, if you'd rather.'

Alan shook his head. 'Thank you – I need – need to –' His voice tailed. He needed to be alone with his grief, but he stared fearfully at the house; at the abyss.

It would be better once they went inside. He would switch on all the lights, turn up the heating. A slight panic was seizing him because he was already unable to picture Sarah clearly; her image kept slipping from his mind and he could only recall sections of it: the texture of her hair, the shape of her mouth; the colour of her bare shoulder; he was even having problems recalling her voice; just snatches of words, of the way she said his name. She only existed for him in fragments, like pieces of a vase lying shattered on a floor.

He pulled the rumpled handkerchief from his pocket, sniffed and dabbed his eyes. *Oh God, dear God, please bless my darling Sarah and give me strength to cope,* he prayed silently.

There was a sharp click as his father-in-law released his seat belt and slowly eased his bulky figure out of the car. Alan was grateful for the company of the kindly journalist, aware of Hubert Wentworth's own sadness also. They shared an unwelcome common bond: the older man had lost his wife in a tragic way also, many years ago. And now he had lost his only child as well.

Images remained burned into Alan's mind. The surgeon's knife slitting open Sarah's navel, the ribbon of blood following the blade's path. The nurses clamping back the parted skin; the surgeon pushing his gloved hands inside the opening. Then the slimy, wriggling creature, trailing a long white cord, raised into the air.

Their baby! Their baby had been born! God had made everything all right!

Then the silence.

No. Oh God, please no.

The tiny human shape coated in wet blood thrashing like a hooked fish. The mass of misshapen flesh; the empty skin; no nose, no mouth, just the one eye, oddly slanted in the centre of what might be the forehead.

And after that, a merciful blur.

Cars were parked in driveways along the street. Lights were on in all the other houses; televisions flickered through their windows; two kids roller-bladed along the pavement. Life was being lived; but Alan wondered why as they walked to the front door, the cold wind and rain lashing them. It was a Georgian-style door, painted green, with a brass knocker. Sarah's choice.

Alan was grateful to his father-in-law for the silence. He knew that he should have organized a party after the funeral, a wake, they were called. But that sort of thing was Sarah's domain, she had always been good at organizing, and it seemed only yesterday that they had sat together, selecting items for their wedding list, writing out invites. He would not have had the strength to face those same people at the house today.

Merely walking into the crematorium had been an ordeal; there had been a large turnout, mostly faces he did not recognize. Some cousins whom he barely knew had showed up, but that was all the representation from his side of the family. Other than his bedridden mother, who had been unable to leave her nursing home, he had no close living relatives; his father had been dead nearly a decade.

Sympathy. What the hell good was sympathy? As he pushed his key in the lock, all he could see was the brass handles on the coffin on the catafalque; and they weren't even real, just plastic coated to look like brass. A sham, an illusion; they were the regulation: *environmentally friendly*, the undertaker had told him. He saw the blue velvet curtains slowly closing in front of the coffin, closing on his Sarah. Heard the ghastly electrical hum. Then the music, Sarah's favourite piece, 'Oh For The Wings Of The Dove'. He wondered who knew, who had suggested it.

The hall was unwelcoming. As they shut the door behind them, the howling wind seemed to have followed them in and was still blowing. It seemed to be coming from above them. Alan switched on a light and a door slammed upstairs.

Both men glanced at each other, their grief momentarily suspended as they stared up into the darkness of the landing.

93

Hubert Wentworth put a steadying hand on his son-in-law's shoulder. 'You – ah – must have left a window open.'

Alan swallowed, his eyes locked on a framed sampler on the wall which read: 'God Bless This House.' A window open, yes, of course. His grief had been playing havoc with his mind. He had put the newspaper and the morning post in the fridge yesterday. Emptied an entire plate of food he had just microwaved for his supper last night into the dustbin by mistake. Autopilot; he was running on auto and the system had gone wonky.

Both men mounted the stairs. As Sarah's father switched on the landing light, the first thing that Alan saw was the cheery blue and white china sign tacked to the door in front of him: 'Baby's Room.' He had to force himself to grip the handle, turn it and push the door open.

A great weight seemed to be pushing back against the door from the other side and a howling draught greeted him. Then he gasped in shock: the window had been smashed; almost all the glass had been knocked out and lay in jagged pieces on the yellow carpet. A mobile of flying animals spun and clattered above the brand new cot. The eyes of the two mourners met and exchanged a mutual signal of alarm.

Alan had heard about this; callous burglars who read the death notices and raided homes during the funeral. But they wouldn't have done that to him, not the way Sarah – and the baby had died – no, surely?

Hubert Wentworth moved quickly as if suddenly transformed into an athlete, striding out and opening the door to the master bedroom. Alan followed: all the drawers from Sarah's dressing table had been pulled open and their contents strewn on the floor. The wardrobe doors were hanging open and most of the contents lay scattered.

Alan's eyes sprang to their wedding photograph in the silver frame on the windowsill and a strange feeling of relief gushed through him at the realization that the thieves had not, at least, taken that. He registered that the radio was still there and the small portable television and he wondered why. Then he entered the small ensuite bathroom. To his surprise the mirrored door of the medicine cabinet was open and several vials of pills and ointments had been knocked to the floor. The doors of the cupboard beneath the fitted washbasin were open also, and the contents emptied haphazardly.

'Christ – what the hell did they want in here?' Alan shouted in sudden fury. 'Drugs? Is it bloody kids looking for a high?'

The newspaperman was silent. He strode out of the room and went back downstairs. Alan followed. They checked the sitting room, the dining room, the kitchen; none of the downstairs rooms had been touched.

Hubert Wentworth picked up the phone and called the police. When he'd replaced the receiver, Alan said, trembling: 'Do you think we disturbed them? Is that why they haven't taken anything down here?'

By way of answer, Wentworth stood up, climbed the stairs again and went back into the bathroom, staring around thoughtfully. 'Be careful not to touch anything,' he said as his son-in-law joined him.

'Bloody kids!' Alan said again, close to hysterics.

Hubert Wentworth seemed far away. 'Kids,' he said, reflexively. 'Kids.' He knelt suddenly and squinted at a prescription vial on the floor, trying to read the label. Then he looked back up. 'Was Sarah on any medications?'

'What do you mean?'

'Anything – any kind of medication at all. Was she taking anything for her pregnancy; or *before* the pregnancy?'

'Well – yes – yes, she was.' Alan's face reddened and he stammered a little. 'We – we'd been trying for a baby f-for th-three years. W-w-why?'

The newspaperman's expression darkened, just a fraction. Then he said gently: 'Just a wild stab in the dark. I wouldn't wish to jump to any conclusions. We – ah – should – ah – see what's been taken. The police will have some ideas, perhaps. It – ah – it is far too early for conclusions.'

18

London. Friday 4 November, 1994

Seated at the dining table in Charley Rowley's London home, Conor Molloy felt he had entered a totally different world.

The small and elegant Georgian terraced house was imbued with an air of Old Money that he had previously only encountered in books and in the movies. Oil paintings filled much of the limited wall space; some were portraits of ancestors; some, bucolic country scenes and others, stormy seascapes. The carpet was buried beneath fine, well-trodden scatter-rugs, and every piece of furniture was an antique; there were some things that even today's finest interior designers could never emulate, Conor thought, and this room was one. The only way to acquire this effect was to inherit it.

The oval mahogany dining table had the right amount of scratches; the knives had blades worn thin with age, and bone handles that were cracked and stained; tiny mounds of salt sat in blue glass in silver holders, and the cut-glass goblets and tumblers were suitably mismatched. Charley Rowley sat at the head of the table, in a purple waistcoat over a striped shirt, green cords and suede loafers, reaching the punch line of a joke he had already told Conor, and which Conor had heard a year before in Boston.

'And then he said: *I can't remember where I live!*'

There was a roar of laughter, followed by isolated snorts and brays as the others latched on, one brain cell at a time. Conor drained his glass of claret; he was feeling dangerously light-headed and realized he had lost track of how much he had drunk. Champagne; Chablis; now this Forts de Latour. He was feeling bullish, a little over-confident; playing the role of Mr Innocent Nice Guy was coming easily, in spite of the fact that none of the company interested him, least of all Rowley's girlfriend, Lulu, who was overweight and over-bearingly loud.

He picked up his balloon of Armagnac, swilled the amber

liquid around, his thoughts slipping to Montana Bannerman, as they had done repeatedly since his second meeting with her two days ago. He compared the genuine warmth of her smile with the strained laughter of these supercilious young women, and realized he was more smitten than he liked to admit. But he was going to need a lot more help from her with her father's papers, so he was going to have plenty of excuses to meet her again.

He had ceased to bother about his blind date, who had been seated on his right and had not asked him one single thing about . himself all evening. Pretty amazing, he thought, considering she had spent a year in Washington. She had responded to his own attempts at conversation with a mixture of monosyllabic replies and selective deafness. Obviously didn't fancy him. Well, the feeling was mutual, he decided, glancing sideways at her now.

Amanda something-something. Velvet headband, black dress that looked like a corset with her boobs shoehorned in the cups and bulging over the top. And she revolted him by chewing Nicorette gum between every course. 'Just given up, darling,' she had said, addressing him the way she might have spoken to her hairdresser.

'Conor, your turn,' Rowley said, blowing out a cloud of cigar smoke. 'Any good jokes?'

Conor had been wracking his brains desperately for the past ten minutes, trying to think of something appropriately lewd and funny that wasn't a hundred years old. He had come up with only two gags both of which had now been told. 'How about my party trick?'

'What's that?' said the man opposite him.

'I can hypnotize people.'

'Yah?' said the girl at the far end of the table, on Rowley's left. She had long straight blonde hair and a pouting, almost aggressively beautiful face. 'I think hypnosis is a big con; that guy on the television fakes it, you can see he does.' She lit a cigarette with a gold lighter. 'Anyhow, I don't see how you can prove someone's hypnotized – they could just be acting.'

'I could hypnotize you *and* prove it,' Conor said.

'No way. People have tried before. I'm not suggestive – or whatever the word is.'

'You don't need to be. I can hypnotize anyone. It's Camilla, right?'

'Corinthia,' she said.

'OK, Corinthia. You want me to prove it to you?' He was aware of the sudden silence.

'Yah, go ahead – but I apologize in advance for ruining your trick,' she said with a trace of hostility.

'OK.' Conor stood up and walked, unsteadily, around the table. He nodded at his host. 'Charley, mind if I sit in your place for a moment?'

Rowley vacated the chair and Conor sat down; the girl wasn't quite so striking close up; he could see through her make-up that her skin was sallow. 'Want to put your cigarette down first?'

She shrugged and set it down, then stared back at him defiantly. Conor picked up the cigarette and held it by its lipsticky butt. All eyes were now on him. He turned it around theatrically, making an arc with the smoke, then pushed the left-hand cuff of his jacket and shirt up his wrist, exposing his watch and a couple of inches of bare skin above it.

He blew gently on the lighted end of the cigarette, making it glow a fierce red. While it was still glowing, he brought it slowly down on to the skin above his watch. There was a smell of singed hair, then a slight rustling sound as he crushed the cigarette out on his wrist. One of the women gave a tiny shriek of horror.

He continued stubbing the cigarette, rotating it methodically, then held up the blackened, crumpled end for all to see, savouring the shock on their faces.

'Have you got asbestos skin or something?' said a rather arrogant male art dealer.

Conor shook his head. 'Power of the mind.'

'It's impossible,' Corinthia said. 'It's obviously some clever sleight of hand.'

'You must have switched cigarettes,' Lulu said.

'I could do the same on any of you,' Conor said. 'I could prevent you feeling pain.' He smiled. 'Would someone like to volunteer?'

Corinthia looked at him hesitantly. Then she thrust her hand forward. 'Burn me and I'll sue,' she said.

There was a titter of laughter.

'I have insurance for this,' he said good-naturedly, avoiding eye contact and staring instead at the bridge of her nose. 'OK, I'm going to count to ten and you're going to go into a deep sleep; when I want you to come out I'll count to ten a second time and tell you to wake up – OK?'

'Yah, OK.' She gave a bored shrug.

He deepened his voice and allowed himself to become aware of the blur of her eyes, a brilliant emerald, so lurid he wondered if she was wearing tinted contact lenses. 'One,' he said and moved his head a few inches closer, without glancing away. 'Two.' He inched closer again. 'Three . . . four . . . five . . . six.' A couple of inches gained each time. Her blinking slowed right down and her eyes began to close. 'Seven . . . eight . . . nine . . . ten.'

He waited a beat. 'OK, Corinthia, you are now asleep, deep asleep, deep deep asleep. Do you feel awake or asleep?'

Her eyes were shut tight. Her voice sounded like a tape being played at the wrong speed. 'Sh'I'm shleep.'

Conor glanced briefly around the table; all eyes were watching. 'You sure you're not just pretending, Corinthia? You're really asleep?'

'Realshleep.'

'You want me to test whether you're telling the truth or not? You did tell me you were impossible to hypnotize, so how do I know you're not just lying to me now?'

'Realshleep,' she mumbled again.

'OK.' Conor took out a cigarette and handed it to the girl on his left. 'Could you light this for me – just so everyone here knows it's really alight and not some trick.'

The girl put it into her mouth, ducked forward towards a candle and lit the cigarette from the flame. She inhaled, coughed and handed the cigarette back to Conor.

Conor glanced around his audience, then took his subject's left arm in his own left hand. 'OK, Corinthia, you have a beautiful arm. Do you have any scars on it?'

'S . . . no.'

'You sure about that? No cigarette burns or anything like that?'

'No scars.'

Conor held the arm out and rotated it, like a conjurer showing an empty box, so that everyone could see it. Then slowly and theatrically, he brought the lighted tip of the cigarette up to her skin.

There was a crinkling sound, then a crackle like grease-proof paper as the flame pressed into the skin. Someone gasped. Someone else said: 'Jesus!'

Conor pressed harder, rotating the cigarette until it was completely extinguished, then solemnly handed it back to the girl who had lit it. 'Could you check that it's out – I don't want to start a fire or anything.'

He heard an uncertain titter of laughter from two places away. Then he lowered his subject's arm on to the table. 'Right, Corinthia, I'm going to bring you back now. I'm going to count to ten and you'll open your eyes and be awake. Here we go. One . . . two . . . three . . .'

On the count of ten, she opened her eyes and blinked with a confused expression, first at Conor, then around the table.

'Welcome back,' he said.

She frowned at him, darting short, suspicious glances, saying nothing.

'Did you feel anything?' Conor asked. 'On your left arm?'

'Yah – think someone was tickling me with a feather brush or something.'

'Have a look – do you see any kind of mark there?'

She glanced at where he indicated with his finger, and rubbed a fleck of ash off, looking puzzled. 'Mark? Can't see anything.' She held her arm up under the candlelight.

Conor reached over and picked up the crumpled cigarette. 'You didn't feel that being stubbed out on your arm?'

'Come on! You didn't!'

'Christ, Conor!' Charley Rowley said. 'How the hell did you do it?'

Conor smiled and said nothing.

'It just felt like a tickle,' Corinthia said, her voice subdued suddenly. 'Just a tickle.'

'It's a trick,' the art dealer said. 'Bloody clever, had us all fooled.'

'It's not a trick, Julian,' a girl said. 'I saw it. He actually stubbed it out on her skin.'

'I still don't believe I was hypnotized,' Corinthia said, recovering her poise. 'It's obvious you have some trick cigarette you switch with the real one.'

Conor raised his eyebrows. 'That's what you're comfortable believing, right?'

'It's not a question of *comfort*. It's the truth. There's no way you could influence my body just by looking at me and speaking to me. I don't believe it.'

Conor was silent for a moment, glancing around the table. Then he turned to the young woman and said, quietly: 'There's a glass of red wine in front of you, right?'

She looked fleetingly at the cut-glass goblet, then back to Conor. 'Yes.'

Conor focused on the bridge of her nose once more. 'I want you to watch that glass very very carefully, don't take your eyes off it, not for one second, just keep on staring at it.' As he spoke his voice became deeper and slower. 'Keep staring at it, Corinthia, and as you stare you can feel the power growing inside you, spreading through your body, you can feel energy radiating out from deep in your stomach, travelling through your veins, building in your muscles. It's making you feel strong, so strong. You love that glass, don't you, Corinthia?'

She nodded and said, in a slurred voice: 'Sh'yesh.'

'You love that glass very much. It is one of the most beautiful glasses you have ever seen in your life. You covet it, don't you? You would like to have glasses like that on your table at home. The truth is, Corinthia, that you are a little envious of Charley for having these glasses, aren't you?'

'A liddle.'

'Only a little? I have a feeling you might be very jealous indeed. I think you might have a burning hatred for Charley for having these glasses. But there's something you can do about that, isn't there? And you know exactly what it is. Concentrate on the glass. Concentrate all the energy that's inside your body, feel it building up. Centre on the glass. Hate the glass, Corinthia! Hate it more than you've ever hated anything in your life. Are you hating it now?'

'Yes, yes, *hating*.' There was an almost messianic fervour in her voice.

'Hate it more! Now more still. Centre every inch of hatred in your entire body on that glass. Hate it with all your body, with all your heart.'

Corinthia's face was turning red; her whole body was shaking.

'Now release that energy!'

There was a sharp report; the glass shattered in front of his eyes, the bowl fragmenting outwards like a tiny bomb. Shards of glass tinkled as they struck pieces of crockery, silverware, cutlery. A pool of red wine began seeping into the linen tablecloth around the base of the stem, which was the only part of the glass still intact.

There was a moment of stunned silence. Conor caught his host's eyes; Rowley was looking aghast.

'My God!' Rowley's girlfriend said, and began to sprinkle salt on to the wine stain.

Corinthia stared silently at the table, her face ashen, as if she had seen a ghost.

'P-pour some white wine on to it – stops it staining,' a woman said.

'Sorry about the glass, Charley,' Conor said. 'I'll pay you for it.'

Rowley shook his head. 'Wasn't you that broke it.' He relit his cigar with a shaking hand. 'Shit! That's creepy.'

'Got any other tricks?' the girl on his right asked.

'Bit of alchemy or something, Conor?' Rowley said, trying with a nervous smile to make light of it. 'Turn a few base metals into gold for an encore? Or mix some magic potion to cure all diseases?'

Conor winked at him. 'That's the day job,' he said.

19

Barnet, North London. 1946

'Do you want a cage?'

Daniel Judd shook his head.

The shopkeeper in his brown overalls eyed the small, neatly dressed boy with a library book tucked in the crook of his arm dispassionately. 'You need to keep 'em in cages. They gnaw.'

Daniel Judd shook his head again. 'I just need a box to get it home,' he said in a shy voice that was barely more than a whisper.

'You got a cage at home?'

The boy blushed and nodded.

The shopkeeper shrugged, delved beneath his counter and placed a small shoebox on the top. He rummaged around again, produced a skewer, and proceeded to punch half a dozen holes in the lid of the box. He eyed the boy again. 'You want a box of food for it?'

The boy nodded, and glanced nervously at the door, frightened his mother might happen to walk past. He slid his hand into his pocket, pulled out the ten shilling note he had been given by an aunt for his twelfth birthday a few days before, and pushed it towards the man.

The till rang and the shopkeeper grudgingly handed him nine shillings and one penny change, then pushed the box towards him. 'Mind to give it plenty of water.'

Daniel opened the door of the shop, heard the sharp ping of the bell and peered at the busy street in both directions before venturing out. There was another ping as the door closed behind him. A bus went past, then a black Hillman and a grocery boy on a bicycle. He tucked the box under his mackintosh and, half walking half running, hurried home, ducking his head for protection against the heavy late August drizzle as well as to reduce the chances of being spotted.

He went under the railway arch, past a bomb site with one façade of a terraced house still partially standing, and into the tree-lined suburban street. A semi-detached pebble dash. He saw a neighbour, Mrs Cornish, a friend of his mother's, coming out of her gate, and crossed the road to avoid her. A van hooted at him as he ran across its path.

A boy from a few houses up, Jimmy Dyers, was careering unsteadily down the pavement on a scooter and stopped when he reached Danny.

'Want to come and play this afternoon?' he asked.

'Can't, I'm busy.'

'What you got?'

'Nothing,' Daniel said, his face reddening.

'What's in the box?'

'Nothing.'

'Can I see?'

Daniel pushed it further under his coat.

'That a book?'

'I have to get home – my mum's waiting.'

'Can you play tomorrow?'

'I'll see. If I'm allowed.'

'You're scared of your mum, aren't you?'

'I'm not.'

'You are so!'

'I'm *not*.'

'Everyone says you are. My dad says your parents are crazy.'

Daniel hurried on and turned left into an identical street. He could see his house, six along on the right, and stopped behind an elm. He removed his mackintosh and carefully bundled the shoebox and book tightly inside it, then walked on with the package wedged underarm, trying to appear nonchalant.

The rain came down harder as he crossed the road, and he glanced at the bay windows, trying to detect any sign of movement behind the net curtains. He knew that when he left home his mother often watched him from the upstairs front window, checking to see if he committed any sins in the street.

As he approached the low wall that enclosed the rosebed, he first satisfied himself that the coast was clear, then leaned over the wall and pushed the box and the book out of sight at the base of a sprawling Old English rose. Wet petals brushed his face and a thorn pricked his hand; he smelled the heavily perfumed scent fleetingly, then stood up and carried on, with his coat over his arm, unlatching the gate, walking up the driveway, and around to the side door.

He opened it and went into the kitchen. His mother was standing in there pouring cake mix into a row of baking trays, her weekly duty for the church coffee morning; a mournful violin concerto played on the wireless. She looked up at him sharply. 'Why aren't you wearing your coat?'

'I was wearing it.'

She reached out a hand and touched his shirt. Then without warning, she slapped him hard on the face. 'Liar! God sees your lies, Daniel, God hears every one. Understand?'

He nodded sullenly.

'You're soaking, you stupid boy! Go and change at once.'

He watched her resume her work of carefully filling each of the indents in the tray and scooping off the drips. Five more trays, he counted. There was time if he was quick.

He closed the kitchen door, ran across the hall, opened the front door as silently as he could, then sprinted over to the rosebed, picked up the box and book, wrapping his coat around them, dashed back to the house and slipped inside. He eyed the kitchen door fearfully; but it stayed closed.

He raced up to his bedroom, pushed the box under his bed, then sat down for a moment and breathed out. When he opened the door again and peered out there was no sign of his mother; he could hear the wireless still playing. He returned to lean under the bed and slid the box out, prising up one end of the lid and peering in. 'Hello, little fellow,' he said. 'Expect you'd like a drink? Won't be a sec.' He gingerly pushed his finger forward, mindful of having been bitten by a rabbit before, stroked the top of its head, then closed the lid and tiptoed through to the bathroom.

He looked around for a receptacle. There was the white Bakelite tooth mug with the family's three toothbrushes sticking out. Too risky if his mother came in. Then he saw the sponge by the bathtub. Perfect! He held it for a few seconds under the cold tap, then hurried back into his bedroom.

Squeezing some water on to his palm, he held it out and

after a few moments, the baby rabbit licked greedily. 'You're really thirsty, aren't you?' he whispered, thinking hard. There was a bottle of ink in his desk drawer. He unscrewed the cap, squeezed the sponge into it, then put the ink cap in the box with the rabbit, and added a generous portion of food. Stroking the creature's back, he whispered, 'See you later, chappie,' closed the lid and pushed everything back under the bed.

He turned to the book and found the pages he had marked with a tiny dog-ear. He read avidly for some minutes, memorizing the instructions, before pushing it under the bed too. Then he tiptoed into his parents' bedroom, listening for sounds from downstairs, and made his way across to his mother's dressing table.

One of the drawers was full of stockings. Shaking with nerves he pulled a single stocking out and crammed it into the pocket of his shorts; next, he cast his eye at the silver photograph frame on top of the dressing table. There were half a dozen black and white pictures of her, each stacked behind the other; he removed one from the very back, slipped it inside his shirt, and tiptoed back to his room.

He added the two new items to those already under the bed, changed out of his wet clothes and went down for his tea with a broad grin on his face.

He was ready. Now he just had to wait for the right day, according to the instructions. And he had to hope they didn't strap his hands; they had not done so for some weeks now. His only real concern was his purchase from the pet shop – if it started scratching or making any other sounds he was in trouble. Killing it would be the easiest solution, but that would defeat the purpose in having a living creature. It *had* to be alive; it said so very clearly in the book. And he intended to obey the book to the letter.

Some pages had words he didn't understand, but he reckoned he had grasped enough. Somewhere in the book it said that the most important thing was to *believe* it would work. If you believed it would happen then you could make it happen. And Daniel did *believe*.

20

Berkshire, England. Sunday 6 November, 1994

Rabbits scattered in the headlights as Monty gently navigated her MG through the potholes of the cart track. She was tired from a long drive in heavy traffic, and looking forward to being home again after spending a fractious and exhausting weekend in Bath with old schoolfriend Polly Maguire, husband Richard, and their three appallingly spoilt and obnoxious children.

It was the same every time she visited them; a perfect tonic for any pangs she might feel about not having a family of her own. The radio announced the seven o'clock news. She thought of Polly who would be struggling for a good hour or so yet to get the last of the children to bed, and for a long while after that to get them all asleep. By contrast Monty savoured the prospect of her own tranquil evening ahead, curling up in front of a log fire with the Sunday papers and the television.

Foxholes Cottage was remote, isolated half a mile off a quiet country road, and four miles from the nearest village. Her closest neighbours were the farmer and his wife who lived a mile further down the track, their house out of sight in a dip beyond a row of pylons.

Apart from farm vehicles and the occasional lost rambler, no one ever passed by. She felt secure here, it was her refuge. Only twenty minutes from their old lab on the university campus, it had been perfectly situated. Now, having to commute to London most days, it was less convenient. She had tried using the train, but the journey time was no quicker and it was considerably more expensive than driving. Although she was earning over twice what she had been drawing previously with her father, she was not overpaid and still needed to budget.

She passed the large barn on her right, then saw the silhouette of her cottage ahead, in complete darkness. For a moment she was concerned, because she could clearly remember having left lights on in several rooms. Then she smiled;

Alice, her cleaning lady who came three mornings a week, had been going to pop in today to feed the cats – as she always did – in Monty's absence. Alice was a resourceful woman who journeyed out here by bus and foot, but she could never get it into her head that leaving lights on was anything other than a waste of money.

The exterior of the cottage was in a poor state of repair. The white picket fence urgently needed painting, and some of the clapboard cladding was lifting away from the upper storey, not helped by the tangle of ivy, honeysuckle and clematis which had suckered on to every plank and brick.

Monty had originally been attracted more by the tranquillity and the fine sweeping views than by the actual building itself, which was unexceptional looking – half-timbered, traditional and functional rather than picture-postcard pretty. It had been built in the 1880s to house a farm manager, and was grander than a traditional artisan cottage, with three bedrooms and good-sized reception rooms, as well as boasting a study.

Monty pulled on to the weed-strewn hard standing, climbed out and hauled open the stiff up-and-over garage door. Then she drove the car in, nudging it close to the racks of apples that lined the far wall. A couple of inches either way made the difference between the door closing and not.

She eased herself out into the narrow gap between the car and the wall, savouring the pungent smell of apples. It had been a bumper crop this year from the five trees in her back garden, yielding a stock that would last her a few months yet. She was an erratic gardener, but she enjoyed eating her own produce, particularly in the knowledge that it was healthy food that had not been sprayed with toxic chemicals.

The garage door closed with a click and a dull metallic boom, and she cut across to the small porch over the front door, pulled her cigarette lighter from her handbag and, using the flame as a torch, slipped her key in the lock. It was a cold, starry night, cold enough for a frost, she thought, shivering.

Two pairs of emerald eyes stared out of the darkness of the small hallway. 'Hello, boys!' she said, putting her overnight bag on the floor and kneeling down as Watson and Crick, her tiger-striped moggies, came towards her, warily at first, then more eagerly, Watson rubbing himself against her hand.

'Did Alice leave you all in the dark? Poor things!'

She switched on the light and noted that everything looked orderly, the *Mail on Sunday*, the *Observer* and *The Sunday Times* neatly stacked by Alice on the hall table. Monty was something of a news junkie, forever scouring the pages of the national and scientific press for information that might be of use to her father, and even more so when he had a new book out – in the hope of coming across reviews.

She shivered again from the cold, keeping her Burberry on for the moment, and went through into the kitchen, grateful for the cosy warmth of the Aga that greeted her. The red light winked on the answering machine, so she hit the playback button, glancing down to check that there was milk and food for the cats in their bowls.

The first message was from her friend Anna Sterling, suggesting that if Monty was working in London on Thursday they went to the new art exhibition at the ICA. The second was a tetchy one from her father, asking her which days she would be in London and which in their old lab, next week. He always sounded grumpy on the answering machine, as if annoyed that she wasn't there in person. And there was a third message: from Walter Hoggin, calling to thank Monty for her help in getting him reinstated. He would ring again, he said.

Still full after a late lunch, she decided to have a light supper and opened the fridge to see what needed eating. There was a carton of mushrooms that were starting to look a bit sad and she decided on one of her favourite snacks of mushrooms on toast. She raised the Aga hot plate cover, put a frying pan on to it and dropped in a generous knob of butter. Almost immediately it began to sizzle.

She switched on the radio, recognized 'Love Is All Around', the theme song from *Four Weddings and a Funeral*, and turned it up loud, then went back to the sink and began to scrub the mushrooms. Both cats nuzzled around her legs. It was five past seven; she knew her father always watched the science programme, *Equinox*, at this time, so there was no point in calling him back until after eight; and she'd call Anna later if she had the energy; if not, tomorrow.

She stopped after only four small mushrooms, pinching her stomach, which felt bloated. Putting on weight, she thought grimly. You get past thirty and that's it, all downhill and left on the shelf. Going to spend the rest of my life sitting here by the fire, turning into a fat old spinster with her cats.

Her thoughts flashed suddenly to the American patent lawyer who had come into her office. Conor Molloy. Mr Bloody Perfect. Tall, slim, dishy. And unless she had imagined it, there had been a definite look of interest in his eyes. She shrugged it off; he looked like the kind who flirted with everyone. Probably had some glamorous bimbo in tow – a fledgling model would be his speed. Men who were that good-looking almost irritated her, and this one really *was*.

Crick and Watson suddenly stiffened and turned towards the door. Monty looked down at them, alarmed. 'What is it, boys?' She turned the radio down sharply, and listened. After a few moments she heard the feeble rasp of the doorbell, and a prick of unease went through her: visitors rarely called, and almost never after dark.

She went back into the hall and peered through the spyhole her father had insisted she have installed in the front door. It gave her a goldfish's eye view of a balding, rather meek man in a raincoat. He did not immediately fit her mental profile of what a mass murderer would look like, but she decided to be cautious, and engaged the safety chain before opening the door and peering out.

He was middle-aged and carried about him the persona of someone who has seen better times but is not completely down on their cups. His herringbone coat was well cut, in spite of its present shabbiness, and he was respectably shod in stout brown brogues. His portly figure reminded her of a character from Dickens, and the sadness on his face touched something inside her.

He spoke slowly and apologetically. 'I'm – ah – trying to find Miss Bannerman's residence.'

She kept the chain in place, concerned that she could see no sign of a car. 'I'm Miss Bannerman. Who are you, please?'

'Of course, of course. Forgive me. Countryside, quite right to be wary of strangers . . .' He fished in his pocket for his wallet, extricated a business card and proffered it through the gap.

Hubert Wentworth. Deputy News Editor. Thames Valley Gazette, she read.

'My daughter, you see.' He wheezed slightly. 'Used to work for you – ah – your father's lab. Bannerman Research Laboratories?'

'Daughter?' Monty did not recognize the surname.

'Johnson – her married name.'

Monty brightened. 'Sarah Johnson? Yes, of course, she worked as our book-keeper for about three years. Left about six months ago – to have a baby. How is she? Has she had the b –' She stopped suddenly as she read the expression on his face; the man seemed to have aged a decade in a few seconds. She thought for a moment he was going to collapse. 'Please, come in.'

'Would you allow me? Thank you. Just for a moment, I won't detain you,'

He stepped in with the gait of an old man, although he couldn't be much more than late fifties, she thought.

'Nice,' he said. 'Nice house. Beautiful, the countryside. Always wanted to try it myself – but – ah – Françoise –' He lowered his head as if he were having a problem composing himself.

'May I take your coat?'

He had noted a painting on the wall; a simple country landscape of a field and a barn, and a solitary oak tree. 'May I enquire the artist's name?'

She blushed. 'It was me.'

He peered more closely. 'Such talent; do you exhibit?'

'I'm afraid not. I haven't for years – I don't have the time.'

'Yes, time, the Ancient Enemy.' He smiled sadly.

'Would you like a drink of something? Coffee, tea? Beer?'

'Just a glass of water would be fine. I parked at the end of the lane by the way – didn't know if I'd be able to turn.'

She hung his coat up then looked at him again. He was wearing a crumpled grey flannel suit, a white shirt and green

111

tie with a dull logo in the centre. A few strands of hair stood on the top of his dome like lone pines on a windswept hillock.

'Come through to the kitchen; afraid I only just got home myself and I haven't put the heating on yet.' She still kept her own coat on.

'I won't detain you long,' he said again, noticing the simmering butter, then eased himself on to one of the wooden chairs.

Monty removed the frying pan, closed the lid of the Aga, and provided a glass of water. Somehow she managed to do it all in one movement.

'So,' the visitor lifted his eyes up to Monty, 'so you didn't hear – about Sarah?' He shook his head as if not really expecting a reply. 'Of course, no reason why you should've done; but she died, you see, in childbirth.'

Monty sat down herself, shaken. 'Died?' she echoed uselessly. 'God. I'm sorry. So sorry.'

'Thank you, you're very kind. She always said you and your father were so kind.'

'She was a lovely girl – I liked her very much. I can't believe she's –'

'Terrible,' he said.

'How's her husband? Alan, isn't it? Is he coping? And the baby?'

Wentworth cupped Monty's tumbler in his hands, trying to draw warmth from it. 'The baby was too badly deformed to survive.'

Monty thought about the quiet, hard-working girl who had come in to tell her she was leaving to concentrate on being a mother. 'How awful,' she said. 'I'm really sorry for you, Mr Wentworth, and for Alan. I'll write him a note.'

'Yes, thank you. Thank you – but – ah –' He glanced up at the electric light bulb in its yellow shade, as if it might provide him with the answer to some cosmic question. Then he looked down at the small pine table again. 'Alan – ah –' He paused and seemed to crumple a fraction, like a collapsing balloon. 'He couldn't take it, you see. Killed himself the day after the funeral – he – ah – he – in his motor car, you see, in the garage – with a hosepipe.'

Monty sat rigidly still, barely able to absorb all the bad news. Death scared her; it was OK when people much older than she died, she could accept that, but she got very spooked when it happened to people her own age or younger. She began to wonder where this was leading, why Sarah's father had made so much effort to bring her the news.

Reading her mind, Hubert Wentworth said: 'I would have tried to telephone you – to save such an intrusion, I – you see –' His eyes roamed the room for a moment and lighted on another of her paintings. 'One must be careful of phone lines; so easy to tap or to bug, if you understand what I mean?'

She frowned, asking herself if he had become a little unhinged by his tragedy.

'Cyclops,' he said, looking up suddenly and staring directly at her. 'Cyclops Syndrome. You've heard of it?' He raised his eyebrows quizzically.

'No . . .?'

'It's a rare genetic disorder affecting babies; ghastly thing, quite ghastly.' He sipped some water. 'Misshapen head, no features at all, no mouth, no nose, no nothing. Except one eye in the centre of the forehead.' He tapped his own forehead. 'Sometimes hair on the body as well.'

'Oh God,' Monty said, as the hideous image gripped her imagination. She shuddered inwardly. 'That's what happened?'

He looked up at the light again, then at the oven. 'An Aga. Such a comforting thing to have. No country kitchen complete without one. Heats the water as well?'

'Yes,' she said quietly. 'At least the kitchen is always cosy.'

'Of course. So important. My wife always wanted a house with an Aga.' His voice tailed. 'Rambling; I'm sorry. Tell me I'm being a nuisance and I'll go.'

'You're not being a nuisance,' Monty said gently.

He tapped the side of the glass with one of his fingers. 'Never had the edge, you see, not that hard edge you needed to make it to Fleet Street. I should have done something else, but you get into a way of life and you stay there.' He gave her a smile that was as sad as bereavement itself. 'Forgive me, I'm always rambling. Good reporters listen, bad ones talk.'

113

Monty smiled, her patience holding. It was her visitor who glanced at the butter congealing in the pan.

'I won't keep you from your supper, you must be hungry. Two cases a year in the British Isles, that's the average incidence of Cyclops Syndrome over the last thirty years.'

'That's two too many,' she said.

Wentworth let out a deep breath, then inhaled slowly. 'An average of one every twenty-six weeks.' He hesitated. 'So it may be noteworthy, perhaps, that there have been *three* cases in the past two months?'

Monty thought for a moment. 'I suppose things do go in clusters sometimes; there might be long periods with none.'

'Of course, of course, you're quite right. One mustn't jump to conclusions. Shock and bereavement can make a person lose their judgement.' The faintest trace of a smile etched his features like the first lines of a brass rubbing. 'But so easy, also, to allow things to escape one's attention.'

She watched him, expectantly.

'So easy to dismiss so much as coincidence, would you not agree?'

'Coincidence.'

Crick nuzzled Hubert Wentworth's leg. He leaned over and tickled him. 'One Cyclops case here in Berkshire. One in Birmingham and one in Edinburgh. In each case the mother died shortly before or during childbirth from an unidentified virus.'

'Does a viral attack on the mother normally accompany Cyclops Syndrome?'

The cat began purring, and Wentworth continued stroking him. 'No, not at all.' He sat upright again, pressed his lips together and shrugged. 'Coincidence, of course, could so easily just be coincidence.'

Monty felt a sudden deep unease. 'That's extremely bizarre,' she said slowly.

Wentworth scratched one of his large, overhanging eyebrows. 'We have a bright young lady reporter on our paper; Medical Correspondent, she's called. Her first job. Zandra Wollerton. I don't have the time, you see, for investigating; takes a lot of travelling, a lot of patience; charm, guile. Zandra

114

is a girl with guile; tough too. You'll see her name in the nationals in a few years.' He paused and drained his glass.

'More water?'

'No, I must go. Your supper. You must have your supper.' He paused to collect his thoughts. 'Zandra, yes, such a bright girl. She's found a link, yes, a connection. Just a small one, a tiny one, probably nothing at all, a red herring.' He went on. 'Bendix Schere, the company that's taken your father's lab over, they manufacture a fertility drug marketed under the brand name of Maternox, yes?'

'It's one of their biggest selling products. I think it's the biggest-selling fertility drug in the world.'

'Of course. That's why one can't jump to any conclusion. But it is interesting that all three of these women had been prescribed Maternox prior to falling pregnant.'

The unease Monty had been feeling began to evaporate. For a moment she had thought he was going to come up with something that would really shock her, but instead it seemed that he was clutching at a thin straw. 'It's certainly a strange coincidence, Mr Wentworth – but I think you'd have to look at it in context. One in six women in the world suffer from infertility problems. A vast number of them in this country take Maternox at some point – and world sales are phenomenal. For just three cases – however awful – it seems – I mean –' She raised her hands. 'It's strange, I agree, but not very conclusive.'

'Of course, of course. You're quite right. But there is one more detail, you see. Again small, again inconclusive.' He turned his empty glass around in his hands. 'This reporter, Zandra Wollerton. I suggested to her that she contact the Medical Liaison Officer of Bendix Schere, and enquire if they had any prior knowledge of a link between Maternox and Cyclops Syndrome.'

'And did they?'

'None whatsoever. They were quite emphatic.' He leaned over and began stroking the cat again. 'But just three days later Zandra Wollerton's flat was broken into; turned upside down and inside out.' He looked back up at her. 'Nothing was stolen. Not a single thing.'

'Professionals?' she said.

'Oh yes, no doubt of that. Not a fingerprint in the place. Nothing. The police said it seemed as if someone knew exactly what they wanted.' He paused. 'You see, there's something else curious. On the afternoon of Sarah's funeral, her home was burgled, ransacked. Alan could find nothing missing at all.' He frowned. 'Burglars are normally after consumer goods, jewellery, silverware, cash. These ignored all that. Possibly they were disturbed, but it seems strange that they found time to riffle through the medicine cabinet in the bathroom, wouldn't you think?'

She said nothing, a tight lump forming in her throat.

'Now you understand, perhaps, why I decided to come and see you in person, and not risk a telephone call?'

Monty nodded bleakly. The man was irritating her slightly and yet there was something about him that prevented her from dismissing him totally; sincerity. 'You are making some very big suppositions, Mr Wentworth.'

'Yes, and I might be quite wrong. Let's hope I am.'

'And how can *I* help you in all this?'

'I need someone inside Bendix Schere to dig out more information. Sarah used to talk to me about you and your father's integrity. I hoped perhaps – under the circumstances – I – ah – might persuade you to have a go for me? In confidence, of course. No names, nothing to connect you.'

She sat, thinking hard for some moments, trying to organize her thoughts. She looked back at him, suddenly feeling very apprehensive, as if the darkness outside were pressing in hard all around her. 'Tell me what you need,' she said. 'And I'll try.'

21

London. Monday 7 November, 1994
Shortly after ten o'clock, Monty drove the MG down off the Westway ramp, the small wipers clumping away almost

116

uselessly against the rain. Two politicians were arguing about Bosnia on the radio, and an intermittent dribble of water fell on to her forehead from a patched rip in the roof. She had gone into their old laboratory first thing to search for some files Conor Molloy needed, and had hoped that by driving into London a couple of hours later than normal she would miss the rush-hour jams, but the traffic was still bad.

She felt tired and irritable, having barely slept. Her mood had been swinging throughout the night from shock and sadness at the news of Sarah Johnson's death to confusion about Bendix Schere. Was Hubert Wentworth mad? Paranoid? Or was there something in what he'd suggested?

She knew that, inevitably, with almost every drug on the market there was a downside; there were always a small number of people who suffered side-effects. It was perfectly understandable that the newspaperman was distraught about what had happened to his own family, and would clutch at any explanation for the horror – but was the discovery that two other people had experienced similar symptoms going to prove anything at all?

And there was a deeper moral issue beyond this: even if there was a link to Maternox, millions of people around the world had been helped by the drug: there were numerous healthy children in the world who owed their existence to it. With all pharmaceuticals, it was a question of weighing the good and the bad and making cold, hard decisions. Percentage chances. It was easy to look at percentage chances when you were dealing with anonymous statistics. Much harder when it was a real human being whom you loved – and difficult to accept the risk if it involved someone you loved.

But if the newspaperman was right in connecting the break-ins, that pointed to something altogether more sinister. She needed more information, she decided, before she did anything at all; it was far too early in the Bannermans' relationship with Bendix Schere for her to start making waves – she was having enough problems preventing her father from upsetting people, without going around asking awkward questions herself; and she had a horror of suddenly finding her name plastered all over the media.

Mr Wentworth seemed a decent enough sort, but he was a journalist and she'd had enough experience over the years to know that the press considered the pharmaceutical industry – and everyone connected with it – a legitimate target. You had to be very careful indeed with them.

She indicated left and nudged her way aggressively into the clogged near-side lane, returning a furious blast of a horn with a two-fingered flick, then turned sharply into a side street, slowed down and scanned the pavement.

She braked as she saw an empty call-box ahead, pulled over and hurried in, yanking the door shut behind her. She pushed a coin in the slot, opened her diary, turned to the page where she'd written the number Wentworth had given her last night, and called it.

'Thames Valley Gazette,' a woman answered.

'May I speak to Zandra Wollerton, please?'

'Her line's busy – shall I put you through to the News Desk?'

'I'll hold.'

The black digits on the indicator displayed 97p credit left. She tapped the small shelf, and glanced at the business cards stuck to the wall. *Monica. French Masseuse. Soothe away those tensions. Gabriella. Latin lessons and correction therapy. Donyelle. Ebony; skin two.*

She often wondered who these women really were. She had read an article in the *Independent* recently that said a lot of them were educated types making easy money. Through the misting window, she saw a tramp shambling along in a filthy coat, clutching a ragged bundle.

'Putting you through now,' the switchboard receptionist said, interrupting her thoughts.

A moment later she heard a hard, sharp voice that sounded in a hurry. 'Zandra Wollerton.'

'Hello – my name's Montana Bannerman – Hubert Wentworth asked me to get in touch –'

'Right,' the reporter cut in, abruptly. 'He told me you'd be calling. Be best if we could meet somewhere. Some place near your office.'

'Or I can meet you in Berkshire, if that's easier?'

118

'I have to be in London at midday tomorrow. Are you free late afternoon?'

'Yes – I'm flexible – I could fit in with –'

'How about four o'clock? Trying to think of somewhere near you where we could talk. Do you know the Thistle Hotel?'

'No.'

'It's about five minutes' walk. Corner of Mottram and Gower Place – big ugly building, looks like a multi-storey.'

'I'll find it.'

'There's a coffee shop on the first floor, called the Woolsack.'

'Can you tell me what you look like – so I can recognize you?'

'It's OK, got your photo on file from the takeover article. I have cropped black curly hair and glasses, and I'm short, OK?'

'I'm short too,' Monty said.

'Has its advantages. Four o'clock, the Thistle,' said the reporter, and hung up.

Charming, Monty thought. Anyone would think she was doing *me* a favour. She replaced the receiver and change spattered into the slot.

She scooped it up, then as she turned, her heart jumped. The doorway was blocked by a tall man in a turned-up raincoat, wearing dark glasses in spite of the rain. A shimmy of fear ran through her. He was standing absolutely motionless, staring straight at her.

Instinctively she stepped back. Wild thoughts raced through her mind. Could call the police. Just punch 999; her mouth felt dry with panic. The booth suddenly felt like a prison. There was only one way out, and he was standing right in front of it. Thoughts of the break-ins the newspaperman had told her about flashed through her mind. Ruthless, shadowy men in masks and leather gloves stopping at nothing. Christ, hadn't done anything, just spoken to – then she noticed the golden dog beside the man, the retriever with the short handle to his wrist and she suddenly laughed at her stupidity in panicking and pushed open the door.

'It's free, sorry to have kept you,' she said. 'I'll hold the door for you.'

The blind man murmured his thanks and stepped carefully past his dog into the booth.

Monty walked along the corridor, peering in through each lab window in search of Jake Seals. She finally saw the Chief Technician in a small, otherwise empty laboratory at the far end, where a number of her father's experiments were in progress.

Wearing a protective suit, gloves and glasses, he was standing just beyond the massive chromium head of an emergency shower, carefully hefting a blue bucket out of a Perspex-fronted fume cabinet labelled; DANGER! BIO-HAZARD!

He placed the container on a white speckled work top, unscrewed the lid and set it down; then lifted out an amber half-gallon Winchester bottle that was covered in a protective film, and set that down on the work top, using all the care and respect that the handling of corrosive and toxic substances required.

Monty waited until the bottle was standing safely, then said: 'Good morning, Mr Seals.'

He turned and looked at her, removed his glasses and shook his long, lank hair away from his face. 'How you doing?'

'OK, thanks. Did you have a good weekend?'

'It was all right,' he said, with a sly grin. 'You?'

She shrugged, feeling awkward under the intensity of his gaze. His eyes seemed to be X-raying her as if he was trying to pry out any secrets. He did this constantly and it irked her. His whole manner irked her. 'Reasonable, I suppose. What's in that bottle?'

'Bendix Soup.'

'Oh yes? What do you have with it – croutons?'

'You can have croutons if you want. Problem is they'd dissolve before you got a chance to eat them. So would the spoon and most of your face.'

'Nice!'

'I can think of a few people I'd like to serve it up to.'

120

'I'm sure you can. Does it have any other name?'

'BS93L5021.' He raised his eyebrows.

'Sounds a mouthful.'

'You don't want to know it; it shouldn't even be here – ought to be in an isolation chamber. Typical of the kind of shit Bendix Schere produces. It doesn't even officially exist.' He shook his mane of hair. 'Ever read Kurt Vonnegut's *Cat's Cradle*?'

'Yes – it's one of my favourite books.'

'Remember the chemical *Ice Nine*?'

'The stuff that was developed for the Vietnam war or something? If you dropped it in a swamp the whole caboodle would freeze over?'

Seals nodded. 'This is about as potent. Dump a gallon of this in a swimming pool and it would strip your hide off in seconds if you jumped in. It's really horrible. Get it on your bare skin and there is *nothing* you can do – there's nothing that will neutralize it. It's the most highly carcinogenic substance in existence; it dissolves flesh and absorbs into the blood stream simultaneously, causing almost instant internal haemorrhaging and destroying the lungs. It's the foulest concoction I've ever come across. If I told the Department of Environment about this stuff they'd cordon the whole building off, and I'm not exaggerating.'

Monty was used to being in the vicinity of toxic substances, but even so this made her uncomfortable and she edged slightly back from the cabinet. 'Presumably it has a use?'

He gave her one of the withering looks that always made her feel like an imbecile. 'I'm sure Bendix Schere would have made it just for fun, even if it didn't.'

She smiled, a little uncertainly.

'Actually, although it's horrible, it is clever stuff. Still under development, so nothing's been done about registering or patenting it. Part of our existing work here is the area of genetically engineering resistance to pollutants in crops and simple life forms. Right now toxic-waste levels are rising in the oceans all the time and getting in the food chain. A lot of natural substances are being turned carcinogenic by pollution.' He tapped the jar. 'What this little darling does is replicate the effect of toxic waste, with a high magnification factor.'

She glanced up at the massive head of the shower bolted to the ceiling a few yards behind her, wondering how effective water would be if any of the toxin got splashed on to human skin, then back at the bottle. 'What's my father using it for?'

'Quite a few applications – basically it speeds up lab experiments when you're examining the effect of carcinogens on susceptible genes.'

'I'm surprised he's allowed it in here – he's got very definite views on these kind of substances.'

'I've noticed,' Seals said. 'Actually, I think he shares a few of my opinions about this company.'

Monty hesitated. 'Last week you hinted there were things you wanted to tell me about Bendix Schere, and said we should have a talk some time, away from here?' She looked back at him. His face was expressionless for a moment. 'Are you free for lunch in the next few days?'

'Free today,' he said.

They sat in a gloomy pub with blaring rock music, too close to a speaker for Monty's comfort. Jake drank his way steadily through his second pint of beer; Monty had only taken a few sips of her glass of white wine.

'I've never heard of Cyclops Syndrome,' he said and tossed his hair back. He shook a Marlboro out of a pack, without offering her one, and lit it with a book match. 'Three cases doesn't sound much.'

'Number thirty-two!' a voice called out.

Monty looked at the ticket in front of her. 'That's us, I'll get them.'

She went to the counter, collected the sausages and chips for Jake and the tuna salad for herself and took them back to the table. 'Want any mustard or ketchup?'

'Ketchup,' Jake said.

She brought the ketchup over, together with knives, forks and napkins, and sat down again.

'Maternox is made at several different sites,' Seals said. 'At Reading, Plymouth and Carlisle here in the UK. In Connecticut, Maryland and Hawaii in the US. In Korea, and I think in Cape Town and Melbourne. There's also a plant making it under licence in Russia. There's always a chance of a rogue batch – but the quality-control procedures make it pretty improbable that it would ever reach the retailers.'

He drew again on his cigarette, stubbed it out, then shook some ketchup over his chips. 'There are a whole series of monitoring tests done throughout the manufacturing process: control of the physical form, the biological form, control of the formulate – everything, right through until it's packaged. From every lot and batch number Quality Control put random capsules aside, break them open and test them.'

'What kind of test?'

'Chromatography analysis. A moving solvent produces a unique fingerprint – or pattern – of the materials, in a sample which is read through dyes or ultraviolet light.'

'Is there any way at all a rogue batch could get through Quality Control?'

He picked up a chip with his fingers and ate it. 'There is a flaw with our chromatography system as it is set up – it will only give us info on what we are looking for; the method won't show up anything we are not looking for.'

'Such as?'

He shrugged. 'If someone has added something they shouldn't have done.'

'Why would they do that?'

'I've known it happen; a company wants to alter the design of a drug, so they quietly slip a few batches in among the existing product and watch to see what happens; saves messing about with early-stage clinical trials with animals.'

She stared at him, shocked. 'You've known it happen?'

'Yes.'

'Maybe abroad in some unscrupulous labs, perhaps, but not with a company like Bendix Schere, surely?'

He raised his eyes. 'You're talking hundreds of millions of pounds in revenue a year on some formulae. If a company like Bendix can knock three years off its research, that's another three years in which it can be earning from the drug.'

'But the dangers are phenomenal – they just couldn't take the risk of getting caught.'

He held up his right hand and rubbed his forefinger and thumb together. Monty could read the signal clearly. *Money, bribery*. Even so, she felt a little heretical when she asked: 'Is there any way you can check batch numbers of the Maternox these three women took?'

She justified the question by telling herself that if Jake could get the batch numbers and they could then test a few samples, it would conclusively prove to Hubert Wentworth that there was nothing wrong with the pills. And it would nip in the bud any possible risk of bad publicity for the company.

He speared a stack of chips with his fork, then raised them up over his plate, to let the steam escape. 'I know Rick Wilson who's in charge of Quality Control at Reading – we were at college together. I can have a word with him, see if he can identify the batches for me. They always retain a few samples from each batch in case of problems – I might be able to persuade him to run a check on those – or I could get him to send me over the release specification and I could do it myself.'

'I'd be really grateful,' she said.

'Anything to put the boot into Bendix is fine by me,' he said, and pushed the tangle of chips into his mouth, chewed, then gave her a smug grin. 'End of the month I'm outta here. Going to Cobbold Tessering with a fifty per cent rise. I'll see Bendix Fucking Schere in Hell.'

Monty sipped some more wine. 'Why – what is it that you have against them?'

His eyes shot towards the door and she saw a sudden flash of fear in them. A deep, intense fear that transmitted to her, sending a chill wisp of air curling through her gut.

Anxiously, she followed his gaze to a man who had just come in, solidly built in his late thirties, in a brown anorak. Then across to another man, with sandy hair and freckles, who was seated reading a newspaper, only a few chairs away from them and well within earshot. She wondered why she hadn't noticed him when she had brought the food over.

Probably because there were dozens of people she had not glanced at. She looked quizzically at the lab technician. His face was drained of colour and he looked even more pasty than normal.

'You OK, Jake?'

He nodded, mouthed a silent warning at her, sipped his beer, then said, breezily and loudly: 'So what hobbies do you have when you're not at work?'

22

Bill Gunn sat, stunned, in front of the wall of monitors in the enhancement room. Only one, the thirty-six-inch high-density screen in the middle, was switched on.

An audio tape screeched as he touched 'Rewind' and watched the digital counter on the control panel, pressing the 'Stop' key as it hit the mark. Then he eased several level controls forward, further filtering out the background sound, and played the tape again:

'*I've never heard of Cyclops Syndrome.*' Jake Seals' voice. There was the sound of a match flaring. '*Three cases doesn't sound much.*' Jake Seals' voice again.

He stopped the tape, quivering not just with anger but with shock. Where was the leak? Where the hell was the leak?

'*Number thirty-two!*' a background voice called out.

'*That's us, I'll get them.*' Montana Bannerman's voice.

'*Ketchup.*' Seals' voice. '*Maternox is made at several different sites. At Reading, Plymouth and Carlisle here in the UK. In Connecticut, Maryland and Hawaii in the US. In Korea, and I think in Cape Town and Melbourne. There's also a plant making it under licence in Russia. There's always a chance of a rogue batch – but the quality-control procedures make it pretty improbable that it would ever reach the retailers.*'

Gunn's cup of coffee in front of him had gone cold, but he didn't even care; he listened through to the end of the tape, then played it one more time. *Got you this time, my friend*, he thought. *Got you by the scruff of your nasty little neck.*

He hit 'Stop', leaned back in his chair and pressed the video sync button. On the screen in front of him he could see, in black and white, Jake Seals and Montana Bannerman seated in a pub having lunch. Bill Gunn did all his monitoring in black and white. Colour might be prettier, but black and white gave better definition, particularly in low light. He glanced at the red digits of the clock of the panel, and then, as if he did not agree, checked his Rolex. 7.45.

'Shit!' He had promised Nikky he'd be home in good time to take her to the theatre. Shakespeare. She was studying literature at the University of London. He didn't mind a bit of culture now and then. He was taking her to *Othello* at the Old Vic tonight. It was a play full of intrigue and he liked intrigue; if Othello had only had as efficient an eavesdropping system as the one he ran at Bendix Schere, Desdemona would never have died.

Nikky was a good kid. Twenty. Two years since he'd divorced *the bitch* who had ruined his life for a decade. Even now it hurt him to say her real name, the wounds were that deep; so she remained the anonymous *bitch*. Nikky would grow up, get bored with him, find someone closer to her own age and settle down one day. But in the meantime it was good, it was what he needed. Wild sex, few questions and unfettered hero-worship. There had been worse times in his life. A lot worse.

He picked up the external phone and punched the number stored in the machine's memory. Nikky answered after the second ring.

'I'm delayed. Jump in a cab; leave my ticket at the box office and I'll see you inside.' Without waiting for her reply he hung up and looked back at the video in front of him.

Speed. When you had a situation like this, speed was essential. There were two people who were real danger: Charles Rowley and Jake Seals. He had advised getting rid of Rowley a long time back, but the Board had decided Rowley knew too much about the company's genetics work and didn't want to risk him moving to a competitor – which he almost certainly would do if he left Bendix; any pharmaceutical company would snap him up. So, instead, Gunn had been charged with keeping him under close watch. Putting the new American, Conor Molloy, with him was a bad move, Gunn believed. If pressed, he couldn't have explained why. It was just instinct; and his instincts were usually good.

His advice on getting rid of Seals had also been turned down for much the same reason – too much risk of Seals moving to a competitor. Now the ball game had changed.

Cyclops Syndrome.

Jesus.

He played the video again from the top, turning the audio up a little louder and listened to the first part of the conversation again:

'I've never heard of Cyclops Syndrome. Three cases doesn't sound much.'

Who had started this conversation? Seals or the Bannerman woman?

He replayed the earlier tape from the lab.

'Last week you hinted there were things you wanted to tell me about Bendix Schere, and said we should have a talk some time, away from here? Are you free for lunch in the next few days?' Montana Bannerman's voice.

He sat in thought. He had put a twenty-four-hour surveillance order on Seals, but the stupid fools had missed one of the key moments: what the hell had happened between the Bannerman woman coming to see him in the lab and the start of the conversation in the pub? The goons on Seals' tail had missed some vital bits at the start of the conversation. Had the Bannerman woman instigated it? Was it she who had expressed the interest in Cyclops Syndrome? Or was it Seals trying to poison her loyalty? That was a question to which quite a few people were going to want an answer, and Gunn didn't have one to give them, not right now. But he would get one. In the meantime, urgent damage limitation was needed.

He picked up the internal secure phone, punched in his access code, then a number.

23

Daniel made an effort to be good on Saturday. A very special effort. It was Saturn's day and he could not afford to miss the chance.

He had learned each of the days by heart. Luna was Monday. Mars, Tuesday. Mercury, Wednesday. Jupiter, Thursday. Venus, Friday. Sol, Sunday.

Saturn's day. The book said he had to do it tonight. He could not risk having his hands strapped to the bed and having to wait another week; anyway, he didn't think he could get away with hiding the things he had gathered and fashioned for another week, particularly as the rabbit had already eaten its way out of two boxes.

He had offered to help his mother in the kitchen, but she'd told him to go away, that he was already beyond redemption and only months of reading nothing but the Bible and constant prayer would give him any possible hope of salvation.

It was a perfect night. Clear with a waning moon; the waning moon was essential, the book said; a sabbat would have been even better, even more powerful, but the next sabbat was weeks away and he couldn't hide the rabbit any longer.

He stood in his dressing gown and observed the moon through a gap in the curtains, watched it hang above the rooftops at the end of the garden, felt the cold glow of its light on his face like a draught, and tried to feel the energy the book said it would give him. Then he squinted at the big round clock on his mantelpiece, and could just make out the time: 11.10. Obeying the instructions in the book, he had bathed with a handful of salt added to the bath water; now he was clean, purified.

His parents had been in bed for an hour. He was desperate to urinate but had forced himself not to go. Silently he opened his door and peered out at their bedroom a few feet across the narrow landing, checking for a telltale band of light below the door, but there was none. Darkness. They were asleep.

He closed the door, shaking with nerves, and carefully laid his candlewick bedspread like a draught excluder along the bottom, pressing it tight so that no light would show through on the other side, then draped his dressing gown over the top of it. It was time to begin. Had to go ahead with this now. Was *determined* to do so. In spite of his terror of being caught.

He started by removing the candle from under the neat pile of his shirts in his dresser. It was a lumpy, uneven object he had fashioned himself from melting down a household candle in a tin over the stove when his mother was out, and mixing it with boot polish. It was not a perfect black, more a blotchy charcoal grey, but it was the best he could do.

He struck a match, glancing nervously towards the door as it flared and shadows jumped around the room, then lit the candle. He waited for the flame to take hold, then tipped the candle to allow some drips of wax to fall into a saucer, and stuck its base down firmly. There was a funny smell, sharp, like burning paint, which he assumed must be the polish, and he hoped it would not wake his parents.

From beneath his mattress he removed the large square of black cloth cut from a blackout curtain that had been inside a trunk in the attic, then a discarded brass poker he had come across on a bomb site and had polished up, followed by a mug of salt and a cup of water he had taken from the kitchen. He draped the cloth over the small table by the window and set the candle on top of it. Beside the candle he carefully placed his penknife with the large blade, sharpened to a razor's edge, open; and then the poker, which was his ceremonial sword.

Next he took the piece of white chalk which he had stolen from school, tied a two-foot length of string securely around it, and with a thumbtack he pinned the other end of the string to the centre of the floor. Keeping the string stretched tight, he drew a circle four feet in diameter. It should have been nine feet, according to the books, but the room was not big enough to allow it. Less scientifically he drew a pentagram inside the circle.

Taking the mug of salt, he carefully poured a small amount

all the way round the circumference of the circle, leaving no gaps. When he had finished, he put several pinches of salt into the cup of water, closed his eyes and blessed it with the end of the Lord's Prayer, then sprinkled the water across the floor, the walls and the curtains, covering every section of the room.

Finally he took off his pyjamas, stepped naked into the centre of the circle, closed his eyes and began to sway rhythmically, arms held out above him, ignoring the goose pimples that broke out on his cold skin, and quietly began to repeat his name, counting mentally each time.

Daniel Judd Daniel Judd Daniel Judd Daniel Judd Daniel Judd . . .

He stopped, as the book had instructed him, at exactly ninety-nine and opened his eyes. The flame of the candle guttered in the draught from the window. He was giddy and a little disoriented, but he could sense the power rising in him. He went to the bed and removed the black book from beneath it; he read once more, for reassurance, the title that was written in strange script: *The Master Grimoire of Magickal Rites and Ceremonies*.

He opened it at the place he had already marked and began reading aloud, in a sharp whisper:

> 'I curse thee once, I curse thee twice,
> Three, four, five, six; I curse thee seven times,
> And then again seven times seven times.
> Be damned! Be damned!
> My power is cursing you,
> My power is hexing you,
> You are completely under my spell.
> Be damned! Be damned!'

Then he stood on a chair and from the top of his wardrobe lifted down a shoebox and put it on the floor. From inside it he removed his mother's stocking and her photograph and laid them both on the black cloth in front of the candle. He turned to another section of the book he had marked with a paper tag, raised the candle, and, whispering the words of the curse again, with a trail of molten wax he copied as best he could the

130

inverted cross symbol on the page: first on to the stocking, then across his mother's forehead on the photograph.

He should ring a bell now three times, the book said. But he had to ignore this instruction, hoping the rite would work without it. Back on the chair, he lowered the cake tin with the perforations he had skewered in the lid. The scrabbling sounds inside became frantic as he set it down on the floor.

Cautiously, he raised the lid a few inches and peered in. 'Hello, little friend,' he whispered. 'How are you? OK? You're a gorgeous fellow, aren't you?'

Two frightened eyes glinted back. It had already bitten him once, but he bore no malice. 'Gently now, don't be frightened, just going to take you out. I love you, yes I do!' He pushed his hand into a thick woollen sock, then raised the lid again, reached inside and firmly seized the rabbit.

It wriggled wildly and he nearly dropped it. 'Relax, little fellow, we're going to be good friends, you and I, we are!'

Must not kill it! It must be alive, he thought as he stroked the back of its head, trying to calm it. He carried it across to the window and held it over his mother's stocking on the black cloth, and whispered the crucial words again, concentrating as hard as he could on the photograph of his mother.

> 'Be damned! Be damned!
> My power is cursing you,
> My power is hexing you,
> You are completely under my spell.
> Be damned! Be damned!'

Then, with his free hand he held his penis and squirted a small amount of urine first on to the stocking, then across the photograph. The rabbit wriggled again, hard. He gripped it tighter, holding it a foot above the stocking, and whispered: 'It's OK, you gorgeous fellow, it's OK, calm down, I love you so much!'

Then he picked up his penknife, located the base of the rabbit's neck with the point of the blade, then sharply rammed it in, being careful not to push too far and lance his own hand. He twisted the blade hard, then cut sharply down into the creature's heart.

Tiny droplets of bright red blood sprayed on to his mother's stocking. The rabbit jerked, then the wriggling faded and the droplets increased into a steady, thin stream accompanied by black droppings as its bowels evacuated.

He drew a ring on the stocking with the blood, then an inverted cross over his mother's forehead, and he hissed the curse loudly and more venomously than before. Then he stepped back into the middle of the circle, closed his eyes, and concentrated. Concentrated on the image of his mother's face; of her head.

Some moments later he heard a sound that he thought at first was one of the air-raid sirens he remembered throughout the war. A low, deep moan that rose slowly into a high-pitched banshee howl. It lasted for a minute, maybe more, and sent shivers racing through him. It was followed by another. Then another. Then a curdling scream of pain.

'My head! My head! My head!'

His mother's voice.

'Owwww! Owwww! Owwww! Oh my God, do something! Oh please help me, someone help me, pleeeeassssse! Help! Help! Help!'

The scream worsened. 'Ohpleasehelpme oh Godddddd!' Then another scream, so terrible it sounded as if it would rip the very darkness from the night.

Daniel stood rooted to his spot, his mouth wide open in shock and disbelief.

24

London, Tuesday 8 November, 1994
Zandra Wollerton's face was gentle and cheerful, in contrast to her voice on the phone yesterday. Hubert Wentworth was right in his assessment, Monty thought; she would make a successful journalist. Strength of character, determination and professionalism showed in the way she conducted herself, as

they faced each other across the small white table, her shorthand pad, thick file and mobile phone laid neatly beside her teacup.

Curly black hair cropped short. A sensible navy two-piece smart enough to wear into court, and a pair of specs; a freckled face with a snub nose, and cheeks that dimpled when she smiled. The lurid green varnish on her fingernails was the only residual hint of adolescence. She couldn't be more than twenty-one, if that, Monty thought, finding herself envying that little wild streak as she stirred the milk into her own tea, feeling distinctly middle-aged in spite of having tried to dress youthfully today in a man's denim shirt over a white t-shirt, narrow black trousers and Chelsea boots.

Zandra opened her file, removed a sheaf of papers clipped together and handed them across to Monty. 'Medical records of Sarah Johnson.' As before, her voice was tough and to the point.

The first page Monty glanced at was a photocopy of a row of index cards, each with tiny, scrawly handwriting. A doctor's patient record notes, she realized after deciphering only a few lines.

She looked up, feeling guilty at prying into someone's personal history, and glanced furtively around the almost deserted coffee shop, afraid that someone might be watching them. A bored-looking waitress stood checking receipts by the till and another was straightening out chairs. Two Arab businessmen occupying a table three away from them were deep in discussion, and a woman in a cashmere jumper was absorbed in a conversation on her mobile phone. The place was inadequately lit and had a gloomy, inert feel; the walls were painted with a childlike frieze depicting scenes from the wool-manufacturing industry and 'Island in the Sun' was playing, barely audibly, on the Muzak system.

Monty looked back down at the records. 'How did you get these?' she said to the reporter.

'I never answer questions like that,' Zandra Wollerton replied in a way that made Monty feel slightly foolish for having asked.

133

'So much for medical confidentiality.'

'She's dead.'

'Would it have made any difference?' Monty retorted testily.

The reporter looked evasive for an instant, then shrugged. 'I have to do a lot of things that aren't very nice, Ms Bannerman. It goes with the territory. I'm looking for the truth and that's often not very nice either.'

These words made her seem much older, suddenly, Monty thought as she listened.

'Three women die in labour suffering from an unidentified virus that looks like a cross between shingles, measles and psoriasis, and each gives birth to a Cyclops Syndrome baby.' The reporter paused to drink some of her tea. 'In their medical records, the only thing connecting them is that they were each treated for infertility problems with a drug manufactured by Bendix Schere, called Maternox.' Then she cocked her head sideways and raised her eyebrows.

'They didn't take anything else?'

'No other drugs at all – at least, nothing prescribed by their family doctors and nothing was given to them by their obstetricians, I've checked that.'

Monty thought for a moment. 'There's been quite a bit in the papers recently about a spate of infant deformities being blamed on polluted sea water. It's possible, I suppose, they might all have been to the same holiday resort. Could they have picked something up there?'

The reporter shook her head. 'None of the women left their home area during the course of their pregnancies. I've checked.'

'You've been very thorough,' Monty said admiringly.

The reporter ignored the compliment. 'There's something else that might or might not be significant: all three women got their Maternox from Price Saver DrugSmart stores.'

'So what?' Monty asked.

'Bendix Schere owns them.'

'You're kidding? I didn't know that!'

'Not many people do – they like to keep the fact well hidden – that way they get to push their own products and make it seem like endorsement from the stores; a smart marketing concept.'

Monty looked reflective. 'I don't quite see why it's significant that the Maternox capsules were purchased at DrugSmart as opposed to anywhere else,' she said.

Zandra Wollerton shrugged. 'May not be, but it's another link.'

Monty stirred her tea. 'Have you talked to any of the dead women's doctors?'

'I've tried; no dice – but that's hardly surprising – the Hippocratic oath and all that.'

Monty stared back at her, wondering how she had managed to get the records. Had she broken into the surgeries? Had the seemingly mild newspaperman, Hubert Wentworth, hired someone to see to it? 'Doctors are supposed to file reports on any side-effects from the drugs they prescribe, aren't they?'

'They're *supposed* to, sure, but many of them don't bother. They're *meant* to fill in a form which goes to the Committee on Safety of Medicines and the Committee on Dental and Surgical Materials, and they *should* inform the Medical Information Department at the company – but it's a lot of paperwork. There's also an official government Confidential Enquiry into Maternal Deaths monitored by regional assessors – but it's controlled by the Department of Health Central Office and information takes two to three years to filter through.'

'You've had no joy?'

'I'm still working on it.'

'What about the Medical Information Department at Bendix Schere – surely they'd be interested?'

The reporter laughed, cynically. 'The first time I tried I got a smooth Sloane in the PR department who gave me the brushoff, so I went straight to the Head of Department, an ice bitch called Linda Farmer. She said they'd received no reports from any doctors and gave me the party line about Maternox – all the crap about forty million women worldwide having taken it and never a single side-effect reported.'

Monty picked at a damaged thumbnail. 'How did you make

135

the connection originally – you know – find out about the three cases?'

'By making about a thousand phone calls to hospitals and coroners' offices.'

'But what made you do it in the first place?'

'It was a brief from Hubert. He asked me to find out how many cases a year would be normal.'

Monty felt her way. 'Do you think he's a bit obsessed about Bendix Schere?'

'He has a thing about them, definitely – I think to call it an obsession may be a bit strong. I guess if you lose a daughter you're going to want to move hell and high water to find out why.'

'So is that it? Just a distraught man trying to make some sense of his daughter's death?'

The reporter shook her head. 'There's more.'

'What makes you say that?'

She hesitated, then leaned forward and peered into her tea as if she was looking for something she had dropped in it. 'It stinks,' she said.

'You really think that?'

'Yup. Just my instincts and maybe I'm totally wrong – but I wouldn't be surprised if it was someone from Bendix who rolled over my flat. I don't have enough to go to press on – *yet*. I'm waiting for one more pregnant woman to die in labour from a virus and give birth to a Cyclops Syndrome baby, then I'm going to sit on her family doctor's tail round the clock for a week until he bloody well talks to me.'

Monty continued to worry her nail. 'Nothing was taken from your flat, Mr Wentworth said. That right?'

Zandra Wollerton shook her head, then stared back at Monty with a faintly bemused expression. 'Well – there was one thing. Maybe the bastard who broke in is a closet pervert. There's a pair of cotton panties I thought I had in the wash box – can't find them anywhere.'

'Panties?' Monty said, surprised.

'Uh huh. Had flowers on them.'

'Seems very weird,' Monty said.

'There are some very weird people in the world,' the young reporter told her.

25

'So what do you think?'

'It's the bizz.' Charley Rowley stared approvingly around the living room, walked to the wide front window and looked out down the quiet tree-lined avenue one floor below. He freed the catch and raised the heavy sash a few inches. Then he listened for a moment to the faint hubbub of the Fulham Road traffic two hundred yards away. It was not intrusive, you could barely hear it.

At the far end of the room, Conor stared through the smaller window down at the sun deck and the well-tended garden which belonged to the ground-floor flat below. 'Seems like a reasonable rent, don't you think?' he said.

'Paying a premium for the area, but it's not bad – considering it's virtually Chelsea here. What about the rates and service charge? Want to watch those – that's where you can get really stuffed,' Rowley said, lighting a cigarette. 'And you'll need to do something about these windows – draughty as hell.'

Conor re-read the letter from the estate agent that he had clipped to the particulars. It was as bitterly cold in the flat as it was outside and they both kept their coats on; Conor his long blue Crombie, Charley Rowley his battered green Barbour that had long lost its wax sheen. 'Seems OK.'

'The Bendix Schere Legal Department will do the conveyancing for you – just make sure they let you know what you're in for with the extras.'

'Sure,' Conor said, barely listening. He wanted this apartment, had fallen in love with it when he had first seen it on Saturday with the sunlight streaming in the windows. It had a good feel – in truth, with its high ceilings with their plaster mouldings, and the large marble fireplace, it had something of the feel of Rowley's house. A few old rugs and antiques and some pictures on the wall and it would make a really classy English pad.

There was only one bedroom, but it was a good size, facing

south like the living room, so it would get plenty of sunlight. The bathroom was spacious, also, with a wild old-fashioned bathtub with lion's feet, a huge faucet and genuine brass taps.

The kitchen was a bit cramped but there was a cosy dining alcove off it, beneath an arched niche, which more than made up for it. He could imagine candlelit dinners in there, maybe with Montana Bannerman. He had a meeting with her late tomorrow morning and was looking forward to it. He had thought of her a number of times over the weekend, and there was a warmth about her that kept on coming back to him.

He found himself comparing her to that brainless girl he'd been seated next to at Charley Rowley's dinner party last Friday – Jesus. She came from a titled family, Rowley had told him, but it still hadn't altered his views about her, and he had no intention of bothering to try and see her again; and anyhow, he reckoned, the feeling was very probably mutual.

Rowley looked at his watch. 'Meeting some friends in the Duke of Boots at seven – going to join us?'

Conor nodded; he had no other plans. 'Thanks.'

'I'm going to have a few jars. Get Lulu to run me into work in the morning.'

Lulu was Rowley's girlfriend. Conor had not got the exact hang of the relationship. She had done the cooking at the dinner party and generally seemed to run his domestic life, which included, as far as he could ascertain, if not actually living with Rowley, certainly being a permanent fixture. But in Rowley's mind and conversations, she barely seemed to exist.

They went out on the landing and Conor pulled the door shut, locking up with the tagged keys. 'Have to drop these through the estate agent's letter box tonight – they're just round the corner.'

'No problem.' Rowley glanced at his watch, then followed Conor down the wide, dingy staircase into the lobby, past a couple of chained-up bikes, and out into the street.

Conor walked along the pavement to his BMW. He pointed the key fob, pressed the button and the indicators winked at him. Rowley stopped and admired a girl walking by on the other side of the street.

'Man, that is seriously nice,' he said. 'I like that a lot; do you think if I asked her very sweetly she'd be willing to have my children?'

'Maybe you should start with something a little less ambitious,' Conor said, easing himself into the driver's seat. 'Try a cup of coffee or something, for openers, you know, and gradually build up to the kids over the next couple of years. Don't blow it by rushing it!'

Rowley watched her disappear through a door, and his face dropped. 'Too late, chance gone. Story of my life.'

'One door closes, another opens,' Conor said.

Rowley climbed into the passenger seat, grunted noncommittally, and tugged his seat belt over his midriff, fumbling for the stalk.

As Conor put the car into gear, Rowley leaned forward and pressed a button on the radio. 'Just want to catch the news – see what the market's done today.'

'Do you play it?'

'Dabble a bit. Peter Rawlings, who was at dinner, is a shit-hot broker – if you ever need someone, I'll give you his number.'

It did not take Conor much arithmetic to work out that after he had paid the rent and outgoings on the flat, plus the cost of furnishing it, there would not be a lot of income left for playing the stock markets. 'Thanks,' he said. 'Bear it in mind.'

Rowley had found the news station on the radio.

'. . . pharmaceuticals giant Bendix Schere announced they have agreed terms for taking over the US-owned Morgan-Pheltz. In turnover this will make British-based Bendix Schere the fourth largest pharmaceutical company in the world. In an interview earlier this afternoon Chairman Sir Neil Rorke announced that a substantial part of Morgan-Pheltz's manufacturing would be moved to a proposed new plant in Glasgow, creating an estimated three thousand jobs. And now sport, and in the . . .'

Rowley gave a low whistle and shook out a cigarette, then offered the pack to Conor. 'This calls for a fag. Want one?'

'No thanks. Did you know about this takeover?'

'Not a dickey. The Bendix brass keep things pretty close to their vests.'

'Have you met any of the main Board Directors?'

'Yah,' Rowley said. 'Met Rorke, he's OK – one of the good guys. But he's not really in the frame, he's only part-time – couple of days a week – I think they wheel him in and out as the sort of acceptable face of pharmaceutical capitalism. I'm not so wild about Crowe.'

'Why not?'

Rowley shrugged. 'Just a hunch. He's a manipulator, and a scientist himself, which makes him pretty unusual for a chief exec.'

'I didn't know he was a scientist.'

'Molecular biologist – he started out in clinical research. You don't get to move from the lab to the chief executive's chair by being a good scientist – you get there by being cunning and ruthless. He has a reputation for being a total S-H-I-T.'

'So do most successful guys,' Conor said. 'I guess Rorke's an exception.' He turned out into the Fulham Road. The location was great, he thought; dozens of shops and restaurants, buzzing with life. It reminded him of Georgetown.

'Hey, you know those tricks you did at dinner, Conor? The hypnotizing stuff?'

'Yup?'

'Have you ever tried using hypnosis for anything else?'

'Such as?'

'Quitting smoking. Or getting a job?'

Conor grinned.

'Why not? You have an incredible power at your disposal if you can really do what you did to Corinthia. Presumably they were tricks, right? Breaking the glass and stubbing the cigarette out?'

Conor drove on in silence, then pulled over to the kerb outside the estate agency.

'Yup,' he said finally. 'They were just tricks.'

26

London. Wednesday 9 November, 1994
Jake Seals stepped out of the lift at the sixth floor, clutching the vinyl hold-all he used as an attaché case, crossed the deserted reception room, entered his smart-card and access code into the door lock then walked swiftly along the corridor to the lab. The only sound was the squish of his rubber-soled shoes, the steady whoosh of air from the climate-control system and a hum like a trapped insect from a faulty fluorescent.

He yawned, feeling leadenly tired as if he had taken some drug which had not yet worn off. Needed to be extra careful when you were tired, that was when accidents happened, he knew. Then he stopped in his tracks beside a fire extinguisher on a wall, as the sharp twinge of a muscle in his forehead made him wince. It was a new pain, one he had never had before, and it startled him. It happened again and he clapped a hand to his head; it felt like an insect the size of an earwig was crawling along inside the skin just above his eyebrows.

Tired, that's all. Absolutely shit-tired, he thought, yawning again deeply and gulping down air, then stared furtively up and down the length of the wide corridor. All the lights in the labs and offices were off, with only the corridor illuminated. The whole floor was empty, as he had hoped; apart from the security guards downstairs and a few computer engineers on night shift, he imagined the entire building to be deserted at this time of the morning.

His watch read 5.35 a.m. Miss Bannerman should be here any moment. With luck they would have a clear two hours before anyone else showed up. Ample time. He shivered and rubbed his hands. It was a cold morning outside, and not much warmer in here. The heating sensors should have picked up his presence and adjusted the thermostat; it would warm up in a few minutes.

He went into his tiny office at the far end of the corridor, which was more a cubicle with a desk, computer terminal, phone and shredder, and laid his hold-all on the solitary visitor's chair. There was the usual morning smell of citrus from something the cleaners used and he was glad they had already been, probably earlier on during the night. No interruptions. His forehead twinged again and lights sparked inside his head. He stood motionless for a moment, waiting for it to pass. No sleep, that was all, that was the problem. And stressed out as hell.

He removed his anorak and hung it on the back of the door, but kept his jacket on and pulled his protective overalls over the top. Then he went to the vending machines in a recess by the entrance to the washrooms a few yards along the corridor, selected extra strong coffee, extra milk and a large dose of sugar.

As the machine chuntered away, the Chief Technician realized his legs suddenly felt unsteady beneath him, as if they were about to buckle. He leaned against the wall, head swimming, and unexpectedly broke out in a heavy sweat. Closing his eyes for a moment, he took several deep breaths. *Maybe picked up some bug*, he thought.

He had intended having an early night in preparation for this morning, but he had been persuaded by a mate to go out for a couple of beers. Two beers had turned into four, then six, then they had got chatting to a couple of birds who had persuaded them to go to a disco, and at half one in the morning he had found himself parked in a massive housing estate somewhere in Hounslow, trying to get a leg over in the back of his car. Without success.

He was regretting now that he had said he would help the Bannerman woman. Posh little bitch. He wasn't sure why he had agreed at all, and it had entailed a hell of a lot of work to get everything ready for a conclusive test – but the early indications from his findings did show something a little odd, and had intrigued him enough to want to go on. He tossed his hair back from his face. His eyes felt like sandpaper and his brain was only working at half speed.

Picking up the hot cup, he carried it back to his office, opened the hold-all and began setting the contents out methodically on his desk. Six small white vials labelled with batch and lot numbers, each containing Maternox capsules.

Beside them he laid the copy he had obtained of the correct pattern of compounds that should show up in a thin layer chromatography plate. Then he read the number on the first vial again: BS-M-6575-1881-UKMR.

The digits and numbers all had a significance, primarily so that in the event of any quality problems the exact site and time of manufacture could be pinpointed. Over one hundred thousand women a year in England alone took Maternox. Two capsules had to be taken four times daily for fourteen days in each month, for a minimum of six months, and the average length of use before conception was five months.

Miss Bannerman had asked if he could find out the batch numbers of the Maternox taken by the three pregnant women who had died. On Monday afternoon after his lunch with her he had rung his friend Rick Wilson, Head of Quality Control at the Reading plant, and given him the prescription details from the dead women's doctors. Instead of being his normal friendly, helpful self, Wilson had become quiet and absurdly formal, informing Seals that such a request could only be processed through Dr Linda Farmer, Director of Medical Information and Liaison.

Wilson owed him a debt going back a few years. Seals had stored it away, knowing there would be a pay-off one day; he did not really want to use it up on this Maternox business, but he dropped a mention of it into the conversation all the same. Wilson did not seem to pick up on it and was antagonistic, so Seals had not pressed it.

Then to his surprise on Monday night, a brown envelope was pushed through his letter box accompanied by a brief, unsigned note with a request at the end for it to be destroyed. The note, in handwriting which he presumed to be Rick Wilson's, stated that the three dead women had each had their prescriptions fulfilled with Maternox from the same batch number, BS-M-6575-1881-UKMR, which had been made at Reading. Along with the vial of these capsules, in the envelope were five further vials, enclosing other batch numbers taken at random.

The dead women had lived, respectively, in Reading, Birmingham and Edinburgh. It seemed more than an odd coincidence that out of the thousands of different batches manufactured at the three UK plants each year, these three women, in totally different geographical regions, should all have been given Maternox from the same batch.

Seals glanced at his watch. 5.45. She was quarter of an hour late. He pushed the vials into the pocket of his overalls, picked up the reference chromatogram and his coffee, and carried them into the lab across the corridor, which was the one he used for the experiments he supervised directly. The lights came on automatically, activated by sensors. It felt very still, and the silence was broken only by the faint hum from the flow hoods and incubators.

As he walked between the benches of white speckled work tops, he paused to check on a couple of important experiments he had been running, and whose results he intended, illegally, taking with him to his new post at Cobbold Tessering next month. In one test tube a cluster of cells lay in a very weak solution of the toxic acid BS93L5021 that he had nicknamed Bendix Soup. He could see, even with his naked eye, that there had been no reaction during the night.

The solution was too dilute, he decided, setting down the coffee and plate and quickly pulling on his protective gloves. He should put on his protective glasses, he knew, standard company safety policy, but with his muzzy head he did not think he could cope with the clamminess of the glasses – and there wasn't anyone around right now to see him setting a bad example.

He walked down to the Perspex-fronted fume cabinet marked 'DANGER BIOHAZARD', reached in and carefully gripped a blue plastic tub with a screwtop lid, containing a half-gallon Winchester bottle of the acid.

Then suddenly, just as he had taken the weight of the tub and raised it a few inches, he felt a blinding pain behind his right eye as if a knife had been plunged through his temple. At the same moment there was a deep, throaty snarl, followed by another, even more loud and vicious, and a wolf, its jaws wide open, its teeth yellow, sharp, slimy with saliva, hurtled from out of the back of the fume cabinet straight at him.

As he screamed in shock and disbelief, his legs buckled,

collapsing under him as if the bones had been ripped out of them. Everything seemed to go into slow motion. His eyes swelled in their sockets in horror as he watched the blue bucket rotate in mid-air above his head, saw the lid drop off and the amber half-gallon Winchester bottle inside tumble out, head first, down towards him.

The cap of the bottle had been removed.

He saw to his utter terror that the chemical inside was gushing out, seemed to be gathering pace and hurtling at him with the speed and force of a fire hose.

It struck him full in the face and chest, with a sharp stinging sensation on his cheeks that momentarily made him cry out, before he began to contort, clutching at his face, the stinging turning to searing agony as the molecules of the acid began ripping the proteins of his skin apart, burning away the pupils and irises of his eyes, stripping off his lips, dissolving his protective clothes.

Monty heard the faint warbling of an alarm as she stepped out of the lift on the sixth floor. She had been cursing herself for oversleeping – she never ever overslept and did not understand how she could have done so today – and had driven like a lunatic on the frosty roads all the way here. She should have got out of bed the moment the alarm went, she knew, but she had tried to snatch a few more precious seconds of doze, and instead had fallen asleep again. Jake was not going to be at all happy with her.

She stopped in her tracks beside the empty security desk and glanced fleetingly at the blank closed-circuit monitors, listening. Definitely an alarm. She pushed her smart-card and punched in her pin number, then opened the door; immediately she could hear the alarm warbling more loudly, and could see a red flashing light outside the end laboratory opposite Jake's office.

She launched herself forwards, sprinting down to the lab door and peered through the glass. She could see nothing. Quickly she inserted her card, punched in the code and pushed the door open.

As she did, burning, acrid fumes engulfed her, stinging her

eyes, searing her throat and lungs, and she coughed, called out for Jake Seals, tore her shawl from around her neck and held it over her nose, then went on in.

For a moment, through unprotected eyes, she could see nothing out of order. Then she heard a hideous, yelping sound that shook every nerve in her body; it reminded her of a dying dog she had once found, its entire rear half crushed flat by a truck. It had died in agony in her arms.

'Mr Seals?' she shouted, then coughed violently again as the awful fumes choked her. Crouching low, she stepped a few paces into the laboratory. 'Mr Seals?' The alarm warbled fiercely above her head. There was a sharp, caustic reek in the air that seared her nostrils and the back of her throat.

Something moved in front of her. She stepped a few paces nearer and called out again, her feet crunching on broken glass. Then her voice dried as she was suddenly able to see the apparition in front of her more clearly. A whinnying scream got trapped in her gullet.

A human form, recognizable as Jake Seals only by the few strands of long brown hair that still hung from one side of his smoking cranium, and by his cowboy boots, was lying on the floor beyond the work benches. He was writhing like a dying snake beneath the massive chromium head of the emergency shower, alternatively groaning and yelping in pain.

His face was a featureless mass of black, smouldering pulp; it was changing shape even as she watched, small sections of skin sloughing off and dropping to the tiled floor.

She backed away, mouthed his name silently, tried to say something to let him know she was there, but her mind was momentarily paralysed by shock. *Water for burns*, she thought, staring at the shower. Water was OK for some things, but not for others. What the hell did he have on him? Acid? Water was OK for acid, diluted it.

'Jake, my God, what is it, what's on you?'

A pitiful incoherent cry emitted from his melting face. It twisted towards her and a gap opened where his mouth should have been and made a sound.

She stared back. 'Wolf? Did you say *wolf*?'

'Wolllffff.' The sound faded into a dull moan.

'What do you mean? Is it some chemical?'

He gave out another dull moan, then a sudden, ghastly screech of pain.

She had no idea what he meant, and there was no time to keep on asking. She gripped the massive ring pull. Thoughts skidded wildly through her brain. She tried to calm down, to recall a first aid course she had been on a decade back, tried to remember what the elderly district nurse had told them about chemical burns. Water. You had to dilute with water. She yanked the handle sharply down and a million clear droplets hurtled instantly from a nozzle the size of a dinner plate.

They struck Jake Seals with an eruption of steam as if a boiler had exploded. She heard an agonized shriek, then Jake disappeared completely inside a densening cloud that was turning a vile greeny-yellow colour.

As the water gushed down, the cloud became denser, more choking, spreading outwards, engulfing her too. Monty stepped back quickly, scared and useless, too shaken to think straight. *Must not breathe it in.* Stared at the gushing water, unsure whether it was making things better or worse. She coughed; her eyes were watering with tears. Then she heard a hollow frothing sound; it was coming from inside her own chest. She remembered what Jake had told her.

It dissolves flesh and absorbs into the blood stream simultaneously, causing almost instant internal haemorrhaging and destroying the lungs.

Panicking, she backed away further, turned, raced down to a phone on the far wall, grabbed the receiver. She was having to fight for air now, heard strange noises in her throat, felt her lungs tightening inside her chest. Closing down. They were closing down on her. Her vision was blurred and she could barely see the numbers on the buttons. Getting harder still to breathe. A friend at school had nearly died from an asthma attack because she had forgotten her inhaler. Monty had never forgotten the sight of her lying on the tarmac of the playground, clawing at the air, hissing like a punctured tyre. It was happening to her now; her throat was constricting, her lungs would not work, would not draw anything in.

She pushed her face right up against the buttons, punched out 9–9–9, her ears ringing with the gurgling inside her own chest which almost drowned out Jake's hideous screams. She had to cover her ear with one hand in order to hear the emergency operator's voice as she struggled to stay upright, to stay conscious. *Have to keep breathing*, she thought as she crashed down on to the hard, tiled floor.

27

Barnet, North London. 1946
'It died.'

The pet shop owner gave the small boy a withering stare, dug his hands firmly into the pockets of his brown overalls, pursed his lips and ran his tongue along the inside of his gums. It was the standard defensive stance he adopted when confronted by irate elderly ladies complaining that their cats would not eat the new food he had persuaded them to buy. 'Healthy enough when it left here, it was.' His eyes narrowed. 'Did you give it water straight away when you got home, like I told you?'

'Yes,' Daniel Judd said quietly.

'And you took it out of the shoebox and put it in a proper cage?'

'Yes.'

'You gave it food?'

Daniel nodded solemnly.

The man studied him closely. He looked a decent enough kid, neatly dressed, well spoken, timid; not the type to maltreat an animal, although he wasn't too bothered about what happened to rabbits after they left here. Dull, beastly little things that would give you a sharp bite if you gave 'em half a chance, could never see the point in them, except they were popular with kids. And there were a dozen different reasons why they would die spontaneously when they were babies. No resistance, that was the real problem.

Now *chameleons*, for instance. They were different. A chameleon was a pet worth having. Except, he thought glumly, he hadn't seen one at a wholesaler's since before the war. Hitler had a lot to answer for. No bananas and no chameleons. 'Suppose you'll need another shoebox?' he said grudgingly.

The boy proffered a sixpenny bit and looked back at him hopefully. 'Please, sir.'

The man softened at the word *sir*. Respect. He liked a bit of respect; he had begun to notice faint beginnings of a decline in respect ever since the war.

Daniel understood about respect. He knew that the best way to get what you wanted from an adult was to proffer respect. It made them feel important.

'Nothing wrong with her,' Dr Hawksworth had declared. *'Perhaps a touch of migraine, but nothing to worry about.'*

Daniel had listened outside his parents' door.

'Like a knife, Doctor,' his mother had said. *'It was like someone had stuck a knife in my head and twisted the blade. I felt sick, giddy.'*

'I prayed to the Lord for her,' his father interjected.

'And how do you feel now, Mrs Judd?'

'All queasy, shaking all over. God's wrath for something. He knows our sins. He punishes us in His own way.'

'You have classic migraine symptoms, I'm afraid, Mrs Judd. Have you been under much tension recently?'

'Doctor, when you have a child as impure in heart as Daniel, you are under strain all the time. We have to save his soul from eternal damnation before it's too late. He tests me, Doctor, he tests us both so hard. The Lord is punishing us for bringing him into this world the way he is. It was a difficult birth, you remember, don't you? How he nearly killed me then?'

'I'll give you a couple of tablets to take now, help you go to sleep, and I'll write out a prescription for your husband to get in the morning. Stay in bed tomorrow and try to rest your mind.'

Daniel had hovered on the landing as Dr Hawksworth, tall and bendy with his droopy moustache, emerged from the bedroom with his father.

'*And how are you, young fellow?*' he had asked.

'*He's fine,*' his father had answered for him.

'*Glad to hear it.*'

'Dr Hawksworth, I think you should know that my wife has never had a migraine before in her life.'

'There's always a first time for everything, Mr Judd.'

Daniel had crept back into his room before the doctor left, and checked once more that everything was tidied away. He had been scrupulously careful. But even so, tonight, a month later, the faintest trace of the pentacle he had chalked on the carpet was still just visible to his eye when he looked hard enough, which made re-drawing it easier now.

He had no way of knowing whether it was anything more than coincidence with his mother. Just lucky timing that she had got her bad head whilst he was doing the spell? In his mind, he had come to believe that was all it was. Yet he continued to nurture a spark of hope that somehow the magic really worked. Tonight he would find out.

There was one big mistake he had made with his magic workings during the spell he had tried to cast on his mother. He had found this out afterwards when he had read through the grimoire again: he should not have kept going in and out of the circle. Once he had entered the circle, he should have closed it and conducted all the workings inside it until he had finished. He would not make the same mistake again tonight.

He flashed his torch at the large round clock on the shelf. 11.15. There was a good waning moon, and it was a fine, clear sky. Perfect. It had been too scary, keeping the rabbit concealed for three days last time; he was better organized now.

He tiptoed to his door, opened it gradually, and listened for any sounds from his parents' room. Silence. Just the steady tick of the long-case clock in the hall. Then he began his preparations.

As before, he laid his bedspread, then his dressing gown, along the bottom of his bedroom door to blot out the light, then draped the black cloth over the table by the window, and placed the black candle on top. From the back of his wardrobe he removed a sock he had taken from his father's drawer – the grimoire said that any item of clothing was suitable – and a photograph of Mr Judd wearing a bowler hat, which he had slipped out of the family album.

At midnight he undressed, lit the candle and began the ritual. He repeated exactly the words and the procedures he had used a month ago, completing the ritual by drawing a circle on his father's sock with the rabbit's blood, then an inverted cross on his forehead in the photograph. He hissed the portentous words once more, loudly and venomously:

> 'Be damned! Be damned!
> My power is cursing you,
> My power is hexing you,
> You are completely under my spell.
> Be damned! Be damned!'

He stepped back into the middle of the chalk and salt circle, closed it with his ceremonial sword, then shut his eyes tightly and concentrated. He tuned everything out of his mind except the image of his father's thin face, hard as iron, above his starched white collar and his correctly knotted, mean little tie.

Silence.

Nothing was happening.

He repeated the words of the curse again, hissing them even more loudly. Then he listened hard. But there was no sound anywhere in the house.

Daniel remained inside the circle for an age. The grimoire said that the power of the spell kept its strength as long as he remained inside the circle. After a while he began to feel freezing, but made no attempt to leave the circle and put his pyjamas back on. His legs began to ache and his body sagged with tiredness. He sneezed, catching his nose and stifling it as best he could.

Finally, at 2.15 in the morning, he was too tired to stand any longer, so he squatted down inside the circle, tucked his legs under him and, lolling his head forward, lapsed into a doze.

At 3.00, exhausted and frozen, he gave up. Despondently, he blew out the candle and began to tidy away the objects. He would bury the rabbit in the garden tomorrow when his mother went out to her church coffee morning, and he would put his father's sock into a neighbour's dustbin. The candle and the black cloth he would keep; the candle had taken a lot of work to make and maybe he would try again soon. Perhaps he should have changed the spell? Maybe there was a different one for a man?

But most likely, he knew, as he lapsed into a gloomy and troubled sleep, it had never worked at all, and never would. You had to be a magician to make it work. And now God was really angry at him for what he had done.

He was jolted awake by the sound of his door crashing open and banging against the wall. Bright daylight flooded into the room. Overslept, was his first immediately guilty thought, as he saw his mother's demented face looming over him, her hair loose, hanging long and wiry like a witch's, her eyes bloodshot and blurred with tears.

Something was wrong, but he did not know what. Frightened, he instinctively withdrew his hands from under the bedclothes, clasped them in front of his face to commence his morning prayers and to ward off her first blow. He closed his eyes again, tightly, bracing himself.

But there was no harsh slap across the face. And for a moment no sound either. Then his mother began to scream hysterically.

'Dead! He's deeaaaadddd! Daniel . . . Daniel . . . your father! Oh God! He woke up about midnight with a terrible headache. He took aspirin, just aspirin. I can't move him, can't wake him, he's cold, son. God has taken him. God is punishing us for your sins. Please, Daniel, help me wake him!'

28

Conor decided the only way to get through his workload was to start coming into the office much earlier in the mornings, and continue through until late at night.

At a quarter to seven, as he drove bleary-eyed up the Euston Road, listening to Michael Heseltine under attack on a news programme, trying to get a handle on British politics, he saw a blaze of strobing blue lights ahead. As he got nearer, he saw two fire tenders and a saloon car with a blue light outside the Bendix building. A small knot of firemen were standing on the pavement, chatting. Conor could see no sign of any urgency as he turned right and pulled up by one of the security guards' windows in front of the barrier.

He had seen this particular guard, a dour man in his mid-thirties, a good dozen times in the past three weeks, but there was no hint of acknowledgement or greeting as Conor showed him his pass card.

'What's happened?' Conor asked.

'Chemical spillage,' he said, as if it were a routine occurrence.

'Where?'

'In one of the labs,' the guard added dismissively, opening the barrier and curtly signalling him through.

Conor parked in his space and climbed out. Even in the low grey morning light he could see the grime on the BMW's paintwork and wheels and made a mental note to take it to a wash tonight if possible, mindful of the penalty otherwise. He walked to the front entrance of the building, curious to find out more about what had happened.

The entrance atrium had its normal quiet, early-morning feel in spite of the presence of a uniformed fire officer and a senior-looking police officer in conversation by the security desk. A man carrying a briefcase was stepping into a lift. Conor glanced at the solitary security guard on duty and was pleased to see it was the most friendly of the five regulars.

He was a sickly-looking black man whose face, beneath a grizzle of greying hair, had begun to shrivel, prematurely, into hard walnut-like wrinkles. It was difficult to put an age on him – somewhere between mid-fifties and sixties, Conor guessed. The name on his lapel badge said: 'W. Smith. Lobby Security.'

As Conor showed him his card, he asked quietly: 'There's been some kind of accident?'

The guard nodded. Conor noticed a sadness in the man's yellowing eyes. 'Yes, sir, there's been a chemical spill, sir.' The voice was courteous and servile, but its owner did not look anxious to say any more.

'What kind of spill?'

'I don't know that, sir. It's up on the sixth floor, sir.'

'Anyone hurt?'

A hesitation then a nod. 'Mr Seals, the Chief Lab Technician. He's very bad – I don't think –' W. Smith halted, uneasily, in mid-sentence. 'Ambulance took the young lady as well. I don't know how she was. The fumes, they said.'

'Young lady?'

'She's very nice. Come here with her father – he's very famous. Dr Bannerman. Won the Nobel.'

Conor felt as if a bucket of cold water had been swilled into his guts. 'Miss Bannerman? She's hurt? You don't know how bad?'

The guard shook his head. 'The ambulance men didn't say. She was on a stretcher with oxygen.'

'Shit! Where's she gone? Which hospital?'

'I don't know that, sir.'

'Paddington.'

Conor turned, startled; the fire officer was looking at him. 'Took 'em both to University College Hospital.'

'How do I get there from here?'

The fire officer gave him directions. Conor thanked him, then went back outside and ran across to his car.

The Accident and Emergency department of University College Hospital was quiet, with rows of empty seats and only a handful of people waiting. There was a strong, astringent smell of disinfectant, mingled with coffee that had been stewing for too long.

The window of the reception counter was unattended, and Conor had to wait whilst a woman keyed information into a computer, her back to him. Finally, he called out: 'Hello?'

She continued to ignore him for some moments, before turning and coming across to the window. 'Sorry to keep you, dear, we're short-staffed this morning. Can I help you?'

'You had a casualty brought in by ambulance about an hour ago – Miss Bannerman – could you tell me how she is?'

She glanced down at a list on the counter, then frowned. 'Are you a relative?'

He heard the wail of a siren approaching outside. 'I – I – I'm her brother,' he lied, hoping to hell she didn't have a brother who was here already. In the States, unless you were a relative hospitals wouldn't give you any information; he assumed the same was true here.

The woman went to the back of the room and picked up a phone. She spoke briefly into it, then came back to Conor. 'Someone will be round to see you in a moment. Take a seat.'

Conor wondered how long he was going to have to wait and whether he should bring his briefcase with his laptop in from the car and do some work. But a door opened behind him and a white-coated woman with short streaked hair came through and looked at him.

'Mr Bannerman?'

He stood up. 'Yes, hi.' He had no difficulty in saying it quite brazenly.

Her name tag read: 'Wendy Phillips. A&E Ward Manager.' She had a pleasant, efficient air, in spite of her eyes being red with tiredness. He wondered if she had been on duty all night. 'You are Miss Montana Bannerman's brother?'

'Yes.'

'Would you like to come through and see her?'

'How is she?'

'She's on a respirator at the moment.'

'Suffering from fumes?'

'We hope it is just fumes and not anything worse – her mouth and throat seem all right but she was frothing from the

155

lungs which could indicate burn damage. But it's too early to tell yet whether there's any long-term internal effect; I understand it's something highly corrosive she's breathed in.'

'What chemical was it?'

'It's not any known substance apparently – something undergoing lab trials.' She walked ahead of him through a wide corridor, lined on one side with trolleys, stretchers and bottles of gas. Two orderlies hurried past them wheeling an empty stretcher.

A pager clipped to Nurse Phillips' breast pocket bleeped, and she raised a hand to Conor, signalling him to wait as she lifted up a wall phone, spoke briefly into it, then replaced it and turned to him. 'There's a neutralizing agent on its way to us under police escort from the company's lab in Berkshire.'

They had stopped outside a room packed with monitoring equipment. Inside, Conor could make out a woman lying on a trolley with an oxygen mask over her face. From the sprawling frizz of blonde hair he realized it must be Montana. A nurse was standing beside her, reading orange digits off a dial and logging them on a sheet attached to a clipboard.

Conor had seen the expression in the patient's eyes once before in his life, in his own mother's eyes, and had never forgotten it. Shock. Total rejection of reality.

'Hi,' he said softly.

There was a faint nod in response.

He smiled down, trying to be reassuring. 'You OK?' It was a dumb remark, he knew, but he could not think of anything better.

There was another nod.

Instinctively he reached down, balled his fist and touched Monty's cheek lightly; its cold, clammy touch startled him, and he tried not to let that show. She wasn't good, definitely wasn't good. Two orderlies came into the room, followed by a serious-looking man in a grey pin-striped suit.

'Dr Goode, this is the patient's brother,' Wendy Phillips said.

Conor felt a twinge of embarrassment and waited for an awkward question as the doctor studied him briefly, but his manner was polite and gentle. 'We're going to take your sister up to X-ray. We are also going to give her an MRI scan which will help us look at the inside of her lungs. I gather it's a pretty invasive substance she's inhaled fumes from, so we need to find out the exact extent of any damage.'

'Do you think it's serious?' Conor asked quietly.

They had moved a few steps away from Monty. 'There's no burn damage to the lips or internally in the mouth, nostrils or the upper larynx, which is a good sign, but she was unconscious and barely breathing when the paramedics got to her; as we don't know anything about this chemical we've no way of telling at the moment what internal damage it may have caused.'

Conor looked worriedly back at Monty. 'How's the other person who was in the lab?'

The doctor stiffened, glanced at the ward manager, then indicated that Conor should follow him out into the corridor. Two nurses walked past them as Dr Goode spoke quietly. 'I'm afraid there wasn't anything we could do for him.'

'He's dead?' Conor said, incredulously.

'He was dead on arrival. Completely covered in this acid. One of the ambulance crew suffered burns and breathing problems from it as well – God knows what the hell they were brewing up there.' The doctor glanced at his watch. 'The tests are going to take a good couple of hours – I can put you in a room, if you like. I gather someone from the company's on their way and there's a neutralizing agent for this chemical being sent down as well – although I'm told it isn't very effective.'

'I guess there's nothing much I can do right now. But maybe I can come back later?'

The doctor brightened. 'I think that would be the best thing. Phone us around lunch time – ask for Nurse Phillips or myself, and we can let you know how things are.'

'I'd appreciate that.' Conor thanked him and left.

As he drove back to the office, thoughts churned in his mind. He had arrived at a quarter to seven, which was pretty damned early. Miss Bannerman and the technician had already long been taken to the hospital, so they must have been in a good half hour earlier at the very least. That would have put the time around six to a quarter after six. Six o'clock in the morning was one hell of an hour for anyone to be at work. So what were they doing?

Something they did not want anyone else to know about, for sure. It was further evidence that his instincts about Montana Bannerman were correct. She was going to be of use to him. Very definitely. He hoped to hell she wasn't too badly injured.

29

Monty's throat felt as if it was on fire, and her eyes were smarting.

'We're going to take your mask off and see how you feel without oxygen, all right?'

She stared up at a stocky man with a thick-set Neanderthal face and an unkempt tangle of wiry, thinning hair; more hair sprouted from his neck and over the top of his shirt collar. He was flanked on either side by nurses, and there was a cluster of people behind him.

A hand descended, something slid around the back of her head, then she saw a Perspex mask being lifted away and she had a moment of panic as it suddenly became harder to breathe. Her lungs were raw as if she had smoked too many cigarettes, and there was a vile, bitter taste in her mouth.

Something in the doctor's expression worried her. She took several fast breaths, afraid suddenly. Perspiration broke out on her skin as she thought of the damage she might have done to herself; irreparable damage. She remembered vividly Jake Seals' words a couple of days ago in the laboratory.

Dump a gallon of this in a swimming pool and it would strip your hide off in seconds. It's really horrible. Get it on your bare skin and there is nothing *you can do – there is nothing that will neutralize it.*

She saw Seals lying on the floor. His body disappearing in the explosion of vapour when she'd turned on the shower. She remembered going to phone the ambulance, struggling with the dial, then nothing more. 'How – how is – he?' Her voice sounded strange, much higher than usual, squeaky.

'Your colleague?'

She nodded, hoping desperately there had been some miracle.

'Not good,' the doctor said gently.

'Is he – alive?'

The reply seemed to take an age. 'I'm afraid he didn't make it.' Pause. 'You did everything you could.'

She bit her lip, which felt puffy. 'No, I – I –' She tried to think, to go back to the lab, to replay the scenario in her mind. She'd left him lying there, hissing and screeching under the shower. Eaten alive by acid.

She could taste the coppery tang of blood and the sharper, sourer, sulphurous taste of the chemical; could smell it in her nostrils. It was eating its way through her, too. That's why there were so many people looking at her. Medical students; they had been brought along to watch her die in agony. Like Mr Seals, but more slowly.

'There was nothing more you could have done,' the doctor said. 'You did all the right things.'

She thought fleetingly of the defiant, arrogant Jake Seals in the pub on Monday, suddenly clamming up and refusing to talk any more about the company, as if something had scared him. He had not seemed like a man to be easily scared. Then yesterday, quietly telling her he had got the pills she wanted, still looking scared.

What had happened to those Maternox? Were they destroyed by the acid, or still lying around in the lab somewhere? Could she get a message to Mr Wentworth before she, too, died?

'How does your throat feel?' the doctor asked.

She looked back at him and swallowed, testing it. 'OK – a bit sore.'

'The scans we've done have shown up a small oedema in your lungs, but it's nothing to worry about – it's more a reaction to the irritant – there's no sign of any permanent damage. You may have suffered a tiny amount of burn and scarring to some internal tissue, which will cause you some tenderness for a while – but it should heal up in a couple of weeks. You need to take it very easy for a few days.'

Her first thought was not relief but that he was lying. Even if he was telling the truth, how could he be sure? He didn't know how destructive the acid was; no one did.

She breathed in again. The metallic smell was sweetened suddenly with the scent of flowers. She turned her head and saw a large bouquet on the table beside her, and suddenly noticed her father sitting by the bed. His presence immediately comforted her.

Dressed in a white polo-neck sweater and tweed jacket, absorbing everything that was going on, giving the impression he was presiding over the room like a tribal chieftain, he winked as he caught her eye. And the simple gesture flooded her with warmth and a burst of confidence.

'You were very brave, darling, trying to help the poor chap,' he said.

'I did the wrong things. I shouldn't have put water on; I should have stayed with him.'

'Water was the right thing; there wasn't anything else you could have done.'

'I'll come back in the morning,' the doctor said. 'See how you're getting on.' He turned to her father. 'Good to see you again, Dick.'

'You too. I really appreciate this.'

Monty watched the two men shaking hands, then, as the entourage moved off, her father leaned over to her. 'Gordon Lanscomb. He's the top respiratory man in the country. I worked with him on that government genetics advisory board a few years back – you couldn't be in better hands.'

She smiled her acknowledgement. 'What's the time?'

He glanced at his watch. 'Half past four.'

The news surprised her. 'Four? In the afternoon?'

'You've been asleep for a while, darling. How are you feeling?'

'OK,' she said flatly. 'I'm OK.' She watched him for a while. 'You don't need to stay – it's nice that you're here, but you have a lot to do – tonight – you have something on, don't you?'

160

'I've got that talk at Sussex University – I'll have to leave in a sec. I'll be back in the morning.'

'How long do I have to stay in?'

'Gordon thinks a couple of days – they want to let your lungs settle down, keep you under observation.' He squeezed her hand. 'Don't worry, you're a tough little thing.'

'It's that chemical that worries me.'

'The healthy human body's a pretty resilient thing. They've given you a cocktail of anti-carcinogen drugs that are pretty effective – they're used in the nuclear power industry for workers who have accidental radiation exposure – you'll be fine. Dr Crowe rang me a short while ago – said if you'd prefer they could arrange to have you moved to one of the Bendix clinics. They're superb hospitals, but I think with Gordon Lanscomb being the consultant, I'd rather you stayed here. Up to you?' He raised his eyebrows.

'I'll stay here.'

'Sensible.' Then he frowned. 'Tell me what actually happened, darling. And why on earth were you in so early?'

Monty tried to collect her thoughts, not wanting to say too much to her father. 'Mr Seals said he was leaving in a few weeks and wanted to have a blitz on getting everything straight for us before he did. We thought the best thing was to have a few really early mornings, get in before the phones started.'

'Were you there when the accident happened? Did you see it?'

She shook her head.

'That's the danger of doing anything when you're over-tired. He must have tripped, I suppose – but surely to God the man had more sense than to carry a chemical that lethal with its cap removed? And no protective eye-wear?'

'He said something about a wolf.'

'Did you say *wolf*?' her father echoed.

'I didn't understand either.'

The scientist looked at her quizzically. 'Wolf?' He took Monty's left hand and examined it thoroughly. 'You didn't get any of this stuff on your skin, did you?'

'No.'

'Well, I don't think I've noticed too many wolves wandering around the building. Have you?'

She managed a half-smile back. 'I think he – he was delirious. I just heard an alarm ringing when I got out of the lift and ran straight down. He – he –' Her voice faltered.

'It's OK, don't talk about it now.' Dr Bannerman turned towards the flowers, changing the subject. 'Wonder who these are from? A secret admirer?'

Monty turned her head towards them, fighting back tears. She reached up an arm. Anticipating her, Dick Bannerman pulled the envelope off the top and handed it to her. She opened it carefully and read the short message inside.

'I understand you were extremely brave this morning. Our thoughts are with you for what you have been through. We are all very proud of you. Neil Rorke.'

The note cheered her, and she passed it to her father. 'I think that's very kind, don't you, Daddy?'

'About the least he could do. Probably trying to fend off a lawsuit from you.'

She chided him. 'That's a bit harsh! He's a really nice man – he did keep his word about Walt –' She bit her lip. She had not told her father the news about Walter Hoggin being made redundant and then reinstated.

'Walt?'

'I – I really do like Sir Neil,' she said hastily.

'I prefer him to Crowe. Not that there's much of a contest.'

There was a sharp knock on the door, then it opened and a man looked in. 'Miss Bannerman?' he said, without apologizing for his intrusion.

'Yes?'

His appearance instantly told her he was not a medic. He possessed more the air of a bank manager. In his mid-forties, he had a smoothly good-looking face with neatly delineated features beneath close-cropped black hair. A raincoat was neatly folded over his arm.

'Detective Superintendent Levine,' he said by way of introduction in a crisp voice that carried a faint Scottish burr. Acknowledging her father's existence with only a cursory nod, he walked across to the bed, fished from his breast pocket a wallet, which he opened in a slick one-handed motion to show Monty his warrant card. 'I wonder if I might have a few words with you?'

'Of course.'

'Could this not wait until tomorrow?' Dick Bannerman said, a trace aggressively.

'It's OK, Daddy,' Monty said.

Bannerman looked at the detective, stood up then leaned down and kissed Monty. 'You sure?'

'Yes.'

'Right – I'll leave you to it. I'll come by first thing in the morning.'

'Don't, Daddy, there's no need – you have so much to do at the moment.'

He squeezed her hand gently and looked into her eyes. 'You matter more than any of it, darling. OK?'

She kissed him goodbye. 'Thank you,' she mouthed.

The policeman waited until the scientist had closed the door behind him, then sat down, resting his coat on his lap. Sharp grey eyes studied her carefully and perfect white teeth transmitted to her the fleeting illusion of a smile. His skin had the kind of light tan acquired from sun-beds, and his trim physique suggested a man who kept himself in shape, perhaps obsessively. There was something altogether rather clinical about him, Monty thought, which was furthered by his very formal way of speaking.

'I won't take up much of your time, Miss Bannerman, but as you are the only person who saw what happened you'll appreciate my need to talk to you.' He sat very straight, with perfect posture.

'Of course.'

'Would you like to tell me as much as you can remember?' Again the teeth hinted briefly at a smile before gliding back behind thin, straight lips.

Monty told him exactly what had happened from the time she stepped out of the lift. He listened in silence, without taking any notes. When she told him Seals had shouted something about a wolf, he frowned.

163

'Are you sure you heard correctly?' The idea seemed to perturb him.

'Yes.'

'I don't know if you are aware, Miss Bannerman, but it appears your colleague was intoxicated when he came to work. He had a blood alcohol level of twice the legal limit for driving. That might explain his extraordinary carelessness.'

'It seems out of character.'

The detective superintendent parted his hands as if he were opening an invisible book. 'It might also explain any strange remarks. I understand he'd had a night on the town and was with a young lady until two in the morning. If he'd drunk a lot, it's very possible his blood alcohol level was still high at a quarter to six in the morning.'

Monty heard what he was saying, but it astonished her. Then she realized she barely knew Jake Seals. Maybe he had even been on drugs as well, hence the wolf hallucination.

Levine fixed a penetrating stare on Monty. 'A quarter to six seems very early to go to work, Miss Bannerman. Is that your normal routine?'

She thought before responding, not wanting to say anything that could enable him to probe deeper. 'When you work for someone like my father, you have to put in those kind of hours just to keep up with him.'

'Of course.' There was no reaction in Levine's face and his eyes did not leave hers. 'And that is the time you start work every day?'

'I used to in our previous lab,' she lied. 'I hoped it might be easier here, with more assistants, but it isn't. We're still winding down our old premises, so I'm trying to be in two places at once. I decided to start coming in early from today.'

'And is it customary for Mr Seals to come in so early?'

'I wouldn't know.'

His eyes continued to scrutinize her. 'I thought it was the police who drew the short straw on unsociable hours.' This time there was a trace of warmth in his smile.

'It's not from choice,' she said. 'I can assure you.'

He stood up. 'You've been very helpful, thank you. I

164

won't take any more of your time now. If you don't mind, in a few days I'll arrange for someone to come and take a formal statement, and I expect you'll be asked to attend the inquest.'

'Yes, of course.'

After he had gone, she lay back thinking. Detective *Superintendent*. She did not know much about police ranks, but that sounded senior. It struck her as strange that someone so high up should be sent to investigate an industrial accident, but maybe that was the kind of respect Bendix Schere commanded – or insisted on.

She closed her eyes, feeling tired, and lapsed into a troubled doze.

'Do you think you can manage a little something to eat?'

Monty opened her eyes with a start to see a nurse in blue uniform laying a tray on a swing table over the bed. 'I brought you some tomato soup, steamed fish and ice cream.'

Monty looked at it queasily. 'I – I don't think I'm really very hungry.'

'Try to eat a little.'

Monty started to sit up. The nurse cranked up the head rest and shifted her pillows. 'There you go. Would you like the television on?'

'OK, sure.'

The nurse switched it on, then gave Monty the remote control. A man and a woman were arguing loudly in a pub on the screen. As the nurse reached the door she said, 'Oh, hello, you have a visitor!'

Conor Molloy came into the room holding a spray of flowers and a massive wicker gift basket of fruit. 'Hi,' he said. 'You about to eat? I'll come back.'

'No – stay, please. Hey, what's all this?'

He blushed. 'I – er – I –' Then he grinned. 'I mugged an old lady in the lift.'

She grinned back. 'They're gorgeous – thank you.'

'I'll ask the nurse – see if I, if she can get a vase or something. How you doing?'

'OK – apart from my voice.'

'Yah – you sound a little like Donald Duck – kind of suits you.'

'Thanks a lot!'

'You're welcome.'

Monty had been feeling exhausted a few moments ago, but the appearance of the American charged her up instantly. She wondered suddenly if she was wearing any make-up, wished she'd had a chance to look in a mirror before he'd arrived and do something with her hair. She felt a total wreck.

'You look better than this morning,' he said. 'Much more colour in your face.'

'It was very sweet of you to come by then. I'm afraid I wasn't very –'

He shrugged, then edged back toward the door. 'I'll go find a vase.'

Monty dunked a piece of dry toast in her soup and lifted it to her mouth. The taste of it kindled a small appetite, and brought back a memory of her mother; when she was a child, her mother had always given her Heinz tomato soup when she was unwell. Still today it always gave her a feeling of reassurance.

Conor Molloy returned, accompanied by a large glass vase which he filled from a tap in the tiny ensuite bathroom. He pushed in his flowers, and asked Monty where she wanted them. She pointed to her bedside table, and he put them down, moving Rorke's bouquet to a table by the window, then seated himself in the chair beside her. There was a moment of silence between them that felt very comfortable to Monty – as if they were old friends easy in each other's company.

The American was looking tired, she thought. His complexion was very pale and there were bloodshot streaks in the whites of his brown eyes, as if he had not had enough sleep last night. Then she glanced away with a faint smile of embarrassment as he returned her gaze.

There was something very solid about him. She liked the way his short tangled hair was swept back and a few locks had tumbled over his forehead; there was more than a trace of the modern Hollywood breed of actor in his looks. But there was something that went beyond, which she liked more than anything; it was the habitual quiet, haunted expression that attracted her. As if there was another layer beneath the tough, good-humoured veneer; something that was both vulnerable and mysterious.

'You're OK?' he asked.

'Yup. I think I inhaled some of the vapour which wasn't too clever, I suppose.'

'Not from what I've heard about it, no. So what exactly happened – was this guy mixing something up or what?'

'I don't know – I just heard the gas alarm as I got out of the lift.'

'What time was that?'

'It was about five to six. I was late –' She stopped. Telling him she was late had been a slip of the tongue.

'Late?' he quizzed gently. 'It was five to six this morning and you were *late*? What time do you normally get into the office?'

She wiped the remains of the soup from the bowl with the last piece of toast, her hand shaking. 'I – I – it varies.' She avoided meeting his eyes, 'Mr Seals was leaving at the end of the month; there was a lot of stuff he wanted to get finished for my father – he – he suggested a blitz of coming in early – before the phones start – you know.'

Conor watched her carefully. It might be the truth but it did not feel like it. Jake Seals was someone who'd had access to a vast raft of highly secret information. If he had given in his notice, it was probable he would have been sent home instantly and not allowed back on the premises.

'Don't let your food get cold,' he said to her.

'I'm not really very hungry,' she said, picking up a fork and spearing a tinned carrot which tasted sweet and overcooked. A subsequent mouthful of fish turned out to be equally soggy.

'Want me to go to a takeaway and get you something decent?'

She grinned. 'Not tonight, thanks – but I might start getting desperate if they keep me in! Have you eaten – would you like my ice cream?'

He shook his head. 'Thanks, I'm fine.' Their eyes met and they exchanged a grin. 'So tell me, what was the real reason you were in at that hour?' He gave her a quizzical frown. 'I mean, forgive me if I'm trespassing on some kind of – you know – personal ground between you and Mr Seals.'

Monty felt herself tensing and tried not to show it. She spoke nonchalantly. 'There was nothing between Jake Seals and me – I'm afraid we didn't even really get on terribly well.' She speared another carrot, her hand shaking, and was aware she was blushing. She tried to look anywhere but at the American, yet found her eyes drawn back to his. 'Truly,' she said, noticing the look of amiable scepticism.

He smiled again, his eyes twinkling. 'Sure. Listen, I apologize – I'm not trying to interrogate you, you can tell me to go stuff my face in a brick wall if you want.'

She laughed, then winced in pain. 'No, don't do that.'

Conor Molloy indicated his mock relief, then spoke again. 'Do you think it actually was an accident?'

She wondered whether to repeat Detective Superintendent Levine's comment about Seals being drunk, but felt somehow that was unfair on Seals. 'No.'

The spontaneity of her reply startled Monty as much as it did the American.

30

'We seem to have two problems: firstly, the man who gave Seals the Maternox capsules. We need to –'

'He's not a problem,' Bill Gunn said abruptly. He stared across the japanned desk which, like the rest of Vincent Crowe's furnishings, always struck the Director of Security as more appropriate for a boudoir than an office. Although it did rather suit Crowe's effete side, he supposed. The black papier-mâché frog which dominated the front area of the desk stared back at him with its red jewelled eyes, partially obscuring his view of the Chief Executive.

Frogs. It was meant to be an in-joke. Every Director of

Bendix Schere had been issued with a decorative frog for their office by Crowe. The one Gunn had been given was a soft-toy Kermit wearing Walkman headphones; he kept it in a bottom drawer of his desk. In Gunn's view his surveillance work was too important to be illustrated in joke form. The removal of all frogs from display in Directors' offices was one of the very few recommendations Gunn had made in his time that had been rejected.

'Why is this man no problem?' Crowe's cold grey eyes, bird-of-prey eyes, came into view behind the frog. The lighting in his office was always low, giving the impression of a grey winter dusk even on summer days. Everything about Dr Vincent Crowe was cold, even his handshake. Gunn respected the Chief Executive and was beholden to him by a bond which went way beyond the mere walls of the Bendix Schere building, but he remained awed by the man and always would do. Crowe was the most frightening human being he had ever met in his life; and he had met many contenders.

'Richard Wilson is one of three Quality Assurance supervisors at Reading, sir,' Gunn said. 'Seals asked him to obtain Maternox samples from batch M-6575-1881. He told Seals to jump in a lake. Then the surveillance team on Seals saw Wilson turn up at Seals' flat that night and post a packet through the letter box. Turns out he owed Seals a favour going back a few years – Seals used to cover for him whilst he was having an extra-marital affair. Seals was calling in the debt.'

'And threatening to tell Mrs Wilson if he didn't play?'

'Precisely, sir.'

'The packet contained batch M-6575–1881 capsules?'

'Yes.'

'Where are they now?'

'We retrieved them from a work bench in Seals' laboratory this morning, before the police and Department of Health inspectors got there.'

Crowe nodded but showed no relief at the news. 'How did this man Wilson have access to them?'

'Quality Assurance hold the retained M-6575–1881 batch samples the same way as all other batches, to avoid suspicion.'

'Why haven't they been substituted with capsules from another batch?'

'That's not my remit.'

'Anything to do with Bendix security is your remit, Major Gunn.' Crowe still referred to him by his old service rank.

'I appreciate that, sir, but I can only work in areas where we have people I can trust and I don't have anyone inside Quality Assurance – there's never been any need to. The plan was, and is, to feed the Maternox batches into the system without raising any eyebrows, so M-6575–1881 is simply one of four hundred batches put into the distribution system at Reading. I wasn't briefed to anticipate the problem we are experiencing.'

'I have always understood, Major Gunn, it is your role to advise us of any potential danger areas.'

Gunn saw the line of arguing wasn't going to get him anywhere. He had warned Crowe that there could be problems if the batch led to any reported side-effects. But Crowe had been dismissive, stating that they could deal with any side-effects if and when they were ever traced back to the Maternox, which he very much doubted. Now, this seemed to have happened.

'I apologize, sir, but I'm not a scientist. I had been led to understand that due to the time lag between the Maternox prescription and any subsequent birth it was extremely improbable any connection with Maternox would be made.'

'You appreciate the importance of security on this trial, don't you, Major Gunn? You are aware of quite how much is at stake?'

'I am always aware, Dr Crowe,' he said, riled at the innuendo.

Crowe rested his elbows on his desk and entwined his long marble-like fingers. 'Mr Seals asks his friend Wilson to obtain a specific batch of Maternox. Within hours of delivering them, Mr Seals is dead. If you were Mr Seals' friend, would you not be just a touch suspicious?'

'In some circumstances I might be,' Gunn said. 'Not here: firstly, Seals' death was an accident – all employees are or will be made well aware of that. Secondly, if Seals used emotional blackmail, I don't think Wilson will be inclined to pursue a connection – particularly as it would mean he'd have to admit to breaching company regulations in removing the samples. I've had Wilson under surveillance since this morning and if I feel there's a need to take any neutralizing action I will, but I don't think it will be necessary.'

'You'll watch him round the clock for a while?'

'Of course.' Gunn glanced at his watch. Crowe regularly worked late and kept his secretarial staff late also. From the time logs Gunn monitored, it was not unusual for Crowe to leave well past midnight and sometimes closer to dawn; and he was always at his desk by 7.30 in the morning. Gunn wondered how much sleep the man needed.

The time now was a quarter to eight. *Shit*. On Monday when he should have joined Nikky for *Othello* at the Old Vic, the playback of the recorded conversation between Jake Seals and Montana Bannerman in the pub had caused him to arrive halfway through the third act. Tonight she had wanted to see Olivier's *Henry V* which was showing at the National Film Theatre and he'd promised on his life to be punctual, and take her to Poons in Covent Garden afterwards, where she loved watching the kitchen through the glass wall. Culture. Christ, he'd never seen so much damned Shakespeare in his life. Although it wasn't entirely a waste of time; the old bard had a devious mind; there were always useful things you could learn about manipulation from him.

'The other problem is the Bannerman woman,' Crowe said. 'She worries me. What was she doing arriving in the building at that hour?'

'Meeting Seals, no question.'

'So who made the connection with the Cyclops deaths – her or Seals?'

'I don't have an answer to that yet, sir.'

'Is she going to believe Seals' death was an accident?'

'She won't have any reason not to.' Gunn smiled. 'I mean, it was a genuine accident, wasn't it?'

Crowe raised his eyebrows a fraction. 'What's her condition?'

'Improving.'

'You have her under surveillance in hospital?'

'We've put a bug in but it's faulty.'

'What do you mean, *faulty*?'

'It's not picking up – either it has a dead cell, or it's been moved or damaged. We're working on it. But she's in a private room; we need to be a little discreet.'

'Are you keeping tabs on her visitors?'

'Absolutely.'

'Anyone of interest showed up yet?'

'Conor Molloy just tipped up.'

'Who?'

'Group Patents and Agreements. Young hot-shot American patent attorney. Been drafted in from Washington to work on the Bannerman patents.'

Crowe delicately scratched a cheek. 'So he has contact with Miss Bannerman at work?'

'Yes.'

'Natural for him to drop by and see how she is, then?'

Gunn hesitated. 'Yes.'

The phone rang. Crowe answered it with a curt: 'Is this urgent?' Then he listened for some moments. 'You have her name? Right.' He picked up a slim gold pen and wrote something on a sheet of notepaper, then replaced the receiver and looked back at Gunn. 'The press,' he said.

Gunn nodded. 'PR have been under siege most of the day about Seals – I have that under control, they've been well briefed.'

'This isn't about Seals,' Crowe said gravely. 'This is about Maternox.'

Gunn only just managed to check himself from swearing aloud; Crowe had a loathing of foul language.

'They would like to know if I am aware of the connection between three recent Cyclops deaths.' The coldness in Crowe's eyes had turned to coals of fire.

Gunn's brain began spinning. 'Which paper?'

'Some rag I've never heard of,' Crowe said contemptuously. '*The Thames Valley Gazette*. Know it?'

Gunn stiffened, and chose his words carefully. 'Yes, it's small fry – a free evening paper, forty thousand circulation in the Reading-Slough area. A total rag, mainly small ads and not much news.'

Crowe glanced down at his notepad again. 'A reporter called Zandra Wollerton.'

Gunn nodded. 'She was asking questions about Maternox a couple of weeks ago.'

'She was? Why didn't someone tell me?'

'We checked her out at the time; she didn't seem to have any information worth worrying about.'

Crowe's eyes were really blazing now. 'Who made that assessment?'

Gunn swallowed. 'I did, sir – I didn't think it was worth troubling you.'

Crowe's fingers visibly whitened as he squeezed them together. 'I'm not convinced you are handling this whole thing very well, Major Gunn. I trust there is nothing in your private life distracting you from your duties?'

'No, sir,' he said coolly, wondering at the back of his mind how the hell he was going to pacify Nikky. On the subject of private lives, he had often wondered about Crowe's. The Chief Executive was married but childless. Gunn had met Ursula Crowe on a number of occasions; a ferociously intellectual, humourless woman as frost-bound as her husband; they were welcome to each other. 'I'll get on to this Zandra Wollerton immediately.'

Crowe sat back in his chair. 'I would suggest you find out who owns this newspaper. The chances are we spend money advertising with the group.' He looked at the Director of Security again and raised his eyebrows.

'Of course, Dr Crowe.' Gunn smiled. 'I get your drift.'

31

Conor stared at Monty, quietly elated by her remark. Her stock had just risen dramatically in his view, and he had to make an effort not to reveal his excitement. Aware of the possibility someone might be listening, he lowered his voice:

'You mean that? You really think Seals' death was no accident?'

She took a few moments to gather her thoughts, wondering if she ought to retract before she dug herself in any deeper. She did not know this American, had only had one real conversation with him before, and had no idea where his loyalties lay. Until just a few moments ago she had presumed they lay with the company, but something in the way he had asked the question made her realize she was wrong. The suspicion in his voice had been as unmistakable as her reply had been spontaneous.

She felt suddenly very frightened, the implications gusting in her mind like the first hints of an oncoming gale. She shivered. Thought about the journalist, Hubert Wentworth, Deputy News Editor, distraught at his daughter's death. The bolshy young female reporter, Zandra Wollerton, who'd had her flat broken into by a pervert who had stolen her knickers. Jake Seals covered in acid. The detective, Levine, who had said Seals was drunk.

Was there enough there to justify an accusation that Jake Seals had been deliberately killed? Logic told her that there was not, that she was emotional from tiredness, fear, stress, that what she had said to Conor Molloy was just a knee-jerk response. 'I – I –' she found herself being drawn into his warm, hazelnut eyes as she replied. *Trust me*, they were saying. *Trust yourself. Trust your instincts!* 'I don't know why I said that,' she stated finally.

Something flashed across his face, just a fleeting change of expression that was gone almost before she had time to register it, and she realized then, beyond any doubt, that he knew something he was holding back from her. But what? She eased the plate of fish away with trembling fingers; it was distracting her.

Conor saw the confusion in her eyes, aware that he had pushed her. But not too far. The confusion was real; there were doubts, he could read them loud and clear.

God, she was attractive, he thought. Even without make-up and with all she had been through today, she looked lovely. Her skin had a fresh, clear lustre, the blue of her eyes

174

shone in gorgeous contrast with the colour of her hair; he looked at her slender white neck disappearing into the slack folds of her hospital gown, looked back at her face with its cute curl of a nose and its generous mouth that gave her an appeal that was increasing with every moment he spent in her presence.

I want you, Montana Bannerman, he thought. I really want you. I even adore your crazy name.

He tried to concentrate his mind on the real purpose of his visit. Then she smiled at him and his resolve weakened as he could almost feel her warmth engulfing him.

'I don't know what I believe right now. I need a night's sleep to clear my head,' she said, still unsure what to make of him. She was in shock, that much she did know, and shock could play havoc with your emotions. But something about this man made her feel so comfortable that she did not want him to leave, wished they could simply change the subject and chat about something different. She regretted her remark now, but couldn't find a way to retract it without looking foolish.

God, if he started telling people in the company she believed that Jake Seals had been murdered, what then? She did not imagine Sir Neil Rorke would take too kindly to her spreading that kind of rumour. She could end up out on her ear, and her father damaged by implication.

'Look,' she said again, 'I – I don't know why I said that.'

'Perhaps because you meant it?' he prodded gently.

She shook her head. 'No. It was a tragic accident – it must have been. Anyhow, with all the security, no one could have got in and attacked him. And who would have wanted to?'

Conor Molloy said nothing, waiting for her to go on.

'Animal Rights fanatics? We had problems with them ourselves in Berkshire,' she said. 'They broke into our animal house one night and released all the rabbits and mice. They sprayed slogans on the outside walls a couple of times. But surely they're not organized enough to break into a building like the Bendix?'

'I don't think so,' he said.

'What do *you* think?'

'In any normal company there'd be all kinds of rumours flying around by now,' he said. 'In Bendix Schere there aren't any; just a wall of silence. All I heard is that he tripped holding a half-gallon Winchester bottle. So if he tripped, why didn't it just fall on the floor? How the hell did he get it all over his head?'

'He fell and the bottle fell on to him?' she suggested.

'Was the bottle smashed when you saw it?'

'I – I didn't look for the bottle. There was glass everywhere, though, so I presume it must have been.'

'If the bottle fell on to him, surely he'd have cushioned it, and it wouldn't have broken?'

'It could easily have bounced on to the floor.'

'Sure,' he nodded in agreement, then drew a breath. 'For the acid to have poured over him, the cap must have been off. Do lab staff normally carry chemicals that lethal with the cap off?'

'No.'

'So doesn't it strike you as odd that Seals did?'

'I hadn't thought about that.' She wondered if the information the detective had given her that Seals was drunk had got round the company yet. 'Maybe if he hadn't been feeling well – perhaps he wasn't concentrating?' she said, testing.

'You knew the man,' he said. 'Would that have been in character?'

She hesitated. 'No.'

'Was he the sort of person to have turned up drunk?'

Their eyes locked. She thought carefully before replying. 'No.'

'I can see you're tired,' he said. 'Let's talk about this when you're feeling better – maybe I could buy you lunch one day next week?'

'I'd like that,' she said.

He smiled. 'So would I. Very much.'

As he stood up, she said, 'Mr Molloy – will you – not tell anyone what I said, you know, about – about it not being an accident?'

He raised a finger to his lips. 'Not a soul.'

*

Some hours later Monty was awoken by a click and saw a pool of light spill into the dark room. A shadowy figure came in, a nurse, she presumed.

'Whrs thrrr?' she said sleepily.

The figure stood in front of the bed, as if checking to see she was all right, then seemed to duck and fiddle with something. A few moments afterwards the door closed again.

32

London. Thursday 10 November, 1994

The presenter was urbane, his face caked in stage make-up to give the illusion of a tan. He addressed the camera quizzically, as if it was an uninvited guest at a party: 'Genetic engineering – a good or a bad thing? If you were born with the gene of an illness that might disable you or kill you in later life, would *you* want to be told? If you were informed that the baby you have just conceived is carrying the gene of a fatal or crippling disease, would *you* want to abort that unborn child?'

He stepped forward into the studio audience and thrust his microphone into a woman's face. 'Susan Bennett is a carrier of the cystic fibrosis gene; she and her husband have made a conscious decision not to have children because of the risk of passing it on to them.'

Monty lay back in the hospital bed, her head cushioned by pillows, enjoying the rare luxury of watching morning television. The subject of genes was everywhere, she thought. You could barely open the papers, turn on the radio or television, without coming across a new discovery or a debate, and she found that exciting. The part she enjoyed most about working for her father was the feeling of being a privileged insider on the hottest scientific topic of the age.

She felt better today; her head was clearer, although her eyes still smarted a bit, and her throat and lungs were a little raw.

The *Daily Mail* lay folded on the tray in front of her. There was a small piece on page 15 about the death of Jake Seals, under the heading 'Lab Death Horror', in which she was mentioned. *Montana Bannerman, 29, daughter of Nobel Prize winning genetics scientist Dr Richard Bannerman, was detained in hospital suffering from shock and respiratory problems.*

Apparently several reporters had tried to see her yesterday but her father had fended them off, and left strict instructions that only friends and colleagues were to be allowed to visit. The room smelled like a conservatory. Three more bouquets had arrived in the past hour since breakfast, one from her friend Anna Sterling, one from Polly and Richard Maguire with whom she had stayed last weekend in Bath, and one from an uncle and aunt – her mother's sister – whom she realized, guiltily, she hadn't seen for a couple of years. Ever since her mother's death her father had been unable to cope with the relatives on that side; they reminded him, particularly his sister-in-law, too painfully of what he had lost.

There was a brief knock, then her door opened. Monty looked round, expecting to find a medic and was surprised, instead, to see the young reporter, Zandra Wollerton. She was clutching a small tape-recorder. Her fingernails were still painted green.

'Ms Bannerman! Hello!' She closed the door as if she owned the place, then sat down beside Monty, ignoring the television. A red AIDS awareness ribbon hung from her lapel.

'Hello,' Monty said politely, but not pleased by the intrusion, particularly as she was interested in the debate on the television.

'I heard the story down the wire and came straight up here yesterday, but they wouldn't let me see you.'

'How did you get in this morning?'

'I told the battleaxe down the corridor I was your private secretary,' she replied proudly, switching on the recorder and holding it angled towards Monty. 'You were the first person to arrive on the scene, I gather?'

Alarm bells began ringing in Monty's brain. The reporter was acting as if she was in the midst of a feeding frenzy. 'Yes, I was.'

'I understand you cradled the dying man in your arms while you were waiting for the ambulance?'

'No I – I didn't do that. Not exactly.'

'But you did injure yourself trying to save his life, didn't you?'

Monty shook her head. 'That sounds rather more heroic than it actually was. I'm afraid I didn't do much at all. By the time I got there it –'

'There's a rumour that Mr Seals was drunk. Would you say that he appeared so?'

The question angered Monty. 'No, I would not! He was a –'

She hesitated, telling herself not to rise to the bait. She needed to stay calm. Anything she said could be twisted in print. It had happened to her before and she had learned some bitter lessons. 'Mr Seals was a professional in a highly responsible position. It's inconceivable that he would have come into work drunk.'

'That isn't what I've heard from the police,' Zandra Wollerton said.

'Seems like you know more than I do,' Monty replied tersely. It riled her that after their serious talk on Tuesday the only thing the reporter now seemed interested in was scoring a few Brownie points with a speculative sensation.

Zandra Wollerton stopped the tape. 'The police took a statement from a girl Mr Seals took out Tuesday night. She said he had been drinking heavily and was extremely drunk when he left her at half past two in the morning.' She started the tape again.

'It was some hours later that the accident happened,' Monty said, feeling a little relieved. If it was true that he'd been drunk after all, then it made the chances that it was all a ghastly accident more probable.

'He was at work very early. Did he always do that? And you?'

Monty took a deep breath, buying time, feeling battered by the relentless questioning. 'I often go in early, yes. I'm under pressure at the moment.'

'Do you feel there might be any connection between Mr Seals' death and the fact that three women have died giving birth to Cyclops Syndrome babies after taking the Maternox fertility drug manufactured by Bendix Schere?'

Monty stared wonderingly at the sincere face in front of her. *Dangerous question*, she thought. Aloud she said, 'I can't see any possible grounds for making such a connection.'

There was an uncomfortable silence between them. The reporter switched off the tape. 'Is there anything you'd like to talk about off the record? I mean, I thought perhaps you might want to be a little more helpful . . .'

'That's all I have to say, I'm afraid.'

The girl pulled a card out of her pocket and handed it to Monty. Her voice softened, changing from interrogator to friend. 'If you think of anything else at all relevant, my direct line, home number and mobile are on this.'

Monty laid it on her tray without looking at it. 'Of course.'

'Nice talking to you again, Ms Bannerman. Hope you get better quickly,' she said chirpily.

Monty smiled at her. There was a good girl under there, beneath the 'tough reporter' carapace. Wentworth was right about her, she would go far. But not at the expense of the Bannermans' goodwill at Bendix Schere.

The reporter hitched her bag jauntily on to her shoulder. 'I haven't finished my investigations into Bendix Schere,' she said. 'Not by a long chalk.'

33

Barnet, North London. 1946

Daniel Judd, standing naked, closed the circle with an arc of the poker he used as his ceremonial sword. He had moved his bedroom table into the centre of the circle earlier, and draped it in black cloth. It was a few minutes to midnight and his mother had gone to bed a couple of hours ago; he was pretty certain she was asleep.

The first month after his father's funeral had been good; his mother had been subdued, numbed by shock. For the first time in Daniel's life – except for a blissful fortnight when she'd been sick with flu – she had been no trouble at all. Then the shock had begun to subside and anger replaced it.

Her anger had, naturally, been focused entirely on himself.

It was his sins, she said, that had brought God's wrath on the family. God had killed Daniel's father because He was angry at Daniel. God had taken her husband to punish her for producing such a wicked son: a son who was insolent, who dared to question the existence of the Almighty. Who questioned everything around him.

He remembered her face four days ago, after church, when he had questioned the vicar about Satan. He had read a book in the library written by a man called Aleister Crowley that said Christians had killed hundreds of thousands of people for not believing in their religion, but that Satanists had not killed any for not believing in theirs. It had been a simple question, he thought. He had merely asked the vicar why that made Christians better than Satanists.

His mother had almost torn his ear off. She had dragged him all the way home by it, twisting it like a dishcloth, then had slapped him in the face until he could barely see. After that she had forced him to wash his mouth out with soap, and locked him in his bedroom whilst she read biblical tracts aloud on the other side of the door.

On the table inside the circle lay the page of a grimoire he had torn from a library book, a small ball of dough he had taken from the pantry, a row of his mother's hairs that he had combed from her hairbrush, a safety pin, a length of twine, a pair of scissors and a shoebox. A black candle was burning and he had already purified the room with salt and water.

He closed his eyes, visualized his mother's face, then opened them again and whispered the words of the incantation printed on the page before him. He finished by saying:

> 'Be damned! Be damned!
> My power is cursing you,
> My power is hexing you,
> You are completely under my spell.
> Be damned! Be damned!'

Next he rolled the ball of dough between the palms of his hands, making it elongate. Pulling a strip off he elongated that as well and pulled two lengths from it. The *arms*, he thought. Then he created the legs, the head and the torso, and assembled the effigy. Using the point of the safety pin, he sculpted features in the face, then pressed the hairs on to the skull, cementing them in place with more dough.

'Mother,' he whispered, proudly staring at his handiwork. 'You are under my spell now. Oh yes, you are!'

He took the opened safety pin, pushed the point through the lower and upper lips he had just fashioned and closed the pin. Careful not to break or pull them off, he bent the arms back then, using some of the twine, tied them together.

He picked up the effigy, raised it in the air and held it aloft whilst he read out more incantations written in a language he did not understand, hoping that he was pronouncing them correctly. After this he laid the effigy in the shoebox, the inside of which was lined with a strip of black satin. Like a coffin.

He opened the circle with his sword and stepped out of it. Then, Daniel Judd stood on a chair and placed the box safely out of sight on top of his wardrobe.

34

London. Thursday 10 November, 1994

The Chief Executive's intercom rang, one muted warble. He lifted the black receiver without breaking his concentration on the report from Conor Molloy that he was reading. The report summarized the prospects of successful US patent applications for Dr Bannerman's work on identifying and controlling the genes of a string of chronic diseases, including psoriasis, arthritis, asthma, arterial disease and stomach ulcers, as well as a key gene involved in the human biological clock.

'Yes?'

'Dr Crowe, there's a Ms Zandra Wollerton waiting downstairs in the lobby to see you. She has no appointment and won't say why she's here.'

Crowe laid the report down on his desk, recognizing the name instantly from his meeting with Major Gunn last night. He swivelled to face his computer terminal, still holding the phone to his ear. 'How do you spell her name?'

As his secretary gave him the spelling, Crowe typed the reporter's name, then hit the search key. Gunn had wasted no time since last night: on the screen appeared her full name; age 21; curriculum vitae and family history. This was followed by details of the circulation and ownership of the *Thames Valley Gazette*. It came under the umbrella of the news conglomerate Central & Western Publishing Plc.

Bendix Schere had spent just over one hundred thousand pounds advertising its over-the-counter pharmaceuticals, baby food and hospital services with Central in the previous twelve months alone. A reasonable spend, he reflected, but less than he'd hoped to find. The threat of withdrawal of advertising might work – no one liked to lose advertising revenue; but for a company the size of Central, it was not a major amount, and the ploy could backfire.

He had half an hour before his lunch appointment. Bringing Rorke in on this might be sensible, he thought. Rorke knew everybody and if the chairman of Central was a friend of his they might be able to kill the story dead in the water.

'Bring her up,' he said into the receiver.

'Major Gunn rang while you were on the line. He's in his office.'

Without acknowledging his secretary, Crowe disconnected, then got the Director of Security's internal secure line.

'Good morning, sir,' Gunn said when he heard Crowe's voice. 'I thought you'd like a quick update on Bannerman's daughter.' He took Crowe's silence as a cue to continue. 'The reporter we were talking about last night went to see her in hospital this morning – we'd fixed the bugging problem and heard everything. Miss Bannerman's fine, in my view; she wasn't rising to any of it. My assessment is that it was Seals who told her about the Cyclops connection – and Seals also stirred it up with this Wollerton woman.'

'You'll have your answer if she tries to get any more of the Maternox batch, won't you?' Crowe said sharply.

'Yes, sir.'

'So keep close tabs on it.'

'I'll find a way, sir.'

'Miss Wollerton is on her way up to see me now,' Crowe said.

Gunn sounded worried. 'Want me in with you?'

'No, I can handle her.' Crowe replaced the receiver and behind the glossy black expanse of his orderly desk and the squat back of the papier-mâché frog, he carefully composed his thoughts.

A few moments later his secretary ushered a young woman into his presence.

Crowe watched Zandra Wollerton walk towards him without raising his chin from the bridge of his interlocked fingers. 'Take a seat,' he said dryly, fixing his eyes on one of the two wing chairs in front of his desk.

The reporter sat down, crossed her legs, switched on her tape-recorder and faced him defiantly.

'So what can I do for you, young lady?'

'Are you aware, Dr Crowe, that three women who took your company's fertility drug, Maternox, have died during childbirth, and that all three gave birth to babies deformed with Cyclops Syndrome?'

'You took the trouble to inform our Medical Information Department of this a fortnight ago, I believe, Miss Wollerton. Do you have something new to add?'

'I'm interested in your opinion as Chief Executive of Bendix.'

'We monitor any reports sent to us from doctors on possible side-effects from our pharmaceuticals. I understand we've received no such reports from the doctors of these three women, and would assume therefore that they do not share your view as to any connection. Do you have medical training yourself?'

'No.'

'You may be interested to know that worldwide last year, thirteen million women became pregnant thanks to Maternox.

The drug has been on the market for nine years without one single side-effect notification from any doctor anywhere in the world.'

'Fifteen million women if you include sub-licensed versions.'

Crowe was surprised by her thoroughness, but did not let it show.

'Dr Crowe, a Chief Lab Technician in your Genetics Research Division died yesterday morning,' she continued. 'Presumably there is no connection between his death and that of the three women? I mean, I understand that he was originally a senior technician in the lab where Maternox was developed.'

'I would be very careful, Miss Wollerton.'

'Ms,' she said with a disarming smile. 'And I'm always very careful. Now, you are presumably aware that all three women who died had taken Maternox from the same batch number: BS-M-6575-1881-UKMR.' She recited it like a child in class.

Crowe was aware that he was crushing his knuckles together, despite himself. 'On what information are you basing that statement?'

'I happen to know it's accurate,' she said, with an arrogance that made him want to shake her.

She glanced round the office, at the grey walls unrelieved by any photographs or prints that would give anything away about its occupier. 'Don't you find it oppressive in here without windows?'

'I'm not interested in discussing architecture, *Ms* Wollerton. Perhaps you could answer my question?'

'I never reveal my sources.' She widened her eyes in defiance.

Crowe made a mental note to phone the Legal Department the moment she left and have them contact her paper. This young woman was a wild cannon, dangerous. Too smart for comfort. And what the hell *was* her source? Seals? It must have been. Employees knew the strict rules forbidding any contact with the press other than through Public Relations.

'You are aware, I assume, Dr Crowe, of quite how rare Cyclops Syndrome babies are in Britain?'

'I'm afraid I'm not a walking encyclopaedia of medical statistics.'

She smiled, unfazed by his aggression. 'Then I think this will interest you: there's an average of two a year. So three within two months is a little startling. Particularly when the only link between them is that the mothers all took the same batch of your fertility drug.'

'And you would like to infer something conclusive from that?'

'No, but it's enough to go to press on. And the death of Mr Seals, with his connection, adds some interest to the story.'

He sat up straight and laid his fingertips very lightly on the edge of his desk. 'And that's why you wanted to see me, to tell me this? I would have thought if you were so confident in your story you needn't have bothered.'

'I'm very confident. I just thought it would be fair to give you the chance to comment. Bendix Schere is obviously concerned – if they weren't they wouldn't have threatened the publishers of my newspaper with advertising withdraw- al.'

The remark almost pulled the rug from under him. Who the hell had been on to the paper? Gunn! His thoughts flailed. What the hell did that jumped-up paratrooper think he was playing at, barging in like that! Gunn's judgement used to be good – more than good, in fact – brilliant. But if he was losing it now . . .

With great effort the Chief Executive of Bendix Schere switched to a conciliatory tack, and his vermilion lips parted into a smile. Creases appeared like cracks in the porcelain white of his face. 'Maternox has helped many millions of infertile women to enjoy motherhood, and neither they nor their babies have suffered any above-normal percentage of health problems. If you want to go to press with wild allegations for no other reason than to gain column inches for your career, I advise you to think hard about the greater consequences.'

Ms Wollerton stared closely at her tape-recorder, checking that it was running, then pointed it in his direction again. 'Dr

Crowe, at this moment there's a pregnant woman in Intensive Care at University College Hospital suffering from an unidentified virus, accompanied by a psoriasis-like rash, and her condition is deteriorating. She took Maternox for infertility problems – from the same suspect batch number. It will be interesting to see if her baby is all right, won't it? They're planning a Caesarean section next week if her condition hasn't improved. I shall be at the hospital.'

He waited some moments before replying, 'I have fond memories of University College Hospital,' he said. 'From my post-doc days.'

She switched off her recorder and stood up. 'Let's hope they stay fond,' she said. 'The *Thames Valley Gazette* might bow to threats, but Fleet Street won't.'

She turned and walked out of the office. Crowe immediately pressed his intercom button.

'Sir?'

Crowe leaned forward and spoke to his secretary quietly, not that there was anyone to overhear him. 'I need a photographic print of that young lady. Just her face.'

'I can have one pulled off the security video in the lobby, sir. Would that do?'

'It would do nicely,' Crowe said.

35

The clock on Bill Gunn's screen told him it was 4.32 p.m. He raised a cup of coffee to his lips and blew the steam off; he had lost track of how many cups he had drunk since arriving at the office at 6.50 that morning, having left it only three hours earlier. He closed his eyes for a few seconds to try to relieve a throbbing headache. Then he scrolled through the report that had just come through on his computer screen, checking it carefully.

The thirty-four hours since Jake Seals' death had been a

nightmare, and he was in no mood for another lambasting from Crowe. Privately Gunn had to admit the Chief Executive was right – up to a point. It was true that he had been distracted by Nikky, and was distracted by her again right now, this moment, as an image of her long auburn hair draped across one of her bare breasts flashed into his mind, making him, in spite of his tiredness, and in spite of having made love to her for an hour when he had finally got home early that morning, feel sharply horny.

Nevertheless he pressed the line button through to Crowe, and picked up the receiver. He was rewarded almost instantly with an irritable 'Yes?'

'I've found out how this Wollerton woman got her info on Maternox, sir.'

There was a pause as Gunn waited for a response. When none was forthcoming, he continued, awkwardly. 'The information was supplied to her by an employee at Reading called Walter Hoggin. He's the one who was Chief Lab Technician at Bannerman Genetics Research and who was moved to our Reading plant. He's been put on Quality Assurance there.'

'An outsider? You let an outsider come straight on to Quality Assurance?'

Gunn lifted the receiver away from his ear as the Chief Executive's voice raised in pitch to a near scream. 'Have you taken complete leave of your senses, Major Gunn?'

The Director of Security did not like being attacked unjustly, but at the same time he wanted to avoid a confrontation. He reverted to the time-honoured ploy of passing the buck. 'I'm afraid it was Sir Neil Rorke's instruction, sir.' Gunn moved on quickly. 'We've questioned Mr Hoggin and he claims he's never heard of any Zandra Wollerton.'

'The man's lying.'

'I don't think so, sir. He claims he was asked for the info by Dr Linda Farmer, our Director of Medical Information. We checked with her, and she had not made any such request. I took a look at her phone log and she was telling the truth – there were no calls from her office to Mr Hoggin. But when we checked the incoming log at Reading, we found two calls to

Hoggin from a mobile phone registered in the name of the *Thames Valley Gazette*. The receptionist logged both calls as coming from Dr Farmer. Gunn eyed the report as he spoke. 'My conclusion is that this reporter duped Mr Hoggin – she saw Dr Farmer a couple of weeks back, so she would have known her voice and a little bit about her.'

Crowe calmed down a little into a tone of quiet fury. 'Hoggin is a senile old fool. Sir Neil wanted him reinstated somewhere to appease the Bannerman woman, but it was totally against my advice.'

'It seems you were right, sir,' Gunn said unctuously.

There were a few moments of silence, then Crowe said tersely, 'I think you'd better come up to my office.'

36

After her meeting with Vincent Crowe, Zandra Wollerton's office called on her mobile, telling her to get an interview on the problems of toxic waste with the London secretary of the National Farmers' Union.

She finally left town after seven, and found herself in a stop-go jam on the Westway. The newspaper's white Ford Fiesta pool car was brand new, with 238 miles on the clock. She wound down her window and breathed in the damp, misty air, then closed it again rapidly as a truck pulled alongside, belching diesel fumes.

She pressed the buttons on the digital radio, trying to fathom how to tune it, heard a smattering of foreign languages, the hiss of static, then the tail end of a commercial for a life assurance company. There was a tape sticking out of the cassette slot and she pushed it in, then ejected it rapidly as she heard the twang of Dolly Parton singing country and western.

'Yech!' she said to herself, wondering which of her colleagues had left it there.

The car clock showed 7.38 and Zandra was becoming increasingly anxious. The traffic showed no signs of easing and she had a date tonight with Tony Easton; *the* Tony Easton who had his own current affairs chat show on Radio Berkshire. They had met while covering the toxic-waste story on Monday afternoon, and next morning he had rung her at the office and asked her out. He was dishy, popular and successful. And, she thought, really nice.

He was in his early thirties, and she had never been out with anyone so mature before. He was taking her to dinner, to a Thai restaurant – she had even bought a new dress, a knitted black piece that clung to her body and looked, she had to admit, pretty good.

He was picking her up at eight from her flat, and she had no way of contacting him to let him know she was going to be late – and at this rate very late. *Shit!* Would he bother to wait if he turned up and got no reply? No, of course not. He'd think: *Stupid bitch, she's stood me up!*

Had to get off this carriageway and try the back roads; if she drove like stink and got lucky with the traffic, she could still make it. The car inched forward. There was a large road sign ahead pointing to Ickenham and Ruislip. Then the traffic stopped again.

Come on, please come on, don't do this to me! She drummed on the steering wheel with the palms of her hands. *Shift it, you morons!* She revved the engine uselessly; a siren wailed somewhere in the distance. *Why the hell does someone have to go and have an accident now?* she wondered irrationally. *Why the hell couldn't they have it some time when there's no traffic? Stupid, selfish senile bastards!*

Christ, calm down, girl, she thought.

The image of Dr Vincent Crowe's face suddenly flashed into her mind involuntarily. *And I'll get you, you smug bastard*, she thought. Get the lot of you.

She thought about the young woman, Montana Bannerman, wondering irrelevantly why she was named after a state in America.

There had been a distinct change in Montana Bannerman's attitude when she had last met her. The first time, on Tuesday afternoon, she had got the impression of a woman who was guarded but genuinely interested in what she had to say to her. At the end of that meeting, Montana Bannerman had promised to let her know if she heard anything that might be of interest regarding Maternox.

But at their second meeting, this morning, she was quite different, unwilling to say anything. Perhaps that was because she was in shock; or maybe it was because she was *afraid* – that seemed much more likely. Zandra had picked up distinct fear vibes. Montana Bannerman knew more than she was letting on and was scared to talk. *Give her time*, she thought. Give her a few days to calm down and she would have another go at her.

There was a story here that went way beyond a simple lab accident; all her instincts were telling her to dig further. And she needed a good story that could hit the nationals, needed to build up her portfolio to make the leap to London. Bendix Schere could, if she played it right, be her first really big break. Crowe looked like a man who was hiding something.

And anyhow, it wasn't merely her own hunch, not just the wild whim of a twenty-one-year-old cub. It was her news editor who had put her on to the story. Hubert knew something was going on. He *knew*. Three deaths from Cyclops Syndrome. The lab technician. It stank.

The slip road finally came up and she turned on to it, then navigating with her *A-Z* drove madly down the side streets, heading towards the end of the suburban sprawl and the start of the Berkshire countryside.

7.46. She was ducking and weaving down a straight dual carriageway. Jumped a light that was just turning red, then another, then to her dismay saw the traffic backed up for what looked like miles ahead.

Shit.

She braked hard, turned left into a side road and floored the accelerator. The engine was sluggish, tight, still too new and the speedometer needle climbed agonizingly slowly. 40 . . . 50 . . . 60. *Come on!* It was a 30 m.p.h. limit, but she ignored it, hurtling at over seventy, then screeched up to a roundabout and saw the sign she wanted. 'High Hamnett.' She took the exit on to an unlit rural road that was almost free of traffic.

7.51. Might just make it yet. Might! Tony was bound to be a few minutes late. People always were, it was polite.

She fumbled with the unfamiliar controls, switched on the wipers and cleared the smeared mist from the screen, braked as she bore down on the tail lights of a car in front, checked it wasn't police, then accelerated past it. The speedometer slid past the 85 mark. She switched on the wipers again, and as they completed their first arc, her heart banged inside her chest and she let out a small cry of shock.

A hideous horned face was staring in through the wind-screen, solid, three dimensional, like a hologram. It was part human skull, part emaciated goat.

She jammed her foot on the brake and slewed to a halt. There was an angry blaring behind her, then a car flashed past. She closed her eyes for a fraction of a second and when she reopened them the face was gone.

She gulped, shaking uncontrollably. 'Jesus!' The wipers made a second arc, then a third. It was cold suddenly, bitterly cold. A slick of fear slid down her spine. It felt as if there was something in the car with her, an unseen presence on the rear seat. She glanced fleetingly in the mirror but could see nothing.

She thought back to Dr Crowe seated opposite her across his desk. That venomous smile. For some inexplicable reason the face she had just seen – or imagined – made her picture him. She hesitated, afraid to look behind her for a moment, then steeled herself and turned her head.

Nothing.

She drove off again, accelerating as hard as she could. The speedometer climbed; she drove over the brow of a hill then down a long straight. 80. 85. 90. A shadow slid across her rear-view mirror and her scalp constricted in fear.

She slowed her speed a little, looked in the mirror again, turned her head, but could see nothing.

Lights flashed at her. A horn blared. The lights of an oncoming car; she had veered out into the middle of the road, she suddenly realized, and she tugged in panic on the steering wheel, swerving back to the left.

Then she saw the mask-like face again in front of her.

Pressed hard against the glass of the windscreen, the features squashed out, distorted like a crazy mirror in a funfair.

'Go away!' she shrieked, petrified, banging the wiper switch. The wipers made another arc; she switched them to maximum speed. But there was nothing there, no face, just the dark road ahead, and two red lights flashing in the far distance.

She looked in the mirror once more. As she did so there was a tremendous bang in front of her face. Something dark, like a massive ball, exploded out of the steering wheel, striking her in the chest, flattening her back against her seat. She felt agonizing pain in her head, as though two daggers had been plunged into her ears.

The ball deflated.

Air bag, she realized. Jesus Christ, the air bag had inflated. For no reason.

Two flashing red lights strobed across the windscreen. She saw a sign, a triangle with a picture of a train on it, saw it much too late. Stamped her foot on the brake, her mouth jamming open in a silent scream. Locked tyres scrubbed furiously across wet tarmac beneath her. The car slewed to the left, heading towards the large warning circle in the centre of the barrier arm. She saw yellow to the right through the trees; hundreds of yards of winking lights; packed carriages; commuters heading home.

She thought of the black dress she had laid out on her bed that morning before setting off. Thought of the handsome radio presenter who would be ringing her doorbell in a few minutes' time, as the car jolted crazily and the barrier exploded into matchsticks in front of her eyes.

Going-to-make-it. Going-to-make-it. Going-to-make-it.

She was gripping the steering wheel as helplessly as if it were the grab-handle of a roller coaster.

Going to be all right.

The car juddered violently, then halted. Her ears filled with a screaming howl. Lights were bearing down. *Got to get out, get out!* She scrabbled for the door handle. Couldn't locate it; she still wasn't familiar enough with the car. Her hand slid uselessly up and down. Found it, yanked it, bashed the door open with her elbow. Wind and rain lashed in. The light was getting brighter. A horn blared. A wall of thunder was hurtling down towards her.

She tried to get out of the car, but her seat belt jerked her tighter into her seat. She fumbled for the buckle, felt the belt go slack; she pushed the door, threw herself out. Something grabbed her foot, jerked it sharply up and back, and with a scream of pain she fell flat on her face, her foot trapped inside the car by the strap of the belt. A demonic wind ripped at her face, her hair. A cacophony of horns blared right above her. Mouth open, whinnying in terror, she stared upwards, mesmerized like a rabbit by the glare of the oncoming lights.

Somewhere nearby a voice was screaming: 'Run! For God's sake, run!'

37

Berkshire, England, Sunday 13 November, 1994
Monty laid two beech logs on the open fire, kicked her slippers off and curled up on the sofa, balancing her plate on her thigh. It was seven o'clock and she was looking forward to the luxury of some television followed by an early night. She pressed the channel selector on the remote control and the title sequence of an Equinox programme on genetics appeared on the screen. Keeping a watchful eye on it, she bit a slice of warm buttered toast and dug her fork into the scrambled eggs she had made for supper.

She was feeling fine now, if a little tired, and was anxious to get back to work tomorrow, in spite of the doctor's advice that she should take a week off; all the rawness had gone from her throat and lungs, and her eyes were no longer smarting. The hospital had discharged her on Saturday morning and her father had driven her home. She had rung him a few minutes ago to remind him that he had to pick her up in the morning, as her car was still in the Bendix parking lot.

Jake Seals' funeral was on Wednesday but the request was for family only and she had arranged for flowers to be sent. Monty was a little surprised by how quickly the coroner had released the body. Presumably he had no reason for holding on to it, but something disturbed her about that, as if any chance of finding out further evidence would disappear with his cremation.

Evidence of what?

She had half expected the American to visit her again in hospital and had been a little disappointed when he had not. But she remembered that he had suggested lunch this week and she looked forward to that, wanted to pry further behind the shutters, to find out what exactly he was insinuating, and what he knew. Was it something about the company? Or something about Maternox?

That made her think, with a sudden chill, about her friend Anna Sterling. Anna and Mark had come by this morning, on their way to a lunch party, to make sure she was all right, and had brought a mass of edible provisions for her.

The three women who had died in childbirth had died a month or so ago; she did a quick calculation backwards. That meant they had become pregnant in January or February. As they had resorted to Maternox, they must have been suffering from infertility for some time; she had heard a figure that the average length of time of taking Maternox before becoming pregnant was five months. She recalled the conversation she'd had with Anna about a year ago, when Anna had confessed that she was infertile.

'*The doctor wants to put me on a drug called Maternox.*'

Monty remembered those words clearly as she swallowed a mouthful of egg. Anna would have started taking the drug at around the same time.

She was distracted from this thought by what sounded like a car outside. She looked at the window, listening hard, but could hear nothing now. It was dark out there and bitterly cold. One of the things she loved about living isolated in the country was the luxury of not having to draw the curtains, and through the reflections in the glass she could see the pinprick of the North star above the woods at the far end of her garden.

There was a crackle and a sharp pop from the grate and a burning ember catapulted across the brick hearth. Crick raised a sleepy eye, while Watson, curled in a ball, slept on undisturbed.

Monty glanced at the red bloom of the poinsettia which Anna Sterling had given her several years ago and which always flowered at this time of year. She wondered whether to warn her friend of the possible danger from Maternox, but at the same time she did not want to worry her. Three cases of Cyclops Syndrome. Three out of the hundreds of thousands – millions – of women who were helped to become pregnant by Maternox each year. Three cases – that was statistically so slight as to be meaningless. The press were trying to whip up a scare out of nothing. Typical. She would keep an eye on the situation, she decided, but she would say nothing to Anna unless she heard considerably more evidence against the drug.

Putting her glass of Australian Chardonnay down, she continued eating. There was another burning pop, then another, and she shot a wary glance at the fireplace. The image of Jake's smouldering, melting face came to mind and she felt a sudden bolt of alarm. Her eyes swung warily back to the window and the blackness beyond, and she was aware of her throat tightening. Nothing out there? Nothing to be afraid of.

Calm down.

She reached for the unread stack of weekend newspapers on the thick cream carpet beneath her, selecting the Weekend section of the day before's *Times*.

As she skimmed through it she saw to her surprise the genial face of Sir Neil Rorke beneath the small headline: MY PERFECT WEEKEND.

Rorke was pictured wearing a battered Barbour coat and Wellington boots, holding the handles of a wheelbarrow; there was a broad grin on his face as if he did not have a care in the world. His perfect weekend, he declared, would be spent on his Scottish estate, walking with his wife and their dogs, listening to Mozart, drinking Glenlivet whiskey and Le Montrachet '78 white Burgundy and Chateau Margaux '37 claret, and eating Scotch salmon and rare beef. The things he would be most pleased to leave behind, he said, were his neckties and his correspondence. A warmth emanated from him, and he struck her as seeming quite out of place with the slickness of Bendix Schere and coldly arrogant people like Dr Vincent Crowe and his like.

Suddenly something caught her eye and she started. Bright light streaked momentarily across the garden, then it was gone. Car headlights. Fear crackled her skin like static. She padded over to the window, pressing her face against the glass.

Then her doorbell rang.

For an instant Monty froze. She turned down the volume on the television and her heartbeat resonated in her ears. Her mouth was dry. She was not normally this jumpy, she admonished herself.

She walked to the front door, then switched on the porch light and peered through the spyhole, gripping the safety chain, ready to ram it home. Through the distorted fish-eye image, she recognized immediately the balding middle-aged man in the shabby raincoat, and relief washed through her.

She opened the door and cold air engulfed her. 'Mr Wentworth? Good evening.'

The newspaperman stood blinking at her apologetically through his square, rimless glasses. 'Miss Bannerman, so sorry to disturb you.' He wheezed a little as if he was out of breath. 'I didn't want to use the phone, too risky. Is it possible to have a quick word?'

'Yes – come in,' she said, still savouring her relief.

'I won't keep you; no one wants an unexpected visitor on a Sunday evening.' He paused and studied the faded runner that lay on the threadbare hall carpet. 'Persian. Every one tells a story; clever; so many legends. Metaphors.'

Monty looked at him blankly. 'Metaphors?'

'The design. The trellis work round the edge – it's the lattice through which souls pass from one dimension to another. You'd be surprised at the stories works of art like these tell.'

'Really?' She looked down at the rug, which she'd bought in a car boot sale years ago, surprised at his knowledge.

He pointed. 'Ah yes. Dark and light borders represent the succession of night and day.' He nodded like an ancient sage.

'It never occurred to me that it was symbolic.'

'Yes, yes, the eight-petalled flower marking the centre of the universe, you see it? The eight petals are the main compass points. In the centre is the hole in the sky marking the gateway from earth to heaven.' Then he smiled at himself. 'Come on, shut up, Hubert Wentworth, this good lady doesn't want to hear the ramblings of an old man.'

'You don't look that old,' Monty said gently.

'Fifty-nine is old enough.' He nodded at his own remark. Then he asked after her, 'Are you better? I heard you were in hospital. Bad business, that.' He peeled off his coat at her gesture. Beneath he was wearing a crumpled suit and tie. Monty wondered if he had been to church.

'I'm fine, thank you.' She hung the coat on the Victorian stand, pointing him through into the living room. As she came into the room herself, Wentworth was standing in front of a painting of a Greek harbour at sunset.

'Is this you?'

'Yes,' she said. 'Ithaka, about five years ago.'

'You should be an artist, you know, not a chemist.'

She smiled wistfully. 'You're very kind.' She sat down on the edge of the sofa, a little embarrassed by the sight of her supper tray on the floor and pointed to an armchair. 'Please, sit down. May I get you a drink?'

As before, he would only accept a glass of water, which she fetched from the kitchen. When she came back she thought he looked exhausted by the sheer effort of sitting. He put his glass down on the coffee table, but continued to hold on to it as if it were a lever he might need to pull in order to extricate himself from the chair.

'Bad news,' he said and nodded his head as if to underline the gravity. 'Perhaps you heard? You saw yesterday's paper? The *Gazette*?'

'No, I'm afraid not . . .'

'I told you about our young reporter, Zandra Wollerton?'

'Yes, I met her a couple of times – on Tuesday and on Thursday.'

He looked across at her, surprised. 'You met her this past Thursday?'

'Yes.'

'Here?'

'No – in hospital –' She was still wondering what the latest bad news was.

'A lot of deaths all of a sudden, Miss Bannerman. Far too many,' he said. 'Our good friends Bendix Schere tried putting commercial pressure on my editor not to pursue this Maternox story – did Zandra tell you that?'

'No – she didn't. I – I'm afraid I was very tired the second time; we didn't talk for long.'

Crick stood up, walked over to Wentworth and rubbed himself along his ankle. The newspaperman leaned down and stroked him. 'So Zandra Wollerton probably also didn't tell you that this unfortunate technician, Mr Seals, had succeeded in obtaining the Maternox information that we're interested in? Plus samples.'

'No!' Monty said, her mind racing along now.

He nodded. 'She was keen to go ahead and publish, but I told her she had to hold on, needed more evidence to make the story stand up. You can't rush into print on supposition; you need facts.' He looked at Monty and his expression darkened. 'I take it you've not heard the news about Zandra Wollerton?'

Monty shook her head and braced herself, knowing that whatever it was, it was serious.

'A railway crossing. She drove straight across in front of a train. Tragic.' He raised his hands in a gesture of futility. 'Such a terrible waste.'

Monty was speechless. She had not prepared herself for this.

'She died on Thursday night. I thought you should know. It seems to have been an accident, just an ordinary terrible accident, but –' Again he gestured with his hands. 'Hurrying. Perhaps she thought she could beat the barrier. Who knows?'

Monty felt as if a small bomb had exploded inside her. An image of the young reporter striding determinedly into the hospital room came back to haunt her.

'I can't believe it,' she said in barely a whisper. 'I –' Her voice tailed and she gave in to a feeling that reality was slipping away from her. She thought of tough, cynical Jake Seals suddenly peering around the pub like a frightened child, could hear the voice of the ambitious female reporter as she chased her story.

She stared at her painting of Ithaka, at the warm Sanderson fabric covering her furniture, at the dancing flames in the grate, at the blackness of the night beyond the window.

'Another accident,' Wentworth said, as if trying to reassure her, and himself.

'Was it?' she said. 'How many deaths do there have to be before –' She bit her tongue, her thoughts fragmenting.

Wentworth drank some water, then cupped the glass in his hands as if he were drawing warmth from it. 'Miss Bannerman, I shouldn't really be dragging you into this, you're a decent person, my daughter Sarah always said you and your father were good people. I should just walk out of here and let you get on with your own life.'

'You're not dragging me into anything. I'm in it already.'

Her visitor stared ahead of him. 'Positive and negative. Yin and Yang. Good and evil. Light and dark. Perhaps they are forever interwoven, like on your beautiful rug. *The light can only shine in darkness* – such a simple truth.' His eyes suddenly revealed a hard, focused expression when he spoke again in less mystical terms. 'Pharmaceuticals. Drugs to relieve pain, to cure cancer, drugs to retard the ravages of senility, to curb infant mortality. So many good things produced by the pharmaceutical industry. So much improvement to the quality of life.'

'When that industry's run by caring people,' she replied.

Her words brought the shadow of a smile to his face. 'Ah yes, indeed, wise words.' He patted his jacket, then rummaged inside his breast pocket and removed a crumpled envelope, which he handed to her.

'Would you have a look, my dear?'

Inside was a photograph that looked as though it might have been taken in a passport booth. It was of a strikingly attractive Indo-Chinese woman in her mid-twenties.

'Beautiful, don't you think?'

'Very.' Monty looked up at him, wondering who it was.

'My late wife,' he said.

She tried to contain her surprise.

'We met in Vietnam – where I was a correspondent for Reuters and she was a reporter for *Paris Match*. One day we were with an American platoon heading towards a village where they suspected Vietcong were hiding out. A US air patrol mistakenly attacked us. Françoise was in a jeep a hundred yards ahead of me and was burned alive in front of my eyes; there was nothing I could do.'

Monty read the sadness in his eyes, and let him go on.

'Thirty-three years later I sometimes have difficulty recalling her face. But I can still smell her burning and I can still hear her screams – just as clearly as if it were only a few hours ago.' His eyes dropped towards the carpet. 'There are some chemical substances that no one should ever make. But someone will. Someone always will.' He shook his head from side to side. 'Profit, you see. There's the devil.'

He looked up suddenly, and grimaced. 'I watched Françoise get out of that jeep and run across a paddy field like a human torch, covered head to foot in a burning jelly that had been manufactured by Bendix Schere for the United States Air Force.' He blinked slowly. 'The same company that manufacture creams for the relief of burns and which you can buy over the counter. The same company that makes pain relievers for arthritis, that makes suntan lotion, that donates millions to charities and to research. A Bendix Schere product made my wife's skin slough off her body in front of me and I could do nothing to prevent it.'

Monty found this man's bitterness almost chilling in its intensity. 'I'm sorry,' she said. 'I had no idea.'

'The pharmaceutical industry has so much potential to do good, Miss Bannerman, but mostly it's in the business of the ultimate alchemy: turning death into gold.'

Wentworth heaved himself slowly to his feet, looked up at the ceiling as he did so and then dabbed at his eyes with his index finger. 'Wooden beams. So good to see a room that still has them.' He turned towards her. 'I'm taking over this story myself, Miss Bannerman. I'm writing it from now.'

'I'll help you in any way I can.'

He ambled out into the hall. 'You are very kind, but I'm not sure it's wise for you to remain involved.'

She was quiet for a moment, thinking, and then told him that she was already far too involved just to walk away now. 'But I don't know how much use I can be.'

'All I need to know at this stage is whether there's a connection through Maternox between my daughter Sarah and the other two women who died.' He hesitated. 'You see Zandra Wollerton telephoned me on Thursday morning and told me she'd established that all three women *had* taken Maternox from the same batch. But I don't know how large the batches are. I don't know if that batch was different from the others. It obviously worries me very much that the two people involved in finding out more have both died within a day and a half of each other.'

'That *may* be a tragic coincidence and nothing more,' Monty offered.

'Of course.'

'Give me the batch number and I'll keep working on this; I'll be in touch as soon as I have anything.'

'A word of warning,' Wentworth said after he'd jotted down the serial number she needed. 'Be careful about using any phone inside the company.'

'Do you think they're bugged?'

'Put it like this, I'd be very surprised if they were *not*.'

'Seriously? Every conversation?'

'There are very sophisticated methods of monitoring such things. Possibly even employees' homes.' He stared pointedly at the telephone on the hall table. 'Use a pay phone to contact me. I gave you my office and home numbers last time?'

'Yes, I have them,' she said, staring at him incredulously, his paranoia striking her as a little absurd.

'Thank you for letting me barge in on you this evening.' He looked down at the floor. 'Such a fine carpet, what a beautiful thing to own. You are very fortunate.'

She helped him into his raincoat, picked up a torch and opened the door. 'It's dark, I'll show you to your car.'

Both cats slunk past them and ran off into the garden. She

switched on the torch and shone the beam on the small Nissan parked in the lane.

Wentworth turned back to her. 'I don't want you to feel in any way obliged. If you wake up tomorrow and change your mind, I'll understand. You're young, with everything in front of you; I don't want to be responsible for damaging your future.' He eased himself into the driver's seat.

'I'm not put off.' She smiled.

'Please think about it carefully.' He pushed the key into the ignition. 'You know the Chinese proverb about revenge?'

'No.'

He was looking at her intently. 'Before you seek revenge, first go out and dig two graves.' Taking his time, he started the engine. 'It's different for me, you see, Miss Bannerman. I've no choice but to do this – you have no motive.'

'You're wrong, I do have a motive,' she said. 'I care very much about the pharmaceutical industry; I want it to be moral and responsible. If something foul is going on, I want it stopped. Sir Neil Rorke is a wonderful man. He would be appalled if there was something wrong in Bendix Schere, right under his nose. He'd not stand for it, I can tell you that, and I can go and see him any time.'

'Don't rush into anything. It's always good to know one has an ally, but keep him in reserve for the time being. Let's try to progress one step at a time.'

She agreed and directed him with her torch to a clearing where he could turn, then watched his tail lights disappear towards the main road until only the dark ribbon of the empty track stretched out in front of her.

Shivering with cold, Monty called out to the cats, then went back inside and locked the front door, checked that the back door was locked also, and began to check in turn each of the windows.

Two people she had known, who were alive last week, were now dead. That really spooked her. It wasn't possible that Bendix Schere could be involved in anything illicit, surely? Hubert Wentworth was just a sad case clutching at straws.

Then she realized with a chill that in thinking that, she, too, might be clutching at straws.

38

Barnet, North London. 1951

Daniel Judd had noticed the skull in the window of the junk shop many times from the upstairs window of the bus he took to school, which often stopped at the traffic lights just beyond.

The shop was in a drab but busy thoroughfare, sandwiched between an ironmongery and a credit draper. The frontage was in peeling black paint, and the grimy glass of the unlit window displayed a haphazard assortment of books, decorative plates, cutlery, Toby jugs and general bric-à-brac.

But what had really aroused his curiosity, beyond the fascination of the skull itself, was that he had also noticed a number of candelabras, chalices, figurines and ceremonial daggers – athames – which he thought he recognized from his library books as occult artefacts.

He stood, hesitantly, on the pavement outside, and waited for a bus to pass. It was his mother's coffee morning at church, but even so he was nervous she might for some reason come by. Or that one of her friends might see him.

She had been much less violent to him in the five years since his father had died, and although he was no longer terrified of her, now that he knew he had the *power* over her, he still tried to avoid incurring her wrath. She had long ceased tying his hands to the bed, but there were still occasions when she hit him. Sometimes, bruised and in pain afterwards, he had contemplated using the ritual to kill her, but one of the main reasons he did not was because he found her a good subject on which to experiment, so he allowed her to continue to think, as he approached his seventeenth birthday, that he was still no different from the child he had always been.

He could use her to test the strength of spells which would induce nausea, spells that would make her lose her memory, ones that would get rid of her anger (only for short periods), ones that would bring her down with ailments, and even ones that would make her buy him particular presents for his birthday or Christmas, although some of the latter were a bit erratic.

He had managed to get her to buy him the *Encyclopaedia of Modern Science*, and a copy of *Darwin's Theory of Evolution*, both of which she had previously always refused to have in the house, believing science to be evil and calling Darwin's theory a hideous blasphemy. But his attempts at putting a message into her mind to buy him a candle-making kit, so that he could fashion effigies, had been a disaster: she had instead bought him a plaster of Paris modelling kit of famous British warriors.

His biggest failure of all had been the spells he had cast to turn her against God. He had tried very hard, holding his own private black masses at home, using communion wafers secreted out of church, which he defiled with urine, excrement, semen and even, on one occasion, menstrual blood, which he had obtained from a sanitary towel he had retrieved from the bin in the bathroom.

There was another reason to keep her alive. If she was dead or incapacitated, either of which conditions he was confident he could bring about quite easily, he would have to go and live with an uncle and aunt and share a room with his cousin, which was no good at all. Privacy was essential to his plans.

Important exams were coming up over the next four years, and it was vital for him to work hard on the development of his powers. He practised obsessively, into the late hours every night, and sometimes right through the night; he had discovered that with proper control over his mind and body he could survive on only a couple of hours sleep a day for weeks on end.

Early experiments on his teachers had been moderately successful, but the exam papers crucial to his future plans, the ones that would see him, gain a scholarship to university, would be marked by total strangers, whose names he did not even know. He would have to design talismans to wear, would have to cast spells on the ink he used, and stay in mental communication with that ink to reach through it into the minds of the examiners. It could be done. Anything was possible.

Do what thou wilt shall be the whole of the law. Love under a strong will.

The needlework words stared at him from the small sampler on the wall as he entered the shop. A bell pinged sharply as the door swung shut behind him, and Daniel felt suddenly very enclosed. There was a slightly sweet smell he recognized as incense, and he stared around in awe at the treasure trove of curios in the strange, church-like dark, his eyes alighting on a sword decorated with chains, a sinister wood carving on a plinth, a shelf of large, dusty volumes.

Behind the counter an emaciated, beaky-looking woman, with dead straight hair pulled back in a ponytail, watched him with tiny, insect-like eyes.

Blushing, Daniel turned away, reached behind a George VI Coronation mug and picked up a copy of a book called *High Magic's Aid* by one of his heroes, Gerald Gardner. He opened it at random, aware of the eyes absorbing him like blotting paper.

'You have a sharp aura for such a young fellow.' The voice washed as gently as a wave of music through the silence.

Startled, Daniel stared back at the counter. It was a man, he realized, not a woman. He had never seen a man with a ponytail before. 'Thank you,' he replied nervously, putting the book back.

'I haven't seen you here before.'

He noticed the pentacle on a silver chain hanging over the man's black shirt. 'I haven't been here before.'

The man watched him in silence for some moments with a humorous glint in his eyes, then smiled warmly. 'I would have noticed your aura if you had been here before, see.'

Daniel was not sure how to take the remark, but the tone of it was friendly. 'Thank you,' he said again.

'Do you have a name?'

'Daniel.'

'God is my judge.'

Daniel stared at him blankly.

'That's what Daniel means: *God is my judge.* All names have a meaning. Is *God* really your judge?'

The question penetrated a nerve deep inside Daniel. He shook his head. 'No, God is not my judge.'

'I did not think so. Good! Daniel. *Daniel*.' The man smiled and tilted his head back so that he was addressing the ceiling, and declaimed: '"A second Daniel, a Daniel, Jew! Now, infidel, I have thee on the hip."'

Daniel looked bewildered.

'*Merchant of Venice*? Not read Shakespeare?'

Daniel shook his head once more.

'No? Well, there are more important things to read, for a boy with your aura, and you have been reading *them*, I'm sure, haven't you?'

Daniel nodded. As he did so, his eyes went to the shelf above the man's head and picked out the title in gold lettering on the spine of a large green book: *Barrett. The Magus*. The words sent a *frisson* of excitement skittering through him.

'But who's been helping your development, Daniel? You have an adept?'

He noticed the man's fingers; they were bony, almost skeletal, the fingernails protruding an inch from the tip and painted black; above them a mass of bracelets were entwined on his wrist. *Adept*. He tried to think what the word meant, his eyes drawn back to the green book.

'I'm sorry – I don't understand what you mean.'

The man watched him again, then a light seemed to sparkle in his eyes. Daniel could not tell whether it was humour or anger. He shifted his position on his chair, like a bird squatting on a perch, touched his forehead and said: '*Ateh*.' He winked.

Daniel understood, and beamed; a warmth, deeper than anything he had ever felt in his life, flooded through him at this sudden, intense communion with a total stranger. He touched his chest and responded: '*Malkuth*.'

The man touched his right shoulder. '*Ve-Geburah*.'

Daniel touched his left shoulder. '*Ve-Geburah*.'

The man clasped his hands in front of him. '*Le-olam*.' His eyes glazed as if he were in a trance. '*Eko, Eko, Azarak*.'

'*Eko, Eko, Zomelak*,' Daniel responded.

'*Eko, Eko, Cernunnos*.'

'*Eko, Eko, Aradia*,' Daniel said.

The man took a deep breath then looked hard at Daniel. 'You have no adept; but you want to learn? You want to develop? Is that why you're here? You've come in quest of knowledge?'

'Yes.'

'How badly do you want it, Daniel?'

Daniel faced his questioner with a confidence he did not know he possessed. 'I want it very badly.'

'You want to develop more than anything in all the world?'

Daniel thought, for a brief moment, about God. But there was something about this man that made him feel instinctively safe. As if he had met, for the first time in his life, someone who might understand his interest in the arcane, someone with whom he could discuss it with no fear of it getting back to his mother, someone he could trust.

He needed that badly. There were many times in the past few years when he had sat in church and thought back to the night his father had died. Sometimes he really believed he had killed him, and he was glad. Other times, he became scared of what might happen to him. God was everywhere; they worshipped God in school, in Sunday school, on the wireless, in the newspapers. It seemed to him that everyone else in the entire world, except himself, loved God. Maybe his mother was right, and maybe his father had been right. Perhaps he was a sinner and would be condemned to eternal damnation.

He had tried to bring up the subject of the occult and of alternatives to God with the vicar, but the vicar had looked shocked and merely spouted the same kind of biblical quotations as his mother. But here, now, in this shop with this strange-looking man, he experienced a deep sense of kinship. He had no fear and no guilt. He felt only a profound sense of having come *home*.

'Yes,' he replied. 'I do want to develop more than anything in the world.'

'You would like to join a coven, wouldn't you, Daniel?'

He nodded.

'Good,' the man said. Then he smiled. 'I'm sure I can help you there. More than you know. Give me your hand.'

Tentatively, Daniel proffered his right hand. The man took

208

it, turned it over and studied the palm for some moments, then he closed his own fingers tightly into it. He squeezed hard and Daniel winced, stifling a cry of pain. Then the man released his grip and gave him a gentle squeeze on the shoulder.

Daniel stared at his palm in shock. All five of the man's nails had made tiny, half-moon incisions, through which blood was beginning to rise. But he felt no anger, only overwhelming gratitude; it was as though, by this act, the man had signalled he was accepting him.

'You have very good blood, Daniel,' the man said. 'It flows fast and the colour is rich.' He smiled again. 'Do I make you nervous? Do not be afraid. Only those who have God by their side need be afraid.'

'I'm not afraid.'

The man turned, pulled *The Magus* off the shelf and laid it on the counter, then gestured Daniel to have a look at it.

Daniel approached the thick, green tome, holding his breath in awe. Then he solemnly raised the cover and turned it over. On the inside was written, in pencil, the price. '£3.10*s.*'

A fortune, Daniel thought. His pocket money was sixpence a week. He did a quick calculation. At twenty shillings to a pound, three pounds and ten shillings was seventy shillings. He would have to save for one hundred and forty weeks – nearly three years.

'Would you like to buy the book? It's an original – 1801. Very rare; if it was in better condition I would have to charge much more for it.'

'I'd like it very much, but I can't afford it at the moment. I only have seven shillings and four pence saved up. My father left me a little money but I can't have that for another six years – when I'm twenty-one,' he said wistfully, and turned to the index, hurrying in case the man took the book away again. *Celestial Influences, The Occult Properties of Metals, Herbs and Stones. Alchymy, or Hermetic Philosophy. Talismanic Magic. Cabalistical Magic. Conjuration of Spirits.* His heart began beating faster with excitement. It was all here, all in this book that he had read so much about.

'Take it.'

'I beg your pardon?'

'I can see how much you love it. How much you need it. Take it. Make good use of it. Go on, it's a gift!'

Daniel looked at him, confused. 'But I – I must give you something.'

'You will, Daniel,' the man said with a smile. 'You will.'

39

London. Monday 14 November, 1994
'You'd had no argument with Mr Seals, then?'

Detective Constable Brine, who was seated on the far side of Monty's desk, looked about twelve years old, she thought. He had a long thin neck on which his head was set too far forward, ginger hair cut in the style of a lavatory brush, and he wore a cheap suit that was too big for him, as if he was waiting to grow into it. His manner was as aggressive as his appearance; he reminded her of an ostrich which had once tried to peck her through the mesh in Central Park Zoo.

It was half past twelve; she had arrived in the office shortly after nine to find that a mountain of calls and correspondence had built up during her absence. She could do without this interrogation right now.

But Brine continued. 'I understand Mr Seals had a bit of a reputation for – how shall we put it? – rubbing people up the wrong way?'

'I always found him very helpful,' Monty snapped back.

'Well, you have to appreciate it seems odd – the pair of you in the laboratory alone, before dawn; then he has an *accident* and dies.'

She drew a sharp breath, the implied accusation both wounding and angering her. 'I suggest you check my statement. You'll realize then that the accident had already happened before I arrived. In my opinion you are over-aggressive and insensitive. I am as concerned as you are to find out the truth, but you're not going to do it this way, OK?'

D. C. Brine looked at her with the insolence of a scolded but unrepentant child, then stood up stiffly. 'I have everything I need for the moment, thank you, Miss Bannerman.'

As he left she contrasted him with the urbane Detective Superintendent Levine of last week, who had at least been courteous. What was this young rookie's game? Levine had told her unequivocally that Seals had been drunk. Why was this man Brine trying to suggest she'd been involved? Nobody seriously considered she might have murdered Seals, did they?

Then she wondered, darkly, if that was the reason an officer as senior as Levine had come to see her? And were they now playing the old one-two; hard cops, soft cops? The rookie deliberately riling her, trying to make her lose her temper and say something on which they could catch her out? She was not sorry when the phone rang, interrupting her thoughts, and she lifted the receiver.

'It's a Mr Best for you. Regarding the symposium Dr Bannerman's attending in Washington next month, and I'm not getting any answer from your father's phone.'

The woman's voice was becoming familiar to Monty; it was one of half a dozen polite, distant voices that spoke to her down the line from the reception pool. She had never met any of them in person and knew, almost certainly, she never would. It was all part of the Bendix Schere philosophy of keeping people apart. *Divide and rule*. It was the principle on which, Monty had once read, Hitler had built up Nazi Germany.

She took the call. The organizer of the symposium – on the morality of patenting genes – was in London for a couple of days. He wondered if there was any chance of meeting up with Dr Bannerman, and also needed to know urgently whether he would like to attend a dinner for delegates, hosted by President Clinton. Monty knew her father was contemptuous of Clinton, as he was of most politicians, and asked Mr Best to let her ring back after she'd asked.

She went into the corridor and peered through the internal window into her father's chaotic office next door. No luck. So she tried his main laboratory, but could see no sign of her father amongst the white coats working there.

She was just wondering whether to go back to her office and

beep his pager when she saw a young female microbiologist walking up the corridor. Monty asked if she had seen her father anywhere and was told he was in Lab 6.

Monty hurried down to Lab 6 with a slight knot in her throat. That was where Jake Seals had died. She had gone there first thing that morning and had had a quick scout round for any sign of the Maternox tablets he'd probably had on him, but without success. It had given her the creeps being in there. She stopped outside the door and could see her father through the porthole, slotting test tubes into the rack of a water bath.

Everything looked calm in the lab. Except as she entered she saw again the blotches of dark blisters on the white work surface, and on the speckled grey floor tiles beneath the shower where Jake Seals had lain. She had to steel herself against the wave of revulsion that rose inside her.

There was an atmosphere of almost studied normality, as if everyone was concentrating more fully on their work than ever, in order to try to blot out the horror of what had happened. She walked quietly between the benches up to her father, and watched his face. As a child she used to love being with him whilst he worked. There was a serenity in his expression when he was concentrating that always made her feel very secure; it was as though, as long as he was a part of science, the world would always be all right.

He looked less robust than usual today, drawn and slightly despondent, and she knew how badly he must be taking Seals' death.

He always felt a deep sense of responsibility for his colleagues, and as he had driven her up to London that morning she was aware through words unspoken that he did not totally believe her reason for being in the lab so early on the fatal day.

He switched on the agitator and the rack of test tubes began to vibrate. Then he turned to acknowledge her.

'I've just had the organizer of the Washington symposium on the line – Mr Best. He's in London and would like to meet up with you for an hour if you have time.'

'If he came over here I could meet him for a quick lunch.'

'He already has a lunch meeting.'

Bannerman shook his head. 'Can't otherwise.'

'I'll tell him it's not possible. Now, hear this . . . He also has an invitation for you from the White House – to attend a dinner hosted by President Clinton during the symposium.'

The scientist peered closely at the contents of the vibrating test tubes. 'I don't want to meet that shyster.'

'I think you should go, Daddy.'

'What the hell for?'

'Because if you don't, people will think you haven't been invited.'

He smiled at her. 'I suppose you've already accepted for me?'

'No – but I intend to.'

He smiled again. 'So I don't have much say in the matter – as usual?'

'Not a lot!'

'Are you invited as well?'

'I'm not sure if I'm coming with you yet – I was going to see how the workload went here.'

'Tell them I want you to come to the dinner too.'

'I'll try.'

He looked up at the clock on the wall. 'Got any lunch plans today?'

'No.'

'Want to come to the canteen with me, about one?'

'Yes, fine,' she said.

He frowned, suddenly. 'Darling – can you be a bit more careful when you take things out of my filing cabinets. I've just wasted half an hour trying to find some of my notes on the psoriasis genes – you'd put them back in the wrong place.'

Monty shook her head. 'I haven't touched your psoriasis files.'

'I don't mean today – last week, perhaps, before the accident?'

'Not guilty. They probably got muddled during the move.'

He looked thoughtful for a moment. 'Yes,' he said. 'Yes, I suppose that's what must have happened. Or maybe I misplaced them myself.' He leaned forward and squinted at the test tubes again. 'Getting older and more confused every day,' he mumbled. 'Promise you'll pull the plug when I've gone completely gaga?'

She smiled, cheered by his irrepressible spirit. 'You've been gaga all my life. How will I know if you've got any worse?'

'Oh, you'll be able to tell – it'll be when I start listening to advice.'

Conor Molloy's office door opened and he could just see Charley Rowley's head, and his daffodil-yellow tie, over the piles of documents that were stacked on his own desk and rising in precarious columns from the floor.

'Morning, Captain America. Good weekend?' Rowley was laden with another bundle of documents and searched the remaining floor space for somewhere to put them.

'OK – I guess. I kind of worked most of it.' Conor shifted a couple of files sideways. 'How about yourself?'

'Ancestor worship. Had to go and see the aged p's.'

'P's?'

'Parents. Thirty-second wedding anniversary, poor old things.' Then he grinned. 'I'm thirty-two – always been a touchy subject.'

Conor grinned too.

'Hey, can't spend all your time working – makes Jack a dull boy. When are you moving into your flat?'

'Wednesday.'

'Good stuff. Need a hand, let me know?'

'Thanks – appreciate it – but I think the Human Resources people have got it in hand.'

Rowley seemed chirpy. 'I'm going down to my cottage in Sussex next weekend – why don't you come? Give you a break from London and see a bit of the countryside.'

'Thank you, squire.'

'Cousin of mine, Mike Keehan, has got the best antiques emporium in Britain – down in Hove. Famous place called Michael Norman Antiques. Kit you out with some furniture for your pad – unless you intend going modern?'

'No, I love antiques – if I can afford them.'

'Mike'll sort you out. You'll be gobsmacked by the place.'

Rowley raised the stack of documents a few inches higher. 'Where do you want all this?'

'What is it?'

'Published data on human trials on the Bannerman dental cavities genebuster.'

Conor stared at it despairingly. '*More* published data?'

'Afraid so.'

Conor shook his head and pointed around the room. 'Did you ever see so much goddamned published data in your life?'

'Got to admire a man of principle.'

'That's one way of looking at it.' He pointed to one of the last remaining gaps on the floor. 'Want to dump it there?'

Rowley put the bundle down and left. Conor turned his attention back to his screen. He had forty eMail messages, and he replied to the thirty that needed an answer. When he had finished, he sifted through the pile of junk mail on his desk, and followed that by flicking through *Human Genome News* and *Scrip*. Then he hit a couple of keys on his computer terminal and punched up the file containing the specification notes he had begun to draft for the first US patent application for Dick Bannerman's work.

He typed a heading: 'Recombinant Protein', leant back in his chair and read through a sheet of notes listing items he needed from Montana Bannerman. Wondering if she was back at work today, he dialled her extension.

A secretary answered and informed him that Miss Bannerman had gone to lunch. She was expected back at two. He looked at the clock on his computer screen. It was five past one. The morning had flown. He logged off, deciding to take a quick lunch break himself and eyed the paper on his desk. You weren't supposed to leave any open documents on your desk even during a lunch break, but there was just too much to clear away. He decided to take a risk on no one checking up, and headed for the lift up to the thirtieth-floor canteen.

It was officially called the canteen, although in style it looked more like a smart brasserie, and in size it felt like the departure lounge of an airport. All the tables were stainless steel, and the chairs were hi-tech tubes of twisted steel. The floor was covered in the usual lush emerald carpeting.

The place was packed, although Conor noticed one or two empty tables, and there was a subdued hubbub of conversation. As he joined the short queue at one of the self-service counters, he saw the blonde frizz of Montana Bannerman's hair right in front of him. She was wearing a navy blazer, a matching short skirt, and he glanced fleetingly down, with a prick of lust, at her shapely legs.

She was talking to a man in his late fifties, with a bald dome and long grey hair hanging down over his collar. Even from behind, Conor recognized the image he'd seen in photographs of Dr Bannerman.

He waited for a lull in their chat, then said, quietly: 'Good to see you back, Miss Bannerman. Are you better?'

She turned and gave him a warm smile. 'Mr Molloy! Hi, thank you, I'm much better. Have you – er – met my father?'

'No, I haven't had the pleasure. How do you do, sir?'

'Mr Molloy's a patent attorney, Daddy, working on the US patents for your research.'

Dick Bannerman shook Conor's hand, eyeing him warily. 'Is that right?'

'Well, I'm not sure how much we're going to be able to achieve – you've sure published a lot of papers.'

'So far as I'm concerned, the less you achieve the better,' Dick Bannerman said sourly.

'Daddy!' Monty said.

'I don't give a bugger about patents,' the scientist said, staring Conor Molloy straight in the eye.

'Nope, well, I guess patenting genes is a pretty contentious issue right now,' Conor replied genially.

They had reached the counter and Dick Bannerman took two trays, handing one to Monty. Conor helped himself to another. He watched Monty's face framed by the bright tangle of her hair as she selected her food and was pleasantly surprised to see that, in spite of her slender figure, she seemed to have a healthy appetite. He found something very attractive about women who enjoyed food.

'Are you eating on your own?' Monty asked him.

'Yup.'

'Like to join us?'

Conor registered the look on her father's face. 'Don't worry, thanks – I don't want to intrude if you're discussing business or something.'

'We're not,' she said with an insistent smile.

'OK, sure, thanks.'

They found a table against the far wall, in front of a floor-to-ceiling video image of a Fragonard painting of an idyllic lakeside picnic. As they unloaded their trays and sat down, Dick Bannerman said: 'I don't understand why the jeepers they can't have windows up here. Bloody daft to be on the thirtieth floor, with magnificent vistas out across London, and we have to look at videos of paintings.'

'I agree with you, sir,' Conor said.

Bannerman stared back at him with undisguised disapproval, as if he'd been hoping for an argument, then liberally shook salt over his salad, without having tasted it.

Monty shot an apologetic glance at Conor, who smiled back. It was evident, from just a couple of minutes in their company, that her father gave her a hard time.

He addressed Monty direct. 'I'm really sorry for you – all you went through last week. It must have been horrendous.'

'It was,' she said. 'Trouble is, no one knows the long-term effect of that chemical. Just have to hope I don't wake up one day and find my arm's dissolved.'

Conor winced. 'Anyone figure out how the accident happened yet?' He watched Monty shake her head in reply.

'Do you think it's morally right to patent genes?' Dick Bannerman barged in without warning.

Conor poured some Coke into his glass beaker. 'I think the whole field of genetic science opens up more questions than it can answer.' He glanced warily at the tables either side, but the occupants were engrossed in conversation. All the same, he lowered his voice a fraction.

'Bendix Schere calls itself *the world's most caring company*. But can any company that genetically engineers and patents a mutant rabbit that gets terminal cancer five days after it's born really be totally caring?'

217

'Do you believe that all control over life should be the sole domain of God?' Dick Bannerman spoke aggressively.

'No, I don't, sir.'

'Are you religious?'

Conor hesitated, caught a sudden stare from Monty and glimpsed a silver chain around her neck, inside the open collar of her white blouse. 'I don't practise, but I guess I have religious beliefs somewhere along the line.'

'So tell me,' the scientist said, his tone overtly hostile. 'If you don't think God should have total control over life, then why are you against genetic engineering?'

The attack threw Conor for a moment. 'I'm not against it at all. It's just that – there's so much scope for abuse that I believe companies have to behave responsibly.'

'Is creating a rabbit that will automatically develop cancer any worse than taking a healthy rabbit and injecting it with carcinogens?'

'Daddy,' Monty said, cutting in. 'Don't you sometimes think the rabbit has a right to an ordinary life?'

'Nothing on this planet has a divine right to anything. We have a moral obligation to treat animals humanely, and I think we do.'

'I sometimes think science is progressing too fast. We don't have time to think about the ramifications,' Conor said, testing him.

'Far as I'm concerned it doesn't progress fast enough,' Bannerman replied. 'Do you like going to the dentist, Mr Mulrony?'

'*Molloy*,' he corrected. 'No, sir, not especially.'

'You ever had cavities?'

'Yes, I have.'

'Ever tried to imagine what it was like going to the dentist fifty years ago, when he had no injection to give you and pedalled the drill by foot? Would you like to have had your appendix out a hundred years ago, strapped to a wooden bench and drunk on cheap brandy? Pharmaceuticals and technology have made the world a better place. You know why? Because they've got rid of pain. Very few people in the Western world have to suffer pain any more. Probably in the

218

next quarter century we will have eliminated it altogether. If a few mutant rabbits is the price we have to pay, I can accept that. I can live with that.'

Conor felt an element of despondency. Bannerman was turning out to be more conventional than he had realized; his potential value was fast receding. It was then that the scientist leaned forward.

'I'm always being misunderstood, Mr Molloy. I'm not against progress or science. I'm against a company like Bendix Schere saying, *Right, everyone, we've identified the genes that cause psoriasis; the genes that cause cardiovascular disease, renal failure, depression, duodenal ulcers, breast cancer, you name it. Now we're going to patent these genes and hold the world to ransom for the next two decades. Pay our prices or die!* There was a gleam of passion in Dick Bannerman's eyes as he spoke now. The sentiments were coming not merely from his heart, but from the depths of his soul.

'Do you realize the power that lies in patenting genes? It's the power of *Life* or *Death*. It's not a question of saying, *OK, we have a better cure than someone else – take the Bendix pills, they're better than Wellcome's, or Pfizer's or Beecham's.* It's a question of, *Look – we know what kills you, or makes you suffer like hell. We alone own the lock and key. You, madam, have a breast cancer gene: we can either switch it off for you or leave you to die, and this is our price.'* Bannerman raised his eyebrows. 'What price any individual human life?'

Conor stared at him and felt better. This man's attitude gave him hope. He had an ally here, if he was careful, a very powerful one indeed. 'You *can't* put a price on it.'

'That's right,' Bannerman said. 'There's no limit to what people would pay to remain alive or to be free of pain. You, me, my daughter, we'd all pay our last cent, and for whomever we love too, no question.'

'But do you think, Dr Bannerman, that a company like Bendix Schere would ever go as far as holding the public to ransom?'

'Let me tell you something: you know the founder – the late Joshua Bendix?'

'Sure – his picture's in the front of the Bendix Bible.'

'Do you know what he used to tell every new salesman who joined the firm? He used to have them come up to his office and he'd say: "I'm not interested in medicine. I'm interested in one thing, and one thing only: *profit*. And if we happen to help a few people down the line – that's not my problem."' Bannerman looked at Monty, then at Conor, with a defiant glare. 'That's the company you and I are working for, and don't be fooled into thinking anything's changed.'

Conor had to struggle to keep a triumphant smile off his face.

40

At a quarter past six, Monty took the lift down to the lobby. She normally left the Bendix Building later, waiting for the rush-hour traffic to die down first, but tonight she had a call to make on her way home.

A trickle of people were filing out through the three security gates. She chose the middle one, pleased to see it was manned by the Jamaican, Winston Smith, the only guard who was remotely chatty.

His permanently forlorn expression always made her want to stop for a moment to try to cheer him up. They had struck up a friendship of sorts when she had first read his name on his badge. She had asked him if he realized that he shared the name of the hero in George Orwell's *1984*. He hadn't, but he had gone and bought the book and enjoyed it, and had since been asking her for other book recommendations; being on late shift, he had plenty of time to read.

He sneezed as she stopped by his desk now. 'Sorry,' he said nasally, pulling out his handkerchief and blowing his nose. 'Are you all right, Miss Bannerman? – heard you was hurt in that business last week.'

'I'm fine, thanks.'

'That was terrible. They don't find out what happened yet?'

'No,' she said.

'I liked Mr Seals. Not many did, but he was OK, that guy was.' He sneezed again.

'You got a cold?'

He nodded. 'This my regular. Going to last me into Christmas.'

'Tried vitamin C, zinc and garlic? It's my guaranteed remedy.'

He sniffed. 'Not no ordinary cold, Miss Bannerman. I get this most of the year round, on and off – reckon that's why they keep me employed here.'

She looked at him, puzzled. 'What do you mean?'

He glanced round the lobby, as if to check it was empty, but still lowered his voice. 'Ever since the tests I did.'

'What tests?'

He lowered his voice even more. 'Ten years ago – 'bout that – they were offering employees a thousand pounds each to try out some new drug they was developing. I more or less got a permanent cold since.'

'What was the drug?' she asked, horrified.

He raised his hands. 'They didn't tell us.'

A lift pinged, the doors opened and various bodies came out and walked across the lobby towards them. Neither Monty nor Winston Smith spoke until they had gone out into the night.

'They didn't tell you what it was for?'

'I needed some extra money – I didn't figure it would be harmful, else they wouldn't be giving it to humans.'

'What happened to the others who took it?'

He shrugged. 'I wouldn't know 'bout that.'

Testing drugs on human volunteers was standard practice. All new drugs were tested first on rodents and sometimes on other animals as well for toxicity; after that there were four stages of human trials, the first with a small group of volunteers who were often paid.

'They never gave you any compensation?'

'Like I say, keeping this job, I suppose. I wouldn't be able to get any other – I have to spend about three months of the year off sick – gets so bad I have to stay in bed.'

221

Monty felt sorry for him, and angry at the company for making him work at all. 'You poor thing. How do you feel about it?'

'I feel bitter, m'am, but there ain't nothing much I can do.' He smiled. 'Read that book you recommended last week. Graham Greene – *Brighton Rock*. That Pinkie sure is a mean fellow.'

'Reminds me of Dr Crowe,' she said.

The security guard chuckled. 'That's good! I like that!' He chuckled again. 'It was Dr Crowe was in charge of them trials – he gave me the pills.'

'Personally?'

'Yes, he took a great interest.'

'I'll have a word with him.'

Winston Smith blanched under his faded facial colour and looked alarmed. 'No – please don't do that. In my contract what I signed, said I wasn't to tell no one. Don't go stirring it up – could cost me my place.'

'OK, don't worry.' Silently she wondered whether it would be worth mentioning to Rorke. But it would still get back to Crowe, she realized. 'I won't say a word.'

'Thank you, Miss Bannerman. You have a nice evening. You think of any more books, let me know.'

She nodded a little distantly. 'Yup. H. E. Bates – ever tried him?'

The guard shook his head blankly.

'*Darling Buds of May*. Forget the television series, read one of the books.'

'Bates,' he said ruminatively. 'I'll go to the library tomorrow.' Then he sneezed again.

She smiled and went out into the car park.

The aftermath of an accident had snarled up the Westway, and it took Monty over an hour to reach the swifter-moving M4. But she didn't really mind, was grateful for the solitude of the dark cockpit of her car, and spent the time wrapped up in her thoughts.

She repeatedly posed questions to herself about Jake Seals' death. Was it deliberate? Was it to do with his new job? But

Bendix Schere couldn't be so ruthless as to kill an outgoing employee, no way, in spite of her father's invective against them at lunch today. She had felt quite embarrassed by the way he'd gone on about it to Conor Molloy, although she had the feeling that the American had some sympathy with her father's views.

The lunch had not exactly been an unmitigated success. Her father had been at his foulest, slagging off, in rapid succession, Bendix Schere, Bill Clinton and the US patent system. Molloy had been remarkably civil, responding quietly and intelligently, and even making her father laugh a couple of times. The more she saw of him the more she liked him, and she wondered whether he would pursue the suggestion he had made in hospital of just the two of them having lunch. She hoped so. Hoped her father had not put him off.

She switched on the radio, punched through a few stations, but found her thoughts were churning too much to listen. Had someone discovered that Jake Seals was going to run tests on the Maternox tablets? And if they knew of Seals' involvement, perhaps they knew of hers also. If they didn't before his death, they certainly did now. Her arriving so early was a give-away.

She thought of the reporter, Zandra Wollerton, and felt scared, even found herself glancing in her rear-view mirror, but she couldn't see much through the cracked plastic window of the soft top, just a bright blur of lights.

Come on, Monty, you're being paranoid.

She took the Reading exit, headed along the ring road a short distance, then pulled into a bus-stop to study the directions she'd scrawled down on the back of an envelope, then drove on. After a mile she turned left at a parade of shops, then checked the mirror. Nothing seemed to be following her.

She drove slowly down a street of modern semi-detached boxes, spotted number 31, and pulled into a space just past it. Two dinky carriage lights illuminated the mock-Regency front door, and the bell played the opening bars of a tune she knew but could not immediately name.

A rotund woman of about sixty, several inches shorter than herself, opened the door, shooing back a ginger cat, and

Monty smelled a strong waft of fried fish. As the woman recognized Monty, she straightened respectfully.

'Miss Bannerman – good evening.' She spoke with a homely Welsh accent.

Monty had only ever met the older woman once before, at their annual Christmas party. 'I hope I'm not disturbing you. You're not in the middle of supper?'

'No, he finished his tea an hour ago – he's just watching something on the telly. Please, won't you come in.'

Monty went into the small hall, her feet sinking into a thick orange carpet. She could hear gunfire, then the squeal of tyres, followed by blaring music.

The woman signalled with her eyes for Monty to wait and rushed through an inner door. Monty, a little embarrassed, could hear the awe in her voice. 'Walter – it's Miss Bannerman – here to see you.' She came back out. 'He's coming right away. Can I get you a cup of tea or something?'

'No, really, thanks – I'm just on my way home. I meant to get here earlier – the traffic was terrible.'

'Well, you're always welcome; we're so grateful to you for getting Walter his job back. He was that unhappy about being made redundant. He always used to tell me how lucky he was to work for such lovely people as your father and yourself.'

Monty blushed under the warm compliment and stroked the cat which was rubbing against her leg.

The television went abruptly silent, and a moment later her father's ex Chief Lab Technician came into the hall. He seemed to have aged in the past couple of weeks, or maybe it was the fact that he looked different out of the white lab coat in which she was used to seeing him.

He was a large man in his mid-sixties, six foot two and amply built, with a softly handsome face beneath neat grey hair. He had always struck Monty as seeming too physically large for his delicate job in the lab, just as he seemed too physically large for this tiny house and his tiny wife. Monty considered him a true gentle giant.

'Good evening, Miss Montana,' he said. 'This is a very pleasant surprise. Back on your feet, I see. I hear you were a brave lady.'

She shrugged. 'I wasn't brave – I was just there and I had to do something.' Then she smiled. 'Look, I'll be very quick.'

'Come on through, my dear.' He gestured her into a living room that was almost completely filled by a bulky three-piece suite and a large television.

She sat on the sofa and sank deep into it. The cat immediately jumped on to her lap.

'Off, Ginger!' Walter ordered uselessly. He lowered himself into a chair. 'Don't think I've thanked you properly yet for getting me my job back.'

'You should never have been made redundant – it was part of the agreement we had with Bendix Schere.' She glanced at the dancing flame lights in the electric fire. 'I suppose these things happen sometimes in large organizations. So how are you getting on?'

'Mustn't grumble. The work's quite interesting – knee deep in red tape, though. Have to fill in requisition forms in triplicate for anything and everything.'

She smiled. 'One of my father's complaints also.' The cat purred loudly.

'How is he?'

'Still settling in. He's got the laboratory and funding of his dreams, but he still has a lot of reservations. I think in his heart he never wanted to change the old lab. I know he misses you.'

'Well, I miss him. Miss everyone.' He shrugged. 'Still, nothing in life stays the same for long, more's the pity.'

She glanced at the old man, feeling responsible, suddenly, for the change that had affected all their lives. 'Walter, I need a favour from you, and I didn't want to discuss it over the phone.'

'In case it's bugged?'

Her eyes widened.

Registering her surprise, Walter Hoggin said, 'There's all kinds of rumours. They say the labs are bugged as well – and that Bendix employ security staff who do nothing all day but spy on the rest of us.' He laughed jovially. 'You probably know already, but I only heard today that employees are not allowed to work on trains or aeroplanes in case of industrial spies! You can get instant dismissal for doing that.'

She nodded. 'They must be the most paranoid company in the world.'

'I got a right wigging the other day for talking to the press. Thought I was for the sack. That would have left me with egg on my face after all the trouble you went to.' He paused for a moment. 'Anyhow, what's this favour you need?'

She drew a breath. 'I need you to do something – to *get* me something.'

He looked pleased. 'Anything at all, you know that.'

'You're familiar with the drug, Maternox?'

He looked uneasy. 'Of course; that's my bailiwick. We're running production of it continuously.'

'I need some detective work.' Monty opened her diary and searched for the page where she'd written the details she'd taken from Hubert Wentworth at their last meeting. 'If I give you the batch number, I wonder if it's possible for you to get me a sample of Maternox capsules. Do you think you could do that? And random samples from other batches?'

He looked at the serial number and stroked the base of his chin; a deep frown creased his forehead. 'I – I don't know if this is coincidence, but this is the same batch I identified for the reporter – the one who pretended to be Dr Farmer.'

Monty stared back at him. 'What was her real name? Was it Zandra Wollerton?'

'I don't know – they didn't tell me.' His frown deepened. 'Rings a bell – maybe they did mention it. To tell the truth I was in a right state. Major Gunn, the Director of Security himself, came to see me and he was not a happy man. I honestly thought I was for it.'

The news disturbed Monty. 'If it's going to get you into trouble, don't worry about it, Walter, OK? I don't want you to risk your job over this.'

'Don't you worry, Miss. If you want a sample of those capsules, I'll get it for you.'

Monty felt a beat of excitement.

'Might take me a day or two, mind – I've got to find a way to do it without arousing any interest.'

'Of course. There's no panic, just whenever you can.' She

felt nervous, suddenly. 'Will you be careful – for yourself, please, Walter.'

'I'll be careful.' He gave her a reassuring smile.

41

London. Tuesday 15 November, 1994

The restaurant was almost empty, and the Thai music whining in the background added a distinctly mournful air to the place. Dark blue tablecloths, pale blue walls, exotic fish drifting in and out of an illuminated grotto in a huge tank. Two waitresses stood with waxen smiles on their faces.

Anna Sterling, dressed in her usual rig of baggy sweater and black leggings, lowered her menu, a vast, laminated card with a marbled front on which a Buddhist temple was embossed in gold foil. She stared at Monty.

Anna had been in a good mood tonight; she seemed happier and more relaxed than Monty remembered for a long time. Her thick, wavy hair had got back its bounce, and in her face the handsomeness of her Latin looks was restored.

'I'm pregnant!' she announced.

'Hey!' Monty said. 'You are?'

'Yes, I am. I really am!'

'That's wonderful! How long have you known?' She was aware, but tried to ignore it, that beneath the happiness she felt for her friend, she also felt a twinge of jealousy.

'I had the confirmation this morning. I was six weeks late – but I didn't want to get my hopes too high.'

'When's it due?'

'Tenth of June.'

'Brilliant!' Monty said. 'That is such good news. We ought to have Champagne to celebrate!'

Anna shook her head. 'I want to keep it low key for a few weeks – until I'm out of the danger period. I'm not going to tell anyone – just you and Mark. I sort of think it might be bad luck to start announcing it to the world.'

Monty nodded. 'So how do you feel? You must be thrilled to bits.'

'I am. But I'm nervous also –' She was interrupted as a waitress came over and hovered, taking their order.

Across the table, Monty was thinking how much her friend had changed over the years, and wondering if she herself had changed also. Anna had been a tomboy at school, both the eccentric artist and the ring leader; and it was Anna who was the dominant one in her marriage to Mark. She was in every way the epitome of modern woman, and yet now, as Monty looked at her, she saw someone very different, someone awed by the tiny speck of human life she was carrying in her womb.

A dark shadow slid across Monty's mind. Maternox. Had Anna been taking Maternox right up to her pregnancy? Was it Maternox that had helped her become pregnant?

Should she warn her?

Warn her of what? That three out of millions and millions of successful Maternox pregnancies had gone wrong? When there was no proof that it was Maternox that had caused the problem – far more cases would be needed before any causal link could be made. Warn her and in so doing frighten her, perhaps needlessly?

Would Anna thank her? Or would she take it as an act of spite? A pique of pure jealousy?

There was nothing, Monty decided, to be gained from telling her, not unless she had a great deal more evidence. So she waited until their drinks arrived, then raised her glass and clinked it against Anna's.

'To the sprog!' she said.

'I want you to be a godmother, Monty. Will you?'

Monty sipped her spritzer and felt the cold of the ice cubes against her lips. 'Sure,' she said. 'Thank you, I – I'd love to. Have you thought of a name yet?'

'Yes, I've chosen them for both a boy and a girl.'

God, Monty thought, *I hope it works out OK for you. I really, really do.*

42

'Any more on the accident?'

Conor was startled out of his concentration by the sound of Charley Rowley's voice.

'Not that I know of.'

Rowley leaned in through his office doorway, looking his normal dishevelled self. His pancake face was puffier than usual, as if he'd had a late night. 'Just wondered – saw you chinwagging with Bannerman *père et fille* in the canteen yesterday. She is worth spending time on.'

Conor nodded in agreement. 'She is.'

'Probably something in the rule book forbidding nooky between employees. But I certainly wouldn't say no.'

Conor found himself resenting the remark, and realized he was feeling possessive. Possessive over a girl he had not even dated. Not yet. 'You already have a very nice girlfriend,' he said, thinking of the ambiguous Louise who had been at Rowley's dinner party and had acted like a hostess, dividing her time between the kitchen and the dining table.

'Lulu?' A rather pained expression appeared on Rowley's face, like someone reminded of a debt. 'Yah, Lulu's all right.' He glanced round at the bundles of documents. 'Fucking stupid to arrive at work drunk,' he said, rapidly reverting to his original subject. 'Unheard of in a company like this. Unbelievable!'

'*Too* unbelievable,' Conor said, but the nuance was lost on Rowley.

The bright mid-morning sunshine did nothing to lift Monty's apprehension as she walked across the car park. The feeling increased as she stepped into the chillier air in the shadow of the Bendix monolith, then entered the cathedral-like splendour of the white marble lobby.

It was half past eleven. She had put in a couple of hours earlier at the old lab, rummaging through some of the archive files for information on her father's published papers that

229

Conor Molloy needed, and she had thick wodges of photo-copies in two Manila envelopes tucked under her arm.

There was a quiet hum of activity in the lobby; a steady stream of employees, like worker ants, escorted visitors in and out through the turnstiles, and the flower-scented air was resonant with the muted bonhomie of power greetings and power partings.

Unusually, all the lifts were in use. Monty waited, staring at her reflection in the beaten copper of one of the doors, but it was too diffused to be of much use as a mirror. Then she yawned, feeling very tired suddenly.

She had slept badly last night, with an endless succession of anxiety dreams about Anna Sterling producing a hideously deformed baby and saying, repeatedly, *Why didn't you tell me? Why didn't you tell me?*

She was distracted by what sounded like the swoosh of a lift descending. The sound faded. It had come from the Direc-tors' lift, which she had been in a number of times during the negotiations for the sale of her father's laboratory, and which was set apart from the rest of the lifts. Must have gone down to the health hydro in the basement, she assumed.

There was a ping and a door behind her slid open. She turned and followed a group of Japanese businessmen in, all of whom stood in obedient silence as the lift rose.

When she arrived in her office she logged into her computer and called up Conor Molloy's full request list. Then she called Conor's internal extension, wondering if he was at his desk, and was surprised when he answered almost instantly.

'Conor Molloy.'

'It's Miss Bannerman speaking. Are you very busy this morning?' she asked, and was pleased by the way his voice brightened when he recognized her.

'Hi! Busy? You kidding? I feel like some Egyptian pharaoh entombed inside a pyramid. You should come up and see the *paper* in here. I never saw files like it in my life! What was your father trying to do – get in the *Guinness Book of Records* for publishing more papers than any other scientist? Seems like every time he goes to the bathroom he publishes a paper about it – I mean I'm surprised he hasn't published his goddamn shopping lists – or maybe he has and I haven't got there yet!'

Coming from anyone else, criticism of her father would have angered her. But she simply smiled. 'He's pretty chaotic – you probably will find several shopping lists in there somewhere.'

'I'm going to need your help on some of this. How was your evening?'

She wondered, with a start, if he was referring to her visit to Walter Hoggin. Couldn't be; there was no way he could know about that; it had to be just an innocent question. 'It was fine, thank you,' she said, a little surprised.

'I enjoyed our Monday lunch. Your father's quite a character.'

'Yes, he is.'

'Are you free for lunch on your own any day this week?'

Take your pick, Monty thought. *I'm free every single day.* But she didn't want him to know that. 'I'll just check my diary.' She waited a moment. 'I can only do today or tomorrow,' she said.

'Well, how about today?'

'Sure. Shall I meet you up in the canteen?'

'I thought we could go out some place – have a change of scenery. There's a little Italian down the road – you go out the front entrance, turn right, cross over one set of lights and it's on the next corner. Called *Il Venezia*?'

'I could meet you down in the lobby. Wouldn't that be easier?'

He sounded evasive. 'Better to go separately. One o'clock OK?'

'Fine.'

'I'll call them, make sure they have a table. Any problem and I'll call you right back.'

When Monty hung up she went straight to the washroom and carefully checked her make-up, then her hair. It had been a cold morning down in the country and she had dressed more for warmth than glamour today, in a black polo-neck sweater and bouclé suit; now she wished she was wearing something a little softer, but it would have to do.

★

231

Conor Molloy was already at *Il Venezia* when she arrived, tucked away behind an alcove table. It was a bustling, old-fashioned place, with tourist posters of Venice on the walls, and the poor lighting gave a small measure of privacy.

He stood up as she approached. 'Hi.'

'Hello!' she said, feeling a beat of excitement. There was a warm smile on his face and his deep brown eyes were focused on her in an expression of pure welcome.

He helped her off with her coat and held her chair whilst she sat down. Then he sat back down opposite her. 'Can I get you a drink?'

She looked at the empty bottle of San Pellegrino in front of him and gave him a grin. 'A large mineral water on the rocks, please.'

'You can have something alcoholic if you want – I'm not going to tell on you.'

She shook her head. 'Mustn't break company rules, must we?'

He looked at her for a moment, trying to figure out whether she was joking, then grinned back. 'They probably have random breath tests in the corridors.'

'Nothing would surprise me,' she said. 'So what's with the secrecy? Why couldn't we be seen walking here together?'

He signalled to a waitress and ordered a second San Pellegrino water, then looked back at Monty. 'Employees are not encouraged to socialize.'

'But surely we're expected to have working lunches.' She smiled. 'Isn't that being a little paranoid?'

'With Bendix Schere I don't think anyone can ever be paranoid enough.'

She stared back at him, remembering with a chill the time that Jake Seals had looked around the pub and suddenly clammed up. But Bendix couldn't watch and follow *all* their employees *all* of the time. Impossible. And why would they want to?

'You look dynamite!' he said suddenly. 'Love your outfit.'

She touched her jacket, surprised. 'This? It's just an old thing I chucked on this morning to keep warm.'

'It looks really good on you.'

'Thank you,' she said, flattered, noting his own modern-cut double-breasted suit. There was something caring and solid about him that made her feel very at ease in his presence.

'Now, tell me about yourself,' he said. 'Do you have a boyfriend?'

Her drink arrived. The waitress poured out half a glass, gave them menus then hurried off. Monty shook her head, feeling very relaxed. 'No one special at the moment.'

He nodded and there was a comfortable silence and air of anticipation between them. But Conor's next words caught her off guard. 'So . . . why do you think Jake Seals' death was no accident?'

'Oh, you mean what I said in hospital? I was probably just in a state of shock at the time.'

'You seemed OK to me. In fact you seemed amazingly rational considering what you'd just been through.' The patent attorney raised an eyebrow. 'Something obviously made you feel things were not right somewhere.'

'I –' She touched the rim of her glass, glanced round then leaned even closer towards him. 'There is something – but it's not much.'

'Tell me. You can trust me totally – nothing you say will go beyond this table.'

She watched his face, studied his eyes. *Yes*, she thought. *You're an almost total stranger to me, and yet I feel that I know you.*

She told him about Hubert Wentworth, about when he had first come to see her with the news of his daughter's tragedy. And about the two other women who had died giving birth to Cyclops Syndrome babies. About how she had approached Jake Seals for information about the Maternox capsules. Then Zandra Wollerton's strange break-in and her subsequent death. Finally she told him of her approach, after Jake's death, to Walter Hoggin.

Her hands were shaking when she had finished. She tried to pick up her glass, but suddenly did not trust herself to hold it. 'The rational explanation is that it's all just coincidence, right?'

Conor had a distant expression on his face now. 'That what you really think?'

233

'It's what I hope.'

The American said quietly, 'Bendix Schere has this benign public face, but none of us really knows *anything* about most of its Directors. We don't really even know who *owns* the company. The only thing we know for sure is that with a best-selling drug like Maternox there are an awful lot of bucks at stake.'

'Enough to kill for?'

'A few years back the World Health Organization publicly accused Bendix Schere of killing more babies per month than the Hiroshima bomb.'

'*What?*'

'Through their powdered-milk sale techniques in the Third World. You didn't hear about that? Bendix Schere never sued. And considering how litigious they are, that seems pretty much an admission of guilt, right?'

She frowned.

'How's this for a very nice little scam. They have teams of salesmen posing as doctors and nurses out in countries like Ethiopia. They approach pregnant women and tell them that in the West we don't breast-feed any more – that it's not hygienic and that powdered milk has more vitamins. And to demonstrate how much faith they have in powdered milk, they offer these women a free supply for the first month after their baby's born.'

Conor sipped his water, then continued. 'So the mothers take the powdered milk for the first month, during which time their own natural milk dries up. They're then stuck having to buy the Bendix Schere powdered milk for the next couple of years. Half of them can't afford it, and so their babies starve; those that can afford it, somehow, mix it much of the time with contaminated water, and rapidly discover the powder doesn't contain the antibodies that their natural milk would. And guess who's around to supply them with the drugs they then need. Get the picture?'

She nodded, horrified.

'So,' he said. 'Take this Maternox business – what do a mere handful of lives matter in that kind of a scale?'

'You really –' Her voice choked. 'You really mean the

company is capable of *murdering* people? Zandra Wollerton, Jake Seals?'

The waitress came over and hovered. 'Couple of minutes, please,' Conor said, then looked back at Monty. 'I don't *think* the company is capable. I *know*.'

'How do you *know*?'

'You have to trust me, Montana. I know.'

Monty was so distracted she barely registered Conor Molloy's breach of company protocol in using her Christian name. 'The powdered milk – the real ethics are horrific – but Bendix probably argue that there's a high mortality rate among Third World babies anyway, and I imagine they can produce statistics proving their powdered milk actually saves lives.'

'That's exactly what they do. But the fact remains that they've never dared sue.'

Monty wondered what exactly drove this man. She glanced disinterestedly at her menu. Maybe his tale was right, but it sounded to her more like student militant rhetoric, the little people versus the Big Institution paranoia that used to be rife on campuses throughout the sixties and seventies.

'If that's how you feel about Bendix Schere,' she probed, 'why are you working for them?'

'I can't give you that answer right now,' he said.

'Oh?'

'You'll understand one day – I hope.'

She smiled. 'You're very mysterious.'

He parried the remark with a fleeting raise of his eyebrows, and leant back in his chair. 'Tell me more about this Jake Seals character.'

'I know very little. He was – I suppose – rather cocky. Definitely didn't fit the Bendix mould.'

'So he might have upset some guys?'

'I'm sure he did. He upset me – I found him difficult at first. But I came to respect him, he was professional and very, very thorough.'

'Do you buy the theory that he came to work drunk?'

'I was sold it by a senior police officer – he wouldn't have made it up.'

'Was Seals conscious when you got to him?'

'Yes – but delirious.' She remembered something, suddenly. 'Is there someone called Wolf in the company?'

'Wolf? As in the animal?'

'Yes.'

'I dunno,' he said. 'I guess it would be easy enough to find out. Why?'

She recalled the pitifully incoherent cry that had come from Seals' melting face, before his voice had faded into moans. *Wolf. Woooolllffff.*

The memory made her shudder. 'He was trying to tell me something. *Wolf.* It was the only thing he said to me.'

The American's eyes narrowed with acute interest. 'Just *wolf*?'

'Yes.'

Without relaxing his eyes, he said, 'Interesting. Very interesting.'

'Why?' she asked.

'They do one helluva good pasta here,' he said, ignoring her query. 'If you even half like pasta it's worth having.'

'*Is* it a person, someone you know of?'

'It's no big deal,' he said.

For the first time since she had met him, Conor Molloy was looking awkward. *Wolf* very clearly did mean something to him, but whatever it was he evidently wasn't about to tell her.

43

London. Thursday 17 November, 1994

Conor pulled into the Bendix Building a few minutes before seven. He was an hour earlier than normal this morning, and it was still dark. As he opened his door, he scanned the almost deserted car park that was floodlit as brightly as a tennis court, looking for Charley Rowley's coupé BMW, and was relieved not to see it.

He hurried in through the lobby, slipped his card into a turnstile, nodding at the guard, the one with the grizzle of grey hair who looked sick, and walked across to the lifts. Moments later he stepped out into the Group Patents and Agreements twentieth-floor reception. A surly security guard with a boxer's face and a crew cut checked his ID in silence, then Conor slid his smart-card into the door and pushed it open.

He was greeted by a dull whine, and down the far end of the corridor saw a Filipino woman hoovering the green carpet. As policy, the cleaning staff had only a minimal grasp of English, and were illiterate. Cleaners were a common tool of industrial espionage.

He walked past the woman, turning right just past a row of notice boards which, apart from a list of statutory regulations, were virtually bare; most notices were posted by eMail. He walked on a few yards past his own office, stopped outside Charley Rowley's slightly larger one, and peered in through the window. The room was dark, the desk bare. Rowley was definitely not in yet. *Good*, he thought. *Excellent!*

He slipped his smart-card into his own office door and the light automatically came on as he went in. The room smelled of polish and looked freshly cleaned. One single night away from the office always seemed much longer, somehow. He hung his Crombie and jacket up, unlocked the metal cupboards and began the first chore of each day, which was to remove the bundles of documents he had put away the previous night, and lay them out, some on the floor and some on his desk. Normally, the next thing would be to switch on his computer terminal and log in, then read his eMail, but today he deliberately left the machine off. Instead, he opened a folder marked 'Acute Pustular Psoriasis Application' and began to read through one of the seven papers Dr Bannerman had published on identifying the genes for this disease.

At half past seven he heard footsteps coming down the corridor and eyed the window. A bespectacled man walked past without looking in. He was an English patent agent, Charley Rowley had told him, who worked in an office next to the vending machines; they had nodded a couple of times but never actually spoken. Conor resumed his reading.

The booming sound of Charley Rowley's voice, greeting someone further down the corridor, interrupted him after about twenty minutes, and he braced himself. A moment later Rowley stopped in his doorway, holding a bulging briefcase.

'Morning, Mr Molloy, how are we today?' he said with the breeziness of a surgeon doing his ward rounds.

'Yup, fine. How about you?'

'Yah. Never better!' Despite the brightness of his voice, Rowley looked, as usual, half dead, as if he had been up partying most of the night. His complexion was white and his eyes bloodshot. 'How did the move go?'

'Good. You must come round – have a drink.'

'Like to.' Rowley twiddled his little finger in his ear. 'Was it this weekend I suggested you come down to the country?'

'Uh huh.'

'Mind mucking in a bit? I'd forgotten we're meant to be doing a spot of paintwork.'

'Sure, no problem.'

'Great.' Rowley eyed the piles of documents. 'Getting on all right? Need help with anything?'

'One minor thing.' Conor stood up and sidled round his desk towards him. 'I have a problem with my terminal – not functioning. I've put a call into Maintenance, but it's going to be a while before they get anyone over. There's an urgent eMail I'm expecting – mind if I take a quick look at my mailbox on your screen?'

Rowley yawned. 'Better do it right now – I'm going to be on my machine all morning. It's just your terminal – the network's not down, is it?'

'No. There's just some glitch in mine.'

'Happens sometimes, affected mine about a year ago.'

Conor accompanied him the few yards along the corridor. He waited as his colleague slipped in his smart-card, then followed him in, manoeuvring himself quickly behind Rowley's desk and to the left of him, so that he had an unobstructed view of the keyboard.

Rowley sat down and switched on the terminal's power button. On the screen appeared the command: ENTER USER NAME.

238

Conor watched the screen carefully as Rowley tapped out, with one finger: **Chrowley**.

Then the command appeared: ENTER PASSWORD.

Like most systems, the password itself would not actually appear on the screen when typed, to prevent anyone else from reading it. Conor was no longer looking at the screen, but at the keyboard, glad that Rowley could only type with two fingers, and that he was only using one of them now.

He scrutinized each key in turn as Rowley struck them: **lu*1*u/**

Conor repeated the sequence silently to himself, committing it to memory. It was a good password, simple, and hard to hack. Rowley had used his girlfriend's nickname as the basis. But he had replaced the middle 'l' with a numerical '1', placed an asterisk either side of it, and for good measure added a slash on to the end. No hacker using a program to scan names, dates or dictionary words would be able to crack it in a hurry.

On the screen appeared: WELCOME TO THE BENDIX SCHERE ELECTRONIC SERVICE. AUTHORIZATION LEVEL 3. ENTER SERVICE YOU REQUIRE.

There were five authorization levels on the Bendix system, which Rowley had explained to him a while back. Level One was restricted exclusively to Main Board Directors. Level Two was for senior management. Level Three was for junior management. Level Four, which was Conor's level, and Level Five, were very limited. Conor could send and receive electronic mail, plus he could access the corporate research library which was on-line, and the company's patents records as well as the Internet, but very little else. Level Five existed principally for the security staff to verify personnel.

Rowley typed: MAILBOX REGISTER.

On the screen appeared the words: WHICH MAILBOX DO YOU WISH TO OPEN

He typed: **C. Molloy.**

On the screen appeared: SORRY, ACCESS TO THIS MAILBOX IS RESTRICTED TO MR MOLLOY. PLEASE ASK MR MOLLOY TO ENTER HIS PASSWORD.

Rowley stood up and indicated for Conor to take his chair. 'OK, Mr Molloy, fill your boots.'

Conor sat down and typed in his own password: **stea<lth**

Instantly his mailbox came up. He had twenty-three messages waiting.

'Just get myself a coffee,' Rowley said. 'Want one?'

'Sure – black, no sugar, thanks. I won't take a couple of minutes.'

'No worries.'

When Rowley had gone, Conor quickly wrote down his password in the back of his diary, then scanned through the sender names in his mailbox. A couple were from Rowley himself, setting dates for meetings; there was one from Montana Bannerman and a couple from her father responding to queries, and one, which he knew would be encoded, from his mother. He would read that one later.

Rowley came back in, yawning again. 'Fucking good club went to last night. Must take you there. Real head-banger of a place.'

'Is that right?' Conor said, trying to mask his lack of enthusiasm. He had never been into clubbing.

'They do some cocktail you get seriously stonkoed on. Bright purple. Absolute killer.'

'What's in it?'

Rowley pinched the bridge of his nose between his fingers for a moment, then gave a conspiratorial wink. 'Oh – I wouldn't know, I didn't drink any myself.'

Conor looked at him oddly for a moment, then twigged: company regulations forbade consumption of alcohol less than twenty-four hours before coming to work. 'Of course not.'

'OK, all finished – get what you wanted?'

'Yup, thanks, appreciate it.' Conor stood up and Rowley took over.

'Right, let's see what the day has to offer. A little dickeybird tells me it's going to be a bummer.'

44

Conor worked through lunch, taking only a ten-minute break when he left the Bendix Building to make a call from a pay phone down the road. At three o'clock he told Charley Rowley that he had to go early, because he was expecting a furniture delivery at his new apartment.

He drove south out of London, down on to the M25 ring road, then turned south again off that on to the M23, past Gatwick Airport and on towards the coast. It was a fine afternoon but the light was beginning to fade rapidly as the car swept up through a deep cut in the South Downs, the sky turning a dark metallic blue. He put on the lights, bathing the dashboard instruments in a crisp orange glow, driving swiftly, keeping an eye on the time.

It was twenty to five as he hit the outskirts of Brighton and pulled on to the forecourt of a pub. Squinting against the shadowy weakness of the interior light, he flicked through the pages of the computer magazine on the passenger seat until he reached the listings section with the name of the company he was looking for, and the directions he had written beside it. He re-read them, then drove on through the town centre, heading towards the sea.

After about ten minutes he passed a forest of domed minarets on his right: the Royal Pavilion, the massive extravagant folly George IV had built for his mistress. This was his principal landmark; now he began looking out for the address he wanted on his left. He crossed a traffic light, then saw the number painted on the column of an elegant Regency terrace. '24'. A large sign hung from the first-floor window: 'Minaret Internet Plc.'

He drove on past it, followed the directions he had been given to the car park. A biting cold breeze was blowing as he walked back along the seafront, past the brightly illuminated pier, clutching his Apple Mac laptop tightly and wishing he had some gloves on. Rounding the corner, he climbed the steps of number 24 and rang the entryphone buzzer.

There was a sharp click and he pushed the door open, walked along a narrow corridor, then up a flight of steps. As he reached the top he was greeted with a warm smile by an elegantly fashionable young woman in her early twenties.

'My name's Bob Frost – I phoned earlier this afternoon.'

'Yes, from Canterbury? Did you find us all right, Mr Frost?'

'Your directions were grand.'

'Come on through. Would you like some tea or coffee?'

'Coffee, please, black, no sugar.' He followed her through a long room that looked like Mission Control at Houston and into a rather chaotic office crammed with desks and computer terminals, at which a bald-headed man, a ponytailed youth and a rather fierce-looking individual with a cigarette gripped in his lips were all working in feverish concentration. Clumps of wiring like mutant spaghetti spewed between the desks into junction boxes on the floor. Keys puttered and lights blinked among the intermittent bleeps, hisses and chimes of modems connecting.

Conor was shown to a chair sandwiched between a desk and a stack of Internet Yellow Pages, and told someone would be with him in a moment. He sat down and stared at a hand-drawn progress chart on the wall opposite him; it was in the shape of a glass tube with an orange line midway between the 7000 and 8000 marks. After a few moments a tall, slim man with long, prematurely greying hair came up to him. Wearing a green jacket over a black t-shirt, and a '&' sign earring pinned to his left lobe, he sported rather conventional glasses.

'Mr Frost? I'm Andy Holyer. What can I do for you?'

The man had 'tekkie' printed all over him, but his manner was pleasant and businesslike.

'I need an eMail address.'

'No problem.' He eyed the computer Conor was holding. 'For a Mac?'

'Yup.'

'Is that a 540?'

'540 colour, yes.'

'We charge a joining fee of £17.75, then a monthly sub of £14.75 – no extras and there's no unit charging. We throw in the manual and the software. The service gives you an eMail account and full Internet access.'

'And I could join up right now?'

'We could add you on to the system at the end of today and get your pack off in the post tonight.'

'I – er – Is it possible I could take the pack with me?'

Andy Holyer looked at his watch. 'I suppose if you called back between six and six-thirty that'd be OK.'

'Sure.'

The young woman who had brought him in came over with his coffee. Andy Holyer turned to her. 'This gentleman wants to open an account, Toni. Could you take the details? He wants to get on tonight, so he'll come back after six.'

'Of course.' She led Conor over to a quieter corner of the room, sat him beside her desk and gave him a form. He laid his laptop and coffee in a gap on the desk and studied the form. It was simple, with spaces for his name, address and method of payment, and details of the system he used.

He filled in his fictitious name and an equally fictitious address in Canterbury, then hesitated at the payment option of cheque or credit card. 'I'd like to pay cash – is that OK?'

'No problem at all.'

He paid for six months in advance, and she wrote out a receipt. 'Do you have the name you want to register for your mailbox?' she asked.

'Yes,' he said with a wry, private smile.

She handed him a form on which he wrote down *eumenides*, then he turned it round for her to read. As she glanced at it, then typed it into the terminal, her face remained expression-less, not revealing whether the name meant anything to her or not. 'So your eMail address will read: *eumenides@minaret. co.uk*. Yes?'

'Yup, that's good.'

'OK,' she said brightly. 'If you'd like to pop back just after six we should have everything ready for you.'

'Do you have an instruction manual I can be studying in the meantime?'

She ducked beneath her desk and produced one, saying, 'You're welcome to wait here, but if you turn right outside the front door you'll find a couple of cafés where you might be more comfortable.'

Conor glanced at his watch. It was only five fifteen. He thanked her and went off in search of somewhere to kill the next three quarters of an hour.

The sight of the lights on in the cottage meant either that Alice had not been today, or that the strict note Monty had left her cleaning lady had got through, she thought as she drove up the pitch-black cart track. So far it had been a losing battle trying to train her daily into leaving the lights on. Coupled with the fact that on winter nights like these it was cheering to come home to a house not in total darkness, Monty thought also that the cats might be happier with some lights on, although she was not so sure about that.

The headlights of the MG picked out the barn, revealing clearly for an instant its corrugated iron cladding and flapping sheeting, before dropping it back into an ominous silhouette. The other thing Monty did not like about arriving home in the dark was driving past the barn; for no real reason it always spooked her.

She turned on to the hard in front of the garage, climbed out, shivering against the sudden cold of the rising wind, heaved up the garage door and drove the car in. She removed her briefcase, containing some papers she intended working on after supper, pulled the door shut, walked up to the front door and pushed the key into the lock.

She was feeling a little down this evening. Lunch had gone so well with Conor Molloy yesterday, right up until the point when she had mentioned that Seals had cried out something that sounded like *wolf*, and then he had suddenly seemed to lose interest in her and retreat into a world of his own.

She'd known he was going to be preoccupied as he had told her he was in the middle of moving; she had been hoping to get a call or an eMail from him today, though, but had heard nothing. Her father had been down in Berkshire and she had gone up to the canteen at lunch time in the hope of running into the American, but had seen no sign of him. A couple of times she had been tempted to phone him on a pretext, but had resisted. *Mustn't seem too keen,* she knew.

The two cats came running up as she entered, the way they always did. 'Crick! Watson! Hello, boys, how are you?' She knelt to stroke them both. As she did so, the phone rang.

Conor Molloy? She hurried through into the kitchen, and grabbed the receiver. 'Yeshello,' she said, a fraction breathlessly.

'Oh – er – Miss Bannerman?'

It was a female voice that was vaguely familiar; Monty recognized the Welsh accent, but could not immediately place it. The woman was courteous, but sounded very distressed.

'Speaking,' she said, a little guardedly, and disappointed that it was not the American; although she remembered she hadn't even given him her home number.

There was a pause. 'Miss Bannerman – I'm so sorry to disturb you – it's Walter's wife.'

'Yes – yes, of course, hello. How are you, Mrs Hoggin?'

There was a longer pause. 'I thought you might want to know – because you asked Walter to do something for you, and you – you might be waiting on it.' Her voice began to falter. 'I'm afraid he had a heart attack at work this afternoon. They –' Her voice cracked completely and Monty held on in terrible silence, fear swirling in the pit of her stomach.

'They – they said they tried to resuscitate him, but that he was dead by the time the ambulance got him to hospital.'

45

As Conor headed north on the motorway, back towards London, the sign loomed up overhead, 'Gatwick Airport', with an arrow indicating the near side lane exit.

Perfect, he thought, accelerating past a couple of trucks, then moving sharply over to the left. He drove up the ramp and stopped at the lights at the top. Amid the blaze of illuminations that marked out the sprawling buildings and perimeter of the airport, he saw several hotel signs high in the night sky.

Any of them would do fine, he thought, selecting the Post House at random and heading down the dual carriageway towards it. He crossed a series of roundabouts, then found himself about to overshoot the main entrance. Braking hard, he swung in without indicating, ignoring the blare of a horn behind him, and followed the signs to the car park at the rear of the building.

Relax, he thought. *Cool it!* He was as tense as hell, and clammy with perspiration. Slowing right down, he cruised the parking lot, and saw a row of empty bays ahead.

He reversed into one, removed his briefcase and locked the car, then walked through a pair of automatic doors into the rear of the lobby and made his way to the front desk. The hotel seemed quiet; a group of businessmen, with their names on lapel badges, stood closely together as if they had been deposited on alien terrain and were waiting to be rescued. Two men in armchairs were engrossed on their mobile phones, and a glamorous brunette sat on her own reading a magazine.

Conor addressed the young woman receptionist. 'Do you have any rooms available – a single?'

'They're all twins, sir, but we have a single occupancy rate of forty-five pounds.' Her voice sounded like one loop of a gramophone needle stuck in a groove.

'Fine, I'll take one.'

She swivelled a pad of registration forms to face him. 'If you could just fill that out, please, sir,' then she turned her attention back to her printouts. Conor wrote the name 'Robert Frost' and his fictitious address in Canterbury, and paid cash in advance for the room.

She handed him a card key inside a tiny folder. 'If you just settle your extras when you check out. Enjoy your stay,' she added with a vapid smile.

Conor got out of the lift on the fourth floor, checked the arrow directions for the room numbers and made his way along to 4122. It was a blandly functional room, with twin beds and a television. Net curtains blotted out some of the glow from the airport, and the double-glazed windows muffled most of the noise.

He found the 'Do Not Disturb' sign and hung it on the door. Then he lifted his laptop, modem cable and the instruction manual from Minaret Internet out of his briefcase, and switched on the computer.

It chimed reassuringly, and as it began booting up he traced the hotel telephone wire behind the bedstead to the socket on the wall. As he'd anticipated, the toggle had been broken off to prevent it being removed, so he levered in a pin, wiggling it until it sprung the catch, and the jackplug slipped out. He pushed in the jack on the modem cable, then connected the other end of the cable to his modem port, opened the desk legs on the base of the computer and set it down beside the television.

He waited a couple more moments for the machine to finish booting up then opened up InterSLIP and typed in a '9', followed by a comma, to the front of the Bendix Schere network dial-in number – so that it would pass through the hotel system. Then he clicked on the 'Connect' button and held his breath. The modem appeared to hesitate for a moment, then made the familiar hisses and beeps.

The words ENTER USER NAME appeared on the screen.

Conor typed: **chrowley**, then hit the carriage return.

ENTER PASSWORD.

Conor typed Charley Rowley's password, **lu*1*u/**, then hit carriage return again.

After a pause, the screen showed the response: WELCOME TO THE BENDIX SCHERE ELECTRONIC SERVICE. AUTHORI- ZATION LEVEL 3. ENTER SERVICE YOU REQUIRE.

Conor glanced at his watch. He had learned as much as he could about the Bendix Schere computer system in the past couple of months, and for such a technologically advanced and security-conscious company, it was a surprisingly old system of networked Macintoshes.

It was due to be updated but not until the middle of next year, which would give him plenty of time to exploit the current system's weaknesses. Principal of these was the fact that it was extremely difficult and time-consuming for

Security to run audit logs – to trace specific illegal entries or uses. And the shorter the length of time he was on now, the harder still it would make Security's task. Although, unless there were any buried alarm triggers in the system, there was no reason for anyone to be alerted by this entry.

The relative antiquity of the system was not as strange as it had at first seemed to him, when Conor understood the reasons: the computer system was run by a sparky thirty-something manager called Cliff Norris; he was well up to speed on the latest technology, but had a definite ego problem. Security was run by a smoothie called Major Gunn, whom Conor had also encountered.

Gunn might have had his high technology training at GCHQ but he had left them a decade ago, and whilst he was well abreast of some of the latest hardware and software, there were gaps in his knowledge through which a supertanker could be navigated. Despite a huge team (no one seemed to know quite how many people worked in Security), Gunn kept everything to do with his Directorate close to his chest, as if scared of revealing his shortcomings. And he did not get on well with Cliff Norris.

As a result, Conor had gleaned, there was a serious lack of communication between the Director of Security and the computer systems personnel.

His plan was simple: to use that situation to his advantage.

First he worked his way through the system until he reached the Superuser entry level commands. Then he implanted his first Trojan Horse, by replacing the genuine command interface with a duplicate false one. Then he waited patiently for one of the system managers with Superuser status to log in. It could be a few minutes or it could be several hours.

Keeping an eye on the screen, he lit a cigarette. Ten minutes passed. Then twenty. He lit a second cigarette, his nerves taut. Five minutes later, as he was stubbing out the cigarette, the word **cliffnor** appeared on the screen. It was the system manager himself logging in!

This word disappeared and was replaced with:
a*l*c/hem> ist.

With a wide grin, Conor copied the system manager's user name and password into his laptop's memory and trashed the false interface. Cliff Norris would have had his entry rejected, and would almost certainly assume he had mistyped his password. Conor lit a third cigarette and watched patiently as Norris logged in again and this time was connected.

Norris stayed logged in for twenty minutes, running a series of routine checks, then logged off again, this time for good, Conor hoped. To make sure, he logged off himself, unplugged his modem, dialled the Bendix Schere switchboard and asked to speak to Norris. After being put on hold for a short while, he was told that Norris had left for the day.

Conor plugged his modem back in and logged in again, this time using the system manager's user name and password. With his new Superuser status, he routed himself through to the network file archive which housed the system software for all the Macs in the building, and inserted a patch virus version of Mac TCP – the software link that handled data travelling between each individual computer and the system. This version held extra lines of program code which would monitor all the lines of data going through the system, pick out any information that Conor specifically requested, and automatically file it away into his eMail box at Minaret Internet. Effectively, he had just inserted a dead letter drop into the Bendix Schere computer network.

On the screen appeared the command: ENTER KEY SEARCH WORDS.

Conor typed MATERNOX, then hit carriage return.

ENTER NEXT KEY WORD OR CARRIAGE RETURN IF INSTRUCTIONS COMPLETE.

Conor pressed carriage return again. Then he logged into Norris's eMail software, and typed out a message to Major Gunn, informing him that an updated debugged version of Mac TCP called 'TETRUS T.G.' had been added to the system and this should be distributed to all workstations in the company, replacing the existing version. It automatically carried the system manager's normal signature.

When Conor logged off his nerves were jangling, but he felt well pleased with himself. If all went well, during the next twenty-four hours Major Bill Gunn would unwittingly become his most valuable assistant.

46

London. Friday 18 November, 1994

The Bitch was taking him for every penny. She already had the kids, now she wanted his money. Bill Gunn sat at his desk sipping his coffee, and read the three-page letter from the solicitors for the second time that day.

> It has come to our attention that you may own shares in the pharmaceutical company Bendix Schere, which information you have not previously disclosed to us or to the Child Support Agency. We would be grateful if you would kindly inform us within seven days of your exact position regarding ownership of any shares in said company.

He read the paragraph again. How had they got that information? The Bitch must have told them. But had he told the Bitch? He must have done, he supposed, years ago, once upon a time when he loved her or thought he loved her. Or had someone been digging deeper?

He was deeply disturbed. Ownership of shares in Bendix Schere was a strictly guarded secret; no paperwork ever changed hands and there was no documentation at all – it was taken on trust. And you never actually *owned* the shares. When Gunn had joined the company, he had been told there was an allocation of two hundred thousand shares in his name. The annual dividend would be paid into a numbered Swiss account for him on 1 May each year. And it had been. In the past ten years the amount in his deposit account at the Zuricher-Mehne bank had risen to just over three million pounds. There were, however, two snags: you couldn't touch the money until you retired; and you forfeited the lot if you left, whether voluntarily or sacked.

He would have to talk to someone in the Bendix Legal Department, let them handle it, he decided. Folding the letter away, he turned his attention to the second problem of the day. Conor Molloy.

Why had Mr Molloy gone to Brighton yesterday?

He studied the printout of the log of the American patent attorney's movements for yesterday, which had been brought to his attention by the data-tracking manager. The log had been compiled from a combination of an audit trail on Molloy's usage of his smart-card to enter and move around the Bendix Building, and the satellite data tracking of his car, which was automatically fed into the computer system.

It did not take Gunn more than a few seconds of studying the printout to realize that the American's trip was a substantial departure from his normal routine. A caveat had been added: on Wednesday Molloy had moved into a new apartment, and therefore, it was possible that yesterday's change in routine might be connected.

Gunn punched a sequence of keys and on his screen appeared a summary of Conor Molloy's movements on Monday and Tuesday, together with Thursday of last week. They seemed routine enough. The American arrived in the office shortly before eight, leaving around seven in the evening. He took a lunch break of exactly one hour, sometimes in the canteen, sometimes going out. He drove straight from his apartment to the office and home again. Nothing out of order there.

On Wednesday he had made two car journeys from his company flat to his new flat near the Fulham Road. That was fine also, the kind of activity to be expected when moving home. So what was yesterday all about?

Molloy had arrived in the office at 6.54 a.m. – an hour earlier than normal. He had taken only a ten-minute lunch break, then he had left at 3 p.m. and driven to Brighton.

Gunn picked up his phone and dialled the data-tracking manager's number. 'Where did Molloy park in Brighton?' he asked the instant the phone was answered.

'A small NCP just off the seafront, near the Palace Pier.'

'Do you know Brighton? Big on antiques, isn't it?'

'Yes, sir. Some people call it the antiques capital of Europe.'

'Used to be the shagging capital,' Gunn said. 'Is this NCP a likely place for someone going antiques shopping?'

'It would be reasonably close to the Lanes and the Kemp Town shopping streets, I suppose. I can find out for certain and come right back to you, sir.'

Gunn hung up and looked at the log again. Molloy had left Brighton at 6.20 p.m., driven to the Post House Hotel at Gatwick, where he'd stayed three hours and ten minutes, then driven back to London.

Three hours and ten minutes in a hotel? Doing *what*? Meeting someone? Maybe a friend from America on stopover? That was possible. Knocking someone off? Possible too, but if he was doing that he would more likely have stayed the night.

Gunn needed something good right now, needed to land a big live fish, and a hunch told him that in Molloy he had distinct possibilities. But there wasn't enough, not yet. He was unhappy about the American's background, he was convinced something on his application form wasn't right, didn't fit, but he still hadn't been able to work out what.

Ever since Molloy had awarded that skunk Mr Rowley two points short of the maximum on the Colleague Data Sheet, and had continued to do so each week, Gunn had been on the alert. Yet Molloy received high marks back from Rowley and from the senior manager of the Group Patents and Agreements Directorate. There was nothing to suggest anything untoward. Nothing but Gunn's instincts.

He debated whether to put Conor Molloy under full twenty-four-hour surveillance, and satisfy himself once and for all, either way. But that was expensive in man-hour time costs, which was how his Directorate's efforts were measured. It was only November and he was already over budget for the year, plus there were several employees in other divisions who needed surveillance at the moment. Chemicals had been disappearing at their Newcastle plant. And Gunn had been tipped off that a new marketing man in the baby-foods division at Reading might be a journalist planning to do an exposé on Bendix sales techniques in the Third World.

Dr Crowe had given him a rocket at the end of last year about the cost of security and poor results. This year had been even more of a bummer. He had not picked up one single instance of industrial espionage, large or small; he had failed to pick up any intelligence on Jake Seals' impending defection, and now Crowe wanted his guts for garters over his handling of the *Thames Valley Gazette* enquiries.

Come on, Mr Molloy, make my day. Do something, you slimy little Yank. Put a foot wrong, step into it right up to your sodding ankles.

Secure in the knowledge that there would be a copy of the log on hard disk, Gunn fed the two sheets of printout into the shredder beside his desk. Then he turned back to his workstation. He re-read the eMail from the computer systems manager informing him that an updated, debugged version of Mac TCP, called 'TETRUS T.G.', had been added to the system and should be distributed to all workstations in the company, replacing the existing version.

His first angry reaction was to phone Cliff Norris, the systems manager, and tell the lazy bastard to do the distribution himself. Then, calming himself down, he remembered it had been his own orders that all software had to be distributed by himself and no one else, and that it was a sackable breach of regulations for anyone to use software that had not been issued personally by him. That was the only way he could be certain of keeping the system free of viruses.

And it had been a damned good system, Gunn thought proudly, as he keyed in the command to distribute the new version of the Mac TCP software to every computer workstation in the whole of Bendix Schere's global empire. At least Crowe could not snivel at him about that.

47

North London. 1951

The Magister Templi opened the front door himself. Daniel stared at him, feeling an immediate sense of disappointment in both the house and the man.

He had been expecting something more imposing, some kind of bleak, turreted mansion, perhaps shrouded by trees and bushes at the end of a long, dark driveway. Instead it was a small semi-detached with mock Tudor beams and pebble-dash rendering, similar to his own, in a quiet suburban backwater ten minutes' bus ride from home.

The Magister Templi was much older than he had expected; and instead of being awe-inspiring he looked, in Daniel's eyes, faintly ridiculous.

He had long iron hair swept back from his brow, a silky beard trimmed like a shaving brush, and a colourless face with faraway eyes. In the centre of his forehead, held in place by a silver band, was a metal five-pointed star, flanked on each side by a pair of real goat horns. From his neck hung a small Baphomet emblem on a silver chain. He was dressed in a white, collarless linen gown and was barefoot, but he carried himself limply with no air of authority. Daniel thought he looked as if he was trying on an outfit that belonged to someone else.

Daniel stared at the Baphomet emblem, trying to conceal his scorn. *When I'm grown up* he thought, *I'll live somewhere grand and be immensely rich. I will never wear silver; silver looks cheap. I'll wear gold. And I will never be merely a Magister Templi. I'll be an Ipsissimus.*

The Magister Templi greeted Daniel without looking down at him, simply staring over his head, and he spoke in a voice that reflected the dream-like quality of his gaze.

'How old are you, boy?'

'Sixteen, sir,' Daniel said. He had read that many covens insisted on that as a minimum age.

'What did you bring with you, boy?'

'My athame.'

'May I see it?'

Daniel unbuckled his raincoat, slid his hand beneath his pullover, removed the sheath knife hidden there and passed it over.

The Magister Templi examined the hilt Daniel had blackened with paint, then studied the blade, turning it over and inspecting the symbols the man in the shop had instructed Daniel to carve on it with a chisel.

'You know these symbols?' he asked, still without meeting Daniel's look.

'Yes, sir.' Daniel's eyes darted quickly around. He took in the large pentacle on the wall, the faint smell of incense, the two black cats that stood watching him.

The warlock pointed to the first symbol, a rough circle with two points rising in a V-shape from the top. 'Tell me what this is.'

'The Horned God, sir. Also the powers of fertility, May Eve, the light half of the year.'

'And this one?'

Daniel looked at the dagger symbol with a pear-shaped hilt. 'The Ankh Cross, sir.'

The Magister Templi pointed to the crude 'SS' marking next.

'The Salute and the Scourge, sir.'

Then he indicated two back-to-back brackets, forming a ')('.

'The Goddess as the waxing and waning Moon, sir.'

'And this one?' He pointed to an 'M' with an arrow rising at the end.

'Scorpio, sign of Death and the Beyond, the *other side* of the God as Lord of the Underworld. Hallowe'en and the dark half of the year.'

'And you are able to recite the words of the Lord's Prayer backwards?'

Daniel did as he was bidden and the Magister Templi listened carefully.

'Good, very good. Do you understand why we say this prayer backwards, boy?'

'We say the Lord's Prayer in reverse to remove the

subconscious fears that Christianity builds in people. By saying it in reverse it shows we are no longer afraid of the Christian God. And if we are no longer afraid, Christians no longer have power over us.'

The Magister Templi nodded approvingly. 'You have begun well. Thoth was right.' Still not looking Daniel in the eye, he added, 'I am Isis.'

'And I am Morgana,' a woman said, materializing from nowhere, also dressed in a white linen robe. She had long brown hair with a striking face, and was much younger than the Magister Templi. Around her forehead was a similar silver band but without the horns; she wore a solid necklace hung with charm symbols and her fingers were heavily adorned with rings. She was the High Priestess that the man in the shop had told him about, Daniel realized.

She stared hard at Daniel with hypnotic brown eyes and continued to stare as he became increasingly uncomfortable under her scrutiny. 'What is your name?' she asked in a voice that was neither warm nor hostile.

He told her, blushing.

'Daniel is not a name for an initiate. Did Thoth not tell you to choose a name?'

He shook his head. Suddenly he was nervous that they were going to reject him and send him home. He was already worried that his lie to his mother about where he was that evening would be discovered. If she rang the vicar and learned he had not turned up to Bible study, she would have one of her mad turns.

His mother had been more violent during the past three weeks, ever since he had met the man called Thoth in the shop where he'd seen the book. He realized it was probably because he had been concentrating on preparing for today, rather than working his spells to keep her restrained. But it didn't matter. As far as he was concerned, today was the most important day of his life. Today he would become a First Degree Initiate.

The distant expression remained in the Magister Templi's eyes, but this time Daniel felt an enormous power coming from them, as if the warlock was somehow drawing out and reading the thoughts inside his head.

'Are you familiar with the name Theutus, boy?'

'Theutus was one of the Vessels of Wrath, sir.'

'Yes, Daniel. The Vessels of Wrath are the inventors of evil things and all wicked arts. Theutus taught cards and dice, he liked to make money and he was good at it.' The Magister Templi smiled. 'I think *Theutus* would be a fitting name for you.'

Daniel tried to engage his eyes to thank him, but the Magister Templi was again staring over his head. Instead he nodded gratefully. The warlock returned his athame, and he sheathed it beneath his pullover.

'It is time,' the High Priestess Morgana said.

'It is time,' the Magister Templi said.

They led Daniel across the small hall, and through a door into a garage which was almost entirely filled by an elderly van painted dark blue. The High Priestess opened its back doors and ushered Daniel into the windowless interior, climbing in after him. Daniel noticed she had a sash in her hand.

'We have to blindfold you now, Theutus,' she said.

Daniel felt a faint prickle of anxiety.

'We're taking you to our temple. You are not permitted to know its location until you become a Third Degree Initiate. It is the Law.'

Daniel nodded and obediently raised his head. He felt the cloth pull against his eyes as she knotted the sash firmly but gently. He heard the clang of the doors closing, then felt the van shake as the engine fired; almost immediately he smelled the stink of exhaust fumes. There was a grinding of gears and a sharp jolt; reversing out of the garage, he realized.

He lost all track of time after a while. The ride was uncomfortable; the van travelled at varying speeds, bumping, lurching, and frequently braking sharply; he did not think the Magister Templi was a very good driver.

Then, after a long run down a straight stretch, the van slowed sharply and he felt it turning to the right. It felt as if they were no longer on a road, but a farm track of some sort. As the vehicle bounced about unpredictably, Daniel had to fight hard to stop himself from throwing up.

Finally the van stopped, and to his relief he heard a clang

that sounded like the rear doors being opened, and suddenly he was breathing fresh air. It was thick with the smell of the countryside and he gulped it greedily, his nausea beginning to fade.

The High Priestess's hand took hold of his wrist and then he was guided out and on to the ground. It felt as though the sun had gone down, and there was a light chill to the late summer air.

'We're here now, Theutus,' the High Priestess said. 'Be careful of the step, lift your foot.'

He did as he was told, walked forward, then heard a door shut heavily behind him. There was a strong carbolic smell. When the High Priestess removed the blindfold, he was in a washroom, with black tiled walls and floor.

'We work sky clad here, Theutus. Please remove all your clothes then step into the shower, we must all be purified before we commence our rituals.'

Red-faced, Daniel complied and the High Priestess took his things into a locker room. When she came out, she was naked as well.

She pointed to the shower and followed him in, turning on the tap. She nudged Daniel gently forward, her own naked body touching his back, until the warm water was spraying hard on his chest and stomach. Taking a bar of soap, she began to wash him, massaging his skin with her fingers, working under his arms, across his belly, then soaping around his penis and testicles and probing the entrance of his anus.

He stood still, unsure what to do and feeling intensely aroused. Fighting with all his willpower, he tried to stop himself from getting an erection; but his penis was beginning to swell.

Mercifully, her hands moved on, down his legs. Then she sponged the soap off him, led him out of the shower and draped a large towel over his shoulders as the Magister Templi, also naked now, took his place.

'I have to blindfold you again now, Theutus,' Morgana said crisply, as if nothing unusual had happened.

Daniel tensed as she secured the sash once more over his

eyes. Then she removed the towel, took his hand and led him forward.

He heard the click of a latch and there was a draught of air accompanied by a strong smell of incense and hot wax. The floor was cold beneath his feet. As he walked ahead, he sensed the presence of a large number of people, all of them silent.

The High Priestess's hand jerked him to a halt. He heard her voice call out, in a loud intonation: 'We bring Theutus here to our temple today and we now prepare him to enter our sacred circle.'

There was a low sound, as if a dozen or more voices were chanting in unison. The chanting slowly grew louder, getting closer. And Daniel sensed fire, also, fire moving closer. He could hear the sound of flames consuming air, cracking, thumping, hissing. An intense heat moved towards his chest; he wanted to step away from it but dared not.

Then he felt an intense heat closing in on his back; then another below his genitals; another against his face. The heat was all around him, he wanted to cry out, had to stifle his voice. There was a crackle and the strong smell of singed hair; he felt some of the hair on his head burn, then some of his pubic hair.

Suddenly the heat went. The chanting ceased abruptly. He heard the clank of a chain, then droplets of icy water were spattering on his face and body. The chain clanked again and more water spattered his body, making him jump.

He braced himself for more, but instead of water a whip lashed across his naked back, making him cry out. There was another stinging lash, on his buttocks this time. Then on his stomach. Then another across his genitals, striking his testicles, doubling him up in pain. The back of his legs; his ankles; neck; right cheek: the lashes rained, one after another. But Daniel stood his ground, fought the tears, determined.

The marks, he thought, with more terror than pain. *My mother must not see the marks.*

At last the lashes stopped. Daniel stood still, his whole body stinging and raw.

'Can we trust you, Theutus?' It was the voice of the

Magister Templi. 'Can we remove your blindfold and let you see our temple and our faces?'

'Yes,' he whispered.

'Say after me: Do What Thou Wilt Shall Be The Whole Of The Law.'

Daniel repeated the words. Then the Magister Templi continued. 'Lo, Jesus of Nazareth, how thou art taken in my snare. All my life long thou hast plagued me and affronted me. In my name – with all other free souls in Christendom – I have been tortured in my boyhood; all delights have been forbidden unto me. Now at last I have Thee, Satan.'

He paused for Daniel to follow suit and then went on. 'I commit my mind, body and eternal soul to Thee, Lord Satan, eternally. And if I shall ever divulge to any living soul of this bond, outside of this Temple, my tongue and my eyes shall be ripped from my living body as my punishment.'

There was a long silence after Daniel had said these final words. Then, abruptly, the knot of the blindfold behind his head was untied and the cloth pulled away.

He blinked as his eyes focused; he was too stunned by what he saw to feel embarrassed or shy about his nakedness. His mouth fell open. He was inside a large barn, the ceiling of which was painted crimson, and the walls completely draped in black cloth. Two black candles, a good four feet tall, rose either side of an altar in the centre of a pentacle painted in gold leaf on the floor. There were many more candles all around, and a row of blazing medieval-looking torches in sconces on the walls.

A dozen people inside the pentacle were staring at him, motionless. Except he could not see their eyes. They were wearing eerie, animal-head masks and were otherwise naked, apart from the silver emblems which hung on chains from their necks.

A pig's head confronted Daniel above the naked body of a man. A cat's face had a woman's body. A snarling wolf and a leering goat also had human forms. Each held their athame pointed upwards and flames glinted off the blades. A young, naked woman lay on her back on a black cloth in the centre of the pentacle, her outstretched arms and legs bound elaborately with cord.

Daniel's gaze went from the eye slits in the animal heads to the naked girl, then back to the animal heads. The way they were looking at him, the way they were raising their athames, filled him with dread.

A trap, he realized. He had been brought into a trap.

He spun round but the door was blocked by the Magister Templi and the High Priestess, both naked as well. The Priestess was holding her athame. The Magister Templi was holding a huge sword high above his forehead as if he were about to strike Daniel. And they were both solemn, unsmiling.

'You have renounced Jesus Christ the Impostor,' the Magister Templi said, staring him directly in the eye for the first time. 'You have renounced God. You have chosen our way instead. You have sworn an oath of secrecy to us.'

'But why should we trust you, Theutus?' the Priestess said in a sneering tone.

'Can we believe in you, Theutus?' the Magister Templi challenged.

'Or would it be better to sacrifice you now, Theutus, and spare you the agonies of physical torture later?'

Out of the corner of his eye, Daniel saw the Magister Templi's sword rise a fraction higher and noticed his knuckles whiten on the hilt. For the first time his courage deserted him completely. He wanted to turn and run, but found he could not move a muscle. His whole body was paralysed – but not by fear. He was being *held* by some unseen force that was more powerful than anything else he had ever experienced. It held him a prisoner, rooted to the spot and helpless.

48

London. Friday 18 November, 1994
Conor hastily washed the last of the shaving foam off his face, then splashed on some Eternity aftershave. 6.58 a.m. Twenty minutes before he needed to leave for work.

He draped the damp towel around his shoulders as meagre protection against the chill – Jesus, this apartment was cold – and walked into the open-plan kitchen area. He made himself a mug of coffee and carried it into the living room where his laptop computer lay. Following the procedures in Minaret Internet's instruction manual step by step, although he was familiar with the software anyway, he logged into his mailbox to see whether his efforts of yesterday had yielded any results.

Almost instantly along the top of his screen appeared the words; TRANSFERRING . . . 1 OF 25.

Shit! he thought, with a broad grin, and dashed to his bedroom to get dressed while the mail was downloading.

As he was straightening his tie, he heard the gong on his computer announcing that the transfer of messages was complete, and went back in to log off. It was seven fifteen. He debated whether to look through them now, which would make him late, or to read them at work.

After a moment's hesitation, he shut down his computer, closed the lid and put it in his briefcase. Having taken half the afternoon off yesterday, he decided he ought to be in on time. He could read the mail on his laptop in the office and no one would know what he was doing. He scooped up his car keys and left, burning with curiosity to know exactly what had fallen into his net.

Monty was having a bad morning. Her father, upset by the news of Walter Hoggin's death, was in a filthy temper, made worse by his being unable to find a particular file. He swore he'd had it in the office only a couple of days previously, but Monty was convinced it must have been misplaced during the transfer from Berkshire. If it didn't turn up she would have to go into their old lab over the weekend to hunt for it, but she didn't relish that prospect. It was depressing enough going there during the working week now, let alone when the building was completely deserted.

Only a handful of their original staff were still there, as the final wind-down took place, and within a month even they would be gone, some tempted into early retirement, others to work at the Bendix plant in Reading where Walter Hoggin had gone. But it was Walter's death, more than the takeover by Bendix Schere, which symbolized the end of an era, and she was dreading the funeral.

When she'd reached the Bendix Building just after ten she'd found a message from Conor Molloy waiting on her voice mail box but, ringing him back, she had in return got his recorded voice and had left another message.

She came back up from the Stacks on the floor below, the nickname given to the massive filing room that served as an archive for all the labs, where copies of all the documents and research notes automatically printed off the computers every weekend were stored in fire-proof cabinets as back-up for the computer files. But her search there had revealed no trace of the missing file either.

She was just inserting her smart-card into her office door when she heard the phone ring. She hurried in and grabbed the receiver. 'Hello?'

'Miss Bannerman. Good morning – we've finally made contact.'

'Mr Molloy. Hello.' The formality struck her as particularly absurd now that she felt an increasing bond of friendship with this man. 'How did your moving go?'

'Fine, no problem. Except I'm still unfurnished.' He paused. 'How you doing?'

'Not great. I –' She glanced through the window into the corridor, saw a technician coming out of the lab door opposite, and pushed her own door shut, lowering her voice. 'Could we meet outside somewhere? I need to talk to you. Can you do lunch?'

'No – I have a meeting here. I've a gap right now, I guess – any good?'

Monty glanced at her watch. It was 11.10. 'Yes.'

'How about the same place we had lunch, in ten minutes?'

'Fine.'

As she hung up, she realized her hands were shaking.

Il Venezia was in the mid-morning lull between breakfast and lunch. Monty arrived first and went over to the alcove where they had sat before, keeping on her coat.

She'd only beaten Conor by a minute. The door opened and he walked in, clutching his briefcase, the collar of his Crombie turned up. The sight of him immediately made her feel reassured.

He walked over to her with a grim smile. 'Hi,' he said, pulling up a chair and sitting down. 'I have something interesting to show you.'

'Oh?' Everything about him seemed so safe, even the way his strong hands flipped open his briefcase and took out his laptop. The Italian waitress came over.

'What would you like?' Conor asked Monty.

'Just a cappuccino.'

'And I'll have a double espresso – and a doughnut. Have one yourself,' he said to Monty, 'they're really good here.'

She smiled at his appetite, the attraction she felt towards him increasing with every moment she was in his company.

The waitress went off.

'Are you OK, Montana? You look very pale.'

Monty watched until the waitress was a safe distance away, then looked back at the American. 'Do you remember on Tuesday I told you I'd asked our old Chief Lab Technician, Walter Hoggin, to see if he could get some Maternox samples?'

'Uh huh.'

She twisted her fingers together nervously. 'He died yesterday. Had a heart attack.'

Conor frowned. 'How old was he?'

'Sixty-six.'

'Did he have any history of heart disease?'

'Not that I know of.'

He was quiet for a moment. 'Where did it happen?'

'At the Bendix lab in Reading where he worked.'

'Where was he taken to hospital?'

'I – I don't know. Why?'

'You don't know if it was a public hospital or a Bendix one?'

'A Bendix hospital?'

'Sure – one of the Bendix clinics – that's where staff usually get taken.'

'I was told he died in the ambulance.'

The waitress brought the coffees and two fat, circular doughnuts, then departed. Conor studied his espresso, then he said: 'You ask Mr Seals to get you the information and the capsules and he dies. The newspaper reporter gets involved and she dies. Then you ask your Mr Hoggin for help and he dies. That's a lot of coincidences.'

'Where does the point come at which you stop believing in coincidence?' she asked.

Now he was eyeing the doughnut. 'When you're a kid growing up, you get to a certain stage where you stop believing in the tooth fairy and in Father Christmas. There's no specific date, no mark drawn on a wall; it's a gradual process, right? You realize, slowly, that things don't make sense any more the way you've been perceiving them, and that's when you start to figure out the truth.'

'I think I'm at that point now,' Monty said. 'I think actually I'm way beyond it.'

Conor picked up his snack and bit a chunk out of it, licking the oozing custard inside, and chewed for a moment. He swallowed, then held the doughnut out in front of her as if it were an exhibit. 'See the glaze?'

'Yes,' she said, a little surprised.

'That's made from the same gel Bendix Schere uses in its labs for testing DNA. They're the largest manufacturers in the world of this gel.'

She looked down at her own doughnut and grimaced. 'Seriously?'

'Uh huh.'

'I'm not sure it looks so appetizing all of a sudden.'

'Didn't you know, Bendix Schere's everywhere.' He put the remaining portion of his doughnut back down on the plate and wiggled his fingers. 'Little tentacles creeping out. They're slowly working towards a monopoly on the world's health. They're already heading towards a monopoly on baby food. Here and there they're making inroads into adult food.' He raised his eyebrows. 'Where do they stop?'

'I don't know. Where?'

He opened his hands and shrugged.

'And you really believe they're prepared to kill?'

'If the reason's good enough.'

'OK, what *is* the reason?'

He raised the lid of his computer and switched the machine on. 'See if this means anything to you.'

He moved his chair so that he was sitting beside Monty, and opened the 'In' section of his electronic mailbox. Moving the cursor down, he double-clicked on one item and it came up on the screen. It was a memo from Linda Farmer, Director of Medical Information to Dr Vincent Crowe, and it said simply: **Confirm we may have 4th Maternox problem. Kingsley C. (Mrs). Under observation. Will report further.**

'Does that mean anything to you?' Conor asked.

Monty stiffened, then suddenly drummed the table with her index finger. 'Where – where did that come from?'

Conor gave her a conspiratorial wink. 'I can't answer that right now. Just tell me if it means anything to you?'

She nodded, the words of Zandra Wollerton, when they had met in the hotel, flooding back to her.

I'm waiting for one more pregnant woman to die in labour from a virus and give birth to a Cyclops Syndrome baby, then I'm going to sit on her family doctor's tail round the clock for a week until he bloody well talks to me.

Conor looked at her expectantly.

'Zandra Wollerton's files,' she said. 'There must be something in her files at the paper.'

'I'm not with you.'

She drained her coffee. 'Give me your home number. I'm going to Berkshire right now and I'll call you this evening.'

He sounded hesitant. 'Sure, I'll give you my home number – but listen – you need to be really careful about saying *anything* on the phone. Use it to arrange to meet, but nothing else. And I think we both need to watch who we talk to from now on.' He sipped some of his coffee. 'I'm going to the country tomorrow – to spend the weekend with my immediate boss, Rowley. Come across him?'

She hesitated. 'I think I may have met him very briefly.'

'He knows his way around the company, and he's OK. If

the opportunity comes up, I'll talk to him to see if he knows anything.'

Monty was precise. 'What we need is to get hold of some Maternox samples from the suspect batch and have them compared to other Maternox capsules.' She gave him the relevant batch number.

He nodded. 'I'll see what I can do.'

She stared at her untouched doughnut, but had no stomach for it.

49

Berkshire, England. Friday 18 November, 1994
Monty found the sprawling Enterprise Park industrial estate off the Reading ring road without difficulty, pulled the MG up beside a large sign listing the companies, and wound down her window. A strong wind immediately blasted her face.

Central & Western Publishing Plc – Thames Valley Gazette. Unit 26, she read and wound the window up again, the car rocking slightly in the gust. She drove on, past a row of modern industrial buildings in identical dark grey livery, then she saw the name of the newspaper emblazoned on a four-storey structure much older and shabbier than the rest.

She parked in a visitor's space, then hurried towards the front entrance of the building, the wind savaging her hair. She'd phoned Hubert Wentworth from a call box after leaving Conor Molloy, and he'd suggested an afternoon meeting. Her watch said 3.15.

In the centre of the lobby a uniformed security guard sat tall behind a desk and politely asked her to take a seat whilst he contacted Mr Wentworth's office.

Monty sat in a low chair and picked up a copy of the *Gazette*, scanning the headline: 'Local Vicar Plans Xmas Visit to Bosnia.'

Christmas, she thought. Only five weeks away and she

hadn't made any plans at all. She was due to accompany her father to Washington at the beginning of December, and wondered if she could persuade him to stay on afterwards and take a holiday; skiing in Vermont?

She used to love Christmas as a child when her mother was still alive. But the only ones she'd enjoyed in the past decade were the two that she had spent with a boyfriend at his family's Yorkshire farmhouse. Then she'd realized she was probably more in love with his large, welcoming family and the warmth they radiated than with the man himself. With the result that she'd let the relationship peter out. But there had been plenty of moments during the past eighteen months when she'd wondered whether she had thrown away her last chance of getting married.

Idly flicking through the *Thames Valley Gazette*, she tried to get the flavour of the paper. It was all local news. Accidents, burglaries, bicycle thefts, weddings and advertisements. Then as she reached the centre pages, a huge photograph of the mangled remains of a car made her freeze.

'GAZETTE REPORTER'S DEATH CRASH MYSTERY: *Remains of the Ford Fiesta in which 21-year-old Zandra Wollerton died.*'

'Miss Bannerman!'

Hubert Wentworth's voice startled Monty, and she stood up hastily. 'Oh, hello! It's good of you to see me.'

He noticed the page she'd left open and gestured at it. 'Terrible business, such a tragedy. Zandra was a bright girl, she would have gone to the top, had all the qualities. Tough. You have to be tough in this game, you see, Miss Bannerman.' He inclined his head as if to underline that when necessary he, too, could be tough.

'No one knows how the accident happened yet?'

He pondered her question before responding. 'I've just spoken to the police. There was a witness, it seems, a man on a bicycle. He says she made no attempt either to brake or accelerate – as if she didn't even see the barrier.'

'Could she have fallen asleep at the wheel?'

He shrugged, his eyes widening into roundels, then shrinking. 'At eight o'clock in the evening? Possible, of course. Who knows? The police experts will be examining the wreckage;

268

perhaps the postmortem will reveal something?' It was almost as if the last remark was a question directed at Monty. Then he glanced at his watch. 'Look, should be quiet in the canteen, a good place to talk. Just one flight of stairs, if we walk it?'

He led the way, greeting the occasional colleague deferentially, as if everyone in the building was senior to him, and yet they all seemed equally respectful back. Monty felt she was seeing a new side to this man.

They went into a huge canteen, served themselves with tea and cheese sandwiches at the counter, walked over to the far end and sat down. The tables were small and narrow and the chairs hard and uncomfortable. Keeping her voice as low as possible, Monty described her approach to Walter Hoggin and his subsequent death.

When she had finished, Wentworth was looking at her with baleful eyes. 'Mr Seals, Zandra and now Mr Hoggin, yes? The tally is mounting. Is that how it seems to you, Miss Bannerman?'

She took a large bite of her cheese sandwich, then chewed and swallowed as quickly as she could. 'Did Zandra Wollerton say anything to you about a *fourth* Maternox case?'

'Another Cyclops Syndrome baby?'

'Yes.'

He shook his head blankly. 'No, nothing at all. But that's not to mean, of course, that she had no leads.'

'Would it be possible to have a look at her files?'

His eyebrows raised like two large, hairy insects preparing for flight. 'Yes! Good idea, I'll take you up to her desk.'

'It's just that, from what she told me I think she did know of a fourth case – or at least a pregnant woman with the same symptoms your daughter had.'

They went up into the large newsroom and walked past desks with computer screens, some occupied, others looking as if they had been hastily abandoned as a result of a bomb scare. They stopped in front of a desk that looked neat and orderly. It was the same as the others, with a melamine wood-grain surface, a blank computer screen, a metal spike with a thick wodge of impaled papers and a stack of untouched *Gazettes*. The only personal object was an oversize terracotta

269

mug filled with pens. A tweed upholstered secretarial chair was pushed tight into the kneehole. Monty felt a lump in her throat at the forlorn emptiness.

The newspaperman reached down and began opening the drawers at the bottom of the desk. The first contained a jumble of spare reading glasses, ruler, scissors and other paraphernalia. The second was packed with lined pads. He lifted one out.

'Can you read shorthand?' he asked Monty.

'No.'

He scanned through the pages himself. 'Looks like there's nothing there.' He took out the next pad and went through that, but again was disappointed. Then he leaned forward and pressed a switch on the back of the screen, bringing it to life. When he tapped the computer keyboard, a series of names and commands appeared then vanished from the screen in rapid succession.

When the word 'Maternox' appeared, Monty looked closely. It was followed by three names: Sarah Johnson. Zeenat Patel. Roberta McDonald. Beside each was the date of death, followed by the name of the certifying doctor. There was nothing else.

Wentworth cleared the screen and typed in a search request. A list! files appeared after a few moments. One was marked 'New Cases'.

He glanced at Monty, then typed in a command to open the file. They both read the screen.

Mrs Caroline Kingsley. b. 14.7.67. 215 Roland Gardens, London SW7. Tel. 071–244–9359.

8 months pregnant. Prescribed Maternox in June 1993, for infertility treatment by family doctor. Dr Paul Corbin, 46 Redcliffe Road, SW10. (Info supplied by husband, Charles, to ZW 12.11.94) Whole-body rash and viral symptoms consistent with previous cases. Admitted Intensive Care University College Hospital 10th Nov. Under consultant obstetrician Mr Gordon Benchley.

Monty felt a knot tighten in her stomach. *Kingsley, C (Mrs)* was the name Conor Molloy had shown her on his computer that morning. 'The name tallies,' she said.

'Tallies?'

'With some information I've come across.'

'Perhaps we should find out how she is?'

Monty nodded.

The newspaperman picked up the telephone on Zandra's desk and called Directory Enquiries. 'University College Hospital, London, please,' he said. A moment later he rang the number he'd been given and asked for Intensive Care. Monty watched him in silence as he went on. 'Ah, good afternoon. My niece, Mrs Caroline Kingsley, was admitted last Thursday. I wonder if you could let me know how she is. Whether she's had the baby?'

Monty continued watching. His face tightened expectantly, then slackened. 'I see,' he said finally. 'I had no idea – I – I was away, you see, just returned this morning.' He shot an expressionless glance at Monty. 'Yes, yes, I'm sure they'll be in touch, of course, such a close family. Just one question. The baby? Would you be good enough to tell me – would it have been Cyclops Syndrome by any chance?' He glanced at Monty again. 'No, of course, I quite understand. Mr Bench-ley, consultant obstetrician. Would he be in the hospital now? I see. I see. Yes, her father, of course, I'll telephone her father. My brother-in-law. Thank you so much.'

Wentworth replaced the receiver and turned to Monty. 'Mrs Kingsley died during Caesarean section childbirth this morning. The ward sister can't confirm to me that the baby, which also died, was a Cyclops Syndrome, but she seemed unsurprised by the question. She told me that was a matter for the obstetrician.'

She stared back at him. 'Christ.' Then Monty read the family doctor's name on the screen. 'Dr Paul Corbin. I'm going to see him. Someone's got to know about this. I'll go now and tell him he *has* to believe me.'

'Shall I send a new reporter?'

Monty looked worried. 'No. It's dangerous and too many people are involved already. I'll go myself.'

'Publishing the story is our best weapon, Miss Bannerman, but I need more evidence. Something that my editor can't refuse regardless of any financial pressures put on him. Something that Fleet Street will run with.'

She looked at him, startled. 'Have you tried to publish something already?'

'No, but my editor is aware of the story. Central and Western Plc, the owners of this paper, have had a warning from Bendix Schere. Threats to withdraw advertising – could be very damaging to the group as a whole. Fortunately my editor's got principles; if we can substantiate the story he'll run it.'

Wentworth had pressed his lips together as if he were sucking a toffee, and now he nodded thoughtfully. 'There's a rather unpleasant character in charge of Security at Bendix who's been creating waves. A Major Gunn.' He smiled. 'I have a contact, an old friend at GCHQ, who's provided me with some information on him regarding his divorce. I could make his life a little uncomfortable, but it's not perhaps the best tactic. You're still prepared to help, in spite of all that's happened?'

'Even more so than before,' Monty said determinedly.

He rotated his teacup in the saucer. 'Tell me something. When you were questioned by the police, did you mention anything I or Zandra had told you – or any of your suspicions?'

'No, I didn't. Nothing.'

He looked relieved. 'How many people know of your interest in this? Does anyone in the company?'

The concern in his voice was deepening her own anxiety. 'No one – just one colleague – and he really approached me.'

He put an arm on her shoulder and guided her out into the corridor. They stopped beside a notice board and he stared gravely at her.

'Bendix Schere is a ruthless company, Miss Bannerman.' He drew a deep breath before underlining this. 'Please be careful.'

'You too,' she said. Her mouth felt dry.

He shook his head. 'My life has been over for a long time. Yours is only beginning.'

She turned her head from him, wishing she was as brave as she was pretending.

50

Brighton, England. Saturday, 19 November, 1994
The saloon bar of the pub was crowded, but Conor and Charley Rowley had found an empty snug tucked away at the rear. They'd just spent the morning at Michael Norman Antiques, so that Conor could kit his flat out, but he'd been too dazzled by the emporium's many treasures to make any choices and had pleaded thirst.

Rowley slurped the head on his pint of Flowers. Conor poured out his Budweiser. 'Charley. The Director of Medical Information – Linda Farmer – do you know her?'

'Met her a couple of times.'

'What's she like?'

Rowley slurped some more beer. 'Ball-crusher.'

'But is she pro Bendix Schere? Like totally loyal, do you think?'

Rowley gave him a sideways look. 'Is the Pope a Catholic?'

Conor grinned, pulled out a pack of Marlboros and offered him one.

Rowley leaned forward to get a light from Conor's Zippo. 'Why do you ask?'

Conor lit his own cigarette and composed his reply carefully. Although he now considered Rowley a friend, and knew that he was scornful of Bendix Schere's petty regulations, he didn't really know how far that scorn went. 'Because it seems there are two kinds of people in Bendix Schere: those who are brainwashed into the company ethos, and those who have an open mind.'

'Dr Farmer is right up there with the brainwashers and the brainwashed,' Rowley said, and took a long draught of beer. 'You just have to accept that ninety-nine per cent of the company are robots, and get on with it. Doesn't bother me.'

Conor finished his cigarette, deep in thought, whilst Rowley went to the bar to collect their food order. When he returned, Conor asked him: 'Would it bother you if the company was doing something illegal?'

Rowley dug his fork into his dish of bolognese and began to eat ravenously. 'Such as?'

Conor shrugged. 'Altering the design of a drug without going through any clinical trials procedures.'

'Do you mean *unethical* or *illegal*?' Rowley asked Conor through a mouthful of food, his face as rubbery and shapeless as the pasta he was shovelling into it.

'Both, I guess.'

'Well, the whole pharmaceutical industry takes short cuts at times. But in principle it would bother me, yup. Why?' He raised an eyebrow sharply.

Conor speared a strip of onion in his tuna salad and chewed it. 'How much do you know about internal security at the company?' he asked, ignoring Rowley's own question.

Rowley chewed another mouthful of pasta. 'Fucking paranoid outfit. No one outside the Main Board could really tell you more. There are all kinds of rumours – wouldn't surprise me if they have more eavesdropping devices than GCHQ. There's even talk about a secret underground floor.'

'You're kidding?'

'Beneath the health hydro in the basement. Meant to be filled with hundreds of dwarves listening in with headphones.'

Conor looked at him in shock, then saw the grin spread across his face. 'You're pulling my leg, right?'

Rowley winked.

Conor asked him, 'Do you know anyone down at the Reading plant – one of your *one per cent* of Bendix Schere employees who aren't robots? Someone you could trust?' Conor watched Rowley's face carefully for any signs of shiftiness that might indicate that he would report him for disloyalty, but Rowley looked totally open, if a little baffled.

'What do you need?'

Conor told him about the three pregnant women who had died, and that he wanted to obtain samples of the Maternox capsules they'd taken and a template of the original specification. But he told him nothing of the possible connection with the death of Jake Seals, nor about Zandra Wollerton or Walter Hoggin. Finally he gave him the suspect batch number.

'Jeez, that's some scenario you've got there . . .'

'I don't want anyone to know –' Conor hesitated, not wanting to tell his friend too much, not wanting to put him in any danger either.

Rowley answered Conor. 'Look, man, I can get you what you want – no problem. But where's this all going next?'

Conor stared at him; there was something very decent about the guy and he suddenly did not feel able to hide the truth from him. 'Charley – I have to warn you of something.'

'I'm already there. You're going to steal the formula and run off with it, right?'

Conor stood up and peered through the snug doorway, but the only people in earshot were four elderly seated gents. He sat down again. 'Look, I think you ought to know – the last two people who tried to get this information are both dead.'

Rowley's eyes widened in mock shock. 'Come again?'

Conor shrugged, made a snap decision, and told Rowley the entire story. When he had finished, Rowley looked shell-shocked.

'Conor, I agree it all sounds seriously weird; but you've just got to be wrong. Bendix Schere is a fucking strange company, I admit – but in my experience it's no different from any of the other pharmaceutical giants. They're all ruthless, and bend the rules when they can. That's the way of the world when there are megabucks at stake.' He drew hard on his cigarette, then blew a long jet of smoke down at the table. 'But as for killing people, no way. No fucking way.'

51

London. Monday 21 November, 1994

The strong wind that had turned into a gale for most of the weekend was still blowing as Monty arrived back in London. She had tried phoning Dr Paul Corbin, the fourth Maternox victim's doctor, after she had left the *Gazette* on Friday afternoon, but he had already gone for the weekend. The woman who answered had not sounded at all friendly or helpful.

After a brief telephone conversation with Conor Molloy on Friday night, Monty had again debated whether she should tell Anna Sterling her fears about Maternox. But it was still only four cases out of hundreds of thousands of pregnancies. And apart from worrying about it, what could her friend actually do? Would a Cyclops Syndrome baby show up on an ultrasound scan? Monty did not think so; surely if it did, the other women would have known and presumably had their pregnancies terminated?

On Saturday she had gone to their old lab and searched for her father's lost file, but without success. On a whim, she had rented the film *Silkwood* from the video shop in Cookham, her nearest town. She had seen it before, a long time back; it was about a woman taking on the might of the American nuclear power industry and being killed for her troubles. Monty had thought she might be able to learn something from it, but all it did was spook her and give her bad dreams.

Now, she parked in a tree-lined side street off the King's Road, then walked, snugly parcelled in her Burberry, back towards the thundering traffic of Redcliffe Road, glad of some fresh air to wake her up after the grind into London through the Monday rush hour.

A clutch of leaves helicoptered in front of her, then a piece of grit stung her eye. She stopped to dab it with her handkerchief. From some scaffolding across the road she heard a clinking of metal, then saw a heavy block and tackle strike the surface beneath the scaffold, making a small crater and spraying out shards of broken tarmac. A car braked hard and swerved.

Christ, she thought, startled, and looked up angrily. If that car had been a few moments earlier it would have been hit. Several hard-hatted faces appeared over the top of the scaffold, looking down. The top of a tower crane hovered behind them. Another workman on the ground was shouting back and gesticulating wildly at something up above. Her eyes followed the direction in which he was pointing but could not see what he meant.

Monty carried on walking, past the once-elegant Georgian terraced houses, counting off the addresses. 52. 50. 48.

Number 46 was like all the others, its white paint dull and faded beneath layers of exhaust grime. She walked up the steps and stared at the list of doctors' names on the bell plate, above which was a polished brass sign: 'Ring and Enter.'

Dr T. Paul Corbin was the third name down. She pressed the heavy, old-fashioned bell, then pushed open the door and stepped into a carpeted hall. There was a welcome warmth as the door swung shut behind her on the wind.

'I'll tell the doctor,' a receptionist was saying in the dictatorial voice Monty recognized from Friday. 'I'm sure he'll call you as soon as he has a moment. I'm afraid he's having rather a busy start to the day.' When she'd hung up she looked at Monty. 'May I help you?'

'Yes – I need to have a very urgent word with Dr Corbin.'

'Are you registered with him?'

'No – I'm not a patient.'

'He's not taking on any new patients, I'm afraid.'

'It's – not me – I mean – it's not actually about myself that I need, er, to see him.' Monty kicked herself for not having better prepared what she was going to say. 'But it really is very important.'

The receptionist looked at her unsympathetically. 'Does Dr Corbin know who you are, Miss – er – Mrs –?' She was fishing for a name.

'Bannerman,' Monty said. In some circles the Bannerman name provided an instant entree, but here it registered a total blank. 'No, he doesn't know me. I actually need to speak to him about one of his patients.'

Just then the door beside Monty opened and an elegant Chinese woman emerged. 'Thank you very much, Doctor,' she was saying.

The doctor followed her down the corridor, held the front door for her, then walked back towards them. He was in his mid-fifties, with a solid but fit-looking physique, and his suave persona exuded an aura of the very finest bedside manners that money could buy.

Brushing Monty aside with a thin smile of acknowledgement, he looked directly at his secretary. 'How many appointments have I got this morning? I really need to go and see Mrs Enright as soon as possible.'

'You have two waiting and another eight booked in.'

'Do you think you could hold them for half an hour if I went now? You could explain it's an emergency.'

'Yes, of course, Doctor.'

The doctor glanced at Monty then back at his secretary as if seeking an explanation for her presence. But the secretary ventured nothing and he turned away.

'Dr Corbin?' Monty said.

He returned and looked at her pleasantly but quizzically. 'Yes?'

'I'm sorry, the doctor is far too busy –' The secretary tried to interrupt.

'I need to speak to you very urgently,' Monty said. 'Just a couple of minutes?'

'I'm afraid I don't have any time at the moment. Can you tell me what it's about?' He smelled lightly of talc and his breath carried a hint of peppermint.

'Yes – Caroline Kingsley.'

His demeanour altered noticeably.

'There's something about her death that you ought to know.'

His expression darkened. 'I have a very sick patient waiting for me. Who are you? The young lady who rang last week from the press?'

'Press?' Monty said, surprised. 'Zandra Wollerton?' Then immediately she wished she had kept quiet. 'Look, if you could just give me a few minutes I'll explain. I can wait until you come back.'

'I have nothing to say at all,' the doctor replied curtly, turned and went back into his surgery.

Ignoring an angry remark from the secretary, Monty followed him in. 'Look, Doctor, please listen to me. I believe that Caroline Kingsley was taking Maternox for infertility problems. I work for Bendix Schere, and there's something you ought to know about Maternox –'

The doctor turned abruptly and rounded on her. 'Let me

278

tell you something, young lady. Allow me to spell it out for you very clearly. Miss Wollerton contacted me some time ago and informed me that there'd been three Cyclops Syndrome birth deformities in the past two months, following symptoms in the pregnant women similar to those experienced by my patient.

'I contacted the Chief Medical Officer at Bendix Schere, a Dr Linda Farmer, to ask if they had any information on this. The next thing that happened was a man turned up here on Friday afternoon with fifty thousand pounds in used bank notes which he offered me on condition I did not ask any more questions. You can tell your damned company that I am not for sale at any price. Now get out of my surgery.'

'Dr Corbin,' Monty said. 'Please believe me, we're on the same side.'

The doctor pulled on a herringbone coat. He turned back to face Monty for a brief moment. 'That is exactly what your colleague said on Friday. I intend speaking to the Coroner's officer this afternoon, and the Committee for Safety of Medicines, and telling them exactly what has happened. Including the bribe that was made to me. Is that clear?' Then he strode out.

Monty followed him into the street. 'Dr Corbin, I'm really pleased to hear you're doing that! Please, listen to me. I'm not a reporter. My father is Dr Richard Bannerman, the scientist. I think there's something *very* wrong with Maternox – let me come along with you in your car and tell you about it –'

He stood at the edge of the kerb, completely ignoring her, waiting for a gap in the traffic, then dashed across in front of a taxi, which braked and hooted. Caught off guard by his recklessness, Monty missed the chance and had to wait for another gap. A terrific gust of wind screamed down the road, almost unbalancing her.

The doctor was hurrying down the pavement on the far side. He stepped out into the road to skirt along the outside of the scaffolding, rather than through the covered walkway. Monty sprinted across and ran after him, gaining rapidly. There was another ripping gust, then high above her she heard a shout, followed by a metallic chime that sounded like a bell. Something hurtled past her face, so close she could feel the air it disturbed, and she flinched, startled, and stopped. Then it hurtled past in the opposite direction. A massive steel hawser, swinging drunkenly, she realized, looking upwards in shock.

There were more chimes in rapid succession, loud, discordant. Something was moving at the top of the scaffolding, swaying. Then to her horror she saw an entire section of gantry disintegrate. Something dark tumbled down and with a terrific dull thud embedded itself, like a meteorite, right into the tarmac only yards from her. It appeared to be part of a pulley.

She looked up again, deeply afraid, suddenly. Something else was plunging downwards now, a short distance in front of her, rotating like a boomerang. An enormous steel hook.

'Dr Corbin!' she yelled at the top of her voice.

It hurtled straight down towards him. But before he even had time to react to her voice the hook struck the top of his head, the force spinning him round to face her.

Her mouth was ripped open by the horror of what she saw: as if in some grotesque conjuring trick the flat shaft of the hook, with a broken shackle attached, had wedged in the top of the doctor's cranium, and the curved point protruded a good eight inches out from his cheek, just below his left eye.

For a brief moment he looked perfectly all right, just a little taken unawares, as if this kind of thing happened to him all the time. Then blood bubbled simultaneously out of his mouth and nostrils. Monty gagged at the sight. He was staring straight at her, his eyes wide open as if he had decided that he would listen to her after all.

All of a sudden his legs buckled and he sank to his knees, his body crumpling forward like a marionette. The point of the hook struck the pavement with a clang, jerking his head back sharply, so he was still looking directly at her, but with eyes that were now sightless. The blood gouted from his mouth, and orange gunge began to ooze out from the top of his skull around the busted shackle attached to the hook. Then he rocked sideways in another ferocious gust.

Monty turned away, clutching the top of a garden wall for support, and gagged again, fighting hard not to throw up on the pavement.

52

People had gathered around Dr Corbin, blocking him from Monty's view. Somewhere close, a woman was screaming hysterically. In the distance she could hear the Doppler wail of a siren.

'I saw it happen,' a man said shakily.

'They've been dropping things all the time – load of cowboys,' a woman announced angrily. 'I nearly got hit by a brick a couple of weeks ago.'

'Don't know what they were playing at with that scaffolding – bloody great metal shackle took a chunk out of the road only half an hour ago.'

'Should have walked under the cover – why did he go round the outside?'

'Move away!' someone shouted urgently from above.

A blue light strobed through the faces. A white car with fluorescent stripes had pulled up and two policemen were getting out. The woman's hysterical screaming continued.

'Are you all right?' a voice said, its owner halting momentarily.

Monty stared blankly at a man in a sheepskin coat, and it took a moment before she realized he was talking to her. The siren was coming closer. Everything else seemed to have gone very quiet. Silent. The whole of London had fallen silent. She touched the brick wall gingerly, for support, and backed a few paces away; then a few more paces, her brain beginning to start working again.

She looked up at the scaffolding; a whole section of the top superstructure was swaying precariously. Nervously she backed even further off and looked around, watched the crowd. Something, bile or saliva, was dribbling down her chin. Fumbling in her handbag, she pulled out a tissue and wiped it.

A voice inside her head was screaming at her to get away. There were enough witnesses already, they didn't need her. *Get away, keep your name and face out of it*, she thought, and backed off a few more steps. The wail of the siren was closer, its pitch altering suddenly to a banshee howl, like a sack of stones being swirled in the air.

She turned and walked quickly on, and clumsily barged into a woman. 'Sorry,' she murmured, and carried on up the street, unfocusing, everything a blur, her brain racing now.

Get away!

She reached the Old Brompton Road and turned the corner, walking past a car showroom then a café, and saw a phone booth ahead. She went in and closed the door behind her, somewhat deadening the roar of the traffic. She took from her handbag the notes she had scrawled at the *Thames Valley Gazette*, and found the number she wanted. She struggled with fingers that were trembling so much she kept dropping the coins, then finally succeeded and pressed the right numbers.

'Morgan Roth Delamere, good afternoon,' announced a very pukka female receptionist.

Monty vaguely recognized the name of the firm as something in merchant banking. 'Could I please speak to Charles Kingsley?' she asked.

'I'm sorry, Mr Kingsley's not in today.'

Monty raised her voice to be heard above the roar of a passing bus. 'Do you know where I could get hold of him – it's very urgent.'

'I'll put you through to his secretary.'

Monty thanked her and waited, then a pleasant woman came on the line. 'I'm afraid Mr Kingsley has suffered a bereavement, and I don't know when he'll be in next.'

'I need to speak to him very urgently – it's in connection with his wife's death. Do you know where I might be able to get hold of him?'

Her tone became cooler. 'Are you from the press?'

'No, I'm not.'

'All I can suggest is that you leave your name and number, and I'll pass them on when he rings in.'

'It's OK,' Monty said. 'I have his home number, I'll try that.'

She thanked the secretary and pressed a new series of

numbers. The phone was answered on the fourth ring by a male voice faintly muffled by crackle.

'Hello. You've reached the London residence of Charles and Caroline Kingsley. We're sorry not to be able to take your call in person right now, but if you leave your name and number and a short message after the beep, we'll get back to you. Goodbye!'

As she heard the beep Monty hesitated, debating. She decided just to leave her name and her home number and say nothing further. But just as she started to speak, she was interrupted by a voice that came on the line.

'Yersss, hello?'

It sounded for an instant like a tape being played at the wrong speed. Then she realized it was the same male voice that had left the message on the machine.

'Charles Kingsley?'

'Yes?'

'I – I'm very sorry to hear about your wife's death. I need to talk to you urgently – I think there might be a medical cover-up going on. Do you think I could come round?'

There was a pause. 'No, I'm sorry, no.' His voice sounded slow and distant. 'I can't see anyone. Not at the moment. Thank you for calling.'

The phone went dead.

'Shit!' Monty hung up, more angry at the man, for an instant, than sorry for him. Her hands were still shaking so much from the shock of what she had just witnessed that she knocked the receiver from the hook; it fell, cracked against the wall and swung from the end of its cord. She replaced it, checked the address on the sheet of paper again, then left the booth and hailed a taxi.

The Roland Gardens address was a Victorian redbrick mansion block off Old Brompton Road in the indeterminate border between South Kensington and Earl's Court, where some streets were bedsitter or hooker country and some were still gentrified. Roland Gardens had the distinct, if faded, air of the latter.

Monty pushed the bell beside the name 'Kingsley', and waited, eyeing the grill of the speaker. There was no response.

She tried a second time and waited for a full minute, but again there was nothing. Except that a tall, elderly woman, all lipstick and rouge, with a cigarette in her hand and a silk scarf around her neck, opened the door from the inside and stepped into the porch in a cloud of scent. Monty held the door for her and the woman thanked her regally, then picked her way carefully down the steps before stopping, looking sharply at her and saying incongruously: 'Not like South Africa, dear.'

'South Africa?' Monty replied, puzzled by the remark, wondering if she had heard correctly.

'Disraeli buggered it all up, of course. He was the man who ruined the postal system. Never been able to get a letter delivered on time since he died.'

'No?'

'One of the problems with islands, dear. Too much sea; too much bloody sea.' Then, shaking her head the old bat wandered off.

Monty went into an old-fashioned hall with a chequered floor and a lift in a brass cage. Somewhere above her she could hear the sound of hoovering. Ordinarily the old girl's dottiness might have made her smile, but today it made her feel uncomfortable, just one more symptom of a world completely out of kilter.

She took the lift to the third floor, pulling the heavy door open with some difficulty when she got there, and stepped out into a corridor of aged grandeur, well in keeping with the downstairs hall. There was a red carpet, carved surrounds to each door, and Art Deco sconces along the walls – several of them with their light bulbs blown.

She stopped outside number 215 and stared, in surprise, at the gaping strip that was torn from the jamb. The thick oak door was slightly ajar, and as she looked closer she saw the reason why: it had been jemmied open, and the solid Banham lock was skewed in its mortise.

She tensed, her nerves sparking as if they were shorting out. Had it just happened? Was the intruder still inside? No, surely not in the middle of the morning. She'd spoken to the occupant only five minutes or so ago, ten at the maximum. It must have happened earlier. Somewhere further down the corridor in another flat she could hear the strains of a violin; its mournful sound made her feel even more uneasy.

Bracing herself for the unexpected, she rang the bell, and rang again when there was no sign of life. After giving it a full minute, she pushed the door further open, listening hard.

Complete silence greeted her. The entrance hall was dark and surprisingly high-ceilinged. Outdoor clobber of umbrellas and Wellington boots adorned an old mahogany coat stand, and a long passageway lined with doorways stretched ahead of her.

She took a breath, then called out tentatively: 'Hello?'

She waited for a response, but heard nothing. Then she walked slowly forward, glancing back at the entrance every few moments, and stopped by the first open door – through which was a good-sized bathroom.

The cupboard doors hung open, their assorted contents scattered on the floor. Monty turned her head sharply, checking the corridor in both directions, instantly vulnerable.

Had the police been? Were they on their way? Fighting an urge to turn and run, she went on to peer through the next door into what looked like a master bedroom. It, too, had been ransacked, with almost every square inch of floor covered in clothing. This had not happened since she'd spoken to Charles Kingsley, she reasoned. Someone had spent quite a while in here.

An impression of new paint came from the next open door; it was a small child's bedroom, with a spotless cot. Monty felt a lump in her throat as she looked at the wallpaper depicting nursery rhymes, at the mobile of coloured shapes above the cot, the pretty furniture, the unused carpet, and backed out. Whoever had turned the place over had not bothered with this room.

There was a grander door, slightly ajar, at the end of the passage. She stopped outside it, held her breath, then she pushed it open very slowly, braced for it to hurtle back in her face, or for a confrontation. But nothing happened.

Still holding her breath, her eyes darting wildly, she went through into a large drawing room, handsomely furnished with antiques, and in semi-darkness due to the curtains being drawn. She could see enough to pick out the drawers of a walnut bureau that lay upside down on the floor, their contents spilled around them. The rest of this room seemed untouched. Then she heard a sharp creak behind her. She turned, her skin crawling, and stood absolutely motionless.

The image of Dr Corbin with the metal shank embedded in his skull came back to her even more vividly than when she had actually seen it happen, and the horror squeezed her stomach like a sponge.

Christ, if I had tried harder to make him listen, she thought. *If I hadn't let him leave his practice. If I had delayed him by just one more second, the hook would have missed him.*

She caught sight of her face reflected in the gilded mirror above a chiffonier and was startled by how pale she looked. Like a ghost, she thought. Then a shadow right behind her, darker than all the others in the room, suddenly moved.

She spun round, a silent scream of terror yammering in her throat, her brain seized up with fear. The shadow was in a chair, a deep, low armchair. But there was nothing threatening in the movement, she realized, after a long moment.

An arm raised itself, slowly, mechanically; there was a brief scrabbling sound, then a click and a weak pool of light from a table lamp that made her blink. She could see a haggard, unshaven face beneath unbrushed hair, staring at her the way a political prisoner long beaten into submission might watch a jailer bringing food.

'I'm – sorry – I did ring – I –' Her apology trailed as she stared at the man in pity now, rather than shock. He was about forty, squarely built, wearing a thick crew-neck sweater, corduroy trousers and moccasins. Black rings as deep as bore holes encircled his bloodshot eyes.

'Ch – Charles Kingsley?' she asked.

'Over the weekend,' he said quietly and disjointedly, slurring some of the words. 'Thrr police said they do it often. They know when there's a bereavement that people some-times go away. I don't know what they've taken; it doesn't matter; I don't care what the hell they've taken.'

A colour wedding photograph in a silver frame shared the

small table beside him with the lamp. It was a happy family group, the men in top hats and tails, the women wearing hats and finery. Everyone was laughing. In the centre were the bride and groom, Caroline and a much younger Charles Kingsley, she presumed. The bride was pretty in a classic English gentry way, her brown hair pinned up in ringlets beneath her wedding veil. He was very much a male equivalent.

'I'm sorry to intrude,' she said. 'But there's something I need to ask. Your wife was taking medication for infertility prior to becoming pregnant, wasn't she?'

He stared back at her in silence for a long while, before speaking again. He did not smell of alcohol and Monty wondered if he was on a heavy dose of sedatives. 'Caroline, she didn't – you see – didn't want – people to know.' He lapsed into silence again. Monty was about to prompt him when he continued. 'She was very shy. She hid the pills. She thought even I didn't know.' He looked up and gave her a helpless, childlike smile.

Monty responded in kind. 'She hid them from you? In a good place?'

He lowered his head and was quiet again. He seemed to be having difficulty holding his eyes open. 'In a spice jar. I don't cook, you see. She thought I wouldn't ever find them.'

'Are they still there now?'

But Charles Kingsley's eyes had closed completely and his breathing became deeper. This time he had gone to sleep.

Monty tiptoed quietly back into the passage. She tried one door, which opened into a broom closet. The next one opened into a large, modern kitchen which had been untouched by the intruder.

She glanced hurriedly around the work surfaces, then she spotted a row of stone spice jars with wooden tops. *Ginger, Garlic, Turmeric, Bay leaves, Chives, Oregano, Rock salt, Cumin, Basil.*

The chances of any of the Maternox still being there were remote, she thought. If Caroline Kingsley had not wanted even her husband to know that she was taking the pills, she was scarcely likely to have kept them throughout the full term of her pregnancy. And yet, Monty knew, she herself had a habit of keeping pills for years after she had finished needing them.

She began to work through the jars, opening the tops of each in turn and rummaging inside. It was as her fingers rummaged deep among the bay leaves that they struck something hard and round.

It was a white plastic vial.

She lifted it out, spilling a few leaves in the process, and shook it. There was a light rattle. The prescription label around it was headed: 'PriceSave DrugSmart, 297 Earl's Court Road.' In smaller wording beneath was printed, 'Keep out of reach of children.' Then: '10ml Maternox, two capsules four times daily with food. MS CAROLINE KINGSLEY, 11 JAN 94.'

On the reverse side of the vial was the product licence number, followed by the batch number. 'BS-M-6575–1881-UKMR.'

She twisted and prised off the childproof lid, and saw six blue and green capsules remaining in the bottom. She replaced the lid with trembling fingers, slipped the vial into her handbag and hurried, furtively, out of the mansion flat.

53

'Mr Molloy, I apologize for disturbing you from your duties this morning, but I'd like to have a word about this report you've produced.' Dr Vincent Crowe tapped the thick wodge of papers on his japanned black desk.

'Yes, sir – about the prior art?'

'Precisely,' Crowe said with a smile as lean as his face. He sat very upright, checked the pink silk handkerchief that bloomed from his breast pocket, and looked expectantly at Conor. 'I was most interested to find out just how much material there is.'

'I've included everything published by Dr Bannerman during the past decade.'

'On what? The whole range of his work?'

'No – this is just on the psoriasis genes. There's about twenty roomfuls of published material on the genetics research he's been doing on other diseases.'

The Chief Executive's lips pressed so tightly together they melded into one thin crimson line. In the chiaroscuro of the overhead spotlight, Conor could almost see the contours of his superior's skull and the labyrinth of veins beneath his alabaster skin.

'You understand the importance of the acquisition of Bannerman Genetics Research Laboratories to this company, Mr Molloy?'

'I think so, sir.'

'The patents of four of the six largest revenue earners for Bendix Schere expire within the next five years. We need to replace them with a new generation of international best-selling drugs that will see us through into the twenty-first century. Psoriatak could be one. One in ten people are affected by psoriasis at some time during their lives. The earnings potential for a drug that will eliminate, through gene therapy, the recurrence of a broad band of psoriasis complaints is, you will agree, very substantial.'

'It won't impress too many dermatologists,' Conor said with a smile that withered rapidly under Crowe's response of stony silence.

'The invention of aspirin and penicillin didn't put too many doctors out of business, Mr Molloy.'

'No,' Conor said, realizing that this was someone devoid of humour, and making a mental note never to attempt a joke with him again.

Crowe's eyes slithered over the piles of papers once more, then returned to Conor. 'I imagine your opinion is that there's far too much published material for us to have any chance of obtaining a US patent for Psoriatak?'

'Well, there's too much published material for us to obtain patents in *any* country. We'd have no chance in the United Kingdom, or the European Patent Office. In my opinion it won't fly.'

Crowe nodded very slowly, his cold grey eyes maintaining piercing contact with Conor's. 'So we have two possible solutions. Either we abandon Psoriatak and flush a substantial part of the purchase price we paid for Bannerman down the lavatory. Or –' His lips formed a tight circle. 'We have to be a little more creative.'

'How do you mean, *creative*, sir?'

Crowe breathed in through his nostrils, weighing Conor up astutely. Then he tapped the wodge of papers. 'By being a little selective with some of this.'

Conor tried to veil his disbelief. 'You mean by "losing" some of it?'

Crowe pressed his fingers tightly together, so that the nails were pointing upwards, and studied Conor over the top of them. 'We are not having this conversation – you understand?'

'You want me to get rid of some published papers?'

'Precisely.'

'But – that would be –'

'Yes?'

'Very unethical. And illegal.'

'You know your way around the United States Patent Office, do you not, Mr Molloy?'

'That's one of my fields of expertise, yes, sir.'

'And you presumably have friends there?'

Conor shook his head. 'I don't know anyone there who is – bendable – if that's what you're suggesting. People seem to change when they start working there. Everyone I know says the same; you can be best buddies with someone at college – but the moment they start working at the Patent Office, that's it; friendship over.'

Crowe ignored this reply. 'The United States patent system works, like the British one, very much on trust, I believe. The US patent examiner will accept what you tell him, am I not correct?'

'He will accept what I tell him, because he knows that as a lawyer, I face being struck off if I'm discovered lying.'

'But unless someone complains and goes to very great lengths, there's no reason why you should ever be found out. Even then, the US examiner would be loath to accept any such complaint, because it would show *he* had been inefficient – again, am I not correct.'

Conor found it hard to believe his own ears – particularly considering Crowe's calibre and position. 'Dr Crowe – may I remind you these are all *published* papers. They've appeared in respected peer review journals – like *Nature* etc., as well as all the usual national newspapers and books. We could shred all *this* stuff, but what about the records, not to mention the thousands – millions, sometimes – of copies that exist in print?'

Crowe remained calm. 'That is not a problem. Once we have the patent, we are in a position of strength. Competitors might try to put out a similar product but they'd face taking us on every inch of the way. They'd have to *find* these published articles, co-ordinate them – and still they'd have no certainty of winning any action.'

He studied Conor. 'It goes without saying that what you are being asked to do is beyond the obligations of your employment, Mr Molloy. If it makes you feel uneasy we could of course relieve you of your duties and assign you to something less demanding.' He raised his eyebrows.

Conor thought quickly. It was vital that he kept his nose clean with the company right now, and not give them any shred of suspicion about his loyalties. He smiled back at the Chief Executive. 'Dr Crowe, I have no worries; my loyalty is to Bendix Schere and I'll do whatever I am asked without question.'

Crowe's face visibly relaxed. 'Good.'

'The problem is going to be Dr Bannerman,' Conor went on. 'He has to sign the declaration for the patent examiner, and my experience of him is that he's kind of flaky – I don't know how we could deliver his signature.'

'That won't be a problem, either. The document he signs will state "Published papers as per attached".' Crowe gave him a knowing look. 'He won't see what you actually submit, will he?'

Conor hesitated. 'I guess there's no reason . . .'

Crowe smiled and stood up. 'I'm glad we understand each other, Mr Molloy. You have a future with Bendix Schere. An excellent future.'

54

Monty walked through the foyer shortly after eleven, feeling nervous about the vial of pills in her handbag, as if she were carrying contraband which the security turnstile might somehow be capable of detecting.

All the lifts were in use and the indicators showed that the one nearest the Directors' express would be the next to arrive. As she waited, she heard a faint whoosh and rumble from behind the Directors' beaten copper door, but instead of stopping the lift carried straight on down. Then, a few moments later, to her slight surprise, there was a second whoosh, followed by a ping, and the Directors' door slid open.

A tall, distinguished-looking man with dark wavy hair streaked silver at the temples, black rimmed glasses, and wearing a camel cashmere coat stepped out and walked swiftly past her.

There was another ping and now the door in front of her slid open. She stepped into the lift, puzzled by the sound she had heard a few moments earlier. She had definitely heard the Directors' lift descend below this floor; surely there wasn't enough time for it to have stopped in the basement health hydro and come back up again?

She was still puzzling over it as she entered her office, then made an effort to switch her mind to the tasks she had to get done today.

A light was flashing on her phone, indicating she had a voice comm message waiting. She put the phone on loudspeaker, pressed the 'Play' button, and took off her coat.

'Hi, Miss Bannerman, this is Conor Molloy. I'm afraid I have to blow out lunch; could you give me a call, please?'

The words left her feeling stranded. All weekend she had been looking forward to seeing him; originally to tell him the news about Caroline Kingsley's death, but now, as well, to show him the Maternox capsules she had obtained. And she wanted just to see him anyway; he seemed like the only rock in her life.

She sat down, biting her lower lip in disappointment, and dialled Conor Molloy's extension. He answered immediately.

'Hi, how are you?' he asked. 'How was your weekend?'

'OK, it was fine. How about you?'

'You sound terrible – what's up?'

'Nothing, I'm – I'm OK – I've had a bad morning.'

'Listen, I'm sorry, I have to rework a report for Dr Crowe which he wants this afternoon. I'm going to have to work through. Are you free later – for a drink or a meal or something this evening, instead?'

The knowledge that he was still on to meet today perked her up again. 'I have to go to our old lab in Berkshire at half four – I'm meeting a man who wants to buy up all our office equipment down there. I could come back up after,' she said.

'No, you don't need to do that. I'll come and meet you somewhere. Berkshire, you said? What's that, about an hour's drive?'

'Yes – depends on the traffic. An hour and a half in the rush hour, forty-five minutes outside it. When will you be through today?'

'I don't know – around seven maybe, with luck.'

'Can I invite you down to my house? I'll cook you something.'

'Home cooking?' He sounded genuinely delighted. 'You know, that's something I've really been missing!'

'You're on!' she said, really pleased at the prospect of seeing him, and of having some company that evening. And she was desperate to tell him her news but dared not over the phone. Instead she gave him directions.

Feeling a lot better, she then went down the corridor in search of her father and found him sitting at his desk in his shirtsleeves. In just the few weeks that he had been at Bendix Schere his large office was already as untidy as the cramped one he used to share with her.

'Hi, darling,' he said, looking up over the top of his bifocal glasses. 'Where've you been? I tried to find you earlier.'

'I – er – had to go to the dentist,' she lied.

'Problems?'

'Just a filling.'

He frowned. 'I've got some more stuff missing, can't find any of my files on the diabetes genes – all the research material we shelved last year when we found the Wellcome Foundation were ahead of the game.' He gestured in despair. 'Can you think what we did with it all?'

She looked round at the chaos. 'Do you leave all this stuff out at night?'

'Of course.'

'You know that's against company rules?'

He grinned at her. '*Nil illegitimi carborundum!*'

'What does that mean?'

'It was an unofficial US army motto in the Second World War. Means, *Don't let the bastards get you down!*'

'I don't think anyone could ever get you down, Daddy.' She paused. 'What do you need the diabetes files for?'

'I've been asked by *American Scientist* magazine for some information on my research – they're doing a feature on progress in identifying the diabetes genes, to tie in with the Washington Symposium.'

Monty looked at him warily. 'Have you cleared this with Dr Crowe?'

'Bugger Dr Crowe.'

She took a breath and spoke wearily. 'Daddy, you've signed an agreement saying you won't talk to the press without the written consent of Dr Crowe.'

'Well, I can't find the material anyway,' he said petulantly.

'Probably just as well.'

He drummed his desk with his fingers. 'I think you're missing my point, darling,' he said. 'The files have vanished – they didn't just walk off by themselves.'

'Well, they're not down in Berkshire; I went through everything there with a toothcomb on Saturday. You've probably been looking in the wrong place. I've put all the files for everything that isn't current down in the Stacks.'

He frowned at her again. 'Are you OK, darling? You look as white as a sheet.'

She nodded. 'I – I saw an accident on my way here. Very nasty, it shook me up.'

'Road accident?'

'Yes,' she said, not wanting to tell him anything about Dr Corbin.

'I thought I might take advantage of these palatial premises and go down to the hydro and have a swim and sauna after work. Want to join me? We could have a bite to eat afterwards? Might do you good to relax.'

'I can't, not tonight. I have to be back down at the lab at four thirty – the furniture chap's coming. I have to haggle a deal with him.'

He screwed up his face. 'I don't think we'll get much.'

'But we're allowed to keep whatever we do get – it's in the contract. Every bit helps.'

'Of course.' He rested his chin on his hand and looked thoughtfully at her. 'You're a good girl, darling. But you've been working too hard recently, you need a bit of joy in your life.'

'I'll go down to the Stacks and have a look for the files for you, just in case they've been put in the wrong place,' she said, avoiding the remark.

'You're an angel.'

She took the lift down to the floor below, and went into the massive archive area. On her previous visits she had always found the place rather eerie: it occupied almost an entire floor of the building, its tall, fireproof grey filing cabinets crammed so tightly that any visitors had to sidle through the narrow gullies of shiny linoleum between them.

This sanctum was presided over by a solitary archivist, a humourless female of indeterminate age who wore her greying hair in a drab bun, and pecked away relentlessly on her keyboard. Like a sentinel she watched, but never acknowledged, anyone who came in. Behind her was a row of computer terminals on which the records were held, as well as microfilm and microfiche booths. Although it was as well equipped as a university library, Monty had never seen anyone else using the Stacks.

She seated herself at one of the terminals and keyed in the name of the material she wanted, just to check it hadn't been moved to a different area. The location appeared on the screen: 'Row M. 2307–15.' Then she made her way down the steel corridors, found the correct spot, pulled open the drawer of the cabinet and checked carefully inside. Her father was right, the files were missing.

She went back to the sentinel and asked if anyone had removed them.

'Nothing is permitted to be removed,' the woman said sharply. 'Not without the written permission of the department head. If a document belonging to Dr Bannerman is lodged here, it requires authorization in writing from him before it can be removed.'

'Would you have a record of anything that's been taken out?'

'Of course.'

Monty showed her the file number. The sentinel entered it into her screen and pressed the return key. A moment later Monty noticed a sudden curious reaction on her face.

'There's no record of them being removed,' she said, raising her head but without actually looking Monty in the face.

She was lying. Monty could read the signals in her body language. Could read it in the sudden rapid blinking of the eyes, the way she seemed to stiffen and to be suddenly unsure what to do with her hands.

'Someone probably put them back in the wrong place,' she said huffily. 'People do that all the time; it can take months to find something when that happens.'

Not wanting to antagonize her further, Monty agreed. 'People can be so careless.'

She spent the next three hours in a fruitless search through the Stacks. It was like looking for a needle in a haystack, but the mindless monotony of her task was exactly what she needed right now, still far too shaken to concentrate on anything more demanding.

She was haunted by what had happened to Dr Corbin. The hook dropping at just the wrong moment. Or was it the right moment? She thought back to the earlier incident on her way to the practice, when a falling block and tackle had narrowly missed a car. *Coincidence.* The word stuck in her mind like a tune as she worked.

There were files dating back to the 1880s: on every disease

she had ever heard of; on every organ of the human body; on scientists; on universities; and on research institutes. She rummaged through them until she ran out of time.

Finally she gave up, thanked the archivist courteously and went back to her office to grab her coat, ready to head for Berkshire. Before leaving, she lowered her handbag under her desk and peered inside. The vial of Maternox pills lay inside a tissue. She pushed it further to the bottom, scooping the rest of the contents of her handbag over it.

It was now nearly three o'clock, and she was not sorry to close her office door behind her. But as she stepped out of the lift into the downstairs lobby she was surprised to see the security guard, Winston Smith, on duty.

She went up to his turnstile. 'You're early today – have you changed shifts?'

His eyes closed for a moment and he pressed a finger beneath his nostrils, stifling a sneeze. 'Got to do extra hours – couple of people off sick, Miss Bannerman.' Then he shut his eyes again and stifled another sneeze, hunting in his pocket for a handkerchief.

'Cold still bad?'

'Always bad, Miss.' He pressed the balled handkerchief against his nostrils, his normal forlorn expression returning to his face.

Then he brightened. 'That book you told me 'bout last week. I went to the library and ordered it. Must be popular – got three people waiting 'n front of me.'

'*Darling Buds of May?* I may have a copy at home – I'll have a look for you.' She smiled. Then she lowered her voice. 'Tell me something. Is there another lift here that we can't see – some goods load that goes down into the basement or something? I'm sure I've heard it a couple of times.'

Beneath the peak of Winston's cap, the large, yellowing whites of his eyes rolled warily to the right and left. He said nothing as two sharp suits, who looked as if they were from Marketing, strode by, then he leaned towards Monty and spoke quietly. She smelled tobacco on his breath and smiled inwardly, pleased to know that he wasn't afraid of breaking the rules.

'Ain't no one gets that lift, Miss.' He zippered his mouth with a finger, and Monty could see real fear in his face.

'Why not?' she prodded gently.

He stared her back full in the eyes. 'This building ain't what you think.'

She returned the stare and gave him a nod of encouragement. 'How do you mean?'

He gave her a knowing look and spoke even more quietly. 'I can't say too much. But you might find it interesting to check out the plans of this building some time.'

'Oh?'

'Ever read Jules Verne, Miss?'

'Yes, I used to love him. Very prophetic writer.'

'*Journey to the Centre of the Earth* – that's the one.' He signalled again with his eyes, then added, 'You mind you have a nice afternoon, now.'

'Thank you,' she said, and walked on past him, out towards her car, deep in thought.

55

Monty pulled out of the Sainsbury's car park into the rush-hour jam on the Reading ring road. As the traffic halted, she stared at a massive illuminated billboard depicting a smiling mother in a cream dressing gown, hugging a naked baby. Along the top of the hoarding were the words:

MATERNOX – **TAKING CARE OF THE FUTURE.**'

And at the bottom was the proclamation:

'**Bendix Schere – The World's Most Caring Company.**'

A fat blob of rain exploded on the windscreen. It was followed by more in quick procession as the skies opened, rapidly blurring the ad. She left the wipers off, preferring it that way, and switched on the GLR six o'clock news.

'. . . renewing hopes of a Christmas truce in Bosnia,' said the newscaster. 'Forty-seven pensioners have been injured in a coach crash on the way to a Christmas shopping spree. And a doctor has been killed in a freak accident on a London street.'

She listened to the rest of the bulletin, which brought all the horror of that morning's drama flooding back, but it said nothing new about the death of Dr Corbin, and did not mention the full gruesome details that she had witnessed.

In an effort to switch her mind to something else, she tried to concentrate on her menu for that night. It would take her about half an hour to get home in this traffic, giving her just enough time before Conor Molloy arrived. She was going to give him coq au vin, followed by some brie and grapes. Not knowing what he drank, she had bought a bottle of Australian red wine and one of white.

Rain thudded on the soft roof of the car. She turned the dial on the radio, blipping in and out of several stations, then found some jazz and stayed with it. Louis Armstrong was singing 'We Have All The Time In The World'. But as she listened her mind switched to the strange conversation she'd had with Winston Smith.

This building ain't what you think.
Jules Verne, Journey to the Centre of the Earth . . .
What the hell did he mean?

Normally Monty loved nothing more than to turn off the main road into the silence of the farm track up to her cottage. But this evening, for the first time ever, the isolation and the bitumen blackness of the night felt threatening, and she found herself driving faster than normal along the rutted surface, fearful something was going to jump out of the hedgerow at her.

She slowed as she passed the large barn, looking hard into the cavernous interior, watching the shadows pushed along by her headlights slide over the two tractors, the trailer, the bales of hay, the broken ancient ploughshare.

The beam of the headlamps floodlit her peeling garage as she pulled into her drive. Normally she would have opened the door and driven in, particularly on a wet night; but, like the darkness around her, the garage suddenly looked enclosing and threatening.

She kept the high beam on for some moments after she had

killed the engine, scrutinizing first the house then the shrub-bery of the garden and relieved that, for once, Alice had actually left the lights on in the living room and an upstairs bedroom.

Without bothering to lock the MG, she hurried through the pelting rain into the shelter of the porch. For some reason, the key would not go into the lock. Cursing, she fumbled with it for some moments, then finally, and clumsily, she managed to push it in; but when she tried to turn it, it wouldn't move.

Puzzled, she tried again, harder, but with no success. She slid it out and pushed it back in again, tried to twist it so hard it cut into her gloved fingers, but still it would not turn.

Then she sensed someone standing behind her.

She spun round, fear pulling at the hairs on her body like a magnet. Nothing there; just the darkness and the thudding rain, and the plat . . . plat . . . plat of water dripping from the guttering. Listening hard, trying to tune out the sounds of the rain, she stepped out of the porch and looked at each of the windows, scanning them for any sign of movement. Then she walked across the sodden grass of the tiny front lawn and around the side, past the dustbins, and stopped dead.

An unseen hand twisted her guts like a tourniquet.

The kitchen door was open. She kept it locked, always kept it locked with both the key and the two bolts, top and bottom.

It was a few inches ajar.

She took a step back, her head turning from side to side, her frightened eyes scooping every grain of light from the darkness. Her first instinct was to run; but it was a long way back to the main road and if anyone was waiting for her they would catch her. The car was the best bet, she thought, and she strode quickly over to it, jumped in, switched on the ignition and pushed the starter button.

The engine turned over but did not fire. She pushed the button again and pumped the accelerator hard. The engine fired then died. 'Come on, please, please!' she hissed through clenched teeth, pressing the starter button again, then again. The interior of the car filled with the stink of petrol. Shit. She knew that the flooded engine could take a quarter of an hour before it had evaporated enough to start.

Fearfully she peered through the rain-smeared windows into the darkness. She switched on the headlights, the beam giving her a crumb of comfort, and thought hard. If there was someone lying in wait, the noise of the starter would have flushed them out, surely?

She wound down the window and listened. Plat. Plat. Plat. It was a quarter to seven. Another hour at least before Conor got here, and probably longer. He was bound to get lost; in spite of her careful directions everyone got lost the first time they visited here.

Shivering with fear and feeling trapped, she climbed back out and stood stock-still.

Got to get a grip, she told herself.

Slowly she walked up to the back door and pulled it open wider, then held her breath. Silence. She took another step forward, then her foot struck something. There was a clink, then a sharp rattle that made her cry out in fright; something skittered noisily across the ground. Her mind worked feverishly, wondering if it was some kind of man-trap device.

Then she looked down at the milk bottles she had just kicked over, and felt a little foolish. She reached inside the door and snapped on the light.

Her eyes scanned the Welsh dresser, the Aga, the fridge, the pine table; it all looked undisturbed, just as she had left it. The small vase of flowers was still on the table; the usual note from Alice weighted beneath a cutglass paperweight. The cats, where were the cats?

Christ, if anyone has harmed Watson or Crick . . .

She felt bolstered by sudden anger. Then her eyes went back to the full vase on the table; a mixture of late flowers she had picked herself on Sunday; in the mild November, several plants had flowered early, or for a second time.

Every flower in the vase was dead.

She stared at them in disbelief. They hung, limp and shrivelled, their stems already turning brown. Couldn't be the heat in here, she thought, surely? Then she realized there was no heat at all; the kitchen felt like a cold store. It was warmer outside than inside. Puzzled, she touched the Aga. It was hot, the black line of the temperature gauge showing normal. Why the hell was it so chilly in here?

Then the door to the hall moved. Her heart thrashed. Four emeralds glinted at her from the darkness of the corridor. There was a snarl, then a hiss. The cats came into the room abreast, stopped in the doorway and looked at her as if she was a total stranger.

'Hello, boys,' she said, her voice trembling.

Crick arched his back and stiffened. Watson hissed again. The sound sent a shiver down Monty's skin. 'Boys! Hello, boys!' She took a tentative step towards them. Both cats took flight, dashing past her and out of the door, as if they couldn't get out of the house quickly enough.

She looked back into the dark corridor, and then, somehow, she walked the few yards into the hall and switched on the light. The morning's post lay neatly stacked by Alice on the table. Nothing seemed to have been disturbed.

Had Alice been taken ill or something? Or perhaps she'd had a mental blank-out, making her forget to lock the kitchen door? Monty peered up towards the top of the stairs, listening hard again, beginning to think that's what must have happened, when her eyes fell on the front door.

A piece of bent wire was protruding from the Yale lock, and the safety chain had been put on.

At once she turned and raced back to the kitchen, slamming the door shut behind her. She looked up at the drying rack above the Aga, saw a heavy Sabatier chopper which she had used on some garlic a few days ago, and picked it up, gripping it tightly. Then she grabbed the phone, half expecting the line to be dead. To her relief she heard the dial tone, and punched out 999.

It was answered almost instantly. 'Emergency, which service please?'

'Police,' she whispered and then had to endure a silence that seemed as long as history. She began to wonder if she'd been cut off. She stared at the open door to the garden. Make a run for it?

'Police,' said an abrupt male voice.

She cradled the phone close to her mouth, clenching the

handle of the chopper, and spoke again in a cramped whisper. 'Please help me,' she said. 'I think I have an intruder in my house.'

56

North London. 1951

'You *can* believe me,' Daniel Judd said in terror as the Magister Templi advanced closer, sword held high as if he were about to cleave him in two. 'You can!'

Rooted to the spot by an unseen force, Daniel stared, pleading, at the Priestess, and at the animal masks of each of the naked people standing silently behind them. Light glinted off the blades of their raised athames. His terror deepening every second, he registered the boar's head on the body of a naked man, an ass's head, a rooster's head. His vision becoming more accustomed to the dimness every minute, he looked again at the living altar of the naked young woman who lay spread-eagled on the floor, just inside the north point of the massive pentagram.

He could see skulls on shelves, the guttering flames of the black candles, the strange occult symbols drawn on the walls, some of which were familiar, others new to him; then he saw for the first time the massive horned half-man and half-goat figure towering over him on the wall beyond the north point of the pentagram. He knew enough to recognize Baphomet, the Goat of Mendez.

'You will give us proof,' the Magister Templi said, advancing another step. He was clad only in his metal headband with the pentagram at the front. He was not wearing a mask, and his grey hair hung lank from his head; his pot belly drooped like a fleshy pouch and his limp penis dangling between his thighs, an enormous thing, awed Daniel with its size.

The Priestess, the only other person in the assembly not

wearing a mask, stepped forward, carrying something in her hands. It was a crude cross, he could see, about eighteen inches long and made from two strips of black wood held together by a single nail.

'Theutus, the opportunity is offered to you to redeem your past. Do you desire to take it?'

'Yes,' Daniel said, his voice feeble and choked.

'Are you prepared to serve Our Lord Satan with your whole mind, body and soul, permitting nothing to deter you from the furtherance of His work?'

'Yes.'

'Do you freely undertake to accept without question all orders that may be given to you by those He has placed, or may place, in authority over you?'

'Yes,' he said, his voice bolder now.

She placed the cross in his hands, and said: 'As proof that you have purged your mind of all false teaching, you will now break this and throw the pieces to the ground, while declaring: *I deny Christ, the deceiver; and abjure the Christian Faith, holding in contempt all its works.*'

Daniel held the cross, struck by a sudden crisis of conscience. For all his hatred of Christianity that the religious intolerance of his parents had instilled in him, he was aware of the historic power and significance of this symbolic object he was now holding. To do what he was bidden meant crossing a Rubicon.

He stared at the cold eyes of the Priestess, at the stern expression in the Magister Templi's face, and swallowed. His grip on the cross tightened. He could throw it in their faces and turn and run.

But why?

And why was he afraid, he wondered? Afraid of this crummy Magister Templi with his silver chain and his old van and his horrid little house? Afraid of becoming like him and nothing more?

But this was just one step. One small step. It was a beginning; things would grow from here. He had nothing to be afraid of. Nothing in the world. He held the key between his hands; held the key to the greatest power in the universe.

He snapped the cross in half and dropped the pieces to the floor. 'I deny Christ, the deceiver; and abjure the Christian Faith, holding in contempt all its works,' he said, his voice loud, confident, utterly certain.

'Now spit on the pieces, Theutus,' the Priestess said.

He knelt and spat ferociously, then stood again.

'Now urinate on them.'

He looked the Priestess and then the Magister Templi in the eye. He held his penis, pointed it downwards and concentrated hard, trying to will himself to perform. It took him some moments before he succeeded in spraying a short burst on to the pieces, then he had to fight to control his bladder to prevent himself from urinating further. He looked back for approval, first at the Magister Templi, then at the Priestess, but saw no expression at all in their faces.

Three naked men stepped forward, one wearing a rat's head, one a raven's head and one a serpent's. The rat was carrying his athame in one hand, and a tape measure and a reel of cotton in the other; the raven held a brass vessel with a hinged lid on which was a thick rubber seal; the serpent brandished a pair of scissors and a sheet of what looked like white blotting paper.

The rat bowed in acknowledgement to the Magister Templi then turned to Daniel. 'Stand upright, Theutus,' he said in a voice as weaselly as his mask.

He measured Daniel with the tape, then unspooled the cotton, placed one end beneath Daniel's foot, stretched it tight up to the top of his head, and cut off the length with his athame. Carefully, he pulled the end out from under Daniel's foot, coiled the length and placed it in the brass vessel the raven held out. Then he turned back to Daniel.

'We have your measure now, Theutus, for your coffin. Remember, won't you, that we have your measure.'

There was no reply to that and Daniel could only nod. Then the man in the serpent's mask came forward, nodded his respects to the Magister Templi, silently took Daniel's right hand and cut each of the nails in turn, careful to let the parings fall into the palm of his own hand. He then emptied these into the raven's brass vessel. Next he cut several small

305

locks of Daniel's hair, placed them in the vessel also, and stepped back.

The Magister Templi now approached. He took one hand off the hilt of his sword, which was still raised above his head, and gripped the edge of Daniel's left ear, pulling it outwards as far as it would go. Then slowly, in silence, he lowered the sword, hilt first, down towards Daniel's face.

Daniel stood, afraid again but unflinching. The blade slid past his nose and became a blur in the corner of his eye. He saw a sudden movement followed instantly by an excruciating burning sensation in his ear and let out a stifled cry of pain.

The Magister Templi stepped back and held the blade out to the man in the rat mask; Daniel could see blood on it. The rat dabbed it with a small square of the white blotting paper, which he then folded and placed in the vessel.

The raven mask raised the vessel up high, and a gong rang, once. The Magister Templi said something in a language Daniel did not understand, and the rest of the assembly responded in unison.

'Hail Satan!'

At this, the rat closed the lid of the vessel and carried it across to the far side of the temple.

His ear hurt badly, and Daniel could feel warm blood trickling down his neck and chest, but the force that had paralysed him earlier was gripping him again now. Anyway he didn't even want to try to touch his ear, for fear of showing weakness.

Three naked women in animal masks were now stepping towards him from different directions, in a ritualized march, as if to some silent drumbeat. One wore a horse's head, one an ass's and one a rooster's, and each of them carried a length of red cord. Daniel watched them, distracted by the pain in his ear, his terror replaced now by a feeling of submission.

A deep, echoing BONG rang out. His eyes swivelled and he saw the huge brass gong suspended from the rafters. A man in the head of a goat stood beside it holding a baton.

Each of the three women bowed in turn to the Magister Templi. Using one cord, they tied Daniel's hands behind his back, firmly but not roughly, then they looped the remaining two cords over his neck so they hung in folds down to the top of his thighs. One tucked the folds beneath his scrotum, then another took up the slack behind his neck. To his shame, Daniel found himself becoming aroused, and was aware that his face was burning fiercely with embarrassment.

The Magister Templi, holding the sword pointing upwards, hilt resting against his shaving-brush beard, stepped to the edge of the circle. He stopped, swept his sword in an arc to open it, and went in, closed it with his sword, then continued into the centre and up to the feet of the naked girl on the floor. He lifted his sword up in front of him and raised the point towards the ceiling.

The strident clang of a hand-bell rang out. As its echoes died away, the Magister Templi, in a powerful voice quite different from his normal speech, called out: '*In nomine Dei Nostri Satanas Luciferi exelsi!*'

As the sound faded, it was replaced with a loud chant from everyone in the temple, in unison: 'Hail Satan!'

The gong was struck and the Magister waited for the echo to fade before chanting, 'In the name of Satan, the Ruler of the earth, the King of the world, I command the forces of Darkness to bestow their Infernal power upon me! Open wide the gates of Hell and come forth from the abyss to greet me as Your brother and friend! Grant me the favour of which I speak! I have taken Thy name as part of myself! I live as the beasts of the field, rejoicing in the fleshly life! I favour the just and curse the rotten! By all the Gods of the Pit, I command that these things of which I speak shall come to pass! Come forth and answer to Your names by manifesting my desires! Diabolus! Thamuz! Samamael! Abbadon! Hecate! Astaroth! Sekhmet! Rimmon! Ishtar!'

The Magister Templi paused, then in unison everyone again chanted: 'Hail Satan!'

The gong was struck once more. And the Magister then prayed in Latin, pausing at the end of each sentence whilst everyone present echoed him.

'*Nema. Olam a son arebil des
Menoitatnet ni sacudni son en te.*

Sirtson subirotibed
Sumittimid son te tucis
Artson atibed sibon ettimid te
Eidoh sibon ad
Munaiditouq murtson menap
Arret ni te oleac ni
Tucis aut satnulov taif
Muut munger tainevda
Muut nemon rutecifitcnas
Sileac ni se iuq
Retson retap.'

Daniel felt a sudden *frisson* of real excitement. It was the Lord's Prayer backwards, he realized, recognizing it from his studies.

Then the Magister Templi intoned again: 'Come forth, o great spawn of the abyss and make Thy presence manifest. Come forth and receive into Thy circle Thy new servant, Theutus.'

Daniel suddenly found himself being pushed forward. He stumbled and regained his balance as unseen hands grabbed each of his shoulders. The cord pulled painfully on his scrotum, sending twinges of pain shooting up his stomach from his testicles. He was propelled to the north-east point of the circle.

The Magister Templi opened the circle with another sweep of his sword, and Daniel was then pushed into the centre, to the feet of the naked young woman. The Magister Templi imperiously rotated the sword horizontally, sealing the circle once more.

There was a sudden silence. The hand-bell was rung again, by a woman in a rat's head. As the peals faded, Daniel heard what he thought was the sound of a baby crying. Aware of the motionless figures all around him, he swivelled his eyes, scanning the darkness, not daring to move his head, but could see no sign of a baby. Then he stared ahead uncomfortably, embarrassed by the sight of the naked woman and the view he had straight up between her spread-eagled legs, but too scared by the Goat of Mendez on the wall above her to look higher.

After more intoning and more choruses, slowly the Magister Templi sank to his knees between the legs of the outstretched girl. He kissed her mouth lightly, almost symbolically, then each of her breasts in a theatrical, symbolic gesture; then her navel; then her vagina.

As he stood again, the hand-bell rang out. When the peals had faded, the Magister intoned: 'Come forth, o great spawn of the abyss and make Thy presence manifest. I have set my thoughts upon the blazing pinnacle which glows with the chosen lust of the moments of increase and grows fervent in the turgid swell. Send forth that messenger of voluptuous delights, and let these obscene vistas of my dark desires take form in future deeds and doings.'

He threw his head back so that he was staring directly upwards, then continued. 'From the sixth tower of Satan there shall come a sign which joineth with those saltes within, and as such will move the body of the flesh of my summoning. I have gathered forth my symbols and prepare my garnishings, and the image of my creation lurketh as a seething basilisk awaiting His release. The vision shall become as reality and through the nourishment that my sacrifice giveth, the angles of the first dimension shall become the substance of the third. Go out into the void of night and pierce that mind that respondeth with thoughts which leadeth to paths of lewd abandon.'

The bell rang again.

Then the Magister stood, held his sword straight out in front of him, and began to turn towards each cardinal point of the pentagram, saying in turn: 'Hail Belial from the north! Hail Lucifer from the east! Hail Leviathan from the west! Hail Satan from the south!' After each compass point, the gong was struck once.

As he turned to face Daniel, the boy saw to his shock that the Magister's massive penis was erect.

Then the Magister intoned: 'My rod is athrust! The penetrating force of my venom shall shatter the sanctity of that mind which is barren of lust; and as the seed falleth, so shall its vapours be spread within that reeling brain benumbing it to helplessness according to my will! In the name of the great god Pan, may my secret thoughts be marshalled into the movements of the flesh of that which I desire! Shemhamforash!'

The reply resounded: 'Hail Satan!'

The gong was struck. Then the woman in the rat's mask began to walk slowly towards the Magister, holding the bell. In her left hand she held a crucifix. As she walked, she intoned: 'My loins are aflame! The dripping of the nectar from my eager cleft shall act as pollen to that slumbering brain and the mind that feels not lust shall on a sudden reel with crazed impulse. And when my mighty surge is spent, new wanderings shall begin; and that flesh which I desire shall come to me. In the names of the great harlot of Babylon, and of Lilith and of Hecate, may my lust be fulfilled. Shemhamforash!'

She stood still as the rest of the assembly, including the Magister, cried: 'Hail Satan.' The gong resounded again.

Then she knelt behind the Magister and kissed his anus. He made a half-rotation, and she kissed the end of his penis. After that she herself turned, inserted the crucifix several inches into the vagina of the spread-eagled young woman, then withdrew it and, still kneeling, held it aloft.

Another woman came forward, intoned the same words, again kissed the Magister in the two places, then took the crucifix, and once more inserted it into the prone female. Daniel watched, agog, as each woman in turn did the same.

Finally the Magister knelt once more between the legs of the young woman on the floor. He gripped his penis with both hands, as if offering it up to a deity, then in a single movement he thrust forward and penetrated her. She let out a single short gasp. He closed his body over her and began to thrust vigorously, his flat bottom pumping like a hammer.

Everyone stood watching. The thrusting increased until the Magister's body tightened and began juddering. He seemed to seize, suddenly, let out a long wail, then lay motionless, spent, on top of his female partner. It was as if they had become fused into one eight-limbed sculpture.

The bell rang again.

'Hail Satan!' the assembly intoned.

The gong sounded.

The Magister withdrew and slowly stood upright, his penis

limp again now. The young woman lay staring upwards, expressionless. Daniel heard the cry of a baby again, and saw a female serpent's head holding a naked boy in her outstretched arms.

Daniel felt his hands being untied, and the cords were allowed to fall to the ground.

The Magister began to intone once more, his head raised towards the black ceiling: 'Behold! saith Satan, I am a circle on whose hands stand the Twelve Kingdoms. Six are the seats of living breath, the rest are as sharp sickles, or the Horns of Death. Therein the creatures of Earth are and are not, except in mine own hands which sleep and shall rise!'

Someone held out an athame to Daniel. It was his own, he realized, which had been taken from him when he had been put in the van. The woman bearing the baby came forward into the circle, followed by another in a wolf's head who was carrying a silver chalice, and the Magister closed the circle with his sword behind them. Then all stood still.

The bell rang three times in rapid succession.

The female in the serpent mask held the baby out to Daniel. He stared into the mask, could see the eyes behind the slits, but could read nothing in their expression. The baby had blue eyes, a light fluff of hair, and was quiet now. Daniel could not tell its age – a few weeks, perhaps older.

He jumped, startled, as a firm hand took his wrist. It was the Magister. Slowly the Magister brought the point of the athame down towards the baby's chest.

Going to cut it, Daniel thought, horrified. The wolf-headed woman held the chalice beneath the baby, as if to catch the blood.

He tried to resist, but the Magister's grip was firm and steady, pushing determinedly, closer and closer. The baby remained placid, even when the tip of the athame's blade dented the skin on the right-hand side of its chest.

The gong boomed, then boomed again, five times in succession. Then, as it boomed a sixth time, the Magister tightened his grip on Daniel's arm and pressed down hard, driving the blade deep into the baby's chest. Daniel gasped in reaction.

The baby's mouth opened as if it had been sprung by a lever. Its arms and legs shot outwards. Its eyes registered only mild surprise, as if it had been expecting a dummy, or food. Blood streamed like red ribbons either side of the blade and down the infant's bare chest. Some fell into the waiting chalice, some ran down its side, the remainder dripped on to the floor.

A cry turned to a gurgle, then silence.

The gong sounded.

Then the wolf-woman held up the chalice to Daniel.

'Drink,' the Magister commanded.

In deep shock, Daniel pressed the metal rim to his lips, then tasted the warm, coppery blood. He swallowed, aware of dozens of eyes all watching him. He saw the Magister nodding approval.

'Shemhamforash!' The gong sounded again.

'Hail Satan!' the entire assembly chanted.

Daniel felt a sudden, strange surge of power within him. With it came an elation greater than anything he had ever experienced. The Magister nodded at him encouragingly. 'Feel the power, Theutus? Do you feel it?'

The boy nodded. He felt as if he could fly.

'Test it, Theutus. You have drunk the blood of power. You have all the power in the world. Test it with a command!'

Daniel thought hard, lowered his eyes, then raised them again towards the Magister and spoke in a voice so loud and strong it startled him: 'O, Lord Satan! I command you to take away from my mother the ability to put her hands together in prayer!'

The gong sounded again. Daniel felt the force of his words carried with it, far beyond the walls of the temple.

57

Monday 21 November, 1994

Monty stayed motionless in the kitchen, the knife gripped in her hand, listening to every sound, watching every shadow through the windows.

Finally, she heard the sound of a car approaching fast, then the slam of its doors. Moments later she saw the beam of a flashlight out in the garden; but it was not until she heard the reassuring crackle of a two-way radio that she began to relax.

There were two policemen; one remained outside, the other searched the house with her, starting upstairs with her bedroom. He opened the large Victorian wardrobe, checked the inside, then locked it again. Raindrops dripped from the peak of his cap all the time and rolled down his heavy blue coat. His name, he had told Monty, was P. C. Brangwyn.

'You're quite sure you didn't leave the front door locked and go out via the kitchen today, madam?'

'I'm quite sure I wouldn't have jammed a piece of wire in the front door lock if I had.' She managed a smile. 'I'm not Houdini.'

He looked back at her thoughtfully, the joke eluding him. 'It's a common technique for professional burglars, locking the front door to prevent themselves being surprised and leaving an exit open for a quick getaway – in your case the kitchen.'

He nodded towards her dressing table, neatly tidied by Alice, and asked, 'Nothing missing?'

'Not that I can immediately see.'

The radio fizzed and crackled just then and a truncated voice said: 'Charley-Victor-ove –' followed by a rasp of static.

Constable Brangwyn nodded an apology at her and pressed a switch on his radio: 'Attending at Foxholes Cottage. On the scene now. Over.'

'Thank you Charley-Victor.'

P. C. Brangwyn looked at Monty again. 'You may have disturbed them before they had a chance to take anything.'

The remark brought her fear swirling back.

'Do you have a routine? Always leave for work and arrive home at the same time?'

'It's changed during the past few months – I used to work in Reading, now I commute almost every day to London.'

'What time do you get home?'

'Normally between eight and nine.'

'And tonight?'

She stiffened. 'Earlier – about half past six.'

He nodded. 'That could explain it. You didn't notice any unfamiliar vehicles along here or parked on the main road recently?'

'No.'

'Perhaps you ought to have a word with the Crime Prevention Officer some time – if you ring the main Reading station they'll put you through. Being as isolated as this, your house is very vulnerable.'

'It's only a little cottage – I wouldn't have thought it was of much interest to burglars.'

He gave her a long, searching look. 'It might only be a cottage to you, madam, but compared to what some people live in it's a palace.'

She smiled wistfully. 'Yes, I'm sorry, I suppose you're right.'

The drawing room smelled of fresh polish from Alice's administrations and nothing was disturbed. Then Monty suddenly noticed her rubber plant over in the far corner, by the window. It had been flourishing for the past couple of years, and had grown to over four feet. Now it looked dead; its leaves were brown and curled at the edges, and the stem seemed to be buckling.

Her eyes shot to her poinsettia, which had been in bloom yesterday. But the flower had browned and withered and the plant looked a goner. Startled, she looked at her palm and her aspidistra. The same story.

'Problem?' the policeman said, sensing her consternation.

'My plants – I noticed the dead flowers in the kitchen and it's the same here.' She pointed at them. 'They were fine yesterday.'

He walked over to the poinsettia, pulled off his leather glove and dabbed the earth with his finger. 'Bone dry.'

'That's impossible! I watered it yesterday.'

He went over to the palm and knelt, digging his fingers into the pot, then raising a pinch of earth. 'Dry as sand – I'm a bit of a gardener myself – these haven't been watered for weeks – months, more like it.' He reassured her. 'Easy to forget these things when you're busy.'

She went over and touched the earth herself. He was right. She darted over to each plant in turn; the soil was bone dry.

Am I cracking up? she wondered.

P. C. Brangwyn's colleague came in, holding his dripping hat in his hand. 'No footprints or anything,' he announced.

Brangwyn removed his own hat, held it dutifully by his side, and spoke to Monty in a new, stiffly formal tone, with his eyes constantly moving as if he were addressing not just her but an entire roomful. As he was mid-delivery, the cats re-appeared and circled his ankles warily. Monty watched them, still puzzling over their earlier behaviour.

'We'll put a call out to all patrols asking them to keep a close eye on your property tonight. You'd best be vigilant, keep your doors locked at all times and an eye out for strangers. If you see any unfamiliar cars down the lane take their number and give us a call.'

'Yes, thank you.'

She stood at the front door, watching them turn around then drive off down the track. As the tail lights disappeared, she felt very vulnerable and closed the front door, sliding the safety chain firmly home. The cats stood and watched her expectantly.

'What's the matter with you two?' she said, kneeling and stroking them. 'Did someone give you a fright?'

She checked to see that the kitchen door was properly locked, turned the central heating up, switched on the porch light, then hurried round drawing the curtains in each room.

When she had done that, she gave her plants a drenching in the hope of reviving them, then laid and lit a fire in the living room. She felt dirty, as if she and the house had been violated, and badly wanted a bath or a shower, but there wasn't time.

She had been planning to casserole the chicken in the Aga, but now she would have to rush and use the microwave; less traditional, but too bad.

Two minutes past eight. Conor would be here any moment, and she hadn't changed, or put on any make-up. She dashed upstairs, hoping the traffic would delay him, and in her rush to get prepared momentarily forgot her anxiety.

She stripped off, splashed on some Issey Miyake cologne, pulled on a black pullover that she knew flattered her figure, her best jeans and her suede boots, shovelled her hands through her hair, then ran back downstairs to the kitchen.

Should they eat in here or the dining room, she wondered. Light a couple of candles and the dining room could be romantic. Maybe too romantic, she worried, not wanting the American to think this was some kind of deliberate seduction scene. They would eat in the kitchen, she decided.

She checked the microwave, but the windowpane rattled in a gust and she turned, nervously feeling a draught like cold breath on her neck, and saw the closed blinds shifting from side to side. She looked at the chopper, which she had left out on the draining board for reassurance, then walked over to the Aga and held her hands over the chromium-lidded hot plate, grateful for the warmth. It was still unaccountably cold in here.

Perhaps she was going down with flu, she thought, parting the blinds and peering into the darkness. Was someone out there now, biding their time? Intruders. Burglars who hadn't taken anything. That was becoming a familiar story lately.

She remembered Zandra Wollerton telling her about *her* break-in. Nothing had been taken then, either, except a pair of cotton panties from her wash box. So far Monty had not actually counted her knickers.

She also remembered, involuntarily, Hubert Wentworth's words that first time he had come to see her here. He'd been telling her about his son-in-law's break-in on the day of Sarah Johnson's funeral.

You see, there's something else curious: on the afternoon of Sarah's funeral, her home was burgled, ransacked. Alan could find nothing missing at all . . . Burglars are normally after consumer goods, jewellery, silverware, cash. These ignored all that. Possibly they were disturbed, but it seems strange that they found time to riffle through the medicine cabinet in the bathroom.

Caroline Kingsley's home had also been ransacked, and the burglars had riffled through her medical cabinet . . .

Outside Monty heard the sound of a car pulling up. She went into the living room and peered through the curtains. Relief surged through her as she saw Conor Molloy walking uncertainly down the path to the front door, his coat collar turned up against the rain.

Don't look too keen, she told herself. *Don't seem too anxious.* She waited until she heard the doorbell, then hung on a few seconds after that before walking through to the hall.

But the moment she saw him all her defences crashed. He had removed his tie and his soft white shirt was open at the neck. Two licks of hair were plastered down his forehead and his face was largely obscured by a bottle of wine and large bouquet of flowers.

Before she knew what she was doing, as he stepped in the door, she flung her arms around his neck and held him tight, tears rolling down her cheeks. 'Thank God,' she murmured, clinging to him as if he were driftwood. Rain lashed in but she barely noticed, feeling the stubble of his cold wet cheek against her face and the reassurance of his arms around her, squeezing her gently.

'Hey!' he said. 'That's some greeting!'

His grip slackened and she stepped back, closing the door behind him. 'God, I've been scared,' she said.

His forehead creased into a frown as he saw her distress. 'What's up – what's happened?'

By way of answer, she led him through to the living room and despite her agitation she noticed him relishing the chintz surroundings. If he observed the dead plants he didn't show it.

He looked at Monty with concern, asking again, 'So tell me what scared you?'

She relieved him of his coat and his gifts, furnished them each with a large Teacher's whisky and collected her thoughts, then began. He listened to everything, interrupting only

317

occasionally to ask for a further detail. She told him first about the intruder; then about her visit to Hubert Wentworth in his office, and the discovery of the fourth Maternox victim, Caroline Kingsley, in Zandra Wollerton's files. About her attempt to talk to Dr Corbin, and then his horrific death. About her visit to the Kingsleys' flat. Finally, she pulled out of her handbag the vial of Maternox capsules she had taken and handed it to him.

He studied the label, then he prised off the cap and shook the capsules into the palm of his hand.

She watched the concentration in his face as he held one of the capsules up to the light. There was something about the seriousness of his expression that seemed to go beyond mere curiosity, beyond mere courtesy to her. It struck her, as she watched the hard set of his grave brown eyes, that she was watching a man driven by some private demon. And as her curiosity about him deepened, so did her attraction to him.

They had both finished their whiskies, she realized, and she jumped up. 'Let me get you a refill?' She wondered whether he would be worried about drinking and driving, but he accepted gratefully.

When she returned, accompanied by Crick and Watson, the American was holding a black notebook in one hand and the Maternox vial in the other; he was so absorbed that he did not acknowledge the refilled glass she put beside him.

'I see it's the same,' he said, his expression very drawn. 'Our old friend, BS-M-6575-1881-UKMR.'

'Yes, I know.' Her mouth felt dry; despite the whisky. 'Do you know anything about the batch-numbering system for Maternox?'

'Uh huh. There are about five hundred batches run off a year for distribution in the UK. Maternox is produced in Britain at three different plants – Reading, Plymouth and Newcastle – and the distribution is regional.'

'Sarah Johnson, who used to work for us, lived in Reading. Caroline Kingsley in London, so I suppose it's very possible they'd have had Maternox from the same plant,' Monty said. 'But one of the other women lived in Birmingham, and the other in Edinburgh.' She thought for a moment. 'I suppose

Birmingham might be supplied by Reading, also. But not Edinburgh.'

'Edinburgh would definitely have been supplied by Newcastle,' he said. 'I checked.' He dropped the pills back into the vial, then he picked up his whisky, rattled the ice cubes and drank some more. 'We need to get a chromatography analysis done on these capsules to see if they conform to the specification or whether –'

His words hung in the air.

'Whether they're a rogue batch?' Monty prompted.

'*Something*'s wrong with them. Dr Farmer, the Director of Medical Information, knows that but she's not doing anything about it – or rather she is – she's covering up. Covering up real hard.'

'Why? Because of the financial damage a scandal could do to the company?'

For a while his expression became unreadable as he examined his whisky, then he began. 'I –'

But he was interrupted by a sudden hiss from Crick. Both of them stared, startled, at the cat. He was standing, with his back arched, staring at the doorway. Watson stood also. Then the two animals stalked determinedly out of the room as if after a quarry.

Monty and Conor exchanged a glance, then followed. Monty saw the cats suddenly sprint down into the kitchen. She walked swiftly after them.

Watson stopped in the kitchen door, his back arched stiffly, spitting. Crick, near the table, raised his paw and swiped at something. A creature jumped, then jumped again.

Monty shrieked and backed away, straight into Conor.

'It's a frog!' he said. 'Just a little frog.'

It jumped once more. Crick had another tentative go at it with his paw, as much in curiosity as anything else.

Conor ducked down, grabbed the frog by one leg, then lifted it up, cupped it gently in his hands and held it out to Monty. 'Poor little thing – I guess it's got confused with all this warm weather. I –'

He stopped, suddenly noticing that Monty had gone sheet white. Eyes bulging, she backed away from him.

'Hey! It's only a harmless little –'

'Please,' she said. '*Don't*. Don't bring it near me, I have a thing about them.'

'About frogs?'

'Please get rid of it.' She darted across to the back door, unlocked it and opened it.

Hold the cats.' Conor deposited the frog outside and hurried back in.

Monty locked the door again. 'I'm sorry,' she said meekly.

He put an arm protectively around her shoulder and gave her a hug. 'It's OK. We all have our phobias.'

She fought hard to stop herself from crying and sniffed. 'Oh boy, my nerves are all shot to hell today.'

They went back into the living room and sat down again. Monty tried to establish a more relaxed atmosphere. 'How was your weekend, Conor?'

'Well, I had some interesting talks with Charley Rowley. He doesn't share my views about Bendix Schere being ruthless enough to kill anyone.'

Monty drank some more of her whisky; she felt it burn first her throat, then her stomach, then the warm buzz spread through her, calming her, making her feel better, stronger.

'Conor, you said on Friday you get to a point where you realize that things don't make sense any more the way you've been perceiving them, right?'

He nodded.

'Well, I think I've run out of my belief in coincidence here. Just what the hell is going on, Conor?'

The wind rattled the panes and the curtains swelled up then eased. 'Have to test those capsules,' he said quietly. 'Need to get hold of the original specification and a template, and see how they compare.'

He added, suddenly, 'Charley Rowley's a good guy, but he's naive as hell. He doesn't have any idea what we're dealing with.'

'Do you, Conor?'

'I have some idea,' he said gravely.

58

Monty pushed her food around the plate. She forced down a few mouthfuls of the vegetables but left the chicken untouched, too many emotions buffeting her for any kind of an appetite to survive. Conor ate hungrily.

She raised her glass, conscious that her voice was slightly slurred, but she didn't care. 'Delicious wine.'

'I'm sure yours would have been better.'

She shook her head and took another sip of the powerful French red. 'This is perfection.' She forked a tiny new potato into her mouth.

He picked a wing up in his fingers and sucked it clean. 'So is this – you're an amazing cook.'

She shook her head, modestly. 'I'm rather hit and miss; I tend to improvise my way through most recipes. Sometimes they work and sometimes they don't.'

'Me, I do a terrific scallops in black bean sauce and stir-fried vegetables. Maybe I could try it on you some time?'

'Yes, please.'

'I just have to get my kitchen sorted out. We'll make a date.'

'Where is it, your new place?'

'Fulham – well, kind of Fulham – just off a road called –' He thought for a moment. 'Redcliffe Road.'

'*Redcliffe* Road?'

'Uh huh. Know it?'

'Yes.' She tapped the side of her wine glass. 'I was there today. Redcliffe Road is where Dr Corbin was killed.'

'Jesus! That construction site down by the lights?'

'Yes. Another coincidence?'

'One I could do without.'

She looked up at him. 'It's a nice area. I like that part of London. How did you choose it?'

'It's within the Bendix Schere approved zone.'

'Within the *what* zone?'

'You don't know about that? You didn't read the Bendix Bible?'

'I have a copy in my office but I've never been right through it.'

'Makes fascinating reading. You and I and your father and everyone else in the company are only allowed to live in allocated areas of town and countryside.'

She shook her head in disbelief. 'Am I OK here?'

'You should check; if not they could insist you move.'

'Let them try,' she said darkly, then grinned at him. 'Tell me about the flat – is it in one of those lovely terraced houses?'

'Yup, really elegant. It's just a one-bedroom, but it has a big living room and walk-through kitchen, high ceiling, with all the mouldings.'

'Sounds gorgeous,' she said enthusiastically.

'Why don't you come and have dinner with me tomorrow and I'll show it to you? Might have to be a takeaway or something.'

'I'd love to.'

He raised his glass slowly and held it in front of his face, and their eyes locked. Then he pushed the glass forward, lightly touching hers. 'I think you're really lovely,' he said.

Monty blushed a fraction and smiled warmly at him; her attraction to him was fuelled further by the wine. 'Thank you,' she mouthed silently, and felt a lump of excitement tingling within her.

'How come you're not married? Or don't have a queue of guys with red roses lined up around the block? Or maybe you do?'

'No, afraid not.' She shrugged. 'I'm just a very dedicated career girl, I suppose.'

He tilted his head a little. 'Are you?'

'Yes.'

He nodded at the painting on the wall, of St Mark's Square. He had noticed the artist's signature earlier. 'Yours?'

'Like it?'

'I think you've got talent. You're wasting yourself in the pharmaceutical industry.'

She shook her head, then in a moment of weakness took a Marlboro from the pack he proffered and let him light it. She inhaled and felt a dizzying buzz in her head, then coughed and had to apologize.

'Sorry – my first in five years!' She took a second, much more cautious drag, and cleared her mind. 'Painting's not important. There are plenty of pictures in the world, thousands of painters far more talented than me, and one more is neither here nor there. But there aren't thousands of people like my father. There aren't even hundreds.'

'Probably not even a dozen,' Conor said.

She took a gulp of wine, then another more daring drag. 'God, this tastes good. You bastard, you're going to get me hooked on smoking again!'

He leaned over, gently prised the cigarette from her fingers and crushed it out.

'Hey! I was really enjoying it.'

'Oscar Wilde once said that a cigarette was the most perfect thing – because it always leaves one unsatisfied.' He looked at her expectantly.

'Very true,' she said.

'So, quit while you're ahead, OK? And maybe the same should apply to Bendix Schere.'

'Quit Bendix?'

'Quit investigating Maternox.'

'Are you serious?'

'Yes. I don't want you to come to any harm.'

She looked at the curled, crushed butt in the ashtray. 'Conor, I don't quit anything easily.'

'That's what I'm afraid of.' He laid his own cigarette down in the ashtray and watched her face. 'I just told you Charley Rowley doesn't have any idea what we're dealing with. Nor do you.'

'What *are* we dealing with, Conor?'

He shook his head. 'I really think you should try to forget it.'

Monty argued back. 'It was you who encouraged me, if you remember. When I was in hospital and you hinted pretty strongly that Jake Seals' death wasn't an accident.'

He picked up his cigarette again. 'It had begun before that for you,' he said. 'I didn't put any thoughts or doubts into your mind that weren't already there. Right?'

It was true, she knew. She wouldn't even have been in hospital in the first place if she hadn't listened to Hubert Wentworth and agreed to help him. She touched the stem of her glass. 'So come on, what is it that Charley Rowley and I don't know about Bendix Schere?'

'Tell me first what you do know.'

She shrugged. 'Not a lot – I –' She hesitated suddenly. 'Actually, I heard something very strange this afternoon. I've become quite friendly with one of the security guards in the lobby. There've been a couple of times when I've heard a lift going down to the basement – but the weird thing is that the sound doesn't seem to have any origin. When I asked him about it he got very nervous. He told me I ought to check out the site plans some time – hinted that the Bendix Building wasn't all it seemed. Then he said that I ought to read Jules Verne's *Journey to the Centre of the Earth*.' She smiled.

He smiled back thinly. 'Sounds like a guy with a pretty wild imagination,' he said, and lowered his eyes evasively to his empty plate.

'Conor, what is it *you* are hiding from me about the company?'

'I don't know, Montana. I just –' He stood up, shaking his head, and walked round to her side of the table. Slowly he leaned over, took her hands and entwined his fingers in them. 'I don't want anything to happen to you, you don't deserve it. And I'm not going to let it. OK?'

She looked up at him, feeling a sudden intense longing for him, and agreed. 'OK.'

He squeezed her fingers a little harder, and lowered his face towards hers. 'I've only just met you and I don't intend losing you.'

Monty felt a sensual excitement. His face filled her view, became a blur of warmth. 'Thank you,' she said softly. 'I don't want to lose you either.'

He was smiling and there was something in that smile that she was finding hypnotic.

'You know, Conor, it's really strange. I feel as if I've known you for ages.'

'Me too.'

Their lips brushed lightly and she felt the sensation reverberate through her whole body. They brushed again, and she shuddered with pleasure, then reached up, spontaneously, and kissed him harder.

He responded increasingly vigorously until she pushed her chair away and stood up, gripped him in her arms and pulled him up towards her. He put his arms around her in response, pulling her even tighter against his frame, kissing her for a long time.

Then their mouths parted for an instant. Their eyes locked in a warm, blurry smile.

'God, I want you,' he said.

'I want you too.'

He touched her lightly on the forehead, and she took his hand, led him upstairs into her bedroom and switched on the heavily shaded lamp.

For a brief moment they stood staring at each other. Then they closed the gap between them and began undressing each other, garment by garment. Thoughts of safe sex flashed through her mind. Condoms, he ought to wear a condom, but she did not want to stop. He looked clean, wholesome, he was fine, fine. He smelled fine too. Anyway, she'd stayed on the pill when her last relationship ended, so there was no problem there.

When he laid her on the bed and entered her, she moaned in pleasure as he pushed up inside her, the firm muscles of his chest pressing against her breasts. Then he made her cry out as he pinched her nipples and kept hold of them, rolling them in his fingertips. She felt him swelling, pushing further and further up into her, felt a wave welling out from deep within, larger and larger, carrying her and flowing through her. As it exploded, firing sparks of pleasure through every cell of her body, she was lost to the world, completely and utterly lost.

Afterwards they lay intertwined, faces pressed together. She opened an eye and saw his eye staring warmly, and could see the edges crinkled in a smile. She smiled back. 'We needed that,' she said.

59

'DADDY! DAADDDDDYYYYYYYY! DADDD-DYYYYYYYYY!' The scream woke Monty. She sat up in wild confusion. It was pitch black in the room, and her mouth was parched. Her nostrils were filled with the rich, animal smells of sex.

'DAAAAAADDDDDDYYYYYYYYY!'

She heard the scream again and fear tore through her like a knife. She had no idea of the time. They had made love constantly during an endless night and she felt utterly in love.

Conor.

She had been making love with Conor.

Beside her he was thrashing and screaming in his sleep.

'Hey,' she said gently. 'Conor, it's OK.'

He screamed again. Then he choked and another scream died in his throat as he stirred and seemed to come round, panting.

'S'shoory. I – sh – shorry. Sh'din't mean to wake you.'

He was trembling. She caressed his forehead which was slippery with sweat. 'What is it? What were you dreaming?'

He recovered himself a little before replying. 'Nothing – just the same –' He stopped abruptly in mid-sentence, and reached out to the bedside table for his cigarettes.

She kissed his cheek. 'You poor thing, you're shaking.'

He lit a cigarette, then proffered it to her for a drag, but she shook her head.

'Do you want to talk about it?'

He inhaled deeply, then blew out the smoke. 'It's – kind of dumb. Just about a bird. A large black bird.'

'Like a rook or something?'

'I guess. Bigger. It's not important, just a dumb dream.'

'Dreams can be very scary,' she said. 'Often they're telling us things.'

'Sure.' The tip of his cigarette glowed bright red as he drew on it again. He seemed to be calming down. 'The tests on the

Maternox capsules, Montana – I could do those myself, in one of the labs if I could get the spec and template.'

'Wouldn't that be dangerous?'

'Maybe over a weekend or something.'

She had an idea and thumped the mattress. 'What about our old lab? Most of the equipment's still there – I sold it off yesterday afternoon, but it'll be there for another month. You'd be totally private.'

'Yup, that makes a lot of sense.'

She felt wide awake and her mind was very clear now. 'Conor, I have a friend who's been taking Maternox and she's now pregnant. I don't know whether I should say anything to her. I don't want to frighten her, and at the same time it would be absolutely horrific if –'

'You need to find out the batch number of the capsules she was taking when she got pregnant, and I need to find out whether there *is* anything wrong with that batch.'

'You're pretty sure, though, aren't you?'

'We need to be certain.'

'And what do we do when we are certain? Go to Sir Neil Rorke and let him know what's going on?'

'Let's get all the facts before we make any decision. OK?'

'OK.' She kissed his shoulder, breathed in the sweet smell of the smoke. 'Conor – you know quite a lot about physics. Are there any atmospheric conditions that can dehydrate plants?'

'How do you mean?'

She told him about the state of the plants when she'd arrived home last evening, and the extreme coldness of the house.

'Weird,' he said, taking a final drag on his cigarette and crushing it out. Then he traced his finger along the silver chain of the tiny crucifix she wore around her neck. 'Are you a Catholic?'

'No. This was my mother's. My father gave it to me after she died, said it would make him feel good if I wore it. It's one of the few sentimental things he's ever done.'

She sensed him rolling it through his fingers as he asked her, 'Do you wear it all the time?'

'Yes – it's become a sort of talisman.'

'Do you believe in God?' he wanted to know.

'Sometimes. Not exactly a bearded man on a cloud, but something. Do you?'

'I believe there's something out there.'

They lay still for what seemed to Monty like several minutes, then Conor slowly began to kiss her again, working his way down her body. They made love and afterwards she slept; deep, dreamless sleep.

60

Tuesday 22 November, 1994

The floor felt as if it was moving and Monty gripped the uselessly small washbasin to keep her balance, feeling suddenly light-headed from her exertions of the night. Her reflection in the mirror startled her; her face seemed to have aged ten years: sallow complexion, and a chin covered in red blotches where Conor's stubble had rubbed.

But her lips spread irrepressibly into a grin. She shook her head at herself. I *feel* good, she thought. The horrors of yesterday in London were locked away in another compartment.

Just don't look at the mirror, it's jealous, that's all . . . But she acknowledged that not having a man in her life, and not being bothered about finding one, had meant her taking less care over her appearance. Now, she decided, she would start doing something about it.

Rain was falling outside, gentle, steady, pattering down. It was 7.30. Still fairly dark out there, but she viewed the approach of daylight with apprehension, not wanting the spell of the night they had just spent together broken.

Conor left for work first, and Monty stood in the doorway watching until his car had disappeared from sight, then she went back inside to make sure the cats had enough food and water before leaving herself.

Unhooking her mackintosh from the peg in the passageway, she decided to wear the Cornelia James printed shawl that went well with it, which she usually kept slung over another peg. But it wasn't there. Strange, she thought, wracking her brains to see if she could remember leaving it somewhere else. No, she was certain it had been hanging there yesterday morning.

It wasn't long before Zandra Wollerton's words came back to her: *Maybe the bastard who broke in is a closet pervert. There's a pair of cotton panties I thought I had in the wash box – can't find them anywhere.*

Was there a snooper with some kind of fetish for women's clothing? Panties and a shawl? The thought churned her stomach, but at the same time she felt a flash of anger. *No one is going to make me afraid of being in my own home.*

She went back inside, phoned the local police and asked for PC Brangwyn. He came on the line after a short wait, and she told him she thought the intruder had taken her shawl. Without mentioning Maternox or the rest of the background, she told him about Zandra Wollerton's break-in, then suggested there might be a connection.

He promised to get hold of the file on that case and to report back to her if his findings revealed anything of interest.

The rain had stopped and stars pricked the dayglo orange haze of the London evening sky. Monty drove her MG slowly down the tree-lined street, looking for Conor's address, uncomfortably aware that she was close to where Dr Corbin had died yesterday.

She looked at the numbers outside each of the elegant if slightly dilapidated Victorian terraced houses, with their columned porches, glancing into her mirror every few moments. 74. She braked, scanning the line of parked cars for a gap, and spotted a tight space about thirty yards ahead. Then she set the alarm, picked the bottle of champagne and the large brown envelope off the passenger seat, before locking the car and walking briskly to Conor's building and up the steps.

She pressed the button for Flat 2. A few moments later she heard a crackly voice, barely identifiable as Conor's. 'Come on up – first floor!'

The lock buzzed; she heaved open the heavy front door and stepped within. At the top of the stairs Conor stood staring down at her, dressed in a faded grey sweatshirt, baggy jeans and beat-up trainers. She had not seen him in casual clothes before and they suited him, made him look very cuddly, she thought.

He greeted her with a hugely enthusiastic 'Hi!' and she fell into his arms as she reached the top step, their lips meeting. She burrowed against him, feeling safe again for the first time since he had driven off from her cottage that morning.

She held out the bottle. 'Brought you a little housewarming present.'

'Wow, Bollinger! My favourite – how did you know?'

She grinned and shrugged. 'Maybe you told me in your sleep!'

He touched the bottle with his hand. 'And it's cold – let's have some right away. I could use a drink.'

'Me too.'

He ushered her into the open-plan kitchen and she looked enviously at the modern units, the large fridge, the Bosch oven and built-in electrical hob. She noticed a wicker hamper, crammed with exotic tinned and bottled foods beside the double sink.

'Charley Rowley sent me this – from Fortnum and Mason.' He picked a few things out at random. 'Quails' eggs. Iranian caviar; peaches in brandy. Kind of essential stuff for stocking a larder.'

'Who needs bread and cheese?'

'Right. Who needs it?'

Monty walked across the room and stared out of the wide front window down at the street below, eyeing the parked cars. 'Conor, this may sound paranoid, but I have a feeling I've been followed today.'

He looked concerned.

'I noticed a dark blue car – a Ford Mondeo, I think – I saw it in my mirror this afternoon when I drove to the Westminster

County Planning Department. And I'm pretty sure it tailed me here.'

'Can you see it now?'

'No.'

'You didn't get a look at the driver's face? Or the registration?'

She shook her head. 'Probably just me – I've been feeling pretty jittery.'

'I'm not surprised after all you went through yesterday. I'd be feeling jittery too. But I wouldn't put it past Bendix Schere to follow employees at random, just for the hell of it.'

'Great!'

He touched her face tenderly. 'Be really vigilant all the time, OK?'

She nodded.

'I mean it.' He frowned. 'Westminster County Planning Department? What goes on there?'

She lifted up the brown envelope. 'These. I've got the plans of the Bendix Building.'

He looked at her oddly. 'Can I see?'

'Yes, I think you should.'

'Right, just let me crack this champagne open and order the food, then I'll have a look. I thought we'd have a Chinese, from the takeaway, that OK with you?'

She nodded and they went through the menu, alternating choices, Monty writing the numbers down. To a list that was already far too long, they then added as an afterthought seaweed and half a crispy duck, which they both agreed were essential.

As Conor phoned the list through, she wandered around the flat, giving herself a five-dollar tour at his invitation. Suitably impressed, she returned and joined him in the kitchen. There she noticed an assortment of books stacked in piles near the window. She knelt and looked through them. The first one was titled: *Joshua Bendix. The Invisible Tycoon*. She picked it up with interest and saw that it was an unauthorized biography of the founder of Bendix Schere. Another, which had the Bendix logo embossed on the front, was titled: *From Invisible Ink to Invisible Profits. The Rise of the Bendix Empire.*

There were a couple more books on Bendix Schere, and then she found a whole section on the occult. Among them was a biography of Aleister Crowley, Colin Wilson's *Beyond the Occult* and an ancient-looking volume with sinister lettering, entitled *The Master Grimoire of Magickal Rites and and Ceremonies*.

'Be about half an hour,' Conor said, walking over. 'I see you've found the library located in the east wing.'

'I've never seen any books on the company before.'

'You wouldn't. Whenever anything's published, they always buy up all the copies before they even leave the warehouses and pay off everyone involved.'

'So how did you get them?'

He tapped the side of his nose and winked. 'A few review copies slip out here and there.'

'Can I read them some time?'

'Sure – actually they're not that interesting. I think the authors and publishers had been threatened with so many lawsuits that they kind of got neutered.'

'You have a lot of stuff on the occult, too.'

He looked awkward. 'Oh – right – yah, I went through a phase of being interested,' he said rather dismissively.

She noticed his discomfort, which increased her curiosity. 'How come?'

He reached for his Marlboros and lit one. 'My mother – I guess it's her Irish ancestry.'

'Is she fey?'

He shrugged. 'Nothing heavy, it's no big deal.' He brought the opened champagne bottle over, filling both their glasses. 'There's a science programme on Channel Four at eight,' he said. 'They're going to be talking about patenting human genes; mind if I just keep an eye out for it?'

She clicked her fingers in annoyance. 'Damn. I read about it – my father wanted me to record it. He might be a brilliant scientist but he can never work his video.' She shot him a grin. 'Something else distracted me last night, though.'

The closing credits on a wildlife documentary were rolling on the screen. A flock of migrating birds blackened the tropical sky. Conor drew hard on his cigarette, then exhaled through his mouth, asking suddenly, 'What did you do with the Maternox capsules?'

'I still have them in my handbag.'

He nodded. 'Tell me something. Last night, did the police take any fingerprints or anything?'

'No, they talked about it, but they weren't enthusiastic. I expect because nothing was stolen or damaged. I got the feeling they weren't intending reporting it as a burglary; probably something to do with the way they massage their crime statistics. But this morning after you left I discovered that something may be missing after all, except I can't be –'

'Hey! Look at this!' he interrupted, grabbing the remote control and turning the television's volume up. Bendix Schere's latest 'corporate imaging' commercial was on the screen. Everyone had been talking about it in the office, but Monty hadn't seen it yet, and she watched with fascination.

The commercial began with a close-up of lava erupting from a volcano. A super-smooth male voice-over said: 'Seventy million years ago the Big Island of Hawaii began as a volcanic eruption on the floor of the Pacific Ocean.'

The camera rose dramatically, revealing the erupting volcano to be at one end of a densely vegetated island. Then it dipped deep into an area of rain forest, showing exotic plants and bird life in microscopic close-up, as the commentary continued: 'The plants of the Hawaiian rain forest have yielded not only sustenance for wildlife and humans, but also one of the richest sources of medicines in all the world.'

The camera cut to a hi-tech Bendix Schere factory plant, surrounded by acres of greenery. 'One company more than any other has been preserving the natural wonders of the rain forest, and harnessing its fruits to create a better world for us all.'

The camera now switched to an Ethiopian mud-hut village. Dozens of young black children swarmed around a visiting European. For the benefit of his audience as he spoke directly into the camera the subtitle appeared: *Sir Neil Rorke.*

'Hello. I'm Chairman of Bendix Schere, and I want you to take a look at these healthy youngsters all around me. Aren't they great?' On cue, he put one arm around a boy, the other around a girl. 'Without the vitamin-enriched powdered milk manufactured by Bendix Schere, I doubt that any of the kids you see here with me today would be alive.' He paused for the camera to sweep over the happy faces.

'Without the chemicals extracted from the acobab tree in the Hawaiian rain forest, this little boy would be a cripple in a wheelchair. Without the root of the Pe-eccu plant, this little girl would be blind by the time she reaches her teens.'

'The camera slowly tracked into a tight close-up of the Bendix Schere's avuncular Chairman. 'My company spends three billion pounds a year on medical research – that's five times as much as the British government. At Bendix Schere we are trying to create a world where there is less pain and less disease.'

Music was faded in, as the camera pulled back, further and further, to reveal that Sir Neil Rorke was surrounded not by a few dozen happy children, but several thousand. Then the caption filled the screen: 'BENDIX SCHERE – THE WORLD'S MOST CARING COMPANY.'

Conor grinned. 'Reckon he'll be up for an Oscar? Talk about one cynical bastard.'

She gently prised the cigarette from his fingers and puffed on it. The smoke tasted good and gave her a buzz. 'Cynical? I rather like him. How much do you think he knows about what goes on in the company?'

'How do you mean?'

She handed him the cigarette back, with some reluctance. 'Well – he's only a figurehead, right? He's Chairman, but he's not Chief Exec or anything. I think he only works two or three days a week for the company, if that. Do you think people like Dr Crowe play on Sir Neil's nice guy image? If there *is* a cover-up going on with Maternox, I can't believe that he would approve.'

Conor drew on his cigarette again and said nothing.

She climbed down from the bed, went into the kitchen and brought back the brown envelope, removing the contents as she sat back down.

'These are the plans I got this afternoon. Of the Bendix London headquarters.'

She unfolded the first sheet: *Garbutt McMillan plans for new Bendix Schere London Headquarters. 1971 Side Elevation.* 'Let's take a look.' She spread the sheet out and stared at it, trying to orient herself. It showed the familiar front façade that faced on to the Euston Road. Then she opened the next sheet.

'That's the west façade,' Conor said, as she rotated it to get it the right way up. Then they unfolded and studied the neat geometric boxes of the floor plans.

After a quarter of an hour, the bed and most of the floor were covered in photocopied plans and there was a strong, acrid smell from the ink and paper. 'What are we actually meant to be looking for?' Conor said.

'I don't know. No idea. I'm just following up what Winston Smith suggested – the security guard I told you about.'

'Oh yeah, the one with the permanent cold and the wild imagination. He didn't give you any clues?'

'He was frightened, Conor. I think he overstepped his mark in telling me anything.'

He rummaged through the sheets and spread out the front elevation again. 'Something's not right here,' he said after some moments.

'What isn't?'

'I'm not sure.' He frowned. 'Hang on, I think –' He began counting the storeys with his finger. Then he turned towards her. 'I make it fifty-six,' he said. 'These are the filed drawings, right? Or just early working drafts?'

'These are the filed drawings. Fifty-six storeys?' she repeated.

Conor counted again. 'Yup.'

'Except – the building is only forty-nine storeys high.'

'Plus the basement.'

'So that makes fifty. There are six more floors on this plan.' Her forehead creased into tight lines and she felt a sudden faint slick of fear run down her spine. 'So *where* are they, Conor? Where the hell are the other six floors?'

'You tell me.'

61

Wednesday 23 November, 1994

Bill Gunn was seated in one of the ornate black chairs in front of Dr Vincent Crowe's desk. He crossed his legs the better to examine the round black mark, courtesy of Nikky, on the bridge of his Hush Puppy. It was the size of a bullet hole.

It had been a token of her appreciation for his arriving three hours later than promised last evening; one sharp stamp of her stiletto heel and she had walked out into the night; and stayed out.

His foot was hurting like hell, and the expression on the Chief Executive's face did not bode well as he glared at him beyond the jewelled eyes of the papier-mâché frog. Their meeting had been interrupted by three incoming calls in succession and they had not yet got further than the preliminaries.

'How could you be so clumsy, Major Gunn? Surely you have people capable of breaking and entering an unalarmed, isolated house without any trace?'

'Yes, sir, of course. They were taken by surprise – she normally arrives home between seven forty-five and half past eight. This time for some reason she got back at half six; they'd had to wait for the daily help to go and for the cover of darkness, so there they were.'

'Cover of darkness?' Crowe said snidely. 'I don't know why they didn't bother signalling their presence with a military band and floodlights.'

'It was very unfortunate, sir. Her early return wrong-footed them.'

'Oh, it wrong-footed them, did it? You're aware of the damage that could be done if she finds out the source of the break-in?'

Gunn nodded.

'And perhaps you would be good enough to illuminate for me, Major Gunn, why you felt the need to break into Miss Bannerman's home at all? Surely you could have obtained what you needed here, with far less effort and risk?'

'I've been uncomfortable about the conversation she had with Seals – which we only managed to record part of,' Gunn said. 'We also know she had a meeting with this Zandra Wollerton journalist on the *Thames Valley Gazette*, and I felt it was important to find out if she had any documents tucked away. She's got nothing in the office, so her home was the next logical place.'

'Hear this, Major. Dr Bannerman is crucial to our genetics research programme, and his daughter is invaluable to him. She literally holds his life together, she's the one person he listens to. Without her influence, we would never have persuaded him to join us.'

'Yes, sir.'

'If he gets upset and walks – there's no one else in the world with the precise knowledge in the gene therapy areas that we need for Medici. If we lose him we lose as much as a decade on the project.' Crowe raised his eyebrows. 'You do appreciate that, don't you?'

'Dr Crowe, I can't do my job if I'm hamstrung by an inadequate budget. If I could afford more surveillance crews and equipment I'd have been able to monitor Miss Bannerman properly and would have known that she was changing her routine. As it is, all my crews are fully deployed and working overtime.'

Crowe tensed with anger. 'I suppose you'd like to employ more security staff than we have scientists, researchers and laboratory technicians put together?'

'All the research in the world is no damned use if we're just doing it for our competitors' benefit,' Gunn retorted.

Crowe inspected his nails. 'I have to tell you that the Board is very unhappy with Security.'

'With respect, perhaps you would tell the Board that Security is very unhappy with the Board.'

'I take it you didn't *find* anything in her house?'

'Nothing. It was clean.'

'Did you bug it? Tap the phone?'

Gunn hesitated. 'No; be simple enough to do so if we decide we have a problem.'

'Good. Don't, unless you really have to, all right? I don't

337

want any unnecessary risks taken with her. And I don't want any of your knee-jerk reactions, such as when you tried to threaten the *Thames Valley Gazette* group with withdrawal of advertising.' Crowe allowed himself a half-smile. 'This does not, of course, mean you should drop your guard on this woman completely. Whatever your failings, Major Gunn, I have frequently been impressed by your instincts.'

Gunn returned the half-smile, feeling a fraction happier, and emboldened. 'Thank you, sir.' Any form of praise from the Chief Executive, however veiled, was extremely rare. 'We do have another potential Maternox problem which I think you should be made aware of. I intend bringing it up at tomorrow's Board meeting.'

'Yes?' The thaw began to fade from Crowe's face.

'We have another employee enquiring about Maternox batch numbers.'

Now all remnants of good humour drained from Crowe. 'Who?'

'Mr Rowley in Group Patents and Agreements. I've always felt that he was potential trouble.'

Crowe curled his hands, squeezing them so tightly his knuckles whitened. 'But he's got no connection with Maternox at all.'

'I know.'

'The next few weeks are critical – particularly if more Maternox problems show up. We need to get him out of the way. And that applies to anyone else sniffing around where they're not wanted.'

'Including Bannerman's daughter, sir?'

Crowe gave him a pained look. 'You have no evidence that she's on to anything?'

'Not yet, sir. But if I came up with some?'

There was a long silence. 'Then we'd have to take a view on it,' Crowe said finally.

There was another piece of information Gunn had in his possession, which he did not convey to Crowe. It might be a handy ace up his sleeve with which to pacify the Chief Executive next time he threw a wobbly, or it might be nothing to get excited about at all. Data tracking of the company vehicles showed that on Monday night Conor Molloy's BMW went to an address in Berkshire subsequently identified as Montana Bannerman's cottage – and did not leave until 8.47 next morning.

62

Big Island, Hawaii. Wednesday 23 November, 1994
Pele was angry. She displayed it by creating a bubbling cauldron of molten lava across the two-mile-wide throat of Mount Kilauea; by hurtling jagged curtains of rock-strewn fire into the sky; by venting brimstone that poisoned the unpolluted air with venomous black and brown clouds; by blotting out the sun and the horizon, drenching everything in a corrosive dew of sulphuric acid.

The lava flowed in a mile-wide stream, two thousand degrees Celsius hot, down to the ocean's edge, relentlessly consuming everything in its path and pushing the Pacific further and further back every day, expanding Pele's domain. Even when the red glow had faded from the lava, leaving a polished sheen of ribbed grey, the temperature only slowly began to drop.

The volcano was the centre of the hot spot in the Ring of Fire, sandwiched by the Pacific Plate, the Indo-Australian Plate, the Eurasian Plate, the North American Plate. Pele's first home had been on one of the minor islands, Niihau, but the goddess of the sea had chased her from island to island, destroying each dwelling that she created. Finally she came to Mount Kilauea and settled, making it her home.

The Englishman watched the familiar but spectacular sight of the eruption from the window of the Learjet as the aircraft made its landing approach at Kona Airport. In the glare of the sunlight his gaze followed the dense plume of smoke bent by the wind and pushed towards the lush vegetation inland. A helicopter hovered around the edge of the erupting crater like a predatory fly. Half a dozen more waited their turn behind it, each packed with tourists who had paid one hundred and fifty dollars for their view of a lifetime.

Occasionally some paid more dearly than planned. Only a few months back the sulphuric acid had eaten through the drive shaft of one sightseeing helicopter and it had plunged with four tourists into the molten lava. Pele had her own way of letting it be known she was hungry.

The Englishman had learned long ago to control his imagination, yet he allowed himself the luxury of trying to picture how it might feel to fall into molten lava. Whether incineration would be instant, or whether there would be time to feel pain, to squeal? Someone had told him, last time he was here, that if you plunged a limb into molten lava it would char into a cinder then snap off. He was not squeamish, but the thought made even him shudder. He could scarcely imagine a worse fate.

It had been a long eruption this time; fourteen months and the volcano showed no sign of quietening. It might help attract tourists to the island, but the sulphuric acid that rained down continuously was not good for the vegetation. Small quantities were insignificant, but a prolonged output like this was another matter. It could have a damaging long-term effect. And you could not switch volcanoes on and off like a tap.

You could not switch people on and off like a tap either. Some hours later the Englishman stood on the terrace of the Ritz Carlton Hotel, his thoughts elsewhere, as the Hawaiian talked earnestly, wanting to please the important foreigner. Small, swarthy, neat, in dainty dress shoes, he reminded the Englishman of a ferret. It was his eyes that did it, furtive little nut-brown creatures that never stopped moving, as if he lived in fear of the Press Gang carrying him off to sea. *You're a shifty little bastard*, the Englishman thought. *You're running some scam and ripping us off, but I don't care. You're like a dog that goes round pissing on every lamp-post, but you always return to your master because you're scared of him and you need him.*

The Hawaiian's tone had altered. 'You are troubled?' he asked.

340

'Troubled?' the Englishman echoed. 'No, nothing troubles me.' He put an arm around the other man's shoulder and patted him reassuringly.

Beyond the terrace, palm fronds, black like cardboard silhouettes against the night sky, clattered in a sudden gust of the rising wind, making a sound like rain. There was a momentary lull in the hubbub in the lounge behind him, and he turned, casting his gaze across the chintzily elegant room.

People stood or sat in groups around the wide sofas and deep chairs. Americans, Japanese, Hawaiians. Most men wore dinner jackets or dark suits, although a few sported gaudy Hawaiian shirts with open necks. The women were in their finery, several in long dresses, others in skirts slit up to the navel, all glittering with jewellery. The Englishman frowned at the mixture of dress codes. He had acquired many airs and graces over the years, and had become the worst kind of snob, as only self-made people can.

An eight-piece band played, good-looking young men in tuxedos, accompanying a peroxided blonde singer in need of a chin lift and liposuction. When the music stopped, the gaggle of dancers looked faintly marooned, like boats caught out by a falling tide.

Midnight. Today marked the twenty-fifth anniversary of the opening of the Bendix Hilo research and manufacturing plant. The band struck up 'Auld Lang Syne' because they thought that was the thing to do. Sentiment. The Englishman acknowledged the potency of cheap music. Yes, humans were sentimental creatures, their emotions easily bought, and their loyalty cheaply held.

They were letting off fireworks, now, in the darkness between the terrace and the shore. Rockets streaked upwards from behind the shrubbery and the palms. Sparks like glittering jewels cascaded on to the ocean.

'We like to believe fireworks chase evil spirits away,' the Hawaiian said, with simple earnestness.

'Ah.' The Englishman nodded. He watched a formation of rockets snake through the sky, making ghost-like noises.

'Superstitious people, my people,' the Hawaiian said. 'Chase away evil spirits and make presents to the gods.'

The air was warm in spite of the breeze, the ever-present Hawaiian wind which the Englishman liked. *Superstitious . . . Presents to the gods.*

The Hawaiian's words interested him for the first time that night.

The people of these islands were modern thinking when it came to business and their daily lives. They were American citizens, had been for three decades, but many had not lost their pagan origins, had not lost touch with the creators of these volcanic islands. Many still considered their gods and goddesses to be personifications of individual forces: Lono, the god of fertility; Kane, the creator of man; Kanaloa, god of the sea; and Ku, the war god. And then a host of lesser gods and demi gods; the most feared of these being Pele, goddess of the volcano and fire.

Pele, he thought and smiled drily to himself. The Hawaiian took the smile as acknowledgement of his statement.

Mount Kilauea had been erupting on and off for nine years. He wondered why he had not thought of it before, wondered why it had taken a drunken Hawaiian plant manager on a hotel terrace to put the thought into his head.

Bendix Schere had taken a lot out of this island in the past two and a half decades. Tri-Zacktol, a rheumatism cure extracted from the bark of trees in the rain forest. The richest source was here on this island, but they were deforesting faster than they were planting. Cyvodenox, a water purifier, came from extractions from volcanic lava. Then there was Phendol-Optyrvac, for reversing bacillus-induced blindness in the Third World. Something needed to be put back and he knew exactly what. He thought about the Sikorsky helicopter that had ferried him from the airport and smiled.

Perfect. Two birds with one stone. Better than perfect, it was exquisitely brilliant. He caught the eye of a waitress and ordered a large Chivas Regal on the rocks.

When the glass came he allowed himself, as a treat, to think again about the terrible agony of human flesh plunging into molten lava. Then he toasted the Hawaiian. 'Tonight we celebrate,' he said. 'To all the gods of Hawaii.'

342

The Hawaiian raised his champagne flute, and his mouth broadened into a sleazy grin. 'To all the gods of Hawaii!' he echoed.

The Englishman felt the refreshing cold of the ice cubes jangle against his tongue as he sipped his whisky. *Especially Pele*, he thought with a private smile.

63

Wednesday 23 November, 1994
Monty arranged for a bouquet to be sent to Walter Hoggin's funeral, which she and her father were going to attend on Friday, then turned her attention to her eMail; there were dozens of internal queries from various names in Group Patents and Agreements, some of whom she had met, but most she had not.

She was now dealing with at least thirty different people in that department, all of them under urgent instructions to get her father's diverse areas of work protected in as many countries as possible, as quickly as possible, and the eMail traffic was getting close to overwhelming her.

Scrolling down the list she noticed a technical query from Conor Molloy and smiled. They had agreed last night that other than matters strictly business there was to be no communication between them at work.

She would be seeing him again tonight. He had invited her to dinner, but she'd told him that she needed to go to her cottage to feed the cats and get a change of clothes. He had immediately offered to come down and she had not resisted, glad that she was not going to have to spend a night there alone. The break-in continued to spook her, but she doubted she would hear anything back from PC Brangwyn.

Her watch said 9.10. She had been in an hour and a long day was still stretching ahead of her. *God, I'm in love with you, Conor Molloy*, she thought.

Trying to overcome her distraction, she finished dealing with her eMail and started on her snail mail – or physical post – scanning everything dutifully.

Then she came to a bulletin sent by a woman scientist she had befriended over the years; Monty had once hoped she might make a prospective girlfriend for her father, but he had shown no interest. The bulletin concerned the publication in France of the gene sequences of lymphatic tumours in rats. A handwritten memo was clipped to the top. 'Thought this might interest your pa.'

She dictated a note of thanks and put the material on the side of her desk. The next item was a small envelope addressed in wonky handwriting that slanted backwards in some words and forwards in others. The sign of a neurotic, she registered without needing a graphologist to tell her the sender's mental state. The address read: *(MS I think) Montana (as in State of US) Bannerman. The Bendix Schere Empire. Euston Road. London.*

Monty slit the envelope open then looked, bemused, at the letter inside:

Dear Disciple of Satan,

Genetic science is the work of SATAN. God made us. Your work of usurping our Lord God is forbidden in the Bible. IN CASE you are not familiar with IT, READ DEUTERO-NOMY CHAPTER FOUR VERSES 15–18:

'You saw no form of any kind the day the LORD spoke to you at Horeb out of the fire. Therefore watch yourselves very carefully, so that you do not become corrupt and make for yourselves an idol like a man or a woman, or like any animal on earth or any bird that flies in the air, or like any creature that moves along the ground or any fish in the water below.'

It carried no date or sender's address, and was unsigned. Monty placed it in a file thick with ten years' accumulation of crank letters. Bannerman Laboratories had had several attacks from Animal Rights activists in the past, and the police had advised them to keep anything that might one day be needed as evidence.

Although probably written by a harmless nutter, the letter disturbed Monty more than usual. There were a lot of strange people out there, many with strong beliefs. Genetics was an emotive subject. She thought about her intruder and the car that had followed her yesterday, and wondered if the letter was connected. She would mention it to PC Brangwyn when she next spoke to him.

There had been a time a couple of years back when her father, in a genetics experiment in the now defunct animal house attached to their Berkshire lab, had accidentally bred a litter of mutant rabbits with no eyes or ears. They had been captured, by freak chance, in an Animal Rights raid two nights later and their photograph made the front page of several newspapers. For months afterwards the entire staff had received threatening phone calls.

She thought a bit harder. It was unlikely that the writer of this letter was the intruder, if it was, surely he – or she – would have pushed it through her letter box at home rather than mailing it here?

She would almost rather think of the intruder as a burglar, or a pervert who stole women's clothing, she decided. Some of the Animal Rights groups were very scary. On a whim, she removed the letter from the file and photocopied it. Then she put the original back, folded the copy and slipped it into her handbag.

A review meeting of the Group Patents and Agreements Department, which had gone on all afternoon and into the evening, finally ended at ten to eight. Conor raced anxiously back to his office, hastily locked all the files away, grabbed his coat and hurried to the lift.

A bitter wind stung his face as he stepped out into the parking lot, as cold as Washington, he thought, digging in his pockets for his gloves. He found his right-hand one, but to his surprise the other one was missing.

'Shit . . .' The gloves were a gift from an old friend and the loss bugged him. He ran back into the lobby in case it had fallen on the floor, and went over to a security guard. 'Anyone handed in a hogskin glove?' He held up its partner.

345

No joy.

They settled with their drinks at a quiet table in a corner of the Plough, Monty's local, and waited for their steaks and fries to arrive.

'Missed you all day!' he said, stroking her arm, making her smile.

'Thank you.' She opened her handbag and handed him the photocopy of the cranky letter. 'Guess what came in the morning post. Probably just coincidental?'

Conor read it slowly, his expression darkening for one fleeting moment then he forced a smile. 'Satan's work, sure, of course, that's what all geneticists are, closet Satanists.' He handed back the letter. 'Always good to hear of lucid new theories about the meaning of life from the Great Unwashed!' His voice sounded strange.

'I wondered if there was any connection with the intruder?'

'Oh, come on, there's a lot of crazies on the bus.' He changed the subject. 'Did you get a chance to ask your security guard friend any more about the missing six floors?'

'He wasn't there. Must have been his night off, or maybe he's sick. Did you speak to Charley Rowley?'

'He was away today, at the European Patent Office in Munich; should be in tomorrow.'

'Can you trust him?'

Conor grinned. 'He drinks and smokes, that's a start these days!'

The barmaid had brought their cutlery and a basket of French bread over. Conor took a piece and began unwrapping a pat of butter.

'I've been feeling scared today,' Monty confessed.

Conor read the anxiety in her face, reached a hand out across the table and clasped hers. He had not planned to feel this way at all, had not reckoned on falling in love with her. 'Look,' he said, 'I don't know what's going on, but we'll get to the bottom of it.' He squeezed her fingers firmly.

'I must be sounding pathetic.'

'No, you'd be very odd if you weren't upset by what's happened.' He smiled. 'Listen, whenever I feel down, there's

346

some Robert Frost that I say to myself. He's my favourite poet.'

'Tell me?'

'*People are inexterminable – like flies and bed bugs. There will always be some that survive in cracks and crevices – that's us.*' He raised his eyebrows.

Monty smiled and squeezed his hand back. It felt as solid as mahogany.

64

North London, 1951

Half past the hour, and on the hour; that was the timetable.

Hilda Judd closed her front door and hurried down the garden path to the gate. Half past the hour and on the hour. A black saloon car lurched down the road in fits and starts, rings of thick grey smoke belching from its exhaust. Two small boys barged past her playing tag.

'Manners!' she shouted after them, furious, but her words fell on deaf ears.

It was raining hard. She wore a mackintosh buttoned to the neck, a rain hat with the tapes tied beneath her chin, and galoshes. In her left arm she clutched her handbag.

She had two minutes, according to the hands of the kitchen clock. God would delay it, if she asked Him. She closed her eyes for a moment, murmured a prayer, then hurried to the end of the block where she turned right, walked past a row of brick façades that were all that remained of a terrace hit by a V2 in 1945.

Sharp needles of rain struck her face and she stiffened her cheeks against them. A red OXO van crossed the intersection ahead of her, weaving and jigging along the tramlines. She heard the clatter of a bell and speeded her pace anxiously, wondering what was wrong with herself recently. She was never late for anything, had never missed the start of a Church mission meeting in twenty years. Now, not only was she in danger of being late, but she had forgotten her Bible.

Forgotten her Bible!

It lay on the kitchen table and there was no time to go back for it; she knew it was there, had been going to slip it in her bag and she could not believe she had left without it.

Forgive me, God.

She felt a sudden panic, could picture her travelling copy of the Good Book with its brown leather cover and gold embossed lettering, could see its fine pages as light as silk lying beside the shopping list and the crystal vase of flowers.

Daniel had made her forget it, she decided. God would punish him for this. There was something wrong with the boy. Ever since his father's death he had been strange, as if there was something malignant inside him. A cancer of the soul. It was grief, she liked to think in rare moments when she was feeling charitable; but she wasn't convinced. He had developed an insolence, an aloofness, as if he was somehow superior to her. He just smiled when she was angry at him and walked away. Sometimes it seemed even as if he felt himself superior to God, beyond the Good Lord's reach. And that had to be knocked out of him.

Knocked right out of him.

If she didn't do it, God would, and God was too busy to be bothered with ungrateful children. Every day she promised God she would step up Daniel's Bible readings, set him specific hours for prayer, and punish him with beatings when he was disobedient. She had asked God for his help in this task, but the help was not coming through.

Week after week she felt sapped of energy, confused, forgetful, clumsy. It was the boy's fault. Every time he came into the kitchen she would break a glass or a dish. Last night she had dropped a full gravy boat on the floor. It was because he made her angry, she knew; just the sight of his face set the furies raging inside her.

Yet he accepted his thrashings without a murmur. And the less he protested, the more vicious with him she became.

She reached the end of the street and her mouth contorted into a tight circle as she saw the High Barnet tram approaching. Not going to get to the stop in time; it was a way off and on the far side of the road. She heard the smooth rumble of the wheels and the erratic ping of the bell.

Daniel. His face suddenly burned into her thoughts as if it had been pressed through the flesh of her brain with a branding iron. Her head felt as though it would split open in agony. 'Daniel!' she gasped, startled and disoriented, suddenly clutching her head in her hands.

A voice whispered in her ear: 'Prayer!'

It was Daniel's voice. Then again, more loudly: 'PRAYER!'

Images of the street all around her began to fragment like reflections in the shards of a smashed mirror. She turned around on her own axis.

'Are you all right, missus?' a stranger's voice said. A helping arm reached out towards her.

'Leave me alone, get your hands off me!' she screeched back. 'I have to get the tram! God is my guide, God is my saviour!'

She stumbled, began to run. A klaxon beeped fiercely and a taxi swerved to avoid her.

'God is with me!' she called out. 'God will stop the tram!'

'PRAYER!' Daniel's voiced hissed intently, like burning, melting flesh.

A shadow slid across the wet tarmacadam in front of her; chromium glinted; another klaxon sounded.

'PRAYER!'

A bell clattered.

'PRAYER!'

Someone shouted.

'We are all equal in God's eyes, Daniel,' she said loudly and broke into a run. 'He *knows*, Daniel. He *sees* you, stupid child. He *knows* you are evil!'

Had to beat the tram. Had to. God would help her beat it. Bearing down, a shadow, streaks of rain, wiper swinging through its arc, the driver's face behind the glass beneath his peaked cap. The Church mission, could not be late.

'I am never late!' she announced to the world.

'PRAYER!' Daniel's voice was a command now. Her son

was so strong, had grown so big, only seventeen years old but he was a man, a grown man now with a penis as big as her –

Oh God, what am I thinking? Forgive me, God, Almighty God forgive me . . .

'PRAYER!'

She outstretched her arms, clasped her hands together, praying as she ran. 'Our Father which art in heaven, Hallowed be thy name. Thy kingdom come. Thy will be done –'

The toe of her rubber boot struck something, pitching her forward. The tarmac rushed up, thumping her hard in the midriff. She lay, momentarily stunned, her arms still outstretched, hands pressed together, and continued the Lord's Prayer in a breathless whisper.

'In earth, as it is in heaven. Give us this day our daily bread. And –'

A shout momentarily distracted her, then she continued. 'Forgive us our trespasses, as we forgive those who trespass against us.'

There was another scream, louder, more desperate. The ground was trembling now. She was aware of the shadow bearing down, but she had to finish the prayer. *Had to . . .*

The voice that came through into her head was her son's voice again.

'O LORD SATAN! I COMMAND YOU TO TAKE AWAY FROM MY MOTHER THE POWER TO PUT HER HANDS TOGETHER IN PRAYER!'

The pain tore her mouth and her eyes open. She heard the squeal of brakes, the grating slither of metal sliding on metal. It felt for an instant as if a filleting knife had scooped out all her internal organs. A shock wave pulsed through her like the cutting of a surgeon's knife.

Cutting through her wrists.

Blood jetted in uneven spurts like water from an airlocked tap. Then the pain shot from her guts to the ends of her arms. She cried out in agony. It was as if white hot pokers had been pressed against her wrists. The pain went as fast as it had come, and was replaced with complete numbness.

She could see her hands, one to her right, the other to her left, upside down, at impossible angles. Blood was dribbling from both of them. They looked like toys, made of waxwork, joke-shop hands. They must be models someone had dropped in the road, lobbed from the open window of a tram as a sick trick.

The metal in front of her eyes had stopped moving now. Someone was screaming hysterically behind her. Someone else was retching. Hilda Judd tried to move her hands, to put them together in prayer, to lever her body up. But all that moved, slowly and raggedly, were the two bloody stumps of her wrists.

65

Thursday 24 November, 1994
Monty was woken by a sharp, metallic chime, followed by a click, then a whirring sound. As she opened her eyes, momentarily confused, she saw a square of green-grey light. Then she remembered she was at home, with Conor. He was sitting up in bed with his laptop computer in front of him.

'What are you doing?' she asked.

He tapped a key without replying, and a moment later she heard the sound of a modem dialling. Then he leaned over and kissed her tenderly. 'Just need to check something. I plugged into your phone socket – hope you don't mind?'

The clock in the top right corner of the screen said 3.55 a.m. She watched curiously as he slid a finger around the mouse pad and tapped another key, opening the incoming mail section of an electronic mailbox. Then her eyes widened in amazement. Repeated all the way down the left-hand column was the word 'Maternox'.

He opened the first eMail. It was a sales report. Monty read the sender's name: **dsmth@bendix.co.au.** (D. Smith, Sales Director, Bendix Schere Australia Ltd). It was addressed to **alowe@bendix.co.uk**. Alan Lowe, who she had met, was the Group Sales Director, and based in the Bendix Building.

On the next line beneath these two addresses, Monty read the letters: **bcc: eumenides@minaret.co.uk.**

The initials 'bcc' usually stood for 'blind copy', and 'Eumenides' rang a bell from her Greek mythology. 'Where did you get this Maternox stuff from?' she asked.

'Bendix Schere very kindly mail it to me.'

'Oh yes?' She caught the humour in his eyes.

'Sure, except they don't know they're doing it.'

'Eumenides?' she said. 'Is that you?'

'Uh huh.'

'Wasn't she one of the Furies in Greek mythology? One of the three merciless goddesses of vengeance?'

'No, it was a name people used for the Furies. It actually means "the Kindly Ones".' Conor clicked on another eMail message and read through it; it contained statistics from Germany showing monthly comparative sales of the percentage market share of Maternox on a trend analysis. Conor closed it and opened another.

'So, you have an eMail box at this company – Minaret?'

Conor frowned in concentration.

'Couldn't the Bendix boffins trace it?'

'Be very hard – they could only do so by a fluke and I've set up a couple of trip wires.'

'Trip wires?'

'If anyone in the Bendix system tumbled this, it would send me a warning signal and at the same time trash the contents of the mailbox.'

She smiled approvingly, feeling very wide awake now. 'So you're not just a pretty face, are you, Mr Molloy?'

He dug a finger into his cheek and his brow furrowed deeply. 'You know your mythology, right?'

'A little. I'm a bit rusty.'

He angled the screen more towards her and pointed at a word.

'*Polyphemus*,' she read.

'Remember who he was?'

'Yes, one of the Cyclops.' It took a brief moment before the penny dropped. 'Christ!' She leaned forward and read the short message. It said simply:

MEDICI FILE: Password change. Note existing password expires midnight tonight GMT. Replace with: poly*phe^mus.

It was signed: **B. Gunn, Director of Security**.

Conor picked his cigarettes off the bedside table, shook one out and lit it. 'So is that name a happy coincidence? Or have we just lucked into the jackpot?'

'I thought we'd decided we didn't believe in coincidence any more,' she said.

'Yup, you're right. That's exactly what we decided.'

Conor had searched his car without success for his missing glove. He must have dropped it somewhere, although he could not for the life of him think where. He had not left the office at all yesterday, and was almost certain he could remember taking his gloves off there and stuffing them into his coat pocket.

He hung up his coat, then sank heavily down on his chair and leaned back for a moment, collecting his thoughts.

It was ten past eight, a little late but just about respectable. It had taken a supreme effort of willpower to drag himself out of bed straight after making love to Monty again that morning. He now felt very tired, but was fuelled with elation both from the night he had spent with her and from his discovery. He was dying to make use of the password he had acquired, but that would have to wait until tonight. It would be foolhardy to attempt anything here.

He went and got himself a black coffee, then logged into his office computer terminal and checked his eMail.

There were twenty-one new messages in addition to another forty from yesterday that he had not had time to deal with. He tackled the easy ones first. There were several from old college chums in Washington, who exchanged eMail with him regularly, mostly gossip, the latest scandal about the Clintons, the latest jokes, and occasionally serious news of developments in genetics.

It was strange how distant Washington seemed and he realized a little guiltily that he had not responded to the last two eMails from his mother yet. It was likely he was going to

353

have to go over soon to deal with the first of the patent applications and he was not relishing the thought much. Apart from being a distraction to his real task, the fact that Crowe had told him to doctor the Psoriatak application worried him very much. If he got caught out, he alone would carry the can; it would be the end of his career, no question. And, more significantly, the end of his mission.

His screen told him he had a fax waiting and he called it up. It was a standard form letter from the US Patent Office informing him that the Psoriatak application had been received and that an examiner would be appointed shortly, who would be in touch.

The appointment of examiners was a lottery; some, he knew from bitter experience, were much tougher than others, although none were pushovers. It would make a big difference whom he got. Crowe was going to be watching this application every step of the way. Most chief executives in the pharmaceutical industry came from business rather than scientific backgrounds. In this respect, Crowe was unusual in having an impressive array of biochemistry qualifications and field-work experience behind him. He was as good a scientist, if not even better, than most of the people who worked for him. No one in Bendix Schere could pull any wool over his eyes in research.

Conor opened an envelope and removed a notification of a forthcoming seminar on the moral issues of patenting human genes. He had attended a lecture given by the same man before, in the States, and had not been impressed. He dropped the envelope and the three sheets of paper into the shredder beside his desk, and dutifully switched it on.

Then he scanned through the last edition of the monthly *Human Genome News*. As he did so there was a rap on his door, and, using his smart-card, Charley Rowley let himself in.

'Good morning, *Mr Molloy*.'

'Hi.'

'You're late again,' his colleague said. 'Rough night?'

'Don't give me grief, *Mr Rowley*, I'm feeling fragile.'

Rowley seemed more serious than usual. 'I need to talk to you. Could we meet for an early lunch – say twelve thirty?'

'Sure.' Conor wondered if he had some information for him, but said nothing.

'There's a pub called the Northerner – you walk past King's Cross station and turn right at the end of the block, and it's just along the road. About five minutes' walk from here.'

'I'll find it.'

'See you then.'

The Northerner was an unprepossessing joint with nicotine-stained ceilings and rock music that was playing too loud. The place had a sour, vinous smell, and its desultory lunch-time clientele consisted of two workmen in thick boots, a man in a cheap-looking suit reading a newspaper, a couple of old men on their own with their beers and cigarettes, and an elderly woman delivering a monologue to the barman.

Conor spotted Charley Rowley seated in an alcove, looking totally out of context in his dandy chalk-striped suit.

As Conor approached him, Rowley drained his glass and stood up. 'I thought they did cooked food here at lunch time – but they only have sandwiches – let's go find somewhere else.' He said this more loudly than was necessary, and without waiting for a response from Conor headed out of the pub.

'I'm happy with just a sandwich,' Conor said, surprised, and wondering if his friend had had an altercation with the landlord. He was even more surprised when Rowley hailed a taxi, bundled him into it, and told the driver to head for the Cumberland Hotel.

As the taxi drove off, Conor turned to Rowley. 'What's up?'

'Stare straight ahead, don't look round, OK?'

'Sure,' Conor said, mystified.

Rowley turned sideways and peered out of the rear window. 'Yup, I was right. The suit in the pub is jumping into a taxi behind us.'

He turned back to Conor, dug his hand inside his coat and pulled out a letter-sized envelope. 'Little prezzie for you. Tuck it away safely.'

'Is this what I think it is?'

'The Maternox template you were after. It has the original spec of the product licence.'

355

Conor pushed it carefully into the inside breast pocket of his jacket. 'I owe you one. Thanks.'

'Donada.' Rowley pulled out a pack of cigarettes and lit one, ignoring the 'Thank you for not smoking' sign on the driver's partition, then glanced surreptitiously out of the rear window again. 'You know that stuff you were on about at the weekend, about the company –' He shook his head. 'Maybe you're not being so paranoid after all. I had one hell of a game getting my chum to agree to part with that template – I've never known anyone get so cagey.'

'What did you say to him?' Conor asked, concerned.

'It's OK, no worries. I gave him some mumbo-jumbo about the Department being asked to look for ways of extending the Maternox patents – see if there's any room to manoeuvre with the design.'

'Would he have had to talk to anyone else?'

'I think that was the problem, particularly regarding the samples you wanted. I've had no joy on that score so far. They're all under some kind of security lock and key. Seems like I must have rattled someone's cage.'

'Which is why we're being followed?'

'I could be mistaken – but I've seen that suit's face around the Building. Seems a little odd that he came into the pub thirty seconds after me, left thirty seconds after me, and got into a taxi going in the same direction.' Rowley glanced at the ceiling of the taxi, as if he were looking for a bug. 'There's definitely *something* not right going on. Don't worry, I'll try again when I get back from Hawaii. I'll pull a bit of rank if necessary.'

'Hawhere?'

'I've just been told this morning I have to fly to Hawaii tomorrow.'

Conor still looked uncomprehending.

'Yup – you know we have one of our biggest plants out there.'

'Aaah, Hawaii Hilo – yes.'

'Something's cropped up – I'm not sure what – but we do a lot of product development out there, and it seems they're on to something pretty exciting. I have to go over and talk about the British and European patent end.'

'There are worse places to be this time of year,' Conor said.

Rowley grinned. 'You could say that.' He sucked on his cigarette. 'Except I'm not big on hot places – wet English summers suit me fine.'

'I'll happily trade,' Conor said. 'Jesus! I'll be thinking of you sitting on your ass sunning yourself, swilling Margaritas and cooling down in the ocean.'

'I'll be doing the first two, but not the last. I can't swim.'

'You're kidding?'

'Nope. Fear of water. Hydrophobia – or whatever it is. I was probably bitten by a rabid dog when I was an infant.'

'Bendix Schere might have a pill that could cure you. I worked on the patent application for a phobia tablet at Merck.'

'Tell you one thing I do know,' Rowley said. 'There's some fucking gorgeous crumpet in Hawaii. Want me to bring some back for you?'

'Tell you what you could bring back,' Conor said. 'The Hilo plant manufactures all the Maternox supply for the West Coast in the States. It would be kind of useful to get a handful of batch samples.'

'Nullo problema,' Rowley said. 'Watch this space!'

The taxi crawled along in the slow-moving traffic; a couple of times the driver looked irritatedly over his shoulder, but said nothing as Rowley continued smoking.

'Let me ask you something,' Conor said. 'When we were talking on Saturday you mentioned some rumour about a secret underground floor beneath the health hydro in the basement. You said it was supposed to be filled with hundreds of dwarves listening to headphones. Where did that story come from?'

Rowley frowned. 'Actually I think it was from the Head of Department when I first started.'

'Gordon Wright?'

'No, a chap called Richard Drewett. Poor bugger died of a brain tumour – at forty-two – only about a year after I joined. Shame, you'd have enjoyed working with him; he didn't give a toss for the company's regulations either.'

In spite of the Bendix Building's ionized, pollution-free, pure-as-the-Swiss-Alps climatic environment, Monty felt badly in need of some daylight and a few lungfuls of real air, however thick with carbon monoxide and diesel particles it might be.

She went out on her own at lunch time and strolled up Euston Road. It was a crisp day, with a clear blue sky overhead. She was feeling tantalized by the fact that Conor was only a few floors apart from her, in the same building, and she couldn't talk properly to him. At least they would spend the whole weekend together and she was really looking forward to that.

She went into a newsagent's to buy a paper and browsed idly through a rack of magazines.

'A RARE AND CANDID INTERVIEW AT HOME WITH SIR NEIL RORKE.'

The headline on the front of *Hello!* magazine jumped out at her. She bought a copy, walked further along until she saw a sandwich bar with a few tables, one of which was free, and went in.

She ordered a prawn salad sandwich and an orange juice and sat down. Opening the magazine eagerly, she flicked through until she saw the Chairman of Bendix Schere. He was standing by a gilded mirror in an elegant period room, one arm resting on the shoulder of a dark-haired woman, who was seated on a Louis XIV chair. She was packaged in dramatic high-necked couture, and her jaw was set in the kind of masked smile that only a face-lift can produce.

The caption beneath said: 'One of Britain's most colourful businessmen invites us into his Kent country home and tells us about his private and public worlds.' And on the facing page the accompanying article began with a quote from the man himself. 'The pharmaceutical industry has awesome power. I feel my responsibility very deeply.'

Rorke seemed such a humane man, Monty thought, it was impossible that he could knowingly be a party to anything sinister. The company was obviously just exploiting his avuncular image, and the real nastiness was being conducted behind his back by that creep Crowe – or someone lower down the ladder.

She thought about the memo Conor had showed her on his laptop from Dr Linda Farmer to Crowe: *We may have 4th Maternox problem. Kingsley C (Mrs). Under observation. Will report further.*

It made her angry. It was she who had convinced her father to sell out to Bendix Schere, and that was because she had believed in the integrity of the company. She still believed in it and was not going to let a few rotten apples destroy its reputation – and tarnish her father's name in the process.

She did not have enough evidence yet. But if the tests on the Maternox threw up anything she would go to Rorke, she resolved, and spill the beans. And she would do that *before* handing over to Hubert Wentworth and seeing the company destroyed by the press.

Monty stepped out of the lift into the lobby atrium shortly before eight. The rush-hour traffic would have eased by now and it shouldn't take her much more than forty minutes to get to her father's house. And she had another reason for staying late.

Winston Smith had been off the last couple of days, and she was hoping he would be here tonight; gambling on the chance that only a few people would be around at this hour, she might be able to have another talk with him.

She was pleased to see that he was seated alone at the security desk, and walked past the white marble fountain up to him. He had lost weight since she had last seen him, his face looking startlingly gaunt, and his mottled black skin had an even more unhealthy pallor than usual. He did not look at all well.

'Hi!' she said.

He nodded at her a little warily. Normally he would have stood up, but tonight he remained seated. 'Good evening, Miss Bannerman.' He seemed very subdued.

'Are you OK?' she asked. 'Haven't seen you for a couple of days.'

The whites of his eyes had a creamy, opaque film, and his left one had a burst blood vessel. 'Haven't been too good, to tell you the truth, Miss.' He wiped a drip from his nose with a crumpled tartan handkerchief.

'Your cold playing up?'

He patted his stomach. 'No – in here – stomach pains. Get 'em some days.'

'It's not rumbling appendix, is it?'

He smiled wistfully. 'No, nothing like that. I wish it was something they could just cut out, but the doctor can only give me pills to make the pain bearable.'

'What does the doctor say it is? An ulcer?'

'I don't know. He don't say too much.' He looked around nervously, then spoke more quietly. 'Tell you t'honest truth, I think it's more serious than they want to let on.'

'How long have you had these pains?'

'About three years now.'

She looked shocked. 'Who is your doctor?'

'Dr Seligman.'

'He's your GP?'

'Well – sort of – he's the company doctor.'

'I didn't know there was one.'

'Oh yeah, he's a nice man. Got a clinic in the basement behind the health hydro. Always very kind. All of us go to him.'

'All of whom?'

'Us members of staff who were used as guinea pigs – for the drugs trials.'

Monty glanced around. 'Listen, Mr Smith, have you ever been to another doctor, for a second opinion?'

'I been to all kinds of docs in the past ten years, Miss. You wouldn't believe the things I've had wrong with me. The rash is the worst.'

'Rash?'

'It's a kind of psoriasis. Get this awful itching all over my body, and I feel real sick for days.'

Psoriasis. The word struck Monty. The psoriasis file was the one that her father had not been able to find. Something felt uncomfortable to her about the connection, but she said nothing about it. 'And what have these other doctors said?'

He shook his head. 'Oh, you know: nothing wrong! All in my mind! I'm covered head to toe in this rash and I've a temperature of one hundred and three and they tells me I must be willing it all on myself – psychosomething.'

'You told them about the tests you did?'

'Uh huh.'

'And you believe their diagnosis?'

'I don't know what option I got, Miss. You go to a specialist in Harley Street and he says there ain't nothing wrong, who you going to believe?'

She looked hard back at him. 'Harley Street? You paid to go there?'

He shook his head. 'No, Bendix paid. When I told Dr Seligman I wanted some second opinions – well, to tell the truth, my wife wanted them – he was very good, arranged the appointments and all, and the company took care of the bills for me. Sir Neil Rorke even stopped to ask me how I was one time. The company's doin' all it can for me, that I'm sure of. But I'm dying, I know that, and it ain't in my head. I'm dying and they don't want to tell me.'

Monty stood tight-lipped. She dug her hands into her coat pocket and realized she was unconsciously clenching her fists. At last she found words. 'My father and I know a lot of medics between us – perhaps we should get someone else to see you?'

'I wouldn't want to do anything to upset Dr Seligman – he's been very good to me.'

Horrified, Monty noted the simple trust in the man's face. 'I'll have a word with my father tonight,' she insisted.

'Well – you're a very kind young lady.'

She glanced past him at the cluster of white marble figurines rising from the fountain, and quickly scanned the entire atrium. They were the only people around. Nevertheless, she lowered her voice to a whisper. 'Listen, the other day, when I asked you about the lift door that never opens, you told me it would be worth checking out the plans of the building, right?'

He looked uneasy, like a trapped animal, suddenly.

'Well, I did check them out,' she said. 'And they don't add up; I think there are some hidden floors. What are they being used for? Animal testing?'

'Don't ask me any more, Miss, please. I shouldn't have said what I did.' He shot frightened glances in every direction, then leaned a little closer to her. 'Please don't tell anyone what I told you.'

She clenched her fists even tighter. 'Mr Smith, six extra floors are shown on those plans – I want to visit them.'

He shook his head vigorously. 'That just ain't possible, Miss.'

'So you admit they exist?'

Beads of perspiration popped on his brow. His eyes darted around like two frightened voles. 'Please don't ask me no more. I don't want to lose my job, ain't no one else would employ me.' He became even more agitated, and his voice got louder. 'I could lose my pension, insurance, everything. My wife's in a wheelchair, she's crippled with Parkinson's, I can't take no risks. I don't know why I opened my big mouth.'

She sighed, bade him a reluctant good night, and walked out into the almost deserted parking lot, deep in thought. As she approached her MG, parked in the shadows of the floodlights against the far perimeter wall and surrounded by empty bays, she suddenly heard footsteps behind her and turned round, startled.

It was Conor.

'Hi!' she said, surprised and delighted.

He raised a silencing finger to his lips. 'Get in the car and let me in.'

She did so and Conor slid in beside her, pulling the door shut. He gave her a quick peck on the cheek. 'I was waiting for you.'

'This is really nice!'

'I won't stop. Listen, I got the Maternox template from Charley Rowley, but he's set off some alarm bells and is being watched. I can do the tests myself but I do need the right equipment.'

'Like what?'

'Like a spectrophotometer, centrifuge, gel box, transilluminator, and a darkroom with UV lighting.'

'We have all that,' she said excitedly. 'At least I think we still do. I can check with my father – I'm seeing him tonight. We could go to the old labs over the weekend – we'd be completely safe there. As long as none of it has been moved to a Bendix lab.' She thought for a moment. 'I'm sure it was on the inventory of the equipment we're selling.'

'Can you find out? I need some chemicals too – some solvent and gel.'

'Tell me exactly what chemicals.'

Conor did so and she wrote them down in her diary. Then he climbed out and walked away towards his own car.

It was not until she was about ten miles from her father's house that Monty realized that the same pair of headlights seemed to be keeping a steady distance behind her. She speeded up dangerously and overtook the car in front. A few moments later she saw one set of headlights leapfrog another in her mirror. On an impulse, she took a sudden right turn into a housing estate.

The headlights followed her.

She took a random left turn.

The headlights followed her again.

She turned right.

The headlights stayed with her.

67

Conor waited in his BMW until Monty had driven out of the Bendix lot, then started his engine and turned left into the Euston Road. The traffic was less congested than during the rush hour, but still bad, and it took him ten minutes to crawl past King's Cross, St Pancras and Euston stations.

Some of Charley Rowley's anxiety about being followed at

lunch time had transmitted to him, and he kept a wary eye on his mirrors, although with the kaleidoscope of headlights and indicators behind him it was almost impossible to detect if anyone was following him right now.

He carried on down the Marylebone Road, up the ramp on to the flyover, and immediately took the Paddington exit. It led him into a broad, terraced street, lined on both sides with hotels, most of them looking grubby and cheap.

He pulled into the left lane, slowed almost to a walking pace and cruised along, until he saw one that might fit the bill. It had a reasonably modern glass door and porch, set unsympathetically into a classical Georgian portico, and three stars beside its name.

A porter in a green jerkin, smoking a cigarette and reading a rumpled tabloid, was seated behind the counter.

'Do you have any single rooms?' Conor asked.

'How many nights?' The man barely looked up, his voice surly and charmless.

'Just tonight.'

'Do you want a bath or shower?'

'Whatever's cheapest. They have direct dial phones, right?'

'All rooms.' The porter looked down a list. 'Shower. Sixty-five pounds.'

'I'll pay cash.'

'Need a credit card imprint if you want the phone connected.'

'OK.' Conor handed him a credit card.

The porter pushed the registration book at him and Conor filled in a non-existent address in Washington. Then the porter handed his card back, and a key. 'Room seven, on the second floor.' He pointed at a fire door. 'Stairs just through there. Continental breakfast in the room or cooked breakfast from seven downstairs. Do you need an early call or a newspaper?'

'Nope, thanks.'

Conor climbed two flights of the narrow staircase, then found himself in a small maze of landings. Checking out the numbers, he spotted his room almost directly in front of him.

He let himself in, then locked the door behind him. The

room was cramped and cold, almost higher than it was long. He drew the curtains, slung his coat on a chair, then pulled the single bed forward to follow the telephone line down to the wall jack. He tried to remove it, but the jack would not budge. He searched in his briefcase, found a paperclip and used that to lever the plug out. Then he plugged in his modem, connected the cable to his PowerBook, opened the top and switched it on.

He lit a cigarette while the machine booted up, then dialled into the Bendix Schere computer system. In response to the prompt: ENTER USER NAME he typed the user name he had previously obtained from Cliff Norris, the system manager, and then Norris's current password: a*l*c/hem>ist.

On the screen appeared a list of options and commands. He called up a search box and typed **Medici File**. Then, holding the cigarette tightly in his lips, he hit carriage return.

On the screen appeared: RESTRICTED ACCESS FILE. ENTER PASSWORD:

Consulting the back of his diary, careful not to make any error, he typed: **poly*phe^mus**. In response, VALIDATING AUTHORIZATION flashed on and off the screen for a couple of seconds, then came a warning:

Information contained here is strictly confidential. If you are not authorized personnel be advised you are committing a criminal offence in breach of the Data Protection Act, 1984, by continuing and you should disconnect immediately.

Type D to disconnect or return key to continue.

Conor pressed the return key. There was another pause, then the heading appeared: MEDICI FILE. And beneath it, a single sub-heading: **Maternox. Phase One Status.**

When he opened the report, it was headed: **Batch no. BS-M-6575-1881-UKMR. Launch date: 31 Oct 1993. Expected result concentration: Sept 94–June 95.** Then came a series of 'case reports'.

1. Johnson. Sarah (Mrs). Course prescribed 12 weeks prior conception. Unidentified rash of pustular psoriasis type at five months. Two weeks duration. Rash returned at seven months spread over upper and lower torso

during following four weeks. Accompanied by temperature fluctuations from 100–104, dizziness and vomiting. Patient admitted to Berkshire General Hospital at eight months. Death from respiratory failure during labour at eight months, two weeks. Baby (m) delivered postmortem by Caesarean section. Symptoms: Cyclops Syndrome combined with acute pustular psoriasis. Asphyxiation due to gross malformation of respiratory organs.

Conor scrolled down to the next name on the list: **Patel. Zeenat (Miss)**.

He read the symptoms. They were identical to Sarah Johnson's. The woman and her baby had died in the Queen Elizabeth Hospital, Birmingham. The third was a Mrs Roberta McDonald. Again the symptoms were identical. She had died in the Royal Edinburgh Infirmary. Then he came to the next:

Kingsley. Caroline (Mrs). This was the woman from whose home Monty had obtained the six Maternox samples. Her symptoms and those of her baby were consistent with the three above. Conor crushed out his cigarette and scrolled on:

INTERIM SUMMARY
Group total: 100
Total conceptions positive to date: 17
Total miscarriages to date: 3
Total deaths to date: 4
Anticipated delivery dates on remaining conceptions:

Hosain. Caroline (Mrs)	24 Dec, 94
Fanning. Amy (Mrs)	14 Feb, 94
Donald. Moira (Mrs)	26 Feb, 94
Symons. Geraldine (Mrs)	14 March, 95
Liddiard. Margaret (Miss)	29 March, 95
Brown. Anthea (Mrs)	22 April, 95
Townshend, Lucy (Mrs)	5 May, 95
Cohen, Sarah (Mrs)	27 May, 95
Sterling, Anna (Mrs)	10 June, 95
Brook-Olsen. Tania (Mrs)	19 June, 95

His eye went back to the name *Sterling.* That rang a bell.

Anna Sterling. Wasn't that the name of Monty's friend? He lit another cigarette, thinking back to the conversation he'd had with her, but could not be certain. Then he looked at the report again: '*Phase One Status*'.

What the hell was going on?

His hand was shaking slightly as he brought the cigarette to his mouth. His original thought had been that Bendix Schere was trying to cover up a faulty batch of Maternox that had been released by accident. But this wasn't an accident he was looking at here, it was deliberate. Something scrupulously planned and monitored. He read further:

INTERIM CONCLUSION: Inherent instability resulting in random mutations. 100% failure rate with identical symptoms. Many positive factors. Strongly urge postponing of the commencement of LATONA Phase One pending further results and analysis. There is insufficient information to date on which to make firm conclusions.

Conor noticed there was no name attached to the report. Very sensible, he thought acidly. He would not want his name on a report like that.

Latona. He read down the rest of the file but could not see the name. Curious, he entered a search for it. After a few moments the announcement appeared:

Latona Phase One file pages under construction. Access not possible. Commencement date scheduled 31 March 1995.

He got up and walked up and down the tiny room a few times to clear his head. He felt like he'd just opened Pandora's box.

He tried searching for further information by entering a series of key words and names, including *Crowe, Farmer, Gunn, Medici Information* and *Polyphemus*, but they yielded nothing.

He saved the Medici file on to his hard disk, carefully encoding it himself in case someone got hold of his Power-Book, then he switched off his computer, disconnected the modem, replaced the phone jack, and pushed the bed back against the wall. He'd had his sixty-five pounds' worth and was ready to leave.

Downstairs in the lobby he settled his phone bill and went outside.

He was so wrapped up in his thoughts that he failed to notice the man in a fleece-lined parka with his collar turned up against the night chill, standing a short distance down the road.

The man waited until Conor had climbed into his car and started the engine, before sauntering casually up the steps of the hotel and into the lobby.

68

Monty tried to keep calm, driving through the housing estate which she had never been to before as if she knew exactly where she was going. She made a right, then a left. The headlights behind did the same.

She looked with growing anxiety at the soft, warm glows in the windows of the houses, some flickering with the reflections of television screens; she glanced at the cars parked outside, recent models, small and mid-range mostly, first and second cars; it was a cosy, affluent little estate.

Turned right again. The lights behind turned right also, following relentlessly. She braked sharply, cursing.

Cul-de-sac.

There was a small turning area dotted with parked cars. The MG's turning circle was not good enough to make it round in one arc. Monty had to stop, reverse, go forward again. Then she stared, surprised, into the orange day-for-night street-lighting.

The headlights had gone.

She halted the car in mid-turn, wound down her window and pushed her face into the cold air. Somewhere close by a dog was yapping. She studied the gleaming silhouettes parked along the kerb as the MG's exhaust rattled against the underside, blotting out any chance of hearing another engine. Her eyes scoured the parked cars, looking for one with a lone figure at the wheel. Complete stillness. No one out walking. The orange light and the emptiness gave a feeling of unreality, as if she were in a ghost town or on a movie set.

She completed her turn and drove at a crawl past each of the parked cars. Approaching a T-junction now, she checked out the last two vehicles. Both were dark and silent.

The lights that had followed her into the cul-de-sac might just have been one of the estate's residents returning home, she realized. But if so, why hadn't he, or she, got out of their car?

She tried to remember the sequence of random left and right turns she had made. She had turned right into the cul-de-sac, she recalled, yes, definitely. She turned left and accelerated. Then right, then right again. Four more turns and she was pulling back on to the main road.

She watched the mirror. Nothing followed her out of the estate. The orange glow faded into the distance and was gone. Nothing was pursuing her now; only the darkness of the night and her own anxiety.

Monty slowed sharply at the 30 m.p.h. limit sign as she came into the suburbs of Maidenhead. She passed the familiar landmarks of a petrol station, a squat concrete and glass church, a parade of shops, and turned left into the leafy avenue where she had lived all her childhood.

The houses were all detached and substantial, set well back from the road, a few with security gates, others heavily screened by mature shrubs and trees. Most of them, like her father's, were Edwardian mock Tudor; but his was one of the least grand. And although it had six bedrooms, most of the rooms were small, so it never really felt like a mansion inside.

Over the past years since her mother's death, Monty had watched the house slowly deteriorate into its present forlorn state. It looked better arriving at night, like this, when you could not see it so well, she thought.

Not for the first time, she wished her father would find someone and marry again. That was what he needed. Then she smiled at the irony of her thoughts. Here she was, worrying as usual about how to find him another wife, when all the time he was fretting that she was nearly thirty and had no steady boyfriend. She was debating whether to tell him about Conor tonight, but felt it was too soon. Her whole world had changed since Monday evening, but she did not feel the time was right to talk about it yet.

She was still, in her heart, unsure about where Conor was really coming from. She was hooked on him, she knew that, totally and utterly; some part of him was present in every thought she had. Yet she did not know the man, and there was a certain air of mystery about him that both excited her and scared her.

Scared her because she could not read him; could not gauge whether this was a wild fling for him that he might in due course burn out of his system. Could it even be that he had a girlfriend, or, worse, a wife, back in America?

She still knew almost nothing about his background, other than that he had been brought up by his widowed mother, who dabbled in the occult and made a modest living as a clairvoyant. Whenever Monty had asked him about his father, he had always changed the subject. He seemed a closed book on so many things; she had not even been able to get him to talk about the scary dream he'd had.

As she parked and climbed out of her car she looked behind her into the darkness but there was nothing untoward. She walked up to the porch and let herself in with her own key.

'Hi!' she called out, noting that the normal musty smell of the house was overpowered tonight by the appetizing aroma of a stew, and she was pleasantly surprised that her father had actually remembered to put dinner on.

He had a daily who prepared his meals, because he was helpless in a kitchen. Dick Bannerman could have split the atom more easily than boil an egg.

'Daddy, hi!' Monty called out again.

In the silence that again greeted her she felt a momentary prickle of unease. The landing light was on, and she looked up the stairwell, then climbed edgily up. She saw that his study door, at the end of the corridor, was ajar.

'Daddy! Hi!'

Silence. Just the faint hum of the computer which he left on permanently.

A board creaked beneath her step increasing her unease. She walked the remaining few paces quickly, pushed the door further open and peered in.

To her relief, she saw her father seated at his desk, engrossed, only the light of the anglepoise and the glare from the screen relieving the darkness of his study. Not wanting to give him a fright, she called softly. 'Daddy!'

He raised a hand in acknowledgement, without turning round. 'Hi, darling,' he murmured, then gave the familiar signal with his hand that he was not to be interrupted.

She walked over and looked at the screen and glanced down the lines of genetic code displayed there, but they were almost meaningless to her. She knew that genes for all living organisms, from plants to human beings, were made from the same four basic compounds, called *bases*: adenine, thymine, guanine and cytosine. And that they were referred to in genetic coding by their initial letters, A,C,G,T. And she understood that every single human gene is a sequence of these bases, some a few hundred long, others several thousand. From there she could grasp that there are three billion bases in the complete DNA block of a human being's forty-six chromosomes. And that every single cell of a human body contains a complete DNA block.

But because of her very elementary understanding, Monty still struggled with much of the field of genetics. Her father had repeatedly explained certain areas over the years, but not everything had rubbed off. She understood the principle, that human genes were the body's blueprint, that they gave the instructions for the embryo human being to develop from a single cell egg, and for the adult body to replenish and repair itself.

She also understood that when she cut her hand, the genes in the cells surrounding the damaged skin gave the instructions for new tissue to grow, the same as they gave instructions for her hair to grow, for her blood to replenish; and she knew that when genes went wrong and stopped functioning, or went into overdrive and functioned too much, people got sick with anything from minor ailments to life-threatening diseases like renal failure or tumours.

Sometimes genes seemed to stop functioning of their own accord, or go crazy after years of working fine; and some which had been dormant for years suddenly got switched on for no explicable reason. Her father believed that sometimes it was life-cycle changes like adolescence, puberty, pregnancy, menopause, that switched genes on and off – and sometimes it was external influences, such as pollution, stress, trauma. Like all genetic scientists he was forced to concentrate on specific fields, but he was a man of sufficient vision, and sufficient impatience, not to get ensnared in one specific avenue.

Despite his obsession with avenging her mother's death by defeating the breast cancer genes, he had always worked on several related areas of genetics simultaneously. And there was an ethos about this field of research that deeply appealed to him: through the Human Genome Project, research scientists in every country were linked to each other, sharing databases by computer, in a co-operative venture the likes of which had never been seen before in the world of science. For the first time, almost the entire world was united on a single scientific project. That communal sharing of information was what excited him most about the entire field of genetics.

As Monty watched him now, he tapped his computer keys and cursed. 'Something doesn't make sense to me here,' he announced angrily.

That makes two of us, she thought. Then she looked fleetingly at the large silver-framed photograph of her mother and herself which stood beside the screen. Looking at her mother's wild frizz of blonde hair, and the way she was giving a cheeky grin for the camera, Monty was startled by a sudden realization of quite how like her mother she was starting to look.

Her father spoke again, without looking up, still exasperated. He was beginning to look old, she observed with sadness; his body seemed to be shrinking; his shoulders were closer together than she remembered and his back looked less muscular.

'Crowe's got it wrong! It's *not* the way to express this gene,' Dick Bannerman said. 'The man doesn't know what he's bleating on about.'

She moved towards him, put her hands lightly on his shoulders. 'How knowledgeable is Dr Crowe, Daddy?'

He tapped in a command, ignoring the question. 'See that? Recombinant DNA! I *told* him we should use liposomes rather than a virus on this experiment. Two whole days of my time he's wasted.' At last he looked at his daughter. 'Bloody man has a lot of opinions based on erroneous research, but he won't accept anything, always wants to *see* it.'

'He doesn't believe you?'

'Treats me like a bloody student! Don't know why he bothered taking me on, half the time. Don't ask me what goes on in his mind – he seems to have some damned hidden agenda, but I'm buggered if *I* know what it is.' He turned his attention back to the screen.

Monty frowned at the words *hidden agenda*, thinking about the missing six floors on the plans, and the Maternox capsules; her mind also conjured up the names she'd seen on Conor's computer screen that morning. *Eumenides. Medici. Polyphemus.* Troubled, she examined the study. It was her favourite room and the only one that felt lived in these days. The walls were covered in pictures – one of them was an autographed black and white photograph of a much younger Dick Bannerman, in a dinner jacket and looking happily sloshed, standing between Francis Crick and Jim Watson, the discoverers of DNA.

In pride of place, surrounded by a large amount of bare wall, was the colour photo of her father, in white tie and tails, being presented with the Nobel Prize for Chemistry. She had travelled to Sweden with him, just two months after her mother had died. She remembered the band playing, the applause, the pride and sadness she had felt for him then, and felt again now, tonight, seeing him so alone, ageing, and growing increasingly bitter towards Bendix Schere – which only a few months ago had seemed to promise him so much.

Hidden agenda. The words resonated in her mind. 'Like me to get you a drink?' she asked.

'I think we'll eat in a minute – I'm hungry. How was the drive down?' He spoke without taking his eyes from his figures.

'OK,' she said distractedly. 'I'll go and get supper ready.'

'Mrs Turnbull's laid it all up – just have to take the stew out of the oven, I think she said.'

'It'll be a little while,' Monty said and went downstairs. She knew full well he would not have read his housekeeper's instructions and would have forgotten something.

The dining room was freezing as always, the dancing flames of the fake coal fire providing the illusion of warmth rather than any actual heat. She sat at one end of the oval walnut table, in her mother's place, and her father faced her at the other.

They ate the oxtail stew in silence for a while. When her mother had been alive, this room had felt quite different, a real log fire always burning in winter, the table laden with food and flowers, buzzing with the conversation and laughter of the distinguished guests they regularly entertained. It was as if when she had died, she had drawn the life from the room and taken it with her. Even the silverware, which used to sparkle on the sideboard, was conspicuously depleted, the best pieces stolen in a burglary five years previously.

Monty was missing Conor. He was in her mind every single minute. After the last three nights it would be strange sleeping alone again; and in her old childhood bed.

'Tell you who really gets my goat at Bendix,' her father was saying, pouring more red wine into his glass.

'Who?' she said.

'That bloody Slick Willy of an American lawyer.'

She felt as if her heart had turned to stone. 'Conor Molloy?'

'You know – that chap from Patents who joined us for lunch last week. I don't know what his bloody game is – keeps hovering around me, picking my brains all the bloody time. Drives me nuts.'

A piece of green bean went down the wrong way and Monty gulped some water, then coughed. 'Probably not his fault,' she said finally.

'I know where he's coming from. He's one of those clever little shysters who've found ways of getting round the patent office examiners. He's into patenting gene sequences – that's why the company have brought him over here. They want to see just how much of human life can be patented – and they think I'm easy pickings.' He put his wine glass down angrily. 'Christ, this Molloy man's a bloody junior, green around the gills – they haven't even got enough respect for me to bring in a major player! Do they think I was born yesterday?'

Monty smarted, wanting to rise to Conor's defence, and groped around for a reply. 'I think you'll find it's Dr Crowe who's the problem, Daddy. I'm sure Mr – Mr Molloy just has to do what he's told.'

'Oh, sure. He's just obeying orders, right? What is he? The commandant of a concentration camp or something? He's a *thinking* human being; no one *has* to do what they're told. I never have.'

Dick Bannerman seemed happier for having said his piece. But Monty had lost her appetite, and she refused when she was offered second helpings.

Her father ladled some more stew on to his own plate, then asked, 'You've had no joy with the missing psoriasis and diabetes files?'

She shook her head.

'I put those diabetes files in the Stacks myself,' he said.

'The archivist says they couldn't have been removed without authorization.'

'Bloody witch, she is. Creepy woman.'

'Very.' She thought for a moment. 'We'll have back-ups on disk or tape, so it's not too disastrous. I'll print them out for you.'

'I'm not worried about replicating the work – I'm worried about who the hell has got their hands on it. I'm happy to share my research with anyone, but I'm buggered if I'm having it stolen.'

Monty waited whilst her father ate again, and sipped her wine. 'Daddy, what are you doing this weekend?'

'Working on this psoriasis stuff – doing my prep for Headmaster Bloody Crowe.'

'At home?'

'Yes, why?'

'I just wondered if you were going into the old lab at all?'

He shrugged. 'Don't have any plans to. Actually, I find it a bit bloody depressing there now.'

Good, she thought silently.

69

Honolulu. Saturday 26 November, 1994

White horses glinted like tin foil on the dark blue Pacific. The pilot announced over the intercom that the line of hotels crammed shoulder to shoulder behind a strip of white sand was Waikiki Beach. Pearl Harbor, he said, was a little further on, around the point. It was twelve noon local time and the temperature on the ground was a warm twenty-five degrees Celsius. He hoped to welcome everyone back to American Airlines again soon, and wished them a nice day in Honolulu.

Charley Rowley sat in his upright seat, belt fastened, last cigarette of the flight crushed into the tiny ashtray, tiredness from the long journey and too many Bloody Marys starting to gain on him. The Boeing bumped a couple of times as it slowly lost height, banked slightly to port, and his view of the island was temporarily replaced by a view of the starboard wing. He watched it with equal lack of interest.

In the arrivals lobby a placard bearing his name was held aloft by a fair-haired man in pilot's uniform. By his side was a short, dark-skinned man, neatly attired in a chocolate brown shot-silk suit and white loafers.

The pilot immediately took his suitcase and briefcase, and the short man held out his hand.

'Mr Rowley? Don Sontaree, President of Bendix Hilo. Welcome to Hawaii. *Ohahu* – as we say!'

Rowley took his hand; it was small and slimy, like his voice. 'How do you do?'

'You had a pleasant flight?' Furtive eyes raked Rowley's face.

'Yah, was OK, thanks.' He was a little surprised to be greeted by the president of the company in person.

'Good! We go straight on. First time in Hawaii?'

Fellow passengers all around him were being draped in garlands of scented flowers. Rowley followed the two men through the throng and into a stretch limousine. It took them on a ride of less than two minutes to another terminal and pulled up beneath the awning. A few minutes later they were out in the bright sunlight again, climbing into a large helicopter that was waiting amid an assortment of executive aircraft on the apron. Heat shimmered off the concrete and the fuselages, but the wind kept the temperature to a level that Rowley, in his linen suit, found comfortable.

In the passenger compartment the president courteously insisted that Charley sit by the window.

'Please, we have very special views in Hawaii.'

They buckled their seat belts and the rotors began turning. 'No one has given me any real briefing – what's this trip all about?' Rowley asked.

The Hawaiian smiled. 'All in good time. I think you are going to find yourself playing a very big part in our future. It is a great honour for you that you are here, you know . . .'

'I didn't know.'

The Hawaiian raised a knowing finger. 'She gives us so much. Such a debt that we owe her!'

Rowley looked at him. '*She?*'

The engine thundered and the helicopter, vibrating furiously, lifted off. Rowley saw a faint trace of fear cross Sontaree's face, then it was gone as they gained height and he appeared to relax.

Pele.' The Hawaiian leaned across him and pointed to a plume of smoke in the distance. 'See – she is greeting you.'

Rowley frowned. 'I'm still not with you.'

'Pele – it is her salute to you.' His breath smelled of chicken that had gone off, and the patent lawyer averted his cheek as far as he could without seeming rude. But he received a further blast. 'Pele! The goddess of our volcanoes.'

'The smoke, right?'

'*Steam*. She is venting sulphurous steam. It is her greeting to you, you see. Her way of saying: "*Ohahu! Welcome to my island!*"'

'I'd prefer her to give me a gin and tonic.'

The Hawaiian looked momentarily puzzled, then roared with laughter. 'Ah, you English! All the same. Your sense of humour! Gin and tonic! You want one now?'

'I could murder one.'

The Hawaiian produced two glasses from a cocktail compartment, a bottle of Gordon's, tonic and ice.

'Cheers.' Rowley sipped the sharp, fresh taste gratefully, then gaped as the ocean slid by beneath them, and the massive crater of the erupting volcano loomed closer.

'Very important,' the president said suddenly. 'This trip is very important.'

'You have a new discovery?'

Rowley had already decided he did not care for this character much; there was something sly, shifty about him; a wheeler dealer. He wondered how on earth such a man had achieved a position of power. Then he tried to rationalize it. Bendix Hilo was an important research and manufacturing plant for the company, but, so far as he knew, it was not a place where decision-making was done. Sontaree might have the grand title of 'President'. But in effect he was probably a glorified factory manager; that was all.

'New discovery?' the man answered him. 'Yes, all the time; every day we are making new extractions from flora and fauna species. Nature is incredible, don't you think, Mr Rowley?'

'Yup.' Rowley was thinking he could have done with a slice of lemon in his drink.

'Over ninety per cent of our flora and fauna is endemic, to be found nowhere else on earth. We have one hundred species of native land birds evolved from just twenty ancestors. One thousand flowering plants evolved from less than three hundred colonizers; and I could go on . . . Not bad for what was once just an atoll of volcanic rock rising out of the ocean?'

'Incredible.'

'Using every living organism on this island, we are now searching for – and sometimes finding – the raw materials to develop new pharmaceuticals for the benefit of mankind. All thanks to the munificence of our goddess Pele.' His eyes widened into an expression of humbled beatitude.

You're serious, Rowley thought with amazement. *You really fucking believe in your fucking goddess!*

The ocean had given way to black sand, then slippery lava cliffs. The centre of the island was a row of mountainous volcanoes; the south side, as far along the coast as Rowley could see, was a solid black desert of lava flows.

Bypassing the dense steam from the erupting volcano, they climbed above an erratic line of dormant volcanic craters. Then as the land fell away on the far side, the scenery changed dramatically to lush green rain forest. Tall, slender trees rose majestically from a green canopy; narrow waterfalls plunged into dense gorges.

When the helicopter began to lose height, the Hawaiian leaned over and pointed. They were descending towards a huge complex of buildings in an almost hidden valley. The complex consisted of one five-sided white central block, and a mass of long, narrow buildings laid out in neat geometric rows around it. The whole site was encircled by a hostile double-wall infilled with barbed wire.

All Bendix Schere laboratories were like fortresses; Rowley knew that. Pharmaceuticals were a sensitive subject the world over; you never knew what offence you were going to cause in your host country, whether you would upset the vivisection-ists, the ecological pressure groups, or now, with genetics, fundamentalist religious groups.

'Looks like the Pentagon down there!' he commented.

'Only one day, it will be much more powerful!' Sontaree boasted.

Rowley looked at him oddly. 'Oh yes?'

Forty minutes later, Sontaree accompanied Rowley to the reception desk of the Waikoloan Hilton and supervised the formalities, ensuring the hotel understood all bills were to be sent to Bendix Hilo. Then he shook Rowley's hand. 'You have time to check in and have a rest. This evening we are having a barbecue in your honour – we collect you at five-thirty.'

'When do we start work?'

'Monday's plenty time enough. See you this evening. Half five!'

'What should I wear?'

The Hawaiian hesitated, then said: 'Beachwear. It will be very warm. Oh – and please be sure to bring a towel.'

A limousine was waiting outside at five-thirty sharp and the chauffeur opened the rear door. Rowley, dressed in a gaudy shirt and Bermuda shorts, carrying a beach towel, slipped into the chill of the air-conditioned interior.

They drove inland, turning on to an undulating road that ran through a volcanic valley surrounded by craters of varying size. It felt like being on the moon, Rowley imagined. The day was fading rapidly and it would be dark in an hour.

They passed a military air base, a surreal site within the lava landscape, and a few miles later the car suddenly turned in between two smart white gateposts and swept up a long drive. As they rounded a curve, Rowley could see an imposing ranch-style mansion ahead. To the left of it in the dusk, he could see the hull of the helicopter and its rotors. It looked, he thought, a little sinister.

Sontaree opened the front door himself and greeted him warmly. 'Mr Rowley! You have had a pleasant rest?'

Rowley stifled a yawn. 'Yes, thank you.' There was a moist smell to the air that he found refreshing after the heat of the coast.

He was led through into a living room, furnished mostly in rattan, with dramatic views down to the coast, and handed a glass of champagne.

'Your health.' Rowley gulped the champagne greedily, feeling thirsty, and the Hawaiian refilled his glass immediately. The man seemed a little edgy, he thought, and conversation was strained. He peered through the window at the view.

'That's Waikoloa, down to the right – and Kona to the left,' Sontaree said.

Rowley suddenly found he was having a problem focusing.

He screwed up his eyes and tried again. The floor felt unstable beneath him. Drunk the champagne too fast, he thought, a little alarmed. Then the glass of the picture window rippled and it seemed as if he was looking at the view through a goldfish bowl.

He turned, startled. The president looked oddly distorted, as if he were melting. He sensed the glass being eased from his hand.

'Need to sit down,' he mumbled.

'We go outside. You can sit in a minute.'

Feeling increasingly strange, Rowley allowed himself to be led out of the house and towards the helicopter, which seemed to be changing shape as he got nearer. The rear door swung open and steps dropped down; like a tongue sticking out, he thought, and was surprised when he stepped on the bottom rung to find it was firm, not squidgy.

He was even more surprised at the figures seated inside. About a dozen people, he guessed, hazily; all appeared to be wearing white robes, their faces obscured by cowled hoods; and there was a cloying smell of incense.

'Didn't realize it was a fancy dress party!' Rowley said light-headedly, looking around, expecting everyone to share the joke with him. Instead there was silence.

As he watched, the white robes seemed to expand, sliding into each other, as if they were dissolving into one amorphic mass. His brain felt as if it was gyrating inside his cranium. Hands guided him into a seat.

Noise exploded all around him. The roar of the engine starting. Vibration. The helicopter lifted off, tilted forward and began climbing. After a few moments it banked steeply. He peered down at the astronomy observatories on top of Mona Kea; in the final glow of the setting sun they reminded him of melting igloos.

They headed east and as the sun slipped behind the horizon they began a long circle around the crater of the erupting Mount Kilauea. At first all Rowley could see was the dense billowing cloud of sulphurous steam. Then as they climbed directly above the three-mile-wide rim, he could make out with increasing clarity the boiling red cauldron of the lava lake inside. It was like a livid, inflamed larynx inside vast jaws, he thought.

Then something closed over his eyes, plunging him into total darkness.

A sudden bolt of fear curdled inside him. 'Hey!' he exclaimed.

A soft object was slipped over his head. Cloth. It was being tightened below his chin. He was having difficulty breathing.

Pitch darkness.

He felt himself thrust face down on the floor; his hands being tied behind his back; then his ankles bound together. His face was sweltering hot; ripples of panic pulsed through him. 'Hrrrgg! Hrrfggh!' he grunted, trying desperately to comprehend, through his drugged haze, what on earth was happening.

The helicopter stayed high for safety, the experienced pilot well aware that an erupting volcano sucked up all the air in its path. It ceased circling and began to hover, the pilot holding it as steady as he could.

Then all the robed men and women began to chant the Lord's Prayer in reverse, in Latin.

> 'Nema. Olam a son arebil des
> Menoitatnet ni sacudni son en te.
> Sirtson subirotibed
> Summittimid son te tucis
> Artson atibed sibon ettimid te
> Eidoh sibon ad
> Munaiditouq murtson menap
> Arret ni te oleac ni
> Tucis aut satnulov taif
> Muut munger tainevda
> Muut nemon rutecifitcnas
> Sileac ni se iuq
> Retson retap.'

Charley Rowley could hear the sound. He wriggled, grunted, suffocating in the cloth hood. Then suddenly he heard the sliding of metal, the roaring of wind, and a blast of refreshing, icy air. His head cleared a little. Some kind of joke? This had to be some prank devised by that shifty little prat Sontaree. It was then that utter terror seized him.

He was being lifted; hands under his stomach, chest, legs. The roar of the wind was getting louder, tearing at his shirt, his shorts, the bare skin of his legs.

Suddenly, he felt himself roll over. The hands were no longer supporting him. He was falling. Going to hit the floor!

Except he carried on falling.

Icy air pressed the hood around his face like a second skin; stinking sulphur seared his lungs.

Dropping.

The red heat was coming up at him; searing, furnace heat; unbearable, blistering heat. He screamed, a brief, muffled cry before his vocal chords were burned away.

From the helicopter they could see the dark figure falling headfirst, like a bomb. It erupted briefly into a ball of smoke as it hit the 2000 degrees hot surface of molten lava, then was gone.

'Take our gift, we pray thee!' the people in the helicopter chanted. 'Hail Satan. Hail goddess Pele!'

70

Berkshire, England. Saturday 26 November, 1994

'We turn right in about a mile,' Monty said, massaging her temples, trying to relieve the splitting headache she had woken with that morning.

As Conor slowed the BMW, she delved into her handbag, pulled out the packet of Nurolief they had just bought in a chemist's and pushed two capsules out of the foil bubbles.

'You reckon those are any good?' Conor asked.

'Best thing I've ever found for a hangover.' She popped them in rapid succession into her mouth and swallowed, eyeing the entwined BS logo on the packet with unease. 'Even if they are made by you know who.'

'I might have a couple as well. Think I overdid the red wine last night.'

'And the champagne and the brandy,' she grinned, then leaned across and slipped a capsule into his mouth, waited for him to swallow, then slipped in the next.

'Some night,' he said. 'It was *some* night.'

She gave his thigh a squeeze in acknowledgement and then she pointed, suddenly. 'OK, that's it, right here.'

They turned, past a battery of signs, into the campus of Berkshire University. Monty directed him to the far end of a large car park that was less than a quarter full.

They pulled up before a faded sign saying 'Space Reserved For Bannerman Labs', and climbed out of the car into the shadow of the massive concrete superstructure of the new science block that was under construction. A piece of loose scaffolding rattled in the wind and Monty turned warily, memories of Dr Corbin still all too vivid.

Weeds grew up through the concrete hard immediately in front of the redbrick building that housed Bannerman Genetic Research, and the window bars made the place look more like a disused prison than a laboratory.

Monty produced a suitably jailer-sized bunch of keys, unlocked the door and stepped in quickly to switch off the alarm. Conor followed and she locked the door again from the inside.

The interior smells had not changed in all the time she had known this building, and they brought a raft of memories back as the click of her heels echoed in the stillness. A calendar hung on the wall and there was a small hatch through to the accounts department, now stripped bare, which had doubled as reception. Bare old wooden desks, metal filing cabinets, mostly empty, peeling paint. She looked at Conor, wondering what he was thinking.

'Lot of character, this place. Must be sad for you to see it go,' he said.

'A few months ago I couldn't wait to get out,' she told him. 'Now I really miss it. I seem to have spent so much of my life here.'

She led him into the main laboratory, with its rows of

wooden work benches still covered in the equipment and apparatus that Bendix Schere had not required, and the peeling Health and Safety warning notices Sellotaped to its walls. 'Welcome to the hub of modern science!' she said.

'Love it! You ought to sell this place to the Science Museum! They could move it lock, stock and barrel into one of their floors as a tribute to your father.'

'I wish,' she said, hugging her chest with her arms against the cold. Her headache was starting to feel a little better already; it was too soon for the Nurolief to be working yet, she knew, probably just a psychological effect.

God, she had hit the booze last night. She had made Conor a meal at home and he had tried to cheer her up with champagne because she had been to Walter's funeral.

She had been deeply depressed by the service. It had been surprisingly cheery beforehand, with many ex-employees there. But as the coffin had slid through the crematorium curtains, the weeping of Mrs Hoggin and her daughters had made the interior of the small chapel feel claustrophobic, and Monty had suffered intense guilt and remorse.

What if *she* had caused his death?

Ludicrous even to think it. It was a heart attack! Mrs Hoggin had told her at the funeral that Walter had a recent history of heart trouble, which he had been trying to keep secret, and was on a waiting list for a coronary bypass. And yet Monty could not shake off the feeling that poor old Walter had gone the same way as Zandra Wollerton and Jake Seals. Whatever way that was.

And in her darker moments, a question was beginning to grow in her mind as to whether she had somehow been the cause of Dr Corbin's death. As well. She had read once, and it had always stuck in her mind, that there were certain people who were *attractors*; their mere presence drew things like poltergeists.

She shivered. Four deaths. Three freak accidents and a heart attack. She reached up and pressed a row of light switches, putting on the overhead fluorescents; the bright light they threw down felt as cold as frost.

She thought about Mrs Hoggin, who had greeted her so

warmly at her front door nearly two weeks or so earlier. Monty had barely been able to face her outside the crematorium chapel. She had dumped on her, dumped on Walter. Dumped on everyone whom she had involved. And she felt a sudden irrational anger towards Hubert Wentworth. It was all *his* fault! If the stupid old fool had never come to see her none of it would have happened.

Monty showed him the cupboard where the requirements he had itemized for her were still stored, beside an empty flow-hood.

'I thought we were coming into a derelict shell. This place is better equipped than a lot of places I've seen in the States.' He hefted his briefcase on to the work surface beside a microscope.

'Yes, and it all works, it's just old.'

'Shame you ever had to sell out.'

'Research funding's a constant nightmare. Scientists aren't valued in this country.'

'Except by commercial organizations.'

She followed him out of the darkroom as he walked round examining some of the other apparatus in the lab. 'You didn't have any computerized gene-sequencing machines?'

'No – I – don't think so.'

He shook his head. 'Probably a couple of hundred thousand dollars' more kit and you'd have been as up to date as any lab anywhere. You wouldn't have needed Bendix Schere.'

'Maybe if my father had patented some of his work we'd have had the money,' she said ruefully.

'You should have tried selling this stuff to a Third World dictator who wants to get into the cloning business. It's amazing what can be done with a full-scale genetics lab.'

'I remember when Bendix Schere sent a couple of lab technicians down they were almost laughing at us. They said most of our equipment looked like it had come out of the Ark.'

'Well, that's because Bendix don't own anything that's more than two years old.' Conor went back into the darkroom and opened his briefcase.

A brown envelope lay inside on his laptop. He removed a

folded sheet of computer paper from it and read the wording: 'Bendix Schere Maternox. Product Code: BS PR65789/0987. Quality Control Analysis Procedure.'

Monty looked at it curiously. She had only ever seen the research side of the pharmaceutical industry, although she had a working knowledge of the production processes. A column of figures ran along the bottom of the sheet; along the top axis was a plot like a heart trace but with no spikes below the baseline.

Conor shut the door. 'OK, I need the capsules. You got the regular ones as well, no problem?'

'I told my doctor I'd been trying to get pregnant for two years without success. He wrote me a prescription then and there.'

He looked at her to see if she was joking. 'Just like that? No tests? No examinations? No specialist?'

She grinned. 'He's a family friend. Actually I told him Father needed some Maternox in a hurry to do some experiments on and it was easier than getting some sent down by the company. I think he knows me well enough to trust me not to swallow them.'

Monty removed two vials from the small, zipped compartment inside her bag and proffered them to him. One contained the capsules she had taken from the Kingsleys', the other, the brand new ones, from a totally different batch number.

Conor removed the lid of the Kingsleys' vial, coaxed one capsule into a shallow glass dish, and labelled it 'A'. Then he replaced the cap, sealing the remaining capsules in the vial and gave it back to her. Next he took a capsule from the fresh vial, put it into an identical dish and labelled that 'B'.

Then he weighed the two. They were very similar. He broke open each capsule and examined the tiny granules with his naked eye, then in turn extracted a single granule from each capsule and examined them under the microscope. They still appeared identical.

He proceeded to pour the contents of the Kingsleys' capsule into a tiny glass tube then, using a pipette, he carefully added water to fill the tube sufficiently to cover the granules, screwed on the plastic cap, then placed it in the clamp of an electronic agitator and switched on.

The contents of the capsule began to dissolve. After a couple of minutes the granules had disappeared completely and the solution was the colour of cod liver oil. Then, using another pipette, he drew the solution containing the dissolved drug out of the test tube and emptied it into a quartz cuvette, which he inserted into a scanning spectrophotometer. He also followed the same procedure with the second capsule.

He worked in silence for some minutes, then switched off the machine and pointed to the Kingsleys' vial in Monty's hand. 'Are you absolutely sure these capsules really are Maternox?'

'I can't be a hundred per cent sure, no. They were in this vial – and they look like Maternox, so I assumed they were. Why?'

He shook his head, pensively.

'It's kind of weird.'

Something about his expression sent a tiny coil of fear inside Monty. 'What is?'

'I'm getting some correlation, but it's only partial.' Frowning, he traced some patterns on the outside of the glass with his finger, then turned to Monty with deep concern. 'There's something else in here. And I don't think it's just some quality fault in the batch: something's been added to the formulation. Deliberately added.'

'Like what?'

'I don't know. Don't even know where to start looking. I'd have to start a series of trial and error tests and see if we get lucky.' He looked at the clock on the wall. It was ten past eleven. 'How's your time?'

'I'm OK.'

'This could take hours.'

'Want me to make some coffee?'

'This isn't going to be much of a Saturday for you.'

'I told you, I seem to have spent most of my life in here. Another day's not going to make much difference.' She smiled, masking another coil of fear.

71

Conor worked for several hours in deep concentration. Monty whiled away the time by reading and re-reading the Medici File on his laptop, by searching again for her father's missing files and then by going for a walk around the campus.

It was growing dark as she came back into the lab. She kissed Conor, who was now wearing the white lab coat she had found for him, but his attention was absorbed in holding a microfuge tube against a vortex mixer.

He switched off the machine and held up the tiny test tube; she watched as he placed the tube inside a small blue bench centrifuge, added a balance tube containing the control sample from capsule B on the opposite side, closed and secured the lid, then switched it on. There was a sharp whine, followed by a deep thrumming sound.

Monty watched it for a few moments, then her gaze wandered along the wooden benches and tables, the silent machinery, the racks of tubes and vials and bottles. Her mind drifted back to the horror of Jake Seals and she shuddered.

There was a click and the centrifuge began to slow down. Conor opened the lid, lifted out the Kingsley Maternox sample and held it up to the overhead light. The contents had separated into three distinct layers; the bottom a yellow liquid; the centre interface a white suspension, and the top a clear, aqueous liquid.

Using a micropipette he drew off the top layer and squirted it into another microfuge tube resting in a rack. Then he added two and a half times the volume again of ethanol, stoppered it, shook it gently by hand, then placed it into the centrifuge, repeated the procedure with the control sample, and switched it on.

He left it to spin for ten minutes. While they waited they exchanged only a few words, the air thick with tension. The timer eventually clicked and the centrifuge slowly came to a standstill. There was a moment of suspense, then Conor lifted out the tiny tube and again held it up to the light. The top three quarters was a clear solution, the bottom a solid white pellet. He drew off the liquid, immersed the tiny pellet in water, capped the tube, duplicated the procedure with the control sample and vortexed them again.

'OK,' he said suddenly, breaking a long silence. 'Moment of truth coming up.'

He walked several paces and stopped beside a flat, clear perspex gel box, a piece of apparatus with which Monty had become very familiar over the years. He mixed gel powder agarose with salt solution and microwaved it for four minutes; then he poured it into a gel tray. While it was still liquid he put in perforated Perspex combs, then, leaving it to set, he checked out the darkroom. When the gel was set he removed the combs leaving sets of slots in the gel, and put the tray into the gel box.

Next he added blue dye to both Maternox samples, and to a calibration standard solution. Then, carefully and laboriously, one drop at a time, he put the Maternox and the calibration standard into adjacent slots. Finally he plugged the machine into a power pack and switched on. Tiny inky blue marks appeared where the solution lay in the gel. Slowly, over the next fifteen minutes, the blue began to migrate towards the right.

'Fancy some fresh air?' he asked Monty, when he was satisfied it was running properly. 'It's going to take about another forty minutes.'

Monty nodded, gratefully. She was ravenous and they headed across to the university's almost empty refectory. Here they sat, comfortably out of earshot of anyone else, with two large bowls of hot goulash.

In spite of their privacy, Monty kept her voice low. 'Conor, I keep thinking there must be a reason for calling it the Medici File. I mean, they've used *Polyphemus*, who was one of the Cyclops, and so the connection there's pretty evident. What's the logic behind *Medici*?'

Conor dug a spoon into his goulash. 'The Medicis were a powerful family in Florence during the Renaissance, right?'

'Yes. Pretty brutal but big patrons of the arts, literature and learning in general.'

He raised the spoon to his lips and blew on it. 'I guess that's probably the significance.'

Monty shook her head. 'I think there's something more.'

'Like what?'

'I don't know. *Polyphemus* is kind of a sick joke, but it has a logic to it. I think we're going to find the same thing with Medici.'

He chewed slowly and swallowed. 'What about the other file, the one that I couldn't access: Latona? Does *Latona* mean anything to you?'

'Latona?' She repeated the word a couple of times. 'Yes! Isn't it in Ovid's *Metamorphoses*? The Roman name of Leto, mother by Jupiter of Apollo and Diana? The legend is that she was insulted by Lycian shepherds who were then turned into frogs.'

Frogs.

As she said the word, she felt deeply uncomfortable, suddenly reminded of the frog that had come into her kitchen the other night. 'God, that's weird,' she said.

Conor gave her a strange half-smile, obviously recalling the same incident. 'You have a thing about frogs, right? They terrify you?'

'Yes.'

'Have you ever been up to Dr Crowe's office?'

She had to think for a moment. 'No – I've only been to Rorke's. Why?'

'I just happened to notice – actually you can't miss it – he has a papier-mâché frog on his desk. It's kind of weird looking.'

'Hey!' she said. 'Sir Neil has a frog on his desk too – looks like gold plate or something. Horrible! It's probably some incredibly expensive sculpture, but it did nothing for me.'

'So we have connections between a Cyclops, a frog and the Medicis. That's some puzzle to be going on with.'

'Maybe someone just has a very bizarre sense of humour,' she mused.

'I would say that humour is very low down Bendix Schere's list of priorities,' Conor replied.

Back in the laboratory, the horizontal cobalt-blue migration

391

lines shown up by the dye were well advanced along the gel box. Conor studied them in silence before unplugging the machine and taking it through into the darkroom.

Once it was placed on top of the transilluminator, which looked like a photographic enlarger, they each put on protective vizored helmets. There was brief darkness when the main light went out, then the room filled with a purple glow from the transilluminator. Monty looked at the gel box and saw, to her surprise, some bands in the gel which were glowing a vivid orange.

Conor took a Polaroid photograph. When he switched off the ultraviolet and turned on the overhead light again, she could tell from his expression that he was deeply disturbed. 'What is it?' she asked.

He turned to Monty, who was watching him anxiously. 'It's DNA; not a protein, and it's about six kilobases long. You saw the migration lines in the gel box? The way they went bright orange under the lamp?' He looked deadly serious. 'DNA does that.'

'You're not saying there's DNA in the Maternox capsules?'

'Yes. They're carrying DNA and some kind of delivery system.' He gave it to her straight. 'We're talking genetic engineering. The Maternox capsules are genetically engineering something into the women who take them. They're carrying a gene complete with delivery instructions.'

Monty opened her mouth in shock, but nothing came out. A curdling chill travelled through her veins instead. 'Wh-what kind of gene?'

'Can't say – this is out of my league. It needs someone really experienced in molecular biology.'

'How experienced?'

'I guess someone like your father.'

She swallowed. 'Conor, I don't know what we're getting into here, but whatever it is I don't want him involved.'

Conor leaned forward and looked into the microscope again. 'Your friend Anna's on that list, right?'

'Yes,' she said bleakly.

He looked back at her and the colour seemed to have drained from his face. 'Monty, I can't even begin to speculate what's going on here. I had a hunch about the DNA, and it proved right. That's all I can tell you for sure.'

'What do you *think* it could be?'

'Remember Joseph Mengele? The Nazi who conducted medical experiments in Auschwitz?'

Monty brought to mind some of the harrowing accounts of the mad doctor's horrific human experiments, in his attempts to serve his Führer's desire to engineer a master race. 'Yes.'

'Well, unless what's in these Maternox is some kind of freak contamination accident,' Conor said, 'there's someone in Bendix Schere who makes Dr Mengele look like an amateur.'

72

North London. 1953
'Where are you going, Daniel?'

'Out.'

'You go out too much. If your father were alive he wouldn't let you leave me like this.' His mother's face darkened. 'Are you going to a sinful place?'

Daniel walked towards the front door.

'God will see you. God will know if alcohol passes your lips. He will punish you for your sins the way He has punished me.' She leaned into the wash tub and pulled out a sheet, holding it pinched between the metal hoops of her two artificial hands.

Daniel just glanced contemptuously at the pewter crucifix that dominated the hall wall, then at the framed Lord's Prayer sampler that hung beside it.

'You don't care, do you, boy? *Fear God and keep His commandments: for this is the whole duty of man.* Ecclesiastes.'

Daniel pulled on his coat. '*My lover is to me a sachet of myrrh resting between my breasts.*'

His mother's face flared. 'May God strike you dead for your filth!'

He stared wilfully back at her. 'Solomon's Song of Songs.

Book One. Verse thirteen.' Then he slammed the front door behind him.

Her voice followed him down the garden path: 'Remember Job, Daniel? Remember?' She was screaming. '*I was eyes to the blind and feet to the lame. I was a father to the needy; I took up the case of the stranger. I broke the fangs of the wicked and snatched the victims from their teeth.*'

Daniel walked blindfolded, guided by unseen figures who each held an arm, gently but firmly. He sensed the terrain beneath his feet change, felt the chill of the night air replaced with the warmth of candle wax and the rich scent of incense.

He also sensed the presence of many people. Tonight was the most important night of his life. They had all come to witness and support him; he could scarcely breathe, scarcely swallow.

Nerves jangled his insides. One minute he felt strong, excited in the knowledge that he was approaching his destiny; the next, he felt unaccountably afraid. Even more afraid than on the first occasion he had ever come here.

He was filled with anxiety about the initiation ritual that lay ahead. He had never slept with a woman; he worried whether he would get an erection, feared they might laugh at the size of his penis, which seemed so small compared to the gigantic phallus of the Magister Templi. And he was very concerned about whether he would be able to contain himself long enough to pierce her virginity.

A group of boys at school had been talking about sex only a couple of days ago. One had an elder brother who had gone with a prostitute but had ejaculated before he'd entered her. Daniel was scared of the shame and embarrassment if the same thing happened to him now.

Through the rope cords that bound his hands, he pressed his fingers together for meagre reassurance. A door closed; bolts clanked home. Then the solitary peal of a gong resounded.

It was followed by a loud male voice: '*In nomine Dei nostri Satanas Luciferi exelsi!*'

The incantation seemed to hang in the air, growing in

394

strength, then, finally turning into an echo of itself, it slowly faded away.

Another voice said: 'Hail Satan, the Ruler of the earth.'

This was the signal for a thunderous chant from all around Daniel: 'HAIL SATAN!'

The gong rang again. Then it was followed by the male voice.

'Tonight Brother Theutus will become the forty-second Initiate, the forty-second Assessor, the forty-second *Adept* of the Temple of the New Order of Satan. If anyone present dares to challenge his application, declare now your objection or forever live in the threat of permanent oblivion. Speak up in the name of Satan!'

There was a long silence. Daniel held his breath. One and a half years. One and a half long years he had waited as an initiate. Now he was finally to become a first-degree adept. Tonight! *30 April; Walpurgis;* the second holiest night of the year.

A hand-bell rang out shrilly.

There were more Latin incantations. Then he felt his robes being lifted from his shoulders so that he was completely naked, except for the blindfold. Soft hands began to rub oils into his skin in sensual upward motions; silken fingers touched his penis, rubbing something on it that produced a burning sensation. He struggled hard for control, aware that he was starting to feel sharp arousal in the pit of his stomach. He concentrated, reminding himself of all the people in the room, but he could feel his penis swelling and beginning, jerkily, to rise as if it had a life of its own.

At this point the Magister Templi's voice rang out imperially: 'His Satanic Majesty commands you, Initiate Theutus, to prove your knowledge by reciting the nine Satanic Statements!'

Daniel waited as he had been bidden in rehearsals. The gong rang. He drew in a deep breath and in as loud a voice as he could muster said: 'Satan represents indulgence instead of abstinence!' *Gong!* 'Satan represents vital existence, instead of spiritual pipe dreams!' *Gong!* 'Satan represents undefiled wisdom, instead of hypocritical self-deceit!'

He waited for the next gong, then said at the top of his voice, free of all inhibition now: 'Satan represents kindness to those who deserve it, instead of love wasted on ingrates!' *Gong!* 'Satan represents vengeance, instead of turning the other cheek!' His voice soared, rolled around the room, came back at him from the walls. 'Satan represents responsibility to the responsible, instead of concern for psychic vampires!'

He felt the vibrations of the gong rippling through him. 'Satan represents man as just another animal. Sometimes better, more often worse, than those that walk on all-fours. And who, because of his *divine spiritual and intellectual development*, has become the most vicious animal of all!'

Gong! Daniel was growing, growing in stature, becoming a man. He could feel his limbs lengthening, knew that his penis was towering over the heads of his audience, knew that they were in his thrall. 'Satan represents all of the so-called sins, as they all lead to physical, mental or emotional gratification!'

He paused long after the peals of the next gong had died, aware that the assembly had no option but to wait for him and it felt good, so good, to have them in his power. His voice soared through the temple, delivering the last Satanic Statement.

'Satan has been the best friend the Church has ever had, as He has kept it in business all these years!'

The Magister Templi's voice said approvingly: 'Hail Satan!'

The chorus resounded: 'HAIL SATAN!'

Gong!

Hands untied Daniel's blindfold. He blinked as it fell away. He saw candle flames, naked bodies, a blur of faces, and nothing but darkness beyond. It was the first time, he realized, that he had seen the members of the Order without masks. High up, shining from the darkness, he could make out the inverted pentagram on the wall. He was standing in the centre of the pentacle on the floor, alone, with a candle flickering on each point. The Magister Templi faced him from the north point, naked except for his crown, a massive, glinting ceremonial sword gripped in both hands and pointing upwards.

Slowly he lowered the sword until it was horizontal, took a

step forward and pressed the tip against Daniel's chest. Daniel felt the sharp prick, but stood, unflinching. Energy flowed from the sword into his body.

The hand-bell rang three times and the entire temple became silent.

The Magister Templi raised his head high and his phallus rose into an erection. 'In the name of Satan!' he pronounced. 'With this mark, o mighty Satan welcome into Your eternal kingdom Your new adept, Theutus!'

His phallus fully erect now, he pushed the sword harder into Daniel, then ripped it savagely upwards, slicing a two-inch rip in the skin across the breastbone.

Daniel gasped as the blade glinted past his eyes; he felt the sting of pain, then glancing fleetingly downwards saw the loose flanges of flesh and the blood trickling down. But *he* could cope with the pain. He was no longer Daniel Judd. No longer a child initiate. He was Adept Theutus. A man! A first-degree adept of the New Order of Satan.

And he was an Assessor. The forty-second and final Assessor; now the Order was closed. Next week he would be presented with his mask; he had been wondering what it would be, had tried to think which creature was missing.

Morgana, the High Priestess, walked slowly towards Daniel. She wore only her crown, the rings on her fingers and a necklace of tiny amulets.

'Hail Adept Theutus,' she said. 'Blessed be thy feet that have brought thee in these ways.' As she spoke she knelt and kissed first his right foot, then his left. Having done so, she raised her head and kissed first his right knee then his left, saying: 'Blessed be thy knees, that shall kneel at the sacred altar.'

Then she took his penis gently in her fingertips. Daniel felt it hardening even more, but he no longer minded. He was proud of it now, proud of its size.

'Blessed be thy phallus, without which we would not be,' she said. Then she kissed the tip with her lips, lingering lightly with her tongue, fixing Daniel with her eyes. Next she stood and kissed his nipples in turn. 'Blessed be thy breast, formed in strength.'

Finally she stared him in the face and said solemnly: 'Blessed be thy lips, that shall utter the sacred names.' She leaned forward and kissed him on the mouth, then stepped aside. As she did so, another woman adept took her place and repeated the same ritual. Each woman in the temple, in turn, followed.

The last one was the youngest by some years, barely older than himself, he thought. She eyed him shyly; a striking, slender girl, with long, fair hair and a gentle smile. A bead necklace rested on the top of her large breasts, and he found his gaze drawn to her ruby nipples. His penis reached out towards her as if it were an uncoiling serpent, and he was aware of her glancing down at it approvingly.

The Magister Templi stepped forward. 'Our virgin initiate, Lileth, will perform the Great Rite with you in the name of His Satanic Majesty. Are you prepared, Adept Theutus?'

'I am,' Daniel replied. His voice sounded oddly disembodied, as if it were someone else speaking.

Two older women came forward and took Lileth's hands, guiding her down on to her back in the centre of the pentacle. They stretched out her arms so that her hands were on the two upper points of the pentagram, then they parted her legs, pushing them wide out, so that each foot was on the next two points.

The gong rang. The Magister Templi began to incant the Lord's Prayer backwards. As he did so, another male adept stepped forward, holding up a communion-wafer host, then inserting it slowly into the girl's vagina. When he removed it moments later, he held it high as he spoke the communion blessing in reverse, then tossed it contemptuously to the floor.

There was a universal call of 'Hail Satan!' Then every person in the temple, except for Daniel and Lileth, took it in turn to step forward and stamp on the host, grinding it into the ground.

Gong!

Two male adepts each took one of Daniel's arms and guided him until he was standing directly between Lileth's legs. Then they eased him down on to his knees.

The gong rang three times. Daniel saw the girl watching him. He saw the soft brush of her pubic hairs, the pink lips of her vagina, felt the power coursing through his veins.

All around him, the adepts began a chant which started low and deep, resonating, carrying with it an energy, a life force, as it rose towards a crescendo.

He knelt, his confidence faltering for a fleeting moment, then returning as the chanting got louder and more feverish every second. The girl reached out her hand, took him firmly and began to guide him into her. He felt momentarily dry resistance, then soft moistness. He pushed gently forward, not wanting to hurt her, then felt resistance again.

His swelling was increasing; his whole body filling with desire. His hands touched the soft skin of her shoulders and he kissed her on the lips, fully aware of everyone watching. He was doing this for all of them. He was performing the Great Rite for his Lord and Master, Satan. For Lucifer, Baphomet, Leviathan. For the Eternal Omnipotent Prince of Darkness. For the other forty-one Assessors.

The chanting was getting wilder, and more demonic. In response, he pushed harder; harder still, felt the girl's pelvis flexing back against him. Pushed again. She let out a tiny gasp that could have been pain or pleasure, then he suddenly slid deep into her.

He was hardening all the time; she was kissing him ferociously like a wild animal, making tiny little cries every few moments.

His whole body had become a pump and the release came like an exploding bomb inside him. Seed gushed like an energy force from him. It kept on, unabating. She was crying out, and so was he.

Then suddenly he was on his feet again, looking down at her. He was towering over everyone now. Twenty, thirty, forty feet tall, the ceiling of the temple pressed against his head. Lileth's eyes rolled up at him and a smile rippled in slow motion through her lips. Waves of energy pulsed through him. He was a giant among pygmies. His blood had been replaced with electricity. He was powerful enough to do anything he wanted.

'*Hail Satan!*' The chant rang out a long way beneath him, like a murmur of approval.

I am Theutus. I was a boy who became a man who is now become a god. I am the god Theutus.

The Magister Templi rose in height also, until he faced Daniel eye to eye. 'You have the power now, Theutus. The power vested in you by Satan. He commands you to use it! Invoke whatever forces you wish. Satan instructs you to demonstrate your power to us all.'

The Magister Templi shrank back in size until he was again lost in the sea of faces that stared up at the giant. Daniel clenched his fists and said the words of the ritual he had learned.

The temperature in the temple began to drop. A mist was gathering around him; cold, swirling, icy. He concentrated hard, forcing the temperature lower, then lower still. Goose pimples pricked his skin. Spurts of vapour rose from the mouths of all in the temple. He smiled and spoke.

'O Thou mighty light and burning flame of comfort, in Whom the great secrets of truth have their abiding, be Thou a window of comfort unto me. Move therefore, and send a servant to appear! Open the mysteries of Your creation! Be friendly unto me, for I am the same! The true worshipper of the highest and ineffable King of Hell! I ask You Lord Satan to make Thy presence known!'

A long silence followed, as if every sound in the temple had been sucked up by the mist. The temperature was dropping further and the coils of vapour thickening. But suddenly there was a low, rippling crackle, then all the vapour funnelled upwards into a vortex.

It gained speed, until it was ripping past Daniel like a speeded-up cinefilm. All the while, the crackle continued, shaking the air like thunder. Then, within it, he heard a scream of real agony. Enveloped within the vortex of rising mist, he could see nothing. The scream was repeated; a woman in terror, piercing his ears like a knife. Then it stopped as abruptly as it had started.

The temple began to return to its former temperature, and the mist thinned into one thin, swirling strand until it was gone. Daniel was back to his normal size. He stared at all the faces watching him. Then he looked down at Lileth.

For an instant, he could not believe that what he saw was real. A shock wave of revulsion ripped through him. He took a step back, panicky suddenly. But the other faces showed no emotion, no expression.

Lileth's head had been twisted almost full circle. Her eyes were bulging and blood trickled from her mouth and ears. Her flesh had been torn open from neck to navel; some of her guts had spilled out and lay in a tangle beside her. The hideous stench filled his nostrils.

The Magister Templi spoke quietly from the crowd: 'It is indeed a great power, Theutus. Greater than any other on earth. You have learned tonight just how dangerous it can be. Use it wisely, and it will serve you well all the days of your life and beyond into the eternal plane. Use it unwisely, and you unleash the most uncontrollable forces in the Universe. It is important to practise, to learn to harness the power, to moderate it and make it work for you. You have the gift of life and of death, now. Satan does not bestow it lightly. Do what thou wilt shall be the whole of the Law. Hail Satan!'

As Daniel gazed in shock at the grotesque female remains at his feet, the chant rang out once more in unison.

'HAIL SATAN!'

73

Saturday 26 November, 1994
'What do I say to Anna Sterling, Conor?'

He watched the two cats eating hungrily from their bowls on Monty's kitchen floor. 'I don't think you say anything right now,' he said, rattling the ice cubes in his whisky and drinking a slug.

'She's going to die, isn't she?'

'We don't know that for sure.'

'We bloody well do.' She took a cigarette he offered without thanking him and lit it agitatedly. 'That information in the Medici File records four deaths to date and no successful births. That's four out of four, Conor.'

He shook his head, holding his own unlit cigarette. 'Four out of *seven*. There were three miscarriages recorded, and no information about the mothers, so I assume they're OK.'

'Great. What do I do? Go round to Anna and punch her in the stomach. Say, "Sorry, this is for your own good"?' She pulled open the freezer door, and peered in angrily. 'I was going to cook you a really nice meal tonight. I hadn't realized how late it is. Have to be a microwaved lasagne.'

Conor glanced at his watch. It was 10.15.

Monty had noticed that the message light on the answering machine was flashing, but she was too preoccupied to bother with it at the moment. Instead she voiced her fears. 'This is too big for us, Conor, we're way out of our depth here. Don't you think we should go to the police?'

Conor looked evasive suddenly. 'I'm not sure that's such a smart idea.'

'Why not?' She put a corkscrew down on the table, and a bottle of red wine.

'Well – I don't think it's really a police matter,' he prevaricated.

'Four women are dead and another ten could die, and it's not a police matter?' She drew on her cigarette. 'Look, the company's broken every rule in the book. They've changed the design of a drug without going through any of the proper channels. Christ, there's *no* mention of animal toxicity tests, *no* approaches to any ethics committee, *no* CTX . . .'

'CTX?'

'Clinical Trials Certificate Exemption.'

'Oh – right,' he said.

'What they're doing is a flagrant breach of the Declaration of Helsinki. This isn't just some minor protocol violation, this is criminal activity. They're doing Phase Four trials without appearing to have done Phases One, Two or Three. There's no mention of any reports to the Medical Control Agency. Nor the Committee for Safety of Medicines. Nothing!'

402

Conor nodded; he was well aware that every new or modified drug had to go through toxicity tests on rodents and sometimes on a range of different mammals. Then the local ethics committee would authorize Phase One tests on a small number of healthy volunteers. If that stage was successful, Phase Two trials would begin on a few hundred patients, to work out the efficacy and optimal dosage of the drug. Phase Three had to involve several thousand volunteer patients in efficacy and safety trials.

If the drug passed Phase Three, the firm concerned could apply to the Medicine Control Agency for a product licence in the UK; or to the Food and Drug Administration, the FDA, in the USA. After the granting of the MCA licence, Phase Four trials had to begin: a post-marketing surveillance study carried out with hundreds of doctors monitoring thousands of patients, lasting around a year.

The success rate was minuscule. Only one in every ten thousand compounds selected ever made it through to a product licence; and it normally took between ten to fifteen years, with a development cost well in excess of one hundred million pounds, to bring a new drug to the market. The cost of failure was horrific; but the safeguards against anyone doing what Bendix Schere now appeared to be doing were stringent. Monty wondered how it was possible for a company the size of Bendix Schere to be up to such tricks, because such a lot of people would know about it.

'Surely Bendix has internal auditors to prevent this kind of thing happening, Conor?'

He picked up the corkscrew and began to open the wine, thinking about the woman in charge of liaison with doctors. Linda Farmer. She had been cold and unhelpful concerning Maternox. He could now appreciate why.

'You're thinking about companies that genuinely care about public welfare, rather than just giving a whole load of advertising bullshit about it. In Bendix Schere the only concern seems to be keeping the lid on.'

Monty sat at the table, feeling exhausted. 'I still don't understand why you're against going to the police.'

'Just think it through for a moment and work out what that

would achieve: *four* seems like a lot of deaths, but break it down into a percentage of the total women taking Maternox, and the annual figures of death in childbirth, and that four becomes very small. Not insignificant, but small.'

At last he lit his cigarette. 'Altering the design of a drug isn't necessarily a criminal activity; it's unethical, sure, but we need to know just what the hell really *is* in those capsules before we have any real ammunition.'

'Surely we could just give the police a copy from your computer of what's in the Medici File?'

'And they could turn round and say it's a matter for the Committee for Safety of Medicines, right?'

'So? We could go to the CSM, couldn't we?'

'What about the consequences of going to the police with a printout I've obtained illicitly by hacking the company computer? For starters, I'm the one who's committed the criminal offence. If we go to the CSM, I'd be out on my ass – and no pharmaceutical company would ever employ me again. And then there's your own position.'

'What's that?'

'Maternox is a wonder drug. Bendix Schere gets almost half its profits from it.' He looked hard at her. 'If a scandal took Maternox off the market, they could go bust overnight. And you and your father would be back to square one.'

'As if that matters now!' She rested her face in her hands. 'God, *if only*. I wish to hell I'd never got us into all this. I should have listened to Daddy – I –'

Conor shook his head. 'You did the right thing. You just picked the wrong company.'

She smoked the stub of her cigarette down to the filter. 'I think the sensible thing now is to go straight to Rorke. I reckon he'd be appalled by what's going on.'

Conor shook his head vehemently. 'Think about it from his position. Look at what options he'd have. If he goes to the police or the CSM, he knows that the resulting publicity will blow his company out of the water. Melt-down. End of Bendix Schere. All the staff out on their asses and the end of your father's funding. With the name of Bannerman tarnished in the process. And –' He looked as if he was about to say something even worse, then stopped for a moment. 'Rorke, for all his Mr Nice Guy image, would realize exactly how he'd come out of all this. He's the Chairman, for Chrissake; and whether he works one day a week or seven, people are going to think him some kind of an asshole for not knowing what goes on.'

She looked at him, astonished. 'Are you really advocating that we do *nothing*?'

'Until we find out just what that DNA is. We have to know that to understand what territory we're into.'

She nodded reluctantly. 'And what's your hunch? What do you *think* that DNA is?'

'I really don't know. Maybe someone in Research and Development is running scared –' He tapped his fingers on the table. 'The Maternox patents start expiring in three years, and they don't have enough new products to replace them. Maybe Crowe's behind all this: perhaps he's given out a load of bullshit to the company's shareholders, and now they're waiting to see some action which he can't deliver. The fastest way to get a patent and to get a drug on the market, either here or over the pond, is to modify an existing product.'

Conor glanced down at the newspaper on the table, distracted by something in it, then addressed Monty again. 'I think the most likely thing is that Research and Development are trying to crash a modification of Maternox through. God knows what. I mean – the whole concept of using infertile women as unwitting guinea pigs is gross, but it does happen in this industry.'

'And you think there might be a legitimate argument for letting sleeping dogs lie? For swallowing the fact that four women are dead and that my best friend might be next? *I'm* not going to sit around and let that happen.'

He squeezed her wrist lightly. 'I'm not going to either, Monty, I promise you that. But we have to get someone to do an analysis on those goddamned capsules before we can make an intelligent decision, and there's one obvious person who can do that.'

Their eyes met. 'My father?'

'Charley Rowley tried to get some more Maternox. He was

spooked by how many waves it created, to the point of reckoning he was being followed? There's *no one* in the company we can trust. Except your father.'

'Don't you have any friends in the States who could do the analysis? Or couldn't we go to some outside lab here in England?'

Conor took out another cigarette. 'In all four of the women who died, an unidentified rash of pustular psoriasis type occurred at five months. So whatever it is that's happening to the mothers, it starts around or prior to that point. Your friend's baby is due 10th June. It's now 26th November. So she's two and a half months pregnant right now. If that foetus is carrying something that's going to transmit to the mother, every new day makes the danger worse – assuming it's not already too late.'

He puffed on his cigarette. 'There aren't that many molecular biologists capable of doing the analysis we need and these tests are a slow process. We're talking about a good fortnight to get any kind of result. Sure I can start looking for someone else – I have to go to Washington some time soon, but we don't have the luxury of time.'

Monty nodded, thinking hard.

He leaned back in his chair and blew a thin plume of smoke at the ceiling. 'Bendix Schere are not about to alert your friend, or anyone else, to the danger, that's pretty evident.'

'Surely the medical profession is going to put two and two together at some point?'

He shook his head. 'You have a very slow reporting system over here. It could take a couple of years before your civil servants reach any kind of connection.' He shrugged. 'Ten, maybe fourteen cases spread over a year. And don't forget Maternox has a brilliant safety record around the world – numerous other factors could be seen as the problem. Like pollution. Even if they had enough evidence, no one's going to stick their neck out and risk a lawsuit from Bendix Schere over a puny number of figures like that.'

'But a journalist like Hubert Wentworth armed with a copy of what's on your computer could.'

They faced each other in a charged silence.

'What you have in that machine is dynamite, isn't it, Conor?'

'Plutonium.'

'Have you got a printout for safety?'

'I've backed it on to a floppy disk which I've hidden in my apartment.'

'Judging from the break-ins that have been going on, don't you think we ought to lodge a printout somewhere, maybe with a lawyer?'

'I haven't actually got a printer – I use the one at Bendix if I need to. Obviously I don't fancy doing that with this, in case anyone sees it. How about giving a disk to your guy?'

'Isn't that dangerous in another way – Wentworth might decide to go to press with it.'

'You think he's on the level?'

'Yes, in as much as I can judge. He's driven by a demon, but I think he's genuine.' She pulled a face. 'I don't really know him – I've only met him a few times.'

'He's not the editor of the paper, right?'

'No – he's deputy news editor.'

'OK – well, that Medici File isn't on Bendix headed paper, there are no names and no signatures. In theory anyone with a grudge against the company could have invented it. For it to stand up as a story, his editor would want pretty strong corroboration from some other source.'

'What sort of corroboration?'

'With something like this, I'd think at least a sworn affidavit from myself as an employee of the company. You see the problem? I'm thinking about our own backs, too, Monty. Just in case the going gets rough.'

She tacitly acknowledged his point.

'Do you have a home number for this Mr Wentworth?' Conor asked next.

'Yes, it's on his card.'

'I think we should try and see him tomorrow.'

She looked at her watch. 'I could ring him now – I don't think he'd mind.'

'No, don't phone from here. We'll use a pay phone some place in the morning.'

407

She looked alarmed. 'You think the phone here is bugged?'

'I checked both your instruments on Monday night. They're clean.'

'You what? You're pretty thorough, aren't you?' She said it half in jest, half in anger.

'We *need* to be thorough, you and I right now, Monty. Your phone's clean, but there could easily be a wiretap somewhere on your line – the cable runs above ground; someone could pick up your conversations just by sitting in a parked car and pointing a beam at the wires. And if the company did have anything to do with the death of one of Wentworth's reporters, they could well be tapping *his* home line; so even from a pay phone, you should say very little. And try to avoid giving your name.'

Monty's head was pounding again, as it had been that morning, and what appetite she'd had was gone. She went over to the answering machine and switched it on.

There was a call from Anna saying there was a play in London she very much wanted to see and perhaps they could go either next week or the week after. There was a garbled message from Alice, her daily, saying she'd lost her key but had found it again now. The last call was from PC Brangwyn. He apologized that they'd had no luck with the lead he had been following up regarding her missing scarf, and he hoped she'd be getting in touch with the Crime Prevention Officer.

Conor, who had absorbed himself in *The Times*, looked up. 'Scarf? Did he say *scarf*?'

'Yes, well it's a shawl, actually – I noticed it was missing after the break-in. Except I can't be sure – I *may* have left it somewhere.'

His face darkened and he looked thoughtful for a moment. Then he lifted the paper. 'There's a piece here about Dr Crowe.'

'Oh – what does it say?' She began slicing tomatoes and preparing a salad.

Conor read aloud:

'*Computer modelling is cutting years off the search for new drugs for pharmaceuticals giant Bendix Schere.*

'Chief Executive Officer Dr Vincent Crowe said: "We were pioneers in the field of molecular modelling. Only a decade ago, scientists were saying it was impossible to replicate chemical reactions accurately through computer programs. We now have the most advanced computerized research facilities in the world and the true benefits will begin to show for our company during the next ten years."

'Bendix Schere's growth, from a worldwide ranking of seventeenth to fourth, has staggered both its competitors and City analysts in the last few years. But how will the company fare when the global patents on its infertility wonder drug, Maternox, and its OTC ulcer drug, Zoxcin, expire in three and four years' time respectively?

'"We're looking towards transgenics as a major future growth area," said Dr Crowe. "We currently hold more gene patents than any other company and we're filing new patents almost weekly. We have the largest genetics research team in the world and are confident of major breakthroughs in the field, leading to the launch of products before the start of the next century that are going to change the face of medicine as we know it, both in diagnosis and treatment."'

'I do not like thee, Dr Crowe,' Monty said.

'The guy has a major personality disorder. Probably due to sharing ninety per cent of his genes with slime mould.'

Monty grinned. 'I thought we all did.'

'No, the rest of the human race only shares seventy per cent.'

Her smile faded. 'I'm worried about the Kingsley Maternox capsules; it seems like it might be near impossible to get any more if I lose them. Perhaps I should ask our family solicitor to put a couple in his safe?'

'Give a couple to this Wentworth guy; they'd be just as secure in the newspaper's safe; probably more so; most papers have security guards these days, but not lawyers' offices. If I was trying to find out what information you had, your lawyer's office would be one of the first places I'd search – after your home.'

'You might be right.'

He curled a finger, summoning her over to him, then reached up and took her hands, pulling her gently down towards him for a kiss.

She kissed him lightly back, then sat on his lap and crooked an arm round his neck. 'I feel so unsure about everything. It's like –' She fell silent.

'Like what?'

'Like nothing is what it seems. Like those six floors below ground that no one has access to.'

'That could always be innocent, just a kind of Doomsday fallout facility.'

'Except my Winston Smith has a panic attack when I ask him about it. You don't get panic attacks over empty basements. I really want to know what's down there, Conor.'

'You could try asking your good friend, Sir Neil Rorke.' He gave her a sideways look.

'That would be putting him on the spot; and he might start asking awkward questions about how I found out about them. I have a much better idea. Could you hack into the personnel files and get me Winston Smith's home address? If we're going visiting tomorrow, we could drop by and see him too. I have a feeling he might talk to me away from the Bendix Building.'

He smiled. 'Do you know any cheap hotels around here? We could kill two birds with one stone.'

'You don't want to stay here?'

'Sure I want to stay here tonight. But you need a phone to call Wentworth tomorrow, and I'll need one to dial into the Bendix computer to get that address. Let's go find a place first thing in the morning.'

'And check in just to make a couple of calls? That sounds extravagant.'

He looked hard into her eyes. 'There's nothing extravagant about trying to stay alive, Monty.'

She felt as if icy spring water was running through her veins. 'What are you keeping from me?'

He said nothing.

'There's something driving you, Conor. There are moments when you seem as fanatical about Bendix Schere as old Hubert Wentworth. Don't you think it's about time you levelled with me? *Eumenides*. Your user-name. A spirit of vengeance. Is *that* what's motivating you?'

410

Again he remained silent.

'You want vengeance, the same way Wentworth does? Is that where you're coming from?' The barb in her next words startled even her. 'Or am I totally misreading you? Is this all a game to you? Are you just a *little* curious, but not curious enough that you're prepared to risk your job for what you believe in?'

He raised his hands and cupped her face in his palms. 'I warned you on Monday to quit this Maternox investigation while you had the chance. And you told me you were a stayer. Don't start fighting me, Monty, we're on the same side.'

'Are we? I know nothing about you. We sleep together, we talk together, and it's wonderful, it really is, but you never tell me anything about yourself. Every time I ask you about your background, you sidestep like a politician. I don't know the *real* you.'

'You will when the time comes.'

'When what time comes?'

74

Sunday 27 November, 1994

Monty sat in the passenger seat of the BMW as they drove away from the hotel they'd checked into less than an hour before. Conor followed her instructions and after a couple of miles they were accelerating on to an almost deserted M4.

The brightness of the morning had gone and the sky was marbled with cloud; the light was already failing and it would be dark within a couple of hours. A blob of rain exploded on the windscreen; it was followed by another. Monty was watching for the exit sign through the sweep of the wipers, thinking how best to tackle her father. How much should she tell him? And, more importantly, was she putting him in physical danger?

She owed it to Anna to act quickly – and to all the other women on the list. One of them was due to give birth in December; could she be saved if her doctor was made aware of the situation?

She thought of Charles Kingsley alone with his grief in his beautiful mansion flat, and of the same horror that lurked only weeks away for the husbands of more innocent women.

She would have to tell her father everything, she resolved. She would have to swallow all the assurances she had given him about how wonderful the company was; he needed to know the score now. He had a great deal of wisdom when he wasn't being stubborn; maybe he'd come up with the best thing to do. That thought made her feel a fraction more comfortable.

Hubert Wentworth's house was in a quiet, unassuming street on the outskirts of Slough. It had brown pebble-dash rendering and mock Tudor beams, a couple of which had sections missing. The property, like its owner, gave the appearance of being in a state of neglect, a little frayed around the edges.

Monty pressed the doorbell, but there was no audible sound. She glanced at Conor, standing beside her with his briefcase. 'Did you hear it ring?'

'No.'

She waited, then pressed it again. Assuming it was not working, she raised the knocker on the letter box and brought it down with a sharp rap just as the door opened; she found herself still holding on to it as she stared into two rheumy eyes.

She introduced Conor, who greeted the newspaperman pleasantly. Hubert Wentworth shook his proffered hand, and returned the greeting. 'How do you do, Mr Molloy. A Baltimore accent, would I be right?'

'You got it.' Conor checked himself from adding *sir*. In spite of his shabby attire, there was a certain air of authority, of elder statesman even, about the man. 'I'm impressed!'

Wentworth ushered them inside. The house was small and poky, and Monty wrinkled her nose at the smell of old fabric, dust and cats. The words 'Bless this House' were hand-painted on a ceramic tablet hanging on the wall. The atmosphere reminded her of visiting her grandmother when she was a child.

Further within, the living room was startlingly neat and clean, with almost every surface bedecked in a forest of framed photographs. There were literally dozens.

At first sight they all appeared to be of the same person, a strikingly attractive Indo-Chinese woman in her twenties whom Monty immediately recognized from the photo Hubert Wentworth had shown her at the cottage. It was his late wife. The pictures made the room feel eerie, she thought. Like a shrine. Then she noticed a series of shots showing a baby girl progressing through childhood into a young adult whom she also recognized. Pretty as an infant, by her late teens Sarah Wentworth – or Johnson, as Monty had known her – was looking very plain. She had the misfortune to have inherited her father's pancake face rather than her mother's high cheekbones; the luck of the gene pool, Monty thought.

She felt a lump of sadness in her throat. She'd just spotted a wedding scene of Sarah standing in a churchyard beside a rather meek-looking man with short, dark hair. Alan Johnson. Dead also. He had gassed himself in his garage. Except for Hubert Wentworth, everyone in the photographs in this room was dead.

The newspaperman left them while he went to make tea. Conor had sat down and Monty joined him. Hubert Wentworth soon reappeared with a tray laid with teapot, cups, milk, and a lardy cake cut into slices.

'Cake,' he said. 'Cake is what we should have for tea. Sarah, my daughter – used to bring me such good ones, much more exciting, I'm afraid, than this.' He raised the pot and began pouring their tea.

'Did you bring up Sarah by yourself, Mr Wentworth?' Monty asked.

'Yes, I did. Françoise died when she was just three. She was a photo journalist, always in and out of Vietnam.' He poured his own tea, then sat down with a heavy smile.

'You see, Françoise was with *Paris Match* to do a photo shoot, and –'

'That's when she was killed?' Conor asked. 'In the war?'

He nodded. '*She* was killed and *I* was sprayed with a defoliant chemical they called Agent Orange.' Wentworth paused, his face tight with thought, then he resumed. 'They sprayed the whole press corps, in a blunder. Seventy per cent of the reporters there that day have now died of cancer. I have to have a check-up every six months. They tell me it's only a matter of time.'

Monty looked at him in sympathy, unsure what to say. She'd heard some of the story before and her mind was boggling at the suffering, directly and indirectly, that the produce of Bendix Schere had caused this man.

'Agent Orange?' Conor said.

'Yes, or a chemical almost identical to Agent Orange. Anyway, it's lethal.' The journalist appeared to address the carpet. 'Like the napalm that killed my wife, it was manufactured by one of the United States factories of Bendix Schere.'

In the silence that followed he offered the cake. Monty didn't want any, but took a small slice so as not to offend; Conor helped himself and began to eat hungrily. 'You might be OK,' he said. 'These things don't necessarily affect everyone.'

Wentworth smiled at him; but it was a smile that seemed to carry with it a trace of envy: envy of Conor's youth and innocence, and of all the life that he had in front of him. 'Time,' he said. 'That's what's valuable to me. The time I have left. I have no fear of death, just a fear of leaving unfinished business. I – I've often thought –' He suddenly checked himself and started again. 'You've come a long way and I should stick to the point. It was fortuitous you rang, I have something you should see.'

He heaved himself to his feet and went out of the room. Monty turned to Conor, wondering what he made of it all, but he seemed deep in thought and did not respond to her.

Wentworth came back clutching a folder. He looked first at Conor, then at Monty, then appeared to make a decision and handed it to Monty. Inside was a wodge of papers. The one on top was headed: 'Confidential Inquiry Into Maternal Deaths.'

414

She looked up for an explanation.

'The government,' he said. 'They've instigated an audit of all deaths in labour. The forms must be completed by the gynaecologist, the obstetrician, the anaesthetist and the pathologist. They're sent to a regional assessor, then to the Department of Health Central Office.' Wentworth looked guiltily pleased with himself. 'I've obtained the reports on the first three women who died after taking Maternox – the fourth hasn't come through yet. And I have an alphabetical list of every woman in Britain who died in labour in the past twelve months – ah – in case we find the need to trawl a wider area.'

'How did you get it?' Conor asked.

Wentworth slowly raised his index finger and tapped the side of his nose with a wry smile. 'A lifetime in newspapers, one acquires connections.'

Monty detected a trace of pride, then it was gone, like the flit of the shadow of a passing bird. She turned to the pathologist's report on Sarah Johnson and scanned through it. Much of it was in technical language, but part of the summary was clear:

' . . . *suggest retention of body fluid and tissue samples for further analysis to eliminate any possibility of a causal link between the acute pustular psoriasis, viral meningitis and the Cyclopism.*'

Feeling a beat of excitement, she turned to the reports on the other two women. In each case the pathologist had made a similar remark. Her excitement increasing, she showed the comments to Conor.

'Someone in the Department of Health is going to start looking for the link, right?' he said, flicking randomly through the dossier. 'But they're going to have a long haul making any connection with Maternox.'

'Without the Medici File,' Monty said *sotto voce*, for Conor's ears.

'None of this material's come to the attention of the press yet,' Wentworth told them. 'I have it in mind to allude to it in an article on fertility drugs, but one must be careful of inferences; I know the pharmaceutical industry is sensitive and litigious.'

Conor's eyes narrowed. 'I wouldn't do anything right now.'

'Mr Wentworth, I think you should hear what we've found out since I last saw you,' Monty said.

'Yes. Do I gather from our rather brief telephone conversation that you have significant news?'

Conor shot Monty a warning glance, then turned to the newspaperman. 'You're not recording this conversation, I hope?'

'Unquestionably off the record, Mr Molloy.'

Hubert Wentworth then listened in increasing shock as Monty reported on her visit to Mr Kingsley, and on the plans of the Bendix Building; then Conor summarized the news from Charley Rowley and the contents of the Medici File.

'Dear God! This is staggering.' Wentworth's hands were trembling in anger. 'Trials . . . human guinea pigs . . . altering the design of a drug . . .' His voice tailed. He turned to Conor. 'You need a fortnight to identify this DNA, you think?'

'About that.'

'And do you have any theories about what it might turn out to be?'

Conor was pensive for a moment. 'Well, there seems to be a possible psoriasis connection somewhere along the line. All four women who died, including your daughter, suffered a rash that appeared similar to acute pustular psoriasis.' He glanced at Monty. 'We happen to know that Bendix Schere experimented on staff volunteers a few years back, some of whom have developed a psoriasis-type rash. And there may or may not be an additional connection, in that Dr Bannerman has had some important research files on psoriasis genes go missing.'

Conor dabbed some cake crumbs off his plate with his finger and licked it. 'We all know that the worldwide patents on Maternox begin to run out in three years' time. If I was in charge of that product, I'd be trying to modify the design in some very small way so that I could re-patent it. If that wasn't possible, then I'd want to give Maternox some kind of added value to make it better than any generic copies coming on the open market.' He raised his eyebrows quizzically at Wentworth, who nodded in comprehension.

'My best guess right now is that the company's experimenting with some kind of bolt-on added value for Maternox. Maybe a Maternox Mark Two that will not only enable infertile women to become pregnant, but will also contain some kind of genetic engineering formula; say, something that will eradicate a number of specific diseases, like psoriasis, from the foetus.' He looked at both Wentworth and Monty. They both seemed a little startled.

'You really think that's what they could be up to, Conor?' Monty asked.

'Sure. It's a possibility. Think what a great selling pitch it would make: we guarantee that your child will never get sick with all the usual stuff like mumps, chickenpox, measles.'

'Medici?' Wentworth pondered, his ears sharper than Monty had realized. 'Medici File?'

'The code name,' Conor said.

'An unpleasant family, the Medicis.' The older man nodded slowly. 'One must be sure. The evidence must be cast iron.' He picked up his cup, then put it down distastefully. 'Cold, it's gone cold,' he said distractedly. He stared down at his lap.

When he looked up again, there were tears in his eyes. 'You must forgive me,' he said. 'I – I don't know what I was expecting, but it was nothing like this. Nothing of this magnitude.'

He closed his eyes and took a deep breath. 'My daughter. They did this to her. They experimented on my Sarah.' He opened his eyes again and stared at Monty and Conor as if trying to remember who they were. 'Much too big for my paper, they wouldn't dare, couldn't afford the risk of litigation against a firm the size of Bendix Schere.' He pulled a large blue handkerchief out of his pocket and blew his nose.

'I've already had words with Fleet Street.' He raised a hand to quell the alarm he could see in their faces. 'Don't worry; just quiet feelers. We could have a front-page splash when we're ready. *If* we can stand it up.'

Conor looked at him stern. 'If we entrust a copy of our material to you on disk, and lodge two Maternox capsules with

417

you, can you give us your word that they'll be locked in a safe in your building until we say so?'

'You have more than my word, Mr Molloy. You have my hands tied behind my back and my mouth gagged. I couldn't possibly run this story without an affidavit from you, and I think a Fleet Street editor is going to want even more corroboration than that.'

'I would think a testimony from Dr Bannerman on the content of the capsules might add some weight,' Conor said.

'A great deal,' Wentworth agreed.

'I'm lodging a personal affidavit with a law firm here in England,' Conor said. 'The guy's name is Bob Storer at Harbottle and Lewis; I've already sent him a disk copy of the Medici File by registered mail and I'm going to instruct him that if anything happens to me, he's to contact you and make the information available to you.'

Monty registered her own private reaction to this speech. Those last words at last made her feel that Conor had finally and incontrovertibly nailed his colours to the mast. She did know where he stood after all.

Minutes later, Monty and Conor left. Wentworth retained the disk and two Maternox capsules, having given his assurance that they'd be secure in the *Gazette*'s safe.

As they walked out into the falling dusk, and reached the pavement, Conor's pace slowed for an instant and he seemed to stiffen. He unlocked the BMW's passenger door, held it open for Monty and said, very quietly, 'Don't look round. Just get in the car quickly. We have company.'

75

'Just keep looking straight ahead,' Conor said, pulling out and accelerating gently down Wentworth's road.

Monty sat stiffly and stared into her wing mirror. She could see nothing behind them.

Conor drove to the end of the street, made a left, then a second left and proceeded down a long residential street. At the end, he made another turn, followed by another which took them back into Wentworth's street, several hundred yards up from his house. Tail lights were disappearing at the far end, in the direction where they had turned not much more than a minute earlier.

Conor drove along the tree-lined road, scanning the parked cars that lined both sides, then stopped, about fifty yards before the newspaperman's house. He pointed to a gap large enough for a single car. 'See that space?'

'Yes,' Monty said.

'It was like that when we arrived, but there was a grey Ford with a driver sitting in it when we came out. Now it's empty again. Coincidence?'

'Did you notice anyone following us on our way here?'

'We were on our own – I was watching real carefully.' He eyed Wentworth's house, glanced in his mirror and frowned.

'Do you think *his* phone might be bugged?' she suggested. 'Is that how they – whoever – knew we were here?'

'Doesn't make much sense to me – if they *knew* we were here, why bother to come down then drive off again?'

'Maybe they were bugging our meeting by using some device in that Ford?'

Conor nodded, and for the first time Monty thought she detected fear in his expression. Her brain spun, trying to recall what details they'd just discussed, trying to work out how much an outsider listening in could have gleaned. 'If they *were* listening, we've just given the game away, haven't we?'

Conor drove on. 'Let's hope they weren't, but it might be smart for our own safety to assume the worst.' He scanned the road ahead. 'We need to move fast now, real fast.'

'Daddy's in Glasgow tonight, giving an informal talk to a group of scientists; he's catching the shuttle to London first thing tomorrow. I'll take him out for lunch and talk to him.'

'Want me to come with you?'

She remembered her father's comments about Conor at supper on Thursday night. 'I think it would be better for me to handle him on my own,' she said tactfully. Then she took Winston Smith's home address in Whitechapel out of her handbag and opened Conor's *A-Z*.

'How do you think he'll react?' Conor asked.

'I don't think it's going to be that easy,' she said. 'I can't just spring all this on him – I'll have to break it to him bit by bit.'

Conor had headed back towards the main road. 'He gave me the impression he doesn't like Bendix Schere one little bit, and would jump through hoops to have a go at them.'

'Yes, I have an idea that's how he's going to react, but I need to make sure he understands the danger.'

It was dark when they arrived outside the East End block where Winston Smith lived. It was an ugly council low-rise, gridded with metal fire escapes and external walkways.

Conor parked in the street and Monty climbed out of the car. Then she leaned in and grinned. 'Make sure no one steals the wheels while you're waiting for me.'

He dubiously eyed the near derelict condition of some of the old bangers on the other side of the street, and nodded.

Monty stared up at Albany Court with a faint shudder; it had an air of squalor, the walls stained and cracked with gangrenous blotches, laundry hanging from makeshift lines, and a swastika spray-painted on a ground-floor wall. Rap music was pounding from a window just above her.

There was a sign listing the flat numbers and levels. Number 27 was on the second floor and there was an arrow pointing the way up. She dug her hands into her jacket pockets, climbed the vibrating metal steps, then went along a walkway cluttered with bins and black garbage bags.

The front doors were all identical, with large frosted glass panels and peeling blue paint. She stopped outside number 27, feeling very tense suddenly, and rang the bell.

After a moment the door shook, then opened. A black woman in her forties stood there on crutches; dressed in a woollen jumper and dungarees, she looked painfully thin and her complexion was waxy.

'I'm sorry to disturb you. Is Winston Smith in?' Monty asked.

The woman studied Monty before answering. 'He's in hospital.'

'I'm sorry. I didn't know that.'

'Friday afternoon, he got took poorly again.'

'I – I work with him – I wanted to have a word with him. I didn't realize . . .'

The woman's eyes narrowed into two slits, like vizors in a helmet. The effect was unnerving. 'Work with him?'

'At Bendix Schere.' Monty suddenly found herself at a loss, and tried to keep her voice relaxed and friendly. 'Which hospital is he in?'

The eye slits widened a fraction. 'The *clinic*. The same one he always goes.' The woman's tone implied that Monty should have known that if she really worked with him.

'The Bendix Clinic?'

'Hammersmith.'

'Hammersmith, right.' She forced herself to ask the next question. 'How – how is he?'

The other woman seemed to be trying to weigh up whether she could trust her visitor. 'He come out in the rash again. The pain's real bad.' She eyed Monty up and down, and said rather disparagingly, 'Are you the scientist's daughter?'

'I'm sorry,' Monty said. 'I didn't introduce myself. Yes, I'm Montana Bannerman.'

The woman nodded expressionlessly. 'You tells my husband about books. He's very grateful to you for that. But you makes him frightened. He tell me you been asking questions. Now he's worried he tell you too much.'

Monty smiled gently at the woman. 'Do you want to talk to me about it?'

Mrs Smith shook her head. Her eyes skittered past Monty, as if terrified someone else was listening.

Monty smiled again. 'I'm just interested in trying to learn a little more about the company – Bendix Schere – it's a very secretive place. I get the feeling there's something Mr Smith really wants me to know. And I just wanted to say that he can trust me.' Monty felt awkward standing in the doorway, having to talk in a low voice. 'Could I come in for a moment and explain? I do want to help your husband.'

Mrs Smith's face contorted into fear. 'Sorry, no; sorry. We are sick people, the company is good to us, gives us free medicines, Winston always has a private room. Please let him be.'

'Did *you* take trial medicines for the company, too, Mrs Smith?'

'Bendix has been very good to us, I don't want to say nothing more. Thank you for coming. Thank you for your concern about my husband's health. I tell him you called.'

She stepped back and closed the door, leaving Monty to walk slowly back to the car.

The Bendix Hammersmith Clinic was a smoked-glass, eight-storey high-rise just west of the flyover. It was conveniently sited for Heathrow, and it attracted a clientele of wealthy Asians and Middle Easterns who could jet in for cosmetic surgery, abortions, infertility treatment, pre-conceptual gender selection, and, more recently, for genetic screening. The Hammersmith Bendix, as it was called, was regarded in medical circles as one of the most luxurious and state-of-the-art private hospitals in Britain, and a range of eminent specialists had attached their names to it.

It struck Monty as more than a little curious that the company should provide such facilities for one of its security guards. Even with Sir Neil Rorke's publicly declared caring attitudes, putting Winston Smith in a £400-per-night bed smacked of guilt. Or something sinister.

Once again, they'd decided that Conor should wait in the car as she went inside. Electric doors glided open, then closed behind her. Triple glazing and white sound completely deadened the roar of London's traffic and the faint scent of flowers recalled the lobby of the Bendix Building.

The carpet was plush, interwoven with a repeat geometric pattern of the 'BS' logo, the walls and ceiling were panelled in pine, and down the corridor to the right were an elegant gift shop, then a florist.

The feel-good factor was an important part of company philosophy. They wanted patients to have the sensation of arriving at an exclusive country hotel, not a hospital. In fact the word *patient* was never used; they were called *guests*.

Monty walked up to the reception counter and asked, as nonchalantly as possible, which room Winston Smith was in.

A platinum blonde in her early thirties, wearing the company's regulation smile as stiffly as its chalk-striped grey two-piece, touched some keys on her computer screen. The smile narrowed, just a fraction.

'May I take your name?' she asked.

Monty was thrown by the unexpected question.

'Surname then initials.' The receptionist's eyes had a cornflower-blue glaze as if she was wearing tinted contact lenses, adding to her automaton quality. She reminded Monty of someone from *The Stepford Wives*.

Monty's brain raced furiously. 'Gordon,' she said, plucking a name out of thin air. 'Mrs Lyndsey Gordon.'

'And your address, please, Mrs Gordon?'

'This is a little unusual, isn't it?' Monty asked.

'It's just a security formality,' the young woman said with unswerving politeness.

'The Coach House, Burnham Beeches Lane, Burnham, Bucks.'

'Post code?'

Monty gave a code to go with the address she'd just made up.

The woman entered it into the computer. 'And your phone number, please?'

Monty felt her face beginning to give her away; 'We're ex-directory,' she said. 'I never give the number to anyone.'

The receptionist typed something else into the computer without commenting, then her next words came like a blow: 'I'm afraid Mr Smith is not permitted visitors.'

Monty detected a change in attitude now; an almost shifty evasiveness. 'When will he be allowed them?'

'I'm afraid I can't give you that information.'

Monty tried, with a warm smile, to appeal to this woman's better nature. 'Oh dear, I've driven two hours to come here. Is it not possible just to see him for a few minutes?'

The receptionist's eyes seemed to focus on some far horizon behind Monty's head. 'I'm sorry, Mr Smith is not permitted visitors.'

Monty parted her hands in a gesture of despair. 'Could you let me have his room number, so I could send him some flowers?'

'Don't worry, Mrs Gordon. If you use Mr Smith's name we'll see that they reach him. She pointed across the foyer. 'You can give your order to our florist right there and she'll take care of it for you.'

There no longer seemed to be anybody home behind the contact lenses.

Monty turned and ambled past the gift shop towards the florist, deliberately taking her time. Two expensively dressed Asians came in as she did so, and went up to reception. Pleased that Miss Cornflower Blue was now distracted, Monty walked quickly into the florist's and bought the smallest bunch of flowers on display, a spray of six tulips, which staggered her by costing five pounds.

She carried them out, glancing in the direction of the receptionist, who was still occupied with the Asians, and went over to the lifts. As she pressed the button, the doors of one opened instantly and she stepped in, then wondered which floor to try first. For no particular reason, she pressed the sixth.

The doors opened on to a wide corridor, with the same plush carpeting as the foyer. Only a metal trolley of surgical instruments and the sight of two uniformed nurses gave away that this was a hospital, and not a five-star hotel.

She turned and walked in the opposite direction to the nurses, past doors each marked with a name card. One was ajar and she slowed as she passed it, peering in, and saw a woman with blackened eyes, her nose encased in plaster, lying in bed watching television.

'A. Gupta' was the name on the next door. Then 'Miss E. Carderelli'; 'D. Patel'; 'H. Wintergarten'. No Winston Smith.

At the end of the corridor was a recessed area with several telephones on a desk and a large planning board on the wall. It looked like a nursing station. Monty glanced behind her, but the two nurses had disappeared. She slipped across and scanned first the desk, then the notice board. Almost immediately she saw a chart marked: '6th and 7th Floor Guest List'.

Nervously, she shot a glance back at the corridor, then read the names on the list. 'W. Smith. 712.' She double-checked to make sure, then walked cautiously back into the corridor. A nurse emerged from a room a few doors in front of her and began walking towards the nursing station. Monty passed her without meeting her eyes. But as they crossed, she heard the young woman speak.

'Can I help you, madam?'

Monty turned, blushing. The nurse was pretty, as all the Bendix nurses were, with an open, freckled face. 'I – er – think I'm on the wrong floor. This isn't the seventh?'

'No.' She pointed to the lift. 'Just go up one floor.'

Monty thanked her, and complied. A few moments later she stepped out on to an identical scene and glanced at the numbers on the doors to orient herself, then turned right. 710. 711. 712.

She noted with some surprise that the card slot on number 712 was empty. It was the only door she'd seen that had no name. She glanced up and down the corridor. A female orderly was pushing a food trolley towards her. She took a breath, then turned the door handle and pushed.

The door was locked.

She tried the handle again, to make sure, then knocked softly and pressed her ear to the door. She knocked again, a little louder. Then a man's voice behind her startled her rigid.

'Are you looking for something?'

Monty spun round and met a cold, hostile expression. She had the feeling she had seen its elegant owner somewhere before, but could not place him. His name tag read 'Dr F. Charles Seligman' and he had dark wavy hair streaked with silver.

She took a breath, anger suddenly replacing fear. 'Yes, I want to see my friend, Mr Smith.'

'Mr Smith is not permitted visitors.'

'This is a private hospital; all guests are allowed visitors. You have no regulated visiting hours.'

The man was studying her face and Monty sensed that he,

too, was trying to recall where they'd seen each other before. Then he suddenly gave a conciliatory smile.

'Mr Smith is not at all well. Receiving visitors is too tiring for him; we can only allow close relatives to see him at the moment. If you'd like to leave the flowers and any message with the floor sister, she'll be happy to pass them on to him.'

He held out an expansive hand and propelled Monty safely away from Room 712.

76

'So, this is where you live?'

Gunn stood barefoot, in his towelling dressing gown, and stared in a mixture of surprise and embarrassment at Nikky, who was standing on the gloomy landing in jeans and a duffel coat, looking totally gorgeous.

'How did you find me?' he said quietly.

'Think I look stupid or something?' She cocked her head teasingly, and her long auburn hair slipped over to one side. 'Call yourself a surveillance supremo? You ought to take a better watchout for someone tailing you.'

He closed the gap between the door and the jamb a few inches. 'Look – I'll call you tomorrow – we'll go see a film or something.'

'Don't I get invited in? I spend three days tracking you to your lair and I don't get a cup of coffee as a reward?'

'Niks . . .'

She tried to look inside and he narrowed the gap between the door and the jamb further.

He hadn't seen her since last Tuesday when they'd rowed, and he'd been missing her like crazy. But he couldn't invite her in, not right now.

'What's in there, soldier? What are you hiding?'

'I'm not hiding anything.'

'Good. In that case, I'll have a coffee.' She pushed the door, but it didn't budge an inch against the solid wedge of his foot.

'Look, soldier, do you have another woman in there? Is that it?'

'*Niks*, I was having an early night.'

'Oh yes, with whom?'

'Niks, come on, I'll see you tomorrow.'

'This is a crummy neighbourhood. I risked my skin coming here and I'm not going back out there alone at this time of night.'

'I'll come down with you, get you a cab.'

She tossed her head petulantly. 'I'm coming in. I want to see who you've got in there. Is she as pretty as me? *Prettier?*'

'I'll get you that cab.'

'I don't want a cab, I want to come in. How many times have you rung me in the past few days? Ten? Twenty? Thirty? How many tons of flowers have you sent me? I took that as a message that you wanted to see me. You let me in that door right now, or you *never* see me again. OK?'

Trapped, Gunn relented, swung the door wide open and gestured with a reluctant sweep of his arm for her to feast her eyes.

She walked in, past an electricity meter and a kitchenette into a dingy bedsit. It was furnished with a single bed, a couple of battered armchairs, a threadbare rug and grimy net curtains. There was no woman in there, nothing; just a blank television, Vivaldi playing on a CD, the glow of a laptop computer screen, and the lingering smell of a fry-up.

As he closed the door she stared at him in utter amazement. 'You *live* here?'

'You want coffee or a drink? Wine? Whisky?'

'I'll have a glass of wine.'

'Red or white?'

'I don't care. This is your home, soldier?' Her initial surprise was fast turning to pity. She walked over to the window, distracted by a rumbling sound, and saw the lights of a train only yards below.

'Look, I don't plan on spending the rest of my life here.

Where did you think I lived – in a palace?' He worked a corkscrew into the cap of the bottle.

'This is why you wouldn't ever bring me to your place? You told me you had a big house, with a pool.'

'You told me material things didn't matter to you.'

'They don't.'

The cork came out with a pop. 'I do have a big house with a pool. The Bitch lives in it with the kids. I'm mortgaged to the hilt and can't sell the house because there aren't any buyers around, and I'm being clobbered by the Child Support Agency. Any more questions?' He scooped out two glasses from the cupboard above the bed.

She was looking at the books stacked on a home-made shelf: *The Encyclopaedia of Psychic Science. The Magician. A Treasury of Witchcraft and Devilry. Beyond the Occult. The Left-hand Path. The Magus. The Golden Bough. The Book of the Sacred Magic of Abra=Melin. The Enochian Keys. The Satanic Bible.*

'I didn't know you were interested in the occult.'

He shrugged and handed her a glass. 'I'm not really, don't know why I keep them. We used to monitor the key occult groups when I was at GCHQ.'

As she turned the pages of a volume entitled, *Spellcraft, Hexcraft & Witchcraft*, fascinated by its contents, she failed to notice the slight veil that the half-truth had brought to his eyes.

'Wonder if I could find a spell in here that would make you punctual?' she said. 'Or horny – no, maybe that would be dangerous, you're quite horny enough already.'

She took the wine glass, drank one sip, then kissed him. 'Let's go to bed, I haven't had you inside me for four days and I'm going crazy from withdrawal symptoms.'

He hugged her hard, burying himself in the scents of her hair and her skin. Nikky looked over his shoulder at the computer screen inches from her face. On it was a long list of names with a peculiar black symbol beside each one.

She read a few of them: *Conor Molloy; Montana Bannerman; Charles Rowley; Hubert Wentworth.* Then she peered more closely at the symbol. 'Are those Christmas trees?' she murmured.

'Huh?'

'On the screen.'

He jolted, as if a bolt of lightning had struck him, broke free from her, turned to the computer, hastily dimming the screen, then shut it down.

'Is that your Christmas card list?' she teased. 'Conor Molloy, Montana Bannerman, Charles Rowley, Hubert Thingie? Hope *I'm* on it somewhere.'

Gunn tried to make light of it. 'Yup, that's right!'

'Conor Molloy, *Montana* Bannerman – that's a funny name – is she American? Another of your girlfriends?'

'No, she's not, and how come you've remembered those names – I didn't know you had a photographic memory?'

'You don't seriously think I spent three days tailing you? I saw this address weeks ago on a phone bill in your pocket and memorized it.' She smiled sweetly. 'There's lots of other things I don't know about you, too.' She kissed him again. 'Bed!'

77

Monday 28 November, 1994

Amongst Monty's morning mail was a thick envelope bearing a Federal Express label, and printed with the wording: 'Washington Symposium of Genetics for Medicine. 9–12 December 1994. Urgent Travel Documents.'

The contents included a covering letter from the organizer, confirming that her father would receive an honorarium of $1000 for attending as a plenary speaker, and inviting both of them to a reception at the White House on the Thursday night. There were two economy-class return tickets from London to Washington, details of the hotel reservation and a programme of events.

Dick Bannerman had seemed pleased when Monty suggested lunch after his flight back from Scotland. So she'd booked a table at the Greenhouse. It was a comfortable restaurant a good distance away from the Bendix Building and she knew they could talk safely there.

She watched her father pick up the Maternox capsule she'd just tipped from its vial on to the tablecloth in front of him. He placed it in the palm of his hand and studied it.

His reaction to all that she had told him was less emotional than she'd expected. His main suspicion was over Conor Molloy's role. Mindful of his previous vitriol about Conor, she had not yet told him they were in love.

'You're certain this is a Maternox capsule and not something else this Kingsley woman might have been taking?'

She nodded. 'The part of the formula that Conor was able to analyse corresponded exactly to the standard Maternox capsules we used for comparison.'

He looked at her sharply. 'So what does this American Johnny-come-lately hope to gain from all this?'

'I don't know, Daddy,' she said truthfully.

'You think he wants to protect his integrity as a patent lawyer? Is that it?'

'Could be.'

Liver and bacon had arrived for her father, and fish pie for Monty. He slipped the capsule back into the vial. 'I could do the tests in a lab at Bendix Schere; it would be much easier for me than using Berkshire. If I'm careful, no one will know what I'm up to.'

Monty shook her head vehemently. 'It's too risky. What about the closed-circuit television cameras in all the labs? We've no idea who'd be watching.'

'They're not going to know what I'm *doing*, for God's sake, girl! I'm running dozens of experiments all the time.'

Monty looked unconvinced.

He checked the date on his watch. 'We're meant to fly to Washington Thursday week for this damned symposium. That's barely ten days if I start today. You think Anna Sterling's life is at risk, which means that every day counts. So I suggest I get going on this as soon as we've finished lunch.'

'But it's *safe* at Berkshire,' she insisted. 'Everyone knows we're still winding the old place down. No one's going to think

430

twice about you going off there, and no one's going to be looking over your shoulder.'

He smiled, warmly. 'Darling, I don't know what these buggers are up to, and I wouldn't put anything past the pharmaceutical industry, but I still find it bloody hard to believe that they'd muck around doing illegal clinical trials with their biggest selling drug.'

'Let's hope you're right,' she said. 'For everyone's sake.'

'And I don't think you need to worry about my safety. We both know damned well why BS took me on board: because I can knock five to ten years, if not more, off their research and development in genetic engineering. They're hardly going to bump me off for running a few tests on a drug that's about to come out of patent anyway.'

She dug a fork into the centre of her fish pie and watched the steam escape. It was like a mini volcano, she thought. 'Let's hope you're right, Daddy,' she said again. 'Let's hope to hell you are.'

78

The jewelled eyes of the black papier-mâché frog on Dr Crowe's desk seemed to be looking at him with a slightly mocking expression, Gunn thought. He stared stonily back at them as he waited for the Chief Executive to finish the phone call which had interrupted their meeting.

After a couple more minutes, Crowe replaced the receiver as delicately as if it were a fine china ornament, and turned his attention back to Gunn. 'Yes, where were we?'

'Mr Rowley, sir.'

'Indeed, poor Mr Rowley. Very unfortunate; a most tragic accident. You have it all in hand?'

'Yes I do.'

'Any interest from the media?'

'None at all, so far. The Hawaiians have been good as gold.'

431

Gunn smiled. 'They can see it doesn't exactly enhance their tourist trade to announce such a dramatic death.'

'Quite so. And the English media?'

'Hundreds of British citizens die on holiday every year; very few make the press and when they do, it's usually at local level. Rowley's parents live in a Sussex village, there's a younger sister in London, and a girlfriend also in London. The parents' local paper might get on to it.' He gestured. 'What are they going to say? The likes of the *Sussex Evening Argus or the Mid Sussex Times* aren't likely to send their cub reporters to Hawaii – even if they have reason to be suspicious, which they haven't.'

Crowe nodded. 'And internally, here?'

'Controlled release. I think the lid is on pretty firmly.'

Crowe looked satisfied. 'You had something you wanted to tell me about the Bannerman woman?'

'This is not so good, sir. On Thursday Mr Molloy from Group Patents and Agreements checked into a small Paddington hotel, where he stayed just three hours then checked out again. My monitoring crew picked his change of routine up on Data Tracking and sent someone to check it out.'

'Was he seeing a woman?' Crowe asked. 'Or did he just not like the wallpaper?'

The information Gunn was about to relate had cost his man a fifty pound cash bribe to the hotel porter but he didn't bother the Chief Executive with that detail. 'Neither, sir; he was on the phone.'

'To whom?'

'To us, sir. To the Bendix Schere computer log-in number.'

Crowe stiffened. 'From a hotel room?'

'It would seem so.'

'Presumably to access something he shouldn't be accessing?'

'That's the only assumption I can make, sir. I got the system manager to run a log audit, but he can't find any trace of Molloy being on the system at that time.'

'Presumably his audit must have shown up the dial-in from the hotel number?'

'Apparently not, sir. Either we have some fault in the system which is temporarily preventing Molloy's activity from showing up, or –' He took a breath, knowing Crowe would not be happy: 'Or Molloy knows how to cover his tracks. Which would indicate that he's a lot hotter about computers than his CV suggests.'

'And here's me thinking that our computer system was impenetrable, Major Gunn.'

'No system is totally impenetrable, sir, unless the hardware and software is updated every single day; that's how fast modern technology is progressing. I believe we've got one of the most secure systems in the world, and we're scheduled to upgrade in the spring. I have to work within a budget, as you constantly remind me.'

Crowe stared at him impassively. 'Go on.'

'Late on Friday, Data Tracking showed that Mr Molloy visited Miss Bannerman's cottage in Berkshire and stayed the night. On Saturday morning, accompanied by Miss Bannerman, he drove to the campus of Berkshire University, spent the whole of the day and early evening at the Bannermans' old lab, then returned to her cottage where he again spent the night.'

'What were they doing in the lab?'

'We weren't able to ascertain.'

'Didn't your man take a listening device?'

'We only have a limited number, sir, because of costs. Miss Bannerman and Mr Molloy are only two out of thirty staff members around the country whom we're keeping under surveillance at present. We've got problems with one of our senior virologists at Northumberland who we think is feeding information to another company. He could do us very serious damage; then there's a dodgy lab technician at Plymouth, four people down at Reading, plus –'

Crowe raised a hand, cutting him short. 'I have all your reports, thank you. Did your man get into the Bannerman lab?'

'No. He was unable to gain access to the premises after they'd left because of the risk of activating the alarm system.'

Crowe clenched his knuckles. 'Don't you think it would have been *worth* that risk, to find out what they were doing?'

Gunn shook his head. 'No, I don't want them to have any inkling that they're under observation. We'll find out in good time.'

Crowe gave him a dubious look but said nothing.

Gunn continued. 'On Sunday afternoon, sir, they drove to a hotel in Berkshire, where Molloy checked in and out within an hour, and where he again dialled into the Bendix computer. Then they visited the deputy news editor of the *Thames Valley Gazette*, who happened to be Miss Zandra Wollerton's boss. After that they visited the flat of one of our security guards, Winston Smith, who was one of our early Beta testers, and who is currently at the Bendix Hammersmith. Miss Bannerman tried to see him there, but was prevented.'

Crowe sat quietly absorbing the bad news. 'It would seem we have a problem, Major Gunn,' he said finally.

'Yes, we do. I want to put both of them under twenty-four-hour surveillance, but I need to take on another fifty men to do that.'

'*Fifty?*'

'For a round-the-clock job on two subjects, that's the bare minimum. M15 use fifty per person on twenty-four-hour surveillance. Three cars, with two per car on eight-hour-shifts – that's eighteen men for starters.'

'Running fifty men costs about one million pounds a year, Major Gunn. I'll have to put it to the Board.'

'Yes, sir. But I can't keep adding to the list of those under full surveillance without adding to my team. Either I have those men or something has to give. Or –' His voice tailed.

They exchanged a brief glance expressing what was left unsaid, then Gunn continued: 'I've never felt comfortable about Molloy, and I'm now convinced the Bannerman woman is on to the Medici Trial. I've been unhappy ever since her lunch with Seals. I have a feeling she's a very tough little cookie, and that we're not going to like what we find.'

'She is tough,' Crowe said. 'Her father hardly dares say *boo* to her. She was a hard negotiator when we did the deal.' He frowned. 'But why would she go to see this security guard? He wouldn't have any information on Medici.'

'I don't know, sir. But I intend finding out.'

434

Crowe pulled a slim black notebook from his inside pocket and jotted something down. 'I'll raise the issue of your financial requirements at this Thursday's Board meeting, Major Gunn. If you could let me have precise details of your revised budget by then?'

'Of course, sir.' Gunn smiled.

79

At ten to five on Monday afternoon, Conor's phone rang. He picked up the receiver. 'Conor Molloy,' he said, and immediately heard the faint hiss of a transatlantic line.

'Hi, it's Dave Schwab.'

The caller had a quiet, serious voice that mirrored his personality. Aged thirty-four, he was one of the younger examiners in the United States Patent and Trademark Office, and Conor considered him a friend.

They had first met doing their PhDs in Molecular Biology at Carnegie Mellon. Their paths had crossed from time to time since, and Conor surmised from the fact that he was getting this call now that the patent application he had filed in the United States for Psoriatak had been assigned to Schwab.

He viewed this as a mixed blessing. Because of their friendship, he might be able to push arguments further with Schwab than with other examiners, and Schwab might take more trouble over the application; but conversely, Schwab was a man of integrity, and in an anxiety not to be seen as granting favours he might well be over-pernickety with Conor's application.

Conor did a quick mental calculation. Washington was five hours behind London. It was ten to twelve there. He could picture Schwab clearly. He would be in his office, back to the window, surrounded by tiers of documents, wearing a baggy shirt, cuffs rolled up and no tie. The guy only ever dressed formally for meetings.

'Dave! Hi, how you doing?'

'OK, how's England?'

'England's good. How's Julie?'

'Julie's good, too.' There was a silence, then Schwab said: 'So – I – got assigned your application for Bendix Schere.' He paused. 'Ah – that's – ah – number 08/190/790; you got that number right?'

Conor grabbed a folder off the floor and frantically scrabbled through it. 'Yup, came through in the confirmation of receipt. That tallies with our docket MA68 1459 01, Psoriatak, right?'

'Correct.'

'You guys have moved fast on this one,' Conor said. 'I appreciate it.'

He was met for some seconds by the static hiss of the line, then Schwab spoke again, his tone cooler. 'I think we have quite a few problems on this one; we're going to need a meeting.'

This news did not surprise Conor. He frankly believed Bendix Schere would be very lucky to get the application through at all, and if they did, it would be heavily modified. But he was paid to fight the Bendix corner, and that's what he was doing. He needed to show Crowe that he was giving it his best shot. 'On which specific areas, Dave?'

'I'm not happy with the prior art, and I think you're asking too much in the application; you're going to have to shave the sides off quite a bit.'

'I understand that. Yup.'

'You're going to have to elect a single group.'

'Time is at a real premium on this one, Dave. I'll be guided by you. How about if we ditch everything except the gene sequence itself?'

'The plasmids and transform bacteria can stay with that, OK?'

'Sure, that would be appreciated.'

'OK, this is getting more straightforward now. I could get you an Office action out within a week.' He hesitated. 'My problem is I'm away the week after next until the New Year.'

Conor glanced at the agenda his department boss had plotted on his wall chart. A tight time scale had been set by Dr Crowe for the filing and prosecution of US patents on Dick Bannerman's work. 'Could we move things forward by meeting before you go?'

There was a pause, then: 'Oh, sure, I guess. But it's going to take me the best part of a week to get this Office action done.'

'If you fax me, I could get the material you need and jump on a plane with it.'

'Let's see, today's Monday. The earliest I could get this out would be the end of the week. I have a kind of crazy schedule. Thursday week, 8th December – if we met in the morning, would that suit?'

Conor agreed to make the journey over but there was another pause and he could sense that something else was coming.

'Conor, I have to tell you even with the reduced application I still don't like the prior art, but I'll see . . . Now, how's the weather over there?'

Conor answered, surprised at the sudden non sequitur. 'Cold. How is it in Washington?'

'Winter's here, we're thinking of moving to Australia.'

'You serious?'

'Who knows? So, you got a girlfriend over there yet?'

'Just playing the field,' Conor said, not wanting to get drawn into talking about Monty.

'Sounds like nothing much has changed.'

'Thanks a lot!'

'You're in the right company, that's for sure; Bendix are really doing the business on Genetics now – they're taking a big lead in the numbers of patents.'

'Yup, they seem pretty aggressive in the field.'

'Can say that again. OK, I have to get on, good talking to you.'

'You too.'

As Conor hung up, America suddenly seemed much further than just five weeks and a few thousand miles away. He made a mental note to make sure he eMailed his mother before the day was done. She must think he'd forgotten her.

A rap startled him and Martin Walker, head of Group Patents and Agreements, glided through the doorway like a fish through reeds.

Walker was every bit the bland Bendix Schere man. Sporting a suit so stiffly pressed it might have been cardboard, he held a wodge of papers in his hand and his expression, wholly devoid of emotion on the previous occasions Conor had met him, was grave.

'Some rather sad news, Mr Molloy; I thought I'd tell you in person as you were colleagues. Mr Rowley has had a very tragic accident in Hawaii over the weekend. I'm afraid he's drowned.'

Walker proffered one of the pages he was carrying. 'Dr Crowe wants this circulated to everyone who knew him. It'll be in the company magazine's next issue, of course.' He laid the page down on Conor's desk.

Conor stared with unfocused eyes at the memorandum. 'Char – Mr – Rowley is *dead*?'

'Super chap. Terrible loss. One of these silly accidents, it seems – the result of high spirits. So unnecessary, but that's how it goes. I'm going to miss him a lot; he really knew his patent law.'

Conor somehow read the sheet. It was headed: From The Chief Executive's Office.

To all personnel:
I regret to have to inform you that our colleague, Mr Charles Rowley of the Group Patents and Agreements Department, is missing, presumed drowned, whilst on a business trip to Bendix Hilo in Hawaii.

Mr Rowley was a highly valued employee who played a key role in the development of Bendix Schere's Genetics Research, and he will be sadly missed by all who knew him.

Dr Vincent Crowe, Chief Executive.

'Do – er – do you know how it happened?' Conor said, his voice faltering.

'I understand it was after a beach barbecue, when Mr Rowley accepted a midnight bet to swim across a bay and back. Apparently he'd been warned about the treacherous currents. I don't quite know what happens about a funeral in these situations – I'll keep you posted.'

'I'd appreciate that,' said Conor on automatic pilot.

'I'm going to have to find someone else to take over his work and liaise with you – not going to be easy – he was very *au fait* with the whole Bannerman situation – you'll just have to muddle along as best you can for a day or two.'

'Sure.' Shock had paralysed Conor's brain, and he felt as if all his intelligence had been sucked out.

'Perhaps we'd better have a meeting in the morning. Come along to my office at nine, all right?' Then he was gone.

Conor sat absorbing Crowe's memorandum for some minutes after Walker had departed. Slowly, his initial numbness began to be replaced with a growing disquiet, as something stirred deep in his memory.

80

Monty stepped out of the lift into the entrance atrium shortly after six and cast a quick glance at the security desks, but there was no sign of Winston Smith. All the guards on duty were occupied with the stream of people leaving the building, making sure they returned their visitors' passes.

She walked over to the lift beside the Directors' express and stood right in front of it, staring at her distorted reflection in the copper doors, and waited, listening, then stepped aside as the doors opened and several figures came out. It was just at that point that she heard a rumble which seemed to be coming from behind the same shaft, but, as before, it carried on down below her and faded.

No mistake. There was definitely another lift in operation, one which did not serve the ground floor.

She looked down at the white marble tiling. The health hydro was in the basement beneath: the exercise machines, squash courts, computerized golf driving range, swimming pool, Jacuzzis, saunas. On an impulse she entered the next lift that arrived and pushed the button for the hydro. A moment later she stepped out on to a plush carpet the colour of grass, and noticed a strong smell of chlorine.

A handsome fair-haired muscle-man in an all-white track-suit sat by the computerized turnstile, fresh towels stacked all around him. He greeted her slickly, with an Australian accent. 'Hi there! You joining us this evening?'

'I haven't been down before – mind if I take a look around first?'

'Sure. Just let me check your pass and you go right ahead. My name's Bud, and anything you want to know, please ask me.' He gave her a winning smile.

Monty walked along a corridor lined with doors to the male and female locker rooms, then came into a busy open-plan space signposted, 'Cardiovascular Area'. Some of the men and women on the rows of gleaming white machines – computerized treadmills, stairmasters, life-cycles – were reading the company magazine whilst their legs pounded.

Across the far end of the room she saw a fire exit sign. Edging past a shell-suited instructor who was showing a middle-aged man how to use a Nautilus machine, she walked over to it. Glancing round to see if she was being observed, she pushed the door open and walked through it into a second corridor lined with a variety of fire-fighting apparatus and, rather sinisterly she thought, hospital trolleys bearing oxygen tanks and masks. There was also a large glass cabinet marked: 'CARDIAC RESUSCITATION – EXPERIENCED MEDICAL PERSONNEL ONLY.'

Another fire door by the cabinet drew her attention. With some difficulty she pushed it open. It led directly into the bottom of an enclosed stone staircase that only went up and which was labelled: 'EMERGENCY EXIT VIA GROUND-FLOOR LOBBY. ALARMED ROUTE TO BE USED ONLY IN EVENT OF FIRE.'

Monty heard a faint whir and looked up; to her dismay she saw a video camera was tracking her, pointing directly at her, its lens rotating as it changed focus.

Quickly, she went back into the corridor which seemed to

follow the edge of the building. She tried every exit door she reached, but all of them led out to a concrete staircase that, again, only went up.

Eventually making her way back to Bud on the front desk, she told him she would think about a personal fitness programme and then she took the lift back up to the lobby. As she went outside, she dug her hands into the pockets of her Burberry against the biting cold of the night air, and pondered.

If the unseen lift didn't stop at the lobby or the hydro, where *did* it start and end? What did it connect to what? And why the hell was it concealed? Maybe it was some kind of service lift, to do with the canteen, or for moving lab equipment around? That was possible; in any normal circumstances, she might even have thought it was probable. But here that explanation did not feel right.

Instead of heading towards her car, she walked right round the outside of the building. She counted eight fire exit doors which tallied with the number she'd counted in the basement, and saw nothing that looked like a separate or concealed entrance.

Disappointed, she unlocked her MG, noticing Conor's car was still in the lot. Good, she thought, checking she had the spare key he'd given her. She had promised to cook him a meal in his flat, and needed time to go to a supermarket first.

She removed her overnight bag and the shopping, set the MG's alarm, then checked the street before walking up to Conor's front door. It had become routine for her to check if she was being followed and she sometimes wondered if she was being over-paranoid.

Lingering traces of Conor's cigarettes soothed her as she prepared a meaty chunk of fresh monkfish for the grill. Then, hoping he wouldn't mind, she picked up the phone and made a quick call to Anna Sterling, to discuss their plans for an evening together later that week. To her relief, Anna told her that Mark had to go to Brussels for a few days on business and she was joining him. Monty had not been feeling comfortable

441

about seeing her friend, knowing what she did and not being able to say anything.

But Anna reminded Monty that she had bought theatre tickets in London for Wednesday week. Monty wondered if her father would have got a result from the Maternox tests by then, and felt guilty that she had not gone down to the lab with him tonight. At least he'd agreed to use their lab, finally. And anyway if she *was* being followed, he was safer alone.

As she began slicing the melon starter, she heard the key in the door lock, and Conor came in, his face ashen. He kissed her distractedly, without his usual warmth, then paced awkwardly around the open-plan kitchen.

'You OK?' she asked, concerned.

He nodded, but said nothing.

'Let me get you a drink – whisky?'

'I need one, a very large one. So will you.'

He eased off his Crombie and slung it on one of the chairs, followed by his red paisley tie, and undid the top button of his shirt. After this, he sat on an arm of the sofa, untied his black Oxfords and tugged them off, leaving them where they fell.

Nervous of whatever he was about to say, Monty grabbed the Glenfiddich and poured a large slug for him, followed by a smaller one for herself.

She added ice, took their drinks over, then sat on the sofa. 'What is it?'

He clutched his glass. 'Charley Rowley. I guess you didn't hear?'

'Hear what?'

'That he drowned in Hawaii.'

She almost dropped her whisky, feeling as if something had just detonated inside her.

Conor rummaged for his cigarettes and lit one. 'I can't believe he's dead,' he said.

'Conor, this is terrible! God, I'm sorry, I'm so sorry.'

'I –' He shook his head. 'Something's very wrong about it; there's something doesn't make sense.'

'Or makes too much sense?'

There was a sudden, uncharacteristic flash of anger in

442

Conor's voice when he next spoke. 'An accident! Every time it's just another goddamn *accident*. Rowley was scared as hell when we left the pub. I remember him in the taxi looking out of the rear window. And this wasn't a guy who got scared of anything.'

It was Conor who looked scared, she thought, his face still drained of all colour. 'Did they give you any details? How it happened?'

'High jinks. He got drunk, tried to swim in the dark – that's what they're saying.'

Monty slipped down beside him and put an arm around him. 'I'm sorry; you really liked him, didn't you?'

'He was one of the good guys; they're thin on the ground in Bendix Schere.'

'They're thin on the ground in life.' She gently prised the cigarette from him, held it with shaking fingers and took a puff. 'Is my father next?'

'I don't think they're going to harm one of their major assets.'

Monty wished she could detect more conviction in his voice.

'One of two things is going to happen, Monty. If your father finds nothing of significance in those capsules, then we've been barking up the wrong tree.'

'And if he does?'

'Then we have to make the decision whether we go to Rorke, or the police, or the CSM –'

A sharp buzzing sound in the hall startled them.

Monty froze. Conor's face stiffened as well. There was another buzz; it seemed louder, more intense.

'Entryphone,' he said, walking back out of the room.

'Careful, Conor, don't let anyone in.'

'I'm not going to.'

Conor lifted the internal phone in the hallway. 'Hello?' Monty watched his face. 'Pizza? No, I didn't order any pizza. What address do you have?' There was a pause. 'This is Apartment Two; you rang the wrong bell. OK, no worries.'

Monty edged her way to the curtainless window and peered

down into the street. A motorcycle was parked outside, the large red words 'PIZZAS PIZZAS' on its pannier.

Firm, strong hands slipped around her waist, moist, warm lips kissed the back of each ear in turn, then the hands held her more firmly. His face nuzzled hers. 'Just a false alarm.'

In the draught, goose pimples ran down her legs and arms and she pressed further back into his body for warmth. 'I'm sorry – I've never been so jumpy.'

'Don't apologize,' he said quietly. 'Being jumpy keeps you vigilant. Being vigilant is smart right now.'

They ate on the sofa, using the coffee table. Conor forked the last morsel of monkfish into his mouth. 'This is delicious,' he said. 'You're a demon in the kitchen! There's a great restaurant I'm going to take you to one day in Washington –' He stopped, suddenly remembering. 'I have to go to Washington next week. Just for a couple of days.'

'Next week? When next week?'

'Guess I'll fly out Wednesday and come back at the weekend.'

'I'm going to Washington on Thursday with my father!'

'You're kidding?'

'No, I'm not. We're having dinner with Clinton no less, and Daddy's talking at a symposium on genetics. Is that what you're going over for?'

'No, I didn't hear about the symposium. *I* have to visit the Patent Office, no less.' He drank some wine. 'Hey, this is good news! First time in Washington?'

'Yessir.'

'December's not the best month to visit. It's too cold.'

'Tell you what, I'd love to meet your mother.' She looked at him brightly. 'Could we do that?'

He nodded. 'I want you to meet her, too. We'll fix it.'

Monty refilled their glasses, then she looked at him again. 'What did your father do?'

Conor tapped ash off his cigarette. 'He was a civil servant.'

'In Washington?'

'Yup.'

'Were you close?'

444

'No, he died when I was eight.'

'What a shame – was it illness?'

Conor drew on his cigarette in silence. Monty sensed she had touched a raw nerve and changed the subject.

That night, Conor had the dream again. The bird dived in a long, sharp zigzag from the sky; it half flew, half plummeted, like a shadow chasing itself. But when it hit the ground it did not look up at him and become his father. Instead it remained still.

A ring of fire began to burn around it, small fierce flames as if someone had drawn a circle with petrol. Then a voice whispered in his ear: 'They shouldn't have done that. They knew he couldn't swim!'

Conor sat up with a start, wide awake, a drumming roar inside his head, his body engulfed in a thick coating of sweat.

'Jesus,' he said. 'Jesus Christ!'

Monty stirred beside him, then he heard her voice in the darkness. 'What is it? What's the matter, Conor?'

'Charley Rowley.' He turned on the bedside light, went over to the closet where he had hung his jacket, and slid his hand into the inside pocket to pull out a sheet of paper. It was the memorandum from Dr Crowe informing employees of Charley Rowley's death. Monty sat up a little and he showed it to her.

'So you didn't get one of these yet?'

'No,' she said.

'We've got the bastards! All these goddamn *accidents*, now we really have these bastards.' He tapped the bottom of the first paragraph with his finger, and read it aloud. ' . . . *missing, presumed drowned, whilst on a business trip to Bendix Hilo in Hawaii.*'

She looked at him. 'Yes?'

'I asked Mr Walker, who brought me this, what actually happened. Like I told you, he said that Rowley had accepted a bet to make a midnight swim. Across a bay and back, I think it was.' He let go of the piece of paper, clenched his hands and pounded the knuckles together. 'Monty, I've just remembered something Rowley said on Thursday, when he announced that

445

he was leaving for Hawaii. I told him I'd be thinking of him over the weekend, sitting on a beach sunning himself, swigging Margaritas and cooling down in the ocean.' He took a breath. 'Charley said he wouldn't be cooling himself down in any ocean, because he had a phobia about water – he was terrified of it.'

Conor began to pace the room. 'So what Walker said is one big goddamn lie.' He stopped, stared at Monty, eyes blazing, and clenched his fists again. 'Charley told me himself that he couldn't swim.'

81

Tuesday 29 November, 1994

The MG's heater whined, and something trapped inside it rattled and clattered intermittently, irritating Monty. Her feet were roasting inside her ankle-length boots and her cheeks were frozen from the air blasting in through a crack in the vinyl roof; she badly missed her shawl, which she normally wore to protect her neck from the draught.

The engine nearly died and she blipped the accelerator hard. The car needed some attention; at least as a result of the Bendix takeover there was some money in her bank account to pay for it. She wondered if the garage could do anything while she was in Washington, but that was only going to be a couple of days.

The brute front end of a juggernaut filled her wing mirror as she stared impatiently at the jammed traffic in front of her, waiting for it to inch forward again. Interchangeable voices droned on the radio, telling her that the capital's traffic this morning was bad, bad, bad. She turned her brain to her own thoughts instead.

Charley Rowley. She had only met the man briefly and could barely remember what he looked like, but she had been unable to get him out of her mind all night. Death by drowning.

What a sorry mess. The Medici File. The buck stopped there, she was sure. And the contents were stored on Conor's computer.

Why Medici? Why name a drugs trial after a Florentine Renaissance family? What was the real connection? OK, the Medicis were immensely powerful and under their influence medieval Florence became the cultural centre of Europe. The Medicis were pretty ruthless, also. But drugs? She wondered if there was some connection between the words *Medici* and *Medicine*, but could not think of anything that made any sense. Medic?

She weighed up again the pros and cons of going to see Sir Neil Rorke. If Charley Rowley had been murdered for getting the Maternox template, or trying to get more samples, they were all at risk: her father, Conor, herself.

Conor was badly shaken. With the death of his friend, the people who had died were no longer just names on a list to him. She thought through his arguments in favour of waiting until her father had the results of his analysis of the capsules. Those arguments applied only so long as they had no hard evidence. With this clearly fictional account of Rowley's end, now they had that evidence.

Someone had not done their homework properly. Presumably Rowley's family and girlfriend would be told the same story; and they'd know he couldn't swim too. Questions were going to be asked. If Monty was a member of his family, she'd be demanding an immediate investigation by the Hawaiian authorities. No doubt that's exactly what they were going to do.

All the more reason to see Rorke and warn him of what was going on behind his back, and the potential disaster for the company.

Monty finally passed the roadworks and the traffic began moving more steadily. After a quarter of an hour she took the exit she wanted, and a few miles later began to recognize some of the landmarks she'd seen in the dark on her trip with Conor on Sunday.

She passed a scrapbreaker's yard of dismembered taxis and found a parking space outside Winston Smith's low-rise. She primed the car's primitive alarm, then hurried up the concrete steps to the second-floor walkway.

Her watch said 9.15. The mountain of work stacked up in her office would have to wait, because right now this took priority. Then she was having lunch with her father in the Italian café up the road from Bendix; they'd agreed that except for emergencies, they would discuss nothing over the phone.

Ducking her head against the beginnings of rain, she rang the Smiths' doorbell. A shadow moved behind the glass pane; Monty heard the metallic sound of a latch, then the door opened a few inches. She saw Mrs Smith, sitting in a wheelchair in her dressing gown, looking up at her with a bleak frown of recognition.

'Hello,' Monty said. 'I'm sorry to be a pest again, but we need to have a talk.'

'He's still in the Clinic.'

'Actually it's you I wanted to see, Mrs Smith.'

'I can't stand up.' The woman's hands were shaking and she seemed to Monty to have lost weight since Sunday. 'It's one of my bad days; can't get out of the chair.'

Monty put on her most beguiling you-can-really-trust-me smile. 'Could you possibly let me in for a few minutes? It might be easier.'

Mrs Smith hesitated, then reluctantly eased back, allowing Monty to step into the minuscule hall from where she could see a little sitting room through to the right. But she was not invited beyond the hall.

Monty took the plunge. 'Look, Mrs Smith – I know you believe Bendix Schere are doing the best they can for your husband, but I think they're using him.'

The seated woman watched her expressionlessly; Monty was not sure what she was thinking, but went on: 'Winston told me that he volunteered for some drug trials about twelve years ago, and that he's been unwell almost on and off ever since. Isn't that right?'

Mrs Smith fixed her eyes on Monty for some moments without acknowledgement. 'I took part in the same trial,' she said finally.

This was what Monty had suspected on her earlier visit. She

448

felt horror mingling with the pity she now felt. 'You did that, and then you got this – this – Parkinson's?'

A tremor seemed to go right through the other woman, rippling her from head to foot. For Monty the effect was as though she was watching a reflection of Mrs Smith in water, instead of seeing her in the flesh; unnerved, she found herself wanting to step back, and had to force herself not to.

'This started six years after,' the reflection said. 'The Doctor Seligman, he can't tell me what's wrong – I been 'ad all kinds of tests. He say I have the same symptoms as Parkinson's, but I don't have Parkinson's.'

Monty frowned. The name 'Seligman' seemed familiar. Then she remembered the name tag of the rather smooth character who'd accosted her outside Winston Smith's door at the Clinic. *Dr F. Charles Seligman.*

'Have you seen any independent doctors?'

Mrs Smith looked furtive, as if she was trying to pluck up the courage to tell Monty something. 'I see the doctor in the health centre just locally, here. He take blood sample and other tests; then when I go back he say the same thing: that it is symptoms like Parkinson's but does not test as Parkinson's, and he say this was too long after the trials and could not be connected.' A tremor, similar to the previous one but smaller, ran through her body. 'He tell me he think it is all in my mind.'

Monty grimaced. 'And your husband, when did you last see him?'

'Yesterday – I went in the taxi the company sent – they very good to us, you see.'

'It sounds like it. How was he?'

She shook her head and her face fell. 'He's real bad.'

'Will you let me get another doctor to see him?'

Mrs Smith looked defeated. 'No, thank you. They doing everything they can for him; I don't think he's got the strength to go through more tests.'

Monty swallowed her frustration. 'Well, will you give him my regards, please.'

'Miss Bannerman?'

'Yes?'

Mrs Smith's eyes had sharpened suddenly, as if focusing

for the first time during the conversation. 'My memory is not so good. My husband, he was a little delirious last night, but he wanted to make sure if you came back I give you this message.'

Monty's eyes widened.

'He wasn't too clear – I should have wrote it down. It was about a car park.'

'A car park?'

'Yes. He said you have to go into the multi-storey car park across the street opposite Bendix. Charles Street? Chalter Street? He say that's where the entrance is.'

'What entrance?'

'He told me you'd understand.'

Suddenly Monty twigged. She nodded vigorously. 'Right! Brilliant! I do understand, yes. Thank you!'

Minutes later she hurried from Albany Court and drove as fast, and as recklessly, as the heavy traffic would permit, towards the office.

82

Conor was surprised to find a three-page fax from the US Patent Office already waiting for him when he arrived at work. Also awaiting him was a warning memo regarding the state of his car, and reminding him of the penalties for not keeping it clean. It was signed: 'G. Snape, Staff Relations Officer.'

The wheels and sides of his BMW were caked in mud from Monty's farm track and he had been too preoccupied to think about it. Irritated by the tone of the memo, he dropped it into the shredder, making a mental note to take the car through a wash before tomorrow. He was going down to Monty's cottage again tonight; getting his car dirty looked like becoming part of the relationship.

Entertaining himself with the pleasurable thought of suspending G. Snape over hot coals and ritually disembowelling him, he skimmed the fax, which was signed by Dave Schwab. As previously hinted, there were a number of factors in the application that Dave was not happy about, and he suggested the interview which they'd tentatively made for next Thursday be brought forward a day – to allow more time to set things in motion afterwards.

Conor's thoughts veered to Charley Rowley. Rowley had not just died, he had been killed. And Conor had to live with the fact that he was the one who'd got the poor guy involved in this whole can of worms. He owed it to Rowley to go hunting some guts for garters.

He made a decision to go out in his lunch break, find a pay phone and try to track down and speak to Rowley's parents. He knew they were a wealthy family. Maybe they had a bit of influence as well. If he could get a song and dance stirred up quickly over this, it might send Bendix Schere's hit squad running for cover.

They only needed a short while. Just long enough to get the results from Dick Bannerman. Ten days.

There was a rap on his door and Martin Walker, Head of Department, glided in. 'Good morning, Mr Molloy, you have my agenda for our nine o'clock meeting?'

'No, I haven't read my eMail yet.' He held up Schwab's fax. 'Been occupied with this.'

Walker looked a fraction less self-assured than normal. 'There seem to be a number of conflicting stories about how our poor Mr Rowley died. I had been led to understand he was attempting an unwise swim, but apparently he fell overboard on a late-night fishing trip.'

'That's quite a difference.'

In a masterful display of self-control, Walker's expression barely altered. 'Well – it reminds me of your Chappaquiddick. All kinds of different stories start flying round when accidents occur.'

'That's because someone was trying to do a cover-up at Chappaquiddick,' Conor said, his eyes fixed on Walker's.

'Yes, tragedy does make people panic, doesn't it? Maybe they all got drunk at the beach barbecue first, and someone made up a story to prevent the skipper of the boat being prosecuted for negligence. The sad truth is that Mr Rowley has drowned, and whatever the circumstances, that remains the case.'

Conor wondered how much all this had cost the company in bribes to the relevant authorities in Hawaii. 'Have they found his body yet?'

'I believe not. From what I hear, with the currents and undertows on that coast, it could have been swept out to sea and lost for ever.'

How convenient for everyone, Conor thought sourly. He pumped more questions at Walker, trying not to show his hand, but got no further information out of him. Changing the subject, he related the substance of Schwab's fax.

Walker agreed to the Washington trip, gave him two names in Human Resources who handled all travel arrangements, told Conor he would see him at nine o'clock, and left.

As Monty drove along the Euston Road she saw the Bendix Schere monolith rising up ahead, on the right. But instead of turning across the traffic and driving up to the security gate, she made a left into the side road opposite and slowed to a crawl. Twenty yards ahead was a ramp leading into a multi-storey car park that she had seen numerous times, but of which she had never taken any notice. Until now.

The orange and black lettering across the entrance said, 'LRG CAR PARKS.' As she drew level, she saw an electronic sign by the lowered barrier that announced: 'FULL, CONTRACT PARKING ONLY.'

She drove on a short distance, turning left again around the block, looking for a meter, then ended up back at Euston Road. Approaching the multi-storey once more, this time she pulled into the kerb, took a chance on a double yellow and ran up the ramp, squeezing past the barrier and into the concrete world of the interior. A closed-circuit camera watched her silently from an indent near the top of the wall.

She thought it was strange that there was no attendant. The ramp curved sharply and steeply, like the chute of a helter skelter: seeing no sign of a pedestrian entrance, she walked up it and around the bend into increasing darkness. Then, ahead of her, she saw a booth and a second much stronger barrier blocking off the ramp beyond.

She approached the booth under the distinctly hostile stare of the uniformed attendant behind its plate-glass window. Her warm smile provoked no change in his expression.

The window facing her was sealed and there was no door. Inside, another attendant was seated in front of a bank of monitors. There was no rate card on view.

'I wonder if you could help me – I'm interested in buying a season ticket,' she said through the security grill.

Unreadable eyes stared back at her. 'We're full.'

'Do you have a waiting list?'

'About three years at the moment.'

Monty thought for a moment. 'OK, I think – I – I'd like to put my name down. May I take a look around first?' She only realized after she had said it, how daft the remark must sound.

He looked at her stonily. 'It's a car park. There's nothing to see.'

She racked her brains for an excuse to get past him. 'You seem to have very good security here. I have an old car – a classic – I'm very concerned about vandalism.' She was making a complete hash of it, she knew, feeling increasingly flustered.

'Nothing gets vandalized in here,' he replied curtly.

'Right. Good. You – er – you monitor them?'

'We have closed-circuit surveillance.' His eyes did not move from her face.

'How much capacity do you have?'

'What's it to you?'

Her face reddened. 'I – I'm curious, that's all.'

The attendant's colleague glanced over his shoulder at Monty and studied her for a moment, as if imprinting her in his memory. In return she tried to look at his monitors, but they revealed nothing more than lines of cars, concrete pillars and pools of darkness.

'What time do you close at night?'

'We don't close.' He was showing distinct signs of losing his patience.

'OK, thanks. If I go ahead and put my name on the waiting list, to whom do I write?'

'You give it to me.'

'Where's your head office? If I want to write in?'

The eyes stared flintily at her. 'If you want to communicate, you do it here.'

She gave him another pointless smile. 'OK, thanks.'

As she went back out into the street, she saw a traffic warden had stopped by her MG. 'Hey!' she shouted, breaking into a run. 'I'm just going!'

The warden was a young woman her own age, with a cheery grin. 'Another thirty seconds and I'd have booked you.'

'Phew!' Monty paused and pointed back at the multi-storey. 'I was just trying to buy a parking contract. Rather a sullen lot in there.'

'Charge the earth, these car parks,' the warden said, then gave her a knowing look. 'But a lot cheaper than getting tickets.'

When she got to her office, Monty ignored the stack of correspondence awaiting her, logged on to her computer terminal and called up the electronic phone directory stored on the company's main archive system. She selected the 'H-M' section for London and typed in a search for LRG Car Parks.

Almost instantly the reply appeared: **Not found**.

She rang Directory Enquiries, but was told there was nothing listed under that name.

Monty hung up and sat back pensively. Fire regulations, she thought, suddenly. Car parks had to be inspected regularly. She tried Westminster City Council and asked for the Chief Fire Officer's department. A female voice answered.

'I'm trying to find the head office of a company called LRG Car Parks, just off the Euston Road,' Monty explained. 'I can't find them listed anywhere, and I thought you'd probably have their correspondence address on file.'

'I'll check for you . . .'

Monty began to scroll through her eMail messages as she waited, noticed an irate one from her father about another

454

missing file, then heard the woman come back on the line. 'LRG Car Parks, 11 Chaltow Street?'

'Yes. That's the one,' Monty said with a beat of excitement.

'We have their head office recorded as 216 Lombard Street, EC3.'

Monty jotted this down, then hung up.

The address rang a bell, for some reason, but she could not immediately think why. *216 Lombard Street*. She stared at it, then suddenly keyed into one of the old files she'd transferred into her computer. 'Bannerman Research Laboratories – BS Acquisition Documents.'

She scanned through it for the correspondence they'd had with the Bendix Schere lawyers, Dean-Wilson. Their City address jumped back at her:

216 Lombard Street. London EC3 6BK.

83

North London. 1953

Daniel squatted in a corner of the temple, his chalice cupped in his hands, and eyed the scene in front of him with distaste.

His fellow adepti lay sprawled on the floor variously and enthusiastically engaged in sexual congress from fellatio to intercourse to sodomy. Mostly they were in pairs, but one group was copulating in a threesome and one in a foursome. This period was not just the highlight of the week for them, it was the highlight of their existence.

Bringing the chalice slowly to his lips, Daniel drank a tiny amount, still uncertain after eighteen months as an adept whether he liked the bitter, metallic taste or not. It was not long ago, he reflected, that he had been so in awe of these people he had longed with all his heart to become a member of their coven; now he was experiencing disillusion.

He could still clearly remember the pride – and the shock –

of his initiation. But more, far more, he could remember the acquisition of the *power*.

The taste of that power.

The incredible energy, strength, ability that it promised. Where was it now? Everyone here had, once, gone through the same ritual as himself, all had tasted that same power. But what were they doing with it? Just squandering it on a few moments of repetitive pleasure.

For it was always the same, week after week. Only small variations in the ritual on certain important dates of the calendar. Nothing else changed here. And after the ritual had ended, the masks came off and the party began.

The sacramental potion was the only drink offered; it contained a potent mix of red wine, gin, cloves, cinnamon, and blood. On festival dates, small quantities of urine and semen were added.

Daniel usually drank only a few sips, making the contents of his gold initiation chalice last the night. Those sips were more than enough to give him a lift and to blur his already well-heightened senses. The drinking was accompanied by shared sandwiches, sausage rolls and cakes. Then after the food came the sex.

It had taken him aback to learn that his first duty as a new initiate was to copulate with a different female member of the coven every week, until he had covered each one. After that, it was a free-for-all.

Of the twenty-one women, Daniel found three quite attractive. There were a further six he could just about cope with; they were neither ugly, nor too old, nor smelled unpleasant, and with sex still a novelty and his urges strong, he was reasonably able to enjoy his couplings with them. But the rest, in varying degrees, filled him with disgust. And even worse had been the two occasions when he'd been taken from behind by other men in the coven, once on his own, once whilst he was actively engaged in intercourse with a woman. As a junior adept he had no option but to comply.

On the nights when his luck was down in the pairings he would drink the entire content of his goblet and sometimes refill it more than once. The result was always the same: he would stagger home with his focus and co-ordination gone, knock everything over and wake his mother who would smell the alcohol on his breath and scream abuse at him.

But it was a long time since he had feared her abuse. Now it simply amused him; so much so that there were times when he had to struggle not to burst out laughing in her face. Even before the accident when she had lost her hands she had turned from an object of fear into a guinea pig on whom he could test his powers. He no longer even regarded her as his mother, but as his caged laboratory animal.

He drank some more of the potion, pleased that he had been quick enough at the end of the ritual workings to slip away before the scramble for pairings started. Three women were absent tonight due to illness, but there would be no shortage of volunteers coming for him in ten minutes or so when the first couplings had ended. He intended to be sufficiently drunk by then not to care.

'You seem very quiet recently, Theutus. Something bothering you?'

The Magister Templi's voice startled Daniel and he looked up at the naked man; saw his flowing hair, the silver chain, the flabby bowl of his paunch, the massive penis limp and spent – glistening with fresh fluids. This apparition sat down beside him and placed an arm around his shoulder.

'Do you want to talk about it?'

Daniel drank a little more and it gave him confidence. 'I don't always want to squander my energies in sex, Magister. I want to preserve my energies for higher work.'

'And what kind of higher work do you have in mind?'

'I want to control the world.'

The Magister Templi's hand remained on Daniel's shoulder. Eventually he said: 'Anything is possible, Theutus, if you want it enough. To control the world is both a big and a small ambition. Why not set your sights on a higher realm?'

'Because I know this one,' Daniel answered simply. 'If both the Great Impostor and His Satanic Majesty place such importance on it, I believe the portal to any higher realm must lie here. I think perhaps it can only be reached by the

457

unification of the whole world under the rule of His Satanic Majesty.'

The Magister Templi marvelled at the boy's mind and vision, and turned towards him. 'I knew when I first set eyes on you that you would outgrow us all one day, but I had not realized it would happen so fast.' He smiled. 'I have often looked at you and wondered how much ancient wisdom is locked in your young mind, how many lives you have led before this one. I will help you and guide you all I can on your ambitious path, but ultimately you will have to help yourself.'

'Yes, I know that.'

'You will need a lot of money and much time. I presume you intend to become a magician?'

'I intend to become *the* Ipsissimus,' Daniel replied, contemptuous of this man's limited horizons.

'You will become the Godhead, Theutus?'

'I will.'

There was a silence between them as the implications sank in, then finally the Magister Templi said: 'Yes, you will need a great deal of money to get on that road, Theutus. You must start on a journey of total purification. From now on you must wear robes made only from the finest linen. You will need to make your own tools from base metals of utter purity, and you will have to cast these yourself in the foundries.'

Daniel watched the heaving, tossing, moaning sea of flesh in front of them, nevertheless concentrating intently on the Magister Templi's words.

'I can give you the right contacts, Theutus, but you will have to work hard to impress them. You are still a teenager now and you will not be permitted to become a full magician until you are thirty-three. But you'll need all of that time and more. Are you prepared to train for such a long period to the exclusion of all else?'

'Yes,' Daniel said without hesitation.

The Magister Templi nodded. 'The right quality of linen will cost hundreds of pounds a yard. Then you'll need brass for your censers, gold for your athame and for all your tools. I warn you, a single ounce of pure gold costs as much as a motor car.'

'The money's no problem.' Daniel looked back at him confidently. 'No problem at all.'

84

Conor faced Monty across the small table in the snug of her local pub. 'Bendix Schere *own* it?' he said. 'The multi-storey car park?'

'Do you have a better theory? The address of the registered office is the same as the Bendix lawyers'. Seems too much of a coincidence to be anything else. And the guys in the booth looked more like security guards than car park attendants.'

'I guess –' He pushed his Budweiser a few inches across the table as if moving a chess piece. 'Maybe there aren't enough spaces in the lot and they needed some more. You know – could be some kind of executive privilege to get your car parked indoors – nicer in winter.'

'Crowe and Rorke both have chauffeurs. And the other Directors' spaces have been in use most of the time I've passed them.'

He pushed his hands through his hair. 'So what exactly did this Mrs Smith say again?'

Monty told him.

Conor echoed the crucial words back at her. '*He say that's where the entrance is*. And you think that could be the entrance to our six missing floors? So whatever's down there can only be accessed either by lift from the Directors' floor or through the multi-storey car park?'

'So it seems.'

He offered Monty a cigarette, clicked his lighter for her, then lit one himself. 'Maybe it's where the Directors go to watch porno movies,' he replied.

She grinned. 'They must have a big supply if they need six floors.'

'Perhaps it's only five – doesn't the hydro count as one?'

'Maybe. OK, so five then,' she said.

He studied Monty for a moment. She was dressed in a loose black jacket, white blouse and black short skirt. She looked immensely attractive and very vulnerable. He reached across the table and squeezed her hand. 'That was brave of you, taking a snoop, but I don't know if it was too wise.'

'No one saw me,' she said. Then she hesitated, thinking about the two attendants themselves, and their monitors. Then about the camera that had panned down at her in the fire-exit passageway behind the hydro. 'I mean – I'm an employee – I'm entitled to go down to the hydro, there's no regulation forbidding that.'

'We're beyond regulations, Monty. We're already sticking our heads inside the jaws of the tiger; when you're doing that it's not too smart to squeeze its balls at the same time.'

She smarted at the rebuke, then tapped ash off her cigarette, unnecessarily. 'I'm intrigued. I'm more than intrigued, I –'

'Yes?'

She tried to tap more ash off. 'I'm sorry, maybe I was out of order, but I – had a hunch, I suppose.'

He said nothing.

'Don't *you* want to know what's down there?' she asked. 'Aren't you curious?'

'I want to know a lot of things, but digging around some place that Bendix Schere has gone to a great deal of trouble to hide is not going to get us anything except unwelcome attention. Until your father comes up with a result, it's vital to keep a low profile, OK? We want to be invisible. We're just good company employees doing our work.'

'Like Charley Rowley?'

He swilled the beer around in his glass. 'Charley Rowley bucked the system all the time.'

'And they tolerated it until he went too far and started snooping into Maternox?'

Conor picked up his glass. A beer mat stuck to the bottom of it detached itself after a few seconds and tumbled into his lap. He pointed to it and said, 'See that? Same thing here. Was he pushed or did he fall?'

'It's an amazingly fast change of story.'

'And so very plausible,' Conor said. He smiled sourly. 'The problem of the non-swimming Charley Rowley neatly side-stepped.'

'Did you speak to his girlfriend, or any of his relatives?'

He opened his arms in a gesture of frustration. 'I spoke to his mother. She's very sweet, but I couldn't get a word in edgeways. She was under the misapprehension I was calling to explain the mistake, and she told me someone from the company had already been to see her about that. She's just devastated by her loss. Full stop. Says she fully understands how the details went awry, particularly in a foreign country.'

'Hawaii's hardly a *foreign* country. It's a state of America.'

'You want her number? You try talking to her.'

'I will.'

He shook his head. 'You won't get anywhere – think it through. BS will have its ass covered by now. Maybe if you sent a private detective out there for six months with a couple of hundred grand in cash, he *might* uncover a wrinkle. But the moment he did, he'd go the same way as Rowley.'

'You really think the company's that thorough?'

He gave her a look of feigned surprise. 'Good evening, pretty girl, what planet are you on tonight?'

'I'm on earth but I think I'd rather be somewhere else.'

'You'll find Washington a good substitute.'

'Yeah, I'm looking forward to going.'

'Nice city, shame about the people. One in every ten humanoids there is a lawyer; the other nine are either muggers or politicians, and the only way to tell them apart is that the muggers are less crooked.'

'I'm surprised Bendix don't have an office there.'

'They do. Well, close by in Maryland – their largest plant in the US. Stick a pin, blindfolded, in a map of the world and you'll probably hit a Bendix site.' He smiled and drained his glass. 'My Washington meeting's come forward a day – I'll be leaving for it on Tuesday. You're coming out Thursday, right?'

'Daddy's worried about getting finished by Thursday – and he can't leave the analysis unattended. He's prepared to cancel Washington if necessary.'

Conor stiffened. 'You can't do that, Monty, you have to come.'

She smiled, uneasy suddenly. '*Have* to? I mean, I'd really like to – and I'd love to be over there with you, but this is more important, surely?'

'I was followed down here tonight,' he said quietly. 'When I stopped to find my cigarettes, I saw a car sitting back a few hundred yards that wasn't there when I pulled up. I noticed it drive past ten miles later when I stopped for gas. Then I saw it behind me again when I stopped on purpose.'

'Where is it now?' she said, alarmed.

'Lurking out there in the night, somewhere,' he said.

'What a horrible feeling,' she said. 'It frightens me.'

It was Monty that Conor was frightened for too, not himself, but he didn't want to say so, didn't want to spook her more than she already was. She was taking everything pretty well at the moment, staying calm, protected by a deep reservoir of her own resources. She needed her senses to be sharpened and alert, not blurred by fear. 'That kind of thing doesn't frighten me,' he said. 'It annoys me. Makes me bloody angry. I don't like my privacy invaded.'

'Nor me.'

He covered her hand with his own, pressing it firmly, and looked directly into her eyes. 'Monty, you have to come.'

She sensed something that she could not identify, as if her antennae were picking up the scent or vibration of danger. 'Why?'

'Do you trust me?'

She hesitated, then more emphatically than she really felt at that instant, said, 'Yes.'

'Then please believe me.'

85

Wednesday 30 November, 1994

Click. The channel changed. A siren wailed, tyres squealed. Click. The channel changed. 'But I love you, Edward,' a woman implored. 'I've always loved you.' There was a bang as a handgun fired. Click. The channel changed. The roar of a crowd. 'Lineker has possession, he's passing it across to –' click. It changed again. Two women were screaming at each other in Italian; subtitles ran along the bottom of the frame.

Click. The screen went mercifully blank and silent.

'God, there's such dross on television.' Nikky slung the channel selector down on her bedside table. She gulped some wine, picked up her Mario Vargas Llosa novel, read one paragraph, then closed it noisily and rummaged through the pile of crumpled magazines strewn across the bed, which they had not removed before making love an hour or so earlier.

Gunn, part of his midriff covered by a sheet, aware that he had drunk too much, lay engrossed in his thoughts, trying to ignore Nikky's irritating attempts to distract him. Conor Molloy and Montana Bannerman were becoming an increasing problem and it was bothering him greatly.

The Bannerman woman had been sniffing around behind the health hydro. She had circumnavigated the exterior of the building. She had been to Winston Smith's home again. Then she had gone into the multi-storey car park. She sure as hell had not done that by chance.

He did not like it, did not like it one little bit. Maybe tomorrow he'd get the budget he was after, but he had his doubts. In the meantime he was having to run a makeshift surveillance using overtired staff on overtime. What he wanted was a tight, invisible web, not a team who were so exhausted they were likely to make mistakes. Bugs were now in place on the subjects' home phones and their office phones were on full monitoring. It was vital they did not know they were being followed; he wanted to do nothing that would put them on their guard.

463

Whatever it was they were up to, he wanted to be able to deliver it on a plate to Crowe. He not only wanted to score a few badly needed points, he was also keen to see how the Chief Executive would react to the news that his darling scientist's precious daughter had been a very naughty little girl. He liked the idea of Crowe being forced to take action that he did not really want to take. Crowe revelled in making other people squirm. Give him a week or two, and he would have Crowe squirming nicely all by himself.

The computer systems manager Cliff Norris had still not come up with any trace of Conor Molloy having dialled into the Bendix system. Gunn suspected the bastard was not looking very hard, if at all. He had recently overruled Norris on some new hardware he wanted, and the systems manager was not a happy bunny about that.

Norris was a breed that Gunn did not like or understand. An arrogant anorak. Most of the tekkies were like that and he had little choice but to live with them. Crowe had accused Gunn of losing his grip and he was right. He had been losing it, but he was feeling a lot more positive now. He had a feeling that Molloy and the Bannerman woman had come along at just the right time for his career prospects.

He was losing his grip on Nikky also, but he was less sure about how to deal with that, or how much longer he could cope with all her demands. Except that he was still hopelessly besotted by her.

'Gosh!' she said suddenly. 'This guy – drowned in Hawaii.'

He turned towards her, startled, and saw she was reading the latest issue of the Bendix Schere in-house magazine.

'Where the hell did you get that?'

'Your briefcase,' she said simply.

'You picked the lock?' he said.

'It's only a dumb combination; a child of four could handle it.'

He snatched the magazine out of her hands. 'That's confidential – employees only.'

'Lucky employees, it's really exciting reading! *Bendix Schere building new factory in Malaya. Maternox sales up sixteen per cent in Brazil. German director of Research and Development raises five thousand marks for Bosnia in bicycle charity race.* This is sphincter-gripping stuff, soldier.' She snatched it back. '*Sir Neil Rorke states that as a tribute the company will donate twenty-five thousand pounds to Mr Rowley's favourite charity.* Well, well, how much more exciting can a magazine get?'

'Read enough now?' Gunn asked her drily.

'Sated. I'm utterly sated. What more could a girl ask? Two terrific orgasms followed by a night in bed with the Bendix Schere magazine; you really know how to treat a girl, soldier.' She slipped a hand under the sheet and fondled his genitals. 'Not much activity left down there. How about going out for a curry – no, how about Mex? I really fancy *fajitas.*'

'I'm bushed.'

'Some food'll perk you up. I'm feeling hungry and horny.'

'Well, you could always sit on the street with a cardboard sign hung from your neck: 'Hungry and Horny – Please Feed and Shag Me.'

She thumped him in the stomach. 'I *don't* think that's funny. Now, come on, let's get up.'

'Niks, it's a quarter past eleven. I'm shattered and I have to be in at dawn to finish a report for Dr Crowe.'

'For such a big, tough guy, how come you're so frightened of this Dr Crowe?' She tugged a crushed copy of the *Evening Standard* out from under Gunn, which was folded open at a picture of Crowe in the business pages. 'Look at him, he's such a weedy thing, and he's got a face like a sick rattle-snake.'

Gunn grinned. 'That's flattering him.'

She stared at Crowe again and screwed up her face. 'Yech, he gives me the creeps. How many people did he kill to get to the top of the heap?'

He turned to face her, electrified by the remark. '*What* did you say?'

'Well, looks like a killer. Did you ever kill anyone, soldier?'

'In the Falklands.'

'And in Belfast?'

He shook his head. 'I'd have liked to kill a few there, but I didn't get the opportunity.'

'And since?'

'I've been in communications ever since. You don't get to kill people in communications, you just monitor them.'

She studied his face closely, with a teasing grin. 'Are you telling me the truth, big boy?'

'What the hell do you mean?'

'Oh, it just seems an odd coincidence. This Charles Rowley's name was on your computer screen with a black Christmas tree beside it, and now he's dead. Just wondering, that's all.' She looked testingly at him for a moment, then kissed him on the cheek. 'Right, more important matters! Tonight's entertainment and the choice is yours: you have ten seconds to get a hard on or we go out for Mex.'

86

Sunday 4 December, 1994
'*The overall objective of this collaboration is to see if eis – and trans-acting components from bacteriophase lambda – can be utilized in mammals to mediate site-specific integration of plasmid DNA into a unique chromosomal alt site.*'

Conor lay sprawled on the sofa in Monty's living room, wearing only his towelling dressing gown, absently sipping coffee; it had gone cold but he barely noticed as he concentrated on the document. A branch of kindling crackled in the grate and spat at him, but he didn't even register it.

'*The assumptions are as follows:*' he read. '*First, in order of priority, we must consider –*'

A kiss on his cheek broke his concentration. 'How many pieces of toast?'

He noticed, suddenly, the smell of grilling bacon and realized he was starving. 'Two, I guess, thanks.'

Conor put the report down as Monty left the room, picked up his laptop and opened his eMail folder. Methodically he began working his way through the last 236 messages, all containing the name 'Maternox', that had been picked up by his Trojan Horse and placed in his Minaret Internet dead-letter drop. He had collected this material yesterday afternoon from yet another hotel room. But now he came across nothing relating to the Medici File, nor anything else of interest; just routine eMail traffic, mostly sales reports and marketing memos.

Monty whipped some eggs in a mixing bowl, then immersed four slices of bread, turning them to soak up the egg evenly, and dropping them in turn into the frying pan. Her eyes drifted to the window. It was a beautiful day; a heavy frost had coated the garden and fields in a snowy whiteness that sparkled in the light of the winter sun, but she ignored Nature's special effects as she kept her eyes peeled for any unfamiliar movement out there.

She had been followed home on Friday night, she was certain. She'd called in at the old lab to find out how her father was getting on, and had sensed a car tailing her afterwards. A pair of lights which had been maintaining a steady distance behind her had suddenly disappeared when she'd turned off on to her cart track.

She had slowed right down a few yards up the track, watching the main road in her mirror for those lights as they went past, but she'd seen nothing. Even when she climbed out of the MG and ran back down to the road, there was only the blackness of the night. Then, later, when Conor arrived, he'd seen a small saloon on the verge with its lights off and a silhouette behind the wheel.

Several times during the past two nights she had got out of bed, walked to the window and peered through the curtains. Conor was leaving for Washington on Tuesday and she wished they could go together on the same flight, but her father did not expect to have a result before late Wednesday night at the earliest.

She was deeply nervous for Conor. Charley Rowley had gone to Hawaii and had been killed. She was afraid something similar could happen in Washington. And she felt uncomfortable at the thought of being on her own in the middle of nowhere for two days.

With her fear for Conor's safety in America in mind, Monty

decided that she should at last go and approach the Chairman, talk to Rorke off her own bat.

Ribbons of smoke rose from the pan. 'Ready!' she called out.

Conor came into the kitchen. 'Wow, French toast – my absolute favourite breakfast!' She served him his two slices, with the rest of the plate stacked with bacon, then sat beside him. There was maple syrup and a jug of fresh orange juice on the table. 'I'm dangerously hungry!' he said, pouring syrup over Monty's toast, then over his own.

'Will you still fancy me if this makes me fat?' she joked, eyeing her own portion appreciatively.

'I guess I could always have the guys in the Bendix Transgenics Division clone a thinner version of you. So even if I didn't fancy the actual *you* any more, I'd still fancy your genes, OK?'

She gave him a dubious grin. 'So what changes shall I make in a cloned version of you?' She slipped a hand inside his dressing gown, and pretended to make for his groin. 'Think there could be room for improvement down there?'

'Thanks a lot!'

She leaned across and licked the sticky syrup off his lips affectionately. 'No I don't really want to change anything. I like every single bit of you.'

And I'm deeply frightened for you.

They wrapped up warmly and set off for a walk after breakfast. As they crunched across the hard, frosted grass on the back lawn, a faint tinge of smoke from Monty's fire hung in the air.

'God, it's beautiful here,' Conor said, looking round in awe. 'Just incredibly beautiful.' He sighed. 'You know, sometimes I find it hard to believe this whole world was created simply by two bits of dust colliding out in space and causing one tiny spark.'

'Does that mean you believe in God?'

'I believe in forces of the universe. I don't like to use the word "God" – more some kind of intelligent energy out there. Something of far greater power than man.'

Monty stared at the watery half-crescent of the moon, still suspended in the noonday sky like a ghost. A red helicopter clattered by, heading in the direction of the military airfield a few miles to the south. She turned her head suddenly towards Conor, and spoke. 'I love you,' she said. Then added meekly, 'I'm sorry.'

'Sorry?' He smiled back, a tiny glint on the far hill catching his eye at the same time and distracting him.

'Yes – I – I can't help it. I love you. I really do.'

Conor said gently, 'You don't have to apologize.' He looked back at the hill, not wanting Monty to see his concern. After a moment, he saw the glint again. Binoculars, or a telephoto camera lens?

Unaware that danger was closer than she thought, Monty continued, 'I – I'm so scared of something happening to you to us.' He touched her shoulders lightly with his fingertips and kissed her forehead. Strangely, the words of his mother over a couple of months ago, on his last night in Washington, echoed in his mind.

You don't have to go. There are other companies – right here . . . You just don't know what you're getting into. Maybe I've taught you too much, given you false confidence. Believe me, I've seen it for myself, I've experienced what they can do. Think again while you still have the chance.

Maybe she was right, but how could he have lived with his conscience if he had just not tried? And anyway if he had not come here, he wouldn't have met Monty.

He squeezed her shoulders, and told her, 'I love you too. More than anything in all the world.'

87

Tuesday 6 December, 1994

The alarm went off at five in the morning in Conor's flat. He sat up immediately and switched on the light. He had to get up early in order to finish some work before catching his flight to Washington.

'Want me to make you some breakfast – eggs or something?' Monty offered.

'It's OK, you go back to sleep,' he said quietly. 'I'll get some coffee in the office.'

She heard him showering, then rooting around packing last-minute bits and pieces into his suitcase. Then he kissed her on the cheek. 'Call you this evening – you're not going down to your cottage on your own?'

'I'll stay here, like we discussed.'

'Promise?'

'Promise.'

'Good.'

She reached out and took his arm. 'You will be careful, won't you, Conor?'

'Washington's my patch, I'll be fine. Just get over and join me as fast as you can.' He kissed her again, then she heard the click of the door and he was gone.

Wide awake now, she rolled out of bed and walked naked through to the living room, which was tinged with orange from the street lighting. She watched Conor emerge from the front door, put his briefcase and hold-all into the boot of his BMW, and hoped he might look up so she could wave, but he didn't.

To her horror, as he pulled out, so did a Ford saloon a hundred yards further back. Keeping its lights off, it followed Conor's car down to the junction at the end of the street, then turned right, after him.

She felt a stab of panic, unsure what to do. Conor was going to the office and it was early in the morning: all she could think of, suddenly, was Jake Seals.

Wishing to hell that Conor had a car phone, she dressed in her clothes of the night before, grabbed her coat, checked that she had the spare keys to the flat, then threw herself out of the door into the morning darkness.

The MG's screen was misted on the inside; she cleared a small patch, then drove off far too fast, taking several lights on amber and one on red.

There was little traffic as she raced up Warwick Road, across the White City roundabout. But once she was on to the Westway, she found herself overtaking car after car, constantly hoping that the next set of tail lights would be Conor's, but disappointed each time.

She saw the BMW in the almost deserted Bendix lot as she drove in through the security gate. Keeping up her pace, she ran into the entrance lobby, noticing only that Winston Smith was still absent, and took the lift up to Conor's floor.

It was too early for any security guard to be in place on the floor itself and she emerged from the lift to find an empty desk and blank screens. Using her smart-card, she let herself through and ran towards Conor's office. She stopped in her tracks. He was walking down the corridor towards her, still with his coat on, a coffee in his hand, a look of surprise on his face.

'Hey!' he said. 'What's up – what's happened?'

She stood for a moment, belief making her breathless. Then she glanced warily around, mindful of their agreement not to talk on the premises. 'A – a couple of files, I thought you might need for your trip – I suddenly remembered where they were.'

He frowned, not cottoning on for a moment, until he saw the urgent signalling in her eyes.

Checking there was no security camera directly on her, she opened her diary, scrawled in large, shaky letters, 'You were tailed from the flat', and held it up briefly to him.

He nodded for her to follow him, led her into the men's washroom, checked the cubicles were empty, then turned on all the taps in sight. 'We have to assume we've got company all the time right now,' he said quietly. 'But if they wanted to bump us off, they'd have done it last weekend down at the cottage. They're watching us because they're not sure what we know. Just keep calm; when you get to Washington it's going to be OK, I promise.'

'Have you got Clinton laying on the National Guard?'

'Something far better. Trust me.'

She saw the concern in his eyes, and regretted their parting even more acutely than before. 'I do trust you,' she said heavily. 'I'm just scared as hell.'

'Stay that way,' he said. 'Stay scared as hell but keep your head.' Then he pointed at the door.

She left the washroom and went down to her own floor, feeling a little foolish for having panicked, and tried to think clearly through her tiredness. Her head ached with a slight hangover from too much wine last night; and whisky, she remembered; and brandy. Christ. She pressed her fingers against her temples to ease the pain. To cap it all, the next two days without Conor stretched out in front of her like a chasm.

When you get to Washington it's going to be OK, I promise.

Why? What was going to happen in Washington that was going to suddenly make everything hunky dory. It was like some global version of a treasure hunt – *proceed to Washington and find the next clue.* Except Conor wasn't a man who played games.

Was he?

She got herself a coffee then knuckled down to work, re-reading the schedule that had arrived from the symposium organizers and running through the checklist for her father. In addition to his main address on Friday evening, he was expected to chair a discussion panel the next day, and had been asked to submit notes for circulation to the other panellists by the beginning of this week. And there would be interviews about his book.

Monty wondered if he had remembered; almost certainly not. She would remind him, but it was too early yet. She yawned and glanced at her watch. 6.20. It was going to be a long day, very long.

Then, impulsively, she did something she had not done for years: slipping her hand inside her blouse, she pinched her tiny silver crucifix in her fingers, and closed her eyes. *Please God*, she prayed silently, *let Conor be safe and let Daddy be safe.*

She had held off phoning Sir Neil Rorke yesterday, torn between her desire to do so and a feeling that it would be letting Conor down. But now she regretted her indecision. Washington was the mugging capital of America. Someone could easily get killed without too many questions being asked.

At 8.30 Monty rang Sir Neil Rorke's extension. She did not

know what days of the week he came in, and kept her fingers crossed.

His secretary answered. 'I'm afraid Sir Neil's in Malaya for the opening of our new plant in Kuala Lumpur. He should be back on Friday. Would you like to leave a message for him?'

Monty hesitated, wondering whether to contact him in Malaya. But trying to communicate over a phone line, not knowing how secure it might be, was a non-starter. 'No, thanks, it's not important,' she said.

Next she dialled her father's office on the intercom; after two rings the call was routed through to his message box. She hung up, and went to see if there was any sign of him on the floor.

The neat and tidy appearance of his office told her he had definitely not yet come in. For good measure she checked out the labs but no one had seen him. He was most likely down in Berkshire working on the Maternox tests, and she debated whether it would be safe to phone him. But when she did call their old number, it rang five times then she heard her own voice informing callers that the number had been changed.

It was quite possible her father *was* there and just not answering, but all the same she felt anxious. She redialled, got the machine again, and announced herself then waited. She was hoping he would hear her voice and pick the phone up, but there was no joy. And it was the same story when she rang his house.

She worked on, then tried phoning again. It was half past ten. Conor would already be at the airport now, she thought, feeling a deepening sense of isolation. With it, her concern for her father increased. If he'd had an accident in the lab, there was no one to help him. And she needed to get some discussion notes faxed or eMailed to Washington today. She would give it another hour.

The campus parking lot was almost full, and it was not until Monty was almost outside the laboratory that she saw her father's rusting grey Toyota in its usual bay. She relaxed a fraction, but as she climbed out of the MG she looked round carefully. It was hard to tell whether she had been followed or not; all the way down she'd been accompanied by heavy traffic and she had no way of sussing whether any particular vehicle had been tailing her or simply going in the same direction.

She let herself in, surprised to find the front door left unlocked, and hurried upstairs to the main laboratory, into the familiar chemical smells.

Dick Bannerman, in white lab coat, was leaning over a Petri dish and dictating into his tiny voice-activated recorder. A rack of test tubes rattled in an agitator beside him. Monty took the scene in, watching, not wanting to break his deep concentration.

Eventually, choosing her moment, she kissed him lightly on the cheek, but it still took some moments for him to register her presence. He murmured something into the recorder, switched it off and turned to her:

'Lost a whole day's work – the cultures died,' he said ruefully.

'Why? What happened?'

'My fault.' He grimaced like a guilty child. 'Just stupidity. Put in the wrong nutrients. I'm not used to doing everything on my own.'

'You look tired, Daddy. Want to take a break and come over to the refectory? It's one o'clock.'

He shook his head. 'Can't leave this until it stabilizes. I'm going to have a problem with Washington now that I've lost a day. I might not be through until Thursday.'

'Daddy, you *have* to be there for Thursday evening – you've only got dinner with Bill Clinton, and he's only President of the United States.'

'Bugger Clinton.' He squinted at the tubes in the agitator. 'I can't just stop this in the middle; I'd have to scrap it all and start from scratch again – so we'd lose the best part of a fortnight. Do you want to take that risk with Anna?'

'There's nothing I could do to keep things going? If you gave me instructions?'

He smiled away the suggestion. 'I'm afraid not. I think what we should do is bow out of the symposium altogether. We could apologize, say I'm ill. It's not that important.'

She twisted her fingers together, gathering her thoughts,

then said, 'If you think you can get the tests finished by late Thursday, then I'll fly out as scheduled that morning, go to the Clinton bash . . . and make your apologies. You can come over on the Friday: they've sold out for your talk – six hundred seats.'

'OK,' he said. 'We'll do that.'

Monty looked down at the Petri dish. 'Apart from your disaster with the cultures, have you been making headway?'

'Yes, but I won't have a clue what might be in the capsules until Thursday night.'

'Remember not to talk about it over the phone,' she said. 'Whatever the news is, tell me when you get to Washington.'

He zipped his lips with his fingers.

Monty smiled. 'Now, I'm going to get us both a sandwich.'

As she stepped out of the building she stood still, nervously scanning the car park. Strains of music, 'God Rest Ye Merry Gentlemen', drifted through the air. Three weeks to Christmas, she thought. Christmas fever was everywhere, in the shop windows, on advertising hoardings, in the fairy lights strung across the streets.

The realization gave her a sudden flash of anger. *This is England, for God's sake*, she thought. Democratic, civilized England. Not some Orwellian nightmare of a Third-World dictatorship or junta. If Bendix Schere was operating outside the law, experimenting, snooping, killing, they needed to be stopped in their tracks.

A name came irresistibly into her mind: Detective Superintendent Levine, who had come to see her in hospital after Jake Seals' death.

She went into one of the phone booths outside the refectory, got the number for New Scotland Yard from Enquiries, then called it and asked if they could tell her where she might be able to locate Levine.

To Monty's surprise, without a moment's hesitation the receptionist said: 'Putting you through.'

There was a click, then Monty heard another woman's voice, pert, efficient. 'Detective Superintendent Levine's office.' And within a minute of introducing herself she'd been put through to the man himself.

'Marcus Levine. Miss Bannerman, very nice to hear from you. Are you fully recovered?'

'Yes, I hope so,' she said. 'I just have to keep my fingers crossed there are no long-term effects.'

'Perilous industry, pharmaceuticals,' he said good-humouredly.

'I'm beginning to think that myself.' There was an expectant silence which she took as signalling the end of the pleasantries. 'There's something I think you ought to know,' she said. 'It may have a bearing on your investigations into Jake Seals' death.'

There was another silence and for a moment she wondered if she'd been cut off. Then the detective's voice calmly said: 'I'm listening.'

'Is it possible to have an off-the-record conversation with you? What I want to say is still speculative.'

'Of course, Miss Bannerman. 'Would you prefer to meet?'

'Could we? Today, if possible?'

'Would you like to come here? Or would you be happier with somewhere more neutral?'

The quiet efficiency in his voice reassured her, and she began feeling safer and more comfortable. She was doing the right thing, she now knew it for sure.

'In case I'm being followed, I'd rather not come to Scotland Yard – could we meet in a pub or a café?'

'Are you familiar with the Strand Palace Hotel?'

She thought for a moment. 'Yes – in the Strand, on the opposite side to the Savoy?'

'There's a large lounge tucked away behind the foyer that's pretty anonymous. I'm going to be tied up for a while this afternoon. Would a quarter to five suit you?'

'Yes, thank you,' she said. 'Thank you very much.'

88

When Conor first began studying patent law at Harvard University, his tutor had explained to the class what exactly being granted a patent meant: it was, simply, he said, the government purchasing an invention.

The inventor sold their invention, whether a design, product or process, to the government, for which the payment was a grant of seventeen years' exclusivity – twenty years in some countries – during which no one else could use the invention in competition without the inventor's permission.

Governments granted patents in order to encourage re-search, to safeguard inventions in their own country, and to secure the revenue from them. But if the applicant had already made their invention public domain, either by lecturing about it or by publishing papers on it, before patents had been applied for, then a patent office would take the logical view that what was being offered was no longer unique, therefore not patentable.

This was the problem facing Conor as he sat in his Club Class window seat in the United Airlines Boeing 757, his computer on his lap, a stack of documents rising out of his open briefcase on the empty seat beside him.

He knew about Bendix Schere's security paranoia: to the effect that it was a sackable offence to work on any form of public transportation, whether train, bus or aeroplane. But this aircraft was half empty and there was no one in the vicinity who looked remotely like an industrial spy. And, besides, he still had a lot of preparation to complete before his meeting with Dave Schwab at the Patent Office in the morning.

Most of his work consisted, at Crowe's bidding, of organiz-ing the documents in such a way as to pull the wool over Schwab's eyes. It was easy for Crowe, because if it did backfire it was Conor's reputation – possibly even his licence to practise – his *number* – as it was known, that was on the line; not the Chief Exec's.

The scam he was pulling on Schwab was the most basic one in the book: because of their workload, US Patent Office examiners were given a strict time limit to spend on each application. Dave Schwab had ten hours in which to read the two hundred pages of documents of the application itself, plus five thick packs of prior art – all the papers and articles that had been published by Dick Bannerman – which might relate to it. In his suitcase in the baggage hold, Conor had another enormous bundle of prior art to dump on Schwab's desk tomorrow, knowing full well the guy would not have time for it.

Almost all the published material in the bundle was innocuous; most of it talked in very generalized terms about the research Dick Bannerman had been doing on isolating the genes responsible for the psoriasis group of diseases. But buried in amongst it all was one single-page leaflet that Bannerman had handed out to a select group of some thirty genetics scientists at a talk last year. That leaflet contained enough of the specific formula of the Psoriatak product to prevent the patent being granted if the examiner wanted to take a tough line. And Dave Schwab always took a tough line.

Conor had positioned the leaflet in the middle of the bundle, confident that Schwab would have to rely on his word as to what was there and would not check everything. Because of the paper load involved, much patent work was done on such trust.

The captain's voice broke through his concentration, requesting passengers to prepare for landing. Conor glanced out of the window and thought about Monty, missing her, and wondering what she was doing now. It was half past three in the afternoon. Half past eight in the evening, London time.

He hoped to God she was all right.

The plane came in low over Chesapeake Bay. It was a clear, sunny afternoon, and even in late November the Maryland countryside looked green and lush, the Potomac twisting through it with a glistening reptilian sheen. The pitch of the engines changed and the aircraft bumped through a string of air pockets. Then the captain's voice came on again.

'We know you have a choice of airlines and we're grateful to you for choosing United. We hope you have a pleasant evening in Washington and that we'll see you again real soon.'

The traffic on the freeway was heavy, and it was half an hour before the long, low grey-brown wall of the Pentagon came into Conor's sight through the trees. The cab drove under a short tunnel, then made a right turn into a familiar wide, grassy avenue that was lined on either side by the modern high-rise buildings of Crystal City.

The people who lived in these high-rises often worked in offices in the same area; if they wanted, they could spend their whole lives indoors, moving like moles through a web of underground corridors that interlinked the massive complex of shops and restaurants.

It was not a district Conor cared for much, but because it housed the Patent Office it was where the company expected him to stay. And right now he wanted to be seen to be doing exactly what the company expected and nothing else.

The eighth-floor room at the Marriott was a good size, furnished in dark wood and plush carpeting, with a view of the open scrubland stretching away into the distance beyond the high-rises.

Conor removed his coat, jacket and shoes, poured a whisky and ice from the mini bar, plonked himself down in an armchair and lit a cigarette. He pondered whether it would be wiser to make his calls from a pay phone down in the lobby, but decided that the precautions he had taken would be sufficient to escape the Bendix Schere eyes and ears. On arriving at the hotel, he had checked in and requested a different room from the one allocated to him. He had then slipped out of a side entrance of the hotel, re-entered and checked in for a second time, selecting a different receptionist, to a room he had previously booked in the name of Mr C. Donoghue. His original room on the sixteenth floor, booked for Mr C. Molloy, now lay empty, with a DO NOT DISTURB card prominently displayed.

He took a slug of the whisky, then lifted the receiver and called the number he knew by heart.

His mother answered after a couple of rings with a gravelly, 'Hello?'

'I'm here,' he said.

'She with you?'

'She'll be arriving Thursday.'

There was a short pause. 'What the hell mess have you gotten yourself into, Conor?'

'I don't know. I thought I could handle it, but you were right.'

'Call me when she's here, OK?'

'I will.'

He replaced the receiver and downed the remainder of his whisky. Then he called the number of his apartment in London.

The phone rang, unanswered. He checked his watch. It was a quarter to five. A quarter to ten in England. He tried again, in case he'd got a wrong number, but immediately heard the same tone again. You could almost tell from the way the phone rang when a place was empty, he thought. He hoped he had not made a serious mistake leaving Monty on her own, and that she was simply out for the evening. He had reckoned they would all be safe until Dr Bannerman had finished his tests on the Maternox. After that, he had a feeling things were going to get very rough indeed. That hadn't started already, had it?

A quarter to ten. Something did not feel right. What the hell had happened to her?

89

Gunn sat at his desk, sipped his Styrofoam cup of sugarless tea and screwed up his face at the taste. Nikky had been making comments about his girth and, as usual with her, he had been unable to tell whether she was joking or not.

He tensed his stomach muscles then rapped his solar plexus

480

several times with his balled fist. Hard as iron. Flat. No damned paunch at all; no flab. OK, perhaps if he let the muscles go slack, completely slack, then there was a bit of loose flesh. But heck, what middle-aged man didn't have some kind of a –

Shit. Middle aged! That was the problem. He was judging himself against other men of his own age – not those of *her* age.

Hence no sugar in the tea; hence the cottage cheese salad he'd had for lunch, and the hour he'd booked for himself in the hydro that evening.

A flashing icon on his computer screen told him he had a new eMail message. It had been flashing at regular intervals throughout the afternoon, but he'd been too occupied to respond. He hit the key to open his mail box, then ran his eye down the idents of the senders and the summary lines, checking for those he was particularly expecting, and stopped at the third one down.

Jon McLusky. Re: Search Molloy

McLusky was his counterpart in the US, based at Bendix Schere's Maryland plant. He moved the cursor and double clicked.

Major Gunn:

Reference your request check qualifications of Mr Conor Molloy: you informed me the following: 1981–7 Stanford University. Biochemistry degree followed by Masters in Organic Chemistry. 1987–9 Carnegie Mellon. Molecular Biology doctorate.

1989–92 Harvard Law School. Bar and Patent Office examinations.

1992–4 Group Patents and Agreements, Merck Pharmaceuticals Corp.

Something strange here: Merck checks out as does Harvard Law School, but previous biog does not: Carnegie Mellon and Stanford have no record of Molloy.

Ascertained also that no records exist of him in any of the background information supplied by you, nor can I find any tallying records of birth in the Public Records Office. Seems like you could have a problem. Please advise what further action you require.

Gunn cursed, wishing to hell he had acted on his original gut feelings about Conor Molloy. Something had felt wrong about him from the beginning.

It was company policy to take a minimum of two references from previous employers or academic institutions, plus two professional referees. The references Molloy had had from Harvard, and in particular from Merck, were outstanding. Gunn knew he should have checked further back at the time, but Merck were an immensely professional company and he figured they would have done all that when they'd first taken the patent attorney on, and if the guy was good enough for them, he was good enough for Bendix Schere.

He pulled out Conor Molloy's file: attached to the letters from Harvard and Merck was a sound personal character reference from a Baltimore lawyer called Michael Clovis, and another from a physician named Dr Robert Melville in Charlottesville. He scanned both documents into the computer then eMailed them back to Jon McLusky asking him to check out the two referees.

An hour later McLusky came back to him: Michael Clovis had indeed been a partner in a law firm in Baltimore. But he had died four years before the date on Conor Molloy's reference. And Dr Melville had died one year before the date on his testimonial.

Gunn stared bleakly at the eMail. He now had two major problems on his hands. The first was Conor Molloy himself. The second, and the one that was worrying him every bit as much, was how to ensure Dr Crowe did not find out about this blunder.

Angry at himself, and taking it out on McLusky, he hit the keys hard tapping out his reply:

Find out who the hell Conor Molloy really is.

90

Monty's guilt about going against Conor's advice increased sharply as she walked into the elegant foyer of the Strand Palace Hotel.

She had been churning over the pros and cons, and each time she arrived at the same conclusions: that she'd *had* to go to the police, and that she would be able to convince them to act discreetly.

As she walked towards the rear of the lobby in search of the lounge, she heard her name called and looked round, recognizing Detective Superintendent Levine instantly.

He was striding towards her. His close-cropped black hair and small facial features gave him the air of purposeful efficiency she recalled clearly from their one previous meeting in her room at the hospital.

He held out a hand. His grip was robotic, and he retained Monty's own hand for several seconds, staring her straight in the eye as if deploying a salesman's technique.

'Very nice to see you again, Miss Bannerman.'

She found herself feeling awkward now she was actually face to face with him. This was a high-ranking police officer and what she was about to tell him could have dramatic consequences for one of the world's largest companies, and result in prison sentences for those involved.

Levine directed her to a secluded niche behind two massive potted plants and they sat down, Monty in an armchair, the detective on the sofa beside her. A waiter came over and she asked for coffee. Levine ordered tea.

'So, you have some information about the death of Mr Seals that you want to talk to me about?' Monty was given a smile of encouragement.

She remembered the need to be circumspect. 'I – I would just like to clarify the confidentiality aspect – between us – first.'

He raised a placatory hand, and Monty noticed a single gold band on his wedding finger. 'Unless you tell me otherwise, this entire conversation is off the record, all right?'

'Thank you,' she said.

He gestured for her to start.

She told him everything, from the first approach of Hubert Wentworth, the deaths of Jake Seals, Zandra Wollerton, Walter Hoggin, Dr Corbin and Charley Rowley. The break-ins at Sarah Johnson's, Zandra Wollerton's, the Kingsleys' and her own home. Conor's discovery of the Medici File, and the tests her father was now doing.

Levine listened, interrupting her only to clarify the occasional point. Most of all, he seemed intrigued by the discrepancy relating to Rowley's death, and he was particularly interested to know what progress her father had made with his analysis of the Maternox.

When she had finished, Monty sat awkwardly; she wondered whether Levine would take her story seriously.

'Who else have you spoken to about all this?' he asked.

'No one.'

'Just your father, Mr Wentworth and Mr Molloy?'

'Yes. I've been very anxious not to do anything that could jeopardize my father's relationship with the company. I didn't want to cause waves and then find we have totally the wrong end of the stick.'

Levine's face gave nothing away. 'I can appreciate your concerns, Miss Bannerman, and you've done the right thing coming to me.' He glanced at his watch and there was a distant look in his eyes for a moment, as if he was turning his mind to his next engagement. 'It would obviously be unwise to take any action before we know the results of the tests. Until then I don't feel I have sufficient evidence that you're in physical danger to warrant the costs of putting you and your father under twenty-four-hour police guard. But what I will do is put out an immediate request for passing attention on your homes and on your laboratory in Berkshire; and if you let me have your registration numbers, I'll have my patrols keep an eye out for your vehicles. I also have a colleague in the Washington Police Department – I'll make sure you're both looked after when you're over there, and Mr Molloy.'

484

She thought she saw a spark of warmth in his eyes and felt safer. 'Thank you.'

He slipped a card out of his wallet and handed it to her. 'You can get me on these numbers day and night – there's my direct office line and my home number. Don't feel embarrassed about calling if anything frightens you; get on to me immediately.'

He raised a hand to summon the bill, saying, 'If the British taxpayers can't afford to protect you, the very least they can do is buy you a cup of coffee.' He looked so serious as he said it, she could almost believe he wasn't joking.

Monty left the hotel feeling reassured by Levine's promise to arrange police vigilance for her and her father, and Conor.

As she walked round into the narrow Covent Garden street that ran along the back of the hotel, she began to head for the bay where she had parked the MG.

'Monty! Hi! What are you doing here?'

She turned, startled, to see Anna Sterling, laden with carrier bags, hurrying towards her.

'What am I doing? What are *you* doing?' Monty said, delighted to see her friend and at the same time embarrassed by the secret she was still keeping from her.

Anna looked wild, in leopard-skin leggings, her wavy hair freshly coiffured into the style of Struwwelpeter. 'I've been spending!' she said. 'I'm celebrating!'

'Oh yes?'

Anna nodded vigorously. 'I've just been with Mark to Professor Campbell's ultrasound clinic in Harley Street – he's the top guy in London. I had my ten-weeks scan – God, Monty, it's incredible! I actually saw my baby! It's about an inch long – I could see the heart beating, the arms and legs moving, tiny little jerks! He said I'm past the danger point, so I'm going to tell everyone that I'm pregnant now – isn't that great!'

'Terrific . . .' Monty said, trying to reciprocate the same enthusiasm. 'Wonderful.'

'What are you up to?'

Monty shrugged. 'Been window-shopping. I was just about to go home.'

'Why don't we have a drink? Have a bite of supper if you like? Mark's gone to his annual old boys' dinner – he won't be home till late, and pissed as a rat. I know a great Chinese restaurant just round the corner.'

'Sure,' Monty said, glad of the outing, but not at all at ease with her friend.

They'd drunk one bottle of Australian Chardonnay between them and had started on a second; Monty was feeling pleasantly woozy.

Shouldn't drink any more, she knew, because she had to drive back to Conor's apartment, but right now she was beyond caring. She felt really relaxed by the booze, it made her feel more comfortable with Anna, and helped her cope with her friend's incessant bubbling recitals of every single detail of her scan. And it helped relieve the pain of missing Conor.

They'd nearly finished the second bottle and Monty was vaguely aware that she was the one doing most of the drinking; Anna kept telling her the obstetrician only permitted her one glass a day.

It was after eleven when they left the restaurant and parted, Monty airily dismissing Anna's offer of a lift. She climbed unsteadily into the MG. Definitely should *not* be driving, she thought, squinting to get the key into the ignition, then groping hastily beneath the dash for the hidden alarm switch, only just remembering it in time.

The drive to Fulham was a blur. A couple of times she debated whether to abandon the car and take a taxi the rest of the way. But she wound down the window, and drove on with the bitter night air blasting her face, trying to sober up a little.

She suddenly found herself driving down Conor's road with no memory at all of getting there. And it wasn't until she'd climbed out of the car that she realized she'd completely forgotten to look out for anyone following her. But she wasn't bothered; the booze had given her courage, and she glared at the pools of light and darkness in the quiet street with a belligerent expression. *OK, you bastards, come near me if you dare, I'm not scared of you.*

She tottered up to the front door and for the first time

registered just quite how drunk she was. It took her some moments to find the key and insert it, then she was in. A phone was ringing somewhere, faintly, and she looked at her watch. 11.40.

The ringing continued, and seemed to be getting louder. Then she realized that it was coming from Conor's apartment.

'Shit.'

She scrambled up the stairs, fought the key into the lock and almost fell into the hall. The ringing was in stereo now. Phone in the living room, phone in the bedroom. Bedroom was nearest. She lurched towards it, fending off the wall, then stepped through into pitch darkness.

The ringing stopped.

Deflated by the sudden anticlimax, she mouthed a silent curse and put the light on. Working out with some difficulty that it was twenty to seven in Washington, she thought it must have been Conor calling.

The flat felt very quiet and it was strange being there without him. Lonely, very lonely suddenly. The effects of the wine were wearing off, and she needed sleep.

Parrrrp. . . parrrrp . . . parrrrp . . . parrrrp . . . parrrrp . . .

The sound registered first in her subconscious.

Parrrrp . . .   parrrrp . . .   parrrrp . . .   parrrrp . . . parrrrp . . .

Then she sat up in a cold sweat, trying to remember, in the pitch darkness, where she was.

Parrrrp . . .   parrrrp . . .   parrrrp . . .   parrrrp . . . parrrrp . . .

The sound was faint, familiar. You heard sounds like that all the time in London; you heard it anywhere that cars were parked, these days. Except this one was even more familiar.

'Jesus Christ!' She sprang out of bed, stumbled through into the living room weakly illuminated by the orange glow of the street lighting outside. She ran to the window and stared out in disbelief.

The bonnet of her MG was open. A youth with a shaven head was standing by the passenger door looking nervously up and down the street. A companion had his head inside the engine compartment. The noise stopped abruptly; the second youth lifted his head out and slammed the bonnet shut. A tall, gangly boy in his teens with spiky hair.

Monty hammered in fury on the windowpane. 'Hey! Hey!' she yelled.

Stark naked, she ran and grabbed her mackintosh. As she did so, the phone started ringing but she ignored it. Forty seconds later she was outside and launching herself in a blind rage down the steps to the pavement.

The MG had come to life and was reversing backwards, bumping the car behind; there was a tinkle of broken glass, fuelling her rage even more. The engine revved, the tyres screeched and she watched helplessly as her car roared out of the parking bay, snaked wildly, and began to disappear down the road.

She raced after it, barefoot. Catch it at the end. Might catch it at the end if it had to wait to turn on to the Fulham Road, she thought.

Suddenly the car slowed abruptly and seemed to glow from within, as if the bodywork had become translucent. The roof billowed out, then rose eerily in the air, separating from the car and winging its way several feet skywards like a gigantic bat. The cockpit filled with a ball of flames. Both doors flew open.

Monty felt as if she had just run into an invisible wall that had jarred every bone in her body and which halted her dead in her tracks. Her ears popped. All the oxygen seemed, momentarily, to have been sucked from the street. Then a powerful shock wave rippled through her and she felt a searing blast of heat on her face.

There was a deep, booming explosion and fragments hurtled from the MG in all directions. It tilted on to one side, slithered crazily across the road, smashed into a parked car and overturned. She could see the chassis, the exhaust and the smooth boxes of the silencers all bent outwards as if gouged by a massive tin opener. Rivers of flame flowed out all around. Then there was a deep, dull KERRRUMPHH and a column of fire rose thirty feet into the atmosphere.

Monty dived down between two parked cars. She heard a cracking sound and an object blurred past her, bounced once and fell with a clatter into the road. On her knees, gripping on to the nearest rear bumper and feeling as if she was about to throw up at any second, Monty peered out towards the fireball.

Through the flames she could see a motionless, blackened shape lying half in and half out of the open driver's door. It was an outstretched human.

Lights were coming on in the houses all around her. She could hear the sound of windows and doors opening. The terrible whooshing roar of the flames. The thick, pungent stench of burning paint, and a sweeter, more sickening smell of roasting meat.

She gagged, whimpering in shock, gripping the sharp edge of the bumper, clinging to it as if it were a life raft. She gagged again as the stench of cooking flesh became stronger; then she threw up.

Footsteps hurried past her. Voices. Someone was screaming. She stayed where she was. It seemed an age before she heard any sirens. The image of the charred figure reanimated itself and ripped through Monty's mind like a bolt cutter. Something drove past her, blue lights flashing, then another vehicle, then another. Fire engines; tenders; an ambulance.

Demented banshee wails of their sirens. A police car, followed by a second; more sirens.

Then a firm, calm voice through a loud hailer. 'Stand back. Please, everyone stand well back.'

Monty remained in her own small universe, crouched down beside the pool of her own vomit, concealed between the two parked cars, shivering with fear.

Should go and speak to someone, she thought. Should tell them it's my car. But she did not want to admit that the grotesque mangled object burning like a funeral pyre belonged to her.

She was incapable of speaking. Incapable of explaining that whatever had been placed in the car had been intended for her.

91

The keys puttered steadily, click-click-click, pause, click-click-click, pause, punctuated by frequent backspacing and curses. Dick Bannerman pecked away with one finger of each hand, watching the rows of black letters appear on his grey screen

AGT TCA TGG GAA ATC TTA GTA AAG CAA . . .

Groups – codons – of three of the four bases, Adenine, Thymine, Guanine, Cytosine, that were the building blocks of all life. He read them off a long column of horizontal dashes that looked like a strip of barcoding, on a sheet of developed film beside him.

There'd been only one hiccup so far, earlier in the week: his original tests had shown that the Maternox contained DNA, but when he'd tried to incubate it, it had not worked. In subsequent tests he discovered it was not DNA, but RNA. RNA viruses were used sometimes as delivery systems in genetic engineering. It seemed that within the Maternox capsule was contained some form of attempt at genetic engineering. But what?

Through a reverse transcriptase, he had copied the RNA into DNA, from which he had then done a series of vertical gel tests, which were captured on the sheets of film each containing two hundred bases, the first of which he was now entering on his screen. He'd had to think of a suitable name for this test; something by which he could identify it, but which would mean nothing to anyone else.

CAPSULE I. SEQ, he typed.

Then he called up the Internet address of the London Genome Data Bank, the British centre of the Human Genome Organization, entered it and waited for a connection. After some moments, the familiar **Welcome to the Human Genome Resource Centre** greeting appeared on the screen, with a list of instructions and options.

The Human Genome Organization (Hugo) was only the world's most ambitious ever scientific joint-venture. All scientists had free access to its series of international programmes, within which all new genes identified were instantly pooled into a common database. The aim of the project was to have all 100,000 genes of the human body identified and sequenced by the year 2005.

Dick Bannerman called up his Proscan program and instructed his elderly computer to do a database search to try to find a match between the two hundred bases he had just entered and any known existing gene. He pressed carriage return to start the process, then sat thoughtfully back in his chair. These Genome searches could sometimes take several hours.

Nine o'clock. It could be a long night ahead but he didn't mind, he was enjoying being back in his old laboratory, felt comfortable here, far happier than in the damned Bendix Building, in spite of all its equipment and staff.

What a mess, he thought; what a damned bloody mess Monty had got them into. She was a good kid and she had meant well, but he wished to hell he had followed his own instincts and never allowed himself to be swayed by her. Sure they had always struggled with funding before, but they had got by, they had been their own people here. They'd not had to answer to creeps like Crowe, had not had to fill out forms in triplicate every time they needed a new box of pipettes or wanted to go to the toilet.

Crowe was someone for whom he had very little time. It was true that unlike most chief executives in the pharmaceutical industry he did actually have a scientific background – and an impressive one at that – but Bannerman found him conceited and opinionated. Above all, his real objection was that he considered him typical of the breed of businessmen scientists whose only interest in research was the commercial profit.

As he left the lab to walk across the campus for a bite to eat at the refectory, he was wondering how watertight their contract with Bendix Schere was, and whether his solicitor could find some way of getting them out of it before the old lab had gone for good.

Feeling a little brighter after his snack, Dr Bannerman arrived back in his lab and noticed immediately that the figures on his computer were static, indicating it had stopped searching. He sat down and stared at the screen.

There was a line dividing it down the middle. On the left were the columns of the bases he had entered, headed: **TARGET FOR MATCH**. On the right was a fresh set, headed: **CLOSEST MATCH**. Beneath, it said:

PERCENTAGE MATCH: 86%

DEFINITION: Poliovirus
(RNA Poliomyelitis)

He shook his head in disbelief. *Polio*. Was that what the Maternox was doing? Delivering the gene that caused polio to pregnant women? No. There had to be some other explanation. He picked up his voice-activated recorder and dictated this latest finding into it. Then he added some interim conclusions.

'Poliovirus possibly indicates intent to use an oral delivery system. Most viruses can't be used to deliver genetic material orally, because they can't survive in the human gut. Poliovirus can. It is simple to produce a defective poliovirus that cannot replicate.'

He read the words on the screen again. 86 per cent match was close, but not identical. He decided it was essential to put the whole of its sequence into the database.

He disconnected from the Genome Data Bank and began the long and monotonous task of entering a further six thousand bases, one finger, one letter, at a time . . .

It was close to midnight before he had the final percentage match back from the Data Bank but this meant he had the whole sequence mapped.

His data revealed that the first 2000 bases and the last 2000 showed an 86 per cent match to polio. But he was struck by the match of the central 2000 bases. He stared at the screen again.

PERCENTAGE MATCH: 98% OVER 2000 BASES

He had been right in his suspicion. The poliovirus was a

vector, a delivery system; it occupied each end of the string. The fact that it was an 86 per cent match rather than 100 per cent was, he presumed, explained by the fact that the virus had been doctored to prevent it replicating – and therefore infecting the recipient with polio.

It was finally beginning to make sense, although he desperately wished he was mistaken.

He thought of the files that had gone missing from the Stacks – one in particular – and read the unblinking letters that were now spelling out its name on the screen in front of him.

'You bastards,' he said under his breath, struggling to contain his sickening horror in a blast of anger. 'My God, you bastards.'

A reflection glanced off the screen and a shadow slipped across his desk. He spun his chair round, startled, to see Dr Vincent Crowe standing in the lab. Right behind him.

The Chief Executive was immaculate as always, in a camel coat with a velvet collar. He held his hands behind his back as he spoke.

'Good evening, Dr Bannerman. I just happened to be passing – thought I'd drop by and have a chat. Haven't seen much of you in the past week or so.' He gestured towards the doorway, where another figure now appeared. 'I'm not sure if you've met Major Gunn, our Director of Security?'

92

Hubert Wentworth was tired. It was 2 a.m. but he rarely went to bed early. The television flickered silently in front of him and all three bars of the electric heater glowed. He needed to stretch his legs, take a hot bath and then he would hope to drop off for an hour or two. It had been a useful night's work, yes, time well spent.

Time.

Putting his affairs in order.

A time to be born, and a time to die. The words echoed around his mind like a half-remembered tune. *Ecclesiastes*, yes. *A time to plant, and a time to pluck up that which is planted.* Death was close now and he was not afraid. He had never been afraid of dying; there was nothing that could come close to some of the horrors of life. The release, the escape. Not for him, *Do not go gentle into that good night.*

Go, finally, to Françoise, who had been waiting for him for thirty-three years.

He had seen the doctor again last week and the report from the oncologist was not good. An operation was needed; radical surgery. But he was not sure he wanted to go through with it; a few years ago, yes, there might have been a point then. So much unfinished business then. But now it was different; a week, maybe two, that was all he needed. Surgery. Pain. Physiotherapy. Prolonging the agony. No, he did not want that.

He stared fondly at his collection of toy cars; painted lead models a few inches long of the saloons, convertibles, sports cars and commercial vehicles of his childhood. They evoked in him memories of a time when life had stretched out ahead and seemed so full of promise. How very different it had all turned out, he thought, his eyes fixing on one of his favourite photographs of Françoise. She was smiling, so warmly, so happily. Sun-tanned, red scarf tied round her head, sleek black hair underneath, the smile, the one that was for him and him alone.

You'll get over it, they said. *Two years. Time is a great healer.*

They were wrong. Thirty-three years and he had thought of no one else, day and night. He had cared for Sarah, yes of course, their daughter, she had meant the world to him, had been his life. But all the time, in her every movement, every sound, he had seen and heard Françoise. He had often wondered if she'd ever realized quite how much she wrenched his heart.

Dead, too, now. His eyes went to the photograph on the mantelpiece. Sarah and Alan on their wedding day. Both gone. They were lucky, they were out of here. In death they had escaped. Not like him; he had been condemned to a living hell, driven by one obsession that had taken thirty-three years to come to fruition.

They had taken his wife and his daughter and they had never said sorry. They had built the Bendix Building as a monument to their success when it should, instead, have been a headstone for Françoise, except she would never have liked anything so vulgar.

He reached forward and stroked the photograph of his wife. *I promised you I would never rest until I brought them to justice.*

Moist eyes fixed on Françoise, he leaned back in his armchair, then looked proudly at the row of documents, each neatly stacked and labelled, that sat on the floor at his feet. His watch said 2.10. He yawned and raised a hand to his mouth, ever mindful of his manners.

Thirty-three years. He had come close to nailing Bendix Schere on the powdered milk scandal fifteen years ago, but they had got wind of the story, put pressure on his publishers, threatening them with lawsuits and withdrawal of advertising. And, within days, fatal accidents had claimed his two key sources.

For thirty-three years he had watched Bendix, stalked them, scoured newspaper archives for every column inch ever written about them, and struggled his way through every paper published by their scientists. Maternox. Thirty-three years of waiting patiently, waiting for that one time they would fail to cover their tracks. And now here it was.

The Medici File.

He leafed through each sheath of the documents he had assembled, checking them, page by page. He thumbed the files on Sarah's death first. Zandra Wollerton had done a thorough job there, poor girl. Too thorough. He had a copy of the fax she had obtained from Sarah's doctor to Dr Linda Farmer, Director of Medical Information at Bendix Schere, reporting the possible link between her virus and the Maternox. Then there was the report on his son-in-law's apparent suicide in his car, sketchy as the inquest had not yet taken place, but not to be ignored.

He checked in turn each of the files on the other three women who had died in labour after taking Maternox, ensuring everything was in meticulous order. Next he scanned through the printout from Conor Molloy's desk. Then finally, he re-read his own detailed report. All he needed now was the result of the Maternox tests from Dr Bannerman.

He had settled on *The Sunday Times* as the newspaper to whom he would give the scoop. If he could stand the story up, he had been guaranteed the works. The splash and spread. The paper required the results of the test, accompanied by affidavits from Dr Bannerman and from Conor Molloy. When they had those, they would move into action and start hitting Rorke, Crowe and the rest of the Board of Directors with calls.

He replaced each of the documents inside their clearly marked folders and carried them into the hall. Tomorrow he would lock them in the office safe.

Then he plodded back to his chair. Nothing to do now but wait for Miss Bannerman to make contact. A lovely lady, plucky and kind; he envied her youth and energy. He liked the American with her, Conor Molloy. A trifle intense, perhaps, but he was all right. He liked Americans, there had been good times in Vietnam before –

He picked up the channel selector and routinely checked the news headlines on Teletext, which he did every hour or so; it made him feel professional, even though his paper rarely featured national news.

A car bomb had gone off in central London; first reports indicated two people were dead. The IRA were back again, he thought gloomily; too many different warring factions and splinter groups for the ceasefire to hold indefinitely.

He looked at his watch once more. It was old, with a winder that had to be turned by hand, and its face had yellowed. A cup of tea would be welcome, most welcome. A cup of tea, then a breath of fresh air, then –

He was startled by what sounded distinctly like a footstep upstairs. He raised his eyebrows, puzzled, then after a moment stood up, went out into the hall and listened. There was no sound at all; the house was utterly still. Must have imagined it, he thought, walking through into the kitchen.

93

Wednesday 7 December, 1994
Have to get away from here, Monty thought. *Just get right away*.

Shivering from shock and the icy night air, she pushed a hand into her mackintosh pocket, and as her fingers closed round the keyring and the cold, sharp shapes attached to it, she felt a small amount of comfort that at least in her panic she had not locked herself out.

Still crouched down, keys clasped in her hand, she crept back a few paces until she was on the pavement, looking in both directions up and down the street. Reflections of the flames bounced back at her from every window; slivers of blue flashing light slid like disembodied spirits over the roofs of the parked cars; sirens shrieked, wailed, cried, like nocturnal beasts of the urban jungle.

She heard the voice through the loud hailer asking people to move further back, losing its patience now, becoming exasperated. A young man ran past her, clad in a dressing gown and slippers.

This isn't happening. She closed her eyes for a brief moment. *Please God let this be a dream.*

She stood up and walked along the pavement. People were peering out of their doorways, dogs were barking. It felt strange to be walking naked beneath her mackintosh and barefoot in London; but everyone else looked strange also; right now the whole world had suddenly gone out of kilter. She would wake up soon.

The front door of Conor's apartment building was open, and a dark-skinned man was looking out. He gave Monty a nervous smile. 'A bomb? It is a bomb, yes?'

'I – I think so.'

'The IRA,' he said and shook his head. 'The ceasefire was just a sham, a publicity stunt. These people are not –'

But Monty had squeezed past him, stumbled up the stairs, locked herself in Conor's apartment and put on the safety chain. Her watch said 1.45. Been in bed about two hours, she thought, feeling sober now, completely one hundred per cent sober. Goosepimples pricked her skin like thorns, and she shivered. Eight forty-five in Washington, she calculated. Phone Conor, phone him and tell him. Warn him.

No calls from home, he had said. Strictly no calls from home. Have to go out, find a pay phone. She pressed her knuckles to her mouth, jammed them hard up against her teeth. Levine. Detective Superintendent Levine. She thought of the police officer, remembered his words as he had handed her his card.

'*You can get me on these numbers day and night – there's my direct office line and my home number. Don't feel embarrassed about calling if anything frightens you; get on to me immediately.*'

She rummaged in her purse, retrieved the card, made her trembling finger hit the right buttons.

The phone was answered on the third ring and she recognized his voice instantly, even though he sounded very sleepy.

'Yes, hello?'

A siren screamed past the window, making speech impossible for a few moments. As it faded, she heard him repeat, 'Hello? Hello?'

'It's Montana Bannerman,' she said.

Levine suddenly sounded much wider awake, his voice taking on precision-tool efficiency. 'Yes, Miss Bannerman, what's the matter?'

'Someone's tried to kill me. My car has just blown up; a few minutes ago.'

'Are you all right?' he asked urgently.

'Yes, I'm OK. There were two youths – they – they –' Her voice cracked as the horror got to her.

There was a brief pause, then he said: 'Right. I want you to stay where you are, keep the door locked and don't answer it to anyone until I arrive. I'm going to take you into protective custody. Pack an overnight bag and I'll get to you as quickly as I can – take me about half an hour across London. All right?'

'Thank you,' she said, choking as emotion overcame her.

She replaced the receiver and wiped away the tears rolling down her cheeks with the back of her hand. Then, suddenly, she stiffened, feeling as if a bolus of cold water had been injected into her insides.

. . . take me about half an hour across London.

How the hell did *he* know where she was? How did he know she was in London, and not at home in the country? She hadn't had time to tell him.

She felt gripped with panic as the room seemed to shrink around her, the walls closing in on her. *Half an hour. Take him half an hour.*

Jesus.

She ran into the bedroom, ripped off her mackintosh, yanked her small suitcase open and threw on her clothes. She raced into the bathroom, shovelled her wash things and cosmetics into her arms, chucked them into her suitcase, stuffing everything in, glancing anxiously at her watch every few moments.

Five minutes had passed. She put her mack back on, unlocked the main door cautiously and looked down the stairs. The coloured man was still standing in the doorway but there was no one else around. Clutching her suitcase and handbag, she descended, squeezed past him without speaking and ran. Away from the burning car, away from the crowd. Kept on running until she had reached Cromwell Road.

The traffic was light. Breathless, she stumbled for a couple of hundred yards, then in the distance she saw the yellow glow of a 'For Hire' sign. She threw herself out in front of the taxi, raising one hand and waving her handbag frantically. To her relief, the driver flashed his lights in recognition and swerved to a halt at the kerb.

She clambered into the back, gulping air.

'Where to?'

She couldn't think of anywhere. Her mind had gone into spasm. *Where to?* What the hell had she told Levine? Everything, the lot; her father; Conor; Hubert Wentworth.

Where to? The police? Go to Scotland Yard? How many friends did Levine have? How wide was his influence? Had he ordered PC Brangwyn not to find anything when the local lads were investigating her break-in? Had he covered up over Jake Seals' death?

I don't know if you are aware, Miss Bannerman, but it appears your colleague was intoxicated when he came to work. He had a blood alcohol level of twice the legal limit for driving.

She looked urgently at the cab driver. She needed somewhere anonymous with a phone, had to speak to her father as fast as possible. 'Heathrow Airport,' she said. 'Could you head out towards Heathrow?'

'Which terminal do you want?'

She hesitated. 'I'll let you know.'

As the taxi turned away, a police car screamed past them, its siren wailing.

'Must be a fire or a bomb or something,' the cabbie said. 'Down Fulham way; lot of activity going on.'

Monty pressed her face against the rear window, watching the road behind for any sign that they were being followed. The traffic was still light and she could see nothing.

As they headed up the ramp of the Hammersmith flyover, the lights of the Bendix Clinic clearly visible to the right, she asked the driver to find a pay phone. He turned off at the next roundabout and pulled up by a solitary booth outside a garage.

She told him to wait, went into the booth and rang her father's number. She let it ring for a good two minutes, willing him to answer. He was a light sleeper, and if he was at home it would wake him.

Her anxiety deepening, she dialled the number of their laboratory; it was quite possible he was still there; she had known him, on many occasions, to work right through the night.

Please pick up the phone, Daddy, she thought. *Please.*

There was a click, followed by the sound of her own voice on the answering machine. She hung up and hurried back to the cab. 'Where's the nearest car rental place that would be open at this hour, do you know?' she asked the driver.

'Out at the airport, I should think. Avis, Hertz, someone like that. I know the Hertz one there's twenty-four hours.'

'OK, take me there,' she said. 'As quickly as you can.'

94

North London. 1953

The spoon clattered from his mother's metal hand on to the linoleum. Daniel, seated across the kitchen table from her, made no move to pick it up. Anyway, she was fiercely proud and did not want to be helped. God had handicapped her, and now He was giving her the strength to overcome the handicap. She had taken to likening herself to Job.

Lifting objects from the floor was the hardest thing. The two metal hands were rigid, unarticulated, and a small object like a soup spoon was particularly difficult to prise off a flat surface.

A lick of steam curled from her brown Windsor soup as she glared defiantly down at the spoon, then she ducked her head below the table, some stray wisps of hair, which was kept short now, tumbling forward. It gave Daniel immense satisfaction to watch his mother struggle. He listened to the racket as her hands scrabbled, waited for the clink, then the silence as she slowly raised the spoon, with studied concentration.

He would let her get it halfway up, then he would use his power and she would drop it again. The spoon would clatter on to the linoleum in musical discord, and his mother would grimace. All Daniel needed to do was hold his concentration. Keep his mind tuned into her own, keep it focused, and he could play her, the way he did all the time now, like a hooked fish.

Now!

The spoon fell into the bowl, splashing scalding soup over her.

'Owww! Damn, damnit!' his mother cried out, soup dripping from her face. But, immediately, she laid a hand over her heart, pressing it into the pale blue strands of the cardigan she had knitted herself before the accident, and stared guiltily at the Bible beside her bowl. 'Lord forgive me,' she said. 'Lord have mercy upon me.' She leaned down again and, when she was out of sight, the smirk spread across her son's face.

Practise! the Magister Templi had commanded. Daniel obeyed. It was the summer holidays now and he was free all day, to work his rituals in his room. He was finding it easier to summon the power and to control it, but he was not sure where the limits lay. Today he intended to find out.

Money. The Magister Templi had told him he would need masses of it to become a great magician. There was no problem; money would soon be on its way.

He allowed his mother to pick up the spoon this time, and waited patiently as she cleaned it on her napkin, then immersed it in her bowl and raised the soup slowly and carefully towards her mouth. Timing was all. He judged it exactly, watching her edge the spoon towards her lips, saw her eyes focused on it. Peripheral vision. Had to make sure it appeared in her peripheral vision. Her lips parted, she blew on the soup.

Now!

He materialized the rat. A large brown rat that scrambled up the side of the sink, as if it had just emerged from the plug hole, then ran on to the draining board, and paused to survey the scene.

The result was as Daniel had hoped. As she screamed, hot soup splattered on to her chin and inside the neck of her blouse. She stood up in panic, banging the edge of the table painfully with her knee and slopping soup from both their bowls on to the table.

'Get it out!' she screamed. 'Get rid of it. It's the Devil! Get it out of here!'

The rat leapt to the floor and raced towards the pantry. His mother stood in the doorway, screaming hysterically. 'Food! Get it out of there!'

Daniel walked unhurriedly into the pantry and smiled to himself. The rat had vanished, simply because he had released the power that had caused it to materialize, but he said nothing, waiting patiently, biding his time.

She called out: 'Have you caught it? Are you all right, Daniel? Be careful, they carry rabies!'

Daniel nonchalantly ate an iced bun off a tray prepared for the Church Ladies Committee meeting. Then another.

'Don't let it on the cakes I've baked!' she screamed.

Daniel finished his last mouthful and called out, 'Come here, you bastard, come here, you little bastard!' He ran out of the pantry.

His mother's eyes darted wildly around the kitchen. 'Where is it, I can't see it?'

Daniel stopped and stared in mock bewilderment. 'Must have escaped.'

His mother stood near her pyramid rack of pots and he saw his chance. Concentrating hard, he caused the rack to shake; the pans rattled. She turned, half demented, then backed away.

'Under there!' she screamed.

He dropped on to his knees and pretended to look under the rack. 'Come on, little fellow, out you come.'

'Is he there? Can you see him?'

He conjured up a larger rat, sent it hurtling straight at his mother. She ran right out of the room and up the stairs bellowing in fear; he allowed the rat to get halfway up, then released his spell and watched it dematerialize into thin air.

Power!

The power was strong today.

His mother's bedroom door slammed shut.

But the power was draining him. That was the problem, it exhausted him, sometimes left him completely shattered for days; the stronger the power, the more it took from him.

Use it wisely, and it will serve you well all the days of your life and beyond into the eternal plane. Use it unwisely, and you unleash the most uncontrollable forces in the Universe. It is important to practise, to learn to harness the power, to moderate it and make it work for you. You have the gift of life and death, now. Satan does not bestow it lightly.

Daniel used the power to think about the silver crucifix his mother wore around her neck. He concentrated hard. God had defeated Satan. The symbol of the crucifix was the symbol of God's authority.

Not any more.

Yahweh!

'DAAAAANNNNNNIIIEEEELLLLLLL!'

The scream cut through the walls of the house. His mother's bedroom door crashed open and she stumbled towards the top of the stairs, clawing her chest. 'Daniel! Oh, God help me! It's burning!'

Smoke was pouring from her chest. He could see the distinctive cross-shaped burn appearing like a stencil in her cardigan. It was growing in size as he watched it, as he concentrated. The smouldering line spread outwards until it reached from shoulder to shoulder, upwards to the bare skin of her neck, then downwards to her navel. Thickening smoke rose, then flames jumped up through the smoke and her whole front became like a blazing Ku Klux Klan cross he had seen in a picture book.

'DAAAAANNNNNNIIIEEEELLLLLLL!'

Her hair went up in a rush like arid hay. One whoosh, then a fierce crackling roar and it seemed her whole head was ablaze, hissing, whining, whistling, crunching. The flames spread down to her pleated skirt and her nylon stockings beneath.

Then he rooted her to the spot.

She stood at the top of the stairs, her arms outstretched as he fixed her there, like a hideous sacrifice on an altar. She could feel all the pain but she was incapable of moving an inch.

Daniel's nostrils filled with the smell of her burning clothes, the acrid smell of the wood, the stench of the nylons, and the sweet, roasting smell of her flesh.

He had to concentrate harder than ever before, to keep her arms outstretched, to prevent her from charging down the stairs. He wanted her to stay like that, could make her stay like that, just had to remember the words he had been told, had to get the sequence right, had to remember how to draw down the power from his great god, Satan.

The wallpaper was blistering, scorching, searing around his mother now. The bulb from the landing light above her head exploded from the heat, showering her with molten glass. Her flesh was blackening on her face, blistering, peeling off in places, but her eyes were still white, staring at him, screaming silently at him. He could read the words in her eyes.

God Almighty's wrath will come down on you for this, Daniel!
God will be thy judge!

Her shoes were burning now, and the carpet beneath them.
Smoke leaked out of the walls and billowed around her.

'Satan is my judge,' he said quietly, and returned her stare.
'Satan is my Lord and Master and always has been. Hail
Satan!'

A wind roared through the house, fanning the flames that
now erupted all around her. The walls were burning, the
ceiling; the inferno descended the staircase towards him, but
he stood his ground, untouchable, holding her charring,
blistering, bubbling torso in a hideous mockery of the
crucifixion.

There was a tremendous rending sound as the floor gave
way and she plunged through the flames, out of sight. The
house exploded and Daniel was catapulted backwards by the
blast, hurtled through what was left of the front door and out
into the garden.

He lay on his back, stunned, as the windows blackened then
burst, showering glass all around him, allowing flames to leap
hungrily out of each of them into the cool evening air.

Neighbours came running. Daniel felt gentle arms lifting
him, carrying him backwards. He heard a kindly voice say:
'Are you all right, son?'

He nodded absently, watching the thick, black smoke that
was spiralling out of every exit, thinking about his mother's
will which she had tucked away at the back of her wardrobe.
She had left some money to a range of charities and some to
her sister. But the main bulk of her estate she had left to the
Church. Nothing to him.

'There's an ambulance on its way, be here in a moment.
How did it happen? Did you see?'

Daniel shook his head. 'No, I was upstairs when I heard my
mum screaming – she must have set fire to herself in the
kitchen.'

'At least you're all right,' someone else said to him. 'You're
a brave chap, you're going to be fine.'

Daniel smiled. With the will destroyed, he would inherit
everything. Every penny. He had very carefully checked the

law. He was going to be very fine indeed. An identical house a few doors away had sold for good money only a couple of weeks ago. A brand new house built from the insurance money would sell for even more. Both his parents had been prudent with their savings, investments and insurance. Yes, he was going to have all the money he needed, and he had already planned his investment schemes to make that money grow.

95

Washington. 30 April, 1968

She took him by the hand, her face whiter than he had ever seen it before, as white as the face of the clown at the circus on his birthday; except she wasn't smiling, not at all. The skin of her face was tight with anxiety.

'Daddy's in trouble, we have to go to him right now,' she said. Her voice was warbling, trembling, it sounded like it had been wrung out of her throat by a pair of coarse hands.

Her long black hair was clipped to the sides of her head and some of the strands hung messily free. She wore a billowy white blouse clamped to her belly by a wide, studded belt. 'He's in real big trouble.'

'What kind of trouble?'

Without letting go of her grip, she hauled him through the front door of their house in the tidy suburb, into the warm sunshine of the spring afternoon. As she pulled the door shut behind them she said, quietly, so he barely heard her: 'Walpurgis.'

'What's Woppergeese?'

'I knew something was going to happen. I said as much to your daddy. He should listen to me, *you* should listen to me, your momma knows things sometimes, OK?'

'Are we going to see Woppergeese?'

'We're going to see Daddy.'

She unlocked the passenger door of the battered Plymouth

and bundled him in, then ran round the other side of the car, slid behind the wheel and twisted the key in the ignition. As he looked at her face, he saw beads of perspiration rolling down her forehead. She was frightened of something, terribly frightened, and the fear transmitted to him, making him afraid also.

The engine rumbled, ticking over fast on choke, racing like a pulse; she backed into the quiet road, then floored the gas pedal. He felt the surge of acceleration press him back against the softly sprung vinyl seat, and watched the needle of the speedometer creep across the dial with a mixture of excitement and fear. His mom was usually a pretty slow driver, nervous of the road, but now she was driving more like his dad, one hand pressed on the horn and cursing everyone in her way.

'We gonna see Woppergeese as well as Daddy?'

'Woppergeese? What's with these Woppergeese? Look, son, we're going to see Daddy because Daddy's in trouble.'

'What trouble?'

'Bad trouble.'

'Why's he in bad trouble?'

'Because he's a good man, and they don't like him.'

'Who's *they*?'

'Bad people.'

He was silent only for a moment. 'What sort of bad people, Mom?'

'Evil. They do the Devil's work. They're pure evil.'

'Why don't they like Daddy?'

A car with two elderly people was dawdling in front of them, blocking the road. She pushed the horn angrily, then answered, 'Because he won't do what they want him to do.'

'What's that?'

'They want him to be untrue to himself.'

He pondered the remark, not really understanding what it meant, then he lurched forward in his seat, bracing himself with his hands against the dash as his mother chickened out of running a stop light ahead and brought the car slithering to a halt.

He followed her anxious stare across the wide boulevard, and up to the right.

'Is that where Daddy works?' he asked, looking at the ugly muddy brown high-rise.

She said nothing. He eyed the building again. In fact it seemed to be two buildings, one growing out of the other. Then he looked back at his mother. He saw that she was muttering something under her breath. It sounded like she was praying.

He felt a knot of tension deep in his gullet, growing every second. He had never seen her like this. She was terrified.

The lights changed. She accelerated and slewed right into a large parking lot directly in front of the brown building. He saw a sign which said 'Parking By Permit Only', but his mother ignored that, skidded to a halt, jumped out and left the engine running.

As he made to follow her, he heard a deep, soft crunch high above him. It was followed by a much sharper *crack*, like a gunshot. He saw his mother stop and her head whiplash upwards. Her eyes bulged and her hand went to her mouth. She made a tiny low moan.

He looked where she was looking. A window was bulging outwards, like a balloon. It expanded further, then further, then suddenly exploded as if it were a down pillow that had been slit open. The air all around it filled with a dense cloud of feathers; as they slowly sprayed outwards, he could see in their midst a gigantic black bird.

It zigzagged down, half flying, half plummeting like a shadow chasing itself, then struck the ground with a heavy thud. It made a terrible snapping sound only a few feet from where he stood. As it did so, its head jerked sharply and seemed to stare straight at him.

The small boy stood, unable to move, his legs welded to the tarmac beneath him, oblivious to the shards of glass raining down. His head began to vibrate uncontrollably in shock. Then a high-pitched whine deep in his stomach rose like the wail of a siren into a piercing scream.

'DAAAADDDDDDYYYYYY!'

96

Wednesday 7 December, 1994

It was ten to four in the morning when Monty drove her rented Vauxhall into her father's driveway and saw immediately that his Toyota was not there.

She felt strangely removed from the shock of what had happened earlier, as if her exploding MG was just part of some freaky game in a virtual reality arcade.

Entering her father's hall, she saw the post neatly stacked by his housekeeper, still unopened. It did not look as though he had been home since yesterday morning and the tidy state of his study and empty wastepaper bin only confirmed this. She had seen enough.

As she got back into the Vauxhall, she had to pull the door hard against a sudden gust of wind. Without more ado, she turned round and headed off towards the university.

She kept a watch on vehicles coming in the opposite direction as she drove, on the off chance that she might spot the Toyota heading home, but the roads were almost free of traffic and she saw nothing familiar. She should stop and phone Conor, she knew, but she did not want to do so until she had found her father and made sure he was safe.

To her dismay, there was no immediate sign of life as she drove into the car park at the old lab. The building itself was in darkness. She walked up to the front entrance and unlocked the door, perturbed to find that the burglar alarm had not been set; it was one of the few things her father always remembered to do.

Everything felt creepily silent and when she looked up the dark stairwell, she felt suddenly scared of what she might find up there.

Please be all right, she prayed, *oh God, please be all right*.

She pressed the light switch, touched the wooden banister rail for courage, climbed upstairs rapidly, and stopped at the entrance to the pitch-dark laboratory. She pulled down all four light switches in rapid succession. Nothing there. No one. Her heart shorting out, she walked slowly towards the office, reached for the handle, afraid to turn it, then twisted it and pushed hard.

An unfamiliar red glow shone out of the darkness on the floor just beneath Dick Bannerman's desk. It was some piece of apparatus he had left on, she presumed.

A creak somewhere behind startled her, and she turned, staring back at the landing. The buzz of the fluorescent above her seemed to be growing more insistent and she tried to tune it out, listening for a footstep, a door hinge, the rustle of clothes. There was another creak; another. Then the window-pane behind her rattled. She breathed out; just the wind, she thought; but it was still some moments before she felt secure enough to turn her attention back to the office.

Identifying which machine the red glow was coming from, Monty was surprised to see that it was her father's pocket dictating machine. He normally carried it everywhere with him and even slept with it beside his bed, recording thoughts and ideas as they came to him.

She picked it up, wondering why the tiny red *record* light was on, then saw it had been left running and the tape had reached the end of the reel.

There was another creak out in the landing. She turned and then snatched a few quick glances around the office for some suitable heavy object she could use as a weapon if need be. If she was going to go down, she was going to go down fighting. A solitary nerve twitched at the base of her throat. Still keeping a wary ear tuned to the landing, she pressed the sliding rewind button with her thumb, let the tape spool back for a few seconds, then released it.

There was a steady hiss of static. She rewound it further. Again static. She rewound it further still, keeping the pressure on the button, watching the progress of the tape. When it was half rewound she listened again, but there was still nothing recorded.

Disappointed, she continued, and as it reached the three-quarters mark, the silence was abruptly broken by the squeaking sound of speech playing in fast reverse. She maintained the pressure on the button for several more seconds, then released it and heard her father's voice, tired and a little faint:

'*Poliovirus possibly indicates intent to use an oral delivery system. Most viruses can't be used to deliver genetic material orally, because they can't survive in the human gut. Poliovirus can. It is simple to produce a defective poliovirus that cannot replicate.*'

The words were followed by a silence broken by the occasional background noises which triggered the voice-activated mechanism: footsteps; a tap running, the coffee machine percolating; the clack of computer keys. Then she heard her father exclaim, softly: '*You bastards. My God, you bastards!*'

She was about to stop the tape to replay the section just before when she heard the unmistakable sound of Dr Crowe's voice:

'*Good evening, Dr Bannerman. I just happened to be passing – thought I'd drop by and have a chat. Haven't seen much of you in the past week or so. I'm not sure if you've met Major Gunn, our Director of Security?*'

'*I'd like an explanation from you, Crowe, as to what the hell you think you're doing with your Maternox,*' her father said.

'*Well, we'd like an explanation from you, Dr Bannerman, as to what you're doing with a Maternox formulaic template owned by the company.*'

Monty presumed this latter voice was Major Gunn's and when she listened on, she heard her father's response.

'*Would you prefer that explanation to take place in a court of law, or in front of the Committee for Safety of Medicines? Now, I'd like you to stop trespassing on my property and leave. If you feel the need to drop in for a chat with anyone else at one o'clock in the morning, I suggest you drop by your lawyers and start briefing them, because by God you're going to need 'em.*'

Monty heard a loud clank after this; her father shouted something inaudible, followed by the sound of a scuffle and a muffled thud. Then came an eerie quiet in which she could make out footsteps and furniture being moved. Eventually calm tones that she recognized, but could not place, took over.

'*Right, just roll up his sleeve and I'll get this into him. Won't give us any more trouble; he'll be docile as a lamb.*'

She listened in horror to a confusion of more footsteps, heavy breathing and shuffling, punctuated by a click that might have been the door, then silence. Just the hiss of static on the tape.

Christ! she thought. *Oh, Christ!* She stopped the recorder, gutted with worry. That Crowe monster had *abducted* her father. She wandered blindly around the office, stopped, leaned on her desk and stared through the frosted glass window into the darkness. What now? Were they going to kill him the way they had killed everyone else?

Her immediate instincts were to phone the police, but she thought about Levine; imagined suave, dry Levine taking charge and shuddered.

Levine, a senior policeman in Crowe's pocket? Or Bendix Schere's? Within hours of seeing him and telling all, someone had blown up her car and Crowe had evidently found out that her father was doing tests on the Maternox. Coincidence? No way. Conor had said some days back that things had gone way beyond coincidence and he was right. How powerful was Levine within the police force? And was he the only cop Crowe had in his pocket, or did he have the whole force stitched up in there?

She stared fearfully at the tape recorder. Evidence, vital evidence; someone might think of it and come looking. *Need to get away from here,* she thought. *Yesterday.*

She jammed the recorder into her coat pocket and ran, leaving the lights on, setting the alarm to aggravate any return visit by Crowe.

Oh Christ, Daddy, where are you?

She locked herself in the Vauxhall and drove for several miles anxiously watching for any sign of a tail, only pulling up at a phone booth when she was satisfied she was clear.

Firstly she called Hubert Wentworth's home number, but it rang unanswered, ignoring her prayers. Letting it ring on, she fumbled in her handbag for her diary, searched for the page where she had written Conor's Washington number; then disconnected from Wentworth, punched in her credit card code, followed by the dialling code for the United States.

Remembering his instructions not to ask for him by name,

she simply asked for Room 807. Moments later she almost wept with relief as she heard his voice.

'Are you OK?' she asked.

'I'm fine, I'm good. I –'

'Conor, we're in danger,' she said, interrupting. 'They've blown up my car.' She was almost breathless. 'They were trying to kill me and now they've taken Daddy and I can't get any answer from Hubert Wentworth. God, I've been such a bloody fool. I went to the police, I didn't listen to you.' Her eyes scoured the landscape in all directions as she talked. 'I went to that smoothie Levine and I think he's in league with –'

'Hey, whoa! Slow down. Calm down, Monty honey, tell me exactly what's happened.'

'. . . OK,' he said finally, when he'd heard it all. 'This Levine's going to be out looking for you with a posse and it's possible he's got every cop in England alerted. Do you have your passport with you?'

'Yes,' she said, glad she'd had the presence of mind to pack her suitcase before fleeing from Conor's apartment.

'Right, you have to quit England. Just get the first flight to Washington that you can. If you can't get a direct flight go via New York.'

'I can't just abandon my father like this, Conor.'

'Monty, you can't stay in England, you won't make it through the next twenty-four hours.' He sounded far firmer than he ever had before. 'You're not going to be any use to your father dead – and they still need him too much to harm him. But they don't need *you*. OK?'

The tone of his voice got through to her. 'Conor, what about you? I'm sure you're in danger, too.'

'I can look after myself. I'm safe until I've finished my business here, I know that much – they badly want me to get this application through.' He spoke more convincingly than he felt. 'You have to come over; I can't protect you otherwise.'

'I don't understand.'

'You will. Now listen carefully. When you get to Dulles Airport go to the main bar in the departure lounge and I'll meet you there – I have an appointment at the Patent Office which should be over by around one, so I'll be there by two, half two at the latest. If you have any problems, leave a message here for me. OK?'

'Please be careful,' she said.

'You're going to do what I've said?'

'Yes.' *Have to ring Anna and cancel the theatre tonight,* she noted.

'You're not going to go chasing round the countryside trying any heroics?'

'I'm beyond heroics, Conor. I'm just really frightened.'

'It's gonna be roses. Just do what I say and it's gonna be roses. See you soon, right?'

'Right,' she said, hesitantly.

'I love you,' he said.

It was only Conor's immense relief that she was unharmed that had stopped him from blasting Monty for her stupidity. *This is one serious mess,* he thought. As in definitely a worst-case scenario.

Had he given Monty the right advice? Was there any other choice? They needed the protection of a fortress right now and the fortress was here. But somehow he had to get them both inside it and that was not going to be easy.

He helped himself to another miniature of whisky from the mini bar, lit a cigarette, then plugged his modem into the phone socket and dialled into the Bendix Schere computer in London.

On the prompt **Enter user name** he typed the user name of Cliff Norris, the systems manager, and then the password **a*l*c/hem>ist**, holding his breath to see if it would be accepted.

On the screen appeared a list of options and commands. So far so good, he thought, he was into the system. Then he called up a search box, typed in the words **Medici File** and hit carriage return.

On the screen appeared: **Restricted access file. Enter password**.

Copying faithfully from the back of his diary, he typed: **poly*phe^mus**. Then he hit the carriage return again. Almost instantly appeared the words:

Invalid password. Access denied.

He tried again, in case he had made a typing error, but the same words came back up. The password had been changed.

Monty was right to be so concerned, he thought. The scumballs had not hung around. He glanced at his watch. It would be 5.25 a.m. in England. Monty had told him the bomb went off around a quarter to two, and that she met Levine beforehand at five in the afternoon.

He did some mental calculations. At five p.m. he had already been on the aeroplane for four and a half hours with three and a half hours to go. From the speed at which it seemed they had acted, it might have been possible for Levine to have had him intercepted at Dulles Airport. But that would have needed some fast footwork this side of the Atlantic, too.

He thought hard about Bendix Schere. They were ruthless, yes, but everything they did was driven by an utterly professional commercial logic. He was not indispensable; they could replace him in days, although they would not find it easy to get someone else prepared to be dishonest with the Patent Office. Provided he carried on his business over here seemingly normally, he had a feeling they would leave him alone, at least until after his meeting with Schwab tomorrow. And that was a meeting he very much wanted to have.

Once the Patent Office had the full set of Psoriatak documents with the concealed prior art leaflet, he would have something else to hold against those bastards at Bendix. If push came to shove, it was going to give him one more powerful bargaining point with Crowe. Provided he could remain alive long enough to use it.

At 9.30 in the morning his bags were packed and he was ready. Leaving everything in his room, he walked down the corridor and through the fire door into the emergency stairwell.

He climbed up to the sixteenth floor, opened the door cautiously and looked up and down. Nothing, apart from a chambermaid's trolley stacked with towels. He walked stealthily down towards Room 1609, and saw that the 'Do Not Disturb' sign was still in place outside the door.

He checked again that there was no one watching him, then crouched to inspect the hair he had glued between the bottom of the door and the jamb.

It was broken.

97

Crowe sat behind his desk, thin lips even more vividly crimson than usual against the pallor of his face, his grey eyes staring straight down the ridge of his nose at Gunn. 'Well?'

Gunn gritted his jaws against a yawn; his body was leaden, his head ached like hell and he was so tired he was close to hallucinating. 'We were very unlucky.'

'*Unlucky?*' Crowe's voice was acidic.

Gunn shrugged. 'Million to one chance.'

'Whatever possessed you to think of a car bomb? We're doing all we possibly can to keep the lid on, and you initiate something that's going to hit every newspaper headline in the country.'

'I think this will change your mind, sir.' Gunn was playing his trump card. He placed in front of the Chief Executive a copy of the midday edition of the *Evening Standard*. The front-page headline read: ANIMAL RIGHTS BOMBERS TARGET LONDON.

Crowe's eyes darted down the article. 'How did you fix this?'

'It fixed itself, sir. The Bannerman woman and her father have had a number of nasty attacks on their Berkshire premises in the past, as well as personal threats. Dr Bannerman once had the windows of his house broken and his tyres slashed. Animal Rights groups are back on the offensive now, targeting everything from farmers exporting live cattle to the pharmaceutical industry; some of them are pretty anarchic. One group has already claimed responsibility, and I'll bet others will for the hell of it. I felt it was the perfect opportunity – *Animal Rights Terrorists Kill Leading Geneticist's Daughter.*'

'Except you killed two joyriders instead. And you can't find the daughter.'

'She doesn't have too many places to go and we know them all.' He gave Crowe a sly smile. 'And we have means of finding her.'

Crowe ignored the comment. 'You think she went back to the lab last night?'

'I went there at half four to tidy up and the alarm had been switched on.'

'I suppose you set it off?'

Gunn blushed. 'That's a very minor detail.'

'Is it?' Crowe pressed his fingertips together. 'Presumably the police rang the keyholders, whom I imagine to be Dr and Miss Bannerman, and found them both absent.' He looked questioningly at Gunn.

'We don't have any worries with the police.'

'No? I think sometimes, Major Gunn, you and I draw our confidence from different wells. Yours appears to have an abundant supply of fresh water; mine is running dangerously dry.'

Gunn said nothing.

'Do you have any more surprises planned? Another pyrotechnic display?'

'No, sir.'

'Have you dispensed with the American yet?'

'I'm waiting for confirmation.'

'And how is the good doctor this morning?'

'Pretty much how you'd expect. Not exactly singing our praises.'

'I can do without the praises. But I want him to sing, very loud and very quickly.' Crowe smiled at the Director of Security.

'Oh yes, we can make him sing, sir.' Gunn was relieved to see a thaw in his boss's frostiness. 'We can make him sing as loud as you like.'

98

Washington. Wednesday 7 December, 1994
Crystal Plaza was a complex of ribbed concrete and glass high-rises from whose bland exteriors it was not immediately apparent where one building ended and the next began. The empire housed at number 2201 advertised its presence to the outside world only by modest-sized gold lettering: UNITED STATES DEPARTMENT OF COMMERCE: PATENT AND TRADE-MARK OFFICE.

There was no alternative public route into the building and besides, Conor thought, the time and place of his appointment was already known to Bendix Schere, and he was pretty sure they would have the place staked out.

As he lugged his heavy suitcase laden with documents towards the entrance, no one revealed themselves as an obvious tail. From the broken hair on his hotel room door, he was primed for trouble, but not here in this very public place; it would come later.

The interior of the building was a labyrinth of pale green corridors housing offices, libraries and the acres of file stacks which contained copies of every patent that had ever been filed anywhere in the world. In the Hall of Fame, seven floors beneath Dave Schwab's office, rows of copperplate portraits honoured those inventors whose ideas had stood the test of time, and sometimes changed the world. Sikorsky who pioneered the helicopter. Frank B. Colton who invented the oral contraceptive. Elisha G. Otis who invented the modern elevator.

One hundred and fifty examiners worked in this building, wielding the power to make or break both small-time inventors and multi-national corporations – by granting or rejecting patents for products as diverse as self-replenishing mouse-traps, steam engines smaller than a grain of rice, prosthetic phalluses, or a pocket-size purifier for turning urine into mineral water.

*

Conor sat in the functional metal-framed visitor's chair in his friend's untidy office, and stared across a desk piled high with bulging folders, all marked with the file number of his application. US Patent Office examiners were strictly discouraged from lunching with patent agents and attorneys. A cup of coffee in the office was all that was permitted before the boundary into bribery was deemed to have been crossed.

Conor had finished his coffee an hour ago, but Schwab still had not refilled the empty percolator next to the crash helmet on the table behind him.

Instead Schwab sat hunched over the desk, picking on trivial point after trivial point. He was as sloppily dressed as ever, wearing a baggy grey and white striped shirt with the cuffs rolled up and a tie at half mast. In deference to modern style, his hair looked as if he had just received a severe electric shock.

Conor was finding it hard to concentrate; Schwab seemed even more pernickety than usual today and they were progressing at a snail's pace. Conor's thoughts were almost entirely about Monty, hoping to hell she had made it safely to an airport and on to a plane.

He glanced at his watch. 11.30. That made it 4.30 p.m. London time. If she'd caught a direct flight at nine in the morning her time, the earliest she'd get here would be midday local time. It would take half an hour to disembark and get through immigration and baggage claim, at the very least. Fine, she'd have to wait in the bar, that would not be a problem. More of a problem was his uncertainty about whether the airport would be watched. But no one would have any reason to suspect she was coming here ahead of schedule, would they? Unless they'd actually followed her to the airport at her end, of course.

A waving hand caught his eye and he looked at Schwab with a start.

'Hello, Conor. Are you on this bus with me?'

Conor smiled thinly. 'Sorry,' he said.

'You look tired – been partying? Old age creeping up? You can't take this gadding around; I can't either. If I don't get in bed by ten-thirty I'm a wipe-out next day.' He looked back down at the document he was studying. Then he nodded at the bundles Conor had unloaded on to the flat table behind him. 'OK, let's move on; so what you got buried in there?'

Conor eyeballed him, trying hard not to look as if he was hiding anything, but his heart was not really in the game. 'Buried? Oh, c'mon, man.' His voice sounded forced and he knew it.

Schwab smiled. 'Hey, c'mon yourself.' He tapped his chest with a massive index finger. 'Do I look like some kind of root vegetable or something? You dump five piles of prior art on me when you know I've only got a couple of hours' reading time left and you're gonna pretend you're not hiding something in there?'

'Nothing important; I'm not going to pull something like that on you.'

Schwab shrugged. 'It's your neck in the noose.'

'I know.' Conor stared out at the dreary view of another high-rise, twenty yards away. He wanted out of here, out of this cluttered office with its lousy view, and its empty coffee machine, and this old friend of his who had grown so goddamn self-righteous.

He wanted to tell Schwab that Bendix Schere stank and he should throw the entire application in the trash can, but this was no moment to start burning his bridges. So he forced himself to sit tight, as if this was a normal meeting like any other.

'Conor, what we need to do now is work right through the application and deal with all the points, and then sort this prior art out.' Schwab removed a bundle from a folder and slipped off the elastic bands holding it together. 'OK, here's the first problem – only a small one. The E-coli – you state here in the application and I'll quote: "Comprising and consisting essentially of . . ."' He looked up at Conor quizzically. 'I'm afraid I'm going to need you to change the wording from *comprising and consisting of* to just *comprising*. It's bad use of language.'

Conor looked at him in amazement. 'But what the hell does that have to do with the actual application?'

Schwab had the grace to look apologetic. 'Yah, I agree, its a nit-pick. I'm afraid it's the Group Director's new peeve – it's really not worth arguing if you want this to get through quickly.'

Conor nodded at a row of certificates on the wall. 'I don't believe this, Dave. Is that what you got those certificates up there for? Good grammar? You get the Split Infinitive Award of the Month or something?'

Schwab grinned and Conor saw a trace of his old friend come through. 'You gonna spend the rest of your life in this place?' he asked him.

'No way – didn't I tell you over the phone when we spoke – couple of years and I'm outta here. Julie and I are heading out to Oz when she finishes her postdoc.'

'Sure, I forgot.'

Schwab leaned forward. 'You're forgetting a lot of things today, man – you OK? I mean you sure it's just jet-lag? You look like shit.'

'I'm OK.'

Schwab looked at him thoughtfully. 'You want to take care of yourself, Conor. Don't go overdoing it. These big companies work the ass off bright guys like you. I've had patent attorneys break down in tears right in that chair where you're sitting. Not worth it. Got to take time out to smell the roses, huh?'

Conor nodded and said nothing.

'Even the biggest bastards in history gave their staff time off, you know. You have to relax sometimes, lighten up. Even the goddamn Medicis gave their henchmen a break.'

Conor stared back at him, startled. '*Medicis*?'

'Yup – and they were real bastards.'

'I forgot,' Conor said. 'You used to be a Renaissance freak.'

'Still am.'

'Tell me something, Dave, did the Medicis have any connection with the pharmaceutical industry?'

'Well, there were plenty of alchemists trying to turn metal into gold and to find cures for disease, but there wasn't any pharmaceutical industry in the fifteenth century.' Schwab rolled his tongue around his mouth, looking pensive.

'Although I guess you could say the Medicis were pretty well up to speed with the medical knowledge of their time.'

'In what way?'

'They used it to their advantage, the way they used everything to their advantage. Like they had a kind of neat trick for keeping their domestics: when new staff first joined, they poisoned them.'

'Come again?'

'Secretly. They gave them a drink laced with a very slow-acting mercury-based poison. Then they gave them the antidote in their food.'

Conor frowned. 'Why do that?'

'Simple; you digest mercury and it stays in your system for life, right?'

'Right.'

'So – the combination of chemicals the Medicis gave their staff could never be eradicated from their systems. But it *could* be contained with an antidote; so long as they took the antidote twice a day, they were fine. But the formula and elements of the antidote were a secret. Ergo the staff could never leave; they needed the antidote, so they were wholly dependent on the Medicis giving it to them. If they left, they would be dead within a few weeks.'

'The Medicis really did that?'

'Yes. It was their way of creating staff loyalty. Has a certain kind of macabre elegance about it, don't you think?'

Conor felt a sudden tremor as the realization struck home. 'Sweet Jesus!' he exclaimed. 'They couldn't do that!'

'They did, Conor – it's documented.'

'I – I don't mean the Medicis.'

Schwab gave him an odd look. 'What *do* you mean?'

Conor glanced down at the floor, unable to continue. 'I – it – it's not important,' he said. 'Forget it.' But his brain was busy racing with excitement, reeling with horror, at the enormity of the implications.

The Medici Trial.

The words burrowed through his mind.

Medici Trial.

How far had Dr Bannerman got with his tests on the

Maternox? Had he identified the DNA? Because if he had, and if Conor was right in his very latest assumptions, there was no question that in doing so the scientist had signed his death warrant. And Monty's, and Wentworth's, and his own.

No question at all.

99

Wednesday 7 December, 1994

At ten past five in the evening, Gunn lifted the phone on his desk and punched two keys for a stored number to Maryland. He was answered by a gravelly voice on the third ring.

'McLusky.'

'Good afternoon, Mr McLusky, I was expecting to have heard from you.'

There was a silence, then the head of the Bendix Schere United States Security Operations said, with a slightly embarrassed laugh, 'Oh – ha – yeah, Major Gunn, I was just waiting for positive confirmation before disturbing you.'

'It's after midday – I thought you were dealing with things last night.' Although the line was secure, Gunn was sometimes guarded in what he said over it.

'That was our plan, but I'm afraid it didn't work out.'

'Why the hell not?'

'I can't answer that right now. Seems like he spent the night other than in the hotel – maybe he was visiting a floozie or something.'

'You mean you don't *know*?'

'He checked in but he didn't spend the night in his room.'

'You lost him, is that what you're trying to tell me?' Gunn thought about the overweight ex-FBI officer with his walrus moustache and salt-and-pepper hair. He was a good operator, dependable and ruthless when required. It was unusual for him to make any kind of error. But he was nudging sixty; maybe he was starting to slacken off.

'No, we didn't lose him, Major, I guess he just gave us the run-around for a few hours. We have him under surveillance right now; he's located in his business meeting and we'll pick him up when he leaves the building.'

'Good.'

'No change in your instructions, Major Gunn?'

'No. I just want it to look convincing.'

'No problem in that division.'

'You also didn't come back to me yet on his background.'

'We're still working on that one. He's a talented guy, knows how to cover his tracks pretty good. I figured since you'd upgraded us from just identifying him to dispensing with his services, there wasn't such an urgency on his background.'

'I always like to know who I'm killing, Mr McLusky,' Gunn said wryly. 'I consider it to be good clinical practice. And good clinical practice is very important to the company.'

100

Washington. Wednesday 7 December, 1994
'This is a breach of regulations, Conor, I don't know if I can do it.'

'You'll have it back in a few hours.'

Dave Schwab shook his head. 'I'm not comfortable about it.'

'Dave – remember that time I covered for you with Julie? When she rang up wanting you and I told her you were crashed out, like stoned out of your brains, while you were shagging that little thing, what was her name – Hollis Emmerson?'

'That was then and this is now, man. Life's changed lanes, this is the real world.'

'And nothing counted then because we were all students and you hadn't taken Julie down the aisle?'

'Yes.'

Conor stared at his friend. 'Well, you were sure as hell scared out of your fucking brains you were going to lose her. Now it's my turn, *I'm* scared and *I* need a favour.'

Schwab looked dubious. 'I could get into all kinds of trouble over this.'

'Dave – come on; get real, like you just said yourself. This is the Civil Service in the United States of America, they can't stop you having friends, they can't hang you over a loan to a pal – one that doesn't have anything to do with business.'

'They might not see it that way.'

Conor was beginning to lose his temper. 'But they're not ever going to know. Jesus Christ, why the fuck should they?'

Schwab raised his hands. 'OK, OK, take it.'

'You'll call Julie, tell her I'll be round for the other helmet and leathers?'

'I'll call her. My leathers are in the cupboard behind you.' Schwab reached wearily behind him, picked up the crash helmet and handed it to Conor; then he dug in his jacket pocket and tossed over a set of keys. 'You take the elevator down to the basement and turn right. You'll see it, a red Suzuki seven-fifty. You ride up the ramp and the doors'll open automatically.'

'I'll drop it off at your place later this afternoon.' Conor took out his wallet. 'And I'll even give you thirty bucks for your cab fare – that about cover it?'

Schwab shook his head vigorously. 'Oh no, definitely not; that would be a bribe, man. I take that and my ass is grass. Just take the goddamn bike and get out of my rug, do what you have to do.'

Conor stood up. 'Always knew you were one of the good guys, Schwab. One day you might even find a certificate on the wall from little ole me.'

The bar in the departure lounge at Dulles Airport was crowded and at first, as Conor approached with Schwab's crash helmet under his arm, he thought Monty had not yet arrived. Then he saw her shock of blonde hair, and his heart jumped. She was sitting, bundled up in her mackintosh, reading a magazine, her small suitcase on the floor beside her.

She noticed him when he was a few feet away, looked up distractedly for a moment, then her face broke into a smile that he wanted to hold in his memory for ever.

He plonked the helmet down on her case and they hugged each other tightly, clinging as if terrified some external force was going to rip them apart. Monty pressed her lips to his and they kissed fiercely for a long time before they spoke.

'Conor,' she said, breathlessly. 'You're here, you're OK!'

In response he expressed an identical concern for her. 'God, I've been so worried about you. You made it!'

She pressed her face against the soft leather of Schwab's biking gear. 'You look cool in this – I didn't know you were a closet Hell's Angel.'

He smiled, curling his arms around her and cradling her. 'First time I've ridden a Suzuki in about fifteen years.' He looked around as he spoke, but there were far too many bodies for him to be able to single out the one that might be watching them. He knew for sure he had not been tailed from the Patent Office. 'No news on your father – or Wentworth?'

'No.'

He kissed her. 'Let's move outta here, we'll talk later.' He tucked Schwab's crash helmet back under his arm, and was stooping to pick up her suitcase when she took a step back suddenly and he saw her expression change; her eyes turning fiery.

'Where are we going, Conor?'

'A place we'll be safe, and where there's someone who can maybe find your dad.'

'Why the mystery?'

He smiled awkwardly, taken aback. 'There's no mystery.'

'You told me a few days ago that you would explain everything in Washington. Well, I'm here,' she said defiantly. 'And I want the explanations now. Right now.'

'Monty, there's no big deal I'm hiding from you, I promise. It's just –' He sighed. 'I guess the truth is just so fantastic that maybe I wasn't sure myself – nor was I sure that you'd believe me if I tried to explain it to you.'

'Try me,' she said. 'Tell me what we're up against.'

'Follow me,' he responded, 'and you got yourself a deal.'

101

Conor swung the motorbike off the Beltway, and on to a wide, quiet road through lush suburban countryside, being careful to keep within the speed limits. He saw nothing following him in his mirrors.

Despite everything, he was enjoying the exhilaration of the ride and the snug grip of Monty's hands round his waist, and felt a nostalgic yearning to own a machine like this again. Maybe when all this evil was over he would buy one, he thought wistfully, and take her on a long trip somewhere warm and safe. If they were still alive and if there ever was a safe place for them again.

He turned left at an intersection and accelerated, his eyes fixed now on the building looming up about half a mile ahead, a massive, bland high-rise. A couple of hundred yards short of it, he pulled into the kerb then killed the engine, jamming his feet firmly on the ground against the enormous swaying dead-weight of the Suzuki, and pushed up his vizor.

Monty climbed off, relieved that her suitcase, perilously strapped to the top of the pannier, was still there, removed her helmet and shook out her hair, then stomped her feet on the ground. She was bitterly cold despite Julie Schwab's fleece-lined leathers which she was wearing over her own clothes.

She followed Conor's gaze and examined the high-rise right in front of them. It was a muddy-brown colour and appeared, at first sight, to be two buildings, one behind the other; but as she looked harder she could see it had been designed in two tiers, the far one several storeys higher than the one which faced them. Its sheer size gave it an air of importance, but Monty thought, in spite of that, it looked ugly and charmless. A gaggle of protesters, gathered outside the main entrance, suddenly broke into a chant as a male figure emerged and crossed the quiet street to a cab rank.

Conor seemed strangely silent.

'What is this place?' she asked.

He put an arm around Monty, and she sensed him taking a deep breath. 'I needed to bring you here,' he said. 'But, believe me, this is the hardest place in the world for me to be.'

He kissed her lightly on the side of her forehead, and she could feel him trembling. 'A lot of people,' he went on, 'are driven by something. They have one thing that kind of obsesses them above all else – like your father and breast cancer research, right?'

The mention of her father sent fresh anxieties for his safety spiralling through Monty. She swallowed and nodded.

'He's a driven man, you told me that yourself – because he's obsessed with identifying and destroying the breast cancer genes. I know what that kind of passion means. You wake up every morning with just one thought on your mind and you go to bed at night with that same thought. With your dad it's because he watched your mother die and that's something he can never forget. Well, I too have something that I can never forget, that's why I understand how he feels. Your dad deals with it his way, I deal with it my way.'

Monty was stunned into silence and on his face she could read only a moving combination of sadness and grim determination.

The building looked even vaster close up, and it was far longer than she had realized. Some of the protesters were still chanting, some waved banners and Stars and Stripes flags, other strutted around wearing sandwich boards. The multi-coloured lettering on one read: KEEP VITAMINS & AMINO ACIDS LEGAL! Another said: ABOLISH THE FDA!

Monty turned to Conor. 'Is *this* the FDA? The Food and Drug Administration?'

He did not seem to hear her as he grabbed her case and they crossed a narrow grass strip that isolated the huge car park in front of the building from the pavement, walking past a rather faded sign that said 'Parking By Permit Only'. Conor's pace quickened so that Monty found it hard to keep level.

'How many people have we talked to who've died now, Monty? Jake Seals, Zandra Wollerton, Walter Hoggin, Dr Corbin, Charley Rowley; we don't know about Rowley, but in each case there doesn't seem to be anyone else involved: Wollerton drives through the barriers at a train crossing; a hook drops on Corbin's head; Seals pours acid over himself; Hoggin has a heart attack. These are all perfectly innocent tragedies when looked at individually. But when you take a collective view the ball game changes. Right?'

'Yes.'

'But there's no conventional force that would make a man throw acid over himself, that would make a woman drive through a barrier in the path of an oncoming train, that would make a hook drop accurately on to a human head.'

They'd reached a massive blue sign sited above a flowerbed that said: US DEPARTMENT OF HEALTH AND HUMAN SERVICES. A flag hung limply above it. They stopped at the base of the building, and Conor set down the suitcase, then craned his neck to see the top floors.

Monty looked up as well, up along the wall of brown tinted glass that towered into the cirrus-streaked sky and mirrored its reflection back at them. There was an uncanny peace, suddenly, but one that suggested a thousand unseen eyes stared down at them. No traffic noise, no wind, just the solitary pinging cheep of a lone bird, then that, too, stopped.

Conor raised an arm and pointed with his index finger. 'You've asked me about my father, and I never said too much, right?'

She looked at him warily. 'No, you haven't.'

'This building does house the FDA – which licenses all pharmaceuticals in the United States.'

She nodded. But the way he was speaking was spooking her; it was as though it was not Conor any more, but a total stranger.

'My dad worked on the eleventh floor. That window up there, see, take a good look.' He pointed up the towering wall of smoked-glass squares above them, and she felt giddy just looking, as if the building were moving through the sky and tumbling forward on to them.

'My mother brought me here when I was a kid,' he said quietly. '*That's Daddy's window,* she said to me. *That's where your daddy works.*'

He fell silent now, for some moments, before continuing.

'I loved my dad. He was a big, good-looking guy – but kind of quiet, I guess. Very deep. We used to go hiking. I can picture him now, walking silently along a trail, dreaming whatever private dreams he had.' Conor bit his lip. 'He always wore a shirt and tie, even when we went to the game. Had a lot of old-fashioned values. One of them was that he believed fervently in the difference between right and wrong.'

Conor had composed himself again. 'He worked as an examiner in the FDA, and was put in charge of a product licence application for Bendix Schere. My mother used to tell me afterwards how Bendix Schere pressured him, offered him all kinds of inducements, before they began getting real mad at him.

'They were wanting to patent a drug, and Dad didn't feel they'd done enough tests. He wasn't convinced it was safe and he blocked it. It contained almost identical compounds to another drug which when it was marketed caused more than five thousand children to be born with horrific deformities. It was called thalidomide.'

'My God,' she whispered.

Conor resumed. 'One day when I was eight, my mom bundled me into the car. She said we had to go see Dad right away, because he was in terrible trouble. She drove here like a maniac, left the car just behind where we're standing right now; I remember it was an old white Plymouth.'

His voice stiffened and he took a breath, then pointed upwards again. 'He fell from that window, that eleventh-floor window. It was like watching a bird fly. That's what I thought it was at first, a massive bird. Then it hit the ground and the head jerked up, and I saw it was my father; there was a look on his face that I have never forgotten. No human being ever could.'

A whole piece of the puzzle in Monty's mind about Conor suddenly resolved itself, but any relief she felt was numbed by her shock. Such sadness; such sadness.

'We went up to his office. It was an unbelievable sight. Like a tornado had hit it: the lights were smashed, paper was strewn everywhere – and I mean *everywhere*; the walls were dripping wet, the clock was haywire. Yet no one else had heard a thing.' He appealed to Monty. 'You and I know there are things that cannot happen and which do happen. You've seen it with your own eyes.'

She nodded and swallowed. The untimely shadow of a bird skittered over the tarmac. Monty jumped as if electric leads had been clipped to her chest.

'All my life I've needed to know what really happened to my dad,' Conor said. 'And to find out who was responsible. Maybe you can understand now what brings me to Bendix Schere.'

102

London. Wednesday 7 December, 1994
No one had had any contact with the Bannerman woman since her phone call to Levine at 1.48 that morning.

Gunn's collar was rucked up around his neck; the damned soft shirts Nikky insisted he wore these days always caused him problems; they weren't designed to take ties. Irritated, he slipped his fingers inside the collar and tried to straighten it out, then he looked at the report on the screen again, which he was halfway through, but he was too distracted to absorb it.

Montana Bannerman had vanished and he did not like the idea of that smart little bitch being left to her own devices. God only knew who the hell she would talk to next. He looked at the clock on his screen. 8.32 p.m.; Nikky would be going ballistic again but that, right now, was at the bottom of the priority scale. Half three in the afternoon in Washington and according to McLusky, Molloy was still in his meeting in the US Patent Office.

Like hell he was, Gunn thought suspiciously. McLusky'd

had Molloy down as being in his goddamn hotel bedroom all night and he'd been wrong. And still no one knew who the little bastard really was. Something had bothered him about the tone of McLusky's voice when they'd last spoken, an hour back. Gunn had detected a chink in his confidence; more than a chink; the man had not sounded at all confident about his claims to have Molloy safely cornered.

The wheels were beginning to fall off. When he'd arrived at Dr Bannerman's laboratory last night, he'd seen a small tape-recorder on the scientist's desk that seemed to be running. In their rush to get the scientist out of the building they'd overlooked it, and when Gunn had returned later to retrieve it he'd found the burglar alarm on – and no tape-recorder.

So whoever had set the alarm had also gone in and seen the goods, then taken them. And there was only one contender in Gunn's opinion.

Montana Bannerman.

What the hell was on that tape? Maybe nothing. There again, maybe everything: both the scientist's findings and an incriminating soundtrack of Gunn's intrusion with Crowe. He tried to gauge where she might go with evidence like that. Probably not the police, something had scared her off the cops, otherwise she would have called Levine again by now.

Slackening his tie, he cradled his head in the palm of his hand. This was nothing short of a Grade One listed balls-up.

His phone rang and he brought the receiver to his ear, hoping to hell for good news. 'Gunn.'

'Where the fuck are you, soldier?'

'Niks, I'm sorry, got some problems here.'

'So many problems you couldn't phone me? We were meant to leave here at seven forty-five. I've been waiting for you.' She sounded genuinely hurt.

'I'm sorry, Niks, believe me.'

'Every day you have a new crisis. Why don't you tell your Doc Crowe to go and jump in a lake and give you your life back?'

A light flashed showing he had another call waiting. 'I've got to go – call you back.'

'When? Tomorrow? Next year?'

'Two minutes, promise.'

'Three and I start burning holes in your clothes.'

'NIKS –' He raised his voice, but she had cleared and he found himself talking to McLusky.

'Not good news, Major Gunn – I thought I'd better level with you. Molloy seems to have given us the slip.'

Gunn looked at the clock anxiously. If Nikky said torches in three minutes she meant it; the girl was nuts. 'Mr McLusky, you are not going to do this to me.'

'I'm real sorry – can't figure it out. He's vanished into thin air.'

Gunn made no effort to mask his sarcasm. 'People can do an awful lot of things, Mr McLusky, but vanishing into thin air is not one of them. They can give the *illusion* of vanishing, but that's as far as it goes.'

'Well, your man's giving us a pretty good illusion right now.'

McLusky didn't even sound sorry; in fact, from the tone of his voice the bastard didn't give a toss whether he found Molloy or not. It was as if the whole task was an inconvenience, a distraction that was keeping him from something more important, like a game of golf.

Gunn reflected about the crass way McLusky had handled the initial reports of Rowley's death in Hawaii. It had cost Bendix Schere several hundred thousand dollars in payola to keep the lid on that. Maybe he was right in his earlier assumption. McLusky was too old, had lost it. But he'd sure picked a bummer of a day to find that out.

'Maybe if you can find out who Molloy really is, you can also find out *where* he is,' Gunn suggested pointedly.

'We're doing all we can.'

Like hell, Gunn thought as he pressed his finger on the cradle to disconnect, then got Nikky with fifteen seconds to spare.

When he had mollified her he walked over to one of his tall metal filing cabinets and slid out a drawer. From it he lifted two sealed folders, laid them on his desk and opened them.

One contained a man's left-hand, hogskin glove, almost

533

brand new. The other, an elegant printed wool and silk shawl with the designer's signature, 'Cornelia James', in the corner. He ran a finger lightly and possessively across both objects, then picked up the phone again and tapped out a number. When it was answered he said:

'Apologies for short notice, but I need some dowsing very urgently. How quickly could you get a team here?'

Half an hour later Gunn left his office carrying the glove and the scarf. Instead of taking the normal lift down, he went through a door to which he alone had access, and summoned a quite different lift.

When it arrived, he opened the doors with a combination of his smartcard and his palm print on an electronic panel; then he keyed six coded digits into a touch panel and waited.

After a couple of seconds the doors closed and the lift began its rapid, near-silent descent.

103

Washington. Wednesday 7 December, 1994
Monty sat numb with cold on the motorcycle pillion. She was shaken by what Conor had just told her, and even more desperately afraid for her father's safety. Her only crumb of comfort was that she was at last beginning to understand what motivated the man she loved.

The twenty minutes or so the journey took seemed never-ending, through suburbs, open countryside and suburbs again. But eventually Conor began to slow, then turned into an entrance way and halted in front of a steel gate, beside which was a security system with a built-in camera. He raised his vizor, pressed a button and called out above the burble of the engine: 'It's me.'

After a moment the gate slid open, allowing them access to a single-storey hacienda-style property, which sat on a small plateau. Two cars were parked outside, a blue Mercedes sports coupé and a grey limousine with a chauffeur behind the wheel.

'It's OK,' Conor said. 'Clients – she warned me they'd be here.' He put his helmet and gloves on his seat. Monty did the same, then turned to him.

'Conor, I don't know what the hell I'm even doing here; I should be in England looking for Daddy.'

Conor cupped her face in his hands. 'Honey, we're going to get your father out of those bastards' hands, but you *have* to trust me. Agreed?' Then he went ahead and rang the bell as if he'd taken her answer as read.

The door was opened a few moments later by a young Latin American maid in a crisp, starched uniform, who gave Conor a shy smile of recognition, and acknowledged Monty with a polite glance. 'Please, you come in, your mother just finish meeting.'

As they stepped into the open-plan, split-level interior, Monty felt as if she had entered a temple or an art gallery rather than a home. Candles were burning in sconces on the walls and in tall wrought-iron holders on the floor. The air was lightly perfumed, either by the candles or joss sticks, and strains of New Age music reminiscent of lapping waves played from concealed speakers. The effect was that of total tranquillity.

The walls were hung with abstract paintings, many featuring religious symbolism, and bizarre sculpted figurines sat on plinths, table tops and in various alcoves. Monty heard voices, then a group of people came round a corner and headed towards them: three men in business suits, and a tall, striking woman in black who gave Conor and herself a brief smile of acknowledgement in which she signalled she'd be with them in a moment.

Monty watched, fascinated by this paragon's appearance. In her mid-fifties, her long dark hair was flecked with silvery streaks that seemed more like highlights than any consequence of age, and her fine, classical features might, when their owner had been only a few years younger, have stared out from the front cover of *Vogue*. In her face and build Monty could see a strong family resemblance to Conor.

'OK, so New Mexico by January, right?' one of the men said, in a Texan accent. 'We'll start the test bores and see what gives.'

'The last twelve months have been very impressive,' another said. 'Have a very happy Chrismas.'

'And a *prosperous* New Year,' replied their hostess.

'With your help I'm sure it will be,' came the reply.

She smiled and inclined her head regally. 'I'll do what I can.'

'You've performed miracles before.'

Her expression clouded a little. 'No, gentlemen, miracles are what we call things we cannot explain, *science* is what we call those we can. I practise science, not miracles.'

The trio departed. As the maid held the door for them, the woman turned her attention to Conor.

'Hi, Mom.' He gave her a kiss on the cheek, which she accepted stiffly and without reciprocating, more as if it were a tithe received from a serf than a greeting from her only son.

'Let me – er – introduce you,' he said, his normal confidence seeming to desert him. 'Montana Bannerman – ah – this is my mother.'

Monty stood, slightly unnerved herself now, unsure whether she should extend her hand. 'It's very nice to meet you, Mrs Molloy.'

The woman shot a glance at Conor then looked, unsmiling, back at Monty. 'It's Donoghue, actually. Tabitha Donoghue.'

Confused, Monty trawled her memory, wondering whether she had made a gaffe. Perhaps there'd been a remarriage and Conor had not told her? Or she hadn't remembered?

Conor blushed, then pushed a hand through his hair.

His mother turned back to him. 'Are you keeping the bike here overnight?'

'No – I promised Dave Schwab I'd drop it back this evening.'

She shook her head. 'I don't want you leaving this house tonight; I intend closing the circle. If you have to get it back, do it now.'

Conor looked at Monty. 'OK – you stay here and have a rest – I'll be half an hour, maximum.'

'I'll come with you.'

He shook his head. 'You look frozen and beat; relax and have a hot bath.'

Although she was feeling exhausted, Monty began to peel off the motorcycling suit with reluctance, on balance preferring to go with him than to be left stranded here with this strange woman.

Tabitha Donoghue said something to the maid in Spanish, who immediately picked up the small suitcase which Conor had carried in for Monty.

'Juanita will show you your room; I guess you'll want to have a little rest and freshen up. Do you like tea or coffee?'

'I'd love some coffee.'

'Join me in the lounge when you're ready, through there, no hurry.' Conor's mother indicated the way with a slender, heavily jewelled hand.

The room was comfortable with a double bed and an ensuite bathroom with expensive fittings. Monty sat on the bed, trying to collect her thoughts, suddenly feeling leadenly tired. Her watch said five to four and it was growing dark outside. Flecks of sleet were falling, and new fears swirled like a mill-race in her knotted, empty stomach. Did she really have to go downstairs and face that cold bitch alone?

She looked at her face in the mirror and was appalled at her appearance, her face puffy from tiredness, her hair crushed shapeless by the helmet; the thought flashed through her mind that the elegant Tabitha must be wondering what on earth her son saw in her.

She had a shower both to freshen up and warm up, put on clean clothes and had a hasty damage-limitation go at her hair and make-up before venturing out.

'You are safe here, Montana,' Tabitha Donoghue said by way of a greeting as Monty found her seated in front of an open fire, smoking a thin cigarette. A silver coffee pot, fine china cups and a tray of biscuits were laid on a quartz-topped table, beside an ashtray overflowing with butts.

There was something in the way she said *safe* that made Monty frown. Nothing she could immediately finger, but it

537

did little to allay her misgivings. 'Thank you,' she replied politely, sitting down opposite her hostess. 'You have a very beautiful home. It's –' she tried to think of a comment that would elicit the reason for the candles, but could not find the phrase she wanted. 'It's so spacious,' she said, aware of her own banality.

Conor's mother poured her coffee. There was a grace in her every movement and Monty again admired her appearance. In spite of a few telltale lines, and a slackening of the neck just visible above her black sweater, she could have passed for someone in her early forties.

'Do you take milk, Montana?' The smell of the cigarette was tantalizing.

'No, thank you.'

'Good; best to avoid all dairy products while this is happening.'

Monty puzzled over the remark but nothing further was ventured on the subject. She glanced round the room, awkwardly. Two Burmese cats sat motionless as marble either side of the fire; tribal masks stared down at them from the white painted walls. Again she sensed the stillness and quietness of a temple.

Mrs Donoghue was now studying her with an expression that seemed to have been hauled up from a well of sadness, and said quietly: 'Some things in life are not worth it, Montana.'

Monty cradled her coffee cup in her lap. 'Excuse me?'

'Life's a compromise; you learn that when you get older.' The older woman stood up abruptly and began to circle the room, looking at the walls, the plants, then straightened a slightly crooked candle, as if she was delaying having to face Monty again.

Monty watched her, wondering about the chore of lighting and replacing the dozens of candles; presumably the maid did it, but why? She noticed, nearby, a framed photograph of Mrs Donoghue standing in the middle of what looked like an oilfield, next to a sleekly handsome man whose face looked familiar.

'That's me with Uri Geller,' Tabitha Donoghue said, evidently having eyes in the back of her head.

Monty was startled. 'What was the occasion?'

'We both located some oilfields for the same company.' She straightened another candle. 'That's my work these days. That's what I do.'

'*Really?* How do you do that?'

'I dowse,' she said matter-of-factly.

'With a divining rod – like the ones used to find water?'

'No; mostly with a pendulum over a map. I go on location occasionally, for very accurate pinpointing, but usually I don't need to; I can get to within a hundred metres or so just on a map.' She turned and smiled. 'The oil companies mostly don't like to admit to using people like me – I think it embarrasses them that I can see off all their hi-tech equipment.'

Monty realized now where her obvious wealth must come from. She was about to ask Mrs Donoghue if she was psychic, when she remembered the rebuke the three suits had received earlier.

'*I practise science, not miracles.*'

'Do you use your pow – ah – skills – for anything else, Mrs Donoghue?'

'I find missing persons for the police.' She shrugged as if to imply there was nothing to it.

'I've read about dowsing, but I don't know how the – ah – science – works.'

Tabitha Donoghue walked slowly back to her chair. 'A great many things work in ways we do not understand, Montana,' she said softly. 'Sometimes we do not want to understand them, and sometimes they are genuinely beyond our powers of comprehension.'

Monty let her go on.

'The thirst for knowledge, for enlightenment, is limited to very few. Most people don't have the time or the inclination to learn. Have you ever thought now ironic it is that such people spend their entire lives with their eyes closed, then die with them open?'

Monty tried to smile. 'I think that is because there are many people who fear the unknown.'

'A fear that is at times wholly justified – as you are now

finding out. But you accept the unknown, don't you, Montana? The occult?'

'I'm not sure.'

'You wear a crucifix, so you believe in God?'

Monty's hand involuntarily went to her neck. The thin chain of her crucifix was buried inside the collar of her blouse, which was inside a pullover; there was no way this woman could see she was wearing it. Any more than she could have noticed her looking at the photograph a few minutes ago.

Had Conor mentioned her crucifix to his mother? That was a possibility, but unlikely. 'I don't see that wearing a crucifix or believing in God means that I necessarily believe in the occult,' she said, thrown.

Tabitha Donoghue studied her face, taking her time. 'Religion isn't some kind of convenience store where you select the goodies you like and ignore what you don't. If you believe in God then you believe in Satan. He comes with the territory.'

Monty shrugged. 'I suppose what I mean is that I'm a lapsed Catholic – an agnostic, if you like.'

'I don't care what the hell you are. It's just better to try to understand your adversaries than to ignore them. And to try to guard against their powers, rather than pretending that they do not exist.'

This sudden vehemence took Monty aback. 'I'm sorry – pretend *what* does not exist?'

Conor's mother looked at her watch, and seemed anxious. 'He should be back by now.'

Monty checked the time herself. Almost an hour had lapsed. 'Maybe he stopped to have a coffee – or he had problems getting a taxi?'

'I go now, good night, Missy Donoghue.'

They both turned. The maid was standing behind them with her coat on, holding a carrier bag. Tabitha Donoghue stood up. 'I'll give you a ride to the subway.' She turned to Monty but her thoughts seemed far away, her words incoherent. 'It's starting, I can feel it. I have to go to him.' She seemed very agitated now.

'Shall I come with you? Monty said, not entirely following, but uneasy at the prospect of being left there alone.

'No, you must stay. You are safe in this house, but you are not safe outside. Don't answer the phone or open the front door, not to anyone.' As she looked at Monty, her eyes became two large circles, like the eyes of a hunted animal, and there was a deep timbre to her voice. 'You spoke of the unknown? You're going to find out about the unknown. You're going to find more than you ever dreamed.'

104

Wednesday 7 December, 1994

The tiny, windowless chamber was enclosed by marble walls, each one displaying an inlaid gold pentagram six feet in diameter. The sole light source was the green glow from the computer screen of the electronic map-reader, which was set into the square malachite table around which they all sat.

Hovering plumb centre over the screen, suspended from a silk thread attached to the ceiling twenty feet above them, was the quartz-crystal weight of a pendulum. It had been honed at the base into a needlepoint.

The only other object in the room was a pure gold scrying bowl cradled in a wrought-iron stand. It was filled with water freshly taken from the baptism font in a local church.

For the moment they concentrated on the screen. One, locked in concentration, held a hogskin glove in the palm of his hand as delicately as if it were a newborn chick. He wore papyrus slippers on his feet and a robe made of finest quality linen; simple, natural clothing that contained nothing to interfere with the energy flow. No jewellery, no mental baggage.

He had evacuated his brain as part of his preparation, concentrating all this thoughts and energy on one speck; one tiny speck in an empty universe. One speck in the void before time had begun. The first speck of dust. Smaller than an atom. Smaller than a neutron. Out there in the void, waiting for him.

Come to me.

It was obeying. Its orbit altered so that it passed close by him.

Come to me.

It was gone, accelerating past him and away, fading into nothingness. In a moment it would return; it was circling the void and would have to return. Coming back now. The speck flashed past him with a glint, then was gone again. From the glove in the palm of his hand he sensed the faintest of vibrations; they clashed with his own, clashed with the vibrations from the speck – the wrong waveband – but he felt a surge of satisfaction. The signal was what mattered and he was picking up the signal.

Come to me, he willed. *Come to me, ah yes, come.*

The speck passed him. It made one complete rotation, then another, each one a fraction shorter than the previous rotation as it traced an invisible path of ever-decreasing concentric circles.

Come to me.

The modulations of the wavebands were beginning to synchronize. The speck turned into an inch-high lump of quartz crystal; the sharp point skimmed the surface of the screen in the table top. On the screen was a map which showed the contours of the Potomac river, Chesapeake Bay and the surrounding land mass.

'Scale,' he called out sharply.

There was a putter of computer keys, then the scale of the map changed from five miles to one inch, becoming one mile to one inch. Grids of streets appeared.

The pendulum began to swing again, in large circles at first, then decreasing again. Finally the point was hovering, in a motion that was almost a quiver, over the north of Georgetown.

He turned to the scrying bowl, staring into the blackness of the holy water. Stared harder, concentrating, willing the image. But it would not come, as if someone was blocking it. Someone who knew how to disturb the vibrations, confuse them.

He concentrated harder still, pitting his mind against the one he could not see, like two wrestling arms locked on a bar table. He thought of the powers he had, the prayers and the rituals and the energy forces he could summon.

I am the Alpha and Omega, the beginning and end, the first and last.

Yahweh.

He focused his mind on the rituals. Focused it on the power of the base metals he had cast with his own hands in the foundry. Silently he called out in the void.

Yahweh.

It was coming. He could see it now, it was working, the arm was yielding, bending, collapsing, caving in. He felt the sweat on his own body, his brow, his chest, felt his energy surging then replenishing, draining then replenishing. Had to keep going, had to summon new strength, had a long, long way to go.

Yes!

A house. Small, badly in need of a repaint. The door was opening, a woman came out first. Yes, he could see it clearly now, as clearly as if it were happening through a window in front of his own eyes. He could see the quarry coming out of the house, giving the woman a quick kiss on the cheek, walking down the drive, getting into the back of a taxi. Yes there was no mistaking, no mistaking at all . . .

'Got you!' he called out, in his excitement momentarily forgetting the protocols of silence. 'I've got you, you smart little bastard!'

105

Washington. Wednesday 7 December, 1994

'Want me to get Dave to ring you at your mother's when he gets home?' Julie Schwab said, as they stood on the doorstep.

Conor thought for a moment. 'No – I'll give him a call later.'

He kissed her on the cheek. 'Good to see you, thanks for your help.'

'No problem. Take it easy, you look beat. They're working you too hard!'

He smiled. 'I guess. Take care.' He turned, hurried down the drive to the waiting cab and gave the address of his mother's house. The sleet of earlier had turned to snow; thick flakes were falling and settling.

Monty was safe; that had been his number one concern. Now they had to get her father out of wherever he was being held. And they had to do it without the police; Monty had proved that herself.

He watched the meter ticking. The driver was a bald black man with the frame of a Sumo wrestler; the steering wheel in his massive paws looked like a toy and he slouched as he drove with an easy, lazy confidence. 'Forecast heavy fall tonight. Gonna be a mess tomorrow, yup, sure is.'

Conor saw the man's eyes in the mirror and nodded in acknowledgement. Daylight was starting to fail and most vehicles had their lights on now.

'Gonna be a real mess, yessir,' the driver repeated.

Conor's forehead twinged suddenly and his focus blurred. He closed his eyes then opened them again, startled, feeling a little giddy. They were accelerating down a slip and joining the Beltway, heading north, moving fast. Snow tumbled towards the windscreen at a sharply raked angle and the wipers clouted it away.

It was the snow that was making him feel giddy, he realized, relaxing a little; it was twisting and turning through the battery of tail lights ahead like a kaleidoscope. A truck thundered past, chucking up slush which hit the windshield with a heavy slap, then he was thrown sideways in his seat as the taxi swerved violently to avoid some unseen obstacle.

He turned and peered through the rear window, but the lane behind was clear. 'What was that?'

There was no response from the driver.

'What was that you swerved for?' Conor asked.

The driver said nothing.

Something was going on up ahead, in the distance. Strobing

lights. Brake lights were coming on. A truck two hundred and fifty yards or so ahead of them was braking sharply. The taxi started accelerating.

Conor frowned, wondering what the driver was doing, waiting for him to jam on the brakes; but he just kept accelerating.

'Hey!' he said, alarmed. 'Hey, you OK?' He looked up at the mirror. The driver's eyes were fixed dead ahead, expressionless, as if he was in a trance.

They were accelerating even harder.

The traffic ahead had come to a complete standstill.

Conor felt a damburst of cold fear. 'Hey!' he yelled. '*Stop* – for God's sake!'

Accelerating.

Hurtling towards the tailgate of the truck. Two hundred metres. One seventy-five. One fifty.

Conor was on a nightmare fairground ride. The truck was still not moving. The gap was closing. Frantically he scrabbled for the passenger handle, yanked it, threw his shoulder against the door, heard the roar of air, felt the velocity against his skin then in one desperate lunge threw his entire body weight against it.

Was he falling? Or was he flying? Tumbling in freeze-frame slowness into the darkness.

A tremendous thump in his chest punched the wind straight out of his lungs as if the entire road had risen up to strike him. He was rolling; rolling. A horn blared. Lights hurtled past him; he felt the heat of an exhaust poisoning his face. Giddy, rolling, rolling. Had no idea where he was. The tarmac trampoline rose up and slammed him in the stomach, then punched him up in the air. It came at him again, smashed him in the chin, then the knees, then the side of his face.

There was a tremendous metallic bang.

He lay still. Two bright lights high above him, bearing down out of the darkness. Coming for him. Angels? No, the hiss of air brakes, the harsh slithering of rubber on wet tarmac. Then total darkness and an echoing roar as if he had entered a railway tunnel; he clutched his hands to his head, pressed himself into the hard road surface in terror as a tractor-trailer hurtled over him.

545

Then it was gone. And he was still there.

More vehicles were coming. He had to get out of the way; a car slithered past him so close its door brushed his jacket. After it had disappeared, he hobbled across the lane on all fours, like an animal.

'Conor!'

The voice of his mother calling out in the darkness.

'Conor!'

He saw a door swinging open, an interior light; a car had stopped beside him.

'Conor! Get in, get in!'

He crawled over the sill like a drowning man heaving himself on to a life raft. Felt the soft leather of the passenger seat; collapsed into another world. Just the glow of the dashboard and the plush smell of the hide, the warm air of the Mercedes' heater.

Ahead, through the wiper and its arc, he could see cars and trucks skewed all over the road; shards of broken glass everywhere. Headlamps were shining on the tailgate of the stationary truck he'd seen half a century ago. Something was sticking out of it like a half-eaten fish in the jaws of a predator. In the arena of lights he could see clearly it was the cab he had just been in. It was wedged, almost up to the rear window, beneath the rear fender of the truck, the roof sheared off and hanging like the lid of a sardine can.

He turned to face his mother, too queasy to speak.

'I thought I was too late,' she said quietly. 'I thought you were dead.'

106

As she heard the distant slam of the front door, Monty regarded the silent cats, the burning candles, the spitting fire, and felt like the spectre at the feast. Only she hadn't actually found the feast bit yet, she reminded herself.

It's starting, I can feel it. I have to go to him.

What was starting?

Curious, she walked round the interior of the house, hoping to spot pictures of Conor as a child, of his father, or anything that would give her further clues about Tabitha Donoghue.

Throughout the living areas, even in the huge modern kitchen, she met the same almost institutional theme of the abstract paintings and the bizarre figurines.

Going through an alcove, she came into an office that was filled with a battery of hi-tech equipment. She saw a rack of computer hardware with a laser printer and monitor, and in the centre of the room what looked like a light-box built into a metal stand the size of a coffee table. Four swivel chairs were arranged around it. A chart lay on top, pressed between two sheets of glass; and suspended directly above it, on a fine thread attached to a hook in the ceiling, was a quartz-crystal weight, the point of which was only inches above the glass.

It was a pendulum, she realized. This must be where Conor's mother did her dowsing.

Feeling a little guilty at snooping, she continued her tour of inspection. Opening a door at the far end of the house, she discovered what she presumed to be the master bedroom, dominated by a king-size two-poster.

Two framed photographs sat on a table by the window. One was a graduation shot of Conor in his cap and gown. The other was a black and white wedding photo showing a younger Tabitha Donoghue beside a shy-looking man in a tuxedo.

Monty was disappointed to find no obvious likeness to Conor. By inheriting his mother's looks, she decided, Conor had definitely got the cream of his parents' gene pool – assuming this was Mr Molloy. Then she shuddered as she looked again and pictured this poor man plunging through the window of an eleventh-floor office and landing at Conor's feet.

Jesus!

Leaving the office, she saw a narrow passageway with a closed door at the end. Telling herself that all their lives were at stake and she had put herself in the hands of strangers, she

547

decided she owed it to herself and her father to do whatever felt right, and she opened the door.

It was pitch dark and she was greeted by the musty smell of a room that is seldom used. She groped on the wall and found a switch. A weak red light came on, from inside a paper globe, and she was surprised by what it revealed.

The room's old-fashioned crimson velvet drapes were drawn shut, and a threadbare Persian carpet covered the floor. In the centre was a circular table with six antique chairs. Several artefacts lay on the table, including an ancient cloth-bound book, a small glass pyramid and an assortment of rock crystals.

Two sofas faced each other from opposite walls, and a collection of more chairs suggested the room was prepared for a group meeting. She noticed the elaborate hi-fi system, and a row of bookshelves.

There was an unsettling, expectant atmosphere, and Monty felt she should not be there, but she wanted to scan the bookshelves before leaving. A vast range of occult and New Age subjects seemed to be covered. Past-life regression, channelling, the power of crystals, black magick grimoires, chakras, herbal remedies, psychic awareness, healing development . . .

She yawned, feeling a wave of tiredness, aware that apart from fitful dozes on the aeroplane, she'd had no real sleep.

As she turned to leave the room, a sharp pain struck without any warning. It felt as if she had been lanced through the temples with a white-hot rod.

She gasped in shock and doubled up. It worsened, disorienting her. She swayed, stumbled forwards, bashed into a chair and fell headlong with it on to the floor. The pain became even worse as if the rod had been twisted. She lay entangled in the chair legs, clenching her eyes shut. 'Conor!' she whispered. 'Conor, help me, please help me!'

A wave of nausea swept through her. She opened her eyes but the room just blurred and tilted at crazy angles. When she tried to stand, it pitched her sideways, unbalancing her.

The pain shot inside the skin of her forehead, into the bridge of her nose and, simultaneously, down the back of her scalp, into the base of her neck. It felt as if the roots of a tree were growing inside her skull, pushing in every direction, forcing their way out through her eardrums, through her eye sockets, through her gullet. Blinding, deafening, choking her.

Panic gripped her. She couldn't breathe, despite trying desperately to suck in air. 'Cnnr. Plsh. Hllp.' The roots were drawing up petrol now, consuming it greedily instead of water, filling her head with a foul-smelling vapour that burned every nerve ending. Then it ignited and the whole inside of her skull exploded into a raging inferno.

'Conor, Conor, Conor, Conor, Conor!' She screamed internally, the pain unbearable. Even so, dimly, she heard a banging sound coming from somewhere. The window. It became louder, frantic. Then she heard voices, laughter. Fighting the pain and the heaving floor, she crawled over, parted the drapes and looked up.

Dr Crowe was standing outside, peering in, his face pressed against the pane. He was telling her to open the window and join him.

In blind panic she tried to scrabble away from him. But an immense force was pulling her towards him, dragging her nearer to the window; nearer; nearer.

Her resistance was fading. She realized now that when she got to the window the pain would stop. Dr Crowe was promising her that. He was there in the darkness beyond the glazing, and had come all the way from England to help her.

'Miss Bannerman, I can stop the pain for you!'

There was a kindness and gentleness in his face that she had never noticed before. Warmth flooded into her body, and the pain began to ease. She stared at him gratefully.

'Trust me, Monty, I can stop the pain. Tell me that you trust me, you have to get away from this house; they want to kill you, to sacrifice you. You have to escape. You are in grave danger here.'

She could see in his eyes that he was telling the truth. And she wondered now how she could ever have doubted him. He *knew* the truth, he *was* the truth.

Then the pain came back, worse, far worse. A cry of agony ripped free from her gullet. Her head was filled with starving ants that were eating her brain; she pressed her fingers into her ears to stop them. But they were attacking her optic nerves now, munching, antennae quivering, biting into the backs of her eyes.

She tried to scream but her throat was blocked with crawling ants. Thank God Dr Crowe was still standing there, so kind, so full of sympathy, her only hope.

'Listen to me, Monty. Do as I say.'

She nodded frantically.

'Your father will die unless you can save him. He is feeling the same pain as you; only you can release him from this pain. Are you ready?'

Yes, yes. She was ready.

'Get on to the table, Monty.'

Crying with pain, she heaved herself slowly, one leg at a time, on to the chair, then up on to the table; she felt it rocking beneath her weight, and the globe lightshade bumped her face, swaying on its flex.

'Now stand!' Crowe commanded.

Slowly she straightened one knee, then the next. The pain was shooting down into her body and the ants were deep inside her eyeballs now; she only had a few moments of vision left.

'Stand! Support yourself with the flex, let it take your weight.'

She steadied herself with one hand, the sole of her left foot flat on the table. Then she pushed, swayed, tottered and was somehow upright, clinging to the flex. The table rocked precariously, almost threw her off, but under Dr Crowe's calming influence she retained her balance.

'Good girl, you are doing so well, I'm very proud of you. We are all very proud of you, we love you very much.'

The pain eased, just a fraction. Dr Crowe was making it better, and she knew that as it eased for her it was easing for her father.

'Now, Monty.' He smiled. 'Now take the flex and wind it three times around your neck.'

She stared at Dr Crowe's face through the gap in the velvet drapes with complete and utter trust, and did what he said.

107

Israel. 31 July, 1985

The helicopter lifted clear of the high plateau's rocky terrain, hovered, then dipped its nose and clattered out over the basin of the Dead Sea into the vermilion ball of the sinking sun.

At the same time two figures in black jellabas scurried like insects out of a crack in the rock, hastily rolled up the two fluorescent strips that had formed the landing mark and, looking furtively around, retreated back into the rock.

An hour later, at the bottom of the crevasse that cut half a mile down and outwards into the bowels of the mountain, the four sentinels of the Holy Tomb of Satan waited silently around the rim of a natural pool the size of a small lagoon. It was reputed to be three miles deep, and the slate grey surface was unruffled by the cascading water that fell, with the din of thunder, two hundred feet sheer into the shallows of its northernmost point.

Between the waterfall and the rock wall behind it, Theutus stood rigid on the Stone of Purification, drenched in spray, his eyes closed, repeating the cleansing incantations he had long ago learned by heart.

When he had finished, the sentinels stepped forward in their black, cowled jellabas, wordlessly dried his naked body with pure linen towels, and led him through a cavity, along a passageway, into a tiny hollow that formed a chamber lit by a single tallow candle.

The chamber was bare except for a row of seven silver aspergilla suspended from hooks by their chains, and a raised slab on the floor, seven feet long and two wide. Fashioned from pure malachite, it had been burnished weekly for centuries into a dull green sheen. Theutus knew from his studies that this was the Altar of Anointment, the second stage of the purification. It was the third stage that he was anxious about, and now it was nearly time. He had been preparing for it for thirty years.

He positioned himself on his back on the altar, closed his

eyes and began repeating to himself the Anointment Keys; the sentinels, their silence never breaking, began the Anointment of the Vials of the Seven Planets.

One took the first aspergillum, a silver, perforated ball, stolen like the other six many years back from the Vatican, and desecrated with menstrual blood, semen, urine and faeces. It contained a saffron perfume appropriated to the sun, mixed together with the pulped brain of an eagle.

Swinging the aspergillum from side to side, the sentinel walked one complete circuit around Theutus, sprinkling droplets of the perfume on to his naked flesh. When he had finished, the second sentinel repeated the procedure, then the third, and the fourth.

The next aspergillum contained a perfume made from the seeds of white poppies and appropriated to the moon; mixed together with menstrual blood. The third contained a perfume of black poppy seeds appropriated to Saturn, mixed with the brain of a cat and blood drawn from a bat. The fourth was to Jupiter; the fifth was appropriated to Mars, the sixth to Venus and the seventh to Mercury.

The same ritual was repeated with each of the aspergilla. Then with a touch of their hands the sentinels gave the signal to rise. Two in front and two behind the anointed one, they proceeded along a labyrinth of passages lit only by the occasional candle, and finally through the Grand Arch into the temple of the Eternal Flame of Satan.

Theutus found himself in awe of the sacred chamber which he now entered for the first time in his life. Its five sides, naturally formed out of the polished rock faces, rose majestically like the walls of a Gothic cathedral up to the summit of the plateau above. Each wall had been elaborately and beautifully carved with Cabbalistic numbers and symbols; but there was no vaulted cathedral roof above their heads, just a small pentagram of rapidly darkening sky.

Forty-two Assessors stood, backs pressed against the walls, completely encircling the room. Silent as statues, they were dressed in pure white linen robes, and their identities were concealed behind the gold face mask of the beast of their choice.

The flames of an intense natural gas fire leapt from a hollow in the floor, the centre of a series of intricately carved concentric circles. The fire had been lit, according to legend, by Satan Himself as His final act of defiance when He was defeated by God. Only Satan could extinguish it, and on the day He did so, He would rise through the ashes to wreak vengeance on God. And in the centre of the fire lay a massive granite crucible. The impurities in the molten gold that filled it to the brim were bubbling to the surface like volcanic lava.

Between the spot where Theutus stood and the fire was an anvil, and a stone slab displaying the heavy tools of a blacksmith and the delicate ones of a goldsmith. Of the many rituals which Theutus had learned in the past thirty years, the work of the foundryman and of the goldsmith had been among the first. Having been instructed that it was necessary for a great magician to cast his own vessels, and to fashion his adornments by his own hand, he had mastered both skills.

But today he had come without his jewellery and without his crown. He came naked into the temple, bringing nothing of the old world with him that might carry a taint that could diminish his powers. Here, in front of his peers, from the crucible's smelted gold, he would forge new vessels – a new crown, new rings and a new pendant.

The gold had come from the vessels and adornments of the outgoing Ipsissimus, the previous elected figurehead of the forty-two Assessors – an 87-year-old banker who lay slowly dying of bone cancer in a private clinic in Switzerland.

It was the same gold that had been smelted down from each preceding Ipsissimus for nearly two thousand years, the same gold that had once formed the chalices and plates used by the great Impostor Jesus Christ and his evil followers. Those chalices had been recovered from the Cave of Qumran where they had been concealed after the crucifixion.

From his early twenties, Theutus had ceased to believe in the existence of the biblical God who had made his childhood such hell; and he did not believe in Satan as a deity either. He considered today's procedure to be mere mumbojumbo, but that did not diminish its value for him. God and Satan had both existed once, of that he had little doubt, but they had been mortal humans, as real as himself, no more and no less.

They had been simply magicians, shamans, alchemists, who happened to have understood how to harness the energies of the universe to their own ends. The power they'd had was within the reach of all mortals, but access to that power was a secret shared only between the forty-two Assessors and their predecessors. It was the power of mind over matter. The ability to project, coerce, influence by sheer willpower, employing the forces of charisma, telepathy, astral projection.

It was a power that went back thousands of years. It was the power to create wealth, political dominance, control. The power to succeed totally in every conceivable worldly way. It was the greatest power known to man.

Theutus knew the individual identity of none of the forty-two silent Assessors here. He knew only that they had selected him with more care, more secrecy and more ritual than the processes by which the Vatican appointed a new Pope.

He was aware that they were all men of immense standing on the world's stage. One was a cardinal from the Vatican. One, an eminent scientist. One, a United States senator. One, a British cabinet minister. Each had been selected from covens all over the world for their psychic abilities, their business influence, their political influence – and their impeccable outward respectability.

Mental control ruled. All verbal communication was forbidden. All had been summoned solely by telepathy. They communicated in silence, they would depart in silence. They shared one common bond.

Power.

Give me a firm place on which to stand and I will move the world.

And they had elected *him* to be their leader; their new Ipsissimus; their Magister of Magisters. The invitation had come out of the blue. Yet not a total surprise. They had been watching him for forty years. He had been aware of what was coming, he had received the signs. Now he had to prove himself able.

If he succeeded, this same group would assemble only once more, ever: for the final initiation ceremony in the Cave of

Demons. That meeting would take place eighteen days after the death of the outgoing Ipsissimus. There would not be another such assembly, Theutus knew, until he, too, was on his deathbed. That might be here in the bowels of this table mountain in twenty, thirty, forty years' time. By then many of those here would be dead also, replaced by younger blood that was just as carefully chosen to share the same knowledge, the same secret.

He had come a long way, Theutus reflected, since the day he had purchased that first rabbit from a pet shop in High Barnet. But he still had far to go. Tonight was the twelfth Ordeal and he had yet to pass it. And beyond that, to come, was the thirteenth Ordeal, with its infamous trek to the Cave of Demons. There had been others who had come this far in the past, and failed; there were rumours of terrible humiliation and agonizing death. To allow any such fears to distract him now would be to court disaster beyond imagination.

Mind over matter.

They were watching, waiting.

Mind over matter. The supreme concentration. He had walked barefoot over blazing coals. But that had been easy. He had spent ten minutes underwater holding his breath, his arms and legs weighted with stones; but that, too, had been easy.

None of the rituals were hard once you understood the secret of control. *Mind over matter.* Most humans used less than twenty per cent of their brains. The secret lay in the other eighty per cent, and none but those assembled here would ever find the key to unlock it.

The heat seared his flesh from a distance of ten paces, and the foul sulphurous fumes invaded his lungs. He stared up at the sky far above. It was darkening and the first stars were coming out.

Stars rule man, but a wise man rules the stars.

The rim of the full moon was appearing over the lodestone high above him. When he could see the moon in its entirety he would begin.

Closing his eyes, he cleared his mind and began to speak the only words he was permitted: 'Hail Zoroaster!' Then he raised his head to the sky. 'Hail Alnath! Allothaim, Achaomazon.' He continued to hail, in turn, each of the twenty-eight mansions of the moon.

Then, bracing himself, Theutus stepped forward until he was inches from the rim of the fire and declared aloud: 'I am Alpha and Omega, the Beginning and the End, which is, which was, and which is to come, the Almighty. I am the First and the Last, who am living and was dead, and behold I live for ever and ever; and I have the keys of death and hell.'

He took a breath, ignoring the heat and the fumes, and worked on his mind, focusing on one thought and one thought only.

No pain. There is no pain. I feel no pain. I am as cold as the deepest waters of the universe. I am untouchable by heat, by pain. I am the supreme master of my body and of all elements. I am now going to use the heat of the Eternal Flame of Satan to burn off all impurities from my skin, but it will not burn the skin itself.

Then he stooped forwards without allowing himself the grace of hesitation and plunged both arms, right up to the shoulders, into the molten gold in the crucible.

And held them there.

His brain was locked on water. Fire could not burn water. He counted. Thirty seconds. One minute.

Water.

Two minutes.

Water.

Five minutes. He felt heat, pushed it away in his mind. The pulse of a clock beat in his head; he was tuned into the clock of the universe. *Water.* Seven minutes. Eight. Nine. Ten.

He lifted his arms out and raised them above the crucible. Molten gold slid like globules of mercury from his skin back into the vessel, and within seconds his hairless arms were completely clear. There was not a mark on them.

He stepped back. There was to be no applause, no congratulations. It was what had been expected of him, no more, no less.

The Chief Assessor, in his Goat of Mendez mask, solemnly lifted the sacred branding iron from among the tools on the slab, placed it into the flames beneath the crucible and held it there for a full minute. Then he removed it and held it aloft, the narrow strip of Cabbalistic numbers and symbols glowing red hot.

Theutus braced himself.

The Assessor turned, and with a solemn nod pressed hard against Theutus's right arm, six inches beneath the shoulder.

This time Theutus felt the full searing sting of the burn, but still he did not flinch. He held his head high, oblivious to the stench of his own charred flesh, and silently began, with intense concentration, to work through the difficult words of the next incantation.

108

London. Wednesday 7 December, 1994
There was a wall in front of him. It was covered in soft grey dimpled paper. A television that was switched off sat on a white shelf. A framed picture that had been irritating him hung on the wall near it. It was a childlike painting of sunflowers in a vase and the name of the artist eluded him.

It was maddening Dick Bannerman more every moment as he tried to claw the name from his memory banks. An Impressionist. Like Monet; Cézanne; Degas; that crew. The name was on the tip of his tongue but just would not come. No ear. The fellow with no ear, he'd cut it off . . . G – G –

It was as if part of his own brain had been cut off. He could see, hear, feel, smell, but nothing else. Couldn't move a muscle. He closed his eyelids slowly then opened them again to test that out. No problems. But the rest of him was locked solid.

He could see the blurred silhouette of what he took to be a nasogastric feeding tube protruding from his nostrils and could sense an obstruction in his mouth; drip lines were connected into his left hand. He could hear the steady clunk-puff of a ventilator. A light source indicated that there might be a window over to his right but he couldn't turn his head to find out. It might just be an electric light. He had no idea what the time was, whether it was day or night, and no idea where he was.

Someone had been in a couple of times; a tall, sun-tanned man in a business suit whom he recognized but could not place. For all he knew this character might still be in the room, out of his range of vision.

He could see the bedclothes beyond the end of his nose rising and falling in tune with the ventilator. He was aware that he had been catheterized and he sensed he was lying on an incontinence pad.

His memory was foggy. One minute he had been in his laboratory, his old premises, and now he was here. He couldn't remember why he had not been in his new lab at Bendix Schere. Perhaps his mind was playing tricks. He wondered if he'd had a stroke. Where was Monty? Why hadn't she come to see him?

I'm a bloody vegetable.

He stared at the painting again. *G. Who the hell was that chap?*

He tried to think back clearly. Two men. But got no further. He eyed the painting again. *Van Gogh. Yes, Vincent Van Gogh!* He felt, suddenly, elated by his small triumph. The first vegetable that knew its art history.

109

Wednesday 7 December, 1994
The plastic-coated flex felt cold against the skin of Monty's neck, but the grip was good, secure, almost snug; it was holding her steady, helping her balance on the unsteady wooden table.

'Now lower your hands, Monty,' Dr Crowe said. 'Place them by your side.'

She hesitated for a moment, then saw the kindness in his expression, felt the sincerity deep inside his heart, and knew she could trust him totally; if he told her to put her arms down, it was safe to do so.

Slowly she lowered them. The flex bit sharply into her neck as she swayed, but it helped to steady her, took the strain of her weight. The flex felt good, it would stop her from falling. Safe. She felt utterly safe. Dr Crowe was her new protector and he was a wonderful man.

'Good!' he said. 'Very good! We're all so proud of you, my dear.' Dr Crowe smiled and Monty felt a thrill inside, glad that she was pleasing him, glad to be making amends for all the bad thoughts she'd had about him in the past. That was all forgotten and they had a new understanding. What was it Conor had said? *That was then and this is now.* Something like that. She understood now what he meant.

'You don't need the table any more, Monty, it's getting in your way. Push it away with your feet, push it hard! Get rid of it!'

Obediently she pressed down hard with the soles of her feet. The table began to rock. Dr Crowe smiled, approvingly. 'That's right,' he said. 'Push it.'

The howl of slithering, locked tyres. Headlights momentarily lit up the interior of Tabitha Donoghue's Mercedes, then another car careered past them, rotating sideways like something that had broken free on a fair-ground ride. There was a sickening bang, followed by a deep, hollow rumbling, like a hundred oil drums rolling along corrugated iron. A truck had hurtled into the pile-up and something beyond it, almost instantaneously, exploded in a ball of fire.

A solitary horn blared. Tyres shrieked like wounded animals. Cars were slewing to a halt all over the highway. One slammed into the central reservation and overturned; another cannonballed into it, sending a small bundle, which might have been a baby, catapulting out.

Conor saw one car with its roof shearing off like a discarded skin. At the same time there was a faint, high-pitched whistle. The pitch changed, dropping then rising again, becoming rapidly louder. A siren. He stared through the windscreen of his mother's Mercedes, urgently wanting to get out and help, but something was holding him back; a signal, weak at the moment, but growing stronger every second.

Monty.

Another car rammed into the wreckage ahead of them. At least four cars were burning. He could hear screams as well as sirens. But all the time there was something else.

Monty. Distress. The signal was growing.

People were running towards the wrecks, trying to free jammed doors; one man in a bus driver's uniform began squirting a tiny fire extinguisher at the inferno raging in an upturned car. Traffic on the far carriageway was moving at a crawl, the occupants rubbernecking the scene.

Monty.

The sirens were close now. The police cars had screamed on to the scene. But surely this wasn't the way pile-ups happened, not so quickly as this. This had to have been staged, maybe they were shooting a movie, or the emergency services were rehearsing the scenario for –

Monty.

Monty.

Monty.

A bolt of fear suddenly swathed through Conor's guts. He saw her face; a cord around her neck; saw her legs dangling, kicking in the air. Gotta get back to her.

'Ma! Mom!' He shook his mother into life.

She gestured at the carriageway ahead, which was completely blocked. 'We're not going anywhere.'

He twisted, peering out through the rear window at the traffic backing up solid behind them. 'Reverse – go up the shoulder, there's an exit about half a mile back.' As he spoke he saw the lights of an emergency vehicle weaving down the shoulder past all the slewed cars. 'Please,' he said. 'Something's happening to Monty.'

Galvanized by the urgency in his voice, she waited until the flashing lights had passed, slammed into reverse and stamped on the gas pedal. The Mercedes jerked backwards, snaking wildly. Another emergency vehicle was coming down, making her swerve, then they were hurtling at the exit, and down the ramp. Conor sat panicking, his mother's house keys ready in his hand, until they pulled up in front of the porch. He threw himself out of the car, sprinted to the front door, unlocked it and burst through.

'Monty!' he screamed.

His voice was ripped away as a wind exploded from nowhere with the force of a hurricane, hurling him outside again and on to his back. The door crashed shut with a splintering crunch.

Dazed and dimly aware of a foreign smell in the air, he met his mother's eyes as she walked past him into the porch, then opened her purse and rummaged inside it. After a moment, she removed a folded square of paper that he had seen many times before, and opened it out. Then, making an imposing figure in her full-length black velvet coat, she closed her eyes and began to murmur the barely audible words of an incantation.

When she had finished, she thrust the door open and strode in, braced to wedge it with her body if necessary. Out of the howling maelstrom inside, a small glass paperweight hurtled past her head, shattering a window in the Mercedes. The gusts blasted her hair so that it trailed from her like reeds in a flood tide, but she stood her ground, eyes blazing with anger.

Conor felt the wind tearing at the roots of his hair too, but already he could sense it was less strong than before. It was beginning to wane under his mother's commands.

Head down, he forced his way in, pushing into the hall through air that felt as dense as water, grimacing at its vile smell. There was a cacophony of rattling furniture and fittings. All the candles had gone out; a painting suddenly detached itself from the wall and hurtled straight at Conor. He ducked, then heard it smash something behind him.

'Monty!' he bellowed. 'Monty!'

The wind seemed to find new strength. It caught him, sent him reeling sideways, and he fell over. But his mother had found the eye of the storm and she stood upright.

'Out!' she commanded, her voice deep. 'I order you to leave this house before I throw you out!'

The smell was worsening; the foul, putrid stench of sour milk, decaying flesh and excrement, the reek of pure, malevolent, evil.

Conor rose and pushed his way forward, moving in slow motion as if he was in a nightmare where he was trying to run, but his legs would not work. Christ, where the hell was Monty?

He yelled her name again and again. And then, suddenly, he had her! Was picking her up clearly, knew exactly where she was. He broke into a loping run, reached the door he was seeking, grabbed the ball-shaped handle and turned it sharply. It sheared clean off.

In disbelief, he hammered on the door instead. 'Monty? Monty!' He stepped back and charged the door with his shoulder. It did not yield.

He kicked it hard, then again felt the door shaking but not giving. Again. Blam! Hyperventilating with panic, he charged it once more, striking it with his full weight behind his shoulder. It splintered open and he lurched through into the gloom. It was some seconds before he realized he was not alone.

Monty was hanging by her neck from the ceiling light flex, her head lolled forward at a ghastly, unnatural angle, her eyes wide open and sightless.

110

London. Wednesday 7 December, 1994
Dick Bannerman heard a door open then close, and sensed someone in the room. Moments later, Dr Crowe strode into his line of vision. He was accompanied by a figure in a navy suit, who wore black-rimmed glasses. The geneticist tried to place him.

Both men stopped at the end of the bed and studied him for a moment, as if he were an exhibit of marginal interest in zoo. Crowe stood at ease with his hands behind his back; the other man walked along the bed and reached above Dick Bannerman's head, apparently adjusting something.

Crowe produced an envelope. 'Sir Neil Rorke asked me to bring this to you, Dr Bannerman. He was most upset to hear of your illness and asked me to convey his best wishes for a speedy recovery. Would you like me to open it for you?'

Dick Bannerman tried to nod, and to his surprise found he was able to move his head a fraction.

'You'll be able to breathe normally in a couple of minutes; then Dr Seligman will remove your ventilator tube and we'll be able to talk.' Crowe flipped open the envelope, and held a 'Get Well' card in front of Bannerman's face. The message inside was handwritten and said simply:

'Strokes are beastly things but I'm sure you will make a complete recovery and be back with us soon. Neil Rorke.'

The scientist's heart sank. That was it, his worst fears confirmed; he'd had a stroke. Struth, how bad was it? Total paralysis? And *yet* – something felt wrong about it. Something was stirring in his mind. Last night? Dr Crowe, and another man. Gunn? Yes! That was his name, the Director of Security. The memory was foggy. They had come to his old lab, now he had woken up here. God, if they had not been there he might be dead. But what had they wanted?

His thinking was becoming more focused every second. He'd been working on the Maternox, had identified the DNA in them. 'M – M – M' his voice was coming back. Then he choked and coughed violently from the obstruction in his throat. The breathing tube, he realized.

Crowe was looking at his watch. 'Just a couple of minutes, Dr Bannerman. Don't try to speak with the tube in.'

He could feel his hands again, his feet. He wiggled his toes. He was able to move his head a little, then more; until, suddenly, he could rotate it completely. Could see where he was: in a bland hospital bedroom. Windowless. Like the Bendix Building.

He tested his body as he waited, working on each limb in turn, flexing the muscles, raising, lowering, to test his motor control. He was relieved to discover there was movement in all areas, even if only very local at the moment. As long as there was movement, it could be worked on; physiotherapy; he had read somewhere that it was vital to start physio as quickly as possible after a stroke.

Maternox. Last night was becoming clearer all the time. The results of his tests! Anger simmered inside him.

'Just going to slip your ventilator out now,' Seligman said, reaching forward and beginning to pull.

Bannerman felt a choking, tickling sensation in his gullet and for a moment panicked as he could not breathe; finally, he saw the long, white plastic endotracheal tube slowly appear, and then he was breathing freely, gulping down deep draughts of air, his throat feeling swollen and parched.

The ventilator hissed one final time then fell silent.

'How are you feeling?' Crowe asked calmly.

'I've had a stroke?'

'I'm afraid so. A very minor one. You've been lucky.'

'That's not what I call lucky. I'm only fifty-eight.'

'Well, they can happen at any age. You're in good hands here. I believe you may have met Dr Seligman, Director of our Clinics?'

The geneticist raised his head to watch Seligman twist a flow valve.

'You are comfortable, I trust?' Crowe asked.

'Bugger being comfortable! Where the hell am I?'

'You're in the Hammersmith Bendix.'

'How long for?'

'That will depend.'

'On what?'

Dick Bannerman watched Crowe's face become evasive; his expression was communicating the wrong signals. Was the stroke worse than he was telling him? Was he about to have another?

'Dr Bannerman, in modern medicine a very great deal is down to the patient's attitude.'

'Where's my daughter? Has she been told?'

'Someone is trying to contact her. We believe she may be in America.'

The geneticist cursed as he remembered. 'What day is it?'

'Wednesday.'

'Damnit – I – I have to be – the White House, Friday. I have a speech, I –' He glanced round for a phone and was surprised not to see one.

'They'll understand,' Crowe said sympathetically. 'Don't worry, it's all taken care of.'

Dick Bannerman was thinking. About Maternox. He had to get his information to Monty in case he had another stroke and went gaga; or died. Ideally he ought to get confirmation that Crowe was involved, but warning bells were starting to ring. He glanced at Seligman and decided he did not like the look of him either. Saying nothing, he tried to shift his body and sit up but could not make it; it was as if half his internal connections had been switched off. He saw Seligman watching his efforts with what looked like a faint smirk on his face.

Meanwhile, Crowe moved slowly around the room, his eyes alighting, bird-like, on one object then another. He stopped beside the television, picked up the remote channel changer, and commented as if at random, 'So many wonderful things in modern technology, don't you think, Dr Bannerman?'

'Yes and no is the answer to that. Like a lot of my colleagues in genetics, I fear some lunatic may go too far one day. Just imagine, for instance, what the work of one isolated madman could do to Bendix Schere's long-term corporate strategy.'

Crowe went over to the Van Gogh painting of sunflowers and tapped it with his finger. 'This is the work of an isolated madman. A tortured genius who died in anguish and poverty. Now his paintings sell for more than the gross national product of some countries. In their lifetimes the Impressionists were ridiculed as charlatans because they dared to be different. In the judgement of posterity, they were the geniuses who liberated painting from the shackles that were strangling it.'

Dick Bannerman was perturbed by the Messianic gleam in Crowe's eyes as he spoke, and wondered if he should have led the conversation on to such dangerous ground. He was acutely aware that being confined to a hospital bed did not give him an equal battle station.

'Half of history's heroes have been branded either madmen

565

of heretics.' Crowe had found his soapbox. 'Copernicus, for saying the earth went round the sun; Galileo for backing him up; then there was Charles Darwin. I could list ten thousand names. I dare say you'd even be on it. Look at you, you have a Nobel Prize yet you're ignored by the mainstream scientific community and until we came along you spent most of your working life knocking on doors with your begging bowl.'

'At least I never did anything illegal or immoral.' Bannerman was not willing to hedge his bets any longer.

But Crowe shrugged. 'The truth is, is it not, that in our field we sometimes have to do things that may seem a little unpalatable, for the greater good.'

'And is that what you're doing with Maternox, Dr Crowe?' This time Dick Bannerman took his courage in both hands. 'By using it as a cover, what you're really trying to do is genetically engineer a psoriasis gene into the germ-line of the foetus. At some point in the future, when that foetus, that baby, becomes an adult, it will develop psoriasis – and it'll pass that gene on to its own children in turn. Right?'

Crowe nodded as if he'd found a convert. 'Very perceptive.'

'I presume you're doing so in order to develop a future market for your drugs?'

'Precisely. It's a new strain of psoriasis, of course, for which we'll have new pharmaceuticals lined up, ready to market. But not just psoriasis, Dr Bannerman. We're working on the development of genes that will produce a whole range of new chronic diseases in future generations – new cardiovascular disorders, new areas of renal failure, new forms of clinical depression, new stomach ulcers – all of which will require the right medication. We deliver the genes into the germ-line via the mother, and then we make sure the drugs are ready to patent and launch in twenty, thirty, forty years' time, when the diseases begin to manifest. Rather elegant, don't you think?'

Bannerman was stupefied. 'Elegant?'

'Do you know of any other business in the world where a company is in a position to create a biological need for its products?'

'Yes. The narcotics cartels of Colombia.'

Crowe wrinkled his nose. 'A crude and inefficient example that does not begin to compare.'

Dick Bannerman studied the madman before him, praying he was one of the isolated variety. 'You're serious, aren't you?'

'One in six women around the world requires infertility treatment, and most of them take Maternox, Dr Bannerman. In twenty years' time, their children will have started to become adults with symptoms of new strains of psoriasis, of depression, of arterial or renal disease, of whatever. As a result,' and now Crowe began to sound like a triumphant sales rep building up to the moment that was going to clinch the deal, 'by the first quarter of the next century, around one fifth of the western world will be dependent on pharmaceuticals manufactured by Bendix Schere. And we don't intend limiting the genetic engineering of new diseases solely to Maternox; no, we're hoping to use many of our other household products to deliver disease genes. All we have to do is get the gene delivery method right.'

'And delivery of the psoriasis gene is not working in your Medici Trial, is it?'

'We are experiencing a few teething troubles,' Crowe said.

Dick Bannerman appealed to him. 'Don't you have one shred of morality in you? Not one tiny speck of humanity?'

Crowe stood square, facing the geneticist, eyeing him coldly. 'Dr Bannerman, do you believe in God?'

'What does God have to do with *this*?'

Crowe glanced fleetingly at Dr Seligman then replied, 'God has a very great deal to do with it. We live in a world running increasingly out of control; and why? Because it's in the evil clutches of a despot who's reigned unchecked for thousands of years. A charlatan, an arriviste poseur, a sadistic bully and a mass murderer. His name is *God*, Dr Bannerman. *The Holy Father. The Almighty.*'

The tirade continued. 'How many human beings has this monster murdered in his name? Can anyone total the combined deaths of the Crusades, the Holy Wars, the Roman Catholic Inquisition that reigned in Europe from 1229 until 1834? Not to mention the numbers put to death in the past thousand years as heretics . . .'

Crowe's eyes were blazing. 'Name me a land where there is bloodshed that is not caused by the Great Impostor and his son, and I'll name you two where there is! Well, we're going to change all that, Dr Bannerman. We've finally realized where God is coming from. The conspiracy is out. Now we're taking charge of our own destiny, entering a new age, and I want to offer you the opportunity to join us. Work with us!'

Dick Bannerman dismissed him in one. 'Count me *out*, Crowe.'

Incongruously Crowe's voice was quiet and friendly when he spoke again. 'There's something you need to understand, Dr Bannerman. It's not profits that interest us – it's control. Over the next quarter-century we're going to dominate the pharmaceutical industry: we will control the manufacture, distribution and retailing of most of the world's medications. We will be able to control pain and, more importantly, reproduction. Think of it . . . we will have more power than any known political party.'

Once again Dick Bannerman's reply was succinct. 'You're off your trolley, man.'

Dr Crowe didn't bat an eyelid. 'Oh, I'm sure that given time to reflect you'll begin to see our point of view. In fact I'll level with you, Dr Bannerman. You see, we need your help; we really need it quite badly.'

'Yes, you do! You've got problems delivering the psoriasis genes via the Maternox because you're using the wrong methodology. You've made one very basic flaw, which probably only three people in the world could spot; I'm one of them.'

Crowe looked at him brightly. 'Ah? Perhaps you could enlighten us?'

'I'd rather see you in Hell.'

'Perhaps you would, my friend. But I'm afraid you won't be permitted the luxury of that choice.' He signalled to Seligman, who leaned across and adjusted a flow valve on the drip stand.

Almost instantly, Dick Bannerman felt the paralysis returning to his muscles. He tried to speak, but found it was all he could do to draw breath.

'One of the major features of Bendix Clinics is their total privacy,' Crowe was saying. 'We can ensure that our guests are never disturbed – ever, if need be.' He smiled. 'Do you understand?'

The geneticist grunted something inaudible.

'No?' Crowe was solicitous. 'Allow me to be a little more specific: either you can help us now, or we can keep you alive and conscious, in a totally immobilized state for as long as you like – ten, twenty, thirty, perhaps even forty years. I don't know how long you'll be able to take it, without reading, writing – just lying there staring at the walls. I imagine you'll find it rather like being buried alive, although not quite so claustrophobic. You can let me know if I'm right because we're going to intubate you again now, and give you the opportunity to think about it for a day or two.'

As Dick Bannerman grunted a protest, Seligman reached above him and made a further adjustment. Within seconds, his entire body seemed to have locked solid. He saw the doctor's fingers prise open his jaw, then the curved white spout of the endotracheal tube approaching, like the bill of an oyster-catcher.

A few moments later he was staring at the Van Gogh and listening to the steady clunk-puff . . . clunk-puff . . . clunk-puff of the ventilator. The room was empty.

111

Washington. Wednesday 7 December, 1994
Conor felt as if his heart was going to tear in two. 'Monty,' he mouthed. 'Oh my God, Monty.'

He grabbed the edge of the fallen table, jerked it upright beneath Monty's feet, scrambled on to it, grabbed the flex just above her head and pulled with all his strength.

It ripped away more easily than he had expected and her dead-weight sagged against him, unbalancing him. He flung his arms around her, cradling her, trying to shield her as they both spilled down on to the floor.

Her body felt soft, she had not yet gone stiff. He touched her cheek. It was still warm.

Screaming out to his mother to call an ambulance, he tried desperately to recall the first aid drill he had learned at school. *Airways*. Airways was the first. The flex was cutting into the skin of her neck, but it unwound easily. Her complexion was blue and there was a ghastly, sightless expression in her eyes. He put a hand beneath her nose, then in front of her lips. Nothing. She was not breathing.

Recovery position. He remembered that next. Then, *mouth-to-mouth resuscitation*. Oh God, he needed six of him. Tilt back her head, free her airway, press his mouth to hers, make a seal with his lips, pinch her nostrils shut, and blow hard three times. Immediately, he removed his mouth, located the spot directly beneath her chest diaphragm and pressed both his hands down together three times. *Darling, come on, don't be dead, please don't be dead.*

As he brought his mouth back down to repeat the procedure for the fourth time, he noticed a flicker in her left eye and his heart crashed loose inside his chest. 'Monty? Monty darling?'

One tiny, slow-motion blink. A short shimmying of her lashes; flickering; both eyelids closed then opened again.

Warm air. Coming from her mouth. Her lids closed. She was breathing. She was alive!

More chest compressions. His mother came running into the room. He looked up at her, shouting, 'Ambulance? Did you call them? Where are they?'

His mother knelt beside him, examining Monty's face.

'She was hanging,' he said. 'From the light flex, she wasn't breathing. Get an ambulance, for God's sake, please.'

Tabitha Donoghue stared at her. 'She's going to be all right. Keep going. Keep doing what you're doing. Don't stop.'

Conor repeated the compressions, then the mouth-to-mouth, until Monty's breathing was noticeably stronger. Normal colour was even beginning to return to her face. Then his mother took over. She knelt on the floor, held her hands palms down, a few inches above Monty's chest, then began moving them in a slow, circular motion, up over her neck, her face, then back down.

'You're going to be all right, Monty,' she said quietly, continuing the steady movement of her hands. 'You're back with us now, just relax, you're safe now.'

Monty opened her eyes and stared at them, blankly at first, confused. Her fingers curled, then opened like a newborn baby's.

Conor took her right hand and kissed it, then held it, squeezing it gently. Suddenly he felt just the faintest pressure from her fingertips. She was responding, he realized. She was trying to squeeze his hand back! He closed his eyes with joy.

'Where's my father?'

Conor looked up with a start; he had been sitting at Monty's bedside for the past two hours whilst she slept, going over and over the past days in his mind, working on his plan. He leaned over and kissed her. 'How are you feeling?'

She raised an unsteady hand to her neck and touched the livid red weals. 'I don't know,' she said. 'I – I –' Her eyes closed again. 'What happened, Conor? Please tell me what happened.'

'Try to sleep. Don't worry about anything right now. Just rest.' He watched her anxiously. They should have driven her straight to hospital after she'd come round but that was too risky; she needed protection.

'Where's Dr Crowe?' she whispered.

'He's not here, it's OK. He won't come back. My mom's making sure of that. He's not going to harm you.'

She shook her head. 'Outside. He was there. I was dreaming, it was horrible; he was looking in through the window; he wanted me to stand on the table and try again, he wanted –'

Conor squeezed her hand and nodded at the floral drapes. 'They're drawn tight; no one can see in. We're gonna be here with you all night, you don't have to worry.'

'My handbag. There's a tape-recorder in my handbag. Play the tape.'

'Try to sleep, darling.'

'Play the tape, please.'

Conor found her bag and saw the small Sony dictating machine. He took it out, pressed 'Play' and adjusted the volume as the words crackled out.

'. . . *we'd like an explanation from you, Dr Bannerman, as to what you're doing with a Maternox formulaic template owned by the company.*'

'*Would you prefer that explanation to take place in a court of law, or in front of the Committee for Safety of Medicines?*'

'Wind it back,' Monty said. 'Play it from the start.'

The door opened and Tabitha Donoghue came in holding a steaming mug; she stepped carefully over the trail of salt that lay across the doorway, and which skirted the entire bedroom. 'I brought you something to help you get your strength back. Could you manage to drink it, Monty?'

'I – I don't think so.'

She sat down on the bed. 'Just let it cool for a few moments and then try, OK?'

Conor wound the tape back to the top and the three of them listened in silence. When it had finished, some of the returning colour had drained from Monty's complexion again and she was looking very distressed.

'Please,' she said. 'We have to find my father. Couldn't we try the British Ambassador? Or Dr Crowe will –' She shivered suddenly, too frightened to speak her thoughts.

'Do you have anything that belongs to your father?' Tabitha asked. 'Something personal that he's worn or touched recently?'

'No – I – don't have anything, not here.' Then suddenly she corrected herself. 'I – what about – the tape-recorder? That's his, he carries it round with him all the time.'

Conor handed it to his mother. She cradled it in the palm of one hand, passing the other lightly over it. The door moved a fraction and one of the cats pushed its way into the room, followed by the other, and they joined the trio.

Closing her eyes, Tabitha had begun to concentrate.

'Want to dowse on your pendulum, Mom?' Conor asked.

'I don't need to do that,' she replied without opening her eyes. 'I can feel him very strongly, I know where he is, I can visualize him. He's a fine-looking man; he has very little hair on top, but it's long and silvery-grey over his ears and at the back.'

Monty stiffened in amazement. Then she realized that her father's picture was frequently in the international press and it was quite possible Conor's mother had seen him and remembered his appearance. Except that she did not look like a woman who needed to lie. 'Yes,' she said. 'That sounds right.'

Still with her eyes shut, Tabitha Donoghue continued. 'He's alive, but he's kind of not alive. I don't quite understand.' Monty watched her anxiously. 'He's lying down, there's something in his mouth, like a breathing tube; but he's not unconscious, and his brain is alert.'

'Is he paralysed?' Monty said.

'He's in a small room, electronic machinery around him.'

'What kind of a room?' Monty asked.

'It has no windows.'

'Christ,' Conor said. 'How many storeys high is the building?'

'About eight.'

'Eight?' he said. 'You sure it's not higher? It sounds like the Bendix Building.'

'Eight,' she said firmly.

'The Bendix Hammersmith,' Monty said. 'The Clinic. That's eight storeys high! Oh God, why is he there? He must be injured.'

'I don't know what's going on, but I don't feel any injuries. I feel this man's body is intact.'

'Please, Conor, we have to do something,' Monty pleaded.

'Tomorrow, hon, tomorrow,' Conor said. 'I know this much. They want your dad alive, they need his knowledge. And I know exactly what we have to do; you're just going to have to trust me. OK?'

She gave a single nod, her face a mask of fear, and squeezed his hand weakly for comfort.

112

London. Thursday 8 December, 1994

'It's her, isn't it?' Nikky said. She lay naked on the floor, slouched against the side of the bed, chewing an olive. She took a slug of her dry Martini and washed the olive down with it, then took another from the bowl and popped it in her mouth. With her free hand she poked around with her pubic hairs, pulling them straight, one after the other.

'Who?' Gunn said, lying back on the bed, his laptop on his thighs.

She peered down between her legs. 'Do you think my pubes are too long? Should I have them trimmed next time I have my hair done?'

'Your pubes are fine,' he said, distractedly.

'At least they're red, like my hair. How many girls have you been with whose pubes are the same colour as their hair?'

Gunn grunted noncommittally, trying hard to keep his eyes open. It was one in the morning and he had been home less than an hour. He looked at the phone, waiting for it to ring. Waiting for that cretin McLusky in Washington to phone him with confirmation that Molloy and the Bannerman woman were both dead. Things were getting back on to an even keel, finally, but there were still a lot of loose ends to tie up. At least the goods were delivered and with luck he had Crowe off his back for a while.

'What did you say?' she asked.

'No, I never met anyone who had the same colour pubes.'

'You're not just saying that?'

'No, I'm not just saying that. Niks, I have to work, give me a break, I need ten minutes of quiet.'

'"Niks, I have to work, give me a break, I need ten minutes of quiet,"' she mimicked and shoved another olive in her mouth. 'Do you think it's decadent to drink Martinis at one in the morning?'

Gunn did not respond. He was studying the checklist of names, deep in thought. *Zandra Wollerton. Hubert Wentworth.*

Charles Rowley. Conor Molloy. Montana Bannerman. Dr Richard Bannerman.

Dr Bannerman. He was still an unresolved problem. He drank some of his Martini and stared at Nikky's mane of dark red hair. She was a problem, also. Ever since she'd looked at the names on his computer. She was a problem that was going to have to be dealt with.

Loose ends. You could never leave loose ends. Like chickens, they always came home to roost.

'It is her, isn't it?' she said again.

'What are you talking about?'

'Christmas trees.'

'What?'

She looked round the bedsitting room. 'Not many days left to Christmas, soldier. What are you doing about decorations in this palatial dump?'

'Niks, *please*.' He tried again to focus his mind.

'"Niks, please,"' she mimicked again, and ate another olive. '*Her*. Your friend. The one on the Christmas list.'

He drained his glass. 'Any chance of not talking in riddles?' He glanced up at the television which was switched on, with the sound mute. Mariella Frostrup was speaking and there was a twinkle in her eye; he tried to lip-read, but she was no more intelligible than Nikky. Mariella Frostrup disappeared and was replaced by a slimy, bug-eyed monster; it was holding what looked like a dismembered arm in its claws. 'Hey, Niks, look at that! Your twin sister's on the box.'

'Looks more like your ex, soldier.' Without glancing round, she passed the *Evening Standard* over her shoulder. '*Her*,' she said. 'The front-page splash. Your friend.'

He reached forward and took the paper. The headline read: LONDON CAR BOMB HORROR KILLS TWO.

He stared at the photograph of the mangled MG, then he scanned the article. '*Police are still trying to ascertain the identity of the two victims . . . may have been the bombers . . . believe the bomb may have been planted by Animal Rights terrorists . . . intended target was Montana Bannerman . . . daughter of Nobel Prize-winning scientist Dr Richard Bannerman, who is on life support in hospital after suffering a massive stroke . . . trying to contact Miss Bannerman who is believed to be overseas on business . . .'*

'Montana Bannerman,' Nikky said. 'She was on your list with the Christmas trees. The same list that had your colleague Charley boy on it, the one who drowned in Hawaii. You seem to be awfully careless with your employees, soldier. Don't think I'd like to work for you. Bit risky.'

113

Washington. Thursday 8 December, 1994
Monty was awoken by a sound in the room, a faint, slippery thud; she stared into the darkness, startled.

Two eyes stared back.

Bulging, iridescent eyes, watching her with mild curiosity, from a few feet away. Moments later they were joined by another pair, then another. More began appearing every moment, filling the air with the sour smell of their reptilian skin. They were silent at first, then a solitary croak echoed through the chamber.

'Rrribbbettt.'

Silence.

Then out of the silence, a response. 'Rrribbbettt.'

Trembling with fear, Monty tried – very quietly – to edge back, but she was already flat against the unyielding wall. The door was on the far side of the bitumen blackness that was alive with blinking eyes and the growing chorus of croaks. As she took the first tentative step towards it, her foot squelched deep into a slimy, wriggling carpet.

She jerked back in horror. Something thudded into her chest; then something wet and streamlined struck her cheek. The creatures were leaping on to her out of the darkness now, their webbed feet dabbing at her hair, her chest, striking her shoulders, her stomach; then they covered her face, blinding her, pushing their legs into her eyes.

'Noooooo! Uurrgggghh!' She clawed desperately at them,

hurling them away; even more flung themselves out of the darkness at her, their legs flexing, coiling. 'Uurrgggghh!! Oh God, help meeeeeee!' They were falling out of the ceiling on to her in droves, going to knock her over with their sheer collective weight. 'Help me! Please, someone help meeeee –'

'MONTY!'

The voice came from somewhere else; another planet.

'Monty! Darling! Hon!'

It was Conor's voice, calm, soft, whispering. 'Monty, darling, it's OK, wake up; come on, wake up!'

She opened her eyes slowly, blinking in the sudden brightness of the bedside light, confused, checking out the room carefully, looking at Conor's anxious face. They were in a hotel room. In – in –? She could not remember where. Not Conor's apartment in London? No, America? Yes, Washington. But then all the relief she felt as the dream receded was ripped away as the memory of last night returned.

Washington.

Conor's mother's house.

She had tried to strangle herself.

Her neck was hurting; she gingerly touched her flesh; it hurt even more under the lightest pressure. Dr Crowe! Dr Crowe had tried to make her kill herself.

She looked up at Conor's eyes, inches above her own, blurry, concerned. His hair was tousled; such warmth in that face; such kindness. 'Don't leave me,' she whispered. 'Please don't leave me.'

He kissed her lightly on the forehead. 'Don't worry, I'm right here. What were you dreaming?'

She hesitated, as if scared that by mentioning it she would bring the dream back, or somehow make it real. 'Frogs. I dreamed the room was full of the damn things and – they – they were attacking me.'

'You have a thing about frogs, don't you? I remember that one that got in your kitchen and really freaked you.'

She swallowed. 'Ever since childhood. It's stupid and I'm sorry I woke you, but –'

'You told me. It's not stupid. Everyone has something they're afraid of.'

'What really happened to me yesterday, Conor?'

'You were psychically attacked. Dr Crowe somehow got to you – he hyptnotized you into hanging yourself.'

'How is that possible?'

'My mother's the expert – she's been involved with this kind of stuff all her life. There are some people who are able to focus their minds, to harness energies, to project. It's kind of like the same power some shamans have, or the power of voodoo. And it's very real.'

'And Dr Crowe has that power?'

'It would seem, yes.' He hesitated, wondering whether to tell her about his narrow escape in the taxi. He decided against.

She touched his cheek with her hand, to reassure herself that he was real. 'Is this how it's going to be from now on, Conor? Are we going to be in constant fear?'

He said nothing.

'God, I thought Bendix Schere was a dream come true. I thought it would solve all our problems and give me the chance to lead a normal life.' She laughed bitterly.

'Did you ever live a *normal* life?' he asked quietly. 'Does anyone?'

She sighed before replying. 'I did once, when I was a child, when my mother was alive,' she said wistfully. 'It felt good in those days. I did the same things as other kids, we did the same things as other families. That's what I mean. How about you? When you were a boy?'

'That was all a long time ago. That was then and this is now.'

'You always say that.'

'It's a universal truth; nothing stays the same. And the way we measure things changes, also. The yardstick I had for normality when I was a kid of seven is different from the one I have now.'

Monty contemplated and knew, in one way, that he was right. She snuggled closer to him, saying, 'Whatever happens, I hope we have some time together. I hope that more than anything in the world.'

'So do I.' He kissed her. 'Want to go back to sleep?'

She shook her head. 'I'm wide awake.'

'Our time clocks. We're on UK time.'

Restlessly she looked around the plush, rather bland room. 'Is this the house you grew up in?'

'It was a lot smaller. About a quarter this size. Mom keeps adding bits on.'

'She makes her money dowsing for the oil industry?'

'She makes a fortune.'

'Did she ever remarry?'

'No. She's a pretty strong character – not too many men are able to stand up to someone like that.'

She watched his face. 'Why do you and your mother have a different last name?'

'I figured Bendix Schere would remember my pa's surname and it might start ringing bells when I joined the company; so I reinvented myself; that's all.'

'Makes sense,' she said, relieved by his answer.

Conor lit a cigarette and gave Monty a drag; it made her cough, and her thoughts returned to the present. 'What am I going to do about this dinner at the White House, and Daddy's talk tomorrow?'

'Don't even think about them. Unless you want to announce that the speaker's been kidnapped.'

'Hey, you know!' she said. 'That's not such a dumb idea. I could do that – we have the tape, right? That would cause all hell to –'

'No,' he said calmly. 'That's too dangerous.'

'Why?'

'Because Bendix Schere are very, very smart. And because you want to get your father back, not get him killed.'

'I don't understand.'

'Just believe me.'

114

'Organizer's Office, how can I help you?'

'Is that the World Genetics Symposium?' Monty asked.

'Yes, it is.'

'It's Montana Bannerman speaking. I'm calling regarding my father, Dr Bannerman, who's meant to be talking tomorrow, and –'

'Yes,' the male voice interrupted. 'We are very sorry to hear about Dr Bannerman's stroke. We have him down as cancelled.'

'*Stroke?*' she echoed. 'Did you say *stroke?*'

'That's the information I have. We were informed by fax – is there –?' His words hung in the air.

'I – I'm sorry – I think, I – I didn't realize someone had already been in touch.' She thanked him lamely and hung up.

'Stroke,' she repeated automatically to Conor. 'Someone from Bendix Schere has rung the Symposium office and told them Daddy's had a stroke.'

Conor was working on his laptop which had arrived in his suitcase by taxi from Dave Schwab's home a short while ago, and he barely looked up. 'They'll have it all in hand, you can be sure as hell of that.'

'But, Conor –'

'Your father has not had a stroke.'

Monty turned round, startled, to see Tabitha Donoghue striding into the room, dressed, as yesterday, all in black.

'He's being held against his will but he's not sick and he's not injured,' she said. 'I can't tell exactly what they're doing to him, but I would guess he's been doped.' Then the tone of her voice changed, and she jerked her head towards the window. 'We have company.'

'Like who?' Conor said.

'I just took a walk down to the gates. Two guys in a blue Chevrolet parked a hundred yards down the hill; third time I've checked – they've been there all morning.'

It felt as if the temperature in the room had suddenly dropped. Although Monty had been expecting a tail, the confirmation scared her.

Tabitha sat down beside her and examined the weals on her neck for a moment. 'They're doing fine. I'll lend you a turtleneck to hide them when we leave. We're booked on a seven o'clock flight to Heathrow.'

'*We*?'

'I'm coming with you.'

Monty had come to accept Tabitha, for all her strange aura, and she was gladdened by this news. Not least because there was safety in numbers. Wasn't there? She glanced at her watch. It was midday. 'We can't get – there – there's no flight sooner?'

'Nothing that's going to make much difference. As we're being watched, I think it's smarter to wait here and leave after dark. I've also made smokescreen reservations in our names on other airlines to Los Angeles, Rome, New York, Hong Kong and Sydney.'

'Dark or not, we're going to have a problem with the guys outside the gates when we leave,' Conor contributed.

His mother smiled. 'That's taken care of. I have a good friend in the local police. I just have to call him an hour beforehand. He'll have those creeps tied up every which way to Sunday in a stolen vehicle check, and he's going to give us an escort right to the airport and on to the plane.'

She turned to Monty next. 'As for you, my dear, we're going to have to make sure you use all the protection protocols. This Crowe character has forged a very strong link through to you; when a channel like that has been opened once, it can be reopened very easily. Any dairy products will heighten your emotional responses, particularly fear. We need to damp your emotions right down so they become harder for anyone outside to manipulate.'

Monty frowned; she found it hard to believe that milk or butter could make any difference. It was her life she was worried about, not her diet.

But Tabitha had not finished. 'Do you wear your crucifix for any special reason?'

'Yes, it's sentimental; it belonged to my mother. Do you think it can help?'

She looked at Monty reproachfully. 'I've never understood why people think carrying the symbol of Christ around is going to act like some magic shield. We're talking about psychic attack, not religion, OK?'

Monty nodded, rebuked.

Tabitha tapped her head. 'You do realize that we're dealing with the occult here, don't you? And the occult is about harnessing the powers of the planet, of the universe, of the human mind. It's about living forces, not dead gurus.'

Monty already felt out of her depth; but there was more to come.

'Satan is a logo, Monty. A brand name, a product packaged and sold by the Church; a big stick to beat the flock with and keep them in line. And the Church's very convenient bogeyman.' Tabitha Donoghue looked at her solemnly. 'The people we're up against aren't interested in that kind of mumbo-jumbo claptrap. They may use all the black imagery, but what they're about is *power*. And power comes through control: the control of the physical, the control of the mind. The power that can enable a man three thousand miles away to persuade a rational young woman to stand on a rickety table and wind a wire around her neck.'

Monty was genuinely intrigued and just wished that the drama they were talking about had a different cast. 'Where does this power come from – and how is it harnessed?' she asked.

'It comes from the natural energies of our planet, our universe, our minds and our bodies. I think we may find the answer one day in quantum mechanics. The old scientists used to believe that the mind and the universe were separate, and that the universe was greater than either any individual human mind, or the sum of all human minds. But right now no one understands or can define the real extent of the powers of the human mind.'

Monty nodded; she could accept that.

'I will give you as much protection as I can, Monty, but I can't guarantee it's going to be enough,' Tabitha continued.

'You need to take salt-water baths to purify your auras. Anyone under psychic attack must work from the outside in. Salt water will help shield you from Crowe's attempts to project to you.' She lit a cigarette, and gave Monty a smile of encouragement. 'You see, they have to make a dent in your aura before they can attack. When you feel under attack you have to try to visualize your aura as a shield.'

Monty remembered in a scientific magazine once seeing photographs of people's auras; they looked like psychedelic space-suits. She tried to picture her own aura as a shield, but the image was elusive. 'How often do I have to take a salt bath?'

'Daily. And I'm going to give you a visualization to do.' She glanced at Conor, then looked back at Monty. 'I want you to think of a gold cross in your solar plexus and another at the base of your skull. Not religious crosses, just two pieces of gold intersecting. These are the two mega-nerve meeting points in the body.'

Monty looked down at the area of her own solar plexus, then touched the base of her skull with her fingers. The movement hurt her neck muscles.

'Have you ever studied martial arts, Monty?'

'No.'

'These are the points in martial arts to go for. If you visualize strongly enough you get them radiating gold, and if the attack is very violent you can make them radiate white lights. You can't maintain it for long, because you'll get violent headaches if you try. But whoever's perpetrating the attack cannot maintain their energy level for long either. Remember that.'

She tapped some ash off, then drew on her cigarette again. 'You need to have salt with you all the time. Wherever you are, make a circle of salt and stay inside it. Nothing can live in salt, and nothing of a psychic nature can pass through it.'

She opened her handbag and removed from it a small piece of paper folded inside a zipped freezer bag, which she handed to Monty. 'Conor already has one of these.'

Monty opened the clear bag, took out the paper and unfolded it. It was covered in a mass of letters and symbols.

'You keep it in the bag because you mustn't wet it – it can cause havoc if that happens, like something electrical shorting out. It's called a Lumiel square and it'll be your protective talisman. Keep it with you and it'll protect you physically and mentally. It will also protect your soul.' She nodded reassuringly, as if trying to dispel Monty's scepticism.

'I used to have a young woman in one of my development circles when I worked as a medium. She always carried one of these. Well, she was in a real bad car smash. Of five kids, three were killed, and one is in a persistent vegetative state. But she got out with just a few scratches.'

Accepting the Lumiel square, as she was accepting everything right now, Monty thanked the older woman warmly.

Tabitha leaned back reflectively. 'And to think I believed I'd left all this stuff behind years ago. I never intended, ever, to get back into all this shit.'

'I don't think any of us *intended* –' Monty began.

Tabitha cut her short. 'Uh oh. Conor very definitely *intended*. From the day his daddy died it's been there, chewing him up, the thought of those big bad guys who harmed his pa. It's driven his whole life.' She smiled sadly. 'I've tried for twenty-six years to talk him into letting it go; tried to tell him that he doesn't understand the power of what he's up against. Now, at last, I think he does understand. But perhaps just a little bit too late in the day.'

'Whatever the reasons, Mrs Donoghue, he's done the right thing. Wasn't it Edmund Burke who said, *All that is necessary for the triumph of evil is that good men do nothing*?'

Tabitha stared at her with dark eyes that combined respect and anguish. Monty felt the first hint of acknowledgement of a bond between them.

'My mother was a medium and a healer, Monty. She spent her life rescuing people who had gotten caught up in the occult.' Tabitha took out another cigarette. 'You did your history at school?'

'Yes.'

'Remember when people laid siege to a walled city? Very few attackers ever won by knocking those walls down. They

584

won by patience, by tactics, by infiltration, getting inside knowledge, inside help, sneaking inside with the wooden horse of Troy, attacking from within, opening the gates from the inside.'

'That's exactly what we've been doing,' Conor said, looking up.

'Bullshit!' Tabitha said. 'How long have you been there? Less than two months and you've caused mayhem. You tried to knock down the castle walls in one go and now they're swarming out at you, mad as hell. You're not going to beat them this way, Conor, no way in Hell.'

'I'm going to beat them,' he said quietly. 'You'd better believe it.'

His mother looked at him in silence with an expression of such sadness on her face that it made Monty feel for her. 'That's what your daddy said. Those were his exact words.'

115

Thursday 8 December, 1994
Nikky Fitzhugh-Porter listened, eyes closed in an attempt to return to sleep, through the sequence of Gunn's morning ablutions. The ringing of his long, hard stream of urine; the vigorous shower; the scraping of his razor; the hiss of his deodorant spray. Footsteps; the rustle of clothes.

Then she was aware of him standing over her, could smell his indifferent Yardley cologne, felt the brief touch of his lips on her cheek.

'Call you later,' he said.

She heard the door open and close. A train rumbled by outside. She opened her eyes and squinted at the clock-radio. It was 6.45. Too early, much too early. She should wait until after nine, she decided, but in her agitated state, brain whirring, she was unable to go back to sleep. She passed the time by trying to concentrate her thoughts on the term paper she had done on Graham Greene and which she was scheduled to discuss with her tutor at midday.

At 7.30, unable to lie still, she got up and showered. When she towelled herself, the crummy bedsitting room felt even more cold and draughty than usual. Perhaps it was her nerves.

When she had dressed, she walked across the threadbare carpet to the door and peered out at the landing. No one there; no footsteps; he was an efficient man and she had never known him return home because he'd forgotten something, but even so she did not want the embarrassment of being caught.

Satisfied the coast was clear, she began a hasty search of the room: cupboards, drawers, careful not to disturb anything. Then she looked under the bed, and even under the carpet, but she found nothing. What she was looking for was stored safely away on the hard disk of his laptop computer which he had taken with him, as always, in his briefcase.

But there was a small copy of it still stored inside her own brain. Not much, not enough to provide her with any answers, but enough to provide plenty of concern.

The phone had rung at three o'clock that morning. Gunn had answered it, whispering, and she had pretended to be asleep. The conversation had been brief and Gunn had sounded furious.

Molloy? And the Bannerman woman? They're not? What the hell's going on over there? You have them nailed down? In a house? Can't you go in and neutralize? Why not? – is it a house or is it fucking Fort Knox?

Molloy and the Bannerman woman. Two names on the list that'd had black Christmas trees marked beside them on Gunn's computer. She went into the tiny kitchenette to make herself a cup of coffee. The atmosphere stank permanently of the fry-ups on which Gunn lived when she didn't cook for him. For some reason she found that the lack of fresh air stimulated her. She could picture that list clearly.

Charles Rowley had been on it. He had drowned in Hawaii, she had read in the Bendix Schere magazine. *Molloy* had been there too. And so had *Bannerman*.

The Bannerman woman's MG had been blown up by a

bomb. After what she had listened to during the night, she figured it did not need a degree in rocket science to work out that her soldier boy had been instructing someone to kill.

She left the bedsit for Ealing Broadway, and passed the next hour by having a café breakfast. Then she went off in search of a pay phone.

A woman's voice answered, brisk and efficient. 'New Scotland Yard.'

Nikky glanced warily through the windows of the booth. There was no need to be scared, she knew, there was no way that Gunn was suddenly going to appear. So why had she got the shakes? 'I want to report something suspicious,' she said.

'Could you give me a few details so I can put you through to the right section, please.'

'Yes,' Nikky said, her eyes scouring the passers-by and then the traffic. 'It's to do with the car bomb the night before last – and the pharmaceutical company Bendix Schere. I – I think that two of their employees may be in danger.'

'Can you hold one moment, please.'

There was silence for about thirty seconds, followed by a click, then a man's voice. 'Detective Superintendent Levine,' he said. 'How can I help you?'

116

Friday 9 December, 1994
In the mêlée surrounding the baggage carousels of Heathrow's Terminal One, no one noticed the trio who had been camped for three hours in one corner of the hall behind a clutch of phone booths.

Conor, wearing his Crombie coat over casual clothes, shifted his position, his backside numb from the hard shell of his Samsonite which he had been using as a seat, his concentration barely faltering as he worked furiously on his laptop. The power indicator was low and the display had already dimmed; he was on the last of his spare batteries and had maybe another thirty minutes' usage, if he was lucky.

Tabitha Donoghue, seated on her folded coat and leaning back against the wall was reading her way through a series of pamphlets and publications. Monty was trying to study a book on Satanism which Tabitha had lent her, but really she was keeping a steady eye on the crowds for anyone who might be watching them.

She felt more together today; she had phoned the Bendix Hammersmith Clinic a couple of hours back and tried to speak to her father without success. She had then asked for the doctor in charge of him, and had been told that Dr Seligman was off duty.

Seligman. She remembered the smoothie with the suntan who had all but ejected her from the Clinic when she had gone there to see Winston Smith. She had been tempted to tell the snooty receptionist that she was organizing a neurologist to see her father, and that she was going to have him transferred, but she didn't want to stir up a hornet's nest that might result in Bendix Schere killing her father in panic. She also had not wanted to stay on the line too long in case the call was traced.

Next she phoned the *Thames Valley Gazette* and asked for Hubert Wentworth. The receptionist informed her that he was not in. Deeply anxious, she had twice rung Wentworth's home number, but there was no answer.

She had also rung her own home number and checked her answering machine. There was a garbled message from Anna Sterling who sounded quite distraught. Monty had called her back immediately, but only got her machine. Had Anna had another scan? Had something hideous showed up on it? Or had she started the first manifestations of the virus that would eventually kill her?

Now she was watching Conor examine the small dictating machine he had bought at Dulles Airport last night, which he had used to make several back-up copies of her father's tape. He held it up to his ear, playing something and simultaneously typing as if making a transcript.

It was 11.30. By Tabitha's reckoning, the last flight from Washington should have landed a good couple of hours back.

Anyone watching for them in Arrivals should have given up by now. But even so they continued to wait, to improve their chances of leaving undetected by another hour.

Conor had said very little since yesterday morning; every time Monty had opened her eyes during her fitful sleep on the cramped airline seat, he had been hunched over his screen entering rows of digits, letters and instructions which she'd recognized as some form of programming code.

Conor had a plan.

She had a plan also. Her enthusiasm for it had waxed and waned, but it was still there. Sir Neil Rorke.

He was a universally respected figure. He sat on charities of which the Queen Mother and Prince Charles were patrons. He had been knighted by the Queen. He was the chairman of a government think tank and had been photographed with John Major. He would be appalled by what was going on in the company of which he was nominal chairman.

He would have to be, because he was the one constant to which her hopes kept returning. The one person with enough connections to be able to circumvent any influence that Levine had within the police. And surely he was the sort of man to put morality first? Regardless of what personal shareholding he might have in the company?

But before she went to Rorke, she needed Wentworth safely in place in a national newspaper's office with a copy of the tape and a printout of the Medici File. Which meant *her* plan was academic for now. So that left it all down to Conor.

He had stood up and was trying to catch her eye. 'OK,' he said. 'We're outta here.'

The three of them exchanged glances, then Conor hefted his suitcase on to a baggage trolley and left. Five minutes later, Tabitha Donoghue did the same. Monty waited a further five minutes, then wheeled her own suitcase out.

She went through the Green channel in the customs hall, and as she emerged Conor and his mother had already gone.

She made her own way by taxi to her pre-booked room at the Sheraton Skyline. She intended to register there for appearances only, and after that she was a free agent.

*

589

Thirty minutes later she was on the M4, driving a small maroon Rover hired from Thrifty Car Rental. It was a fine sunny day, unseasonably warm, she thought.

She felt a sudden sharp twinge in her head and for a moment was afraid that she was coming under attack again. Then it softened into a dull, throbbing ache. Tiredness, that was all, she thought. Probably a little dehydrated as well; her mouth was parched and she was longing for a drink. She settled for lowering her window. Soon be there now.

Hubert Wentworth's blue Nissan was on the carport in front of his garage and the sight of it relieved her; except that she was a little surprised to see that, at two o'clock in the afternoon, the living-room curtains were drawn. She pressed the bell; no response. She raised the brass knocker and rapped. No response.

Monty walked round to the back door. Two pints of milk stood by the step. She rapped loudly; then, on a whim, she tried the door handle. To her surprise, it opened.

Hesitant at intruding, nevertheless she stepped in and was surprised to hear conversation. She froze, listening. A man whose voice she did not recognize was expounding on human relationships and physical attraction. 'What we do not realize is quite how much has to do with our own parents. For instance, even the attraction in the colour of skin. We take for granted –'

Television, she twigged. She took a breath and called out: 'Mr Wentworth? Hello?' A used plate lay in the sink and some fresh tangerine peel sat on the draining board. He had to be here.

Puzzled, Monty tried the living room. It felt uncomfortably hot. The television was on, and all three bars of the electric fire were blazing, giving the impression someone had just popped out for a moment.

She closed the door and looked reluctantly up the stairs, nervousness setting in. After calling out a couple more times, she began climbing towards the gloomy landing.

'Mr Wentworth?' Her own voice sounded strange, higher than normal. She knocked on a door, then opened it slowly, fearfully. But the room was empty; just a small study. Then she knocked on the next door along, which was slightly ajar, and waited.

A stench of excrement was coming from this room.

Her stomach knotted tight, she pushed the door open a little further, holding her breath against the smell.

The first thing she noticed was a wooden chair lying on its side. Then she saw what at first, for one fleeting second, she was convinced must be a dummy. It was hanging from the ceiling light flex, a plastic bag over its head, its almost hairless torso naked apart from a lace brassiere, matching knickers, suspenders and fishnets.

Oh God in heaven, no! Please! A low whine of terror shimmied from her lips.

NO.

Oh God, Dr Crowe, she thought, you sick bastard. You sick, sick bastard.

Trying to compose herself, using every ounce of her reserves, Monty stepped forward and touched Hubert Wentworth's bare arm; it was stone cold and the flesh felt like putty.

Thinking fast, she backed out, ran downstairs to the phone and called 999. When the operator answered, she placed the receiver on the floor, saying nothing – aware from a magazine article a while back that if an emergency call was made and no one spoke, the police would be sent to investigate. Then she left the house by the same way she had entered.

'Hello? Hello, caller? Can you speak, caller? Hello, caller?'

117

Brighton, England. Friday 9 December, 1994
'Ah, Mr Eumenides!'

Conor smiled at the greeting as he entered the chaotic hi-tech offices of Minaret Internet. He recognized the man who was standing behind the desk in the bay window with his arm outstretched, and tried to recall his name.

Long, prematurely greying hair; a face like Nick Nolte after a long fast, green jacket over a purple t-shirt, silver '&' sign pinned to the left earlobe; glasses.

Andy Holyer, he remembered just as he shook hands. 'How are you, Andy?'

'OK.' He smiled. 'I like the Eumenides bit. The Furies, the merciless goddesses of vengeance, right?'

'Right.'

Andy Holyer tilted his head to one side in concentration. 'I think what I like most about those ladies is their concept of punishments that continue after death.' He pointed to a chair. 'Sit down, Bob – it is Bob, isn't it? Bob Frost?'

Through the window Conor could see the domed minarets of the Brighton Pavilion sparkling in the early afternoon sun. Down at the street, he could also see the Ford he had rented from Avis at the airport parked on double yellows. 'Yup, Bob Frost,' he said, repeating the name he'd given when he had opened the eMail account. He sat down and put his briefcase on his lap. 'Tell me something, do you guys have any kind of international connectivity facility here?'

'How do you mean exactly?'

'You have a working relationship with Internet access providers in other countries?'

'Well – I suppose you could call it that – I mean, sure, we communicate with quite a lot, regularly.'

'Where? The States? Europe? Asia?'

'All of those.' Andy Holyer shrugged. 'China, Russia – particularly Russia, there are some cool types there. If you speak Russian I can give you some terrific Web sites.' He sat down, tapped something on his keyboard, then twisted the monitor on his desk so that Conor could see it. The ball-shaped purple logo of the company had expanded into a rotating virtual globe. In almost every country on it, tiny lights winked. 'See those lights,' he said enthusiastically. 'Each one represents an Internet point-of-presence.'

He tapped his keyboard again. The globe disappeared and was replaced by a list of cities: Vienna; Moscow; Vladivostok;

St Petersburg; Paris; Cape Town; Warsaw; Hong Kong. The names were endless.

Conor pressed. 'From here, you could set me up with an Internet account in any of these cities?'

Holyer nodded. 'Be expensive, but we could do it. How many were you thinking of?'

'Two hundred.'

Holyer blinked. 'This is a joke, right?'

'I'm not joking. How fast could you do it?'

'Just accounts set up, yeah?'

'Just accounts.'

Holyer reached for his cigarettes. 'OK, look, no guarantees but I would guess a week to ten days.'

'Is it business that you'd like to have?'

'Sure, very much.'

Conor nodded. 'OK, here's the problem. I don't have ten days. I don't have a week. I appreciate the factor of varying time zones and all that, but I need everything up and running inside twenty-four hours.'

'All two hundred accounts?' Holyer asked in horror.

'All two hundred.'

118

London. Friday 9 December, 1994

Monty drove to Winston Smith's address in a daze, the image of Hubert Wentworth superimposed on her every thought.

Traffic thundered past. Cars, vans, lorries. Normality. Normal life. Friday afternoon. There were people out there who were living lives untouched by Bendix Schere, people who would soon be heading home to begin their weekends.

Not her father, she thought bitterly.

Not Hubert Wentworth.

She'd already tried ringing Rorke but had learned from his secretary that he was away from the office, spending a long weekend in the country. Hunting, shooting, fishing, she supposed bleakly. Well, those were three things she had a mind to put in hand too. And with any luck she was about to stock up on vital ammunition.

Second floor, she remembered as she reached the Albany Court low-rise an hour later and tackled the latticed metal steps, then made her way along the walkway to number 27.

Somehow she had to persuade Mrs Smith to open up, to tell her more. And maybe, she hoped, Winston might be back home.

She rang the bell and a few moments later a shadow moved behind the frosted glass. The door opened a few inches then stopped. Tired eyes, raw and bloodshot, stared from a sallow black face. There was a hint of recognition, but no welcome.

'Hello, Mrs Smith,' Monty said, alarmed by her appearance. 'I – how's Win –'

'Will you come in, please?' There was an urgency in the request and Monty responded to it by stepping into the tiny hallway immediately. Mrs Smith, supported by crutches, gestured her through into the living room.

When the older woman next spoke her soft voice had a tremble. 'You didn't hear, then, Miss Bannerman? My husband died on Monday.'

For Monty the news came as a shock, and she had to school herself to utter the right words. 'I'm sorry,' she said. 'I'm so sorry.'

There was an awkward silence, broken by the new widow. 'The funeral was yesterday. Just family. They cremated him. Strange, because he always wanted to be buried, not that. But the doctor who was with him in his last hours said he made it very clear he'd changed his mind. The nurse said so too.'

Cremated, Monty thought. Of course, don't want to risk an exhumation and forensic examination. No doubt that was Crowe's doing, she decided bitterly. 'There was no postmortem?'

'No, nothing like that.' Mrs Smith reached over to her mantelpiece and produced a white envelope as she spoke. 'But

594

there is something Winston said for *you* to have. I didn't know how I was going to get it to you.'

Monty took it with a frown. 'Thank you.'

There was an object inside, something thin, hard and flat; Monty wondered whether to open it in front of the bereaved woman or whether that would be distressing for her. She decided to wait until she was outside. She could see that Mrs Smith was making an unnatural effort to hold herself together simply because she had a visitor, and she knew she should go so that the poor woman did not have that extra strain.

Wordlessly, she put an arm around Mrs Smith's shoulder and wordlessly Mrs Smith acknowledged the gesture, both of them heading back to the front door where they parted solemnly.

When she was back in her hired car, Monty opened the mysterious envelope and removed a folded sheet of plain white paper.

Taped to it was a white plastic smart-card with a band of computer striping, identical in appearance to the one she had herself been issued by Bendix Schere. A short, undated note in shaky handwriting said:

Dear Ms Bannerman.

   The pin no. is 0626.

   The card will let you more places than your own. Anywhere in the building you wish to go. Even Room 101!

   All you got to do is look confident and nobody won't question you. My friend Roger is there Monday to Friday. 8 a.m. – 4 p.m. He will show you all you want to see. You can trust him. I am sorry I never had the courage myself.

   Winston Smith.

She dabbed away tears with the back of her hand and looked at the card, thinking hard.

Anywhere in the building you wish to go . . .

119

The pain struck as suddenly and savagely as it had before. Monty tore her hands from the steering wheel and clamped them to her head, pressing the sides of her skull, trying to crush all sensation. A horn blared behind her; blared again, longer, angry. Jammed in the Park Lane traffic, she jerked on the handbrake. This time it felt as though a huge insect was trapped inside her brain, swirling round, buzzing, trying to rip its way out with claws and mandible. Her vision blurred. Feeling a giddy wave of nausea, she had to open the door of the Rover and lean out, retching.

Gold cross.

Gold cross.

Tabitha had warned her that this could happen when Crowe tuned back into her, trying to locate her.

Gold cross.

Needed to visualize it at the base of her skull and in her solar plexus. She was close to her destination. Just had to fight the pain off until she could get there, Marble Arch was right ahead now, going to make it. Got to! The horn blared again.

Go to hell.

She closed her eyes, concentrated, two intersecting lines of gold; felt them there; felt the light radiating. The pain in her head was subsiding; she opened her eyes.

'You all right, lady? D'you need an ambulance?' A man was looking down at her; leather jacket, thick jumper.

A short distance behind him Monty could make out a white car. It had a box on the roof. A man in uniform was getting out. He was walking towards them, fast, urgent strides. A police officer. The sight of him panicked and galvanized her.

'No, I'm fine.' She slammed her door, rammed the car into gear and lurched forward; her head was clearing of its own accord, the buzzing had stopped. She looked anxiously in the mirror and could see the police car in the next lane, about three cars back.

Coming into Marble Arch, the traffic was thick but moving. She forced her way into the next lane, but the police car made no attempt to do the same. Then to her relief she saw it turn off. A couple of minutes later as she drove down Bayswater, she saw the stark grey edifice of the Royal Lancaster Hotel rising twenty storeys into the falling dusk.

She pulled up on the forecourt. Telling the doorman she would only be a couple of minutes, she hurried inside and up to the reception desk. Yes, the young woman told her, Mrs Robert Frost had checked in; she was in suite number 1111.

Monty went to a booth, picked up a house phone and asked to be put through to the suite. A moment later she heard Tabitha Donoghue's edgy voice. 'Where the hell are you, Montana?'

'I'm here, in the hotel. I'm coming up.'

'I don't know what's going on. Some kind of a sick joke . . . they put us on the *eleventh* floor!'

'Is that significant? I'm sorry – I – I don't understand –'

'My husband – Conor's father – don't you see? He fell from the eleventh floor. They've done this deliberately. I warned Conor; these people are too powerful for us. Whatever you do, don't come up here, Monty; it's too dangerous and I can't protect you.'

Monty knew a case of hysterics when she heard one. 'I'm on my way,' she insisted.

She raced across the foyer to the lifts. As she stepped out on the eleventh floor, she hurried down the corridor. 1103 . . . 1105 . . . 1107 . . . 1109 . . . 1111.

She rapped to gain entry and was greeted by a white-faced Tabitha Donoghue wearing a blue towelling bathrobe.

Monty pushed past her into a plush hall and saw Tabitha kneel and carefully straighten a line of what Monty assumed to be salt, on the floor.

'Where's Conor? Is he here?'

'No. But he phoned an hour ago from the hotel at the airport. He said he's going to have to work through the night. He asked how you got on – the newspaperman?'

'They've killed him.'

Tabitha looked despairing now. 'Yes, they'll kill everyone.

It's too strong here, Montana.' She was wringing her hands. 'We're too close to the source; it's beyond my powers to contain it.'

'You're just going to have to try.'

'It's not possible, Montana. Not without . . . months.'

'Months?' Monty repeated.

'Months – of working through rituals; we'd have to assemble a whole coven. We don't have enough energy with just the three of us. And I'm too out of practice.'

Monty dug her hands into her mackintosh pockets. 'Mrs Donoghue, we're dealing with a bunch of sick perverts and right now we just have to keep our nerve. I'm going down to park my car and sneak my bags up. Then I suggest we camp here for the night and wait for Conor. OK?'

She took the lift back down to the lobby, went out to the Rover, and pulled out into the crawling traffic, looking for the nearest car park. In Washington, Tabitha had seemed so calm and strong. Her present condition frightened Monty and she didn't want to leave her on her own for long.

She waited in line at the traffic lights just beyond the end of the hotel. When they turned green, she turned right along the rear façade of the Royal Lancaster, merging with the dense Bayswater Road traffic, stopping and starting.

Then, suddenly, with no warning, not even the flicker of a shadow, there was an ear-splitting bang on her roof. The car lurched sickeningly, the top pressing down on her head.

Startled, Monty saw that the front windscreen had sprung from its twisted frame and was sticking out over the bonnet like a jaw.

For a moment she wondered if a tree had fallen on to the car. Then her mouth flew open in a silent scream as she saw the female hand dangling in front of her eyes; each manicured finger displayed.

She scrabbled to open the door. It would not move. She tried harder, striking it with her shoulder, but still it would not move. A wide band of blood had started to slide down the window. Breathing in short, hard bursts, she scrambled across the passenger seat and got out of the door on that side.

Other people were getting out of their cars all around her, as if responding to a cue. Someone was pointing. A child was screaming.

At first Monty could only watch the shocked faces of everyone else, unable to find the courage to turn and follow their gaze. The whole of London seemed to have come to a halt. Then she did turn round, and every ounce of warmth drained from her flesh.

A half-naked body lay spread-eagled across the crumpled roof of her Rover, inadequately covered by a blue towelling dressing gown that had fallen obscenely open, exposing the wearer's backside and grotesquely twisted legs.

High above her, Monty could see the spidery cracks and a jagged hole in the wall of glass on the eleventh floor of Tabitha Donoghue's hotel. A new kind of fear, more intense and more chilling than anything she had ever experienced, slipped quietly inside her, like a ghost.

120

'Don't move her!' a woman called out. 'Nobody move her!'

A man in a herringbone coat jostled past Monty, blocking her view. 'I'm a doctor,' she heard him say. Then after a few moments he spoke again, more quietly. 'There's no pulse. Looks like the impact has snapped her neck.'

Monty backed away; everything was blurred. Had to get away, she thought. Before the police came; they would want her to go to the station and Levine might be waiting there.

She ran, handbag swinging from her arm, along the Bayswater pavement, her surroundings almost invisible to her. She reached Marble Arch panting hard, took the underpass, and ran on, up a teeming Oxford Street and all the way to Tottenham Court Road.

Something was drawing her along, pulling her to Great Russell Street and the gold and black gates of the British

Museum. She needed the British Library that lay within its colonnaded façade and she *had* to get there before it closed for the day.

'Hmmmn.' The librarian in the reading room dug his hands into his blazer pockets and jiggled some change in response to Monty's breathless request. 'What area of the occult?'

'Satanism.'

The word was absorbed without any visible reaction, and Monty was directed to a stack of bookshelves.

A quarter of an hour later, she had eight books which she lugged across the reading room and piled on an empty desk. The musty smell of old leather rose up to her as she opened the top volume: *An Illustrated History of Magik*. Its thick pages showed engravings of strange symbols, mummified corpses, creatures that were half human, half beast, and the eerie mask of a human skull wearing a bearskin wig: *I scare you, you scare me, I scare me, we scare ourselves*. She turned through these pages then stopped at a passage headed 'Working Spells'.

From earliest times, magic appeared to be a more economical means of destroying an enemy than combat . . . She read on through a range of spells and magical weapons; through chapters headed, 'Ritual Murders', 'Blood and Sacrifice', 'The Cabbala', 'Alchemy and Alchemists'.

Here she stopped and began reading the text: *According to the alchemists, the world is not completely separate from its Creator, since it possesses a 'living soul', the* 'Anima mundi' *which is linked to Him 'in the same manner as a woman to a man'. This 'spirit of the world' is a remnant of the ancient notion of the Mother Goddess and the cult of Isis in Egypt.*

Monty frowned. *Alchemy.* Was it possible that the chief executive of a modern international pharmaceutical giant was really dabbling in the ancient practice of alchemy?

Over the page in a chapter headed 'The Devil Incarnate', a hideous black and white photograph caught her eye, making her shudder. It was a goat's head mask, with curled horns and a flowing beard, atop a human form in a white robe. The caption beneath said it all.

Magicians, particularly in the West, like to call up the devil, especially where they are concerned with 'black' magic or sorcery. Those who practise 'black' magic like to believe that the earthly form assumed by the devil is that of the goat.

But it was the next photograph that really leapt out at Monty. It was a mask in the form of a frog's head, complete with glistening skin, a smug, sinister smile and an expression of pure evil in a pair of hideously bulging eyes. The man whose head it concealed was wearing a white, richly embroidered robe. Seated in an ornate chair, he was holding a strange, curved object in his hands. The photograph was captioned:

The Baphomet – Goat of Mendez – is not considered the only symbol of the devil by occult practitioners. Some cults represent him in the carnation of other beasts, as the illustration here shows, of Daniel Judd (better known as **Theutus***), Grand Magister of the New International Satanic Brotherhood.*

As Monty looked back at the photograph she trembled – the eyes of the frog seemed to be focusing on her, coming out from the page towards her. Almost involuntarily, she shut the book to get away from them, and reached for the next volume on her pile: *From the Crusades to the Internet: The Black Agenda, A History of Modern Satanism.* She began reading the Introduction.

Since the uncovering of the Dutch secret intellectual society of the 11th Century – The Illuminate – conspiracy theories have thrived. Is there a small group of people, an international intelligentsia, who secretly manipulate and control the world? And who have been doing so for the past eight hundred years? And if so, who are the members?

One day in the year 1622, the inhabitants of Paris woke to find their city walls covered with posters bearing the following message: 'We, deputies of the principal College of the Brethren of the Rosy Cross (Rosicrucians), are amongst you in this town, visibly and invisibly, through the grace of the Most High to whom the hearts of all just men are turned. We are here in order to save our fellow men from the error of death.' This was considered by most people to be a joke, but we should remember that the Rosicrucian Brethren were credited with possession of the following secrets: the transmutation of metals, the prolongation of life, knowledge of what is happening in distant places, and the application of the occult sciences to the discovery of even the most deeply hidden objects.

Eliminate the term 'occult', and you find yourself confronted by the powers that modern science possesses or is on the way to possessing . . . According to the legend, already firmly established at that time, the Rosicrucians claimed that man's power over nature and himself would become limitless, that immortality and control of all natural forces were within his grasp, and that he would be able to know everything that happened in the universe . . .

Let us consider this notion of a secret international society composed of those of the highest intelligence, spiritually transformed by the profundity of their knowledge, desirous of reserving the right to use their scientific discoveries at the right moment, or else to conceal them for a number of years – such a notion is both an extremely ancient and an ultra-modern one. I would even dare to state that, on a certain level, such a society exists today.

Though there is nothing to prove that a secret Rosicrucian society existed in the seventeenth century, we have every reason to believe that there is a society of this nature today and that there is bound to be one in the future.

Scientific research has reached the stage where we can envisage a form of genetic engineering that will 'improve' living beings, including man himself. The aim of the alchemist's research was the transmutation of the operator himself; perhaps it is also that of the modern scientist.

After this passage, Monty flicked through several pages on ritual magic. Halfway, her attention was arrested. It was the frog's head again.

This time it was a colour picture, and the robed figure wearing the mask was standing on the rim of an ornate pentacle on the floor of a temple. On the wall behind his head black candles burned in sconces. The caption beneath simply said:

Theutus. (Daniel Judd.) Grand Magister of the New International Satanic Brotherhood.

The photograph was one among several; others showed an altar; a naked man and woman, each wearing crowns, the woman holding a chalice; a sinister chiaroscuro image of Aleister Crowley holding his magic wand; a group of women standing in a desert in chiffon gowns, amid steaming cauldrons on tall tripods, their arms raised; a naked man straddling a naked woman inside a circle; and there was a still from the film of *The Devil Rides Out*.

Monty turned to the book's index and looked up 'Daniel Judd'. There were three references, and she located the first.

Daniel Judd (Theutus) was already an adept in the New Order of Satan when he was initiated into the New International Brotherhood of Satan – probably the most secretive of all the Satanic covens in existence today, and whose roots go back to the past century and possibly further. It is known that Hitler, Himmler and several other leading Nazis belonged to lodges of this coven. Its spread today is a matter for speculation.

For years rumour has claimed that politicians, high-ranking clergymen, powerful businessmen – as well as members of the police and the armed forces – are numbered among its initiates. But no such evidence exists. There are even rumours of a Satanic Vatican, variously located in the desert of Saudi Arabia or the foothills of the Andes.

Daniel Judd, the son of fanatical religious parents against whom he rebelled, was recruited into the coven when in his teens. He then had a spectacular rise during the late 1950s and early 60s, becoming its United Kingdom Grand Magister in 1968 at the age of only thirty-four. Strangely, he cannot be traced beyond 1969, the year in which he published The Master Grimoire of Power and Success Through Satanic Workings. *By his thirty-fifth birthday, he seems to have disappeared off the face of the earth. Judd, or 'Theutus' as he preferred to be called, claimed that he had magical powers and could make himself invisible, or could shape-change, at will. Rumours abound that he transformed himself into a beast or a fowl, that he went to another planet, that he dematerialized and became part of the energy force of the cosmos, and, more prosaically and even less probable, that he abandoned his occult life and went into industry.*

Monty checked back to the picture she had already seen of Daniel Judd wearing his frog mask. Then she began to search for the second index reference, on page 138. To her surprise, she found the page was missing. Looking more closely, she could see a sliver of it remaining; the page itself had been carefully cut out. By a souvenir hunter? she wondered.

The frog mask gripped her, despite herself. Like a lot of people, Monty was slightly drawn to the thing that most scared her. Daniel Judd? Theutus? She had come here to learn more about occult workings, to find out more on what Tabitha Donoghue had tried to teach her, to protect herself and Conor. But some instinct told her not to ignore Judd. Or was it just the coincidence of the frog mask?

She looked at her six remaining volumes and realized that one of them was Judd's own oeuvre: *The Master Grimoire of Power and Success Through Satanic Workings*. She began reading the author's introduction.

Since the dawn of time Occult Masters – Adepts – have possessed the power to influence people, to change events and to command whatever they desired to happen. Many of these men and women have been quite ordinary looking, possessing no special physical qualities, and attracting no undue attention towards themselves. It was said of them that 'Things seem always to go their way.' But whilst most of these Adepts have led lives far removed from the spotlight, some have been among the most famous personages of all time. To the well-informed reader it will be no news that much of human history has been shaped behind the scenes by the secret machinations – good and evil – of the very powerful men and women of the magickal arts.

Nothing happens 'by chance!'

Things that mystify, baffle or terrify us are always caused by someone or something. This is not only axiomatic of magick, but of every true science also. With Ceremonial Magick you can learn to control your destiny, rather than being controlled by it. This choice is now about to be yours in the pages of this grimoire.

On the back cover there was only a woodcut of a frog's head inside a circle, with a small pentagram above. So Monty turned to the contents page and found a list of illustrations, including several of the author.

When she looked up the first one she saw that it had been removed. The next illustration was also missing, and the next. Every single page which carried an illustration of Daniel Judd, except for one, where he was wearing his frog mask, had been cut out.

Increasingly puzzled, she began searching through the indexes of the other books she'd found. Judd's name was in most of them, and in three, references were given for photographs of him. She searched for them with no success.

Every single page that should have shown a photograph of Daniel Judd's face had been removed with surgical precision.

A shadow fell across Monty and she looked up, startled. The duty librarian who had helped her earlier was looking down at her. 'I'm sorry,' he said. 'It's seven now, and we're finished for the night.'

Monty nodded reluctantly. 'Would you like these –?'

'Just leave them on the desk. They'll be collected in the morning. Are you going to want to come back tomorrow and look at any again?'

'Yes – I – might do that.'

'I'll have them kept out. Come and see me when you get here.'

Monty thanked him and made for the deserted lobby. Her boots clicked on the marble floor as she walked, bringing back memories. She had always loved the British Museum, it had been her favourite expedition as a child and she had spent many afternoons exploring it with her father. But right now, like the whole world outside, it felt alien and menacing.

The security guard pushed the door open for her, and the cold draught of the night air struck her face. Then she stopped in her tracks at the top of the Museum's steps. Saw the white car speeding in through the gates, a blue light on the roof and fluorescent stripes down the side.

It pulled up just beyond the bottom of the steps, the rear door sprang open and the interior light came on, revealing he neat, close-cropped profile of Detective Superintendent Levine.

121

Monty stood, panic-stricken. Make a break for it across the courtyard? But she didn't know how fast Levine could run. She made a snap decision. Better odds, not good, but better, she calculated. She turned and hammered on the door, signalling frantically to the guard who had just let her out. 'Forgotten something!' she mouthed.

He opened up again, and she barged past him. 'Sorry! I left something really important!' Then instead of heading back to the Library, she turned left and sprinted up the wide steps to the first floor of the British Museum.

'Hey!' she heard him call. 'Hey, m'am, it's closed. The Museum's shut!'

She kept going, up into the darkness, reached the top of the stairs and saw the shadowy statue of a kneeling man and beast that she remembered marked the entrance to Prehistory and Roman Britain.

She ran forward into the first of the Roman galleries; it was pitch dark here, too black to see, just the faintest shimmer from a dim, overhead light source. She slowed to a walk; the only sound she could hear now was the click of her own heels and her breathing.

Keep going straight, she thought, trying desperately to remember the geography of the place. After Roman Britain she should be entering the Early Medieval room, and then she could turn left into the long gallery that led to Ancient Iran.

Instead she stopped dead with a jarring thump that knocked all the wind out of her. She had walked straight into a display cabinet, she realized, feeling its contours, edging around it. There was a shout behind her now, quite dose. Then the beam of a flashlight streaked past her and for a brief moment she could see ahead, and get her bearings.

She broke into a run; keeping as best she could to the left-hand side, avoiding the centre displays. The beam flashed again, striking a Roman head on a plinth directly in her path.

She dodged sideways, then was suddenly dazzled by the beam of another flashlight shining straight into her eyes.

The beam lowered and as she blinked she could make out the silhouette of the guard blocking her path. Before he had a chance to speak, she yelled urgently at him: 'Did you see them? Two men? They just broke into one of the offices; I chased them this way, they must be here somewhere!' Monty was gambling and she knew it.

'Heck, no – No I didn't!'

'Give me your torch a sec.'

As he held it out, with slight reluctance, she snatched it and raced on. With the beam guiding her, progress was far easier and she tore at full sprint down through Ancient Iran into Babylon. Then the Royal Tombs of Ur. As she rounded the Tombs, another guard appeared at the far end of the gallery and she could hear an alarm siren. 'That way!' she shouted at the guard. 'They went that way!'

'No one came past me, miss.'

'They must have done!' She ran on again, without waiting for his further response; then in her panic she missed the right turn-off she needed and found herself among the Egyptian mummies. Silent bandaged figures stared at her from behind glinting glass. She spun round, disorientated. Twin torch beams were jigging down towards her. She raced back at them, saw the open entrance into Coptic Art, tore through, then down the staircase at the far end into the small North Entrance lobby. A guard was standing by the door.

'Quick!' she shouted at him. 'There's been a break-in in Oriental Antiquities. The police are outside, let them in!'

He hurriedly unlocked the door, pushed it open, and peered out expectantly into the night. Monty squeezed past him, looked quickly both ways, then rocketed along the pavement of Montague Place, across the dark, terraced square of Bedford Place and into the bustle of Tottenham Court Road.

She saw a free taxi, hailed it frantically and clambered into the back, pulling the door shut with a slam; then fell into the seat panting so hard she was unable to talk for a moment.

The driver slid back the glass partition. 'Where to?'

She coughed, gulped down more air. *Anywhere but here*, she

thought. 'Just drive on for a couple of minutes, then I'll tell you.'

She checked through the rear window, but with the thick wedge of traffic behind it was impossible to tell if she was being followed. Ahead they were fast approaching Euston Road. The Bendix Building was less than a mile away to the right. She leaned forward. 'Turn left at the Euston Road,' she said, wanting to put as much distance between herself and the building as possible.

Then she leaned back and closed her eyes, thinking hard. Tabitha Donoghue had been through all the protection protocols with her. Purifications. Salt. Lumiel square. Visualization. Incantations. But there was one thing she had not done; in fact, she had poured scorn on it. Right now, Monty decided, anything was worth trying.

She addressed the driver once more. 'Do you by any chance know a church that stays open all night?'

122

Saturday 10 December, 1994
It's an alms house. They have a soup kitchen in the crypt for the homeless. Never shuts.

That's what Monty's taxi driver had said, and that's how she'd come to spend the night in the house of God. With the intermittent company of a ponytailed clergyman who had worked his way round all the troubled souls sleeping on his pews, and prayed with them. But come morning, her father was still in the wrong hands, and the mother of the man she loved was still dead.

She admired the grand entrance enviously. She'd taken a fast train to Tunbridge Wells from Charing Cross and then travelled by taxi to the Kent village where Sir Neil Rorke had his country residence. The gates were open and a gravel driveway lined with laurel bushes curved away towards the house, which was not visible from the road. At this stage she chose to make her approach by foot, and as she rounded the first bend, the house appeared about a hundred yards ahead, behind a formal grass circle in the driveway – in the centre of which lay an ornamental pond.

It was just as she'd expected from the photo-feature she'd seen a couple of weeks back in *Hello!*, an imposing, if rather cold-looking property. The front façade was Georgian, square and handsomely proportioned, with grey walls, a slate roof and an elegant white porch. An immaculate black Range Rover was casually parked to one side, and Monty skirted it.

As she walked up to the porch, she heard frenetic barking coming from inside the house. The sky had darkened in the last few minutes, and an icy gust tossed flecks of sleet around her. She was all too conscious that her presence was uninvited, as she pressed the bell.

Instantly the barking intensified, then she heard a familiar baritone voice booming: 'Bartholomew! Simeon! Sit! Sit!'

The door opened and she saw Sir Neil Rorke himself, in a silk paisley dressing gown and black leather slippers, semi-kneeling, holding the collars of two huge, frisky, mastiff puppies, and struggling to keep his balance.

For one fleeting instant there was an expression of complete hostility as if he was angered at having the privacy of his weekend disturbed, Monty assumed. She suddenly remembered one of the captions she had read in *Hello!*:

'With his business and charity commitments, my husband spends most of the year travelling. We try to keep our country home as our one sanctuary.'

But before she could fully register it, all traces of hostility had vanished and Rorke's eyes twinkled with what seemed like genuine delight.

'Miss Bannerman! What a lovely surprise!'

'I'm really sorry to disturb you at the weekend, Sir Neil.'

'Not at all; always delighted to see you, my dear. Come in, please.' The dogs began barking again, and he bellowed at them to be quiet. 'You'll have to forgive my appearance – I

609

was just having a bath and change – got to attend a local Christmas charity.'

The hall had a flagstone floor scattered with Persian rugs, oak-panelled walls hung with tapestries, oil paintings and gilded mirrors, and a wide, elegant staircase leading up from it. He closed the door and released the dogs, which jumped up excitedly at Monty, almost bowling her over.

'*Quiet!*' he bellowed again. 'Bartholomew! Simeon! Baskets!'

The two dogs seemed to take this as a cue for a game and both leapt up at him simultaneously, catching him off-balance. The rug skidded under him and he made a lurch for the nearest secure object – a bentwood hatstand. As he leaned against it, he stretched an arm back to smoothe his wavy hair. The action caused his dressing gown to slip off one shoulder for a moment and Monty saw, to her surprise, a line of numbers and letters there, about a quarter of an inch high and two inches wide; the skin around them was scarred, as if they had been branded on.

'Bloody dogs!' Rorke was saying, making light of the incident. He had straightened his dressing gown, seemingly oblivious of what had just happened. 'Tea, coffee – or a glass of sherry?'

'Coffee would be great.'

He led her through into a room she also recognized from the *Hello!* feature, a fine period drawing room, elegantly furnished, with rows of Christmas cards on the marble mantelpiece. She thought again about the strange markings on Rorke's shoulder, puzzling; then realized, with a chill, what it must be: concentration camp branding.

She sat on a sofa. The Nazis had branded all the Jews. Rorke must be Jewish. Yes, she thought, he could be with his dark wavy hair and his heavy face, there were definitely Semitic traces in his features. But was he old enough to have been interned? He must be in his late fifties, early sixties. Yes, he could have been, as a child.

She was distracted by the ping of a telephone, as if a receiver had just been lifted or replaced. But she had to focus on the way she planned to tackle Sir Neil. She removed the dictating machine from her handbag and checked that the tape was wound back to the start.

A few minutes later Rorke reappeared, apologizing for the absence of his wife. He had changed into a suit and striped shirt and was carrying a tray laden with coffee and biscuits.

He put the tray down, raising his eyebrows at the dictating machine, then eased himself on to the opposite sofa, leaned forward and pushed a coffee cup, then milk and sugar, towards his guest. 'Right, my dear,' he spoke good-humouredly. 'Are you going to interview me?'

She smiled thinly, feeling very nervous. 'No. There's something on this tape I want you to hear. I'm afraid it's going to shock you.'

Rorke listened intently to the tape and to Monty's story, which she made as detailed as she could. He looked increasingly incredulous, but also receptive. Monty had the feeling throughout that it was almost as if he was waiting for proof of something he already knew.

He stood up decisively when he had heard everything. Instead of wasting time expressing his horror, he was ready for action. 'The immediate priorities are to find your father, to protect you and Mr Molloy, and then to see what we can do about your Anna Sterling, and all the other women on that evil list.

'One of my closest friends is Sir Patrick Norton, Chief Commissioner of the Metropolitan Police. Whoever this little squirt Levine is, he can't have that much influence. Obviously we need to move quickly; if you're being watched, they'll know you're here now. I'm going to call Patrick at home immediately. I want to see Crowe under arrest by the end of today. And that's just for starters!'

As she watched Rorke stalk out of the room, Monty suddenly felt sorry for him, and strangely guilty at having been the one who'd had to break the grim news to him about the company he chaired.

She heard the ping of the phone again, then, less than a minute later, a second ping. That had been a short conversation, she thought. Then she realized that the number might have been engaged and he was trying again. She slipped the dictating machine back into her handbag, feeling drained. She heard the phone ping a couple more times.

Rorke came back down after ten minutes; he seemed to have aged ten years, and he had a coat slung over his arm. 'Right, let's get moving. Sir Patrick's arranged for the Chief Constable of Kent to be here in person in about five minutes. He's going to take us to the Bendix Hammersmith with an escort.'

Monty was impressed by the level of Rorke's contacts; the big cogs were turning now. If only she'd done this earlier, she chastised herself, instead of trusting that creep Levine.

'Your lunch?' she said suddenly. It was 1.30. 'Aren't you expected?'

'I phoned,' he said curtly. 'Dealt with it.'

After that there was an awkward silence between them; the situation had gone beyond words, Monty acknowledged.

The doorbell rang and generated fits of barking which sounded muffled now, as if the dogs had been locked in somewhere. Rorke stood up to walk out into the hall, and Monty followed. Through the window, she could see the front half of a black Mercedes with smoked windows, waiting in the drive.

Rorke opened the front door with a flourish and gestured for Monty to go first. She took one step forward and stopped dead.

Doctors Crowe and Seligman were standing inside the porch, shoulder to shoulder, completely blocking it.

She spun round in terror, looking to Rorke for help. His face was a mask of cold, white fury. A second later she realized his anger was directed not at the two men, but at herself.

'You snivelling, filthy, trouble-making little bitch! How dare you behave the way you have?'

She felt a sharp prick in her thigh, like a wasp sting. She had time to notice that Rorke's face suddenly looked oddly distorted, as if it was melting. Then her legs started to buckle.

123

Conor crawled the rented Ford up Euston Road towards the Bendix Building. He sat in a cocoon of numbed grief.

Dead. His mother was dead.

His ears rang with the echo of her words on the night before he had left Washington. *Think again while you still have the chance.*

If he'd heeded her, Bendix Schere would have gone on, unchecked. And he would not have met Monty.

But his mother would still be alive.

And where the hell was Monty? In that bastard Crowe's clutches?

He could see the windowless monolith of the Bendix Building rising ahead to the right, and with it rose all the hatred he had been harbouring for twenty-six years.

He swung the car into the Bendix lot, pulled up at the security gate and handed his pass through the window.

The guard peered at the windscreen. 'Where's the tag?'

'Tag?'

'Your parking ID tag. Can't bring an unauthorized car in.'

'Fuck you!' Conor exploded. 'This is a rental – my car's in dock.'

The guard closed the window, sat back behind his desk and picked up a mug of coffee. In front of Conor, instead of the customary green light, a red light flashed accompanied by words on a screen: **ENTRY REFUSED. REVERSE AT ONCE. YOU ARE TRESPASSING**.

Conor had to reverse back into the main road, and park on a meter around the corner. As he walked back he noticed the tail of a black Mercedes disappearing up the ramp of the car park that Monty had told him was owned by the company.

The automatic doors slid open and he walked into the white marble atrium and up to the security desk, which was manned by just one guard, a black man in his fifties. Conor almost mistook him for Winston Smith, Monty's friend.

'Hi. I need to contact Dr Crowe urgently. I guess he's not in, right?'

The guard's voice was neutral, neither pleasant nor hostile. 'Sometimes come in Saturday mornings but I ain't seen him today.'

Conor continued awkwardly. 'Look this is something that can't wait – do you have an emergency number for him? I'm one of his patent attorneys.'

'Got identification?'

Conor showed him his card.

The guard nodded and with some reluctance said: 'Got a couple of numbers I can try. Ain't going to be too pleased to be disturbed at the weekend.'

'It's an emergency.'

The American was unshaven, his eyes were bloodshot and his clothes were dishevelled. The guard looked at him and wondered if he'd been drinking. *Mr Conor Molloy.* That rang a bell. A definite ding-dong. He glanced down at his computer workstation and was about to tap the name in, when to his shock, he saw it was already up on the screen.

He swallowed and gave the American a nervous smile. Of course! The name had been up there all day. *Mr Conor Molloy.* He smiled again, in a way that he hoped was reassuring, then, trying to look as nonchalant as possible, he rang the number of Major Gunn's mobile phone.

124

There was an eerie stillness inside the Mercedes, which was accentuated by the artificial darkness from the black windows. The rich smell of leather filled Monty's nostrils, as the car glided silently through the London traffic.

Sandwiched on the back seat between Crowe and Seligman, her body felt set in cement. For a time she must have been asleep or unconscious, she realized, but she was awake again now, and confused. They were driving up Park Lane. *Came here last night,* she thought, and tried to remember why. They drove around Marble Arch. Of course. They were heading down to the Marylebone Road, then the Euston Road.

Her fear returned, quietly but insistently, like the scrabbling of tiny paws of a creature trapped inside her chest. The traffic and the buildings and people slid past the windows, a sinister, unfamiliar London dark as a nuclear winter.

Need to wave, she thought. Need to shout, to attract someone's attention. But no one could see or hear her in here.

They were driving along Euston Road now, past Euston Station. The Bendix Building rose up on their right, but instead of moving into the right-hand lane the Mercedes moved over to the left and began to slow. It turned into a wide road lined on both sides with high-rise office buildings, accelerated briefly, then swung sharp left into the entrance of the multi-storey car park.

She stared in terror at the orange and black sign on the wall: LRG CAR PARKS. Then at the bold red sign by the lowered barrier that was now rising: FULL. CONTRACT PARKING ONLY.

The Mercedes rose up the steep, curving concrete ramp; she heard the wheels rattle over a loose drain; saw the attendants' booth ahead, recognized an unsmiling face inside it. In front of a second barrier the chauffeur reached out, pushed a card into the pod beside him.

The car park was far larger than she had imagined; most of the bays were empty. Of course. It was Saturday. The Mercedes made a sharp right then stopped beside a bank of lifts.

The chauffeur opened Crowe's door and held it for him. Seligman indicated for her to follow him, and she slid across the seat, her body heavy and leaden.

Crowe slid a card into a grill in front of the lifts and keyed in a sequence of numbers on a touch pad. Immediately one of the doors slid open and he waited for Monty to step in, then followed her with Seligman. They sank rapidly downwards then stopped. The door opened to reveal a grey marble lobby presided over by two uniformed security guards behind a console.

Barely acknowledging them, Crowe walked to a heavy metal door, pushed in his smart-card and keyed in his pin number. The door slid open on to a long, empty, brightly lit corridor.

She followed Crowe, too groggy to do anything but obey.

You snivelling, filthy, trouble-making little bitch!

Those words weren't an act; they came from the heart. The mistake was hers; she had again gone against Conor's advice. But still she could not totally believe it of Sir Neil Rorke; surely not him, too?

She glanced at Seligman, who was walking along at her elbow. Behind him the corridor was empty. A camera winked silently. Escape was one option: she could make a dash for the lift; but she wouldn't have enough time, not unless she knocked Seligman and Crowe out – and with what? The only weapon she had was her soft leather bag that she was clutching tightly. And besides, she thought suddenly, they might be taking her to her father, or to Conor.

They might also, she knew, be taking her somewhere to kill her.

They passed a row of vending machines then several laboratories, most with their doors shut. The walls were bare of notice boards and warning posters, which added to the sinister anonymity of the place.

They reached another metal door at the end of the corridor. Crowe again inserted his card and keyed in his pin number, and opened it on to a concrete stairwell that disappeared into blackness. 'Just one flight. We might as well walk.'

It was icy-cold, and dimly lit. Monty peered around her into the gloom and frowned. The stairs led down only, not up.

'The fire escape interconnects only the basement floors, Miss Bannerman,' Crowe said, answering her unspoken question. His voice echoed slightly. 'No fire could spread from here to the upstairs floors: there are nine metres of concrete separating us.'

'So how would people get out in a fire?'

'The entire area is covered with a halon gas system. Any fire would be extinguished instantly.'

Monty stared at him. Halon gas extinguishers smothered the fire by releasing an inert gas, forcing out the oxygen. They were highly efficient – but lethal: an effective system would remove all the oxygen in a room in seconds, asphyxiating anyone present.

'Isn't that dangerous for your staff, Dr Crowe?'

'It concentrates their minds.' He gave her a thin smile, then walked on down the stairs.

On the floor below, Monty followed Crowe into a small anteroom. A security guard with dark rings beneath his eyes and blotchy, discoloured skin stood behind a small console and a bank of television monitors. Crowe strode past him, through a locked steel door and along a wide corridor that reeked of disinfectant. She began to notice another, familiar stench that always made her uncomfortable. Damp animal hair and straw. They had come into the animal house.

She followed Crowe into a dim, cavernous room lit by ultraviolet lights. The smell of animals was much stronger here. A console of monitors and computer equipment ran down the centre and glass-fronted cages lined both sides of the room floor to ceiling.

They walked past cages of dogs, monkeys and rodents, many of them wired up to monitoring equipment, then Crowe stopped by a window and beckoned to her.

She could see that it was an incubator; inside lay a tiny inert form, intubated and on a ventilator, electrodes taped to its shaven head and cannula lines from neck, wrist and groin; a catheter ran from its tiny penis. The creature's eyes rolled wildly in their sockets. A hairless monkey, Monty thought at first, then, as she looked closer, she realized with shock and revulsion that it was a human baby boy.

She stepped back, reeling. 'What – are you –?'

'Impressive, don't you think?' Crowe said.

'It's *human*!'

With a broad sweep of his arm he gestured at the walls of incubators. 'These are all human, Miss Bannerman.'

Monty approached the windows cautiously. Floor to ceiling, racked six deep on either side of the room, were rows and rows of babies, naked and identically wired. She stared goggle-eyed at Crowe, then Seligman. 'Are these clones? Is that what you're doing here?' Her voice came out as a whisper.

'Not exactly, Miss Bannerman,' Seligman said smoothly. 'These have all been reared *in vitro*.' He smiled. 'There's no need to be so shocked. They are only *technically* human beings, after all.'

'*Technically*?'

'They're brain dead, kept on life support. We deal with that at birth. None of them will ever experience human consciousness; they're no different from a vegetable – or perhaps something of a lower order – such as a sea anemone.'

She pressed her face against a window, her insides heaving with silent fury, then turned back, barely able to control herself. 'You can't do this,' she managed. 'You don't have – the – right.'

Crowe's tongue flicked momentarily between his thin, ruby lips. 'We get dangerously precious ideas about rights and humanity, Miss Bannerman. We have to adapt for our needs. If we don't, we become extinct.'

She thought, suddenly, of the Bendix Schere television commercial in which Sir Neil Rorke was pictured in an African village hugging the little children. 'BENDIX SCHERE – THE WORLD'S MOST CARING COMPANY.'

She looked at another baby. 'Who works here, Dr Crowe? What kind of staff do you have here? Do they just accept this?'

'Some are very well paid, Miss Bannerman. And some are not in a position to leave.'

She turned back to him. 'What do you mean?'

He smiled. 'You cannot always buy loyalty in staff. Sometimes you have to create it.'

'Create?' Then it dawned on her. Winston Smith. They hadn't been experimenting on the man at all. They had simply turned him into a terrified, medication-dependent slave. Like the rest of the security staff here, doubtless.

'You seem to be distressed, Miss Bannerman. I think we should continue our tour. Perhaps you will find our aquarium more – ah – to your taste.'

They took the lift down one floor. Somehow she was going to get out of here. There had to be *someone* more powerful than Rorke and these men who could see what was going on and tear the company to pieces. She closed her eyes, praying that her father and Conor were all right. Conor had a plan. But his mother had been part of that plan.

To her surprise, as they stepped out into a dingy corridor, there was no security guard evident, just a closed-circuit camera.

A short way down the corridor was a door with a small glass porthole and thick rubber flanges. Crowe inserted his card, keyed in his number and the door swung open with a hiss. They went through into a cramped airlock chamber. As the door closed behind them, Crowe said, 'You live in the countryside – I presume you are interested in wildlife, Miss Bannerman?'

'Wildlife?'

'Mother Nature? Our great provider?' He pushed open the second door into almost total darkness; a blast of foul-smelling, damp, warm air engulfed them. It carried the smell of stagnant water and pondweed.

Monty followed Crowe on to a slatted metal grid that stretched ahead of them and to either side, the size of a football pitch. Banks of infra-red lights hung from the ceiling, pumping out a weak glow and an intense heat. She looked down and saw inky water, then pinpricks of reflected light. Light reflecting from the eyes of hundreds of invisible creatures below them.

Something jumped right beside her and she shrieked, stepped backwards on to Seligman's feet.

It jumped again. Then again, straight at her.

'Get it away!' she shouted, stumbling backwards, pushing the doctor out of the way.

It jumped again, bounced off her chest, fell to the floor. Then again, something cold and slimy brushing her hand.

'Ribbettt . . . ribbbettt . . . ribbbettttttt . . .'

It jumped again, thudded against her skirt as if angered by her intrusion.

She flapped it away, windmilling her arms. 'No, uggg – no!'

It jumped up, struck her face, wet, rough, slimy skin. She batted it away frantically with her hand. 'Help me!' she screamed. 'Please help me!'

Crowe turned. He ducked down sharply, snatched out both his hands then lifted them slowly up in front of her eyes.

'What's the matter, Miss Bannerman?'

She stared, transfixed, at the shiny creature he was clutching between his fingers, its legs flexing, its mouth opening and closing, its hooded eyes blinking.

Her eyes were becoming accustomed to the gloom, and she could see Crowe's prize more distinctly every second. A shudder rippled through her: it was the size of a cat.

'You don't like frogs at all, do you, Miss Bannerman?' Crowe's teeth glinted. 'I wonder why not? This little chap is such a good friend to us. In twenty years' time he will provide one of Bendix Schere's most profitable drugs.' He held the frog out towards her and she cowered back, pressing against the chamber door.

'Please,' she said. 'Please, don't.' All around she could hear the hollow moans, croaks, occasional splashes.

Crowe inched the frog towards her. 'This creature is a miracle of Mother Nature, Miss Bannerman. She is one of the rarest creatures in the world. *Rheobatrachus silus* – the Gastric Brooding Frog. We have the largest hatchery in the world here, right in this room – over four thousand of them – and we're building a new one this very minute near Slough, where we'll breed one hundred thousand.'

He moved the frog closer as he spoke, savouring her terror. 'The human stomach is a wonderful thing, is it not? Think what it digests: starches, minerals, all kinds of proteins. Have you ever wondered why it is that our acidic juices don't eat away our own stomachs? An interesting question, wouldn't you agree, Miss Bannerman?'

She stared in silence.

'Well, I'll tell you. The stomach walls are made up of unique cells that are impervious to ammonia and carbon dioxide.

These cells are all that stand between us and a painful death from auto-digestion. Clever, isn't it? Which brings me to our little friend here.' He stroked the frog tenderly. 'Most living creatures either lay eggs or bring up their young in their wombs. Not this lady. She brings up her babies in her stomach. So how do they survive? Why are they not digested by her gastric acids?'

Monty swallowed, perspiration streaming down her body.

'You see,' Crowe continued, 'she releases a substance that inhibits acid secretion immediately after the eggs are ingested, and this persists throughout brooding. We have identified the human genes responsible for producing the cells that are impervious to ammonia and carbon dioxide. With your father's help, we plan to introduce the genes into the foetus through Maternox. When the babies grow up and reach puberty, the hormonal change in their bodies will activate the genes and they will cease producing these cells and start digesting their own stomach linings. Without corrective medication for the rest of their lives, they will die painful deaths.'

'And – and – y-y-you are going to m-manufacture the treatment using these frogs,' she stammered.

Crowe lifted the frog away from her face. 'Correct, Miss Bannerman,' he said with a look of profound pleasure on his face. 'Absolutely correct! The ailment will be diagnosed by doctors as a new kind of stomach ulcer, brought on by the stresses of modern living.' He smiled again. 'We already have our drug designed and waiting, but we shan't even file the parents for another twenty years, just around the time when the ailment will first start to appear.'

He stroked the frog's forehead again, as if it was a prized pet. 'Did you know, Miss Bannerman, that the frog and the human being share one very similar organ?'

Monty said nothing.

'The eye. You did not know that the frog and the human eye are very similar? We believe that if a human being had his – or her – eyes replaced with those of a frog, they would still be able to see very adequately. And, of course, vice versa.'

Crowe looked down at the frog and then suddenly stared

very pointedly at Monty. 'I expect you are wondering why Dr Seligman has come along with us. Let me explain. Although he is now our Director of Research and Development, Dr Seligman trained originally in Switzerland as an eye surgeon. He has carried out a great deal of research into the human eye and he believes genetic engineering may eventually enable many forms of blindness to be cured. Of course, this requires much lab work, does it not, Dr Seligman?'

Seligman inclined his head.

Crowe continued his gentle stroking. 'I am unclear, Miss Bannerman, exactly how much information on the Medici Trials you or your father or Mr Molloy have in your possession and to whom you have passed it on. I don't need the information now, you understand, not this minute. We are going to leave you in peace for a while to think about what you would like to tell us.' He paused for a moment. 'I am sure that when you have – ah – helped us with our experiments, your father will become far more willing to assist than he has been to date. In the meantime, I can think of no more appropriate place for you to contemplate how it will feel to see the world through the eyes of a frog. That's if the operation is successful, of course.'

He turned and lobbed the frog into the darkness.

'Please don't leave me in here,' Monty pleaded. 'Not here. I can tell you what I know – but it's very little.'

Crowe studied her face thoughtfully for a moment, then rested his hands gently on her shoulders. 'I want you to think very carefully about every little detail of what you know and whom you have told. You have caused us a lot of anxiety, my dear, a very great deal.' He smiled.

Then, brutally, he kicked her legs away from under her and pushed her backwards. She fell with an agonizing jar on to the metal floor, letting out a gasp of pain and shock.

There was a sharp click as the door closed on the two men. She was alone with the croaking of the frogs and the splashing of water. The croaking seemed to be getting louder, more frogs joining in as it rose to a crescendo. In her terror it sounded as if the frogs were massing around her for an attack.

Then she remembered something.

125

Conor paced restlessly around the atrium. Monty was here; he could feel her fear in his bones. He looked at his watch: zero minus four hours and seven minutes. *Worst case scenario.* It was in place and the clock was running. If all else failed, he would have done what he came here to do. But at what price?

He stared angrily at the security guard behind the desk. Come on, come on. He clenched his hands in anguish and frustration. Don't let it be too late, please, please, don't let it be too late. He walked back to the desk. 'What the hell's happening?'

The guard flinched, said nervously, 'Any minute, sir; should be on the telephone any minute.'

Fifteen minutes had elapsed since Conor had arrived. Still plenty of time. Enough to get the message across; not enough for them to do anything about it. They would have to release Monty, they would have no choice.

'OK, you go see him now. You take the Directors' express lift.'

Conor turned, startled by the guard's voice, and stood up. 'Directors' express? He's in the building? In his office?'

'Yes, sir, seem that way.'

Conor looked at him belligerently. Dr Crowe had been here all the time?

'Got to let you in.' The guard walked alongside Conor down to the lift and slipped his card into the panel. The doors opened immediately. Conor stepped inside and was surprised when instead of going up, as he had been expecting, the lift began to descend, dropping rapidly for some seconds. Then it stopped and the doors opened on to a small anteroom with an unoccupied security desk with a closed steel door beyond it. He stepped out and the doors shut behind him. Monty was down here; he could feel her even more strongly now.

He waited some moments then looked again at the desk. It had a built-in keyboard and a monitor that was switched off. He tapped a few keys but nothing happened, then something on the ceiling caught his eye and he looked up. It was an orange strobe light beside a complex arrangement of fire sprinkler nozzles. Beside them was a warning plate:

DANGER. HALON GAS AUTOMATIC EXTINGUISHER SYSTEM. WHEN LIGHT FLASHES EVACUATE ROOM INSTANTLY. KLAXON INDICATES FIFTEEN SECONDS TO ACTIVATION.

They had to be paranoid about fires to have that kind of system in a room used by people rather than machines, he reflected.

Minutes passed. His anxiety increasing, he tried the steel door behind the security desk, inserting his card once, twice, but the door's red touch pad – something he had not encountered on the upper floors – would not operate with his code.

He sat down on the edge of the desk. Ten minutes passed. Twenty. What the hell was going on?

Time was starting to run short. He paced the room desperately, shouting at the walls, 'Dr Crowe, read your eMail! Don't fool around with me, you don't have time! *Read your goddamned eMail!*'

126

'*Soldier, I don't like this game any more.*'

Gunn chewed his thumbnail.

'*Soldier, I mean it. I really don't like this game any more.*'

Nikky's face, framed by her long red hair. Looking up at him as she lay naked, strapped down on to the altar six floors beneath the atrium.

That moment when her expression had changed, when she had realized it wasn't a kinky sex game and they really were going to cut her heart from her chest while she was still alive; he would carry that moment with him to his deathbed.

Now they had to deal with the Bannerman woman.

Flanked by two guards, he stepped out of the lift and walked along the corridor to the hatchery. Damnit, he didn't like this game any more either. Seals, Rowley, the reporter Zandra Wollerton – they'd got what they deserved. But Nikky was different. Hell, he'd really loved her.

And now the Bannerman woman. *You're losing it,* he thought. *Losing your fucking nerve.* He went through the airlock into the hatchery, into the cloying humid air, the stink of pondweed, the echoing croaks, his feet changing on the slatted metal grid, and stared into the infra-red darkness.

She wasn't there.

127

Monty watched the three men, through the slats of the louvred door, come running back down the corridor towards the hatchery. The one in the suit was speaking urgently into a two-way radio, but his words were drowned by the din of the huge pump pressed against her.

All you got to do is look confident . . .

The suit and one of the guards took the lift; the other retraced his steps slowly up and down the corridor and stopped right in front of her, staring at the slats. She could see his face clearly; thick, rubbery lips, hooded eyes, mean.

Monty braced herself, beyond fear now, gripped with just one desperate thought: survival. Somehow she was going to do it, get out of here, tell the world.

The guard gripped the handle. Her heart banged in her chest. Surprise was her only weapon; if she kicked him hard between the legs, snatched at his eyes with her fingers, she might have a chance –

He shook the door, testing to make sure it was properly shut, then walked away. Stunned with disbelief, she remained motionless.

Several minutes passed and he did not return. *All you got to do is look confident* . . .

Easy to say. She gripped the thin plastic card Winston Smith had given her. His note had said it would open every door in the building and on this one, at least, it had worked; it had got her out of the hatchery.

Cautiously, she pushed open the door and peered out. The corridor was empty. She looked around her: no signposts, arrows, area names. A television camera pointed in her direction. Got to move, keep moving, get away.

Roger. The name on Winston Smith's note. *My friend Roger is there Monday to Friday, 8 a.m.–4 p.m. He will show you all you want to see. You can trust him. I am sorry I never had the courage myself.* If she could find Roger maybe he could help her, get her out. Except it was Saturday today, she realized. But there was still a chance. She remembered that Winston Smith's shifts seemed to change randomly.

Bearings. Get my bearings. She tried to calculate what floor she was now on. The lift was an option, but risky; it could stop at any floor and there would be a camera in it. Best to stay with the corridors and the stairs. And she might just find Roger.

She scanned the corridor again. A clicking sound was coming from the left and she hurried in that direction, hopes rising, then stopped, disappointed to see only a rest area with washrooms, drinks vending machines, and a table and chairs. It was the hot drinks machine that was making the clicking sound.

She checked out the washrooms in case there was a concealed exit beyond them, but could find nothing, and ran back down the corridor.

A few yards on the corridor dog-legged to the right, and as she rounded it, she saw to her relief a steel door with a keypad. She slid the card in carefully, then tapped out the pin number Winston Smith had given her. 0626. The lock clicked and the tiny red flashing light turned green.

She passed through the door, into the concrete stairwell. Her eyes darted nervously up into the gloom above her, then down. There was just one flight below her and she could see clearly where it ended, at another door and a blank wall.

A sharp crack rang out, making her jump. She spun round and saw the door closing and locking behind her. She looked up, and was relieved to see no signs of life. Was there a hiding place here? But she could see no recesses, or closets.

She paused, trying to collect her thoughts. Got to go up, got to work her way upwards. Then she froze as a door opened two levels above. Saw a shadow; heard urgent voices.

No time to get the card back in. She fled down the stairs, winding round and round, then crouched in the darkness at the bottom and listened, praying they weren't going to come down here.

Footsteps descended then stopped just above her. There was a sharp click, then silence. She breathed out but stayed crouched, peering upwards, until she was sure they had really gone.

A couple of cigarette butts and a discarded polystyrene cup lay on the concrete floor in front of her; she found the sight of the butts oddly reassuring, as if it was a secret signal that there were rebels to the Bendix creed down here. Then she slipped her card into the slot, keyed in the numbers, and tentatively pushed the door.

It opened into a small anteroom, with a small console behind which sat an elderly, black security guard, who looked up, straight at her.

She froze.

Then she heard more footsteps coming down the stairwell above her. In desperation she lunged into the room. The guard was of a similar age to Winston Smith, his hair greying and the skin of his emaciated face blotched with large patches of red scales. There was something in the way he looked at her, with kindness not hostility, that made her know, instantly, who he was. 'May I see your identity, please, madam?' he said.

Glancing nervously at the door behind her, she tore Winston Smith's letter from her handbag and handed it to him. He unfolded it, read it and thrust it back at her with a shaking hand. He looked quickly up at the ceiling then leaned towards her and whispered, 'I can't help you. I want to but I can't. It's not possible.' His eyes went again to the ceiling, widening with fear.

She followed his stare up to the television camera and panic rose inside her. There was a door right behind him. She had to go through it. 'Roger, Winston Smith is dead. They could have cured him but they didn't, they killed him. They could make you better but instead they give you drugs to keep you bad. Please help me get out of here. Let me go through. Tell them you didn't see me.'

The door behind him burst open. Two guards came in, the one she had seen through the slats and another, followed by the suit. There was a loud click as the door automatically locked behind them.

128

'I trust you are comfortable, Dr Bannerman?'

A drip line still ran from Dick Bannerman's wrist, but he was no longer intubated and was breathing unaided. He was aware that during the night he had been moved, in very doped state, from the Bendix Hammersmith Clinic to this small, sparsely furnished and windowless room.

He was awake and alert, although his body felt leaden and it was an effort to raise an arm a few inches or flex his fingers. He slowly rotated his head towards the door and saw Dr Crowe standing there, dressed in green scrubs, a surgical mask hanging below his chin.

'Where the hell am I?'

'I wouldn't clutter your head with details of geography, Dr Bannerman. You have more important matters to consider.' Crowe closed the door and walked to the bed. 'I would have preferred it not to be this way; one rarely gets the best out of people by threatening them, but sometimes there is no alternative. Do we understand each other?'

Bannerman eyed him levelly. 'I don't think you understand me at all, Crowe. You can do anything you want to me, but I won't help you or your stinking company one iota. Is that clear?'

The Chief Executive inclined his head. 'I think you might change your mind.' He turned and looked pointedly at a television set in the corner of the room and said, 'You see, Dr Bannerman, it's not *you* who we're going to hurt.'

He switched on the television. An operating theatre appeared on the screen. A gurney was being wheeled in by two people in scrubs. They moved it into position beneath the massive octopus lamp, pulled the brake lever, which retracted the wheels, then stepped out of sight.

As they did so, Dick Bannerman could see very clearly that it was his daughter lying on the gurney. She was restrained by leather straps around her legs, arms and neck. The camera zoomed in, as if for his sole benefit, to show in full close-up the stark terror on her face.

'We'll talk later, Dr Bannerman,' Crowe said. 'Give you a chance to think things over.'

The door closed and he was gone.

Conor stared in desperation at his watch. The bargaining time he had calculated was fast running out. His knuckles were raw from pounding the walls and he brought them to his mouth, sucked them, tasted the coppery tang of blood.

The door opened. A guard came in holding a gun. 'Dr Crowe would like you to see something, Mr Molloy,' he said, with a smirk.

'I have to speak to Dr Crowe,' Conor said. 'I have to speak with him right away. Can you take me to him? I *have* to speak with him.'

The guard shook his head. 'Sorry, no can do.' Keeping the gun pointed at Conor, he inserted a card into the workstation and with one finger tapped four numbers on the keys. Moments later the monitor came to life. Swinging his gaze from Conor to the keyboard and back to Conor, he tapped more keys. There was a pause, then on the screen appeared a clear image of the inside of an operating theatre. Conor saw Monty lying strapped to a gurney, with several people in scrubs gathering around her.

Conor gaped in horror. 'What's going on? What the hell's going on?'

629

'Dr Crowe thought you'd like to see this,' the guard said smugly.

He stared at the screen again. He could see the terror in Monty's face. It was difficult to make out the other people. Crowe – he could see Crowe adjusting his mask over his mouth and nose, and beside him a smooth-looking man pulling on surgical gloves. 'What in God's name are they doing to her?'

The camera zoomed in close on to Monty's face, then pulled back to a wide angle. Something caught his eye on the ceiling, right at the top of the monitor, only just in frame; an orange warning light and nozzles of a fire extinguisher system, the same as in here. Halon gas.

He stared at the guard, straight into his eyes. The guard returned his stare smugly. Conor stared harder, harder, concentrating, desperately concentrating in spite of his blind panic, concentrating, pouring all his energies into those two round beads. Kept on staring. The guard's smile was slackening, his jaw dropping. The hand holding the gun began to lower. The guard's eyes were glazing now, losing their focus, he was drifting. Drifting . . .

Now!

Conor leapt at him, grabbed the wrist of his gun hand with his left hand, heard a bang as the weapon discharged, slammed the knuckles of his right fist as hard as he could into the guard's nose and fell against the desk with him, bringing his knee sharply up between the man's legs. He punched him again, then again, gripped his gun and jerked his arm down on the edge of the desk, sending the gun clattering to the floor.

The guard flailed with his free arm, catching Conor's ear a glancing blow. In blind fury Conor grabbed him by the hair and smashed his face into the keyboard. 'Where is she?' He smashed the guard's face down again. 'Where is she, you motherfucker?' He smashed it down again, then again.

The guard screamed, 'Please don't! Stop. Please stop.'

Conor twisted him round by his hair. 'Where is she? Tell me *now*!' He jammed a hand into the guard's groin, squeezed hard.

The guard howled in agony.

'Where? Tell me or I'll rip your fucking balls off.'

'Le – level two.'

Conor squeezed again.

'L-l-lift. Lift. Level two.' The man was panting and blood trickled from his mouth and nose. 'T-turn right. Sign. Signed.'

Without letting go of his hair, Conor pulled the card out of the slot on the workstation and held it up in front of his nose. 'Do I use this?'

The guard nodded.

'Pin number? What's the fucking pin number?'

'Zero six two six.'

'You're shitting me and I'm coming back for you, you understand that?'

The guard signalled with his eyes.

Conor gripped the card in his teeth, pulled the guard's head as far back as he could, then slammed his fist up into the base of his chin. The guard's eyes rolled. Conor released his hair and he fell motionless on to the floor.

Conor knelt and grabbed the gun and raced to the lift.

129

The room smelled of antiseptic. Monty blinked in the glare of the lamp overhead. Her arms and legs felt as if they were being gripped in a vice. She tried to raise her head, to turn it, but that, too, was clamped tight.

She stared at the tiled walls, terror rising in her throat. A group of people in scrubs were gathered to one side with their backs to her, occupied with something they were blocking from her view. They turned occasionally to glance at her, and only their eyes were visible above their masks. Crowe. Seligman. Linda Farmer, whom she had met only once, the Director of Medical Information – and another woman she did not recognize.

There was a clatter of an instrument. She saw Seligman hold a tiny bloody object up to the light in long-handled forceps and examine it carefully. After some moments he lowered the object and raised a second. There was a murmured exchange of words, then several members of the group turned again and looked at Monty.

She began praying, silently, desperately. She tried visualizing a gold cross; thought of the Lumiel square in her handbag. Then, despairingly, of Tabitha Donoghue's smashed body on her car roof.

The woman she had not seen before was walking towards her, slowly and carefully, holding a metal tray out in front of her as if she were presenting an offertory to an altar. A large frog crawled pitifully across the tray. Where its eyes should have been she saw raw and bloody empty sockets.

Monty's throat muscles went into spasm. She gurgled in terror.

The woman moved the frog closer, so close it almost touched Monty's nose. Shaking, gulping at air, she could smell the creature, could see the loose skin beneath its neck pulsing as it breathed. She shut her eyes tightly. They could not make her watch, she still had that freedom.

When she opened her eyes again, the woman was moving away. Monty swallowed. Moments later the woman returned with another tray, which she again presented close to Monty for inspection. Neatly arranged on a bed of crushed ice were the frog's bloody eyeballs.

Her insides corkscrewed in panic. She jerked her wrists, her legs, her neck against the straps.

Someone wheeled a rattling trolley up to her. The group were gathering around her now. Seligman leaned over her, rummaging in the instrument tray, selecting first a small, gleaming scalpel which he raised in one hand and inspected, then an instrument with a long, thin handle and a flat round steel scoop on the end.

'Nooooooooooooo!' she screamed.

Seligman rotated the scoop between his finger and thumb. Light glinted off it.

'No!' she said. 'Please, no. Anything. Anything you want. Not my eyes, not –'

'I will be quite quick,' Seligman said to her, with no trace of

632

emotion at all. 'It is very important with the eyes to be quick, because the optical nerve endings die so very fast.' Then his expression hardened. 'The frog is a cold-blooded creature, Miss Bannerman. Cold-blooded creatures feel very little pain; did you know that?'

She stared back at him, voiceless now.

'I did not use any anaesthetic on the frog, so I am not going to waste precious time using any on you.' He reached up and made a small adjustment to the angle of the lamp.

Then Crowe's voice: 'Have you thought of anything you would like to tell us before Dr Seligman begins, Miss Bannerman? Or shall we remove one eye first and see how things go?'

'Nothing,' she gulped out. 'There's nothing. We – I – only spoke to Mr Wentworth – Zandra Wollerton; no one else. I didn't talk to anyone else and they – they are dead. I didn't, I promise, I swear.' She knew she was incoherent now.

'What about Mr Molloy? To whom has he talked, Miss Bannerman?'

'I don't know.'

'I think you do.'

'Please. I don't. I really don't. I haven't – seen him – not since – I don't know where he is.'

There was a brief silence, then Crowe said, harshly: 'Take the first eye out. We'll talk to her again when you've finished. A little pain might concentrate her mind.'

The woman who had presented the trays leaned over Monty, pressed her fingers deep into the base of Monty's throat, at the top of the strap, forcing her head back. Another pair of hands pressed down on her forehead.

Panting in terror, Monty could only watch as Seligman's gloved fingers came down towards her right eye. She closed her lids, squeezed them tightly shut, fighting with all her strength to resist the pressure of his fingers as he tried to prise them open.

She was losing. First her lashes, then the rubber of his gloves rubbed painfully against her eyeball; then she saw a watery haze of light as he succeeded, the pressure from his fingers relentless, as if he were used to this, did it every day of the week. He had the lids peeled back now, wide open.

'Retractor,' he said calmly.

Gloved fingers appeared holding a tiny wire hinge with rubber edges. Monty saw it coming towards her eye, felt the acute discomfort as it was inserted, forcing her lids wider.

'Right,' Seligman said. 'I'm now going to cut through the conjunctiva.'

No, please no, you are not going to do this. Please no. Monty stared into Seligman's eyes, pleading desperately, pleading with all her heart. His brow furrowed in deep concentration as he leaned forward, until his masked face was inches from her own. A flash of light bounced off the gleaming blade of the scalpel as it came slowly, rock steadily, down, then blurred out of focus a fraction of a second before it made contact with her flesh.

130

Level 2 . . . turn right . . . signed . . .

Conor barged out of the lift before the doors were fully open and found himself in an empty anteroom identical to the one he had just left.

He slid the card into the door, keyed in the number, pushed it open, then looked, wildly, both ways down the corridor, holding the gun out in front of him. The corridor was deserted. He sprinted down and after twenty yards he hit an intersection with a battery of signs. He tore down to the left, towards the door marked Theatre 1. Then on. Another ten yards.

Theatre 2.

He pressed his face to the glass porthole in the door. They were in there. Green scrubs clustering around the gurney. The surgeon bending over Monty . . .

The key card fell from his shaking hand as he pushed it against the slot. He knelt, tried to get his nails under it, but it stayed stuck to the floor as if held by a vacuum. *Jesus, come on!*

Frantically he prised it off the floor then rammed it into the slot and hammered in the numbers. The light flashed green and he charged the door with his elbow. It did not budge. He tried again and it bucked but did not yield.

Was it locked from the inside? He pushed again, then pulled and it opened immediately, a large, heavy door on a weighted spring. Someone looked round, a woman he did not recognize.

'*Don't touch her!*' he screamed, swinging the gun at all of them. 'Move away from her. Move away from her or I'll shoot! Move! I'll shoot, I'll goddamn shoot! Move!'

For an instant everything froze, as if a pause button had been hit on a video.

Crowe spun round. Conor saw the cold grey eyes above the mask and in that instant he wanted more than anything on earth to pull the trigger. He had never fired a gun in his life but he could do it now, do it easily. But the bullets might go astray, might hit Monty. *Monty. Had to get Monty out.*

All eyes were on him.

'Move! I said move!' The gowned figures started moving, backing away. He swung the gun again, watching them like a hawk, then fixed his stare on the surgeon. 'Drop the scalpel.' He jerked the gun forward, gripped it with both hands, aimed it squarely at the surgeon. The scalpel clattered on to the tiled floor.

He remained in this position, half in and half out of the doorway. He glanced over his shoulder. Corridor still empty. He was thinking clearly surprisingly clearly and he felt calm. He was in command. One step at a time now. He caught Monty's eye.

'Hands on top of your heads, all of you, put them up.'

They obeyed.

Glanced behind him again. Nothing. Looked up at the ceiling, at the television camera, directly above him at the fire extinguisher system, back at the camera. Other people would be watching, reacting. No time to waste, not one second.

'You!' He yelled at a gowned woman, pointed the gun squarely at her. 'Push that trolley here. The rest of you stay still; anyone moves they're dead.'

The hatred was exploding inside him. The hatred he had been storing for years. Had to release it, had to, before it destroyed him. The woman was pushing the gurney towards him now, wheeling Monty towards him, bringing Monty back to him. Her face was white but she looked OK, not hurt, she was OK.

Got to stay calm. Come this far. Hold it, got to hold it.

Come on, Crowe. Make my day. Give me the excuse to shoot you. God, I want to shoot you, you goddamned piece of shit.

He stared down the barrel at Crowe. Seligman. Linda Farmer. Short, hard, bangs of anger exploded inside him like firecrackers. He felt the energy surging from him. He stared at the octopus lamp. Crowe. Seligman. Farmer. The lamp again. There was a flicker. A bulb blew. Then another.

Crowe was staring hard at him. Conor quickly looked away. *Got you, you bastard, I'm not letting you go, oh no.*

He stared back at the octopus. Felt the energy shooting from him like rockets. The remaining bulbs exploded simultaneously. Flames sheeted out of the lamp and thick acrid smoke rose from it, spread out across the ceiling. The lamp was on fire, burning, crackling. Conor smelled the acrid reek of the smoke. Then a streak of brilliant orange light suddenly flitted across the room.

It was followed by another.

Then another.

Conor's eyes shot to the ceiling. The rotating warning light of the halon gas extinguisher system had come on. Crowe and Seligman looked up in alarm and took a step forward, towards the door.

'Back!' yelled Conor. 'Get back!' Flashes of orange streaked their faces as the mirror in the lamp housing revolved. One end of the gurney was within reach now. Conor grabbed the metal rim behind Monty's head with one hand, and with the other jabbed the gun at the woman in scrubs who was staring, petrified, holding the gurney, her eyes moving from him to the light and back again.

Conor yanked the trolley back towards him, then rammed it hard forward, smashing it into the woman's midriff, sending her backwards on to the hard floor.

Then six loud klaxon bleeps sounded. They were followed by a digitized warning voice:

'FIRE EXTINGUISHER HAS BEEN ACTIVATED. EVACUATE THIS ROOM IMMEDIATELY. FIRE EXTINGUISHER HAS BEEN ACTIVATED. EVACUATE THIS ROOM IMMEDIATELY.'

Panicking, Crowe, Seligman and Farmer all moved forward.

Conor threw a glance at the flashing light and screamed, 'Don't move! Don't move another goddamned inch!' Swinging the gun hard on them, he moved backwards through the door, hauling the gurney into the corridor and rolling it aside to let the door swing shut. The instant the lock clicked home he rammed one end of the gurney into the door, swung the other end across the corridor and wedged it against the wall, barely giving Monty a second glance. It was a perfect fit. No way that door was going to open.

A warning light flashed on the outside wall. Monty was staring at him in shock.

The digitized voice was still audible. 'EVACUATE THE ROOM. EVACUATE THE ROOM. TEN SECONDS TO ACTIVATION. NINE . . . EIGHT . . . SEVEN . . .'

There was frantic pounding on the door. He saw a fist hammering on the porthole, trying to punch through the glass.

'FIVE . . . FOUR . . .'

Crowe's masked face pressed against the glass. Their eyes locked. Conor felt the venom, the hatred, burning through the glass. Felt Crowe willing him, felt the power drawing him like a magnet. Drawing him towards the door.

'THREE . . . TWO . . .'

He tried to look away but could not. Tried desperately to break away from the grip of those eyes. Imagined a gold cross. It dissolved. Imagine another. That melted into black liquid. His hand went to the edge of the gurney. The door was shaking as if a battering ram was pounding it. Tried to look away. Saw only Crowe's grey eyes, felt their pull, willing him to open the door. His head was bursting and he felt nauseous. The gun fell from his hand.

Gold cross.

Gold cross.

Crowe was speaking to him now through the glass. 'Move the gurney, Mr Molloy. This isn't the way to carry on! We can deal with this in a gentlemanly way. Man to man.' Crowe was suddenly his best friend in the world and he wondered why he hadn't realized that before and why he was trying to hurt him now. Why, he *loved* his best friend . . .

He turned and put both hands on the gurney, saw Monty frantically shaking her head, then caught Crowe's stare again through the window. No. This wasn't right. He thought of his father. Saw the huge black bird hanging motionless in the sky, its wings outstretched. Saw it hit the ground and jerk its head sharply up and stare straight at him.

The way Crowe was staring at him now.

Thought of his mother. Stared back into those grey eyes. *No. No way, no –*

There was a piercing banshee scream.

Crowe's face disappeared. The light through the porthole dimmed. Conor heard a tremendous rush of air. He pressed his face to the glass. A snowstorm was blowing. It was the halon gas forcing out the oxygen, dropping the temperature to below zero, turning all the vapour to ice.

He peered through the glass. The four people inside looked as if they were performing a ritual dance, ripping away their masks, mouths open, cheeks sucked in, eyes unnaturally wide in shock and fear.

The woman he had knocked down was lurching across the floor, pounding her chest with her fists, her face shrivelled like a deflating balloon. She stumbled and fell, pummelling the tiles with her hands and feet.

Linda Farmer was ducking and lifting her head, her face a contorted mask of desperation. Seligman, all composure gone, was stomping round and round in a tiny circle, his body buckled, maniacally jigging his balled fists up and down.

Crowe's face reappeared at the window, blocking it, mouthing frantically to Conor. Conor turned away, looked at Monty and leaned forward, blocking her view of the porthole. There was more pounding on the door. He waited until it stopped.

638

When he turned back Crowe was still there, a hideous marionette with a purple face, bulging eyes and veins pushing out of his forehead. He was shaking as if plugged into an electrical socket, frantically trying to communicate with Conor. Conor turned away again.

'What's happening?' Monty said.

Conor pressed his hand against her cheek and said nothing. He waited a good half-minute, watching the corridor in both directions, before turning back to the porthole. Crowe's face had gone.

He looked through. Crowe lay on the floor just beyond the door, curled up, choking and shaking violently, still staring up through the glass. Dr Linda Farmer, Seligman and the other woman lay contorted, convulsing, arms outstretched towards the door, eyes bulging and sightless.

'Conor!'

He turned as he registered the alarm in Monty's voice. Two guards were racing down the corridor. The gun. Where the hell was the gun? He saw it on the floor, ducked down, grabbed it, then threw himself across Monty, trying to shield her, waving the gun so they could see it clearly. 'Stop!' he yelled.

They halted, two nervous-looking men in their late fifties, and backed away, raising their hands.

'Right!' he yelled. 'Now listen to me! I want Sir Neil Rorke on the end of a phone line. Right now, right this minute, do you understand?'

'Conor –' Monty tried to interrupt.

'You hear me? One of you stays here with us and the other goes and finds Sir Neil. I don't care where the hell he is or what he's doing –'

'Conor!'

He glanced down at Monty, the urgency in her voice reaching through to him; she was staring at the corridor behind him. He saw a shadow leap along the wall and a split second later felt an explosion inside his head.

131

The gun flew from Conor's hand. As he slumped sideways he dimly saw it spinning on the floor beyond his reach on the other side of the gurney. An arm clamped around his throat; his neck was jerked violently up, his legs were kicked away and he was brought crashing to the floor on his back.

A moment later someone was on top of him, a burly guard he did not recognize. He heard footsteps. Shouting. Someone yelled: 'Move that trolley, move that fucking trolley! Open the door, get the fucking door open!'

Dazed, Conor struggled to free himself, but his arms were battened down by the guard's knees. Then he saw the muzzle of a handgun, inches from his face.

'I can't move it!' someone shouted. 'It's stuck! Jesus, it's wedged tight, gimme a hand, get out of the fucking way!'

The guard climbed slowly off him, keeping the gun on his face. 'Stand up. Quick.'

Conor staggered to his feet and lurched sideways, colliding with the wall. Guards were appearing from all directions. Two of them were frantically pushing and pulling at the gurney. Conor was relieved to see it still had not budged; the pressure from the halon gas in the operating theatre would be forcing the door outwards, jamming the gurney even harder.

'Lift it!' one of them shouted. 'Lift it from beneath! C'mon!'

'Get the fucking woman off it!'

They tore off the straps and tipped Monty on to the floor, then climbed beneath and tried to push it upwards. It still did not budge. Monty crawled on to her knees, white and shaken. Conor moved towards her but the guard jabbed him away with his gun.

A hard-looking man in a suit appeared around the corner at the end of the corridor, walking rapidly, jacket open, tie flapping. Conor recognized him instantly: Major Gunn, Director of Security. Then, following a yard behind, he saw the unmistakable figure of Rorke, looking highly agitated.

With a loud metallic scrape, the gurney finally swung free.

One of the guards inserted a card, tapped the keypad, then pulled open the door. Conor felt a powerful blast of cold air. Rorke charged through into the theatre. Gunn, pausing for a second to stare at Monty and then Conor, followed him.

Conor exchanged a glance with Monty. She was shaken, but on her feet. She looked fine. Half a dozen guards now blocked any possible escape path in either direction.

There was a long silence. He stared at the partially open operating theatre door. There were more footsteps; two men raced down the corridor dressed in lab coats, one carrying a large black bag. They swept through the open theatre door.

'How you feeling?' Conor asked Monty.

'Shut it,' the guard said, jabbing the gun at him. 'I don't want a word from you. Not one word from either of you.'

Conor looked at him. 'I need to speak with Sir Neil –'

The guard raised the gun and tightened his grip. Conor said nothing more.

Ten minutes passed. Then the theatre door opened wide and Rorke came out, ashen faced. Gunn followed him. Rorke looked at Monty, then Conor, then turned to Gunn, and said, in a quavering voice: 'Take that creep somewhere and shoot him. And that little bitch – and her father. They've done enough damage. Get rid of them.'

Gunn shot a glance at Conor, then turned to the Chairman. 'With respect, sir, I think we do need them.' He met Conor's eyes.

Conor took his cue. 'Sir Neil,' he said, more calmly than he felt, 'I sent Dr Crowe an eMail, but I don't think he read it. I think you'd better have a look at it – you –'

'I don't care what you think, Mr Molloy. I'm not interested in what you have to say.'

'Dr Crowe did read it,' Gunn said, curtly. 'He copied it to me. I've spent the past hour and a half working on it.' He turned to Rorke. 'I'm afraid you're going to have to listen to him, Sir Neil. If you don't, in three hours' time you won't have a company.'

Gunn closed the door of the Chairman's office, and Rorke, white with shock and anger, switched on his computer terminal, logged on then stepped aside. Gunn tapped a command on the keyboard. Conor stood beside them and watched impassively as the words came up on the screen. Monty watched, fascinated.

x-Sender: eumenides@mailhost.minaret.co.uk
Date: Sat, 10 Dec 1994 11:48:56 + 0100
To: crowe@bendixs.co.uk (Dr Vincent Crowe)
From: eumenides@minaret.co.uk

Attachments: Audio
Subject: Re: MEDICI FILE

Hi, Dr Crowe.
This is Conor Molloy. You'll be interested, I'm sure, to see the following file that I came across on a restricted access level on the Bendix Schere computer system. No doubt you are familiar with its contents?

MEDICI FILE
Maternox. Phase One Status.
Batch no. BS-M-6575–1881-UKMR.
Launch date: 31 Oct 1993.
Expected result concentration: Sept 94–June 95

There followed the case reports of Sarah Johnson and the other three deaths to date, Zeenat Patel, Roberta McDonald and Caroline Kingsley, and the list of the remaining women who had conceived after taking the doctored Maternox, and their expected delivery dates. The symptoms of the dead women and their babies were identical and damning: severe pustular psoriasis and death from respiratory failure in the mothers; Cyclops Syndrome combined with acute psoriasis and death due to gross malformation of the respiratory organs in the babies.

Conor's eMail continued:

I'm sure you'll be interested, Dr Crowe, to see the following transcript of an audio tape recovered from Dr Richard Bannerman's laboratory in Berkshire on the night he was kidnapped whilst working

642

on analysing Maternox capsules. The voices have been identified as those of Dr Bannerman, yourself and Major Bill Gunn:

Dr Bannerman: 'Poliovirus possibly indicates intent to use an oral delivery system. Most viruses can't be used to deliver genetic material orally, because they can't survive in the human gut. Poliovirus can. It is simple to produce a defective poliovirus that cannot replicate.'

(*Pause.*)

'You bastards. My God, you bastards!'

Dr Vincent Crowe, Chief Executive of Bendix Schere:

'Good evening, Dr Bannerman. I just happened to be passing – thought I'd drop by and have a chat. Haven't seen much of you in the past week or so. I'm not sure if you've met Major Gunn, our Director of Security?'

Dr Bannerman: 'I'd like an explanation from you, Crowe, as to what the hell you think you're doing with your Maternox.'

Major Bill Gunn, Director of Security, Bendix Schere: 'Well, we'd like an explanation from you, Dr Bannerman, as to what you're doing with a Maternox formulaic template owned by the company.'

Dr Bannerman: 'Would you prefer that explanation to take place in a court of law, or in front of the Committee for Safety of Medicines? Now, I'd like you to stop trespassing on my property and leave. If you feel the need to drop in for a chat with anyone else at one o'clock in the morning, I suggest you drop by your lawyers and start briefing them, because by God you're going to need 'em.'

Major Bill Gunn, Director of Security, Bendix Schere: 'Right, just roll up his sleeve and I'll get this into him. Won't give us any trouble; he'll be docile as a lamb.'

Dr Crowe, you will find the complete audio duplicate of this recording on an icon marked DR
BANNERMAN ABDUCTION, which will have automatically been placed on to your hard disk memory. If
you click on the icon it will play the sound.

This same eMail message and audio attachment
is being stored on 200 eMail file servers around the
world at this moment. For verification, among the
locations where you will be able to find and read it are
the following: Vienna. Moscow. Paris. Cape Town.
Zagreb. Warsaw. New York. Washington. Chicago.
Los Angeles. Rome. Vladivostok. St Petersburg. Hong
Kong. Sydney. Brisbane. Reykjavik. Gothenburg.

At the end of this mail are the eMail addresses of
the above so that you can verify for yourself.

For Bendix Schere's protection, this information
is encrypted. However, unless I personally inter-
vene, at 7 p.m. tonight GMT, one of these servers
will automatically unencode and begin mailing
copies of this information to all 9500 current news-
groups on the Internet. Another server will commence mailing copies to the President of the United
States, the British Prime Minister and all other
heads of state and military around the world with
Internet addresses. A third server will mail this
information to all newspapers, television and radio
stations in Britain, the United States and elsewhere
around the world which have eMail addresses.

I have written a program interlinking each of
these 200 servers. Should you attempt to deactivate
any single one, the remainder will instantly mail out
all the information to everyone I have itemized
above, and, through a worm virus, continue, ultimately distributing copies to every single person in
the world connected to the Internet.

Knowing your fondness for killing people who
irritate you, such as Jake Seals, Zandra Wollerton,
Walter Hoggin, Dr Corbin, Charley Rowley, Hubert

Wentworth, not to mention both my parents, Edward Donoghue and Tabitha Donoghue, I would suggest that killing me would be unwise. I am the only person who can issue commands to stop the information going out and have taken precautions.

To guard my long-term safety, this command will have to be reissued by me at 7 p.m. GMT every Saturday for the next twelve months. As an added precaution I have distributed photographs of myself and passport details to each of the operators of these file servers. They will only accept the stop command if I turn up in person to enter it. If any date is missed, automatic irreversible distribution of the information commences.

Rorke looked, questioningly, at Gunn. The Director of Security stared back at him gravely. 'I'm afraid it's correct, sir. Our Systems Manager and team have been on to it since Dr Crowe received the message. He appears to have done what he says.'

Rorke was silent for some moments. 'So what are our options?'

Gunn glanced at his watch. It was ten to four. 'Where do you have to be at seven tonight, Mr Molloy?'

'An hour and a half's drive from here.'

Gunn scratched the back of his head. His eyes flicked to the monitor, then to Conor. He turned back to the Chairman, and said grimly, 'I don't think we have any options, Sir Neil. I'm afraid that Mr Molloy seems to hold all the aces.'

132

Rorke went out of the room with Gunn.

Conor and Monty stared at each other in silence, and she understood from the signal in Conor's eyes to say nothing. He slipped his arms around her and she held him tightly, struggling to control her fear. She knew that now at this moment, perhaps more than ever before, she needed to be strong.

They sat down at a conference table. Monty remembered the first time she had been in this office with Rorke and Crowe just over a year ago, and how happy and full of hope she had been. She looked at the squat gold frog on the Chairman's desk and thought about the frog in Crowe's office, made of black papier-mâché, with jewelled red eyes. The frog –

Her thoughts were broken as Rorke and Gunn came back into the room. She avoided meeting Rorke's eyes.

Gunn closed the door and stayed by it. Rorke walked a short distance across the room, then turned to Conor. 'So what is it you want? I assume you've thought about it carefully.' There was no rancour in his voice; it was as if this was a minor problem he wanted to get out of the way before turning his mind back to more important matters.

'What's happened to my father? Where is he?' Monty asked before Conor could reply.

Gunn shot a glance at Rorke and answered for him: 'Your father is here in this building. He's fine.'

'*Here?* Why's he here? I thought he'd had a stroke.'

Gunn's voice was polite and courteous. 'Your father is in good health. 'He –' He shot a glance at Rorke as if for help. 'He's under sedation.'

'I want to see him,' Monty said. 'Now. Take me to him.'

Rorke looked anxiously at his watch.

'This meeting goes no further until we've seen Dr Bannerman, Rorke,' Conor said. 'I also need my briefcase, which I left down in your charming hospitality suite.'

Gunn and Rorke exchanged another glance. Something in their expressions made Monty deeply uncomfortable.

'I'll take you down,' Gunn said.

The sight of her father's pallid complexion, and the drip lines and monitoring equipment had been a shock to Monty. But even in the few minutes they were with him, after the flow of anaesthetic and sedatives had been halted, he had shown noticeable improvement. The young doctor in charge of him had assured them that Dr Bannerman would be on his feet within a couple of hours.

Back in the Chairman's office, Conor took a seat at the head of the conference table, put his briefcase in front of him and opened it. Monty sat to his right, and Rorke and Gunn sat facing her to his left. Monty watched the Chairman's face for a few seconds, disquieted by his air of confidence.

'The first myth we need to dispel, Rorke, is the one of your role with the company.' Conor removed a sheet of paper and laid it on the table for them all to read. 'Bendix Schere has always maintained total secrecy over its shareholdings. Not surprising, is it, Rorke, since you actually own one hundred per cent of the stock?'

Monty looked, astounded, at Conor then at Rorke.

'Sure,' Conor went on. 'You give pieces of the action to your Directors. You are fair and democratic. You split forty-nine per cent of the equity of the company and the votes between them, but they never get any documentation for-malizing it. It's valid only for as long as they remain with the company – but it's a big incentive. Your average annual dividend runs from a few hundred thousand to a couple of million pounds per head. Nice work if you can get it, Rorke, but I don't think the qualifications for a seat on your Board are entirely straightforward, are they? You require something in addition to business and scientific skills from your acolytes, don't you?'

Conor pulled a folder from his briefcase and tossed it on to the desk. 'You thought you were pretty thorough in covering your tracks. You had your minions work their way through every library and publishing house in the world. You even had two slightly less-than-helpful photographers killed.' Conor leaned back. 'You went to a lot of trouble to hide your past. Plastic surgery would have done the job much more effi-ciently, but perhaps in 1969 that wasn't so good as it is now?'

Rorke appeared unmoved.

'You see, Rorke, my mother used to be an authority on the occult. She collected every book that was ever published.'

Conor opened the folder, which was filled with large photographic prints, and spread them across the table.

Monty looked at one, a page of a book, with a black and white photograph of a man kneeling in a white robe in the centre of a magic circle. A series of artefacts including a skull, an athame, several chalices, censers and statuettes had been placed around the circumference. The man was in the process of having a mask in the shape of a frog placed over his head.

The caption beneath read: 'Daniel Judd (Theutus), being ordained as the Forty-Second Assessor of the New International Satanic Brotherhood.'

As she looked closer, Monty could clearly see the face of the kneeling man. He was much younger in the photograph, maybe thirty years younger. The face had since fleshed out and the hair was much longer, but the features had not altered. There was no mistaking him. It was Rorke.

For some moments she could not take her eyes away from the picture. She looked up at the Chairman and her skin crawled. She selected another page, also removed from a book, with three photographs. The young Rorke was present in two of them. As she leafed through the collection of prints she realized with increasing certainty these were the same pages that had been missing from the books in the British Library.

'Daniel Judd,' Conor said, his voice acid now. '*Theutus*.' He pointed at the pictures on the wall, of Rorke sharing a joke with Prince Charles, of him standing arm in arm with Clinton. 'All your friends in high places. You murdered your father and your mother, didn't you, *Daniel Judd*? You tortured your mother first; you cut her hands off, then you tormented her, then you killed her. Your charm knows no bounds, Rorke. *Sir* Neil Rorke. How did it feel when the Queen knighted you?'

Rorke looked at him with hatred. 'Why don't you stop this charade and tell me what you want, Molloy?'

Conor nodded. 'Sure. I have it right here.' He pulled another folder from his briefcase. It contained a thin sheaf of documents, which he separated into four identical piles. He pushed one set to Rorke and another to Monty, ignoring

Gunn for the moment. 'Want to tell me where your secretary keeps her coffee machine while you take a read?'

Rorke looked at the papers in front of him. 'There isn't time to read all this now.'

'You'll manage,' Conor said, and pushed the fourth bundle to Gunn. 'Guess you should take a look also. It affects you too.' Then he stood up. 'Anyone take milk? Sugar?'

Thirty minutes later Rorke replaced the last page of the final document in his bundle then stacked the pages tidily, looking at Conor with incredulity. 'You want me to make over my entire shareholding to Dr Bannerman, Miss Bannerman and yourself?'

'It's a good deal for you,' said Conor smoothly. 'In exchange, you receive a guaranteed pension of one hundred thousand pounds a year for life, plus the same fifty-one per cent of the profits of Bendix Schere that you currently get, for life.' He paused a moment. 'The remaining forty-nine per cent will be distributed annually to medical research foundations and charities. You've always called Bendix Schere the "World's Most Caring Company" – well, that's how it's going to be from now.'

'And you also expect me to sign the document resigning as Chairman.'

'Dr Bannerman, Miss Bannerman and I will appoint a new Board. I don't intend keeping too many of your existing playmates.'

Rorke caught Gunn's eye, frowning. 'And is there anything else, Molloy?' Rorke said, turning back to Conor. 'Any more surprises tucked up your sleeve?'

Monty looked anxiously at Conor. There was no way Rorke was going to swallow this. And she desperately needed to tell Conor what she had seen in the subterranean laboratories. It would get out, it had to, and when it did the company would be finished. Was that why Rorke was so calm? Was Conor unwittingly offering him a golden get-out?

'Yes,' Conor said, 'there is. I want you to take me to the Cave of Demons.'

'*What?*'

'Just the two of us. Alone.'

Rorke smiled, visibly relaxing. 'You're not serious, Molloy?'

'I've never been more serious.'

'You wouldn't last five minutes in there. I'm sorry, you're talking about something way out of your depth.'

'Am I?' Conor flared.

Rorke sat looking at him for some moments. 'No one goes to the Cave of Demons unless they have been summoned, Molloy. It isn't possible.'

'You have the power, Rorke. You are the only human being on earth who is permitted to go.'

Again Rorke stared at him in silence for what seemed an eternity. Then he shook his head. 'No. No way, Molloy. What you want is not possible. It has never been done.'

'It can be done,' Conor said. 'It is written in the Great Law.'

'No one has ever done it. Not in two thousand years.'

'You are permitted to return there once,' Conor said. 'It is one of the Sixty-Three Privileges you hold.'

'It would take months of preparation. It's madness to even think about doing it unprepared. No, Molloy. If you go to the Cave of Demons you will die.'

Conor shook his head. 'No, I won't die, Rorke, because you're going to protect me. I'm bad news for you dead.'

'I could give no guarantee that I could protect you. I don't think you fully understand the forces that exist there.'

'Then you'll have to work very, very hard, Rorke. You've never put a foot wrong in your life – so far. Why start now?'

Rorke watched him silently.

'If I live, Rorke, you will still have your fortune intact. If I die, you either face catastrophe or you take your money and spend the rest of your life in hiding. I don't think that would suit you somehow.'

'Molloy, you give me no choice. I'll take you to the Cave of Demons. If you survive, then we'll sign the documents.'

Conor gave him a wry smile, opened his briefcase again and removed another document. 'I'll meet you halfway.' He put the document on the table. 'I've already signed this. It's an irrevocable instruction to my lawyer, Bob Storer at Harbottle and Lewis, who should be waiting down in the lobby right now. He will hold the only copies of the documents in existence in his office. If I make it back, he gives them to me. If I don't, he gives them to you.'

Conor looked at his watch and stood up. 'It's non-negotiable, Rorke.' He handed Monty a piece of paper on which was written a telephone number and said to her: 'I'll be waiting at that number at five to seven. I want to hear you and your father both telling me Rorke has signed. Then I'll issue the stop commands.'

He turned to Rorke. 'Major Gunn will witness your signature. You have the company seal here?'

'You won't come back, Molloy. You don't seem to understand that.'

'That's your problem as much as mine, Rorke.' He closed his briefcase and picked it up. 'I want you to make a call to have the company jet ready for take-off from Gatwick Airport at eight o'clock tonight, with a flight plan filed for Tel Aviv. You'd better hurry; you have some serious packing to do. Now I'm going to have a word in private with Miss Bannerman. I'd appreciate it if you would arrange for the lift to take us down to the lobby.'

Monty and Conor travelled down in silence. A man in a suit was waiting on one of the reception sofas with a large attaché case beside him and Conor introduced Monty to him, briefly, then went out into the car park with her and they climbed into his rented Ford.

'I know what you're going to say,' he said.

'Conor, you don't. You haven't *seen* what they're doing down there. I can't begin to –'

Conor raised a calming hand. 'There's a lot of stuff we're going to have to deal with, hon, a lot. But I want to be able to sleep easily in my bed at night. So do you and your father. I don't know how many of Rorke's piranhas like Detective Superintendent Levine are swimming around out there beyond these walls, and I don't intend taking my chances with them.'

'Is it true, what Rorke said? That you haven't a chance?'

He took her hand and squeezed it. Monty felt the pressure of his fingers, tense and nervous. 'I have a chance, and I have to take it. We don't have an option. There is only one way I'm ever going to be able to feel safe, and only one way I can ever hope to protect you and your father.'

'Isn't what you've done on the Internet good enough?'

'No, it's bullshit and he knows it. They'll crack the code eventually. All I've done is to buy us a little time. Now I have to try to buy us our lives.'

133

It was nearly nine o'clock when Monty and her father approached the outskirts of Maidenhead. In spite of everything that Rorke had agreed and the documents he had signed, Monty kept a wary eye on the headlights that appeared in her mirrors.

'What do I tell Anna Sterling?' she asked.

'The truth,' Dick Bannerman said simply.

'Conor told me not to.'

He was quiet for some moments. 'How many more women have had Maternox from this batch and are still at risk?'

'Ten. That's the number I counted on the Medici File.'

'Over what time span are they due to give birth?'

'Between now and June next year.'

'Molloy really told you not to tell Anna the truth? Doesn't that go against what you and I have always agreed, darling?'

'Conor said if the truth about Medici got out it would destroy the company.'

'Yes, I don't doubt it.'

'And we have to wait, anyway, till Conor's back, Daddy.'

'You know,' he said at length, 'I'm surprised at Molloy being prepared to go along with any sort of cover-up. I'd been starting to admire him. Didn't like him when I first met him, but he's been growing on me. Watched his antics on the television monitor – he's a dab hand with pyrotechnics. Didn't seem such a bad bloke after all. Underneath.'

She smiled, then her fear for Conor's safety ran a deep black stain across her meagre relief. 'No, he's not. He's not a bad bloke at all.'

She pulled up outside her father's front door and switched off the engine. The darkness filled her with foreboding. It was three hours since Conor had left with Rorke.

They went inside and Monty walked quickly through to the kitchen, snapping lights on as she went. She stared at the telephone for a moment then picked it up and dialled Anna Sterling's number, unsure whether she would even be in on a Saturday evening. It was answered on the third ring.

'Sterling.' A man's voice. Anna's husband, sounding very depressed.

'Mark,' she said. 'It's Monty.'

He perked up a fraction. 'Monty! Hello!' His voice sounded slurred, as if he had been drinking.

'Are you guys all right?' She tried to sound normal. 'I tried to ring but things have been a bit – ah – hectic. Is Anna OK?'

There was a long silence, which made Monty deeply afraid. 'Mark? Are you there?'

'She lost the baby.'

'What? What *happened*?'

'Thursday morning. Three o'clock. They took her to hospital. I was away on business.'

'Christ. How is she?'

'Sh'all right. Depressed. Coming home tomorrow. I'm collecting her.'

The sense of loss in his voice resonated through her. She felt for him intensely, felt for both of them, knew instinctively the pain and anguish they had been through.

She squeezed the receiver in her hand, held it close to her ear, her heart pounding. 'Will you give her a message?' she said, her voice choked, unsure whether she was sad or relieved. 'Will you tell her – just tell her I'm so sorry.'

134

Israel. Sunday 11 December, 1994

The rim of his Panama shaded Conor's face from the furnace heat of the sun; his suit and sodden shirt clung to his skin as heavily as if he had been swimming in them.

Water.

With growing desperation he stared at the mountains that walled off the desert ahead of him. A sudden blast like thunder ruptured the sky and he ducked instinctively. Two jet fighters roared past overhead; he could see the red balls of their afterburners, then they were gone, leaving only their rumbling echo.

His mouth was parched, his lips leathery. He had drunk nothing since breakfast in the hotel this morning and it was now mid-afternoon. Out of the corner of his eye he saw the movement of Rorke's arm slipping inside his jacket, then heard the sound of the cap of the water bottle being unscrewed. The greedy swigging; Conor could imagine the liquid going down, cool and clear, pure as spring water. Rorke had not offered him any and he was too proud to ask.

Too proud and too angry. And he wanted nothing that would put him in Rorke's debt.

He did not understand why he had not brought water for himself. How could he have set out into the desert without water? There had been plenty of time for Rorke to warn him. He had told him he would need a hat and rubber-soled shoes. He had not told him they would walk for six hours through the searing noonday sun and that he would need to bring water with him.

But why the hell hadn't *he* thought about it?

Conor felt dizzy. The tiny camera in his pocket he had bought on the way to the airport last night weighed down like a brick in his pocket. The desert tilted suddenly to the right; then to the left. He stumbled off the track into deep, hot sand which poured inside his shoes.

Water.

Something stirred in his mind. He could remember *buying* canteens of water in a shop. Had he left his in the shop?

Rorke was plodding steadily on without waiting for him. A camel train moved across the track miles ahead in the distance; it would be long gone by the time they reached it. Conor stumbled forward, struggling to keep his brain clear, to keep his focus, to remember why he was here. Put one foot after the other, had to remember that, just keep moving forward, right foot, left foot, just keep going.

For his father. For his mother. For Monty. Rorke was messing up his mind. Rorke was playing his games. Rorke had deliberately deprived him of water and now he was depriving his mind of the ability to focus.

Water.

There was no water. He had to get used to the fact that there was *no water*. Imagine water instead. Yes, he could do that. He needed to focus his mind on water, imagine he was drinking it, imagine it moistening his lips, imagine gulping it down his throat. Rorke had stopped and was drinking again. It seemed only a few moments since the man had last drunk. Except the mountains were closer now, the sheer faces of sandstone that rose above them into the sky dwarfing the figure of Rorke with his massive bag slung over his shoulder.

He had bought a bag also. A knapsack; he was certain he had bought a knapsack. He had bought a knapsack to carry the canteens he had bought in the shop. But where was it? Had he left it in the taxi?

Yes, Rorke must have made him leave it in the taxi.

Later, Conor wasn't sure how much later, they were climbing up through the rocks. Rorke led the way, picking a steady route up through the ever-steepening wall of rock that rose above them and dropped sheer beneath them into the valley.

There would be water on this mountain, Conor thought. His hopes rose with each turn, expecting to see a spring or a pool, but there were none; only arid dust and rock. Once or twice when he let down his guard Rorke taunted him by making him see an imaginary lake or spring, which disappeared when he scrambled towards them.

The sun was no longer high in the sky. Only a few hours of daylight remained. Then it would be cooler. Then he could suck the moisture from the leaves of –

Anger tore through him like a sudden gust. *I don't need water, Rorke. I don't need anything. I can cope. I will survive. It's all a state of mind. You think you can blunt my mind, Rorke, but you're wrong. You're sharpening it every second. Sharpening it with hatred.*

I don't need water. Unlike you.

I don't need anything.

They climbed for another hour and a slight, fresh breeze picked up. Conor followed Rorke up a narrow ridge, and as they rounded a curve at the top he saw a stake, old and weathered, set into a crack, from which hung a short length of frayed, broken rope.

Rorke stopped and gestured with his arm at the mouth of a cave just beyond the stake. The entrance was about twenty feet wide, shrouded by a deep overhang. From its position set back from the ridge Conor realized it would be invisible from both the valley beneath and the air above. A strange noise came from inside sounding like radio interference.

'This is it, Molloy.' Rivulets of perspiration were pouring down Rorke's face and he was panting with exertion. He pulled out the canteen of water and drank hungrily.

Conor wiped the sweat from his eyes with his sleeve and stood still. They were near the summit; the desert was a long way down. The sun was already low and soon it would be dark. Conor's mouth was dry and his lips sore and cracked.

'Not much from the outside, is it?' Rorke said, replacing his canteen. Then he wheezed, and took several breaths before speaking again. 'You know, you're a smart young man, Molloy. Too smart to die. Why don't you join me instead of fighting me? Work together with me?'

'I'm not for sale.'

'Everyone has a price.'

'I don't.'

Rorke mopped his face with a large handkerchief. 'You may like to think you're different, but you're not, you know.'

'You killed my father and mother, Rorke. You really think you could buy me?'

'Parents are nothing, Molloy. Just transporters of your genes. I wouldn't get sentimental. Sentiment is a cheap and dangerous emotion.' He smiled. 'You ought to drink, Molloy. Dehydration is dangerous in the desert. Why aren't you drinking?'

Rorke was staring hard at him. Something caught Conor's eye. Bright red. Nylon. A strap. A strap over his right shoulder. Then he saw the strap over his left shoulder also. He reached behind his back and felt his knapsack.

Jesus Christ. He had his knapsack! Had had it all the time – how the hell –?

Rorke. Rorke had been playing with his mind. He heaved the bag over his head, pulled the buckles open and pulled out one of the two canteens inside, felt its weight, solid, heavy, filled with water. He unscrewed the cap, brought it to his mouth and swigged hard. Almost instantly he spat it out, coughing and retching.

It was petrol.

He put the cap back on, tried the second canteen. Petrol. *How?* What was going on? He remembered the shop where they had bought the canteens; he had filled his himself from the cold tap at the back. He had put them in his knapsack and kept it with him. There was no way Rorke could have put petrol in them.

He glanced at Rorke's face, saw his eyes watching him, and knew. Knew Rorke's game exactly. He raised the canteen defiantly to his mouth again, careful not to inhale, to breathe in the smell, then tilted his head back, braced himself and began drinking.

The taste was horrendous. He gagged. Forced it down, kept his lips clamped around the neck, swigged, swallowed, swigged, swallowed, kept going, forced himself. He drank until the canteen was drained, and wiped his mouth with the back of his hand. The taste of petrol had gone now. It was water, pure fresh water.

He put the cap back on and tossed the empty canteen back into his knapsack, feeling some of his strength returning.

657

'You're right, I did need a drink.' He looked straight at Rorke and then turned and walked towards the entrance of the cave. The whistling shriek of radio interference rose to a cacophony as he approached, and a stench came out to meet him. Bats, he realized with disgust. The cave inside was alive with a vast colony of them. He could see them hanging, hear them rustling, jostling, squeaking.

The cave itself was small, unprepossessing; this was not it, could not be, he thought. Was it a trap? Then, thirty yards across the floor, he saw the second entrance. This was just an anteroom, he realized as he crossed the first cave, ignoring the noise which had become more frenetic with his intrusion. He went through the second entrance and stopped in his tracks, awestruck.

The cave was vast, Far, far larger than he would have believed possible from the outside. Thirty, forty, maybe fifty times larger. None of the few sketchy descriptions he had come across had even remotely done it justice. There was a cathedral-like stillness, but it was many times the size of any cathedral, or indeed of any building he had ever been into. There were bats in here, too, but they were higher up and their sound less intrusive.

Every inch of the walls that he could see was carved with symbols and hieroglyphics, and the stone floor was dominated by a pentagram, thirty metres across. In the centre of the pentagram sat an imposing carved stone chair. The Throne of the Incumbent, Conor remembered from his readings.

The light was meagre and fell rapidly away into darkness. At the far end of the cave, tiers of stone formed a natural auditorium, like an amphitheatre.

He was aware of a power, a force that felt truly demonic, colder, more hostile, more sinister than anything he had ever experienced before. His scalp prickled with fear and he shivered, his shirt clammy on his back. He was cold, bitterly cold. He took a few tentative steps forward. The Cave of Demons. The place where the final confrontation had been fought. Where, according to the legends, God had defeated and banished Satan. And where the demons waited, biding their time for their fallen Master's return.

Rorke walked past him and stopped at the edge of the pentagram. He removed a ceremonial sword from his bag, opened the circle with it, then stepped through, turned and closed the circle with his sword behind him. Conor watched as Rorke moved towards the stone chair, sat down, then slowly unpacked his artefacts and arranged them around him. A gold censer. A gold athame. A chalice. Several more vessels. An ankh.

'Brought your toys with you, Rorke?' he called across, his voice less confident-sounding than he had intended.

'What have you brought with you, Molloy?' he replied, calmly, lighting incense. 'What's your secret weapon, Molloy?'

Conor believed that there were immense forces of energy in the universe, which had collected in some places, and which could be harnessed. That was what Rorke and his followers had done. The rituals were mumbo-jumbo, he knew. Just a device for focusing their minds, that was all.

He looked in silence at Rorke. There had been a battle in this cave many years ago – a fight between forces of good and evil – when good had won. God had defeated Satan. The good forces had long gone, but the evil still remained.

Good could win again. The secret was in the Bible; it was there, quietly and unobtrusively, but plain for all to see.

'Decency,' he said, finally. 'That's what I believe in.'

Rorke stood up and walked slowly over to face him, remaining inside the circle. His face was shiny with a patina of grease, his hair damp and matted. 'Decency, Molloy?'

'Yes, Rorke. I believe in decency. That's my weapon.'

There was a smirk of contempt in Rorke's face which suddenly faded. 'You know, Molloy,' he said quietly, 'everyone thinks they can handle this thing – this power that you're trying to wrest from me here tonight.'

Conor said nothing.

'I thought I could, long ago. I really thought then it was just a question of good versus evil. But there's no longer good versus evil in this world,' Rorke continued. 'Good versus evil has become *bad* versus evil. You try to change, but in the end it's you who gets changed, Molloy. Power corrupts, and absolute power corrupts absolutely. Great men are almost always bad men.'

Conor stared at him. 'That's your excuse, is it, Rorke? Is that how you justify murdering my father and my mother?'

Rorke shrugged. 'It's all a matter of perspective. For you what I have done is evil, for me I look upon it as necessary for a greater good. Everything depends on how you look at it, Molloy. You look at me and you see a monster; I look in the mirror and I see a gentleman.' He smiled. 'But I'm sorry we couldn't do business together. Really, I am. You and I are the same beneath the skin.'

He turned and walked in silence back to his chair. Conor watched him sit down and felt a moment of doubt. *Be careful.* Rorke was playing his game; a grand master trying to find a chink in his anger and succeeding.

Almost.

You bastard.

He would see the glow of the setting sun below the lodestone at the mouth of the cave. Three or four minutes, that was all, before darkness began closing in. Conor could feel the tightness in the air. His thoughts strayed to Monty. Nearly twenty-four hours since he had seen her.

He sat on the stone floor. Rorke's head was framed against the orb and a chink of sky was visible now beneath the lodestone. Tiny coils of smoke from the incense rose either side of him. The camera, he remembered. Take a photograph while there's still light. So that I can prove to the world that this place really exists.

He slipped the camera surreptitiously from his pocket and brought it swiftly to his eye, framed Rorke centrally and pressed down. The camera jerked wildly in his hand as if it had been hit by something. There was a smell of burning plastic; the top of the camera was glowing red hot and was melting in his hands.

Startled, he dropped it to the floor; the back sprang open and the film fell out. Thick, acrid smoke rose up as the casing sparked and crackled.

Rorke was looking at him and smiling.

Conor glared at him, struggling hard not to curse. Rorke

wanted to get him angry, to make it a confrontation of force against force. That was how his mother had tried to beat them, and she had lost. She had warned him that their power would be too much and she had been right.

Tonight he was using a different power. The same power, he was certain, that God had used against Satan. It was not brute force, or his omnipotence, that had won, it had been cunning. Whether he could do the same he did not know. He could only try.

Rorke was quiet now, absorbed in his ritual. Conor folded his hands in his lap, closed his eyes and began the meditation of the Thirteen Portals that he had learned by heart. He felt his metabolism slowing down, sensed the darkness gathering outside, drawing the last remaining rays of light out from the cave. The bats had quietened and the cave was silent and still.

The chill air was numbing his body. Suddenly he was standing at the edge of a lake. High above him he heard a scream. Charley Rowley, on fire, was hurtling down into the lake. He hit the water and vanished in a cloud of steam, with a solitary, terrible cry.

Conor's eyes sprang open. Although it was dark, he could sense Rorke smirking. The smell of incense was overpowering. Rorke was messing up his mind, trying to block his concentration. He closed his eyes, willing himself to stay calm.

Resist no evil: but whosoever shall smite thee on thy right cheek, turn to him the other also.

He resumed his meditation. Mind over matter. Mind over body. For twenty minutes he meditated without interruption, gradually slowing down his heartbeat. Counted it down. Sixty-five. Fifty-five. Forty-five. Thirty-five. Down. Twenty-five. Down. Fifteen. Ten. Five. One.

One beat a minute.

Held it there. *One beat a minute.*

He felt a blast of hatred from Rorke, but made no attempt to resist it; instead, he absorbed it like a sponge. Images taunted him. His father plunging through the window. His mother spinning wildly, screaming incantations. Conor absorbed them all, sucked them in, allowing himself no emotional reaction. His ears were filled with a venomous babble of voices, strange tongues, incantations. His father. His mother. Reproachful, crying, frightened, lonely in death.

One beat a minute. That was the only thought he allowed himself. One beat a minute. His mantra. He lost all track of time. Occasionally he could sense Rorke's presence intruding, the rustle of his clothes, his nervous, ponderous breathing. Then, gradually, he began to sense the looming presence of something approaching.

One beat a minute.

There was a new sound, a gusting wind that whistled like the call of a giant bird, rising to a crescendo, then dying. Moments later it returned, rising in strength. It swirled several times around the walls of the cave with a low moaning howl then departed.

It was here.

One heart beat a minute. Outside there was a crackle that sounded like rain. But it wasn't rain, it was wind, shaking the trees, the bushes, hurtling sand and dust and pebbles against the rocks. The crackle increased into a ferocious rending that sounded like thunder, then the wind burst into the cave, came at him from every direction, rocking him, tearing at his hair, trying to rip him from his seat. He moved to cover his face but his arms were frozen to his side; he was rooted.

One beat a minute.

The wind cut through his clothes, blowing harder, colder. Grit stung his cheeks, his hands. It was as if he were in the centre of an exploding bomb.

Then he heard a voice, raised into a screech. Rorke.

'Nema. Olam a son arebil des
Menoitatnet ni sacudni son en te.
Sirtson subirotibed
Summittimid son te tucis
Artson atibed sibon ettimid te
Eidoh sibon ad
Munaiditouq murtson menap
Arret ni te oleac ni
Tucis aut satnulov taif
Muut munger tainevda

Muut nemon rutecifitcnas
Sileac ni se iuq
Retson retap.'

Conor listened, absorbing every word. Though his metabolism had slowed right down his brain was clear, razor-sharp, and he knew immediately what Rorke was doing. The Lord's Prayer, in Latin, in reverse.

More incantations followed. The wind strengthened with each one, rocking Conor. Then a gust, the strongest yet, flung him sideways on to the floor. He lay there, his concentration barely disturbed.

One beat a minute.

Resist not evil. Absorb the energy. *Resist not evil: but whosoever shall smite thee on thy right cheek, turn to him the other also.*

Absorb.

The Bible said to bend with the whirlwind. Bend, not resist. If you allowed yourself to bend, you did not break.

Conor waited where he lay, pliant and absorbent. The wind tossed him across the floor, against the wall, then it picked him up and hurtled him across the cave. He crashed into the far wall with a bang that jarred every bone in his body, then thumped, in agonizing pain, on to the floor.

One beat a minute.

He lay still. A figure loomed out of the darkness, swept down at him, a hideous fluorescent figure in flowing robes with a skull for a face and goat horns rising from his head; it drew its face close to Conor's, staring at him with socketless eyes and breathing fetid breath from its half-jawed rictus grin.

'Conor, why didn't you listen to your mom?'

It was his father.

He shrank back in terror. His concentration slipped. The skull pressed close to his flesh, whispered, 'She warned you, Conor. She warned you so often. Warned you that you did not know what you were getting into.'

His heart was thumping. *Breathing too fast, much too fast! Concentrate! Draw it in, absorb!* He closed his eyes, forced away the image, ignored the wind which picked him up and slammed him face-first into a stone step. Ignored the searing pain in his nose and the taste of blood in his mouth. *One beat a minute one beat a minute one beat a minute.*

One beat a minute.

'What's up, Molloy? No fight? No spunk?' Rorke was yelling at him. 'Come all this way to get battered to pieces? Still conscious, are you, Molloy? Still happy to be here? Thinking about your little floosie?'

Conor drew in Rorke's voice, stored the venom, gave nothing back.

One beat a minute.

'Lot of things you don't know, aren't there, Molloy? I wonder who'll be fucking her after you're dead and gone? I wonder who's fucking her tonight?' Rorke's voice cracked a fraction.

The temperature in the room dropped sharply. The air filled with a banshee shrieking. Incantations in a hundred different tongues, all directed at him. He absorbed them calmly, filled up cavities in his brain with them. He looked into the blackness; could see nothing. There was a sudden rattle and hailstones the size of marbles blasted his head, his face, his hands. The temperature rose, to a searing, choking heat. Then it dropped again. Wind came at him from every direction and he was lifted up, spun around and around in a vortex, slammed into a wall and crashed to the ground.

One beat a minute.

He waited. The wind lifted him again, high up; he felt the beating, spiny wings of bats on his face, felt their claws, their beaks, his ears filling with their buzzing, shrieking, whistling, then he was slammed to the ground again.

One beat a minute.

He clung to the thought; held his heart motionless.

Beat.

Long pause. Held it. Held it deeply, dearly, held that one thought in his mind and no other.

Flames singed his face.

Beat.

Rorke's enraged voice rang out. He was shrieking, venting anger, and Conor absorbed it, took it in, every word. The floor and the walls of the cave shook with a deep rumble like thunder. Then there was a lull. Rorke was tiring. He could feel it. The lull. Silence. *You are old, Rorke. You are old and tired and out of practice. You have relied too much on your henchmen. You've lost the edge, lost your supreme powers . . .*

NOW.

One hundred beats in one second. Conor's heart was exploding like a jackhammer. Every scrap of wind, every ounce of energy in the cave that he had drawn into his body, every incantation, the heat, the cold, every ounce of Rorke's rage, of his own rage that had been building for years, he powered out in that one second, powered at the dark hulk on the chair in the centre of the room, blasted it through the psychic shield of the pentagram.

'*Ayaaaaaayaaaaaaaaaaaaaaaaaaaaaaaaaaaaaaaaaaaaaa!*'

Rorke's scream rang out through the darkness. Moments later a terrific sheet of lightning erupted in the centre of the cave. He saw Rorke glowing a vivid electric blue. Orange and green light arced around him. His hair shot up like spikes. His eyes bulged. His veins popped on his forehead. Fissures appeared in his cheeks. His clothes rippled and came apart at the seams, burst open. His arms flung outward, and cracks appeared in the skin of his chest and belly as if he were made of clay. His intestines began to uncoil like a serpent freeing itself from its nest.

Then a sudden, bright light flashed, as if a bomb had detonated inside him. He glowed translucently for an instant, white hot, and screamed once more, a howl of agony that filled the entire cave and seemed to roar out into the night sky beyond. Then Conor's ears went numb as a massive shock-wave hit them.

In sudden silence he watched Rorke explode into a vortex of wild, jagged streaks of electricity that raced out in every direction through the cave. Then they faded, until they had burnt themselves out.

Then darkness again.

Total silence.

Conor lay still for several minutes. He tried to push himself to his feet but he had no strength. He crawled towards where he thought the door lay and fell sideways, his hand slithering in something wet and slippery. He laid his head down on the stone floor and closed his eyes. He had nothing left to give; he was drained, emptied. Nothing left to do now but curl up and wait to die.

Slowly, sound began to return to his ears. In the distance he heard a babble of strange tongues. Faint, like a whisper at first, then getting louder.

His last conscious thought was of Monty.

135

Israel. Monday 12 December, 1994
A bird twittered.

Slowly he forced his eyelids open. Beyond the outside entrance to the cave Conor could see a pink dawn sky. He lifted his face up off the floor and the movement was painful. His face felt puffy and his nose hurt. His mouth was parched.

He staggered to his feet and swayed, one shoe on, one shoe off. The cave felt warm, quiet; it seemed to be filled with a deep, welcoming glow.

The stone chair on which Rorke had sat had shattered and lay in pieces across the floor. There was a stain on one part of the wall, dark red like dried blood. Near it was a smaller stain. He saw a Rolex watch, the face smashed and twisted almost in half. A solitary sand-caked shoe lay upside down on the far side of the cave. Rorke's. There was more blood beside it and what looked like a piece of splintered bone with skin attached. He saw a ragged strip of pin-striped cloth. Another strip of skin.

Then he saw Rorke's holdall close to the steps where he had been lying. He looked inside. There were two canteens, one full. He drank deeply, then stopped, knowing that he must ration himself for the walk back.

His body, although aching and sore, now surged with energy. He looked around, up into the darkness, at the walls, down at the shattered throne. He was alone, but he did not feel lonely. The forces that yesterday had awed him and scared him now fuelled him and gave him strength. He was wanted here now. He belonged here. He looked up at the symbols on the walls, looked at the steps, then something caught his eye on the floor and he walked over to it.

It was a gold pendant, in the shape of a frog's head, on a chain. Conor picked it up and examined it. There was something rather vulgar about gold, he thought, dangling it by its chain.

Everything depends on how you look at it, Molloy. You look at me and you see a monster; I look in the mirror and I see a gentleman.

No, Rorke, he thought, *no way. No gentleman would ever wear this.* He carried it out through the cave, past the stake wedged into the crack in the rocks and threw the pendant hard out into the valley. He turned away before it had even dropped from sight, walked back towards the Cave of Demons.

His cave, now.

He saw his shoe just inside the entrance, slipped it on and tied the laces. Then he strode confidently into the cave. At first he kept outside the pentagram, then he shrugged, stepped over its outer circumference and walked slowly to the centre, and stood there in silence.

Rorke's words came back to him.

. . . everyone thinks they can handle this thing – this power that you're trying to wrest from me here, tonight . . . But there's no longer good versus evil in this world. Good versus evil has become bad versus evil. You try to change, but in the end it's you who gets changed, Molloy. Power corrupts, and absolute power corrupts absolutely . . .

He walked out of the pentagram, feeling uncomfortable suddenly. It was dawn outside and the air would be cool. There were a good couple of hours before the sun reached its full heat. He should start now, he thought. Right now.

There was a car waiting where the taxi should have been and Conor felt a beat of apprehension. It was a white Mercedes but it did not look like a taxi.

When he was still a good quarter of a mile off, the driver's door opened and a man in a brown suit with short hair and aviator glasses got out and hailed him with a formal, business-like wave. It was Major Gunn, he saw, as he came closer.

Gunn opened the rear door of the car and held it for him, subserviently. 'I thought there might be a problem, sir – if the taxi that brought you here dropped off two people, and only one returned . . .'

'And you didn't know which one it would be?'

'No, sir.' Gunn allowed the trace of a smile.

Conor slumped on to the back seat. The door closed. Gunn started the engine and the cold air of the air-conditioning filled the interior. Conor lay back, absorbing it gratefully, then took the cold bottle of mineral water that Gunn passed him and drank until it was almost drained.

Gunn drove for some minutes in silence. Then he said, quietly, 'I'm glad, Mr Molloy. I'm very glad.'

'I'm pretty glad too,' Conor said, wryly. He lay back in the seat and closed his eyes.

Rorke was wrong. It was possible to change things. If you were determined enough.

He glanced through his lashes at Gunn's face in the mirror. The test lay ahead. Was it possible for bad people to become good? Or for good to become bad?

Grief lay ahead also. He needed to allow himself the time and the space to grieve properly for his mother. And then, some time after that, he was going to sweep Monty up in his arms and carry her off to a quiet corner some place and tell her they were going to marry. It wasn't going to be a question, it was going to be a statement.

He finished the bottle of mineral water and started on another, which Gunn passed him automatically. He cradled it in his hands, pressed it to his cheeks, rolled it around his face, trying to chill off some of the heat from the sun.

His eyes were raw from the glare and his hands were sunburned and hurt badly. He looked down at his clothes: his jacket was ripped in several places, three of his shirt buttons were missing and there was blood on his tie. *Have to get a new suit*, he thought and wondered, with sudden irrational concern, how they would find a decent men's outfitter.

Glancing out of the window again and back at the mountains, he remembered a line from a poem he had read years before. It was from Shelley, he thought. Yes, Shelley.

Sometimes,
The Devil is a gentleman.
He smiled.

EPILOGUE

Saturday 27 June, 2002

'Mack, time to go, we're outta here!'

Mack Molloy looked up for a moment at the sound of his father's voice, then, his face screwed up tight in concentration, he stuck the crayon in his mouth and sucked on it as though it were a pretend cigarette, before adding some touches to his drawing with it.

Monty smiled. Mack was forever making her smile. She watched him in his tracksuit bottoms, sweatshirt, mop of blond hair flopped forward, his face and hands smeared with crayon. He seemed to spend most of his time in a world of his own, quietly observing, drawing, thinking. Sometimes she worried that he thought too much, too deeply for a five-year-old. He bombarded her with questions about how things worked, about who God was, and about death. He was particularly interested in death.

'Mack! C'mon, fella, got to get ready, got Alec's birthday party to go to!' Conor shouted.

Mack grimaced and continued with his drawing. Monty glanced at her watch. 'Darling,' she said quietly, 'Daddy's calling you. You have to get ready. Go and wash and I'll come and help you dress.'

He shrugged, uninterested.

'Don't you want to go to the party? It's Alec, your friend, you like him.'

Deaf ears.

Hurriedly Monty dunked her paint brushes into the chipped coffee mug of turps, wiped them and laid them on the lip of her easel.

It was a fine summer day. The distant sloping field which she could see from her studio window was flecked with puffs of white, and the air was alive with the buzzing of bees and the distant bleating of sheep. Through the reek of turpentine and

670

linseed oil, she could smell the garden, flowers and freshly mown grass.

She liked the dilapidated old barn Conor had had converted into a studio for her. It was her retreat, her sanctuary. The door opened and Conor came in looking livid. 'Mack! Come *on*!' His voice sounded short and fractious, a sign that one of his black moods was approaching.

He had the moods every once in a while and they would last for several days. His temper would be ferocious, frightening her sometimes with its venom, and always they would be followed by several days in which he would be quiet and deeply gloomy.

They had started after his return from Israel. He had never talked about what had happened in the Cave of Demons. Sometimes she wondered quite how much he kept from her. There was a secretive side to his nature, but that had been part of his attraction for her, right from the beginning.

Mack would be six in a couple of months' time, and she was four months' pregnant now. She had miscarried twice in the intervening years and Conor, on the advice of the obstetrician, was insistent that this time she did nothing other than rest and paint until she was safely through the danger period. During the past few months he had been even kinder and more attentive than she had ever known him.

He slipped an arm around her shoulder now and eyed the unfinished painting on the easel in front of her. 'You have the sky good,' he said.

'Thanks. I don't think the colour of the water's right, though. It's too green.'

'It's too flat. You got those clouds overhead, it means there would be wind, a squall. The water should be whipped up into waves.'

She nodded; he was right. He usually was. 'You won't forget the necklace, darling?' she reminded him.

'Nope.'

They were going to the christening the next day of Katy Sterling, her god-daughter. Anna and Mark Sterling's first child. The necklace was being inscribed with Katy's initials. A pretty sterling silver chain with a locket. She had wanted to get

671

gold, but Conor had insisted on silver, he had a thing about gold, an intense dislike that she had never understood, but she accepted it.

She turned and gave him a spontaneous kiss. 'Love you,' she said.

He squeezed her harder. 'Love you too.'

Conor was a good man, she thought gratefully. He was kind, and a tireless worker and although he was Chairman and Chief Executive of Bendix Schere he concentrated much of his energies on charitable work, and on helping struggling research scientists. He earned warmth and respect from everyone who knew him.

Monty had had a huge struggle with her conscience when it came to determining the future of Bendix Schere. In the end she had been persuaded by Conor to accept the shares thus guaranteeing the company's survival. First and foremost was the freedom that the money would give her father for his research. Then there was the vast funding at their disposal to hand out to other research foundations and charities who were in the same position she and her father had been in. And, as Conor pointed out, they knew the truth about Bendix Schere. Could they be sure any other pharmaceutical company they went to for funding would have any more integrity, or any fewer skeletons in the closet? Wasn't it better to stay with the devil you knew?

Her father and Conor had reached an uneasy compromise. Dick Bannerman accepted his one third of the company stock, and the role of Director of Research and Development, on the one condition that none of his work was ever patented. For a man whose career was patent law it was a tough one for Conor, but he accepted it. In seven years Bendix Schere had not filed a single patent. The company was still in the world's top ten league.

Following Sir Neil Rorke's mysterious disappearance, Monty had joined the Board of Bendix Schere as Director of Human Resources, a post she held for three years, with only a short period of maternity leave for Mack. She did the best she could for the sick security guards and the other members of staff who had been held captive by their ailments, and Gunn

672

had been remarkably efficient in helping her to weed out Rorke's erstwhile playmates.

Eight of the remaining nine women who were still pregnant as a result of the doctored Maternox miscarried. The ninth, whose baby was the most imminent, died in a car accident which, Conor insisted, was a genuine accident.

But even now the babies in the basement lab preyed on Monty's mind. Within twenty-four hours of Conor's return from Israel they had disappeared. She wondered sometimes whether Conor was right and she had been hallucinating from the drug she had been given and had imagined them. But she didn't really believe that.

Monty did not, however, regret Levine's demise. The Detective Superintendent had been found in his bedroom, dressed in ladies' underwear, hanging from an electric light flex. The story made all the national headlines, every single one. She had seen to that personally, had drafted the anonymous tip-off herself and faxed and eMailed it to every news editor. She liked to think that Hubert Wentworth would have approved.

The bitterest irony was that Conor had had a plaque put up in the atrium commemorating the deaths of Dr Crowe, Dr Seligman, Dr Farmer, and the other woman, Dr Baines, in a tragic accident brought about by a fire in a laboratory. He had insisted it was important for appearances. At least, she supposed, she did get some measure of satisfaction each time she went into Bendix Schere and saw the plaque. It reminded her of something her husband had become increasingly fond of saying over the years:

Sometimes,
The Devil is a gentleman.

Conor squeezed her again, as if he were frightened of something and did not want to leave her. Maybe, she thought, he was afraid of the dark mood that was looming.

'OK, Mack! That's it! Let's go!' he said.

Startled, Mack jumped up. 'OK,' he said. 'Going. I'm going!' And he scampered out of the room.

Monty and Conor grinned at each other.

'What's he drawing?' Conor asked.

'I don't know – he's been busy on it all morning.'

Conor walked over to Mack's little table and looked down. He stood, motionless, for some moments, the colour draining from his face.

'What's the matter?' she said.

He continued staring at the drawing in silence. She walked over to him.

Mack's drawings always took a while to decipher. This was of a huge black creature that looked half-bird, half-human. It seemed to be falling out of the sky, plummeting towards the jaws of a monster that was lurking in the entrance of a cave.

ACKNOWLEDGEMENTS

I am always amazed at the level of enthusiasm from the people I turn to for help in the research for my novels. And this time there has been a generosity of spirit that has made the writing of *Alchemist* as much a tremendous (and at times hair-raising) adventure as hard work, and there are many people to whom I owe very deep gratitude.

I need to single out in particular Steve Goodman, Andy Holyer, Dr Nigel Kirkham, Joanne Larner, Chris Pett, Maxine Sanders and Dave Schmickel, who all in their individual ways came up with the inspirations that shaped the book and who gave their time warmly, whenever it was needed, for over two years. And I have a very special thank you owing also to my Deep Throat, My invaluable M.

To all the names below I thank you far more than this short space allows: Sue Ansell, David Austin, Don Barrett of Wyeth Laboratories, Anna Beard, Felicity Beard, Mr Robert Beard FRCS, Simon Bell, Nick Bremer, Richard Blacklock, Dr Clive Cohen, Dr Michelle Cooperman of the Imperial Cancer Research Fund, Robert W. Esmond and Evelyn McConathy of Sterne Kessler Goldstein and Fox, Steve Goodman, Drew Granston, Dr Patrick Hall-Smith, Mike Harris of Brighton Police, Dr Stephen Hempling, Andy Holyer, Veronica Hamilton-Deeley, Bill Jones, Dr Bruce Katz, Michael Keen, Joe Kerridge, Dr Nigel Kirkham, Robert Knox, Gary Lane, Joanne Larner, Professor Alan Lehmann, Judy Lehmann, Nigel MacMillan, Roderick Main, Robert Martis, Dr Lyne Mayne of the Trafford Centre, Paul Michaels, John Parker, Chris Pett and Hanna Dzieglewska of Frank P. Dehn, Patent Agents, Dr Ken Powell of Glaxo-Wellcome plc, Blaine Price, Peter Rawlings, Brenda Robinson, Maxine Sanders, Dave Schmickel of the US Patent Office, Martin Short, Ian Stevens, Dr Duncan Stewart, Simon Thornton, Lady Helen Trafford, Michael Stott, Patent Attorney, Canon Dominic

Walker OGS, Dr Jonathan Williams FCAnaes, Dr Richard Wiseman.

I owe an enormous thanks also to the creative team and tireless support of my UK agent, Jon Thurley, and his right hand, Patricia Preece, in whose presence the central idea for the novel first saw light, and to my wonderful editorial team of Richard Evans, Jo Fletcher and Katrina Whone, and my editor Liza Reeves who risked all with her studies to get the book completed – and got a First. And a deep thank you also for the invaluable input of my US agent, Michael Siegel.

And lastly, a debt of gratitude for the endless patience of my wife, Georgina, and to Bertie for not chewing all my floppy disks:-)

Peter James scary@pavilion.co.uk